THE FIRST BOOK OF THE CROWN COLONIES

AT THE
Queen's Command

THE FIRST BOOK OF THE CROWN COLONIES

AT THE
Queen's Command

MICHAEL A.
STACKPOLE

NIGHT SHADE BOOKS
SAN FRANCISCO

At the Queen's Command: The First Book of The Crown Colonies
© 2010 by Michael A. Stackpole
This edition of
At the Queen's Command: The First Book of The Crown Colonies
© 2010 by Night Shade Books

Edited by Janna Silverstein
Cover art by Ryan Pancoast
Cover design by Claudia Noble
Interior layout and design by Ross E. Lockhart

SUSTAINABLE FORESTRY INITIATIVE

Certified Chain of Custody
Promoting Sustainable
Forest Management
www.sfiprogram.org
PwC-SFICOC-272

First Printing

ISBN: 978-1-59780-200-0

Printed In Canada

Night Shade Books
Please visit us on the web at
http://www.nightshadebooks.com

To Kat Klaybourne

Thanks for being my best friend and partner in
the brave new worlds we explore every single day.

Acknowledgments

This novel would not have been possible without the aid of many: Kat Klaybourne for her insights and unflagging support; Jason Williams and Jeremy Lassen of Night Shade Books for taking a chance; my agents Howard Morhaim and Danny Baror for guaranteeing I had the time to do the job; Janna Silverstein for translating me into English, and Reinhold Mai for translating me into German.

1763

CHAPTER ONE

April 27, 1763
Coronet
Temperance Bay, Mystria

Captain Owen Strake stood on the *Coronet*'s wheel deck, smiling as the ship came around the headland. The wind remained steady, but in the harbor the sea lost its chop. The angry clouds that had pounded the ship with nearly incessant storms had vanished, and the rising sun painted the sky blue. A light mist rose off the deep blue water.

Owen's stomach began to ease and his flesh to warm. The crossing to Mystria had not been kind to him. Seven weeks of nausea had left him twenty pounds lighter and intolerably weak. Even disastrous campaigns, battle wounds, and long, cold retreats had never left him feeling so hideous.

The ship's captain, Gideon Tar, turned toward Owen, smiling through weathered features as his steersman straightened the wheel. The First Mate bellowed orders sending men aloft to furl sails. "At least we beat May here, which I had not thought likely when we left Norisle."

"I was counting the days."

Gideon shook his head. "You were counting the *hours*, Mr. Strake. Or, Captain is more correct." The sailor looked him up and down. "As wretched as you must feel, you wear the uniform well. Queen's Own Wurms, yes?"

"Yes, and you're being polite, sir." Owen held his arms out to his sides. "I'm too small for it now. My wife had it tailored as a surprise. She'd be horrified."

"You should have brought her with you. She could have taken it in."

Owen shook his head. "I'm fair certain, Captain, my wife would have enjoyed the company of your wife and the other women on board, but she is delicate. I do not know how she would have taken the passage, but I do not think she would take well to the Colonies. She prefers her galas and society far too much."

"And she was the one to whom you wrote all those letters?"

"Yes, and I would be obliged if you would see them back to Norisle when you sail again."

Tar nodded. "It would be a pleasure. I owe you at least that given your

1

intervention with Mr. Wattling."

"I appreciate how you handled the aftermath, sir."

For the sake of secrecy, since the Tharyngians had spies everywhere, Owen had boarded at night. He had remained largely below decks until they were well away from the Auropean coast. Not even the ship's small contingent of Marines, with whom he had bunked, knew who he was nor his rank until he'd pulled his uniform from his trunk that morning.

Captain Tar had known only that the man's passage was of vital import to the Crown, and that no attention should be called to him. Owen had prevented a passenger from beating his servant to death—a violation of Owen's orders to remain unremarkable. Tar had calmed things with Mr. Wattling, giving Owen time to absent himself.

"What fraud is this I see before me?" Wattling, a rotund man with a bright red face, mounted the deck and strode straight for the officers. "Dressing this man as a soldier will not preserve him. I ordered you to flog him, Captain Tar, and you will do so."

Gideon raised his chin. "Mr. Wattling, may I introduce to you Captain Owen Strake, of the Queen's Own Wurms."

"I am not an idiot, Captain. Red coat with blue facings, the braid: I know the unit very well. A fraud, I tell you, and you shan't get away with it. No, sir." The large man hammered his walking stick against the deck. "You *redemptioneers* all do hang together. I should have known."

"Do you suggest, sir, that I wear this uniform to deceive you?"

"Of course, damn you, I cannot say it more plainly." Wattling's piggish eyes tightened. "A Mystrian in Her Majesty's service, perhaps, but a captain, never! Officers are gentlemen, and you are no gentleman. No Mystrian could be!"

Gideon Tar's face flushed crimson.

Owen stepped toward the angry man. "Mr. Wattling, it has been a trying passage. I shall assume your ill-humor and poor manners are because of fatigue."

"Assume what you wish…"

Owen raised his voice, his green eyes widening for emphasis. "Sir, you are *speaking* when you should be *listening*."

Wattling raised his stick. "I will not have some grubby Colonial speak to me in such a tone. Flog him, Captain!"

Gideon Tar stepped between the two men. "I should remind you, sir, that you are on a ship crewed by 'grubby Colonials' and that it is yet a long swim to Temperance."

Wattling hesitated a moment, then stepped back and barked out a harsh laugh. "You wouldn't dare, none of you. Mystrians haven't the fortitude. The moral defects for which you were shipped here are writ large on you all. You barely eek out an existence in a fecund land, but have neither the intelligence nor courage of true men."

His cane became a scepter brandished. "I know all about you. I've read every word of Lord Rivendell's *The Five Days Battle of Villerupt*. Had to. Set the type myself. I printed it on the very press in the hold of this ship. I know all about Colonial cowardice facing the godless Tharyngians."

"*You* printed that sheaf of lies?" The moment he'd spoken Owen knew he had gone too far.

"Lies?" Rage cast Wattling's expression in iron. Even his jowls ceased quaking. "I set every word as given to me by his lordship directly. Are you saying he lies?"

Owen shook his head. "He was not even at Villerupt. I was—First Battalion, Scouts company. The closest Lord Rivendell got was L'Averne. Gout kept him from walking and his piles left him unable to sit a horse." Owen almost added that medicinal brandy left Rivendell unconscious for the first three days, and hopelessly hungover for the last two, but thought better of it.

"This is an outrage! You slander the man."

"As you slander the Colonials."

Wattling shook his stick. "Are you saying the Mystrian Rangers didn't break on the third day?"

Owen raised his chin and clasped his hands at the small of his back. "I am saying, sir, that they fought as hard as anyone. I was there."

"Then you fled with them. Just another coward."

"Mr. Wattling, have you any practical experience of war?"

Wattling refused to meet his gaze. "The Crown has not required my service."

And you never saw fit to purchase a command. "It rained incessantly during the campaign, sir. The men, Norillians and Colonials alike, were wet and miserable, cold. Half our brimstone was wet, our muskets rusting. Many men were barefoot. This ship's provisions have been far better than any we had in the field. The rains turned everything into a marsh, washed out roads and bridges."

"Soldiers choose their own lot in life, sir."

"They do, so you have to think on the courage of men who, born in Mystria, would answer the Crown's call and board a ship for a land they've never seen. A hundred and eighty men, three companies. Major Forest's had little training or drill, yet by Lord Rivendell's order they were to anchor the left, tight against woods his lordship deemed impassable."

Owen shivered, memories coming back too fast. Brigadier General Richard Ventnor, later made Duke of Deathridge, had fought Rivendell's troops well, pushing hard toward Villerupt. The Tharyngians had given ground and that

4 — MICHAEL A. STACKPOLE

third day, on the narrow plain of Artennes, it appeared the conflict would be decided.

"You should understand, Mr. Wattling, that in the first two days, the Mystrians acquitted themselves well, acting alongside my troops as skirmishers. At Artennes, the Platine Guards Regiment came through those woods on logging trails—wide logging trails. You remember the Platine Guards. They forced Lord Rivendell off the Continent two years earlier."

Owen didn't wait for the man's response. "A battalion of skirmishers against Tharyngia's elite guards. The Mystrians gave three volleys before they broke. Even then, they regrouped and continued fighting, harassing the Guards."

"Be that as it may, they *broke*. They let the enemy through. They should have sold themselves dearly, dying where they stood. But they couldn't have. It's not in their blood. It's not in *your* blood."

"Oh, they fought. Their leader lost half an arm, and his command well over half its number." Owen's hands tightened into fists. "And I hasten to add, Mr. Wattling, that Lord Rivendell's son, John, never answered the call to come to our aid. His inactivity is what doomed the left flank."

"Another slander from a coward's mouth!"

Owen lowered his voice. "It is in deference to Captain Tar that I do not demand satisfaction of you, sir, right here and right now. And because my uncle, Richard, the Duke of Deathridge, frowns on dueling."

"Your *uncle*, sir?"

"My mother is his youngest brother's wife. That would make him my uncle."

Wattling's jowls quivered. "But, sir, your name. Strake is a Mystrian name."

"And so my father was Mystrian, a sailor like the good captain here. He met my mother, married her, and got her with me before his ship was lost to pirates. She later married Francis Ventnor."

Wattling's mouth hung open. "I had no idea, sir."

"Nor could you have, since Captain Tar was under strict orders to keep my identity secret. My orders, you understand, from my *uncle*."

"The Duke, yes, quite." Wattling smiled slyly, his complexion still ashen. "I should have seen through it, of course, your disguise, to your breeding. No Colonial would have stopped me as you did."

"Yes, about that." Owen turned to Captain Tar. "You'll understand, sir, if I prefer charges of assault against Mr. Wattling here. I would make it attempted murder, but I cannot ascertain Mr. Wattling's intent in beating the boy."

Wattling's eyes widened. "You cannot, sir! The boy is a redemptioneer. He is indentured to me."

"I can, sir, and I will, unless…"

"Yes?"

"You cancel his indenture contract and pay him a crown."

"That is an outrage!"

"Captain, if you were to drop anchor here, and we tried Mr. Wattling, what would the penalty be?"

"Fifty lashes."

"You cannot flog me! I am a *gentleman!*"

Owen closed the gap between them in two easy steps. "No, sir, you are not. You are a pompous fool who has made the mistake of insulting the Mystrians who surround him, and will surround him. And let us not be coy, sir. If you were such a success in Norisle, you would not have packed your press and come so far over the sea. You'd hardly allow that Colonials can read, yet you bring a press to serve their need for reading material. Is it to make your fortune, sir, or to avoid paying a fortune to your creditors?"

Wattling shrank back against the ship's rail. His voice barely rose above the hiss of sea against hull. "I haven't got a crown, sir. All those damned pirated editions of *Villerupt*. They ruined me. And now, without a servant, how will I earn money? How will I live?"

Gideon Tar rested a hand on the man's shoulder. "You will live like every Mystrian, Mr. Wattling. You will work hard. You'll be cold in the winter. Hungry, too. You'll marvel at some things and quake in fear at others. You'll sweat, you'll ache. You will live and perhaps even prosper."

The Captain guided the man toward the main deck. "You'll want to get below to finish gathering your things."

Once Wattling had disappeared, Gideon returned to Owen's side. "I don't normally abide flogging, but for him…"

"If arrogance was a flogging offense, he'd have long since grown immune to the lash."

"Doubtless true, my lord."

Owen shook his head. "Don't, Captain. I'm not a noble. My stepfather never adopted me. Out of deference to my mother's father, Lord Ventnor provided me a basic education. He applauded my entering the army, with high hopes I'd die on the Continent."

"And Duke Deathridge?"

"Much the same. My wife pleaded for him to give me this chance."

Gideon slowly nodded. "So the endless war will be expanding to Mystria."

"It's a long way from a Minister's notion to cannons thundering in the wilderness."

"There are times I wonder if the Ministers even know why we fight the Tharyngians."

"Honor? Because they overthrew their King and now the Laureates rule? Because the last generation failed to conquer them, so this generation must?"

Owen leaned heavily on the ship's rail, fatigue both physical and spiritual making his limbs tremble. "They *are* evil. During Villerupt, I saw things no man ever should. You don't want that coming to Mystria."

Tar smiled. "Then I shall be happy you are here to prevent it."

Owen laughed. "I hope, sir, you are right."

Tar looked out toward the harbor. He fished a small crystal sphere from his pocket and held it up to his right eye. The glass glowed with a faint blue light. The man smiled. "Harbormaster is coming out to guide us in."

Owen looked west, but shook his head.

Tar held the crystal out to him. "Use it, if you like."

"Thank you, no. I never mastered the spell that focuses those things for me." Owen held up a thumb. "All the magick they say I need is here."

"Shooting fast and straight has its advantages in your line of work."

"It does, sir, it does."

A shout from a small boat called Captain Tar away to deal with a harbormaster.

Owen remained at the rail, sorely missing his wife. He should have felt relief at finally being in spitting distance of solid land, but in the absence of seasickness, loneliness opened a void in his middle.

I wish you had come, Catherine. At once he realized he was being selfish, because she truly would have been miserable. She would have hated the ship's cramped quarters and found the ship's fare inedible. Aside from Captain Tar's wife, she would have found no suitable companions among the other women. Had she been called upon to actually work, she would have been completely lost.

He smiled, thinking of how she would have whispered about her adventures, no matter how minor. She could make removing a splinter seem like an assault on a fortress. That ability endeared her to him. Her world was so completely removed from his that he could take refuge in it.

And it was her desire to provide him refuge that had given her the strength and courage to beard Duke Deathridge in his own den and convince him that Owen had to be sent on this mission. They both hoped Owen's adventure would allow him to earn enough of a reward that they could take a small home in Launston and live quietly. *She'd even suggested I could write a book about my adventures and make more money that way. And I have just angered a publisher.*

He glanced over at the main deck, where Wattling and the preacher, Benjamin Beecher, stood at the rail. Beecher had seemed harmless on the crossing, holding services every Sunday and not sermonizing for too long. Perhaps Wattling was looking for spiritual guidance, though Owen deemed it more likely that the fat man simply sought pity.

Owen turned his attention to the Mystrian shore. Ancient forests with tall pines, birches, oaks, and other trees he could not name formed a dark palisade warding rolling hills and far distant mountains. Deep in Temperance Bay, the Benjamin River flowed into the harbor. The town had grown back from the water and up over the hills, with buildings mostly of wood and many of stone.

The war in Auropa had lasted four years, consuming men and money with surprising ease. Norillian and Tharyngian colonies provided the wealth that drove the economies and backed the war bonds that paid for the war. If Norisle could cut off Tharyngia's flow of wealth, the Tharyngians would be forced to surrender.

And likewise Norisle if we lose control of our Mystrian holdings.

He understood the wisdom that sent him half a world away to scout Tharyngian territory. It made perfect sense in the world of ledgers and figures. Men and brimstone and guns and uniforms all could be inventoried, then bundled on to ships with weighed-and-measured stores of food. Ministers would invest resources in the war—primarily to deny resources to the enemy—thereby winning that war. It would be a superior return on their investment.

But men were not numbers even though casualty lists suggested otherwise. *Numbers do not scream. They do not cry out for their mothers.* Owen shivered. *Numbers do not beg to die.*

Captain Tar broke through his thoughts. "It occurs to me, Captain, that men like Wattling want to believe they understand the reality of war."

"That is the folly of many men."

"Can anyone understand battle if they have not been there? I've not seen much fighting—fended off a pirate or two—but holding a Mate so the doctor can saw his leg off stays with a man."

Owen straightened up. "Wattling was partly right. Soldiers and sailors, we choose our lot. Seeing a weeping man staggering beneath the weight of his wife's headless body makes you wonder what war would do to Temperance."

Tar turned toward their destination. "It's a long way between New Tharyngia and Temperance Bay."

"Let's just hope it stays that way." Owen gave the man a smile. "And if my mission is successful, it will."

CHAPTER TWO

April 27, 1763
Temperance Bay, Mystria

Owen Strake disembarked from the *Coronet* once the longboats had pulled it to the dock. His papers had been sent ahead with the Harbormaster, bound for Her Majesty's military headquarters. The Prince's Life Guards had been stationed in Temperance, in deference to Prince Vladimir's presence as Colonial Governor-General. The Guards had earned their assignment as a result of their failures fighting the Tharyngians—and hated it.

Though happy to be off the ship, reorienting himself to walking on solid ground presented challenges. Owen stumbled a bit, clearly appearing drunk to a pair of women who hurried out of his sight. Their long, somber grey clothing along with the disgust on their faces suggested they were of the Virtuan sect, which had founded both the Temperance Bay and larger Bounty colonies. While more liberal individuals had flooded Temperance in the pursuit of commerce, the Virtuan influence could be seen in a singular lack of visible public houses or bawdy houses near the wharves.

Both existed in Temperance. The Virtuans had gathered them in the South End, on the other shore of the Benjamin River—swampy land that festered with noxious vapors and biting midges. He had to admire the Virtuans' pragmatic nature. They could not prevent men from indulging in vices, so they guaranteed that torment for sinfulness began at the moment of indulgence.

Likewise their practicality showed in the way the city had been laid out. The hills made a grid impractical, so they began with a hub at the wharves and sent seven spoke roads radiating out. Arcing roads cut across the hills and, further out, new spoke roads kept the space between blocks somewhat uniform. Six bridges crossed the Benjamin, which was one more than the city needed now, and three more than when founded.

Owen enquired of the Harbormaster where the Guards were located and set off on Fortitude Street. He worked his way up the gentle slope, then cut south on Generosity. Shortly, on the left, he found the headquarters. It appeared as nothing more than a house with a small sign in the narrow front yard. Save for the sign, and two Guards standing either side of the door, he could have walked past it without a clue as to its purpose.

The guards, in their red coats with buff facing, and tall, bearskin hats, neither saluted nor seemed to notice Owen at all. He entered and reported to a Sergeant Major sitting in what should have been a parlor. The man bade him wait, then slipped down the hall to another room.

Owen looked about, feeling uneasy. The room had wainscoting, a chair rail and plaster over lathe to finish it, yet had an incomplete quality. Soot from the stone fireplace stained the whitewashed wall, but that was hardly unusual.

Then it struck him. His wife would have caught it immediately. *The room is utterly devoid of decoration.* Back home in Norisle some cherished treasures would have a place of honor on the mantle. A picture of the Queen would have hung on a wall. Other pictures, or a shelf with books, or even a carving on a wooden panel would provide some character. A flag, a hanging of some sort, something to add color at the very least.

It is terribly sterile. He wasn't sure if this was an artifact of Virtuan influence or that Colonel Langford was one of those humorless men who believed that Saturday floggings and Sunday services were the keys to maintaining a ready fighting force. *Were that true, however, there should have been at least one wooden cross to display allegiance with the Church of Norisle.*

The Sergeant Major returned and conducted him to Colonel Langford's office. He announced Owen, then retreated, pulling the door closed behind him.

Owen saluted and the man returned it half-heartedly, never even looking up from his desk. Unlike the bare receiving room, the office was jammed with shelves bowed beneath the weight of books. Papers rose in piles on the desk, held down by a powder horn, two odd skulls, and several stone implements Owen could not identify.

"Sit please, Captain." Langford pointed with the end of the quill, then went on to scratch another line into a ledger. The man's powdered wig rested on a stand on a table by the window. His bald pate was beaded with sweat, and grime soiled his jacket's cuffs.

Owen did as he was bid. "Have you, sir, had a chance—"

Langford hissed at him, looked up for a heartbeat, then scribbled another line. He then sighed and dipped his pen again before sitting back. The man's glasses magnified his tired blue eyes and the bags beneath them.

"I have read your orders, sir. The Home Offices and Foreign Bureau have no understanding of Mystria." Langford made another note and smirked. "I do not like having you here, sir. The wars on the Continent are not something we wish to have spilling over here."

"Colonel…"

The quill flicked Owen to silence. "No, sir, I shall hear none of it. You will follow orders and report home. Let that be the end of this foolishness."

Owen frowned. "I do not understand, sir, your ire."

"I do not expect you do, Captain, nor will you."

"I believe, sir, your perspective in this matter would be helpful to my mission's success."

"Success, Captain? You are as much a fool as those who sent you." Langford set his quill down, then closed the inkpot's metal lid. "Let me put it simply. We have forty thousand troops ready for this summer's campaigning on the Continent. They will fight in an area that comprises roughly one *tenth* of the Crown Colonies—an area that has roads, has been settled for centuries, and is so close to Norisle that children could construct a raft that could easily make the journey. By contrast, it took you seven weeks to get here—and a swift crossing that was. We have three thousand regular troops on this side of the ocean, and can raise twice that in militia. Even if we were to do that, the lack of roads or any other sort of transport means attacking New Tharyngia is impossible. A campaign would also require us to deal with the Nations of Twilight People who inhabit the wilderness. Impossible."

Langford pointed toward the northeast. "You, sir, will be heading into a trackless green Hell populated with infernal beasts and people, and all for naught."

"These are my orders, sir."

Langford snorted. "You are not the first they've sent. Sensible men have remained here and hired accounts written by others. Follow their example, sir."

Owen stood and enjoyed Langford's little fright as Owen loomed over his superior. "I shall assume, sir, this suggestion is a test to see if I will follow orders; and suitable disciplinary actions would have been taken if I agreed to it."

Langford's hand started toward his quill, then he thought better of it. "Yes, a test. Very good, Captain, you passed. Cannot be too careful."

Owen nodded. "I will prepare a list of the things I need. I would appreciate your supplementing it with supplies that would facilitate my mission."

Langford nodded and took his quill up again. "Gladly, sir."

The sooner I am out of here, the sooner you imagine the wilderness will kill me. "There is also the matter, Colonel, of a packet I have for the Prince."

Langford looked up. "You will wish to deliver this to him directly, I assume."

"Those were my orders."

"Very well." Langford scribbled a note on a piece of paper, handed it to Owen. "Sergeant Major Hilliard will send you on your way. I will have your things sent around to your billet."

"Very good, sir, thank you." Owen came to attention and saluted.

Langford slowly rose and returned the salute. "Your mission is futile. Your determination will get you killed."

Owen smiled. "I've no intention to make my wife a widow, sir, but I will fulfill my orders."

The Guards' stable master gave him a bay gelding and directions. Owen followed Blessedness Road around to Justice and out through Westgate, heading west on the Bounty Trail. The route roughly paralleled the Benjamin River for several miles, then diverged as the river dipped toward the south.

The trail deserved the name, since it was little more than a set of wagon ruts flanked by grasses trampled beneath foot and hoof. Most commercial traffic, Owen guessed, came down the river. He passed a number of estates with their own docks; very few of them had a drive connecting to the trail. The river, clearly, served as the primary transportation route.

Owen did not ride as swiftly as he might, despite his urgency to deliver the sealed packet to the Prince. The land's breadth and lack of development surprised him. Back in Norisle there might be great expanses of fields, but walls divided them. All of them lay under cultivation. Forests dotted the land but more as private hunting preserves for nobility than places where no man had yet set ax to tree. Cresting hills and riding down into valleys, he expected to see small villages astride the trail, but none existed. A mile or two outside Temperance and he could have been the last man alive.

Were I slain here, no one would ever know. That thought sent a shiver down his spine and a brief glimpse of his wife in mourning. The black clothes would suit her, her brown eyes glistening with tears. She would dab at them with delicate hands, her brown hair gathered back, her flesh pale, beautiful in her grief.

Owen felt no overt threat, but Langford's comment came back to him. He checked the horse pistol holstered on the saddle. Its presence reassured him, but the realization that he really didn't know Mystria nibbled away at him.

Langford had described infernal beasts and hostile natives. In the capital, Owen had visited displays of stuffed creatures from Mystria, and of drawings revealing the Twilight People in all their savage glory. Many early colonists had perished on these shores because of poor harvests and brutal winters.

His horse pistol would do little to save him from either, or many of the monsters. But if he did his work quickly and well, he'd be back in Norisle before the first snow fell, safe again with Catherine, beginning his new life.

He half-smiled. Most people seeking to begin a new life did so by moving *to* the colonies. He wanted only to explore, then return home. With enough money, he and Catherine could escape his family and know true happiness.

Owen allowed the bright sun and play of butterflies amid fields of red and gold wildflowers to distract him from darker thoughts. His mission would provide enough information that wiser heads could craft a campaign for the coming year. He would complete his survey, carry his report back to Launston, and the Tower Ministers would issue orders that would win glory for some and kill many more.

And I shall be far away with my wife, happy at last.

By mid-afternoon Owen rounded a hill covered in tall oaks and looked down upon the Prince's estate. A small trail broke off to the south between two lines of trees onto the forested grounds. The main house—a massive brick building—had been fashioned after a summer hunting palace, complete with two wings at right angles to the center. Other outbuildings lay half-hidden in the woods nearest the river. Surprisingly little of the forest had been cleared, and in a few places it had made inroads into flat lawns.

Aside from a thin trickle of smoke from a chimney, the only sign of life about the place was a peasant stringing pea-vines up in a small plot near the front door. Owen rode up and dismounted, making enough noise to attract the man's attention. When the peasant continued puttering away, Owen assumed he was old and deaf, so moved to where the man could see him.

Unless he's blind as well.

The man continued working.

"Excuse me." Owen prepared to hand the man his horse's reins, but hesitated.

The gardener wiped his hands off on his thighs, then tipped his broad hat back. He rocked to his feet fluidly—proving he was not particularly old, nor in any way deaf or blind. He smiled. "You would be Strake."

Owen dropped the reins. "Forgive me, Your Highness. I…"

"I admire your restraint, Captain. The last man they sent was a Major who hit me with a crop."

Owen's mouth gaped.

Prince Vladimir laughed. Able to look Owen in the eye, he had a more willowy build. His brown eyes were a shade lighter than his mahogany hair, and a few wisps of white dotted his goatee. Leanness hollowed his face, and sun had weathered his flesh. He looked the very antithesis of nobles at his aunt's court.

Closing his mouth, Owen pointed at the peas. "You were tending peas when I arrived as a test?"

"Come now, Captain, you are smarter than that."

Owen thought for a moment. There had been no way that the Prince could have anticipated the day or time of his arrival. "But, Highness, your refusal to acknowledge me…"

"Yes, *that* was a test. Love to know a man's temperament." The Prince gathered up the bay's reins. "Come along. You'll have a packet for me and I'll need my spectacles."

The Prince led him past the eastern wing and handed the reins to a stable boy. The Prince washed his hands in a drinking trough, then they entered the manor through a door facing the trail. They passed through an interior door into a massive room that occupied most of that wing's ground floor.

The Prince crossed to a large desk set against the interior wall. Owen waited in the doorway. Countless shelves filled the space, lining the walls and segmenting the room. Books filled some shelves, but others held jars in which dead specimens drifted in viscous suspensions. Frogs and fish he could easily recognize, but other things were beyond his ken. A live raven cawed from a cage opposite the desk. Posted on the top shelves, or hung from the ceiling, preserved and mounted alien animals stared at Owen with glassy eyes. The largest of them occupied displays in the corners, save for a huge bear reared up—claws and fangs clearly visible—beside the Prince's desk.

Vladimir removed his hat and hung it over the bear's muzzle. He waved Owen into the room. "The packet, Captain?"

Owen started, then removed the orders from inside his jacket and handed them over.

The Prince smiled as he unlaced the leather wrapping. "Feel free to explore. You may find, here in my little museum, that some of your work has already been done."

CHAPTER THREE

April 27, 1763
Prince Haven
Temperance Bay, Mystria

Owen cautiously approached the work table at the room's heart. Several bound volumes lay open. Pressed and dried flowers had been affixed to the pages of one, with notes penned in an even, feminine hand. They described the flower in every detail, including its preferred habitat and range, as well as its known and suspected uses.

Other books displayed well-drawn images of birds and animals. The writing recorded many of the same details as in the flower book, but in a much bolder hand. Owen suspected that to be the Prince's work. The animal accounts also included hunters' anecdotes. Some entries had numbers beside them which, Owen quickly figured out, referred to specimens in jars.

The pages crackled as Owen turned them. The rough paper rasped across his fingertips. Many of the creatures strongly resembled those back in Norisle, often only differing in color or size. But some other creatures... *Can such things exist?*

He looked up. An ivory skull weighed down a stack of papers: clearly feline and much larger than any wild cat he'd ever seen. The curved fangs were nearly a handspan in length. He traced a finger along the inside edge and almost cut himself on the serrated surface. The teeth had been designed for slicing flesh and sinew.

The Prince glanced over his shoulder and chuckled. "That's a small one. The adult is over there." The Prince pointed toward the corner of the room, hidden behind a tall clutter of shelves. "They've coded this message. I will be a minute. Go take a look."

Owen nodded as the Prince sat at his desk. The soldier squeezed into the labyrinth of shelves, careful not to upset anything. His shoulders brushed books on both sides. Twisting around to the right, he turned a blind corner, then gasped. His left hand came up to fend off his attacker as his right hand fell to where he should have been wearing a pistol.

Instead of the skull he'd been expecting to find, he'd come face to face with a fully mounted and articulated cat of enormous proportions. A few dark spots haphazardly dappled the short, tawny fur along its spine. Tufted ears flattened back against its skull. Its snarl revealed the saber teeth ready to drive deep into prey. Clawed paws reached for him, ready to hook and hold. From its nose to the tip of its stubby tail the creature had to have been at least eight feet long and would've been about five feet at the shoulder.

The glassiness of the creature's dark eyes and its rigidity left no doubt that it was dead, but its lifelike pose made it a creature of nightmares. Owen peered closely at it, both admiring its size and looking for some sign of what had killed it. The creature appeared to be in full health and Owen found no obvious wounds.

The Prince appeared, smiling. "Bravo, Captain Strake. You didn't scream. That was not true of Colonel Langford."

"What is it?" Owen brushed a hand along its back, feeling the fur. "I've been to zoological gardens, but never…"

Prince Vlad stroked the creature's other flank. "It has many names. Some call it a lion or a tiger. It doesn't have enough spots to be leopard. I prefer sabertooth cat. Many Mystrians call it a *jeopard*. I believe it's a play on the words leopard and jeopardy. It's rather accurate so I may give in and adopt it."

Owen shivered. Displays and pictures in Norisle had been completely inadequate. He assumed stories of fabulous beasts had been intended to scare children and credulous individuals who would never set foot on that distant shore.

The Prince smiled. "I apologize for sending you here unawares. I've closed off this little corner of my workshop as a test for visitors. Put it down to my odd sense of humor, perhaps?" He patted the nearby shelves. "I even reinforced the woodwork, since the common Norillian reaction is to flee gibbering madly."

Owen smiled, imagining Mr. Wattling's probable reaction. "Colonel Langford considered me as welcome in his office as he would a jeopard, I think."

The Prince nodded and waved Owen back out toward the desk. "Langford never was much of a field commander. He does well for himself as a glorified quartermaster. I understand he rents his men out for work details and pockets the money."

Owen blinked. "And you have not reported him for this?"

Vlad sat at his desk. "It is a game we play. He knows that I know, so occasionally the work projects are for the common good. Oh, Captain, don't look so surprised. I really have no other alternative."

"Highness, there are regulations and duties."

The Prince nodded easily. "Were I to prefer charges, Langford would be sent to Rivertown, down in Fairlee. General Upton would hold him and send my request for a court martial back to Norisle. Six months later, after Parliament has argued about things, the request would be denied. Langford would return and the cycle would continue."

"That hardly seems…"

"Fair? Equitable? It isn't." Vlad got up, moved books off a stool, and brought it over for Owen. "Sit, please. Norillians who come to Mystria greet this land in one of two manners. Some see it as a land of great riches. They harvest as much as they can, and return home. Some are refilling their families' coffers, others are social climbers. The motive doesn't matter. They each have their personal goal and they strive for it, and nothing more.

"The others, though, they have the spirit of the redemptioneers, even if they are here of their own free will." The Prince hunched forward, his elbows on this thighs. "They see this continent as a place rich in possibilities. A man can be anything he wants to be here. He can be free."

Owen found himself grinning at the Prince's enthusiasm. It struck Owen as incongruous because here he was, sitting with the man who was third in line for the throne of Norisle, and yet there was no pretense. While the man may have tested him earlier, Owen felt accepted as an equal.

Vlad straightened up. "Your reaction to my jeopard and Langford tells me something about you, Captain, but I need to know more."

Owen nodded. "As you desire, Highness."

"Who is it that hates you so much that you were given this assignment?" The Prince tapped the unfolded orders. "The cover letter is rather plain. The phrase here, '…the mission, to be carried out to the best of his abilities,' usually means they won't mind if you don't come back."

"Not enemies, Highness, family. My wife beseeched my uncle to let me have this assignment." Owen sighed. "The Duke of Deathridge, my uncle, allowed himself to be swayed by her passion."

"Your wife must be charming indeed." The Prince's eyes narrowed. "Still, to send you to Mystria… I would guess you're not his *favorite* nephew."

"Far from it, Highness." *If I didn't make it home, his only concern would be getting me a headstone cheap.*

The Prince opened a drawer in his desk and pulled out a crystalline disc. He held it so it fit neatly between the thumb and forefinger of his right hand, tucked deeply into the joint. He squinted for a moment, and the glass began to glow. The Prince stared into it as he traced it back and forth across the pages of coded symbols. He paused in his reading every so often, setting the disc down, making a note in the margin of Owen's orders, then picking the lens up again to continue reading.

Finished, the Prince sat back. "I can see your uncle's hand in the mission document—not literally, of course, but close. While others have come on similar missions, your orders are by far the most complete and show the best understanding of the Mystrian situation. The way to defeat the Tharyngians on the Continent is to beat them here. Your uncle, it appears, understands that fact well."

The Prince got up and pulled a large, scrolled map from atop a shelf. He spread it over the table, pinning down one corner with the jeopard skull and another with a sharpened stone blade. One of the flower books held down the map's left side, allowing the corners to curl in.

"This is the entire continent—at least as much for which I have reliable information. The Tharyngians claim everything north of the Argent River and west to what are called the Four Brothers Lakes. They also claim everything on down the long, wide Misaawa River."

"Misaawa?"

"In the native tongue—or one of them anyway—it means 'life.'" His finger traced a line of mountains to the east of the river, almost halfway to the coast. "Our Colonial charters grant us rights to the land between the ocean and these mountains. A century and a half ago the mountains were deemed impassible, *and* no one imagined we would expand so quickly. The redemptioneers, it turns out, were more fecund and industrious than thought possible. But then, when you have to work to live, and more hands make working easier, you create an interesting cycle of life.

"The Tharyngians have not been so fortunate. The north has a much shorter growing season. They regularly import food from Tharyngia. But because they work more closely with the Twilight People than we do, they're sending a great deal of money back to the Continent. Fur sales finance their war effort. Timber and potash production and even limited amounts of gold contribute as well. To protect themselves, they've begun to establish a series of forts at critical river junctions and on the myriad small lakes in the west. They've chased off our trappers and settlers."

The Prince tapped the Misaawa River with a finger. "I believe the Misaawa River Valley to be every bit as fertile as the best of our lands. If the Tharyngians establish settlements there, like the one they have at the base of the river, it won't be long before their population will meet or exceed ours. Once that happens, we will be trapped. We will face open warfare here, just like on the Continent."

Owen studied the map. The mountains had been sketched in with black ink, and rivers traced in blue—save for the Misaawa. That river had become a long, thick sepia line, looking like dried blood. That same hue had been used to create several other features, mostly in the south and west.

Owen frowned. "Have you just not put roads on the map?"

"Wouldn't waste the ink." The Prince shrugged. "Would you call the track you rode out on here a proper road?"

"No, Highness."

"You're not alone. Colonel Langford cannot imagine how troops could march into battle lacking good roads. And our tiny patches of cleared land are nothing he recognizes as proper battlefields."

Owen smiled. "I remember the Mystrian Rangers fighting throughout the Artennes Forest against the Platine Regiment. The lack of a cleared field didn't seem to bother either unit."

"Good, very good. If you understand that much, then perhaps you *are* the man for this job." The Prince stroked a hand across his chin. "I'm going to make certain you see what needs to be seen. Langford will assign you a couple of his scouts—competent men, but lazy, I'm afraid. It won't do."

"No, Highness."

"I will write him a note telling him that I'm sending my man with you. Langford will protest, but I have dealt with that before."

Owen nodded. "Your man is good, Highness?"

Vlad smiled broadly. "The best. He's the one who killed that jeopard."

Before Owen could ask, the prince led him back to the large cat. He spread the fur on the creature's throat revealing a small hole. The Prince then rubbed a hand over the jeopard's spine. "Went in at the throat, came out there. A hundred yards. One shot."

Owen gasped. "Highness…"

The Prince raised a hand. "First, Captain Strake, I paced the distance myself. And while you're about to tell me that a musket cannot hit a target with a killing shot at that range, a *rifle* can, and this is what Nathaniel used. Fourteen-weight of lead, flying true."

Owen measured the angle between the entry and exit wounds. *The thing was charging at the time, much as it is now.* "That was quite a shot, Highness."

"Two winters ago, very harsh. It got a taste for men, came down hunting. We stalked it." The Prince blushed. "I missed, despite using a fine rifle given to my father by a Seljuk Calife. Nathaniel dropped it and had his rifle reloaded before it had finished thrashing."

"I shall be pleased to meet such a remarkable marksman, Highness."

Prince Vlad looked Owen up and down again. "And I shall be interested in seeing what he makes of you, Captain Strake. In fact, I wish I could join you on your expedition."

"It would be an honor, Highness."

"You're kind, but I would just slow you down." The Prince's face brightened. "But, speaking of honors, I have a favor to ask of you, if I might."

"Anything you desire, Highness."

"Well then, come with me." The Prince headed toward the yard. "I'd like to know what you think of my dragon."

CHAPTER FOUR

April 27, 1763
Prince Haven
Temperance Bay, Mystria

Owen followed the Prince outside and down over a vast expanse of lawn gently sloping toward the river. There, just past the dock, half-hidden by a small stand of trees, lay a broad, squat structure. Rough-hewn timber framed it, and uneven boards sided it. Despite being painted red and having the requisite slate roof, it did not much resemble similarly purposed buildings back in Norisle.

Traditionally wurmrests were built of stone—though it occurred to Owen this might've been because most wurmrests were centuries old. Enormously strong and often clumsier than anyone would wish, wurms smashed through anything less sturdy than stone walls. Bearing this in mind, Owen looked for any signs that the careless lash of a tail had knocked boards loose, but to no avail.

As with all the wurmrests he'd seen, this one was situated close to the river. Come spring floods, water channeling through the wurmrest would thoroughly clean it out. An added benefit to such a location was that the sound of running water and cool breezes coming off the river calmed wurms during uncomfortable summer months.

Something's missing. Owen couldn't identify what was wrong until he reached the building's shadow. *It doesn't stink!*

Wurmrests usually had a rather distinctive odor about them, one that no one described as pleasant. The kindest description had likened the stench to the lingering stink of a battlefield after three days under a hot sun. Wurmwrights developed a strong stomach very quickly, or found another line of work.

"Highness, you *do* understand I am not a wurmwright. If there's something wrong with it…"

The Prince nodded. "You mean the lack of stench? Mugwump has taken to eating some local berries. He still feeds mostly on fish and beef, but follows his meals with the berries. They make him decidedly less fragrant."

"Mugwump? I thought your wurm's name was Gorfinbard."

"It was. Still is in all the official registries." The Prince slipped the bar from one of the two broad barn doors. "Once, the chief of the Altashee—one of the Twilight Peoples—visited. I showed him my wurm. He called him mugwump, or something very close in their tongue. Mugwump actually responded and seems pleased with that name. I have no idea what it means and I'm not anxious to find out, but if it pleases the beast, I will use it."

Owen grabbed the other door and pulled, then followed the Prince into the dark interior. They moved along a raised wooden walkway spattered with dry mud. A waist-high railing on the river side made it difficult for someone to accidentally fall into the wurmpit. The Prince leaned against the rail and nodded. "And there he is: Mugwump."

Owen stared down, admiring. Though the Prince had referred to the creature as a dragon, it was technically a wurm since it lacked wings and could not fly. "He is magnificent."

Being a member of the Ventnor family and then the Queen's Own Wurm Regiment had afforded Owen ample opportunity to study wurms up close. He often spent time on his grandfather's estates caring for his uncles' wurms, though he'd never been given the chance to ride one all by himself. Not being of noble blood nor possessed of great wealth, he could not afford to buy a commission in the actual wurm companies. That not withstanding, he was more comfortable around the great beasts than some of their riders.

Without a second thought, Owen descended into the pit. He kept toward the edge where the mud remained shallow and worked his way toward the beast's head. The Prince, who was better dressed for a foray into the pit, followed him. Owen moved slowly, taking great care not to slip—less out of concern for his clothes than not wanting to excite the wurm.

Ten yards from Mugwump's head he squatted, gathering the tails of his coat into his lap to save them from the mud. He smiled; he couldn't help it. Of the many wurms he'd seen, Mugwump was by far the most impressive.

Forty feet long, perhaps a bit longer, the wurm was covered with black scales. Though the wurmrest's dim light made it difficult to be certain, the scales shone far more brightly than the dull wurmflesh common in the Regiment. The beast's horns and claws appeared more substantial than on Regimental wurms. Moreover, gold and scarlet stripes and dots decorated the scales and horns. Owen had never seen anything like it on a living wurm.

Mugwump lay his lower jaw in a puddle, a leafy branch from some bush sticking out of it. As the men drew close, he opened one golden eye, the tall, slender pupil narrowed slightly, and a semi-opaque membrane nictitated up over the golden orb. The creature raised his head slightly, dark water dripping from his jaw line.

"Captain, beware."

Though Owen knew what was coming, he didn't move.

The wurm dropped his wedge-shaped head. A wave of mud splashed up, coating Owen from the waist down and spattering him above.

Owen howled with laughter and the wurm snorted. The soldier wiped mud from his face and smiled broadly. "My uncle had one that pulled similar tricks. He was vicious at molt. We'd have to wait until he'd almost finished shedding, then deal with him."

Prince Vlad raised an eyebrow. "I thought you said you were not a wurm-wright."

"I'm not, but the Ventnor family wurmwright was a good man. Lost his wife and children to the Black Pox. He took me under his wing whenever I was home from school. Time in the wurmrest kept me out of sight and from having to deal with my cousins. It became my refuge."

"Then, if I might, I would like to avail myself of your experience." The Prince whistled.

Mugwump shifted. Plowing up a muddy berm, the great beast swung his head around and thrust his snout between the two of them. Hot breath came in short blasts from his nostrils, strong enough to almost knock Owen over.

Steadying himself with one hand on Mugwump's muzzle, the Prince moved toward his eyes. "Go over on the other side. You know where the aural canal is?"

"Yes, Highness." Owen advanced, ending up ankle deep in mud just behind the creature's jaw, a couple of feet below one of the golden eyes. The wurm's aural canal sat just behind and a little above the corner of the jaw. An armored scale as big as a dinner plate shielded it.

"Now, if you will, Captain, take hold of the canal cover and try to shift it. Gently."

Owen cautiously slid his fingers under the scale. Dragons had two layers of flesh. One, the scales—hard like fingernails—were anchored in the lower layer. That lower layer felt supple and warm, much like a snake that had been sunning itself. Mugwump's flesh felt normal, reassuring Owen.

He manipulated the canal cover, slowly at first, then with a bit more vigor. It felt loose, like a tooth almost ready to fall free. For contrast he tried another scale, but it held firmly. A third had a moderate amount of give.

"Have you discovered it, Captain?"

Owen moved back to where he could see the Prince. Vlad leaned against Mugwump's muzzle, his elbows and forearms resting there as if the wurm were just a piece of furniture. He paid no apparent attention to the golden-eyed stare. *Or his proximity to a mouth full of razor-sharp ivory.*

Owen frowned. "It was loose, Highness. Scales do fall out from time to time. I don't see any Green Bloom on him. He seems warm. If he is eating well…"

"No sign of molt, Captain?"

Owen shook his head. Wurms periodically shed their scales and spun cocoons of dragon silk. Very strong, it would be harvested and spun into wonderfully tough and lightweight garments. All of the Regiment's Wurmriders had combat uniforms cut from it. The cocoon was a harbinger of a molt, and cutting a wurm prematurely from the cocoon was vital because no wurm survived chrysalis.

When freed from their cocoon, they remained asleep for weeks. Some even slept for months. They sloughed off their skin, which had to be cut away. Men highly prized the outer layer of flesh. The Wurmriders all had boots and gauntlets of wurmleather. Once freed of their old skin, the wurms woke up and within a month had grown new scales. Those trained to war took to the their old duties without requiring additional drills.

"I did not feel any silk, and he has too many scales yet."

Vlad stroked a hand over his chin, smearing mud. "Your observations concur with mine and those of my wurmwright, Mr. Baker. My concern is that the loose scales are distributed over Mugwump in a bilaterally symmetrical pattern."

Owen frowned. "But it can't be a molt since he has not spun."

"Do we know that cocoons are necessary for a molt?" The Prince held his hands up. "I don't mean for you to answer that. It's a question of some minor debate between me and some of my Auropean correspondents. I find the pattern intriguing because birds, to maintain stability in flight, molt in a bilaterally symmetrical pattern. If the ancient stories are true, and dragons could fly, perhaps this loosening of scales presages something more?"

"Highness, that's not a question I can answer."

Prince Vlad laughed. "It takes a wise man to admit ignorance. There can be other explanations, of course. Mugwump has been in the royal stables for centuries, but he's not been fought in the last fifty years. Being as how he's the only wurm in Mystria, there has been no reason to bring him to combat."

"It could be, Highness, that he's about to shed armor he's not using." Owen frowned. "I do have to say, he's the biggest wurm I've seen, and…" Owen traced a finger along some scarlet and gold striping running up the muzzle. "I've never seen markings like these before."

"Nor have I. The Truscian painter, Giarimo, did his portrait just over a century ago. No sign of the markings then." The Prince patted Mugwump on the muzzle. "If only you could talk, my friend, you could tell me. Is it your peaceful life, or it is something else? Your reaction to this land, perhaps, as Mister Baker believes?"

The wurm lifted his head and brought it, dripping, over Owen and back toward the puddle. His thick, black tongue swept out, dragging that branch into his maw, then his mouth closed. Mugwump eyed them for a second, then twisted and rolled down into the center of his wallow. He writhed there, grinding his back into the mud, his four legs reflexively clawing toward the roof. His mouth opened again, his tongue lolled out, and his eyes closed.

The Prince sighed. "Things would be much easier if he shared my love of science and discovery. And forgive me boring you with my inquiries."

Owen held his hands up. "Please, Highness, it was an honor."

Prince Vlad pointed at the gold band on Owen's left hand. "Did you bring your wife with you?"

"No, Highness." Owen smiled. "Though had she known I would be meeting you, she would have endured the journey."

"I'm certain your wife would be delightful company."

"You're very kind, Highness."

The Prince's eyes glittered. "Shall I gather that if I wanted to know any Norillian court gossip, she would have been a good source?"

"Her one failing, Highness." Owen sighed. "She told me a great deal before I left, but I did not pay attention. No matter; it would all be old."

"And given my aunt's often mercurial personality, it would likely have changed, or changed back, since you sailed." Vlad laughed. "There are times when the ocean is welcome insulation from her guidance."

Owen smiled politely, not knowing what else to do.

The Prince waved him forward. "Come, let us get you cleaned up. I can do at least that. Eli, my wurmwright's son, serves as my squire and will get most of the mud off your coat. Those breeches are beyond salvation."

Owen ascended the short ladder onto the walkway. "Please, Highness, I appreciate the offer but will decline. Colonel Langford will take some pleasure in seeing me thus."

"You mustn't tell him that Mugwump did this. The man has forever desired to see the wurm. Petty, I know, but denying him that pleasure is one of the few means I have of irritating him. I suspect that speaks well of neither of us but, as vices go, it is hardly the worst."

"I will tell him I paused by the river and slipped."

The Prince smiled as they closed the doors to the wurmrest. "Clever man. You might actually succeed in your mission."

"Thank you, Highness."

"I think you will find, Captain Strake, that my assessment will make your life more difficult than you imagine."

"Highness?"

The Prince matched his stride as they headed to the front of the estate. "Let me ask you… No, no, let me tell you: You are a clever man. No need to deny it or hide it. You have a goal. You have a reason for coming here, one beyond your orders. You're too smart to be looking at this as a grand adventure—though you do realize it will be the greatest adventure of your life. There is something more there."

Owen shivered. The image of his beloved Catherine swam into focus. "Yes, Highness." He almost continued speaking. He almost told the Prince his reason, but in glancing to the side, he saw a steely glint in Vlad's eyes that told him whatever it was, it was unimportant.

"Mark my words, Captain Strake. Your mission and its successful completion will be the first step in determining the future of the world." The Prince's eyes narrowed. "There will be many who do not want you to succeed, but for the sake of the world, you must."

CHAPTER FIVE

April 27, 1763
Bounty Trail
Temperance Bay, Mystria

Owen stopped by the Benjamin River to wash wurm-mud off his clothes. His jacket and waistcoat had gotten the worst of it, so he scrubbed them as best he could, and washed the grime from his boots. He splashed water over his breeches and, after removing his shirt and boots, waded into the river to clean the rest of him.

Whereas others might have been disgusted, Owen smiled. He almost shouted out happily, but refrained. The unspoiled wilderness didn't need his voice disturbing it.

All the stories he'd heard and read about Mystria had not prepared him for the pure delight of the land. In just one day he'd seen so much. *There will be many more strange adventures before I am home again.*

A crashing in the brush off to his left brought him around. He swam back to shore and reached for the horse pistol. Owen brought the gun up, his thumb resting on the firestone. He looked toward the sound, steadying the pistol with his left hand. Images of stalking jeopards filled his mind.

Idiot. That predator would be the whisper of death.

There, thirty yards away, a massive beast on long legs emerged from the brush and onto a small sandbar jutting into the river. Brown in color save for its long, buff muzzle, its head was crowned with a huge rack of thick antlers. Its stubby tail and brown ears flicked about. The creature surveyed the riverside, then cropped some of the grasses growing at river's edge.

Owen lowered the pistol and released the breath he hadn't realized he'd been holding. At that range he couldn't have hit the beast. No matter. Such was its size that a single lead ball wouldn't bring it down. *Even a jeopard might think twice.*

The monster looked in his direction for a moment, then ambled into the river and swam across the deep center channel. Once it had its feet under it again, the creature strolled toward the far shore, nibbling as it went. It never cast a glance back.

Owen shivered, not so much out of draining fear, as the pure joy of seeing something so different. Yes, it distantly resembled the sort of deer his father and uncles hunted on the family estate, though much bigger. The deer were another product of the estate, more cattle than wild beasts. This, on the other hand, wandered boldly across the countryside as if it were a king.

Definitely regal and apparently fearless.

He almost turned back to the Prince's estate to ask after it, but if that became his pattern, he'd never get back to Temperance before nightfall. He grabbed up his wet clothes, wrung them out as completely as he could, then went back to his horse. He draped the red coat over the back of his saddle, fitting the tails around his horse's tail, and pulled the damp waistcoat back on.

Riding back toward Temperance, Owen looked again at the countryside. The Prince's words resonated in him, so he began his work immediately. If the war on the Continent was to spill over into Mystria, armies would somehow have to be brought together in a cohesive manner and set to battle. It was his job to find a way for that to happen.

Within the first mile, several things became readily apparent. Owen had marveled at, and doubted, the feat of marksmanship that brought the jeopard down. That a man could kill a target at a hundred yards, even with a rifle, strained credulity. Even granting it was during the winter, when trees had been stripped of foliage, Owen wondered how the hunter had even *seen* the target at that range.

The forests he rode through—and it was all forest save for swaths cleared around small farms or the occasional meadow—barely let him see thirty yards. The beast he'd seen at the river could have been moving through the woods parallel with him, and he'd never see it. He might hear it, but manage a clean shot? *Impossible.*

The trail slithered through the countryside and doubtless had its origin in a game trail which many feet expanded. In places where water seeped up, or flowed down from hillsides, the road should have been impassable. In those spots, people had cut trees to shore up the road. They laid eight-foot lengths of log across the path, providing a modicum of stability in what would otherwise have been a marsh of stinking black mud. His horse preferred riding around the makeshift bridges when possible. The logs themselves showed some signs of wagon-wheel wear.

Though caution had been taken in the wettest areas, the rest of the road hardly remained dry. Men and horses might be able to tolerate little uphill jogs and downhill runs, but a team of oxen pulling a cannon or a supply wagon would never make it. The single virtue of fighting in the Low Countries had been a system of well-maintained roads that made transport easier. Here, moving troops and supplies would be a nightmare.

Unbidden came the memories of the last campaign on the Continent. The rain had fallen for days over roads better than this track, reducing them to mud. The Mystrians had taken to the hardship better than most. It struck Owen now that might have been because the only way they could feel superior was by refraining from complaint while their Norillian betters wailed and moaned. And the Mystrians hadn't had any qualms about setting their guns aside to pick up axes and shovels to clear routes and shore up roads.

But this countryside would take a battalion or more of laborers to widen roads and build bridges. While that would make troop movement easier, it made surprise impossible. Reaching an advantageous position from which one could engage the enemy was important. If the enemy could tell from which direction you were coming, chances were they would occupy that position before you ever could.

Of course, that is putting winter before fall. Owen had to wonder if there were any suitable battlefields in all of Mystria. The farms he'd ridden past might have, at most, a dozen acres cleared and most had little more than two. That would be enough ground for a battalion to fight, but battalions do not decide battles.

Aside from the cleared fields making a quilt of the countryside, most of the land was far from level. Farmers had terraced some spots, but mostly left hillsides for cattle and sheep to graze. And the ground was filled with stones, as evidenced by those gathered to form walls at the fields' edges.

No, the land was decidedly inhospitable to war. *But I will find a way around all obstacles.*

Another shiver shook him. He wanted to put it down to a damp vest and the coming dusk, but a profound wave of isolation washed over him. His wife, his beloved Catherine, had always said that he could find a way around all obstacles. She'd intone the words with reverence, and smile at him in a way that made him feel like a god striding the earth.

He shook his head, smiling. *I so hope you are right, darling, for the sake of our future.*

The sense of isolation bled into caution as the world darkened. He drew the horse pistol and weighed it in his hand. Heavy dark wood, brass fittings binding the steel barrel to stock and brass for the stonelock, the pistol was standard issue for cavalry soldiers. Owen's thumb fell naturally to the blue firestone at the barrel's base.

While Owen was considered a very good shot among his peers, the pistol would avail him little against the hazards of Mystria. He could easily bring the pistol to bear on an enemy, invoke the spell that would ignite the brimstone and thereby propel the lead ball at his target. But that horned creature, or the jeopard, would shrug off such a shot.

And so his mission loomed before him, gigantic and possibly insurmountable, just like Mystrian fauna. If he failed, many would expect him to use the pistol to blow his own brains out. It would be the honorable thing to do, after all. Wouldn't be proper to have the family's name besmirched by his failure.

They'd expect me to take a gentleman's way out. Owen laughed to himself. *And then would claim I'd never been a gentleman at all.* In fact, if his uncle had the means to do it, the story would be changed so that a Ryngian assassin had killed Owen. The tale would ennoble his death, allowing Owen to enhance the reputation of a family that had little earthly use for him.

No matter what I do, the Duke will find a way to make it serve his purpose.

Owen laughed again, the sound disappearing into the forest. Since his uncle would turn anything to his advantage, Owen needed to make sure he succeeded well enough that it benefited him and Catherine as well. Only then could he escape his uncle's influence and find true happiness.

He slid the pistol back into the saddle scabbard and looked over Temperance from the hill above it. It struck him that perhaps this new world—so far away from and alien to his uncle—would give him the chance he'd not ever had before. Catherine was certain of it. He chose to believe in her dream, and that had him smiling all the way back into town.

Night had fallen by the time he reached the Guards' headquarters. He slid out of the saddle, surprised. The building was shut up tight with no sign of life. There wasn't even a guard stationed nearby.

A young man detached himself from the shadows. "You'd be Cap'n Strake?"

Owen nodded. "And you are?"

"I'm to take you to your billet. Colonel Langford had your things delivered." The young man shrugged and began walking off along Generosity.

Owen ran after him and caught his arm. "Wait. Where is Colonel Langford?"

"Don't know. Home, I imagine."

"And the guards?"

The man turned. Clean shaven, tow-headed, tall, a bit on the gangly side, he gave Owen a lop-sided grin. "Don't do things here quite as they might across the water."

"Meaning."

"Likely they's down to the Queen and Crown slaking a thirst." He turned again and started walking. "You'll be wanting to come along. Mother's got some supper for you."

Owen ran back, grabbed his horse's reins, but didn't climb into the saddle. He sensed this was what the man expected him to do. First rule of winning any fight was not to do what the enemy expected. He caught up with the young man after a short run.

"I've been billeted at your house?"

"Were it *my* house, you'd not be staying." The man slowed a bit so Owen could pull even. "It's my father's house."

"And your father is?"

"My father is the smartest and the most honest man in this here whole colony. You'll not be treating him like a servant. And you'll not be rude to my mother, you won't beat the young ones, and if you so much as look at my sister…"

"Sir, I am a most happily married man."

"Didn't seem to make no nevermind to t'others."

"So, if I look at your sister, you'll leave me for some jeopard?"

"No, I like jeopards." Despite the adamancy of the man's clipped reply, the hint of a smile crossed his face.

"I shall take it, sir, that I am not the first Queen's officer who has been a guest in your home."

"My father is thinking it's his duty to host officers."

"This guest, he was a noble who was arrogant and rude?"

"The last one, the one before that, and the two before that."

Owen chuckled.

"Being as how you think this is funny…"

"No, sir, I take your warning seriously." Owen forced his smile to broaden. "Those noble officers purchased their commissions. I earned mine on the battlefield. And I've seen Mystrians fight. I was impressed."

"Was you?" The man's eyes tightened, but he nodded.

"My name is Owen." He offered the man his hand.

The man hesitated, then did his best to crush it in a grip of surprising strength. "Caleb. Caleb Frost."

"Pleased to meet you, Caleb." Owen matched his grip firmly, pumped his arm, then freed his hand. He let Caleb see him flexing it. "If I could trouble you…"

Caleb arched an eyebrow.

"On my ride back from seeing the Prince, I encountered a beast, eight foot at the shoulder, dark brown, long legs, huge rack of antlers."

"Bowled or more like branches?"

"Bowled, with spikes coming off them."

"That's a moose, most like."

"'Most like?' There's more than one creature answering that description?"

Caleb laughed. "Have to wonder at the wisdom of the Crown."

"I beg your pardon."

"How is it they send you out here for scouting, and you don't know the first thing about Mystria?" Caleb slapped his thigh. "But you'll just be sitting on your tuffet here while others do your work, I 'spect. Just like the others."

"Did any of the other scouts ride out to see the Prince directly upon their arrival?"

Caleb's brow furrowed. "Don't recall them much leaving town."

"So, perhaps, I'm not much like them."

"Perhaps not."

Owen scowled. "So, how is it you know *why* I'm in Mystria?"

"It ain't as if the Ryngian war is any secret. What with them building forts to the west, we expected something would be done. But more to your point, Sergeant Major Hilliard told my father about you when he brought your things. And Cask and Branch been spreading it around that Langford has hired them to see you upriver. Easy work for them."

"What are you saying, sir?"

"Well, Captain Strake, it works this way." Caleb grinned broadly. "Colonel Langford pays Cask and Branch to guide some Norillian fop around. They take him out into some of the nastiest country they can find. The officer comes back, the boys go out hunting, trapping, trading. They talk to the Twilight People, get told what the Ryngians are doing, and that gets written up in the report. They include maps and the like, which is mostly worthless. And half the Twilight People trade with the Ryngians, so they're not inclined to be telling the whole truth, if you catch my meaning."

"But the Colonel has his duty."

"Sure, to himself. The trading Cask and Branch do is for him. He sends skins back under military impound. A friend in Norisle brokers them for him. No duty on them, you see. I hear tell he has a thousand pounds waiting for him in the City."

And Langford expects I will do the same as the others.

"Thank you, Caleb, for this information."

The Mystrian nodded. "So you'll be enriching yourself, too. Long as you treat my family right, it'll be soft duty."

"No, sir, I did not come here for soft duty."

Caleb shot him a sidelong glance. "You can say that now, Captain Strake, but the road to the Prince's estate, that is about as civilized as Mystria gets. Where you want to go, if there have been a dozen Norillians through there, I'll be surprised."

"But surely men have gone…"

"Mystrians, sure. Maybe a hundred." Caleb grinned glowingly. "Something for you to sleep on, Captain Strake. *Norillians*, maybe a dozen; and considerably less than that made it back alive."

CHAPTER SIX

April 27, 1763
The Frost Residence, Temperance
Temperance Bay, Mystria

Clearly Caleb meant to terrify Owen, but the words hadn't had quite that effect. Owen did not fear for himself. If what Caleb said was true, the wilderness remained truly uncharted. Specifically, the maps back at Horse Guards were worthless. If a strategy was being planned based on them, none of the details would be relevant. Any military expedition would be doomed.

Which makes my mission even more important.

Owen looked up, thinking to ask Caleb a question, but was struck by two things. The first was that a remarkable change had overcome his guide. Caleb had straightened up and moved more tightly—not nearly as loose-limbed and gangly as he had first appeared. He'd also tucked his shirt in, buttoned his coat, and had combed fingers through his hair. The transformation effectively disguised him as a gentleman.

Second, they had come to a house at the top of the hill at the corner of Diligence and Virtue streets. The square house rose to three stories with a captain's-walk atop the roof, and a balcony above the door. The house faced the bay and had been constructed of granite blocks, and trimmed with another, lighter stone at the corners. It had a slate roof and two chimneys, one at either end. A granite wall surrounded the house. Well-tended bushes and a couple trees shaded the front.

Caleb pushed open the dual iron gates and beckoned Owen in. A servant came running up the drive from the side of the house and took charge of the horse. He led it off toward the back of the property where, Owen presumed, a stable and carriage house lay.

Owen hesitated. "This is a grand house."

"My grandfather built it." Caleb mounted the steps and opened the door. "Come on."

Only when he reached the top of the steps, and saw the people gathered in the foyer before the broad stairway leading to the second floor, did Owen realize his coat had ridden with his horse into the stable. He paused on the doorstep, then Caleb grabbed him and pulled him into the house.

"Mother, Father, may I present Captain Owen Strake, of the Queen's Own Wurm Guards. Captain Strake, this is my father, Doctor Archibald Frost."

Owen offered Dr. Frost his hand. "You are most kind, sir, for taking me in. I apologize for my uniform…"

Archibald, a small man with a pear-shaped physique and apple-red cheeks, clasped Owen's hand in both of his. The man's cheeks fought a losing action against a broad smile as he pumped Owen's hand warmly. "No apologies, sir. It is an honor. May I present my wife, Hettie."

Mrs. Frost proved the opposite of her spouse, being tall and slender, even regal. She smiled warmly, though nowhere near as effulgently as her husband. "It is our pleasure to welcome you, Captain Strake."

"You are most kind, ma'am."

Doctor Frost turned and introduced a half-dozen children ranging in age from thirteen to three. Their names immediately fled Owen's memory. He'd take abuse from Caleb when he had to ask about them again. He put it down to still wondering about Caleb, because the man who introduced him to the family was not the same man who had led him to the house.

But, then again, he'd have forgotten the names anyway, because the end of the introductions was when *she* descended the stairs.

Doctor Frost waved a hand impatiently. "There you are, Bethany."

Bethany Frost combined the best of her parents. Slender and tall, with long, golden-brown hair gathered into a braid, she glided fluidly down the stairs. She had her father's smile and bright blue eyes the same shade as his wife's, but decidedly warmer. Her smile broadened as she first saw him, then she missed a step and almost tumbled down the stairs. She caught herself on the railing, then laughed delightedly, her cheeks flushed.

Owen couldn't believe it. Had any Norillian woman come to the stairs late, it would have been with the intent of making an entrance. The stumble would have been taken as evidence of poor breeding and grounds for suicide. For Bethany, however, it appeared to have no more significance than a simple accident would merit.

She reached the bottom of the stairs. "A pleasure, Captain Strake. Forgive my being late, but I was making sure your room had been made up."

"I thought he was sleeping in the stable."

Doctor Frost chuckled. "Yes, Caleb, I'm sure you did."

"Father."

"Caleb, you see, Captain Strake, has some very definite feelings concerning Her Majesty's government and how we are treated. He's at Temperance College, studying for the Clergy. Alas, I fear he is becoming something of a free-thinker."

"He was quite friendly, sir. A gentleman."

Owen allowed himself to be steered down the central corridor and to the right.

A long trestle table had been set for one, with the seat near the fire. Dr. Frost sat at the table's head, with Owen at his left hand. Caleb sat opposite. Owen's host unstoppered a crystal decanter and poured red wine for the three of them.

He raised the glass. "To the Queen's health."

"Her health." Owen drank. "Very nice. Better than I had in Tharyngia."

"I should hope so. My father bought it thirty years ago and it has been maturing in the cellar." Frost set his glass down. "And you have not fooled me by covering for my son. I know him well. He seems to forget that animosity does not excuse one from behaving as a gentleman."

Caleb glanced into his wine. "I apologize if I offended you, Captain."

"No apology required. I found our conversation very informative." Owen turned to Dr. Frost. "And I, sir, would like to apologize for the behavior of the other officers you have hosted. I should like the names of the offenders. I shall take great delight in thrashing them at the first opportunity."

"You're most kind, Captain, but I doubt that will be necessary."

Hettie entered bearing a bowl of stew. Bethany followed, bearing a small basket with sliced bread. Caleb reached for a piece of it, but she slapped his hand. His mother gave him a reproving stare, so he sat back and grumbled.

"You'll forgive the meager fare, Captain. My husband and I were hoping to have a more formal dinner on the Lord's Day, after services."

"Nothing to forgive, ma'am. I've been on a ship for seven weeks. It's been weak broth and hardtack for far too long." Owen smiled, breathing in the aroma from the thick brown stew. "It smells wonderful."

Hettie and Bethany joined them at the table, book-ending Caleb, with Bethany closest to her father. "Please, Captain, eat."

Owen spooned up a carrot, a pea, and a small piece of beef and ate. He closed his eyes, letting the scent fill his head. Things were tender enough he didn't need to chew, but chew he did so he could savor the mouthful. He washed it down with more of the wine, then smiled.

"This is the best I've eaten for over a year."

Caleb arched an eyebrow. "I'd have thought the Wurm Guards would have the finest of everything."

"They do, if they have a wurm." Owen broke a slice of bread in half and dipped it into the stew. "The Regiment has five battalions; one of wurms, one of heavy cavalry, two light cavalry, and one of light infantry. We're the skirmishers. First to battle, last to leave; last to mess, first to leave. Story is they keep us around in case the wurms get hungry—and wurms prefer their food lean."

Mrs. Frost took a salt cellar and pepper mill from the side table and placed them near Owen. "Captain, may I ask if you were at Artennes Forest?"

"Yes, ma'am, I was. I have a lot of respect for the Mystrian Rangers."

Mrs. Frost's smile broadened, but Bethany's slowly evaporated. "Do you remember Major Robert Forest?"

Owen sat back. "Very well, ma'am."

"He is my brother."

"Is he well?"

Caleb snarled. "Isn't much of a one for a handshake, being as how he left half an arm in the forest."

Owen rested the bread on the edge of the bowl. "I ask after him, Master Frost, because I dragged him out of the woods, him still shouting orders to his men. I tied off the arm so he'd not bleed to death, and I fetched him brandy for when the butchers decided the forearm had to go."

Bethany leaned forward. "Did you know Ira Hill? He was in the Rangers."

"I do not recall the name, Miss."

"He was tall, black hair, green eyes, darker than yours."

Owen searched his memory. "I can't promise, Miss, but I recall a man fitting that description. Always had a joke?"

Her face brightened. "Yes, yes, that was him."

"I remember digging beside him as we tried to clear a road. It was raining. He said he'd trade his shovel for a bucket and bail more than he could dig. I didn't know his name, though. Is he a friend?"

"Was." Her face closed again.

Caleb glowered. "He died in those same woods, Captain."

"I'm very sorry."

Bethany nodded. "It's hard not knowing, and people, they say…"

Dr. Frost took one of Bethany's hands in his own. "The Rivendell book, you understand, Captain. Ira had asked for Bethany's hand before he went off and, well, most people are believing the Rangers were cowards."

Owen turned to Bethany. "Look at me, Miss. The Rangers did more than most on that campaign. I got assigned to liaise with them, some folks thinking I was as expendable as they were. The Rangers fought well and hard. Don't believe anything different. What Lord Rivendell wrote is fable beginning to end. He wrote it to make himself and his son look good. You just remember that the Tharyngians feared the Rangers enough that they sent their best against them. They won, but it was a close thing. If there had been *two* Ranger battalions, the war would be over."

Bethany's lips pressed together and tears glistened. She nodded, then kissed her father's cheek. Wordlessly she left the room. Her mother followed her.

Dr. Frost patted Owen's arm. "Eat, sir, don't let it get cold. I appreciate your saying what you did. You have to understand something about us Mystrians—things that not even my son understands. Norisle cast the first of us out because we were undesirable. Some of us were criminals. Some of us thought the Church was too strict. The Virtuans thought it too lax. And some of us were simply thought lazy or stupid and shipped away to die in the colonies.

"Many did, but this land vitalized those who survived. It gave us strength. It gave us opportunity. So now we're like some big puppy, full of energy, and we want to please our master. We do what we can, but getting swatted, it sits poorly."

Owen nodded. "I understand, sir, far better than you can imagine."

Caleb refilled his wine glass. "But it is more than that, Father. The very philosophers and great thinkers you teach about at college, they are saying that the rights of Men are not bestowed upon us by kings and queens. They are our birthright as Men. They say we cede power to the nobility in return for guidance and assistance. When we get neither, they have broken the contract through which they get power."

Dr. Frost slowly rotated his wine glass. "You make it sound so simple, Caleb."

"It *is* simple, Father." He tapped a finger against the table. "It is a simple matter of theft. Power is being stolen from us."

"No, Caleb, it is not that simple. We are born of Norillian traditions. Our laws, the customs by which these colonies are governed, are based in Norillian Common Law. The colonies themselves function with Royal Charters. Our Governors are appointed by the Queen. Her nephew is our Governor-General. Norisle has given us a very great deal. We cannot unilaterally declare any previous debts null and void because we are displeased with the current situation. We would cut ourselves off from our beginnings. If we do that, we forget who we are."

"Perhaps it is time, Father, for us to cease trying to remember, and for us to just decide who we are."

Dr. Frost laughed. "Bravo, Caleb. To parrot so effectively the pamphlets that circulate *in camera* is an art. Captain, what do you think of the rights of Men and nobility?"

Owen looked up from swiping a piece of bread through the empty bowl. "To be honest, sir, the army does not encourage philosophical discussions, nor does it leave much time for them. In the army we revere tradition, so I agree with you there. But, I suppose, were I the puppy, there would come a point where taking a bite out of my master's hand might seem appealing."

"Ha!" Caleb smiled and refilled Owen's glass. "You see, Father!"

"Well now, Master Frost, I'm not saying I agree with you. Men aren't puppies.

A puppy isn't aware that a beating will follow that biting. A man should know better, and know if he wants to invite that beating."

Caleb's eyes sharpened. "But, Captain, is a man a man when he accepts that someone else says he's inferior and never tests that assumption? As my father said, Mystrians were cast upon this shore because we were expendable. Everyone in Norisle would have been happy if we had died. Fact is, we didn't. My grandfather came over as an indentured servant to a miller. Worked his way out of his obligation, then turned to trading. In thirty years he made enough to build this house, endow part of the College, and send ships to every corner of the globe. Yet there's not fishmonger in Highgate or a lowly clerk in the City that doesn't believe himself better than the best of us."

Owen ran a hand over his jaw. He'd seen the same treatment at school and within the army, but there, to react was to be punished quickly and severely. Did curbing his desire to defend himself make him less of a man? Did it stop his shots from hitting targets?

Dr. Frost raised his wine glass. "I submit, gentlemen, that this discussion, which is really the eternal struggle of children to gain the recognition of parents, will not be resolved this evening. Let us, therefore, table it and discuss more pleasant things.

"After all," Dr. Frost's smile wavered for the first time, "if your reason for coming here, Captain Strake, is true, the least pleasant of man's inventions will be coming to our shores. And, I suspect, it is an immigrant which will be most reluctant to leave."

CHAPTER SEVEN

April 28, 1763
The Frost Residence, Temperance
Temperance Bay, Mystria

Owen awoke with a start, reaching out for his wife. His dream had been vivid enough that he sought warmth in the emptiness where she should have lain. Her absence disoriented him. It was several hours past dawn, marking this as the latest he'd slept in months, and it likewise confused him.

He tried to sit upright, but the soft mattress resisted his effort. He surrendered, the feather pillow molding itself to mute bird-calls from outside. He smiled and tried to capture the dream's fleeting images.

Catherine had joined him in Mystria. They attended a ball at the Prince's home. The center of his laboratory had been cleared and the bear and the jeopard took part in the dance. The moose appeared also. Well-mannered, all the animals, enjoying themselves while a regimental band played. The Prince danced with Catherine and she smiled as broadly as ever he had seen. And then she came to him and clung to him and they found themselves in his bed, making love.

Owen might have been tempted to put the dream down to nothing at all, save that Catherine believed fervently in dreams. He had no idea what the presence of the animals meant. He forced himself to remember what he could, so he could write it all down for his next letter home. She could make of it what she wanted.

He closed his eyes again just for another moment, and then remembered nothing until the light tapping on the door presaged its opening.

An elderly valet entered bearing his coat, vest, and breeches freshly washed. Owen pulled himself up against the headboard as the man hung his clothes in the wardrobe. Wordlessly the servant stepped into the hallway again, then returned with freshly polished boots.

Owen smiled. "Thank you."

"It is our pleasure to serve." The old man returned the smile with sincerity. "Doctor Frost awaits your pleasure, Captain."

"Please convey my thanks. I shall be with him shortly."

The valet nodded and retreated, drawing the door closed behind him.

Owen rose and stretched, then washed his face and hands in the bowl on the side table. He dried them with a towel, then pulled on his clothes. The trunk he'd brought from Norisle had been opened and the clothing stored in wardrobe and dresser. Instead of his boots, however, he chose hose and low shoes with big silver buckles.

He descended the stairs and exited out through the kitchen to use the privy. He much preferred the outhouse, despite its being stuffy, to hanging his arse over the heads on the ship. Though the scent of salt air was more refreshing, getting splashed with cold sea spray was not.

Upon exiting he discovered Bethany working a pump to fill a bucket. "Good morning, Miss. May I help?"

She smiled. "Most kind, sir, and far better a greeting than I deserve."

Owen frowned, working the squeaky pump. "You have me at a disadvantage, Miss."

Bethany wiped wet hands on an apron. "You will please forgive my conduct last evening, Captain Strake. Though it has been three years, I find myself still wanting to know of Ira. To discover that you had been there with him… it brought up many memories I had hoped I had put away."

Owen stopped pumping. "Please, Miss, I am the one to apologize. I meant to cause you no upset."

"Nor did you." Her smile shrank. "You were truthful and honest. And kind."

Her implication that some men had lied about knowing Ian—presumably to get to know her better—did not surprise him. Nor did word that many men embraced Lord Rivendell's lies about Mystrians. He'd seen such dishonorable behavior in the ranks, among the highborn and low. *More among the highborn, in fact.*

"I believe you will find, Miss, that very few men wish to take responsibility for their actions and desires. Lying, being tactless, hurting others: all of these are easier than just standing up and being men."

Bethany laughed, but would not meet his gaze. "You sound like my brother."

"Something I suspect he would deny."

She lifted her face, her smile returning. "You have a point, Captain. But do not think ill of him. He's not yet tamed his emotions, so he speaks his mind."

"Seldom a vice, save in the military."

"Always a vice when voiced as loudly as Caleb does." She laid a hand on his arm. "But I delay you when you need breakfast. We have some put aside for you."

"Lead the way. I shall bring the water."

He followed her into the kitchen and deposited the bucket on a counter-top. She directed him into the dining room, where her father awaited him. Owen sat, and Bethany returned to the kitchen to bring him some bacon and biscuits with butter and honey. With another trip she added a pot of tea and two cups, pouring for him and her father.

Dr. Frost slowly spun his steaming cup. "You're up early, Captain."

Owen chewed quickly and swallowed hard. "Sir, it is mid-morning. I should have been awake much sooner."

"Most of our guests sleep in much later, and ask for dinner to be served to them on a tray." Frost passed him a sealed message. "Colonel Langford was up early himself. He wishes to see you by noon."

Owen flipped the message over and back. "Do I need to read it?"

The elder man shrugged. "You will find that while my wife has little time for gossip—or so she says—there is a very quick and efficient spy network among domestics. Your expedition will be heading out at the beginning of the week under the leadership of Rufus Branch. The Colonel will be telling you how long you will be gone and inform you of some of the hardships."

Owen broke a biscuit in half and began buttering it. "Shall I assume there are wagers being placed on how long before I return to Temperance and allow the expedition to continue without me? Not that a gentleman such as yourself would entertain wagers."

Frost's eyes brightened. "You think too highly of me, sir. My father built a mercantile empire based on taking risks. I chose to become a Natural Philosopher, but I also take risks—those of a sporting nature. It is believed you will survive ten days or until you reach Grand Falls. It is also believed you will not run at first sight of the Twilight People; but that the first jeopard will have you screaming in terror."

Owen laughed. "Having seen the one in the Prince's collection, I find that to be a smart bet to cover."

"Captain, I think you underestimate yourself. At least, I hope you do. I have a bit riding on your success."

"Will you tell me, sir, how you are betting?"

Frost thought for a moment, then shook his head. "No. You are the sort of man who would endure much to validate my trust in you. There is no need for you to know; and my fortunes will ride with my judgment of you."

Fully dressed in his uniform, Owen reported to army headquarters and was ushered in directly to see Colonel Langford. As predicted, the Colonel proceeded to outline the hardships in store for Owen, and hinted broadly that he could use a man of Owen's skill in Temperance itself. "To be frank,

Captain, it would be a better use of your skills than getting lost and killed in the woods."

"I am certain you are correct, Colonel." Owen reached inside his jacket and produced a folded slip of paper. "But I do have my orders. Now, sir, if you could look this over, I believe it is all I will need to complete my mission."

Langford read the paper, his eyes narrowing. "You spent a great deal of time on this requisition, Captain."

"Yes, sir. On the passage I studied a Ryngian survey I found in a shop in Launston. De Verace's Survey of 1641."

Langford looked up. "It has been translated?"

"No, sir; I am fluent in Ryngian and Kessian. My grandfather had little tolerance for ignorance." Owen held a hand out. "If you approve, sir, I will go to the Quartermaster and draw these things."

Langford dipped a quill and hastily scrawled his name at the bottom. "I applaud your industriousness, sir."

"Thank you, sir." Owen accepted the paper, stood and saluted. "May God save the Queen, sir."

Langford, without rising from his desk, returned the salute. "And may He be kind on your person and soul."

Lieutenant Palmerston, the Quartermaster, a grizzled veteran with one eye, a handful of teeth, and a couple fingers shy of a fist on the left, studied Owen's list. Then he laughed aloud. "Brimstone, firestones, and shot for two-hundred-fifty rounds for your musket; a hundred for a pistol? Biscuit and dried beef for three months? Clothing, blankets, trade goods, gold? Oh, sir, begging your pardon, but you cannot be serious."

"I most certainly am, sir." Owen's eyes narrowed. "Why would you think I won't need these things?"

The Lieutenant caught himself and aborted a laugh. "Well, sir, it is just that the Colonel already requisitioned supplies for your expedition. Rufus Branch drew it up. I've checked it all proper like. There's more than enough to cover your needs, sir."

Owen stroked a hand over his jaw. The Lieutenant presided over a warehouse that seemed quite well-stocked. In fact, the only thing it seemed to be lacking was men working in it.

"Might I have a look at the requisition?"

Palmerston opened a drawer to his desk and brought out a three-page document. "All signed proper like."

He was correct. Colonel Langford had signed the last page and initialed all the others. And if Owen was not mistaken, the document had actually been written by Langford. Owen studied it and fought to keep his growing anger hidden.

"Might I ask, Lieutenant, about this item here, about the beef for the trip. The charge for services, here."

"Oh, that's just standard, sir." The man scratched up under his eyepatch with a scarred finger. "You see, the cattle will be taken from our herd to Mr. Cask's slaughter house, killed, and butchered. They will smoke it and salt it, you see, sir, so there is your service."

"But, Lieutenant, that will take time and the beef won't be ready to go."

"No, sir, so we will issue beef here from our stores, and then that will replace it." The Lieutenant nodded reassuringly. "Just the way it is done here, sir."

Owen shook his head. "But the butcher, he'll take his customary forequarter, yes? And, forgive me, but don't we have butchers in the Regiment? Shouldn't they be doing that work?"

"And they would, sir, but they have other things to be doing."

"I see." Owen pointed to something else on the requisition. "Here they ask for brimstone and shot to make up five thousand rounds."

"Yes, sir."

"But they also ask for five *hundred* firestones. That much powder and shot only requires *fifty* firestones."

"Well, sir, in the wilderness…"

Owen grabbed the Quartermaster's jacket and yanked Palmerston across the desk. "I've fought on the Continent, sir, in pitched battles from which your unit *ran*. I've put a hundred-fifty, even two hundred shots through a firestone before it needed replacing. Those extra firestones, I would imagine, go for a pretty pence out here. You profit from that illegal trade, don't you?"

"Now see here, sir…"

"No, Lieutenant, you listen to me. I came to do a job. Others may have been convinced to stay here in town while the Casks and the Branches did their work for them, but that is not me. War will be coming to Mystria. My job is to prepare for that war. If you're not helping me do that, you're giving aid and comfort to the enemy. That's treason, sir, and I will prefer charges. Is this clear?"

The Lieutenant nodded. "Yes, sir."

Owen shoved him back into his chair. "Langford is profiteering. I know that. He sends trade goods back to Norisle as military cargo, avoiding tariffs. I shall assume, based on the orders concerning the beef, that the 'service charge' is paid back to him by the Cask family? And that you never quite get as many barrels of preserved beef as ought to come out of the number of cattle sent off to slaughter?"

"Yes, sir. And one of the Casks is a tanner, too, sir, so he gets the hides. The bones are ground for meal, used in the fields."

The Captain nodded. "And one of the reasons that our butchers are not available to slaughter our beef is that Langford has them off working as laborers?"

Palmerston's face closed. "They work for Cask in the slaughter house."

Getting away with hiring troops out as day labor would be simple to hide. Even if the troops reported this activity—and most wouldn't since they were just following orders and didn't know any better—where would the reports go? If the officers weren't part of the deal, rank and file soldiers likely wouldn't be believed. Many of the officers were convinced that the extra work would be good for the scum in the ranks. Even more would consider the whole thing beneath the honor of a *gentleman*, so if there were to be a court-martial, Langford would get off with a mild reprimand.

"How can you hide the loss of brimstone and firestones?" Mystria, for very sound reasons, was prohibited from manufacturing its own brimstone or firestones—both of which Her Majesty's government sought to strictly control. For hundreds to be stolen each year and distributed on the black market could not escape notice.

Palmerston fidgeted. "Well, sir, I am not the one who writes reports that go back to Horse Guards. But if I understand it, the Colonel makes up little operations against raiding Twilight People. He reports successfully repelling attacks, sir, with appropriate expenditures of brimstone and firestone. It seems, sir, that as long as he's winning, no one in Launston has any complaints. He even praises men like you, sir, in his reports; so there are those who say these things happen. If the Colonel likes you, sir, you might even get a medal."

Owen's stomach began to fold in on itself. "Tell me this, if you know it. The other expeditions, the ones the Casks and Branches did. How far did they go?"

The Lieutenant sighed. "I don't know for certain, sir, but I can tell you this. Come spring every year after these expeditions, Rufus Branch's wife has had her a baby. She ain't much to look at, and fear of Rufus would keep most men away if she was. But he hain't beat her for taking another man to her bed, and the children are all ruddy and red like their father. I'd say, sir, most all what's in those reports was dreamed up, and most like while he was sleeping in his own bed here in the South End."

CHAPTER EIGHT

April 28, 1763
The Frost Residence, Temperance
Temperance Bay, Mystria

The arrival of a breathless messenger saved Palmerston from any further interrogation. The Private, straightening his hat as he snapped to attention, saluted abruptly. "Begging your pardon, Captain Strake. The Colonel's compliments, sir."

Owen straightened and returned the salute. "Yes, Private?"

"The Colonel requests you come to Government House straight away, sir." The soldier swallowed hard. "The Prince, sir, is in court and has requested the two of you attend him."

"Very well, Private. Please convey to the Colonel my intention to join him forthwith."

"If it pleases the Captain, the Colonel ordered me to conduct you there without delay."

"Yes, Private. Wait outside for me to join you."

The soldier departed and Owen turned to Palmerston. "You will write up a report concerning Langford's illegal activities. You will make two copies. One you will entrust to Caleb Frost. The other you will prepare for me."

Palmerston's eyes grew wide. "The Colonel, he'd kill me, sir."

"The only way you can prevent him from killing you, Lieutenant, is to prepare those reports. I will release them if any harm comes to you." Owen tapped a finger on his own requisition. "You will prepare my supplies immediately and you will cut the other order down to fifty firestones, do you understand? I will come back and count them."

"Yes, sir." The man sighed. "I wasn't meaning no harm, what I did."

"I understand that, Lieutenant." When the Tharyngian war ended, the army would shrink. Men like Palmerston would be retired on a fraction of their pay. The man likely had no other trade, no prospects, save for what he could put by. Avoiding poverty only made sense.

"You lost your fingers and eye on the Continent, yes?"

"Ryngian ambush. Musket-ball hit my barrel. Took two fingers. Stock splinter took my eye."

"I'm here to see that doesn't happen again. Without good information, the Ryngians will ambush us just as you were ambushed. And from what you've told me, a survey that's over a century old is more to be trusted than the one sent to Horse Guards last year. We can't have that."

The Lieutenant nodded. "No, sir. I'll do what you've told me to do, sir."

"Good." Owen sighed. "Her Majesty will thank you."

"If it's all the same, sir, I'd just as soon she didn't even know I existed."

A man after my own heart. Owen threw the man a salute, then found the waiting soldier outside. They set off and entered the city center from the south, passing beneath the shadow of St. Martin's Cathedral. Like the Frost's house, it had been built of granite, with flying buttresses and a gray slate roof. The bell tower rose to the height of fifty feet and had a cross atop it that went another twenty. It had been modeled on St. Paul's in Launston, but lacked the ornate statuary in niches at the front. The bronze doors were smaller and had been shipped from Norisle, as no native industry could have produced them.

To the west lay Government House. Like the Cathedral, it had been scaled down from its Norillian counterpart. Stone had not been wasted on more than the foundation—local timber had been used to finish it. Three stories tall, it had been built wide rather than deep. It occupied the whole of the western edge of the square and had three separate sets of doors: one for each wing, and the broader central doors toward which the Private led Owen.

Colonel Langford waited impatiently inside the foyer, a relatively cramped space with creaking floorboards and tall windows. He dismissed the soldier with a snarl, then pulled Owen into a shadowed corner.

"What did you say to the Prince yesterday?"

Owen stood tall. "I do not believe the Prince intended you to be privy to our conversation, sir, little of which concerned you."

"Captain, I am ordering you."

"We spoke of my mission." Owen opened his hands. "The Prince then invited me to take a look at his wurm. After that, I returned to Temperance."

"You didn't talk about me?"

"Aside from mentioning that I had reported my arrival to you, no, sir."

Langford pursed his lips. "Very well. Here is the thing of it. On occasion the Prince decides that his being Governor-General requires him to do more than his abominable Ryngianesque researches. He wishes to discuss your expedition."

Owen nodded.

"You are required to be there. You will answer questions *only* if I give you leave to do so. Do you understand?"

"My duty, sir, is to Her Majesty…"

Langford's face darkened. He thrust a finger at Owen's nose. "Your duty, sir, depends upon my support. You will be spending the summer here, perhaps longer. You will need my help. If you know what is good for you, you will do as I tell you to do. You are a *very long way* from Norisle, Captain. Many things can happen here."

"Am I to interpret that as a threat, Colonel?"

"I won't insult your intelligence, Captain. Your success or failure is at my whim. You do not want to displease me."

Owen drew himself to attention, then saluted. "As you say, sir."

"Very well." Langford crossed the foyer. A liveried servant in a wig bowed and then opened the door to the assembly room at the heart of Government House. That central room ran to the back of the building and was as wide as it was deep. Wooden pillars split it into thirds. Desks and chairs had been moved to the walls, but marks on the floor showed where they normally were arrayed as if for a parliament. Owen guessed that a regional legislature likely used the chamber when the Prince was not in residence.

A throne had been centered toward the back and as they approached, Owen barely recognized the man seated in it. The Prince had donned a full wig, with the curled locks falling past his shoulder both front and back. His blue jacket and gold breeches shimmered brightly—the hallmark of their having been woven from wurmsilk. The jacket facings glowed with burnished red wurmleather, and the black buckles on his matching shoes had been carved from wurmscales.

Colonel Langford stopped four paces shy of the throne and bowed. Owen, a step behind him, followed suit. He then retreated to the right, leaving Langford alone before the Prince.

The three of them were by no means the only people in the room. Not only had some people preceded them, but more entered in their wake. They lined up as if the center of the room had an invisible carpet on which they were afraid to tread. Most reminded him of Dr. Frost—well-dressed in clothes stylishly fashioned from homespun wool and linen. The colors perforce ran to blacks and browns since indigo and other brighter hues had to be imported, but here and there a kerchief or vest lent a splash of color.

Down toward the end, barely inside the doors, stood men who looked quite ill at ease. They wore buckskins, with fringes on the sleeves and down the side seams of the trousers. Beadwork decorated some of the clothes, but most showed only stains on thighs, shins, and at the sleeve-cuffs. These men had a rough, unkempt nature and their shifting postures betrayed an uneasiness with their surroundings.

Prince Vlad raised a hand and the porter closed the doors. "Colonel Langford, so good of you to respond to our request so quickly. We trust we drew you away from nothing vital?"

Langford smiled unctuously. "The Queen's work is never done, Highness, but any service I can render you is always paramount."

"And you, Captain Strake, you were not inconvenienced by this request?"

"No, Highness." Owen shivered at the remote and imperious tone in the Prince's voice—so unlike how he had sounded the day before.

"Colonel, I am given to understand that you have retained Rufus Branch to guide Captain Strake."

"I have, sir. His knowledge of the area is unparalleled."

"Is it?" Prince Vlad frowned. "We should have thought Nathaniel Woods had traveled more extensively, especially in the area where Captain Strake's orders require him to explore."

Langford bowed his head. "Of course, Highness. I should have said Mr. Branch's knowledge is unparalleled among *available* guides."

The Prince clapped his hands. "Well, then, Colonel, we have excellent news for you. Mr. Woods is available for this assignment. He will arrive presently, so you will tell your... why, look, he is with us. Mr. Branch, you and your men will not be required. You're free to go."

The ruffians at the far end of the room appeared quite surprised, but Langford's rising voice cut off the dull roar of their conversation. "Highness, you cannot dismiss them."

"Did we hear you correctly, Colonel? We cannot dismiss them?"

"Yes, Highness. They have a contract to provide services. It would be great hardship for them if it were to be set aside."

Prince Vlad's chin came up. "Would it? These men appear to be hale and hearty to me. Could they not avail themselves better by going out and trapping something? We could not be paying them more than they would make trading and trapping, could we?"

"It is a complicated matter, Highness." Langford's face grew hard. "An *army* matter, Highness. Quite outside the things you need worry about."

"We believe you will find, Colonel, that all *your* funding comes through the Ministry of the Exchequer, which is a civilian organization. It is, therefore, of concern to us. The fact is that Mr. Woods—a guide you have proclaimed to be superior to your selection—is available for two gold crowns. We believe this is a considerable savings over your proposed budget."

Langford began to sputter, but the Prince raised a hand. "We are not finished. It has come to our attention that there are rumors of your personal financial involvement with the Casks and Branches, Colonel, as well as other irregularities."

Langford's face flushed. "Do you have proof, Highness, of these insulting accusations? Would you trust rumors over the word of a gentleman that contradicts them?"

"No, Colonel, but I am duty bound to prepare a report and forward it to the proper authorities."

"But it would be baseless."

Owen took a step forward. "Begging Your Highness' pardon; on *my* word as a gentleman, the Colonel's financial dealings are as warped as an old, wurmrest door. If you wish, I shall compile what I have learned so far into a report ready for transport back to Norisle when the *Coronet* sails."

"Your offer is welcomed, Captain, but maybe a bit precipitant." Vlad looked again to Colonel Langford. "In addition to guiding Captain Strake, we shall be asking Mr. Woods to continue his survey of flora and fauna. In anticipation of receiving new samples and new information, we shall be spending most of our time on our estate. You will find us singularly preoccupied, so that filing such a report may well be beyond our means. We shall be forced to take you at your word that you have no financial dealings with these men. Is this clear?"

"Yes, Highness."

"Very well. You are dismissed."

Langford bowed, then shot Owen a venomous glance.

"And you, Captain Strake, I require you to remain here. I insist you dine with me this evening."

"You are most kind, Highness."

"It is not kindness." The Prince nodded solemnly. "There are items in the packet you gave me which need discussing; and the sooner done, so much the better."

Langford and the others withdrew. Once the door had closed behind them, Vlad pulled off his wig, tossed it on the throne, and scratched his head vigorously with both hands. He made no pretense of smoothing his hair again, but turned and grinned at Owen.

"I appreciate your support, though it was unexpected. Langford and I would have come to the same solution. You have succeeded in making yourself an enemy."

Owen nodded. "It would have happened regardless. Out of the five shillings in a crown, two must end up in Langford's pocket, or those of his confederates. It is scandalous, of course, but if Langford's people actually did the things they were overpaid to do, there would be some benefit. As it is…"

"I know, and so do some in Horse Guards." The Prince waved Owen after him, heading for a door in the south wall that opened into a small set of apartments. "I informed Horse Guards that the past reports were unreliable. No one believed me, however, until a spy in the heart of Feris, in the Ryngian Ministry of Colonial Affairs, located two outposts in places where our reports indicated there were none. While my reports are still disbelieved, various friends asked me to arrange for Nathaniel to move through those territories and ascertain the truth."

Owen's nostril's flared. "Did no one believe I would do my duty?"

"On the surface, Captain, no one would. Despite your family's position, you are hardly well regarded. You are a Colonial half-blood who liaised with a Colonial unit disgraced in battle. Need I paint you a more complete picture of why some cautious souls wished to guarantee accurate information?"

"No, Highness, I understand."

"Good." The Prince smiled. "But you and I, for now, shall talk of specifics, and I shall write out some orders for my friend. Then we shall dine and you will go to your home for a well-deserved rest. Your arduous journey will begin very soon."

And it was, as the Prince predicted, an enjoyable evening of roast pheasant and local vegetables combined with valuable lessons that would aid Owen's ability to survive in the wilderness. The Prince delivered each of them as an anecdote, both making them easier to remember and less offensive in the telling. By the end of the evening Owen knew he still had a great deal to learn, but he had acquired a great foundation upon which to build.

He left the Prince with a smile on his face and a warm glow in his belly.

Both of which vanished when, at the first shadowed corner, the butt of a musket cracked against his head.

CHAPTER NINE

April 28, 1763
Temperance
Temperance Bay, Mystria

Owen awakened on the ground, dust in his mouth, a second before a booted foot caught him in the mid-section and lifted him back into the air. The Prince's dinner gushed out, replacing the dry dust with the harsh wet of vomit. He landed on his side, bouncing, then drew his knees up to cover his belly.

"Think you're so smart, do you?" A man's deep-voiced question invited laughter from his confederates. "Think you're better'n us, do you?"

Owen coughed, then spat. His stomach ached and the world swam. He could make out silhouettes—at least half a dozen—but there could have been more. The closest one to him, the man who had spoken, filled most of his vision—and that was a factor of his size, not just his proximity.

"There he is, boys, all curled up. A little Norillian dog, ready to die."

More laughter, until another voice cut in.

"Now, Rufus Branch, don't appear you're making constructive use of your time here."

"You stay out of this, Woods." The large man thrust a finger at Owen. "You know his kind. He wears the red coat. He thinks he's better'n any three of us."

Light laughter came from the alley-mouth. "You ain't never been good at your sums, Rufus, but even you can see there's a mite more than three of you here."

"You want to be evening up the odds?"

"I get to scrapping, ain't going to be even. Like as not I'd shoot you *again*."

Owen shook his head, partially clearing it, then pulled his hands and knees beneath himself. "Three to one? I've fought worse."

Woods, at the alley-mouth, was little more than a tall, slender silhouette with a gun cradled in his folded arms. "Belike that knock in your head scrambled your brains, Captain Strake."

"Not like he has any brains," one of the others scoffed.

Owen got to his feet and staggered to his left. He let one of the men catch him and push him back upright. Owen twisted, burying a fist in the man's gut, then snapped a knee into his face. The man dropped fast. Spinning, he got his back against the building, then jacked his right elbow into the face of the man by his other side. The man's head rebounded off the building and he flopped forward, covering his compatriot's moaning body.

It wasn't the first time Owen had been jumped by a gang. He had one rule for such fights and applied it religiously: do as much damage as you can, however you can, and don't stop.

The man on his left hesitated, but the one on his right came burrowing in. Head ducked and arms wide, he went to tackle Owen. The soldier hit him hard over the left ear, dropping him to his knees, then kicked him in the chest. The man somersaulted back, cutting Rufus' legs out from under him.

Without waiting for the man on the left to act, Owen charged and caught him with an uppercut. Tooth fragments littered the dust. Owen grabbed the man's jacket and tossed him onto Rufus' back.

Another man raised his fists and broadened his stance. Slightly smaller than Owen, he had a confident glint in his eyes. He darted forward, feinting with a left toward Owen's head. Owen's hands came up, leaving him open for the man to drive his right into Owen's stomach.

Pain exploded but didn't slow Owen down. He snapped his head forward, smashing his forehead into the man's face. Bones cracked. Blood gushed over Owen's face. The man staggered back, hands rising to his ruined nose. Owen kicked out, catching him squarely in the groin. The blow lifted the man a foot or so in the air and dumped him, writhing, into the alley.

Rufus roared and Owen spun. The giant had tossed one man off him and rose to his feet. A head taller than Owen, and with shoulders broad enough to fill the alley, Rufus Branch curled his hands into bucket-sized fists.

"You should've stayed in Norisle."

Owen swallowed hard and set himself. He had one chance. A quick kick to a knee, crippling Rufus; then finding something big enough with which to brain him.

All of a sudden Rufus' head snapped forward, accompanied by the sound of a musket-butt being applied as a club. The man staggered and half turned. "Why'd you have to do that, Woods?"

"You're not worth the price of powder to reload." Woods hit him again, catching him in the forehead.

Rufus Branch collapsed.

Woods lowered his gun. "The last of them went running off. He'll bring friends. I'm thinking a retreat's the smart play."

"Agreed." Owen straightened up and felt around his right ear. His fingers came away wet. He stepped over Rufus and followed the Mystrian out of the alley. "You didn't need to intervene."

"I reckon you coulda took Rufus, but he'd agone and busted you up some. The Prince hired me to guide you. Ain't no good if you is crippled."

Owen stopped by a public wellhead and worked the pump, splashing cold water over his head and washing off his face. The shock brought a little clarity, but the aftermath left room for his body to report the aches and pains. Another wave of nausea washed over him, but he choked vomit back.

Nathaniel Woods came around and looked at his ear. "Nasty gash. You'll be needing some sewing to fix half your ear back on. Good thing Mistress Frost is handy with a needle and thread."

Owen straightened up again, sweeping dripping black hair out of his face. "They will be rethinking their offer of hospitality."

"It won't surprise 'em none." Nathaniel shrugged. "Caleb likely told them what to expect after he told me."

Owen looked back toward the alley. "He wasn't…"

"He don't have much truck with the Branches."

The two men moved on through the dark city streets, heading uphill toward the Frost estate. "No love lost between you and Rufus."

"'bout right."

"You said you'd shot him before?"

Nathaniel nodded. "He was needing it. Wanted to shoot him in the head, but it was so far up his hind parts, alls I got was his sitting-down meat."

Owen couldn't tell if Nathaniel was joking or not. He got the very distinct sense that both in the alley and even now, Woods was measuring him. "So, tell me, Mr. Woods. Would you have intervened if it wasn't part of your job?"

Nathaniel Woods stopped in the middle of the street and ran a hand over his angular chin. "I'm thinking I might have. Spoiling Rufus' fun's one of the pleasures of my life."

"You're not afraid of reprisals?"

"Not particularly." Nathaniel started moving again. "I'm thinking he's a lot less favorable on being shot than I am on shooting him."

Owen pressed his handkerchief to the side of his head. "You're not afraid of him shooting you first?"

"He gets close enough to take that shot, I ain't deserving of much more life."

They came to the Frost house. Owen opened the gate and waited for Woods to come in.

Nathaniel shook his head. "Your arrival will cause enough commotion. I'll give you a day to rest, then will meet you at your supply depot."

Owen nodded. "I've already requisitioned supplies."

"So I've heard. We'll get them right when I see you." Nathaniel threw him a brief salute, then backed into the shadows.

The Frosts' front door opened. Caleb held up a lantern and Bethany came running out, skirts gathered in her hands. Though the light only illuminated part of her face, her widening eyes and opening mouth made his head hurt worse.

"Caleb, quickly, help me." Bethany tucked herself beneath Owen's left arm and slipped a hand around his waist. "He's bleeding."

"I can see that." Caleb joined his sister on the other side, and the three of them managed to negotiate the doorway with surprising ease. Without another word between them, they took Owen to the kitchen and sat him in a chair.

The mistress of the house fixed him with an iron stare. "I have seen worse. Bethany, take his jacket, brush it off, and start working on those stains. Caleb…"

Her son held his hands up. "A tot of rum, I know."

"But none for yourself. You're the reason he's in this condition."

Owen shrugged his coat off. "Mrs. Frost, there is nothing Caleb could have done…"

"Captain Strake, I would appreciate it if you do not presume to know Temperance or my son that well. When we learned you were dining with the Prince, we sent Caleb to wait for you. He did not do that."

"He told Nathaniel Woods…"

"I am well aware of what he did." Mrs. Frost took a clean cloth and dipped it in some hot water. She pulled his hand and handkerchief away from the wound and wiped blood away. "I know what a store the Prince sets by Mr. Woods, but that hardly makes him an angel."

She set the bloody cloth down and picked up a needle. She threaded it, then held it in the flame of a candle.

Owen frowned. "What are you doing?"

"What must be done."

Caleb returned and handed Owen a small cup of rum. "Virtuan superstition. You were up to deviltry tonight, so there's demons in the wound. Heating the needle will remind them of Hell's-fire and scare them out of there."

Mrs. Frost scowled. "More than once you've been sewed shut with this needle and have barely a scar to remind you of it, Caleb Frost. Don't be mocking God's work."

"Yes, Mother." Caleb pulled back and mimed drinking the rum at a gulp. "It helps."

Owen tossed off the alcohol. It burned all the way down and exploded in his stomach. He wondered for a moment if he would vomit again, but the rum's warmth soothed things.

Mrs. Frost took the cup from his hand and poured the remaining drops on his wound. "A cup for your insides, a drop for your outsides."

"That stings."

"Good. Let it be a reminder to you next time."

It felt odd to be stitched up. Not that he hadn't before, but never around an ear. In addition to the little pokes and the tugs when drawing the stitches tight, he got to hear the popping of his flesh, and the rasp of the thread going through the hole. Mrs. Frost worked diligently, and put more stitches into that small wound that he'd gotten for a sword-gash on his thigh.

Finally she snipped off the end of the thread, then poured another drop of rum on her handiwork. She fashioned a pad out of some clean cloth, rubbed some green paste smelling faintly of mint into it, and set the cloth against the wound. She secured it in place with a bandage that went all the way around Owen's head twice and tied off over his other ear.

"I should think, Captain, that should do."

"Thank you, Mistress Frost."

"You will thank me by staying out of trouble." She turned to her daughter who was sewing up a tear on his jacket sleeve. "You will get him a pad for his pillow, so he will not bleed on our linens."

"Yes, Mother."

Mrs. Frost's expression eased. "Is there anything else you require, Captain?"

"No, I think, well, perhaps, my writing case."

Mrs. Frost's glance dispatched Caleb to Owen's room. He returned quickly with a boxy leather case. "I'll put this on the dining table."

"Thank you." Owen moved into the dining room, the rum still warming his belly. Caleb had set the case at Owen's place on the table and had lit a candle. He stood at the sideboard pouring himself a cup of wine.

Owen waved away the offer of wine and opened his case. He set out some paper and ink, then used a small knife to sharpen a quill. *But who do I write first?*

He saw no purpose in preparing a report on the incident. Langford would only laugh. He might even send his own version of the incident back to Launston to discredit Owen. Preparing a report and sending it directly to Horse Guards would do him no good. It would just be taken as confirmation of the craven nature of the Mystrians, and confirm him as being stupid for having been ambushed. The report's very existence would be used against him—most likely by his uncle.

And writing to Catherine would not do. She would faithfully read the letter, but would keenly feel every blow. The letter would cause her great anxiety, and that was the last thing he wished to do. Catherine would be pleased and proud of victory, but heartsick at his injury. She would blame herself for his being in such danger.

Bethany came into the room bringing another candle, his coat, and her sewing kit. She smiled. "Please tell your wife that your jacket is in good repair."

Owen blinked. "Excuse me?"

"You must be writing her, to tell her you are well despite things, yes?" She sat and hunched over his coat. "Caleb told me you are married. You must miss her."

"I do, Miss, yes, very much." Owen set the quill and penknife down. "I'm not certain she would care to know what has happened. Not about this, anyway."

Bethany looked up, surprise cocking her head. "When Ira was gone I wanted to know everything, every detail. He wrote some—had someone write I mean—and my uncle wrote. We got letters in bunches, of course. Some long after…"

"I can imagine how much that hurt."

She shook her head. "Not as much as not knowing. Men think that not telling saves us worry, but we know. We know when something is not being said, and that makes us worry more. We know you are not telling us something that will worry us, and that leaves it to us to imagine something truly terrible."

"Alas, my wife is not of a temperament to deal with visceral details." Owen half-smiled. "She could never have done what your mother did."

"I know."

"What?" Owen frowned. "You presume a great deal, Miss Frost."

"No offense intended, Captain." She held up his jacket. "I have noticed an indifferent pattern to the repairs. Your wife is not intimate with a needle and thread."

"You notice my handiwork, I'm afraid."

"I am certain she would want you to look your best, so I shall redo some things." Bethany smiled and got out a small pair of scissors. "Go ahead, write. I love the sound of a quill on paper. I find it very soothing. It is one of the reasons I enjoy writing."

"What do you write?"

Bethany looked up, her eyes widened. "Silly things, Captain. Scraps of poetry. Things that shall never see the light of day."

"You shouldn't be ashamed of what you write, Miss Frost. I am certain you have talent." Owen sighed. "I'm afraid I am a better seamster than a writer, but I shall work at it. But I don't think a letter is the thing. I shall commence keeping a journal. That will be good for this journey. I shall start tonight. Tomorrow I shall have to purchase journals to accompany me."

"It should be my pleasure to find you a stationer, Captain Strake, if you so desire." She smiled. "With one proviso."

"And that is?"

"When you return, I wish to read it all."

CHAPTER TEN

April 29, 1763
The Frost Residence, Temperance
Temperance Bay, Mystria

Owen awoke feeling as if he'd been trampled by horses, then dragged a mile behind them. His head throbbed and his stomach pulsed painfully. It didn't help that he could smell bread baking. It made his mouth water, and his stomach knotted in protest.

He rebelled at the thought of leaving bed.

But leave you must. Laughing at himself, he threw back the covers and levered himself out of bed. The fact was that he *had* once been trampled by a horse, and had been dragged behind others. *That* had been bad. He rubbed his stomach and the purple bruise over it, then pulled on breeches, stocking, shoes, and his second-best shirt.

He traced a small, vertical bit of stitchery on the right side. A corresponding scar twisted his flesh beneath—not having been sewed up as neatly as the shirt. He could still feel a twinge as the lance hit him, feel the pressure as it skittered off a rib, and the triumphant look on the Lancer's face before Owen shot his lower jaw off.

He shivered and unbandaged his head before the round table-mirror next to the water bow. The bandage had remained clean, but blood seepage had stained the cloth over the wound. He used a little water to loosen it, then gently pulled it away.

A little redness, slightly swollen, and a bit warm to the touch, but it looked good. Mrs. Frost's stitchery had been tight and the wound had already crusted over. In a week or so he could clip the stitches and pull them out. Let his brown hair grow a bit and no one would ever notice the scar.

Owen washed up in the bowl, then shaved using that same mirror. He had always enjoyed the ritual of shaving—his having an angular face making it easier than for others. He found something soothing about the routine, about lathering his face, then applying cold, razor-sharp steel to his throat. Hearing the scrape of metal across flesh as the hairs popped reminded him that he was still alive, even when pain made him wish he was not.

He headed downstairs and found Doctor Frost in the dining room reading a broadsheet with the title "Wattling's Weekly" emblazoned across the top. "Good morning, Doctor."

"And you, Captain. I understand you had an eventful evening."

Owen nodded. "Which your wife and daughter did their best to repair."

"Your coat is hanging in the kitchen by the door." Doctor Frost folded the paper. "A new paper."

"Mr. Wattling was on the ship. I am surprised he managed to publish so quickly."

"It's old news from Norisle." Frost smiled. "Nothing of your encounter last night, and no report on the debate at the college."

"Debate, sir?"

"Please, sit. Martha, the Captain will have his breakfast now. I told them to fix you some weak tea with honey and some ginger. Good for the stomach. Bread, no butter." Frost slid Owen's chair back with a foot. "Two stories are circulating concerning your encounter last night."

Owen sat. "Indeed."

"One has you and Nathaniel Woods insulting the Branches and their getting the worst of a thrashing. Nothing for them to brag upon. They've run afoul of Woods before with similar results."

A servant brought the tea and bread. Owen sipped carefully and his stomach eased slowly. "The other story?"

"A group of Twilight People slipped into the city and attacked you, but Nathaniel Woods told them to go away."

Owen frowned. "Why would that story have any currency?"

"You wear the red coat. The Twilight People were of the Ungarakii and in Tharyngian employ. The story serves those who hate the Twilight People. If they are painted as loyal to the Laureates in Feris, reports will get back to Launston and more soldiers will come to drive the natives away."

Owen dipped a corner of the bread into his tea, then took a bite. "I don't see the logic of that. I rode from here to the Prince's estate. There is plenty of unoccupied land."

Doctor Frost sat forward, resting his elbows on the table. "That is a matter of contention, Captain. The Twilight People migrate seasonally, so what we see as open is land they require for hunting, or that might be sacred to them. They do not develop the land as we do. Because they do not engage in animal husbandry or much more than subsistence farming, they require far larger tracts than we do. When someone decides to go out, clear some ground, and set up a farm, the Twilight People take offense. Not close to the city, mind you, but out there, in the wilderness."

"Langford could send troops to punish the raiders."

"He could, but most of the settlers involved are squatting on land claimed by the Crown. Speculators, however, want those lands, so the pressure will increase to destroy the Twilight People." Frost sat back. "That discussion formed part of the debate last evening. The larger question was whether or not Mystria would do better as its own nation, or subject to the Crown."

Owen's eyes tightened. "That discussion could be construed as treason, Doctor Frost."

The older man smiled. "Not the discussion, sir, but advocacy of independence—and no one advocated that. What we did discuss, however, was whether or not the Crown was negligent in its conduct toward us. Benign negligence in the minds of most but, alas, not all."

"I'm not certain I follow, sir."

"Let me give you one simple example. The southern colonies are prohibited from selling cotton to anyone but Norillian merchants. They are paid a price set by the Crown, a price which is considerably below that offered by the Tharyngians."

"The Tharyngians are our enemies, Doctor. You cannot be suggesting we would trade with the enemy."

"No, but Norillian merchants buy our raw cotton, then sell to agents of the Alandalusians at a great profit. They, in turn, sell it to the Tharyngians." Frost raised a finger. "And, more to the point, the cotton that ends up in Norisle is milled there, then shipped back here. The cloth is sold at a considerable mark-up. Because we have ample rivers, we could produce our own cloth here, even more cheaply than in Norisle. We could even ship and sell it cheaply in Norisle, but the Crown prohibits us having any native industry."

"I will admit, sir, that this seems, on the surface, to make no sense, but…"

Frost chuckled and patted a hand against the broadsheet. "It makes perfect sense, Captain, when you realize that it is the men made rich in the various trades who have the Queen's ear. They are the men who sit in Lords or have their agents elected to Commons. They tell the Queen that were we to have our own mills, it would ruin the Norillian economy. They remind her that we are the children of convicts, dissidents, and redemptioneers and, therefore, inherently untrustworthy."

Owen raised an eyebrow. "You argue against yourself, sir. You suggest you are not defectives. If this is true, and you were given industry, you would succeed in your ventures, ruining Norisle's economy. The Crown is either ignorant, or terribly wise."

"I prefer 'unthinking,' Captain." Frost lifted up the paper. "Consider, if a press can be shipped here and set up in two days, do you think it possible that a mill will not be someday duplicated? Might some man ruined by a rival not come here and build one? Might not a Ryngian cede us that knowledge to ruin Norisle?"

Owen nodded. "Either could happen. Each would be illegal."

"If you were given the orders, would you destroy those mills?"

"It would be my duty."

"But could you get *all* of them, Captain?"

Owen shook his head. "They would still be illegal."

"And inevitable." Frost smiled. "Change is an irresistible force, Captain. Progress cannot be hobbled, just harnessed. And, if not harnessed, it will run out of control."

The soldier shivered. "You have given me much to think about, sir. Had my brains not been scrambled, I might have given you a better argument."

"You acquitted yourself well, Captain. This is the joy of being a Natural Philosopher. The world is my treasure. I am free to think and imagine. My passion is illuminating the minds of the young." He leaned in again. "I would ask of you a favor, however."

"If I may be of service, sir."

"You will be going into areas where not many have gone before. If it does not compromise your duty, I would appreciate copies of your charts—the rivers, you see. We huddle on a narrow strip of the coast. If we are ever to thrive, we will move inland, and the rivers are the routes we will follow."

Owen hesitated for a moment. The information he would obtain was for the Crown. By rights, its distribution would depend on his superiors. But Nathaniel Woods could just as easily communicate same to the Frosts—and Colonel Langford would certainly sell them the information. Frost's possession of it was inevitable. *Just like change.*

"It would be an honor, sir."

"Very good, thank you." Frost clapped his hands and looked up as Bethany came in from the kitchen, fastening a light cloak around her shoulders. "Are you come to conduct the Captain about town?"

"Are you done torturing him?" A white bonnet restrained her light brown hair, save for a curl over her forehead.

"For now, yes." Frost slid his chair back and stood. "A pleasure, Captain."

Owen stood and shook the man's hand. "And mine, sir."

"Take good care of my daughter." Frost pumped his arm warmly. "Until this evening. Good hunting."

As they moved through Temperance, Owen studied people with new eyes. His red coat and even his second-best shirt had been woven tightly—more tightly than clothes worn by anyone but the most prosperous. Many men wore breeches that had been patched repeatedly, and often needed yet another patch or two. More commonly they went without shoes or stockings, and few possessed proper coats.

Prior to his discussion with Doctor Frost, Owen had been inclined to put their slovenly appearance down to their nature. Norisle's feckless and destitute—those in thrall to spirits and indolence—dressed similarly. He thought them incapable of rising above their nature, lacking character. Even those brought into the army and trained for better retreated to their baser selves when given any idle time.

"Did you not hear me, Captain?"

Owen blinked. "My apologies, Miss Frost. My mind was off and away."

Bethany laughed easily. "You are like my father in that regard. I should have expected this after his speaking with you this morning."

"He does challenge a man."

"That he does." She opened a hand toward a small alley off Fortitude Street. "You may find the journals you want here, on Scrivener Street; or you might want to obtain logs closer to the dock."

"We should look here."

"Very well. What was it my father had you thinking about?"

"Things well outside my purpose here."

A frown wrinkled her brow. "My dear Captain Strake, do not think me some addlepated girl. I am my father's daughter and capable of handling myself in discourse."

"No offense intended, Miss. We discussed the lack of a native textile industry." Owen jerked his head back toward Fortitude. "Consequently I was noticing what people wore."

"It gets very cold for some come winter." She paused before the door of Burns and Company, Booksellers. "We might try here."

Owen opened the door into a small shop crowded with shelves. A bell tinkled from above the door. A small man wearing spectacles appeared from deeper within the shop. Two large volumes filled his hands. "Good day, Miss Frost. May I help you?"

Bethany eclipsed Owen. "I hope you will, Mr. Burns. Captain Strake desires two journals, three hundred pages each, your best paper, leather covers, and oilskin wraps. He'll need an inkstick and a half-dozen quills."

The man smiled, setting the books on a small, drop-leaf desk in the corner. "I can bind up the journals, send them around to your house, Miss Frost, by eventide."

Owen nodded. "That would be satisfactory."

"As for the quills, well, I have something here you might like better, Captain." Burns pulled a narrow wooden box from the desk and slid the top off.

Two turned wooden cylinders rested on a red velvet bed along with three silver wedges. The man handed one of the wedges to Owen. The metal had been hammered incredibly thin, and curved along its length. It tapered to a point and had been split halfway up the middle.

"Local silversmith, he makes these. They're nibs, fit into these holders. Last longer than a quill and don't need sharpening."

"The work is incredibly delicate." Owen held it out for Bethany to see, slowly turning it in his fingers. "Do you know how he does this?"

Burns shrugged. "Not being *cursed*, I don't know for sure, but he uses a firestone in the process. Has it at the end of a thumb, in a glove you see, so he can work the metal while hammering."

Which is why it's silver. Iron and steel dampened magick, all but destroying the ability of any but the strongest user to make it work. Stories of heroes who could enchant a sword abounded, but Owen had never seen that ability in action.

The bookseller ducked his head. "And no offense meant, Captain."

"None taken." Owen nodded solemnly. "Soldiers greet that appellation proudly. We might be bound for Hell, but we'll send the enemy there to welcome us."

"And we are right happy you do that, sir." Burns smiled. "Will you be taking these?"

"Yes." Owen handed back the nib. "Reckon the bill, please."

"Gladly, sir. Shall I have the pens sent round with the journals?"

"Please."

The man scratched some figures on a scrap of paper. "That will be a crown, three and eight."

Owen slipped a hand into his pocket for his purse, but Bethany laid a hand on his wrist. "That is outrageous. We are leaving now, Captain Strake."

"What?"

Bethany turned on the bookseller. "Mr. Burns, my family has traded with you for many years. We recommend you highly. This should cost no more than a crown and ten, or four shillings eleven."

"But, Miss…"

"Mr. Burns, you are charging Captain Strake more because he wears the red coat—and you just praised him for his defense of our nation. You would charge no Mystrian so dearly."

The bookseller blushed, then looked at his paper again. "Yes, of course, Miss, I added incorrectly. A crown and four. The pens, you see, are consigned. I cannot bargain."

Owen gave the man a gold crown and four copper pence. "Thank you, sir."

"My pleasure, sir." Burns bowed his head. "And good day to you, Miss Frost."

"Mister Burns." Bethany preceded Owen from the shop and moved quickly down Scrivener Street.

Owen caught up to her with a couple long strides. "His price—I would have paid as much in Launston."

"But we are not *in* Launston." She pointed back toward the shop. "His family comes from charcoal burners. His children go round to homes and shops and public houses offering to clean lamps for the black, which is what he uses to make his ink."

"Enterprising."

"It is, and he's a sharp man with his figuring. His prices are the best for his wares, which is why he has our custom." She shook her head. "But to prey upon someone like you."

Owen smiled. "Soldiers are used to having merchants take advantage."

"That hardly makes it right." Bethany shook her head. "He was willing to overcharge you because you are a stranger. You, a Queen's officer, a stranger. Too many men get to thinking like that, and the men of Norisle *will* be strangers. And then, Captain, a bill will be delivered that can only be paid in blood."

CHAPTER ELEVEN

April 29, 1763
Temperance
Temperance Bay, Mystria

Having successfully conducted the tasks he needed to complete, Owen Strake accompanied Bethany Frost on her errands. He suspected that some of them were contrived so they could spend more time together. He imagined she hoped he could remember more about Ira Hill. Regardless, he enjoyed the time spent in her company. Her laughter warmed his heart, and the way she faced the bookseller down appealed to him.

Catherine never would have done that. Instead she would have paid the asking price, then engineered an effort by other wives to utterly ruin the bookseller. The difference in approach was clearly a difference between the two women. It also marked a difference between the societies on either side of the ocean. Mystrians tended toward being direct and open. Though alien to Owen, he found himself warming to this approach.

Owen carried a basket as Bethany picked through bunches of radishes and early carrots. "If you would not mind, Miss Frost, I was wondering what the prevailing attitude about *the cursed* is within the colonies."

She laughed easily. "You should not let Mr. Burns' attitude concern you, Captain. People are quite accepting here. The vast majority of the colonists came from the cursed classes. Having the curse made life here much easier those first years."

That made perfect sense. Magick remained largely benign because users could only effect what they could touch, and because iron and steel were proofed against it. Any warrior armed with an iron weapon could slay a sorcerer with relative impunity. Magick use remained largely hidden down through the years. Anyone suspected of being powerful was either ostracized or destroyed.

It wasn't until brimstone's introduction from the Orient, and the spells that made firestones functional, that magick became important. The nobility bred the curse back into their bloodlines—though common were the rumors that they just revealed what they had hidden for many generations—and the cursed underclasses became valued for their ability to fight wars.

And yet, anyone who appears too adept will quickly earn a perilous assignment.

Bethany placed two bunches of radishes in the basket. "The curse helped not only because hunting staved off starvation, but the Twilight People respect magick. They did not know of brimstone or firestones, or iron, for that matter, but learned very quickly. In return, they shared some of their knowledge of Mystria. Had we neither guns nor magick, I think they would have wiped us out."

Owen frowned as they moved on toward another stall. "Your father said there are some who hate the Twilight People."

"Hate and fear." Bethany nodded. "They want their lands, not to live on, but to hold and sell to others. Speculators. Greed drives them. It's said the Twilight People use the same word for greed as for insanity. I do not think they are far wrong."

"*Are* the Twilight People a threat?"

She laughed and rested a hand on his arm. "I fear, Captain, that what you know of the Twilight People comes from reading books of the same caliber as Lord Rivendell's work. In the northeast we have two very large groupings of tribes: the Confederation and the Seven Nations. The Seven Nations range out further west and are heavily influenced by the Ryngians. The Confederation deals more with us. And yet, within each grouping, the tribes have their own affinities and alliances, which shift on a whim. While I never have felt in danger here in Temperance, there have been times traveling when I have not felt wholly safe."

Bethany spoke so plainly that Owen found it easy to imagine her astride a horse, a pistol in each hand, fighting off marauders and highwaymen alike. He glanced at her hands, but only caught a fleeting glimpse of her thumbs.

She caught his eye, then held her hands out, thumbs uppermost. Her voice sank to a whisper. "Yes, Captain, my family is cursed. I have shot, but not recently, as you can see."

He nodded.

She quickly caught his right hand and brushed her thumb over his rough thumbnail. Each line on it marked a battle, and the smoothness near the cuticle betrayed his long voyage to Mystria. The blood from those battles had long since faded from beneath his nail, but the nail's corduroy surface revealed hard fighting.

"The marks are genuine. I have not *rasped* my way to glory."

"There is none of that here, Captain." She released his hand. "The Virtuans admire courage and hate boastfulness. Lord Rivendell's book was frowned upon mostly because of its tone, not what it said about Mystrians. In Temperance, at least."

"The book had little to recommend it."

"Few here see a use for it."

Owen shrugged. "It will hold a door open in a wind."

Bethany giggled, then selected a small bundle of rosemary and added it to the basket. "So, tell me, Captain, what are you? A Six or an Eight? Caleb is a Six, though he claims Seven."

"I am actually a Thirteen."

She blinked. "Ira was a Ten and the best we had to send."

Owen smiled. "It has nothing to do with my Norillian blood, Miss Frost. My mother's people boast of being Sixes, but they lie and lie badly. Even my stepfather and the Ventnor family can produce, at best, an Eight. No matter. The measure is false."

"How can you say that? You can load and shoot thirteen times before magick exhausts you. This gives you a great advantage."

"It would, Miss, if in battle a soldier could get off more than three shots before the enemy was upon him with bayonet, lance, and ax."

From his basket Bethany took a smaller basket and began to gather a dozen eggs into it. "That was not the impression of battle given by the Rivendell book."

Owen chuckled. "Lord Rivendell saw no fighting. Those whom he later interviewed—including his son—spent time working with a rasp and then embellished their roles greatly."

"You've read it, then?"

"My wife insisted." Owen shivered. "Catherine could not bear to read it, but implored me to do so. She hoped I was mentioned. There was nothing of me in there, of course, though it did please her that Rivendell praised my uncle as if he were the very avatar of some ancient and terrible god of war."

"More of Rivendell's lies?"

Owen frowned. "No. When it comes to war, my uncle has a fearsome talent. What was written of him was likely the only truth in the whole book."

Bethany smiled and put an egg in her basket. "Is she nice, your wife?"

"Yes. We married in the spring before Villerupt. She lives at my grandfather's estate."

"And she chose not to come with you to Mystria?"

"She is not terribly adventurous, Miss."

"I had wanted to go to the Low Countries with Ira, but it would not have been proper, as we were not wed. Some of the other wives did go. My uncle met his wife there, in fact. She was widowed in battle. She nursed him back to health. I find it romantic, but do not say that in front of my mother."

"I shall heed your warning." Owen trailed after Bethany, wondering if he would have noticed her had she come with the Colonials. Likely not, though the way she moved through the market bespoke an energy that would have been welcome in the camp.

"Did Catherine go to the Continent?"

"Yes, but never to camp." Owen smiled. "She is rather delicate and enamored of dances and gowns. She eschews early morning walks because of dew and detests mud. She sometimes suffers from the vapors and to be setting up a tent during a downpour after a swampy march would lay her in the grave."

"Sounds like one of the Fairlee girls my uncle wishes to marry to Caleb." Bethany settled the small basket of eggs in his larger basket, then linked her arm in his. "It is time for us to return home."

Owen looked up and read the time from the clock on Government House. "It is, indeed. I will walk you back, then I have to meet Nathaniel Woods at the Stores Depot."

A shiver ran through Bethany.

"What is the matter?"

"I do not care for the man, Captain Strake. I know the Prince favors him, and he is the best guide in the colony, perhaps *all* the colonies, but that does not excuse his behavior."

"What behavior would that be?"

"I am not a gossip, sir."

Owen patted her hand. "I did not mean to suggest you were, Miss Frost. I apologize for any such implication. Will his behavior compromise my mission?"

"I shouldn't think so. Away from Temperance he should be better." Bethany frowned. "Little help, I know. And don't go asking my brother about him. Caleb all but worships him. But please do be careful."

"I will. I promise." Owen purposefully broadened his smile. "I'm sure my mission shall be as peaceful as this trip through the market, though the company will not be close to so delightful."

Owen found the disconcerted expression on Lieutenant Palmerston's face gratifying, though he wished he'd been the cause of it. Instead of that, he had Palmerston look to him for relief, with an amused Nathaniel Woods watching.

Palmerston held his hands up. "Captain Strake, I did as you asked. I gathered all your supplies and had them done up nice and complete." He pointed to a pile on one side of the depot floor. "But then this gentleman came in and he ruined everything."

Owen glanced at Woods, who was standing beside a much smaller pile. "I thought, sir, we were meeting here at half past two. Did I mistake the time?"

Nathaniel shook his head. "Seen you marketing with the Frost girl. Figured

I'd come down here, see what was what."

Owen looked at the two piles. The larger one contained most everything from Owen's original list, including bolts of cloth, beads, other trade goods, some ironwork, some books, two casks of salted beef, two cases of biscuit, blankets, tack and saddles, and feed for horses.

The other pile looked tiny by comparison. Woods had pulled aside a single musket, a pistol, shot and brimstone, a sextant, a pouch with food, another with pre-rolled cartridges for the guns, a knife, a small ax, two canteens, a single blanket, and a backpack that could carry the extra shot as well as his journals, a small telescope, and a change of socks.

"Lieutenant Palmerston, would you excuse us for a moment?"

The Quartermaster quickly exited the building, closing the door behind him, but not all the way.

Owen completed the closing. "Mr. Woods, I appreciate your association with the Prince. You know your business. But, sir, I have a mission."

Woods leaned back against the wall. "You're to scout out where the Ryngians are and report back. And while you're at it, you'll make friends with the Twilight People and convince them to be fighting for the Queen when the war comes this way?"

Owen hesitated. "Did the Prince tell you that?"

"Ain't no need." Woods slowly shook his head. "Norillians been trying to do that thing since my pap was a boy. Now you're thinking them blankets and that cloth will be a way to buy some good will, ain'tcha?"

"You suggest it won't, sir?"

"Well, now, ever hear of Major Hopkins?"

"Afraid not."

"Tain't much of a surprise. Thirty years ago, Major Hopkins brought the Twilight People blankets tainted with the Blood Pox. Thought the Altashee would just wrap themselves up and die. Didn't happen."

"I was unaware of that."

"Not many are. Know why his plan didn't work?"

"No."

Woods' eyes tightened. "The Altashee ain't idiots. The men bringing the blankets all had pox scars. The Altashee sussed out what was going on. They got them some powerful medicine magicks. You tote them blankets and they'll figure you're out to kill 'em."

Owen shook his head. "They stay, then. The Twilight People, they still trade for cloth, yes?"

"Some. From a post where the cloth has been sitting around for six months or more, and where whites buy it and wear it."

"The horse fodder?"

"Don't need feed for horses we ain't gonna have."

"I see." Owen looked from one pile to another. He had a choice to make. He could demand that Woods justify every exclusion, or he could ask *why* he'd selected the things in the small pile. The latter course would be more productive, though he itched to go through the former. It *was* his expedition, after all.

Or is it?

"How many rounds for each weapon?"

"Two hundred and a half for your long gun; a hundred for the pistol and seven firestones total."

Dust motes danced in the light illuminating the small pile. "That's twice as many firestones as needed."

Woods shook his head. "You ever actually put a hundred shots through a firestone?"

Owen frowned. "More. They were army stones like these and rated for a hundred shots."

"Out here we reckon the man making firestones has a brother in that there Parliament what sends him work. Got paid good for 'em, but he's a long ways away. If one of them shatters after ten or fifteen or fifty shots, you ain't gonna survive long enough to be a-complaining to him."

"You've made your point."

"Out there ain't no Fire Wardens for to sell us a spare firestone or three. The rule is 'a pinch more powder and keep your stone bright.' That'll put your shot where you want it."

"Since you have rejected the foodstuffs, shall I assume we will be living off the land?"

"You can't imagine the bounty out there, Captain." Woods smiled and his gaze became distant. "You'll be glad you don't have weevil biscuits and sour beef. What we can't kill or pick, we'll trade for. We'll even get you some better clothes."

"I think not, sir." Owen held his head up. "I am an officer of Her Majesty's Army. I shall wear my uniform proudly."

"Your clothes ain't going to last."

"It really doesn't matter, Mr. Woods." Owen kept his voice firm. "This mission will take us into enemy territory. If I travel out of uniform and were captured, I would be hung as a spy. I am *not* a spy. I shall not comport myself as one."

Woods had been grinning as if he was going to laugh, but his expression sobered quickly enough. "You're set on that?"

"I am, sir."

"The matter is closed. I respect your conviction, sir." Woods shook his head. "Not sure I understand it, but I 'spect that's a piece of civilization I'm not meant to be comprehending. Will you be adding anything else to your kit?"

"I have a few personal effects. Journals. Pens." Owen thought, then shook his head. "Unless you think there is something else. I am sure there will be room in my pack."

Woods nodded. "I reckon we're covered."

"And Mr. Woods…"

"Yes, Captain Strake?"

"This *is* my expedition, isn't it?"

"It's all yours, sir." Woods gave him a tiny salute. "I'm just along so's you can find your way to the end of it."

CHAPTER TWELVE

May 1, 1763
St. Martin's Cathedral, Temperance
Temperance Bay, Mystria

Owen found himself with the luxury of a couple of hours before the grand Sunday dinner Mrs. Frost had promised earlier in the week. Owen had joined the family at services. Bishop Othniel Bumble had held forth in a fiery sermon about duty to the Crown. After the service, the Frosts invited the Bishop, his family, and his aid, Reverend Benjamin Beecher to join them for dinner.

Owen occupied himself by organizing his journals. He decided one would be a workbook for notes and sketches while traveling. The second would be the mission journal. He would copy and organize things from the workbook to guarantee the information's accuracy.

While this was his intent, in sitting down to practice with his metal nibs, he realized his plan would not work. The workbook observations about Mystria expanded beyond their original scope. He found himself evaluating the people and their customs. Commentary required context, so his writing became voluminous.

He found himself motivated, in part, by Lord Rivendell's book. That Rivendell's tome could be taken as the definitive account of Villerupt revolted him. He wanted his impressions of Mystria to educate readers about the people and their true courage.

This created problems. The assault, for example, did not paint a pretty picture of Mystrian behavior. Owen chose to write things down as plainly as he could. He hoped that his portraits of the Frosts and even Nathaniel Woods would balance any negative impressions gleaned from the actions of people like the Branches.

Owen had filled several pages with an even hand when one of the younger Frosts tapped on his door. Owen pulled on the plain coat he'd worn to church and descended. The dining table had been set up in the kitchen yard, on a green lawn.

The rotund Bishop Bumble regarded him with a flash of displeasure before a smile lit his ruddy face to the point of buffoonery. He threw his arms wide and waddled forward. "So good to see you again, Captain Strake. May I present to you my wife, Livinia, and my niece, Lilith."

Livinia Bumble suffered in comparison to her husband and Mrs. Frost, being slight of frame and colorless to the point of appearing gray. She did make an effort at smiling, but it exhausted her. Owen would have taken her to be entirely timid, but her blue eyes remained sharp and seemed to miss nothing.

Owen bowed and kissed her proffered hand, then smiled at the other member of the Bumble party. Lilith was everything her aunt was not. Tall and flame-haired, the young woman smiled dazzlingly, fully aware of the effect. Though she wore a gown styled as simply as her aunt's, and cut from the same cloth, her bright blue eyes and the spray of freckles across her cheeks rescued her from being drab.

Lilith curtsied as Owen took her hand. "You honor me, Captain Strake."

Owen kissed it, then straightened. "My pleasure, Miss Bumble."

He then offered his hand to the fourth member of the Bumble party. "Good to see you again, Reverend Beecher."

Beecher, who looked a match for Livinia save for being taller, nodded curtly. "I see you fare better on land than on the sea."

"Which is why I serve in Her Majesty's Army and not the Royal Navy." Owen shook the man's hand firmly, resisting the temptation to crush it. Beecher had not been unkind on the ship. More than once he'd joined Owen at the heads, vomiting over the side.

Mrs. Frost called them all to dinner. The Bishop sat at Dr. Frost's right hand, in the space Caleb would have occupied had he been present. Owen sat on the left, with Lilith at his side and Bethany opposite her. Beecher sat at Bethany's right. The children ranged between the young adults and the end of the table where the two matriarchs sat.

The meal consisted of three courses. It began with a fish chowder containing maize and potatoes in a milk broth. Onions and pepper had been added, the latter in a profligate quantity. Owen's throat closed with the first spoonful, but eased after a little wine.

The Bishop noticed. "You will find, Captain, that spices are not as dear here as they are in Norisle. We tend to demonstrate our fortune with their overuse."

Doctor Frost snorted. "And we drink very expensive wine to wash spice away."

"Praise God you can afford it, yes, Archibald."

"Quite, Othniel. To your health, Captain."

A steaming haunch of beef came next. Doctor Frost carved, offering a small lecture on the primacy of red meat as he cut. The Bishop got the King's cut, but the slice that ended up on Owen's plate nearly matched it. The cuts got progressively smaller, save for the last two, which went to Hettie and Livinia.

Bowls brimming with green beans and squash circulated. Never having had the latter, Owen watched how much others took. Butter and more pepper had been used in the squash, so when it came his turn, he served himself a conservative portion. His first taste, however, pleased him so much he kept an eye on the bowl in case there was any left over.

Conversation remained light during the meal. Owen had once been told that a gentleman "is neither a bore nor seated next to one at dinner." Doctor Frost's comments ranged on subjects far and wide, while Lilith remained coquettish and flattering. Owen did his best to cope with each, offering a couple of stories of his time fighting on the Continent. For the most part, however, he kept quiet.

This was not entirely out of manners. Bethany, though she smiled at both men on either side of her, did not appear to be her lively self. From what Owen could overhear, Beecher's attempts at conversation consisted of repeating selections from the great sermons. His delivery would have taxed the patience of a stone.

Bishop Bumble did not speak much to Bethany, save for a few mumbled comments during Owen's tales. Bethany reacted stiffly to the comments. Color drained from her face and she chewed mechanically for a time after that. Though she recovered enough to laugh politely at Owen's stories, Bumble clearly had upset her.

To the delight of the children, a pudding with berries and raisins finished the meal. They were served first, then the women excused themselves and herded the youngsters away. Beecher slid down into Bethany's chair—uttering a sigh Owen would have preferred not to have heard.

Doctor Frost poured a small cut-crystal glass of sherry for each man, then hoisted his in the air. "To the Queen's health."

Owen quaffed the sweet wine. It burned all the way down, but gently, at least to his throat. Beecher appeared to have more difficulty with it, much to the silent amusement of the two older gentlemen.

The Bishop refilled their glasses, then set the bottle in the center of the table. "Captain Strake, I would ask you a question."

"Please, sir."

"Are you not proud of your service?" The question came in a voice that was nine-tenths innocent. "Neither here nor to church did you wear your uniform."

"I am very proud of my service." Owen met the old man's dark stare openly. "I feared that the bright coat, the gold braid, would seem ostentatious and arrogant on the Lord's Day. I didn't wish to disrupt your service."

"I wish you had." Bumble picked up his glass and slowly spun it. Sunlight sparked rainbows. "I would have bid you come forward and sit in the front so my flock could see a proud officer of Her Majesty's Army. Too many people here are given cause to think poorly of our government. Colonel Langford and others set a frightful example."

Archibald Frost smiled. "I think, Othniel, you judge the people of Temperance harshly."

"I wish I could agree with you, Archibald, but the fact is that our people have lost their way. They have forgotten that we are all children of God, and that He has established an order to the Universe. We are to serve His purpose, and His purpose is clear. Our monarch is His ordained representative on this Earth. We believe that because He has granted us the bounty of this continent, we are somehow superior to the men of Norisle. A ridiculous proposition, wouldn't you agree, Captain?"

"I am not a theologian, sir. I pray to shoot better and faster than my enemy."

Beecher leaned forward, raising his glass. "And it is a good thing that God grants you that prayer for you are His agent in the war against the Atheists."

The Bishop and Dr. Frost exchanged glances at Beecher's outburst. Frost could not suppress an indulgent chuckle. "Not all Tharyngians are Atheists, Mr. Beecher."

"Their revolution overthrew God's ordained King and established the rule of the Laureates. They refuse to acknowledge God as their superior."

Bumble set his glass down. "Mr. Beecher, I have suggested you need more precision in your thinking and words. It is vital for your career. Doctor Frost is correct. The Laureates tolerate worship. Many of them are Deists, and most are Agnostics. Only a select few are Atheists. That is their nature. They assign Science the highest order and acknowledge that Science can neither confirm nor deny the existence of God."

"And they shall burn in Hell for that."

"Indeed they shall, but this does not make them Atheists, merely wrong." The Bishop smiled at Owen. "What would you do, sir, if you had a man like Mr. Beecher in your command?"

"That is what we have sergeants for."

Beecher sat back. "I am certain none of them are Atheists, are they, Captain? War not being a thing to promote such nonsense."

Though Owen knew better, he rose to the bait Beecher had so carelessly offered. "To be frank, Mr. Beecher, war is the last thing to promote a belief in God. When you've seen a man's head blown open by a musket-ball, with a chunk of his skull missing, and he sits there reciting nursery rhymes or begging for his mother, you wonder what sort of a God could condone war. And I understand and *believe* that these men will be rewarded in Heaven, but I cannot help but wonder if even an eternity of pleasure is just recompense for sitting with your guts in your lap, or watching a surgeon take your arm off with a saw."

Beecher paled. "I only meant…"

"I know what you meant, sir, and I know the fallaciousness of it. Perhaps, Mr. Beecher, if the opportunity ever presents itself for you to join a military expedition, you will take it. You will learn a great deal about men, war, and yourself."

"Quite right." The Bishop nodded solemnly. "You know, Captain, I offered the blessing before the Mystrian Rangers sailed for Norisle. I gave quite a good sermon but I wish I had heard your words. I would have gone. Perhaps, had I been there, I could have stiffened their spines or, at least, eased their torments."

Until his last comment, Owen was prepared to open fire on the Bishop, too. Genuine compassion issued through his voice, checking Owen's anger. "I believe, sir, both of you would have benefited from that experience. Contrary to what you may have read, the Mystrian Rangers did make you all proud."

The Bishop raised his glass. "To their health and salvation."

Owen drank, wishing for more of one than the other.

Talk turned from things philosophical to local, so Owen excused himself. The Bishop promised to invite him to dinner upon his return. Owen accepted in advance and left them in the yard. He fully intended to head to his room, but as he cut through the darkened dining room, he caught sight of Bethany sitting alone in the front yard.

She looked up as he appeared before her. "Good evening, Captain. Would you like to sit?"

"Thank you." Owen looked at his hands. "I might be mistaken, Miss, but did Bishop Bumble upset you during dinner?"

Bethany sighed. "He has preached from the Gospel according to Rivendell before. While you spoke of the war, he was praising God that Norisle had brave men like you to defend it. You see, most of the Rangers were indifferent about Church and not all of them were sober when he offered his blessing."

"Was your Ira among them?"

She shook her head. "Ira attended every Sunday. At college he was studying for the clergy. The Bishop had offered to go with the Rangers. My uncle put it to a vote. The soldiers said no. They said Ira was the only minister they needed."

Things began to fit together more clearly. "I see. And Beecher, was he a bother?"

"Harmless. A puppy." Bethany smiled. "He's enchanted with Lilith. He'll never win her. Better men have tried."

"Better men like Nathaniel Woods?"

"Woods? Ha!" Bethany shook her head. "The Bishop would have Woods burned for a witch if he came near her. And Nathaniel would gladly jump into the flames."

"I didn't have the impression you disliked her."

"I hide things very well, Captain Strake." She laid both her hands on his forearm. "On your journey you will see many wonderful and dangerous things. But in no greater jeopardy will you be than you were this evening."

"I don't understand."

"You were being measured to be Lilith's husband."

Owen held up his left hand and flicked his thumbnail against the ring. "But I'm married."

"Mystria is home to the ambitious, Captain." Her eyes grew dark. "They find the ends justifying the means, so there are no lengths to which they will not go."

"You suggest many horrible things, Miss Frost."

"More so than you know, Captain." Bethany squeezed his arm. "Be careful, please, as you go, and especially as you return."

CHAPTER THIRTEEN

May 2, 1763
The Frost Residence, Temperance
Temperance Bay, Mystria

Owen got up before dawn, dressing himself by candlelight in his uniform, from his tri-corner hat with blue cockade, to boots with polished spurs. He filled his pack with extra clothes, rolled his blanket and put that on top, and pulled the pack on. He then donned his ammunition pouches, slid the pistol into a holster at his right thigh, and shouldered his musket—the bayonet for which hung from a sash at his left hip.

His duty rituals consisted mostly of caring for his weapons. The musket, when placed with the butt on the ground, ended up three inches taller than he was—the bayonet added another foot and a half. The steel barrel alone was forty-two inches long. It ended in a curved brass fitting made of two pieces. The centermost bit could be unscrewed and removed, revealing a narrow hole at the barrel's base and a hollow in the large brass piece. A firestone would be set in that hollow, then tightened down with the center-bit. A hole in the retention collar allowed a portion of the firestone to protrude, so he could thumb it and magickally ignite the brimstone.

The long gun he'd drawn from stores had seen better days. He'd cleaned it, washing, swabbing,, and oiling the barrel inside and out. He'd also cleaned and oiled the stock, then tightened down every screw he could find and replaced those he could not. He made sure the ramrod would remain in place while he traveled. Without it, he couldn't load the gun, changing the musket into a club.

The Frosts, minus Caleb, had risen early enough to see him off. Mrs. Frost handed him a loaf of bread and some cheese all wrapped up in cloth. Bethany gave him an envelope with two quills just in case of disaster. He thanked them both, his throat tightening.

His reaction surprised him, and it took him a moment to figure out why. Though they were strangers to him, they'd fed him, repaired his clothes, sewed up his wounds, and otherwise seen to his welfare. They'd done it out of a sense of duty to the Crown. *And because they are just nice people.*

Ultimately they had treated him more kindly than his family ever had, and when they wished him a safe journey, he knew they actually meant it.

Doctor Frost walked him to the gate. "I have enjoyed our all-too-brief association, Captain Strake. I very much look forward to your return."

"You and your family have been wonderful. I hope I have not been a burden."

"Nonsense, sir, it has been a delight." Frost drew a small book from his coat pocket. "I know you don't want extra weight on your trip, but I thought you might find this intriguing."

The tiny volume had been bound in black leather with the title "A Continent's Calling" incised in gold on the cover. Doctor Frost smiled carefully. "It was written by Samuel Haste. It inspired our debate on whether or not Mystria would be better off as its own nation. Some of your countrymen would take it as a work of treason, but I hope you find it to be something else. Mr. Haste truly loves this land and dreams of all it can become. You should understand that, and that many people share his dream."

"Thank you, Doctor." Owen slipped the book into his coat pocket. "I expect to be back before September. I would call upon you then."

"Captain, we insist you stay with us upon your return." The man smiled. "In fact, I think Major Forest might be heading north around that time, so I shall see to it that you are reacquainted."

"Most kind." Owen gave the man a brief salute. "Until then."

Owen headed off along Diligence quickly, planning to meet Woods at Westgate as the sun rose. Out toward the city's edge, where the prosperous built their stately homes, no one stirred on the broad streets. Down toward the docks the sounds of the city waking echoed through alleys and crowded neighborhoods.

The day had started with a bit of crispness in the air, but it would burn off quickly. Still, it made for easy walking and Owen couldn't help but smile. His brief trip out of the city had hinted at how much there was to explore, and he was anxious to get started.

"Walk your legs clean off at that pace, Captain."

Owen spun, leveling the musket. "Woods!"

"Thinking I was Rufus?"

"I didn't expect... I thought we were meeting at Westgate."

Wood detached himself from shadows. "So'd some other folks. Word got out."

"I told no one."

"Never 'spected you did." Woods yawned and jerked a thumb to the left. "We'll head over to Justice and go out through the pig yards."

Owen shouldered the musket again. "Are you afraid Rufus is watching us?"

"Ain't 'fraid, just cautious. Careless word here, a word sold there, might be finding trouble we ain't needing."

Owen followed him. "Are you suggesting that the Tharyngians are actively spying in our colonies?"

"Are you believing they're not?"

"No, Mr. Woods, I would imagine they are. I was asking, to be more precise, if you have any knowledge of Tharyngian spies in Temperance Bay."

"Don't suppose I do." Woods looked back over his shoulder at Owen. "Don't know that I care. Ryngian and Norillian fights don't much concern me."

"How can that be?" Owen's eyes narrowed. "What the Ryngians want to do to us should be every man's concern."

"I reckon we'll be disagreeing about that, Captain." Woods picked his way between two barns and around a pig pen. "Mind you, we'll be having plenty of time to gum that to death."

"I should think this is an issue that needs settling more quickly."

"More pressing things to deal with first, Captain."

Owen's guide set off at a trot, crossing the road and heading off through a meadow full of green grass. He trotted toward the dark treeline. His fringed buckskins made him stand out, but he moved quickly enough that he seemed a ghost. He reached the trees a few steps ahead of Owen and promptly disappeared.

Owen got into the trees, then crouched, looking back through bushes toward the city. A few lanterns burned in windows, and dark smoke rose from chimneys, but nothing indicated pursuit. Owen took that as a good sign, though he resented the fear trickling through his belly.

A branch snapped off to his right. Owen spun quickly, trying to bring his musket up. The barrel smacked a sapling hard. The impact unbalanced him, dumping him on his backside as surprise flooded through him.

A dark-skinned humanoid loomed over him. He'd clearly *not* broken the branch. He wore a loincloth and leggings. Save for a beaded armlet from which dangled two feathers, he remained naked from the waist up. His long, dark hair had been gathered into a thick braid bound with leather. His amber eyes, narrowed as they were, reminded Owen of a cat.

The dark man smiled, white teeth splitting a shadowed face.

Nathaniel crouched at Owen's side. "Captain Owen Strake, you'd be meeting my brother, Kamiskwa. He's of the Altashee."

Owen gathered his feet beneath him and brushed leaves from his coat. "He's one of the Twilight People."

"He is." Nathaniel stood and picked a leaf off Owen's coat. "Come sun-up you'll see more green than grey in his skin."

"Does he speak?"

"Only when he has something to say." Nathaniel chuckled softly. "That'll be coming soon enough, Captain. Kamiskwa is always free with an opinion."

Owen offered the Altashee his hand. "Pleased to meet you."

Woods pushed Owen's hand down and away. "The Twilight People don't do things like we do. They're wary."

"Because of Major Hopkins."

"Not entirely, Captain." Woods retrieved the musket and handed it to Owen. "Magick works by touch. Don't know a man, you don't let him touch you. Gives him a chance to hurt you."

Owen nodded. "Of course, no offense intended."

Kamiskwa chuckled, and made a comment. Woods joined him, held a hand up. "Nothing bad. He just said that any who thought you'd be back in Temperance within the week was wrong."

Owen smiled. "Thank you, Kamiskwa."

"Don't be thanking him." Woods patted the Altashee on the shoulder. "He says you have ten days."

The trio took off at a solid pace and made good time even in the pre-dawn darkness. Kamiskwa remained half-invisible as he ranged ahead. The game paths he chose went around hills instead of over them. The tracks doubled-back on themselves, as any animal trail will, but the men moved faster along them than they would have if they'd resorted to bushwhacking straight through.

Woods brought up the rear and stopped fairly often to watch their backtrail. He'd come trotting up, his rifle sheathed in a beaded doeskin case. He always had a big smile on his face. He shook his head at Owen's mute inquiries and urged him on with a nod.

They set a good pace. Owen kept up despite carrying twice as much as either man. Woods had his rifle, shot pouch, a knife and tomahawk. Kamiskwa bore a musket, but his had been cut down into the carbine model the cavalry most often used. He carried a knife and had a length of knobbed wood slung over his back. It had been inlaid with mother of pearl and featured a triangular blade on the back of the knob.

As the sun rose Owen unbuttoned his woolen coat, but refrained from loosening his waistcoat. He shifted the eleven pounds of musket from one hand to the other. The aching of his shoulders and the growing blister where his boots rubbed at his heels reminded him of marching through the Low Countries.

That realization brought him back into his mission. Though they were making good time through the woods, no modern army could have followed them. Having soldiers snake through the woods—even his skirmishers—would guarantee disaster. If they didn't get lost, and many of them would, they'd be strung out and easily ambushed. Because of the Mystrian forest's undergrowth, the enemy could hide until he could reach out and touch a man.

Kamiskwa's caution made abundant sense.

Woods caught up with Owen as they came to a sandy portion of a stream bed. "'Bout time to get something on your insides, Captain Strake?"

Owen nodded and shrugged his pack off. "I noticed that neither you nor Kamiskwa carried food. I will happily share."

"So will we."

Kamiskwa crossed the stream and quickly climbed up into an old pine tree. He disappeared into the foliage. He climbed halfway up—at least that's what Owen judged by which branches were dancing—then lowered two beaded leather bags and two loosely rolled blankets with both ends secured by leather thongs.

As the Altashee retrieved their baggage, Woods tossed aside several stones stacked on the sandbar, then scooped out a pit beneath where they had stood. He reached down into the hole and gingerly teased out three packets wrapped in maize husks. Owen immediately caught the scent of salmon and his stomach grumbled accordingly.

He frowned. "You stayed here last night, cached your bags in that tree, and used the remains of a fire to cook the fish while you came and got me?"

Kamiskwa grunted, which Owen took as a confirmation.

"Pretty much right on the button, Captain."

Owen sat down, pulling off his pouches, and decided to press his luck. "You didn't leave any sign you were here, so you're cautious. Means you think you could be in danger anywhere."

Kamiskwa smiled and retrieved a fish. "*Nahaste.*"

Owen raised an eyebrow as he broke the bread into three parts. "Meaning?"

Woods accepted bread. "You're up to three weeks."

"How so?"

"You're observant and a thinker." Woods stretched out and sucked at burned fingers. "Lots of things get cached hereabouts. Over there, 'neath that rock shelf, we put some firewood. Replaced what we used last night. Anything else we weren't needing, we'd put it there, too. You'll see lots of that. No mark on the cache, take as you like, put back more. Marked, a man won't touch it."

Owen teased open his packet of fish. Steam rose, filling his head. He slid flesh from bone and savored. The velvety fish just melted in his mouth. "This is good."

"Kamiskwa tickled them on out of the wet." Woods nibbled some bread. "That's another thing out here. You travel light as possible. Also, with jeopards and bears about, you ain't wanting to carry things they counts as supper."

Owen looked around. Sunlight was breaking through leaves. The stream gurgled and little breezes rustled foliage. A few birds sang in the trees, and crows flocked to squawk. Outside their little bowl he could see nothing, and found it easy to imagine a jeopard crouched and watching them.

"We will not be wanting for supplies?"

"Ain't enough for an army, Captain, but we ain't no army." Woods pointed off to the northwest. "Fair piece of the ground we'll cover, Kamiskwa and I hunt and trap regular. If you're not too picky, you'll eat. Even if you is, you won't starve none."

Owen picked up his musket. "I can lend a hand hunting."

Kamiskwa laughed.

Woods shook his head. "Not likely."

"I assure you, I am a dead shot."

"Ain't saying you ain't, but you is damned loud of foot."

"It was dark."

"True point, but you'll be needing to be a walking-whisper. Then there's that coat. You mights-well be on fire."

Owen's expression darkened. "We discussed this. I am an officer in Her Majesty's Army. I have my duty and will not be shot as a spy."

"Well now, I ain't too worried 'bout *you* being shot." Nathaniel smiled. "Any Ryngian sees that flash of red and shoots, like as not me or Kamiskwa's gonna catch that ball."

Owen laughed. "Marksmanship has never been a Ryngian strong point."

"Good thing you're a crack shot." Woods pointed to the musket. "You'll want to be loading that thing, and keep it loaded. Your training, you can probably get off four shots in a minute?"

"I've done as many as five."

"Out here, shooting may come on you quick. Likely because someone's already done shot at you."

Owen nodded. "I'll bear that in mind." Standing, he produced a cartridge and began to load his musket. "The Prince said your rifle was fairly special."

Nathaniel smiled proudly and stripped the fringed sheath off it. "This here is one of two dozen or so rifles made by Colonel Apostate Hill up Summerland way. It is a breechloader. I don't have to be stuffing a ball down the barrel just to shoot it back out. It uses a .71 caliber slug—same weight as your musket, just squashed a little. More egg than round. Rifled barrel so's it's accurate out to a hundred yards. It does some killing out there."

"The Prince mentioned you killing a jeopard. Showed me the mounted specimen. That's fancy shooting at range."

"More luck in that shot than there was good." He jerked his head toward Kamiskwa. "Like as not, my shot would have just riled it. Kamiskwa was there to do the killing if it got close."

"And what if he missed?"

"I'da had another shot ready. And if I missed that, I'da deserved to be dinner."

"I look forward to a display of your marksmanship. Perhaps you'll shoot us something for lunch."

"I reckon I could, Captain Strake, but we won't be needing it today."

"You have food cached further along the way?"

"After a manner of speaking." The guide smiled. "At noon we're having supper with the Prince."

CHAPTER FOURTEEN

May 2, 1763
Temperance Bay, Mystria

After erasing any trace of their having stopped, the party moved on at a more leisurely pace. Owen still felt himself an object of study, but also realized his guides were giving him the opportunity to learn. They'd offered the direct warning about the necessity to keep his weapon loaded, then proceeded to give him practical lessons on moving through the woods.

Owen studied Kamiskwa and did his best to ape him. The Altashee moved economically and carefully, preferring to slip beneath or around branches rather than push them aside or hack them off. Going up hills he tended to step on exposed roots, or rocks that were solidly buried. He took smaller steps rather than longer ones that might result in a slip or spill of stones. He moved quickly, but without haste; a distinction that manifested itself in a fluidity that gave him a ghostlike quality.

Woods' earlier comment had been correct. As the sun came up, Kamiskwa's flesh and hair picked up a greenish tint. He remained mostly dark—very much the color of the pine needles. A few spring-green locks streaked his hair. Owen couldn't figure out if this was because of his youth or his age, since the man had no wrinkles and if he bore scars, they did not show up in contrast to his flesh.

What he did have were tattoos. Simple line drawings tending toward geometric shapes and a few animals. They'd been done in black and only showed up in full sunlight. Owen could make no obvious sense of them.

They continued on for another hour, pausing at streams to refill canteens and waterskins. They used that time to listen as well. Though Owen would have laughed at the notion had anyone suggested it, Mystria sounded different than Norisle. Bird song and insect buzzing came tantalizingly close to those of his home, but a few differed mightily. This he found somewhat disconcerting.

A hawk screamed and sparrows, which had gathered around a blackberry bush, immediately took flight. Owen looked for the hawk, expecting to see it perched on a branch and defiantly proclaiming its existence. The only bird he saw, however, was brown, twice as large as a sparrow, with equally nondescript plumage. It landed beneath the bush and started harvesting berries from the lower branches.

Woods pointed at it. "That's a liehawk. The Altashee name for it means 'Little Bird with Big Voice.' Other folks call it the bully-bird. You'll hear that name used on people, too."

Owen shook his head. "Just how different is this place?"

Woods shrugged. "Don't know. Hain't been to Norisle. This here is its own place. What's different to your eye?"

The soldier took off his hat and wiped his brow with his sleeve. "We've been walking since dawn, but haven't seen any signs of humanity in that time."

"This is a big land, Captain, two-three times Norisle. Maybe more. Half the people. Most on the coast."

Owen nodded. "And along the rivers."

"Very good, Captain." Woods smiled. "Ain't going to be many folks out where we're headed. That ain't a complaint."

Kamiskwa grunted his agreement.

The three of them headed off again, and within a short time Owen caught a heavy, thudding rhythmic sound. *Axes.* Kamiskwa slowed them down and worked his way around a level lot where three men labored clearing the land. Two brought the trees down and trimmed the branches. The third used a team of mules to haul the logs through a forest of stumps to a pile. They'd already split and cut a few of the logs, creating a square foundation, onto which they'd erected a tent.

Owen studied the lot. A small stream ran through it on the far border by the tent, promising a good water supply. They'd cleared the better part of three acres and had situated the tent at the base of a hill in the lot's northeast corner. By the end of the summer they'd have gotten up many of the stumps. Within a month they'd be able to do some limited planting and get a harvest before the winter.

Owen started into the open, but Nathaniel held him back. "Squatters. Won't be welcoming us."

"Aren't they afraid the landowner will evict them?"

"Depends, don't it?" Woods withdrew from the edge of the clearing. "The Confederation lays claim to these lands. Her Majesty thinks her issuing deeds trumps that. Name on the deed could be someone back in Norisle, or down in Fairlee or Ivory Hills. They might go to court in Temperance, but ain't many a judge will rule in their favor."

Owen pointed toward the lot. "But those men know that what they're doing is wrong."

"I reckon they ain't thinking it is." Woods spread his arms wide. "When the redemptioneers first came here, it was all wide open. You find a place, farm for a bit, move on when the land wore out. Then the Parliament says that no one can go beyond the mountains. That's fine, still lots of land, but then ministers and their friends bought it all up from the Crown. So you take a man who has worked hard improving the land, and he cain't afford it because some speculator who hain't never worked a day in his life is greedy."

"I would agree, Mr. Woods, that this seems hardly equitable, but theft is not the proper response."

"Ain't theft. More like taking a lend of the land." Nathaniel laughed. "Captain, you heard of the Golden Rule?"

"Do unto others as you would have them do unto you."

"Maybe in Norisle. Round these parts, it's he who has the gold makes the rules."

A shiver ran down Owen's spine. The Royal Army allowed those with money to purchase commissions. A noble—like Lord Rivendell's son, John—with a taste for adventure and no understanding of warfare could buy his way into the command of troops. More than once, such privileged commanders had refused to obey orders issued by a superior but *common* officer. Often they issued their own orders in some vain attempt at winning glory. Their actions would destabilize a line, provide an opening for the enemy, and often transformed a victory into a rout. At Villerupt, had Rivendell's son actually followed orders, the Mystrian Rangers might not have suffered as severely as they did.

Woods' version of the golden rule applied in Norillian civilian life, too. A noble's misdeeds could be silenced with gold, whereas a pauper's offenses would be severely punished. Someone like Lord Rivendell, whose power and prestige legitimized his book, commonly hid moral shortcomings by virtue of charitable gifts and well-placed bribes.

"Is this why you are so hostile toward Norillians?"

Both Woods and Kamiskwa broke out laughing.

"I fail to see what you find so funny."

Woods wiped a tear from his eye. "I ain't hostile toward Norillians. Leastways not specifically. I *hate* all men what is out to spoil this land."

"I'm here to see to it that the Tharyngians do not spoil it."

The Mystrian arched an eyebrow. "Are you really thinking that is the truth of it, Captain?"

"I have my orders."

"You succeed, what happens then? Next year, the year after, war. Don't matter who wins. The Crown prints up more deeds and charters. More people will come to profit. Speculators get richer. Those who value freedom will keep moving west until someone stops them. Like as not that's another one of your Crown missions."

Woods spoke with passionate disgust, but Owen didn't take it personally. His was an opinion born long before he'd ever met Owen. He'd likely trotted it in front of every man he met and judged them by their reaction to it.

Owen lowered his voice. "Could be things will happen as you say, Mr. Woods. I don't know. What I do know is that I am here to do what I can to stop the Ryngians from threatening the colonies. I'm hoping it prevents war. But I have to ask you, sir, that if you hate all men equally, why have you accepted the Prince's commission to be my guide?"

Nathaniel smiled. "The Prince, he makes a try at understanding this place. Some say his methods are a little Ryngian. Could be. I cotton to the glow in his eyes when he sees something new. Iffen I works for him, not many folks will be of a mind to be bothering me. Makes my life easier."

They arrived at the Prince's estate a little before noon, making their approach along the river. They'd crossed the road Owen had ridden before in the heart of the woods. Looking back at the track, and quickly losing sight of it, reminded Owen of how very different combat would be in Mystria. *Anyone who thinks it will not be will suffer.*

They found the Prince at the river, stripped to the waist, washing mud off his shirt. He wore homespun trousers and a floppy-brimmed felt hat, which had a dollop of wurmmud where another might affix a ribbon. He shook hands with Woods, and returned Owen's salute, then turned to greet Kamiskwa.

Neither man exchanged a word. They clasped their hands behind their backs and bowed toward each other. They remained bowing for a handful of heartbeats, then straightened up and smiled. Their ritual puzzled Owen for a moment, then he realized that to the Twilight People, showing an empty hand was more of a deadly threat than clutching a knife. Hiding their hands was a pledge of good behavior and a sign of friendship.

Owen shivered again. It quickly came to him how strange Norillians must have first seemed to the Twilight People. The first colonists wore odd clothes, they spoke a strange tongue. They had iron and steel and guns. They would smile as they offered you their hand. *The first settlers must have seemed to be blood-mad butchers, smiling as they threatened.*

From the other side, the refusal to shake hands was a confirmation of hostility and duplicity. The Twilight People clearly could not be trusted—which is why it would be so easy for people to believe fanciful stories about raids and atrocities. And when it became known that the Twilight People could work magick, they became an even more potent threat.

Owen smiled in spite of himself. *These are insights I need to record.*

The Prince wrung his shirt out, then slung it over his shoulder. "I have instructed the staff to lay out dinner on the lawn. Such a lovely day. And I've done away with tables and chairs. You'll be out there roughing it days on end. This is my only chance to share your adventure."

The four of them retired up the lawn to a level spot that provided a wonderful view of the river, the mountains beyond, and the wurmrest. Servants had laid out several blankets and centered baskets with bread, cheese, and braised chicken parts. Wooden plates had been stacked next to four pewter cups and a bottle of wine.

The Prince unceremoniously plunked himself down. "Captain, I insist you remove your jacket and boots. Your waistcoat, too. I want you to feel comfortable as we eat."

"As you command, Highness." Owen shrugged off his pack, then removed his coat and folded it. He set the waistcoat on top, then pulled his boots off. His stockings showed a spot of blood at the heels.

The Prince shook his head. "Blisters, that won't do. I will package some salve of bear grease and a couple herbs. It will ease the pain and toughen up your skin."

"You are most kind, Highness." Owen sighed. "I lost the calluses on the crossing."

"Not the first." The Prince doled out plates, then poured three cups of wine. Kamiskwa took the fourth cup and poured water from a canteen into it.

"Are the Altashee not allowed to drink?"

Kamiskwa smiled. "I simply choose not to."

Owen's mouth hung open. "You speak our language?"

The native nodded.

"But you didn't say anything…"

"You two used up all the words." Kamiskwa's smile broadened.

Kamiskwa and Woods burst into laughter.

Owen's face burned.

The Prince patted his forearm. "At least with you it was only the morning. On my first journey with them, we were four days out before I knew Prince Kamiskwa could speak our tongue."

"*Prince* Kamiskwa?"

"My, you *have* kept him in the dark, haven't you?"

Woods curbed his mirth and cleared his throat. "No harm done, Highness. We was taking his measure."

"Really, Nathaniel." The Prince arched an eyebrow. "I should have thought you had that the night he flattened those Branches."

"Well, this is true, Highness."

"And the fact that Caleb Frost, despite his best intentions, can only criticize Captain Strake by saying he has a lot to learn about Mystria."

"Yes, Highness."

The Prince held up a hand. "I am serious, Nathaniel. You have to understand that this man is unlike the others sent out here. He is a serious soldier. His reports will shape policy for dealing with the Tharyngians. Mystria's future will depend upon his success or failure."

Woods' expression sobered. "I understand, Highness. Captain, please accept my apologies for any behavior you found offensive."

"No need for apologies." Owen looked at the Prince. "There is something else, isn't there, Highness?"

The Prince sighed. "There might be. A fast packet-boat came into Temperance the day after the incident with Colonel Langford. A messenger brought me some coded messages. Do you know the name Guy du Malphias?"

Owen's stomach knotted instantly. "Yes, Highness."

Nathaniel frowned. "Who would that be now?"

"He led the Platine Guards at Artennes Forest." Owen shook his head. "He's the devil incarnate."

"He's worse." Prince Vlad's eyes tightened. "Two months ago a small Ryngian flotilla slipped past the Channel fleet during a gale. They were bound for Mystria and had du Malphias aboard. He's been in New Tharyngia for at least two weeks. Whatever you find out there, he'll be up to his elbows in it."

CHAPTER FIFTEEN

May 2, 1763
Prince Haven
Temperance Bay, Mystria

Owen's appetite completely vanished. He'd seen du Malphias only once, and that through a telescope during a driving rain. The Tharyngian had been more of a silhouette, really, high on a ridgeline, astride a horse. In profile his aquiline nose stood out and his goatee added a sharp point to his chin. Then he turned to look toward Owen, and the Norillian had had the unmistakable feeling the man saw him and saw through him.

It felt as if the light breeze now came out of the arctic, and even Nathaniel noticed the change. He set a half-gnawed chicken leg on his plate and wiped his mouth on the back of his hand. "The Devil is he?"

Prince Vlad nodded. "A brilliant man, really. A polymath—he has many interests and excels in all of them. He was the youngest man ever made a Laureate. I've read a number of his papers. I have many of them in my library. He was a very hopeful young man, but with the war, that changed."

Owen swirled the wine in his cup, studying it. "We took a few towns that his Guards had abandoned. They'd thoroughly looted them, even down to the point of breaking into mausoleums and digging up graves. In war you see bodies, but that was different. People just torn from their rest, parts hacked off. Lots of missing skulls."

Kamiskwa's dour comment needed no translation.

The Prince made a half-hearted attempt to muster a smile. "It is worse than that, I fear. His transportation here suggests a shift in Tharyngian political power. Du Malphias has been associated with the hardline lions. The sheep have lost their hold. Du Malphias will move to consolidate holdings before we can react."

"Did your dispatches say anything about the Queen's response? Are troops on the way?"

"No, Captain. I gather that prudence and intelligence held sway. The flotilla was not large, so it is believed there can be little military threat in this season. Horse Guards believes that du Malphias will be creating a series of fortifications from which attacks can be launched. He was the architect of the defenses at Villerupt, after all. They will not be easy nuts to crack. Next year, they believe, is when he would move to the offensive, but only if he is substantially reinforced. To prevent that, we will attack into Tharyngia again this year. We'll either inflict the defeat that will make his efforts moot, or tax Ryngian resources such that he will never get the troops he needs to invade."

Nathaniel leaned back on his hands. "I'm thinking that's a powerful lot of iffin' and supposin'. Cold comfort."

"Agreed." The Prince drank some wine. "This is why your mission is even more important than before. We have to know where du Malphias is, how much he has in the way of resources, and what his most likely route of attack will be. I will be frank, gentlemen. If he were to pull together all the regular troops and militia in New Tharyngia and couple them with warriors from the Seven Nations, he would have a large enough force to overwhelm any single colony's defenses."

The Prince came up on his knees and shifted his blanket around. He tugged it up toward the center, then twisted the edges, very quickly constructing a crude topographical map of north Mystria. He broke bread into crumbs, which he placed in strategic points, then plucked blades of grass and laid them out to represent rivers.

"The Ryngians claim everything west of the mountains, including the Four Brothers Lakes, the land of two rivers, and Misaawa River. Up here in the north, Black Lake feeds into the Argent River, so they claim Black Lake as part of the Argent River watershed. But to the south, Black Lake also feeds into the Cool River, which is ours. The river flows south to Hattersburg where it joins the Tillie River. To date neither nation has acknowledged the other's claims. Further west, Lac Verleau has remained neutral, but the Governors of Queensland and Lindenvale have sold deeds to land on its south side. We have settlers moving into that area, creating tension with Ryngian trappers and settlers."

Owen nodded. "If du Malphias brought troops down the Cool River, he'd go to the heart of Lindenvale, capture Hattersburg, then move east along the Tillie River to threaten Margaret Town. That would cut off Queensland, Summerland, and Lindenvale."

Kamiskwa pointed at the crumb marking Hattersburg. "Many rivers meet to form the Tillie before it flows to the big water. He could come down from Anvil Lake in the west to loot and fight a retreat that would draw militia far from home. If he looses his Daskashii allies to raid…"

Vlad pushed his glasses back up on his nose. "A sound point. Thank you, Prince Kamiskwa. You see, Captain, this is why your mission is so very important. We know these rivers exist, and we assume they will be the means du Malphias would use to transport troops, but we do not know how many of the rivers are navigable. A raiding party of two hundred men can move quickly, but an army of four thousand with cannon has an entirely different set of needs."

Owen scrubbed his hands over his face. "You realize this mission is impossible, yes? To survey all of the rivers is the work of years, maybe a decade. Which path to choose? Black Lake seems the easiest route, but the Green River out of Lac Verleau and into the Upper Tillie and tributaries also works. Where to begin?"

Nathaniel pulled his knees up to his chest. "Begging your pardon, but ain't the two of you looking at this ass-end around?"

Owen frowned. "Meaning?"

"You're guessing and call it figuring. Shouldn't look for where he'll end. Look for where he's starting." Nathaniel pointed at the map. "He sailed up the Argent two weeks ago. He'll be stopping in Kebeton to round up men and supplies iffen he's going to be building his forts. Take least a week. The Ryngians, they'll be a-wanting to hear him palaver about something. They'll feast him a bunch. He'll need scouts. He'll hire trappers and traders. We find out who is missing from his normal haunts, we find du Malphias."

Owen smiled at the Prince. "I suddenly understand your liking this man."

"Yes, don't let his rustic nature fool you, Captain. He's smarter than he wants to let anyone know."

Nathaniel laughed, his long hair dangling as he threw his head back. "It ain't no strategizing, it's trapping. Find the beaver lodge, set the trap nearby."

"This beaver will have very sharp fangs." Owen drank to wash the sour taste from his mouth. "This is important enough that you will want reports, yes, Highness?"

"Yes. Encrypted, I should think." The Prince's brows furrowed. "You don't have a crypto-lens, do you?"

"No, Highness."

"Do you know how to work a book cipher, Captain?"

"I fear not, Highness."

"It is fairly simple and unbreakable save the enemy is able to find the book that is the key." Vlad pointed toward his house. "I will find a book, one for which I have the matching volume. To send a message, you write it out and then, leafing through the book, you find a page on which a particular word is printed. You substitute the page number, paragraph number, and word number for the word in your message. If the word 'amber,' for example, was found on page forty, third paragraph, fourth word, it would be written 40-3-4. Furthermore, you will date your notes, and subtract the date from thirty-six, adding the difference to every value. If you are writing on the 30th, the word would be represented as 46-9-10. Is that clear?"

"Yes, Highness."

"Eliminate articles like 'a' and 'the'—they just waste time—and underestimate any numbers by twenty percent. If someone does intercept a message and translates it, they will believe we are fooled. Send things to me by way of the Frosts, please."

"Yes, Highness." Owen smiled and dug into his jacket pocket, producing the Haste book. "Doctor Frost gave me this to read. Could we use it?"

The Prince laughed. "A delicious idea. No one would ever think a Norillian agent was using a seditious text for covert purposes. Splendid."

Nathaniel grinned. "And what would a Prince of the realm be doing with such a book?"

"Memorizing it, actually, and with more haste now, no pun intended. The book is fascinating." The Prince returned the smile. "You should learn to read. You would enjoy it."

"I read honest sign. Man-scratches ain't never honest."

"But they can be illuminating. Perhaps Captain Strake will be good enough to read you selections on your journey."

Owen and Nathaniel exchanged glances. *That isn't going to happen.*

"Captain, I've prepared a short list of things I'd like you to keep your eye out for. Samples, if you can, a description if you cannot. I understand the focus of your mission, but if you would indulge me…"

"As you wish, Highness."

"Thank you." He stood. "How will you travel?"

Nathaniel chewed a big bite of chicken breast and swallowed fast. "We'll go due west up Old Ben as far as we can, then head north. The Altashee will be at Saint Luke, so we'll see what they have heard, then to Hattersburg. From there we go north or west. Probably north. Two-three weeks out from there, weather holds."

"Very good." The Prince opened his arms. "Please, my friends, eat while I get that list. I wish you could stay but your mission, I fear, has an urgency none can deny."

Kamiskwa and Nathaniel fell to devouring the chicken and cheese. Owen forced himself to eat, knowing he'd need it. Both of his companions lived well off the bounty of the land, but either could have hidden behind a scarecrow without fear of detection. Hunting didn't always mean killing, and fishing didn't always mean catching, so they might be days between meals.

He was glad for the relative silence with which they ate. He'd accepted his mission on the mistaken belief that it would be a simple surveying job. It wouldn't be an easy one, but neither would it be terribly complex. He had expected to have the time to complete it and do it thoroughly so his work would not invite criticism.

News of du Malphias changed all that. Though Nathaniel was right that they had to find du Malphias before they could concentrate on what routes he might use to attack the colonies, this perforce meant Owen could not accomplish his original mission. He'd been with the army long enough to know what that meant. Even if his work was critical in defeating du Malphias and driving the Ryngians from Mystria, the results of his mission would be compared against his orders. He would be judged a failure.

That inevitability saddened Owen. The Crown had always rewarded bold explorers who returned with information that would increase the Crown's holdings and wealth. Owen had believed, deep down, that he might discover a pass that could be named after him, or a bountiful lake or river which led even further into the continent's interior. The Queen might see fit to grant him a peerage. If he was lucky, he could use his knowledge of Mystria to make money and gain status that would equal or surpass the Ventnor family. It would be his ultimate victory over his family.

And Catherine would be even more proud of him.

But now that avenue to glory had been walled off, and a malignant Tharyngian Laureate manned the barricade with his Platine Guards in tow. The only glory Owen was likely to win was posthumous, and he didn't find that idea appealing in the least.

And yet, never did it occur to him to abandon his mission. His duty to the Crown superseded his own wishes. Moreover, the information he'd gather would save soldiers' lives. It would even create another opportunity for his uncle to swath himself in glory.

Kamiskwa made a comment in Altashee and Nathaniel laughed.

Owen arched an eyebrow. "What?"

"Kamiskwa called you *Aodaga*. Means 'thunderface.' You're brooding and he reckons you're dangerous when you do."

"I suppose he could be right." Owen popped a last bite of cheese into his mouth and finished his wine. "Du Malphias is someone I'd just as soon have back in Tharyngia."

"I get a clean shot, I'll be happy to send him to Hell. That's fair close to Tharyngia, ain't it?"

Owen laughed. "I expect it is."

The Prince returned and handed Owen the list and a small jar of the unguent for his heels. He gave Kamiskwa a small, leather-bound box. "Your father had commented on my spectacles and I secured him a pair. I thought he might enjoy them."

"You are very generous, Prince Vlad." The Altashee tucked the package into his bag. "He will visit you again when the leaves turn. And now he will find his way easily."

"I look forward to his visit." The Prince started off down toward the wurmrest. "We had a bit of a wind two nights ago. A branch fell and, I'm afraid, damaged your large canoe."

Kamiskwa set off with the Prince. Nathaniel grabbed Owen by the shoulder. "One thing you'll want to be learning about the Shedashee—the Twilight People."

"Yes?"

"Generous people to a fault. Among them, if you say you like something, admiring it like, they'll give it to you. If you refuse it, it's a great insult." Nathaniel nodded toward the Prince. "When Kamiskwa's father was here last, he took a serious liking to the Prince's glasses."

"You're not having me on in saying this?"

Nathaniel shook his head. "I'll still be joking with you about some things, but nothing there's likely to be blood over."

"This mission is very serious. More so now."

"You don't be worrying about me." He smiled. "I told you before I hate all men equally, but I reckon I can muster a bit more for this Ryngian. We'll find him, kill him, and then don't nobody have a reason for ruining my land."

CHAPTER SIXTEEN

May 2, 1763
Prince Haven
Temperance Bay, Mystria

The Prince and Kamiskwa dragged a birch-bark canoe, about fifteen feet long and tapered at both ends, from some brush on the river side of the wurmrest. A small hole punctured the left side just large enough for a child to slip her hand through. The two men turned the canoe upright and lay it on the grass.

Kamiskwa studied the hole for a moment, then walked over to a trio of birches at river's edge. Using his glassy-bladed knife he sliced off a palm-sized bit of peeling bark. He crouched, placed it in the water, and anchored it with a stone.

From within the wurmrest, Mugwump sniffed and snorted. In the dimness beyond the barred opening, a golden-eye glowed.

Nathaniel moved to keep the Prince and Owen between him and the wurm's gaze.

Owen smiled. "You're not afraid of the wurm, are you?"

Nathaniel smiled wryly. "I ain't seeing keeping back from something what could take me in a gulp as much of a bad idea."

Kamiskwa rejoined them. "Among the Shedashee there are stories of these beasts—much larger ones with wings. They are not good stories."

"Wurms can be fierce in battle, but Mugwump is docile." Owen affected nonchalance, letting his lack of concern get under Nathaniel's skin just a bit. "Released in combat he'd be pretty nasty."

"My point 'zactly, Captain." Nathaniel shook his head. "I reckon we can get all our gear in this canoe and not have to drag another."

Kamiskwa grunted, then returned to the river and recovered the wet bark strip. He knelt beside the canoe and held the patch against the outside. The pink inner bark appeared through the hole. Then he placed his right hand over the hole, pressing it against his left hand on the outside. Slowly he began to rub his hands forward and back, introducing an oval motion that picked up speed as he went.

He began to chant in a low voice, in his own tongue.

Owen opened his mouth to ask what he was doing, but Nathaniel held up a cautionary finger. Owen caught a scent, the sweet scent of green wood that's been split open. It shifted a little to become the loamy scent of a forest after a soaking rain.

After a minute Kamiskwa grew silent and stood. *There's no hole.* Owen stepped closer. He could see no sign of the hole. No scar, no discoloration, nothing. Try as he might, he could not see where the hole had been.

He shivered. He'd heard rumors of tailors and seamstresses fashioning clothes without seams for nobility, but when he'd had a chance to view their handiwork, he'd always found that needle and thread had been applied generously. One of the *Coronet's* sailors had always used magic to reinforce sail patches, but he secured them with thread regardless. As good as his work might have been, picking out the patch had never been difficult.

But this, what Kamiskwa had done, it simply couldn't be done. It would require him to be more powerful than any mage in Norisle—and that mage would have been exhausted after accomplishing so much. The Altashee didn't even look the least winded.

The Prince, however, looked delighted. "Every time I see that, it amazes me."

Nathaniel smiled. "Our canoes do seem to be in the accidental way lots around here."

Vlad shot Nathaniel a sharp stare. "Mr. Woods, were I wishing a demonstration, I would prepare one so that I could fully measure what happens and seek to replicate it myself. I am sure that Prince Kamiskwa would oblige me if I asked."

Kamiskwa nodded, but smiled as well.

Vlad held up a finger. "That reminds me." He turned, and scurried off into the wurmrest.

Woods placed his pouches toward the canoe's front end. "Good craft, these. Sturdy and not so delicate as you might be wanting to imagine. Still, you have to be careful. You don't want to put a foot or an oar through the sides."

Kamiskwa went back to where the canoe had been stored and returned with three leaf-shaped paddles. He handed one to Woods, but didn't give Owen the second.

Owen frowned. "I may not be in the navy, but I can paddle."

"The spare is just in case we need it. This canoe only requires two. It would steer funny if you was paddling." Woods pointed toward the middle of the boat. "You're just self-loading cargo, Captain."

"Here is more cargo, for your father, Kamiskwa." The Prince returned with a burlap bag. He pulled out one of Mugwump's scales. "There's four. He'll find something to do with them, I hope."

Owen held a hand out and accepted the scale from the Prince. "Did you have this painted and lacquered?"

"No. I just pulled four from a pile."

The soldier traced a finger along a scarlet stripe. "Wurmriders paint and lacquer scales. Even when they do that, they're never as pretty or polished as this."

Vlad took the scale back and slipped it into the sack. "While you're gone, I shall experiment. I'll leave some in the sun and see if that has any effect. Another mystery to explore. I shall be pleased to share the results upon your return."

Kamiskwa accepted the gift. "The Prince again proves himself to be a good friend of the Altashee."

"Merely returning kindnesses the Altashee have showed me."

Kamiskwa stowed the scales with his other gear, then he and Nathaniel hefted the canoe and carried it down to the river. They slid it into the water, then pulled it around parallel to the shore.

Nathaniel looked Owen up and down. "You'll be wanting to take off your boots and stockings. Your feet will get wet, but will dry off faster. Help your feet heal, too."

That made sense, so Owen went barefoot. The cool water and oozing mud actually felt good as he put his gear into the canoe. A small deck made of gapped cedar planking kept him from thrusting his feet through the canoe. He arranged his pack so he could use the back of it as a desk, and slid his musket in on the right, keeping it close at hand.

Prince Vlad held on to the canoe's stern as the other two men got in, then gave it a shove into the current. He waved from the shore. "Good luck!"

They headed upriver. Though the Benjamin didn't have a strong current, Nathaniel and Kamiskwa paddled steadily to make headway. Both men glistened with sweat after a short time, but made no complaints about their labors.

"I reckon, Captain, you figgered that rivers is our roads. Work fine going up, better coming back. Canoe full of pelts make a man rich down to Temperance."

"I can see that." Owen studied the shore. Mostly forests, with the occasional swampy meadow full of cattails, long grasses, and bright flowers. "Do you know the river's speed?"

Nathaniel shook his head. He'd removed his buckskin shirt, baring his upper torso. The man's muscles worked fluidly beneath tanned skin. A few scars stood out. Owen recognized the raised welts of a whip, a couple of knife cuts, and one gunshot wound, but asked about none of them. If Nathaniel wanted him to know, he'd tell him, otherwise it was none of his business.

"She flows as she flows."

"I need to know speed to calculate rates of movement for troops."

"Miles per hour, then?"

"Yes, that sort of thing."

"You won't be finding that of much use here, Captain." Woods smiled back over his shoulder. "Ain't really how fast the river goes as how fast a man can go on the river."

Owen frowned. "Meaning?"

"Well now, supposing the river goes five miles in an hour. A man going from dawn to dusk could go pretty far."

"Sixty miles. Knowing that, I can estimate how quickly du Malphias could deliver troops to Temperance."

"But if his people all got in canoes and paddled fast, they'd go farther, and your figuring would be wrong."

"Yes, but…"

Nathaniel shipped his paddle and turned halfway back toward Owen. "The Altashee don't worry none about miles. For them it's all 'walks.' Right fine system."

Owen frowned. "Let me be clear. I need to know distances so I can put things on a map."

Kamiskwa cleared his throat. "Captain Strake, how long does it take a man to walk one of your miles?"

Owen looked back at the Altashee. "Flat road, easy pace, a third of an hour."

"And in the rain, no road, through the forest, heavily laden?"

Owen laughed, remembering more than one similar march in the Low Countries. "One in a day."

"Distance does not matter. Speed of arrival does." Kamiskwa smiled indulgently. "We have many walks. Your flat road would just be a walk; though we have no flat roads. A hunting walk would be slower. *Garrahai*—warwalk—much faster. Then there are wet and dry walks, and light and heavy walks. We have words for all of them."

Owen was about to complain that this system was highly impractical, but he stopped. For a people that migrated seasonally, in a land where no roads existed, the system actually did work. And while it seemed impractical to his mind, it suited the land. He might have to calculate distance backward for mapping purposes, but absent a surveying crew, his measurements were going to be inexact. While his sextant would allow him to track latitude, but without a pair of timepieces, determining longitude couldn't be done.

He frowned. "If you measure in walks, how do you measure travel on the river?"

"This river is a two-three: twice as fast as a walk paddling up, three times floating down." Kamiskwa dipped his paddle again. "The system has worked for all time."

Owen nodded. "And the charts sent back from those who came before me? Their distances?"

Nathaniel shrugged. "Made up mostly, I 'spect. Ain't never run into any of the Branches outside Bounty. Only true distance they know is between alehouses and stills."

The Altashee chuckled. "They measure in dizzy-walks."

Owen fell silent and listened to the sound of paddles in the water. A dragonfly zipped over, paced them for a bit, then lighted on a gunwale. Its iridescent wings sparkled in the sunlight. The insect's mahogany body hue reminded him of Catharine's eyes for a moment, then his thoughts abruptly shifted to Bethany Frost. He thought she would be entranced by the insect.

Catharine would want me to save her from it.

The dragonfly took off, zigzagging toward the shore. Owen followed its flight, then looked up and gasped. "My God, what is that?" He reached for his musket.

Nathaniel turned and signaled for him to leave the gun alone. He lowered his voice. "It's a tanner. This range your ball would bounce off."

Owen stared. The creature appeared to be an elk, but one of prodigious proportions. It stood taller than he was at its shoulder, and he was certain he could have lain straight out on its vast rack of antlers with plenty of room for his head and feet. It grazed, still chewing, as it lifted its head to regard them.

"A tanner?" The brown coat with white throat blaze provided no clue about its name. "Why do you call it that?"

"One of the first explorers through here, Blackston, I'm thinking his name was, called it the 'Titan Elk.' Cumbersome name."

"Ti-*tan* becomes tanner, I see." Owen shot Nathaniel a sidelong glance. "And I could hit it from here."

"Hitting ain't killing." Nathaniel nodded toward the elk. "Tanner'd take more than one ball. Wounded, it would run a fair piece. We'd be all day finding it. If it tried to find us, well, we'd run a fair piece our own selves."

The guide sighed. "Now, iffen we was out trapping or hunting, beast like that would be worth the shot. Meat'd feed a village for a week. That hide would cover Reverend Bumble. Worth a pound or three down to Temperance."

Owen dug into his coat pocket. "Perhaps it's on the Prince's list."

The other two men chuckled. "You'll be finding a lot on his list. Half of it don't exist."

"But the Prince…"

"He's a smart man, belike, but some of that learning has come from books that ain't worth the time to open."

Kamiskwa cleared his throat. "My people related stories to early explorers, who paid them with a variety of baubles. The more fantastic the story, the better the pay."

Owen nodded. "How will I know what is real and what is not?"

"Only know what I see, only believe what I touch." Nathaniel smiled.

"I get the feeling, Mr. Woods, that this will be a very long trip."

The other men chuckled and bent to their paddles. Owen continued to watch the elk until it vanished around a river bend. That the creature dwarfed any similar European beast impressed Owen. Its magnificence made him smile. But there was something else there, too. The tanner, and maybe even the way the Twilight People accounted for distance, seemed so primitive.

Others would take primitive to mean backward, but Owen intended a wholly different sense. Mystria seemed a land that slumbered, still young and vital. Norisle and Tharyngia had been worked long and hard. He couldn't have gone a fraction of the distance he'd traveled in either without coming across someone or at least a signpost that indicated people lived nearby.

The earliest Mystrian settlers and explorers had called the natives the Twilight People because they tended to keep to the shadows. They'd been seldom seen except at twilight, and even then only in silhouette. They were part of the land and their reticence to be seen had been explained away as their fear of the white men and their magick.

Owen suspected it was something else entirely. The Shedashee *were* part of the land. They lived with it, reaping its bounty, not tearing its flesh and breaking it to their will. They'd watched that behavior in the settlers and wanted nothing to do with them, thinking them evil or insane.

And greedy, to them, is insane.

That first afternoon, with nothing but the sounds of wind, water, birds, bugs, and fish leaping, made Owen realize how far he was from Norisle. Not just in miles or walks, but in the very nature of the land. Mystria wasn't a place to be broken easily, though war could do that.

And it was his mission to lay the groundwork for that war. He would do his duty for the Crown. He had no choice. War was inevitable, especially with du Malphias somewhere out there. But, if there was a way to mitigate things, a way to save Mystria, he would seek that out, too.

If he did anything less, his failure would haunt him for the rest of his life.

CHAPTER SEVENTEEN

May 6, 1763
Grand Falls
Bounty, Mystria

They continued up the river another four days through country that slowly rose toward the mountains in the west. They encountered rapids around which they had to portage. They brought the canoe to shore, unloaded it, carried it up around the rapids, then reloaded their gear and proceeded on upriver.

Travel was not arduous. They started out at dawn, would rest for a couple of hours during the heat of the day, then push on until dusk. Kamiskwa proved adept at hand-catching fish—what Nathaniel called "tickling"—and Nathaniel shot a tom turkey on the second day out. They roasted some of it, smoked the rest in a makeshift smokehouse, and didn't even think about hunting until they'd finished the bird.

Kamiskwa cleaned and plucked the turkey, and found a use for the various parts. The feathers went into the bag with the wurm scales. The innards got tossed into the river for fish, and after leaving bones out overnight for insects to clean, he collected them up too. Owen presumed they'd be ground for bonemeal and used for fertilizer.

He'd watched Kamiskwa work. The Altashee used the smaller of two knives. Each had an antler handle and a black, glassy stone blade. Though only three inches long, the butchering knife's blade had a triangular shape and two very sharp edges. The point where blade and antler met had leather wrapped around it so he couldn't see how it was joined.

He suspected magick.

Owen squatted next to the Altashee. "What is your knife made of?"

Kamiskwa smiled, never looking up from his work. "Your Prince calls it obsidian. In my tongue it is *chadanak*. It is 'shadow that cuts.' It is traded from far away and very valuable."

"Same stone as the blade on your warclub?"

The Altashee nodded. "I am afforded it by my rank."

"Yes, you are a Prince." It struck Owen as very odd in that moment that he, a common officer, and Nathaniel, a commoner, were being served by nobility. *Is this place so strange that the natural order of things is overturned?*

Nathaniel laughed from where he was building a tiny smokehouse with river stones. "Now Captain Strake, don't be getting your knickers in a knot. Being a prince among the Shedashee ain't exactly like being a prince in Norisle."

"No?"

"See, the Twilight People set a store by magick. They're much better at it than we are. The stronger you are, the better they like it. Tend to want strong men to breed with their strong women. Among them, the child belongs to the mother's family, but there's a bit of sharing. If a warrior got a child on one of Kamiskwa's sisters, it would be expected that he'd return the favor."

Kamiskwa nodded. "It keeps peace between the tribes."

"Kamiskwa is a prince not just because his father is a great chieftain, but because he's proven himself to be strong in magick. They have contests every two-three years for to pick princes. Then the matriarchs start horse-trading with other families and tribes for their services."

Owen shook his head, not quite sure of what he was hearing. "So he will then have a wife chosen for him by tribal elders?"

"Not a wife." Woods took out his tomahawk and chopped some branches off a maple tree to roof over his smokehouse. "It's whoring according to Reverend Bumble."

Owen looked at Kamiskwa. "Is he having me on again?"

"He exaggerates." The Altashee, almost invisible in the growing gloom, looked up. "We have marriage guaranteeing that two people have children together exclusively, or with others by permission of the spouse. If I were to marry, my wife would join my household. Sharing seed keeps all tribes equal in power. It ties us together. No one wishes to go to war against his father's people."

"I see."

Nathaniel laughed. "You will, inside the week, I'm thinking."

Owen left to gather firewood and later, after they'd eaten, he pulled out his journal and began writing. He recorded the information about the Altashee marriage custom and the knife, covering a page. He included a rough sketch of the knife and tucked one of the small turkey feathers into the pages. Though not a great artist, his various drawings looked closer to reality than not.

He realized that he was including a lot more detail than he had expected, especially some concerning his reactions. He mentioned his surprise concerning the Altashee marriage custom, and his great joy at Woods' turkey-killing shot. None of that had any value to his mission, but it pleased him to write it down.

He knew it would please Bethany, too. She was a lovely woman and smart. She was clearly a product of the land of her birth. He found it very easy to imagine her faring well were she with them. She'd tirelessly pitch in, doing a fair share of the work.

Catherine, on the other hand, would be lost completely. *She would hate being out here.* She would have little interest in the flora or fauna, and would be completely useless doing any work around camp. Even trying to collect firewood would likely inspire the vapors, necessitating a long rest. *And we'd need another three canoes for her wardrobe.*

The realization that he was writing for Bethany did not displease him. He would be clinical in the details he transferred into his official transcript, but in his private notes he wanted to record all his thoughts and feelings. Owen felt certain Bethany would appreciate them and, unlike his wife, would not become anxious just reading them.

Having a confidante, even *in absentia*, made the trip much easier. Nathaniel and Kamiskwa clearly had quite a history together, as well as a certain disdain for things Norillian. He'd never fit perfectly with them. This didn't bother him too much. He was well used to being an outsider. Having someone to explain things to eased his isolation.

After cleaning up all sign of their campsite the next morning, they got back on the river. Owen got to see another moose and, later, watched a black bear clawing a bee-tree open to harvest honey. None of the creatures paid them any mind. Owen marveled at their lack of concern and, consequently, felt no fear.

Most often they traveled in silence, mostly out of a reverence for the land and its beauty. The sun dawned and painted the clouds red and blue. The setting sun could flood the sky with gold and deep scarlet. Once an eagle swooped down and plucked a salmon from the river, screaming victoriously and flew off to a nest high atop a tree.

Owen remained silent for fear of breaking whatever spell enabled him witness such wonders. Woods and Kamiskwa would share a silent glance, smiles splitting their faces, as they marveled at things like the eagle. They had so much wilderness experience, and yet the land still surprised them.

This pleased Owen, and scared him. If he were to be successful, he'd have to communicate a sense of Mystria to his superiors. Yet their attitude—based on birth, wealth, and rank—insulated them from understanding. They were already at the pinnacle of society, therefore at the pinnacle of the world. There could be nothing bigger or grander than what they already knew. To suggest otherwise would incite them to doubt their reality. It would be easier to convince them that wurms could fly than get them to see the true nature of Mystria.

On the fourth day they came to Grand Falls. The land rose abruptly for three hundred feet and the water traveled through a narrow gorge above a fantastic waterfall. They unloaded their gear just before noon and rested before beginning the trek through the woods to the upper river.

"We done walked the river 'bout as far as possible. Rest up here, start on foot tomorrow."

"Very good, sir." Owen sat on a rock beside the blue pool into which the water splashed. A bright rainbow glowed through light mist coming off the water. He pulled his journal from his pack and quickly sketched the falls.

"You're getting a mite better, Captain."

He looked up. "Thank you, Mr. Woods."

"I'm not making nothing of your chicken scratches, mind, but you got the falls right." He carried his sheathed rifle across his shoulders and pointed the butt toward the top. "Two years back me and Kamiskwa was up here come spring. Ice jammed up above there, so you could see everything dry. There's a cave back behind the water. Looked as though a jeopard or two laired there down through the years."

Owen glanced at his musket leaning against a tree. "I'd never make it alone, would I?"

"Nope, but this is more bear country. Don't have much of a taste for men. Now an ax-bird would be on you in a heartbeat."

Owen flipped to the back of the journal and unfolded the Prince's list. "A-ha. Ax-bird. Is that just a legend?"

Woods shook his head. "They exist. More to the south and across the mountains. Mild winter, snow early out of the passes, some of them come over. Hain't seen sign for a while."

The soldier traced his finger down the list. "Giant Ground Sloth? Mammoth? Wooly Rhinoceros?"

"Down south, Fairlee and Ivory Hills. Newland and Felling maybe. Ivory Hills got its name from the Mammoths. We might see one of those Wooly Rhinoceroses he wants. Short of having a cannon, there will be no bringing one back."

Kamiskwa made a comment in his own tongue.

"Add a bigger canoe and a bigger river." Nathaniel walked over, slung his rifle across his back, and hefted the canoe with Kamiskwa. They started off through the woods along a well-worn path.

Owen gathered up his things, including the paddles, and followed. Like Woods, he slung his musket across his back. Bringing it to hand would take a while, so he slipped the pistol into his right hand. He kept his thumb off the firestone, but kept watch as they moved.

They followed no trail, just picked their way between trees and over hummocks. Five hundred feet from the river, near a large standing stone, they overturned the canoe in a sandy depression. Woods motioned for Owen to give him the paddles, which he tucked under the canoe.

"You'll just leave this here?"

"Won't nobody touch it." Nathaniel nodded. "Mystrians will know it's Shedashee, and won't want to be caught dead taking a lend of it. The Shedashee will know it's Kamiskwa's and ain't gonna take it for similar reasons."

Owen studied the canoe more closely. "How will they know? There's not a mark on it."

"Not to you and me, but in magick…" Nathaniel shrugged. "As I said afore, the Shedashee is better at magick than we is. Kamiskwa made the canoe, so there ain't no mistaking who it belongs to."

Gathering their equipment, they set off on a trail paralleling the falls. It gently cut back and forth across the face of the foothills. It leveled out now and again, affording them a chance to rest. After about an hour they reached the gorge's far end and made camp in a clearing that had seen much use.

Owen surveyed the river above the falls. Broad and shallow, with lots of rocks and trees that spring floods had tumbled down from the mountains, it was useless for commerce or troop transport. "If du Malphias is going to use the Benjamin, he'd have to start down below."

"He'd be having plenty of eyes on him." Nathaniel pointed south across the river. "T'other side there is Lanatashee territory. They's in the Confederation, though me and Kamiskwa don't have much truck with them. Altashee this side. Iffen he was a-coming, you'd know."

Owen glanced toward Kamiskwa. "Would your people stop him?"

The Altashee looked up. "Wars between white men do not interest us much. You fight to possess things. You want to control land. We wish to live with it. War is too serious to unleash for silly reasons."

"But you would let us know he was coming."

Kamiskwa smiled. "And we would watch you fight."

Owen nodded. "Nothing could induce you…"

"The Altashee, they ain't mercenaries like Seven Nations tribes. Ungarakii would fight for the promise of warm spit on a hot day. Don't 'spect the Ryngians is paying them much more than that."

"Will we be running into hostiles, do you think?"

Kamiskwa laughed. "No Ungarakii has the courage to come into Altashee land. They dream of it, but such dreams become nightmares."

The Norillian soldier smiled. "Very good."

"Don't mean we won't be setting watches." Nathaniel unlimbered his rifle. "Some times them Ungarakii do dream, and takes a dose of lead to wake them up again."

CHAPTER EIGHTEEN

May 7, 1763
Bounty, Mystria

In their first day away from the river, they moved as quickly as practical through the forest, following meandering game trails when they could, cutting through ravines, splashing through streams, or going directly over hills when that shortened the distance significantly. Kamiskwa led them, setting a challenging but not terribly difficult course. Owen sensed in him a desire to return to his family—a sentiment he'd never shared and found himself envying.

Within the first four hours they suffered the first casualty. Though Owen's boots had been issued by a quartermaster at Horse Guards, they split at the seams and the left sole flapped open at the toe. Where the boots weren't falling apart, they rubbed his feet raw. The pain at his heels competed with the burning of his shoulders and thighs.

Owen searched his pack for some cord to bind up the shoe, but Kamiskwa knelt and pulled his boots off. "Salve your feet. Put on more stockings."

Owen did as he was bidden. The salve stung a bit at first, especially on the heel, then a cool numbness spread over his feet. "The salve helps, but I wish I could be dangling my feet in a stream."

Nathaniel leaned on his rifle. "Be time for that later. That salve, it has *mogiqua* in it. That's the numbness." He reached over and plucked a frond from a fern-like plant. "Good for most anything what ails a man."

Kamiskwa applied his smaller knife to Owen's boots. He cut away the lowers, then split the uppers along the seams. He drilled holes around the upper portion's perimeter, then dug leather thongs from his pack. He threaded the thongs, then laced Owen's feet into them. The excess leather wrapped up over his toes, and up the back of his heel, giving him some basic protection.

The makeshift moccasins only required parts of one boot, but Kamiskwa insisted he keep the other half. "These will not last too long."

"Thank you." Owen stood and flexed his feet. The moccasins felt good, but he didn't like being out of uniform. He recalled how miserable the army had appeared during the retreat from Villerupt and hated it. He wanted to show the Tharyngians that pride still existed among the Norillians.

At least I am not barefoot.

Kamiskwa rose, sheathed his knife, and started off again. Following game trails made the walking relatively easy. Bushwhacking caused Owen all sorts of problems. The brush tore at his clothes, whipped his face, and threatened to yank his musket from his grasp. His hat hit the ground more than once.

Kamiskwa seemed to delight in plowing through berry bushes. Since he and Nathaniel wore leather leggings they had no problems. The thorns shredded Owen's pants and stockings. Even being able to grab a handful of berries on the way didn't make up for the clawing he endured.

Running up through streams eliminated the problem with branches and thorns, but caused other difficulties. The leather lacings stretched when wet, so Owen had to pause and tighten them. And while the water did help soothe his feet at first, his feet chilled quickly. He found himself freezing from the waist down and sweating profusely under his coat.

Despite his pain and discomfort, Owen did notice one thing he considered significant. Whenever they reached the reverse slope of some hill and he could get a view of the distance, Kamiskwa had them pointed unerringly in the same direction—north-northwest.

"It's as if Kamiskwa has a compass." Owen offered Nathaniel his canteen during a stop.

The Mystrian drank. "Kamiskwa's sense of direction *is* that good, and he's lived in this area for his whole life, but there are signs he watches for. Sees them with magick."

"That's not possible. Magick only works with things you can touch."

"Could be that's true. Then again, the Shedashee is better at magick than us." Nathaniel pointed at a large rock coming up on the right. "They train people to be pathfinders. Give them magick to mark stones and trees. He can see it or feel it."

"But how?"

"Well, I've given that some thought." Nathaniel swept a hand through air. "You feel the air iffen you do that?"

Owen nodded. "Of course."

"I reckon the air carries the sense of the magick to him."

"Again, not possible."

"No?" Nathaniel smiled. "You don't touch the brimstone when you shoot your musket, but it fires all the same."

"But that's because the firestones are created special to transfer the magick." Owen watched Nathaniel's smile grow and stopped talking. He couldn't deny the logic of Nathaniel's example, but if it were true, then a number of assumptions about how his world worked suddenly came into question. It was a bit more than he cared to think about at the moment.

"Must be because he's powerful in magick."

Nathaniel laughed as they started moving again. "And could be that you're not privy to magicks that would let you see how powerful you are."

"What?"

"Well, Captain, my thinking goes like this: if the Twilight People are more powerful than we are, at least we know how powerful we *might* be. And a powerful man, he might throw his weight around."

"I can see that." Owen ducked beneath a branch and started down the hill after Kamiskwa. "Your point?"

"My point is that magick would have to be controlled." Woods cut between pine trees beside him. "Look at firestones. You can only buy them from Fire Wardens. You use too many too fast, they don't sell to you. You don't bring in an old one for new, you don't get a new one. And if you're caught using a substitute, depending on the magistrate, you could lose your thumbs."

"That's an extreme punishment."

"Granted, but why the limit on firestones? And why do you have to learn magick from a patent mage?"

"They don't want people hurting themselves. You have to know your limit." Owen held up a thumb. "Magick can hurt you, even when used correctly."

"I ain't thinking the government cares 'bout people hurting themselves." Nathaniel snorted. "I'm thinking that they don't care if redemptioneers and beggars die on the voyage over, long as it's not too *many* die."

"You hear stories of people dying from using magick."

"But have you ever seen it?"

"No." Owen snarled. "You seem to take a certain delight in trying to vex me."

"Ain't that, Captain." Nathaniel gave him a solemn nod. "You're a smart man. Them's some questions need a smart man thinking on 'em."

By late afternoon they reached a wide stream and crossed. Kamiskwa led them on for another half-hour, then signaled for them to slow. Nathaniel shucked the sheath from his rifle. Owen drew the pistol. Both of them crouched and followed Kamiskwa into the brush.

They came to a small depression in the ground lined with a carpet of leaves from several autumns. A man's body lay huddled there, knees drawn up toward the chest, but arms not hugging them in. There was no question that he was dead. Maggots writhed beneath his skin, something had gnawed off his ears and lips. Birds had been harvesting hair and a larger beast had begun feasting on his calves.

Owen went to a knee. "It looks as if he's been shot."

Nathaniel poked the body with a stick. "Clothes are practically falling apart. Bullet hole in the vest, but not in the shirt beneath."

Owen pointed instead at the man's head. "I meant his skull."

The other two grunted. The man's skull had a hole in it, not quite cleanly round. A ball had hit at an angle and had gone in near the temple. It had come out toward the back of the skull, still on that side, and had blown a chunk of bone away.

"Who would murder a man out here? Why?" Owen grabbed a stick and hooked the edge of a satchel tucked beneath the body. "And why would they leave this if they killed him?"

"Bigger problem than that, I'm thinking."

"Yes, Mr. Woods?"

Nathaniel stood. "Assuming he fell where he was shot, ain't no point around here high enough to put a shot in at that angle. And if he were shot below, why drag him up here?"

Kamiskwa stood and folded his arms across his chest. "Another problem."

Owen looked up. "What?"

"The wound that killed him. Look close."

Owen did as instructed. He bent down, holding his breath against the stench. "Holy Mother of God."

The bones in the skull: they'd begun to heal.

CHAPTER NINETEEN

May 9, 1763
Bounty, Mystria

Owen carefully poked the skull with his stick. The triangular piece of bone near the exit wound didn't move. Though the fracture lines of the bone were clearly visible, they'd begun to lock together.

"That's just not possible. How did you know, Kamiskwa?"

The Altashee shook his head. "Magick taint. Something evil."

Owen shifted the stick around and snaked the pouch from beneath the body. The right hand came into view and had a bronze ring around the appropriate finger. "Mr. Woods, can you get that ring?"

"I'm not of a mind to be robbing graves."

"Nor am I, but this is a mystery I'd like to solve." Owen untied the thongs and opened the pouch. He pulled out a journal very much like the one he'd been keeping, and a half-dozen pencils. "They're round. Not of Norillian manufacture. Are they made here?"

Neither man knew. "I'm thinking I've seen round in New Tharyngia, but I ain't claiming that's the whole truth."

"No knife to sharpen them. This one was gnawed." He opened the journal. Penciled lines and sketches filled many pages. The text appeared to be in Ryngian, but it didn't make much sense. It also deteriorated over the course of keeping the journal. The letters got bigger and slanted down the page, with sentences occasionally spilling across the gutter onto the next page.

"I can't make any sense of this, but here's an interesting thing. No dates, but there are all these circles that are shaded. I think that's the moon. He didn't know the date, so he drew the moon each night." Owen closed the book. "It is in Ryngian, though. Du Malphias sending out his own scouts?"

Nathaniel reached down and snapped the ring finger off, then pulled the ring off and flicked some leathery flesh away. "Maggots say he's been dead for two days. Flesh and bone, I'd put him at dead six months anyway. That's a mite before your man arrived."

Owen accepted the ring and held it up. A simple signet ring, it had been cast

110

in bronze. The flat surface had the letter "P" engraved into it, and the legend "1/3" below. "First company, Third battalion, Phosphorus Regiment. They were destroyed at Villerupt. If he was there, he's been dead for three years. That's impossible. He must have once served, came to Mystria to start over, and he died here."

Nathaniel nodded. "As good an explanation as any."

Owen stood, slipping the journal, pencils, and ring into his pouch. "The Prince will find the journal an interesting puzzle."

Kamiskwa agreed with a nod, and they set off again. They pushed past dusk, then made a cold camp. They split the night into shifts, with Kamiskwa agreeing to take the last one and rouse them when it was time to move out. Woods took the first, leaving Owen for the middle of the night.

Since they'd not made a fire, Owen had insufficient light by which to read or write. Still, he fished out the dead man's journal and compared the last drawing of the moon with its current phase. Like the presence of the maggots, the drawing suggested the last entry had been three maybe four days earlier. Aside from the head wound, they'd not seen any obvious signs of trauma, so exactly why the man died where he did remained mysterious. And how he got there with that head wound was an even bigger mystery.

Owen found himself less concerned about the circumstances of the man's death, than the location. The man had penetrated very close to the point where the Benjamin River became navigable. If he had been scouting for du Malphias, they could have found the most obvious avenue of attack by accident. That was a very lucky stroke.

The soldier caught himself. Du Malphias could only attack down the Benjamin River if he had the information in the journal in Owen's hands. The most productive idea was to believe that du Malphias had sent out many scouts, and that at least some of them would successfully return with journals describing other ways to get into Mystrian territory. The journal Owen had found might be useful in picking out a path to du Malphias' stronghold, but du Malphias would have to defend against the possible loss of a journal or a scout being captured.

The information in this journal will be very valuable. Owen resolved to pen a note to describe its discovery.

Owen smiled. "Provided, of course, I survive to write that note."

The next morning they continued on, but at a more leisurely pace. While being watchful for trouble, Owen could not help but notice the sheer beauty of the forests. The green canopy glowed with sunlight. Shafts sank through here and there, but green shadows softened edges and warmed the land. He followed the trails Kamiskwa picked out but, as he looked through the trees, countless other trails beckoned.

They paused by a stream to rest, and Owen stared off at a shrouded pathway heading up a nearby hill. Breezes made the leaves sway just enough that shadows shifted. He thought he saw something and drifted toward it. It looked like a child huddled behind a tree, then it vanished. A bit further a maiden appeared wearing the shape of his wife, but with a Shedashee's coloring. And then, a bit further along, his mother beckoned.

A hand landed on his shoulder and he nearly jumped out of his skin. He spun. Nathaniel stood beside him. Kamiskwa stood at the ready by the stream, a hundred yards away. But that can't be. How can I have gone this far?

He looked at Nathaniel and realized the man had a hand over one eye. "What are you doing?"

"You right handed or left?"

"Right."

"Close your left eye and look again."

Owen did as instructed despite knowing it was nonsense. He turned and, suddenly, what had been an inviting trail shifted. Green lights still played through it, but sharp, black shadows predominated. The shape he'd taken for his mother became a bent and angular figure, a nightmare creature made of twisted sticks. And then it blew apart as if hit by a gust of wind, a gust he could not feel nor hear, and which affected nothing else.

"What is this?"

"*Pikwazahk.* It's the winding path." Nathaniel looped an arm over his shoulder and steered him back toward the stream. "The Twilight People believe the forest is alive. There are parts what are ancient. Things live there. There's times they are hungry."

"Is that true?"

"Don't know." Woods shrugged. "I felt the call. Times I wanted to walk into the woods, just keep going. Seems so peaceful you just want to drown in it."

"What is it about covering the eye?"

"Your strong hand is the practical hand, according to the Shedashee. That eye, the practical eye. The other, the soul eye."

"Cover that and you don't see the illusions?"

"'Pears to work."

They rejoined Kamiskwa, but Owen had a hard time shaking the sense of peace. He recognized so many pieces of it. His mother's smile. Catherine's clinging to him with passion just past. Bethany's smile and even the rough camaraderie of soldiers in the field. All times when the world itself had just faded away, leaving him alone but not alone, reassured that things were right.

His companions gave him a little time to collect himself. Kamiskwa kept a close eye on him as they headed out, grabbing his shoulder at one point when he'd stepped off the trail.

"Why is this happening?"

Kamiskwa looked around defiantly. "They want your power. You have great magick. You have fought far away and killed men they have never tasted before. You are sweet to them. New. They hunger."

"Why don't they want you?"

The Altashee laughed. "They do, but they cannot have me. Not me, not my children or their children."

"I don't understand."

"When my father was young his sister went missing on the winding path. All were afraid. Fall had come, an early winter promised. The Old Ones wanted prey before winter, before they went away."

"Into hibernation?"

Kamiskwa shook his head. "Into hiding. There are things that will feed on them, too. My father did not fear. He walked the winding path. They sent many warriors to stop him, but he defeated them all. He took his sister back. He exacted a promise that they would not feed on us for four generations."

Owen's eyes narrowed. He wasn't certain if the tale he'd just heard was true, or another fanciful story like those sold to scouts and other officers who had come on his mission before. And yet, he could still feel their desire. He wondered if the sirens of old Hellenic tales were old spirits hungering for men?

"Such things are long gone from Auropa."

"Are they?" Kamiskwa smiled. "Or do they just now live in other places? Cannot one get lost in your cities, your forests?"

A chill ran down Owen's spine. "There are always stories of children gone missing. In the Low Countries men vanished. We thought they deserted, but, perhaps…"

He took another look around. "This land is even more dangerous than I can imagine, isn't it?"

Nathaniel laughed. "I reckon, iffen that's the case, they done sent the wrong man to be scouting."

Owen raised an eyebrow and fixed him with a stare.

The Mystrian held a hand up. "Didn't say I thought it was true, Captain Strake. I was just supposing. Truth be told, you seen more in just a handful of days than most all your countrymen put together. You ain't whimpering for a return to Temperance, so you's likely the right man after all."

Though he felt no real inclination toward it, he let Nathaniel's remark mollify him. It wouldn't do to get upset over a simple remark, especially when it was based in the truth. Owen had spent a great deal of time in school and the military fighting prejudice based solely on his being half-Mystrian. He was used to it. Being thought deficient for entirely different reasons caught him by surprise.

As he thought about Nathaniel's remark—and reclaimed his hat from where a branch had knocked it yet again—he discovered the difference in criticisms. Norillians looked down upon him for something he could not control: the circumstances of his birth. Mystrians were judging him for something he could control: his lack of experience. Nathaniel and Kamiskwa were even helping him gain experience, and protecting him from perils he had no way of understanding. They might be wary of him, but they were also willing to give him a chance.

He caught up with Nathaniel as they entered a narrow meadow at the base of a wooded valley. "I appreciate all the help you're giving me. I want you to know that."

"That's kind of you." Nathaniel nodded solemnly. "I reckon I been a-judging you by other Norillians, and that weren't quite fair. My apologies, Captain."

"Not necessary, sir."

Ahead of them Kamiskwa slowed as he moved through the waist-high grasses. Nathaniel pressed a hand to Owen's chest.

"What?"

"Iffen we's gonna see a jeopard in these parts, this is the kind of place it likes." Nathaniel pointed off across the meadow toward a tree leaning against another at the edge of the woods. "Like this when we shot the Prince's jeopard. It was perched atop a log like that one over..."

Woods whistled loud and Kamiskwa dove forward. The Mystrian brought his rifle up with no further warning. His thumb covered the firestone. Fire jetted from the muzzle. Thunder roared and smoke blossomed, half-blinding Owen.

But not before he saw a puff of smoke in the distance, heard the blast of gunfire and the hiss of a ball scything through grasses before it knocked him flying.

CHAPTER TWENTY

May 9, 1763
Bounty, Mystria

Owen's musket flew into the tall grasses. He spun away from it, landing on his left hip. Pain jolted through it. He glanced down. The ball had caught him there, but he didn't see a hole or much blood. By rights blood should have been gushing and the pain of a shattered pelvis should have left him screaming.

Keening war cries and another gunshot eclipsed any chance to check his injuries. One of the Twilight People, this one with his face painted black save where a single white eye had been painted on his forehead, appeared at his feet. The warrior raised a warclub and shrieked.

Owen rolled to the left as the club pounded the ground, just missing him. Then in one smooth motion, as the warrior spun and raised the club again, Owen drew the pistol from the small of his back. His thumb covered the firestone. The warrior's eyes widened.

Owen invoked magick.

Had it not been for long hours of drill and hot minutes spent in battle, he never could have triggered the spell. Panic and pain he'd long since learned to shunt away. Almost without thought, he conjured the formula then pumped it out through his right thumb. The energy burned into the firestone, igniting the brimstone.

The warrior's face evaporated. The .50 caliber ball caught him right above the bridge of the nose, shattering bone. Scalp stretched, trapping the fragments, then the ball burst out the back. Blood and brains jetted in both directions. The shot lifted the man off his feet and dumped him in the long grasses.

With no time to reload, Owen snatched up the dead man's warclub and stood. His hip held, but something wasn't quite right. The stiffness didn't matter, as another warrior drove forward. The man backhanded a warclub at Owen. Owen blocked the blow, then tipped his club forward and jabbed. The blade plowed into the warrior's chest.

The Shedashee stepped back, fingers probing the wound, but Owen kept coming. Another jab smashed the hand holding the warclub. As it dropped, Owen buried the club in the man's stomach. The warrior pitched forward. Owen crashed the club into his skull. The warrior collapsed and lay still.

Owen limped ahead. Kamiskwa blocked an overhand club blow with his rifle, then whipped the butt around. His opponent's face crumbled and teeth flew. Woods, rifle in his left hand, snapped his right hand forward. A bloody tomahawk spun through the air, catching another warrior in the flank. He'd been sneaking up on Kamiskwa. The Altashee Prince spun, whipping the rifle's butt around in a blow that dropped his assailant.

Another shot rang out from the same spot as the first. Owen dove for cover. He found himself crouching near Nathaniel with a body between them. From other rustling Owen took it that Kamiskwa had also ducked out of sight.

"The shot came from the fallen tree."

"I saw. I'll get him once I reload."

"Don't, he'll see you."

The Mystrian laughed. "He would if I had to stand to load."

Nathaniel grasped a lever that had previously sat flush in a groove on the stock. He forced it down and the whole firestone assembly at the base of the barrel slid back. A gimbaled cylinder tipped up. Nathaniel stuffed a paper powder cartridge into it, then seated a bullet in the opening. He pushed the cylinder back down, and worked the lever to advance the assembly and seal the chamber.

Owen smiled. "Very quick work."

"Thanks. Kamiskwa, you reloaded yet?"

"By the time you miss I shall be, yes."

Nathaniel grinned. "Reckon I cain't afford to miss."

"I'll draw his fire." Owen heaved himself up and thrashed his way through the grasses. He cut at an angle to the tree so the shooter would have to track him. He bobbed up and down, his red coat contrasting vividly with the green grasses, waiting for the shot.

The sniper obliged him. The bullet whizzed past Owen's head, leading him by a couple of feet. Then Nathaniel shot. Even with his rifle blast still echoing in Owen's ears, there was no mistaking screams of mortal agony from the fallen tree.

Owen cut back to where he'd dropped the pistol and quickly reloaded it. He fed powder from a paper cartridge down the barrel, then rammed the paper and a ball home. He slid the ramrod back into its place beneath the barrel. "My pistol is ready."

"I'm ready. Kamiskwa?"

"I've been waiting on you."

Owen found Nathaniel again. "How do we do this?"

Nathaniel gestured to one of the bodies. "These are Ungarakii. They're part of the Seven Nations. They travel in packs of six or so. We got most all of them. The painted eyes say they were scouting. Probably for the Tharyngians."

Owen looked toward the fallen tree. "Likely a Ryngian or two down there then."

"Most like." Nathaniel pointed at him. "How's your hip?"

Owen took his first good look at it. Wooden splinters peppered his hip and thigh. He plucked one out, then tossed it aside. "Ball must have hit my stock. Long range for a musket shot, so it just broke wood and knocked me down."

"Stiffening up, is it?"

"I'll limp for a bit." Owen paused. "Don't hear anything. He's dead or getting away."

"I reckon we best do something about that."

Setting a pace that had more to do with caution than Owen's limp, they closed in on the fallen tree. Kamiskwa ranged out far on the right flank and circled around into the trees. Owen and Nathaniel, advancing and covering each other, moved in more directly. It took them the better part of an hour to reach the fallen tree.

Owen stared down at the body of the man behind the tree. "Nice shot." The bullet had drilled through dirty leathers halfway between breastbone and navel.

Nathaniel crouched, turned the man's face this way and that. The dead man hadn't shaved in a while and his ears looked odd. So did his nose.

Owen frowned. "What happened to his face?"

"Not sure. Cain't figure why he has a glove on his left hand neither." Nathaniel stood and waved Kamiskwa over. "He look familiar?"

The Altashee nodded. "Pierre Ilsavont."

Owen leaned back on the fallen log. "You know him?"

"He cheats at cards. The shot that hit you was the best shot he ever made." Woods picked up the man's musket. "Fancy gun. New. Must have stole it. Ain't no way he bought it."

"Let me have a look." Owen caught the musket and tipped it up to look at the butt plate. "Arondel et fils, Feris, 1762. Made last year. Maybe your man was lucky."

"He'd have to be really lucky."

"How so?"

"Winter of 1761 came hard in these parts." Nathaniel nodded toward the body. "That's what's wrong with his face. Frostbite. See, Pierre here got drunk. He walked out into a freezing blizzard. Got hisself dead. Spring of '62 Kamiskwa and I wandered into the churchyard in Hattersburg and peed on his grave."

"Are you sure that's him?"

Woods shrugged. "Never did see him planted. And he died with lots of debts owing. Coulda been he figured himself better off pretend-dead and just laid low."

Kamiskwa spat at the body. "*Wendigo.*" He walked away and started to gather dead wood into a small pile.

"What did he say?"

"*Wendigo.* The Shedashee have this legend. Cannibal comes among them, kills and eats them. Pure evil, like a spirit, takes them over. It's supposed to do that during the winter, when food is scarce. He reckons Pierre was dead and the *wendigo* spirit brought him back."

Owen raised an eyebrow. "You believe this?"

"Don't know what I'm believing about Pierre here. Still and all, that same winter, Kamiskwa and me went to Trading Post Number Twenty-three up Queensland. Small place, palisade fence, main gate open, store open, snow drifted in. Five men in there, dead, froze-solid, half-eaten."

Nathaniel looked down, his brows furrowed. "Most folks think it was a bear. Trapper up that way got a bear come spring, said he found a ring in the stomach. That was good enough for most folks.

"But there weren't no bear tracks or scratches at Twenty-three. Weren't no bear awake then. Weren't no hands gnawed off."

He toed the corpse. "I ain't saying it was Pierre here. Like as not it weren't. Don't know what it was. But I am willing to believe there is evil in the world, evil what will make a man crazy. If they want to call it *wendigo*, that's good enough for me."

Part of Owen wanted to dismiss the *wendigo* as superstitious nonsense, but he'd seen things on the Continent that had driven men mad. He recalled having to fetch an officer out of the wine cellar of a chateau. The man had just packed himself into a corner and sat there weeping in the dark. He wasn't drunk; he was just seeing ghosts. That was one kind of madness, and Owen had seen the other, too, the bloodlust that never could be sated.

Wendigo is as good an explanation as any.

"What do we do?"

"Grab an ankle." Nathaniel set his rifle down, and took hold of one leg. "We're going to drag him over to that pile of wood, light it up, and burn the *wendigo* out of him."

They didn't have enough time to burn the body entirely since they wanted to be well away from the spot before nightfall. Kamiskwa said that only the head needed to be burned. Nathaniel produced a stone knife and took the head off a bit more efficiently than made Owen comfortable.

They left the Ungarakii bodies where they lay, but stripped them of all weapons. They also cut off knotted bracelets, one of which each warrior wore. Each seemed to Owen to be of a different style, woven together out of a variety of colored threads and what looked to be hair.

Kamiskwa let a finger bump along a series of knots. "The patterns indicate his family, clan, and societies. The colors are events. Blue for birth, red for battle, black for ceremonies. The hair is from men he has killed."

Nathaniel plucked one from Kamiskwa's hand and measured its thickness against his own thumb. "Two inches, maybe three. That's worth a crown."

"A bounty?"

"That's right, Captain Strake. We get to Hattersburg and the six we collected here means we can live fancy for a while."

"I wasn't aware Her Majesty's Government…"

"It don't." Nathaniel tossed the bracelet back to Kamiskwa. "Frontier settlements have been asking a long time for some of you Redcoats to keep them safe. Them settlements don't have proper charters, so no troops come. Bounty-men will come, though, and hunt all manner of things, including the Ungarakii."

In dealing with the Ungarakii bodies they found the remains of Owen's musket. A ball had shattered the stock. Owen removed the firestone assembly and the barrel, then tossed away what remained of the stock. He appropriated the dead man's musket. It took the same caliber shot as his musket, which saved Owen the need to recast bullets. More importantly it had a shorter barrel, trimming two pounds from the overall weight and a foot and a half from the length.

The barrel, however, was the wrong shape to accept Owen's bayonet. And the shorter length meant it had a shorter effective killing range. In the woods this would not constitute much of a problem, since anything he could see would be well within the weapon's lethal range.

By rights, Ilsavont never could have expected to hit any of us. Owen looked back at Nathaniel as they marched along. "You said he wasn't a good shot. Why did he shoot from that range?"

"Been cogitating on that myself. I reckon he done seen your red coat and got to panicking. A mite skittish he always were."

"That not withstanding, I am still going to be in uniform on this expedition." Owen scratched at the back of his neck. "His action would confirm his being in Tharyngian employ."

Nathaniel shook his head. "Most like, but ain't no love lost 'tween the Altashee and the Ungarakii. Could be his boys seen us earlier and gathered here to get us."

Kamiskwa turned and snorted. "Ungarakii cringe before the Altashee. They would not have dared hunt us. They were tracking the corpse we found."

"Is that so?" Nathaniel scratched his chin. "They was heading in that direction."

Owen frowned. Ilsavont was Ryngian. The Ungarakii were Ryngian allies and knew the area. The dead man's journal had been written in Ryngian and he was a scout himself. It made sense that someone might be sent to look for him.

"If they were hunting the body, how did they do it? Neither of you saw any sign of the dead man's passing, did you?" Owen looked at Nathaniel. "You made a point of this being a big land. How would they expect to find one body in so huge a landscape?"

Nathaniel shrugged. "I wished I had you an answer."

Kamiskwa held a hand out toward Owen. "The corpse's ring, please."

Owen dug it out of a pouch. "Do you think magick is involved?"

The Altashee cupped the ring in his hands. His eyes closed. He remained very still for a moment, then his eyes snapped open. "Strong impressions. The feeble Ungarakii could not track them."

"I don't recall Pierre being so all-fired powerful myself."

"Kamiskwa, can you track this ring back to another impression?"

The Altashee again closed his eyes, then snorted. "Yes."

"Where?" Owen smiled. "It will lead us to du Malphias, I am sure."

"It is faint and fading." Kamiskwa shook his head. "And would lead us back to Pierre."

"Damn."

Kamiskwa grunted. "We should push on. What I cannot detect, perhaps my father can."

Owen rubbed at his hip. "Not sure how far I'm going to make it."

Kamiskwa smiled. "No matter how far it is, we should walk with haste. We have the ring and though the *wendigo* no longer has a head, we do not want his body coming after us."

CHAPTER TWENTY-ONE

May 9, 1763
Saint Luke
Bounty, Mystria

The thought of a headless body trailing them through the woods did create a sense of urgency. They pushed on into the dark until they'd crossed another large stream. They camped slightly upriver of some rapids and Kamiskwa insisted on sinking the ring into the river for the night.

Nathaniel agreed. "Wisdom in action. The ring will make magick ripples in the water. The *wendigo* will follow it down stream and miss us by a mile."

"That will really work?"

Kamiskwa shrugged. "In the old stories something similar has been effective. Now we need to take care of your hip."

Owen hobbled down to the stream's edge. His red coat might have made him a target, but it had cushioned the impact with his musket's stock and had absorbed many of the splinters. He pulled it off, then peeled his trousers down.

As battle wounds went it wasn't that horrible. One splinter had stabbed about an inch deep. The rest had just peppered his flesh. He drew the long one out, starting blood flowing slowly from a hole he could plug with his thumb.

Nathaniel appeared and handed him several of the fern fronds. "Chew."

Owen stripped the leaves off the plant and stuffed them in his mouth. What started as sweet became bitter very quickly. Pieces of stem crunched between his teeth, releasing more sour liquid. He involuntarily swallowed a bit and his throat burned. He couldn't ever recall tasting anything more foul.

Kamiskwa set down a hunk of moss and offered his cupped hands.

Nathaniel slapped him on the back. "Spit."

The frothy green mulch had the look of a freshly smashed grasshopper. Kamiskwa packed it into the wound and smeared it around the hip. He then clapped a hunk of moss over it. Using a strip cut from Owen's blanket, he bound the leg up.

Nathaniel handed Owen a stout length of maple to use as a walking stick. "It's a good day when we kill a handful of Ungarakii and get away with only a scratch. We get to Saint Luke, someone can sew it up proper."

"I apologize for slowing us down."

"No apology necessary." Kamiskwa spread his arms wide. "We are in Altashee territory and we have slain enemies. We are heroes. Any walk is a heroes' walk, and no one will complain about its speed."

Despite their kind offer to let him sleep, Owen agreed to take a watch. The *mogiqua* poultice deadened the pain, but didn't do much to ease the stiffness. Owen wanted to tell himself that his stiffness was only because of the wound, but he knew better. He had marched through the Low Countries with ease, but Mystria presented new challenges. He couldn't wait until his body had adapted to them.

Owen wasn't certain he believed in the *wendigo*, but during the midnight watch, he did keep an ear out for splashing. In the morning, he scouted down along the shore to see if there were any footprints. He did it as quietly as possible, though his injured hip made that difficult. If either of his companions noticed, they said nothing.

Kamiskwa chose a course from that point forward which kept to trails and minimized exertion. Whenever Owen protested that they could go faster and more directly, the Altashee counted that his path enabled them to backtrack the Ungarakii. He went to great pains to point out a variety of signs and over the next four days Owen learned a great deal about tracking.

Toward the end of the fourth day, after slogging their way through a narrow part of a swamp, the three men emerged and climbed one last wooded hill. They paused at the top, giving Owen time to scrape mud off his coattails. At least, that was why he thought they'd paused; then he caught the scent of wood smoke over the stink of the swamp's black muck.

Kamiskwa smiled. "Welcome to Saint Luke."

"I thought the Altashee migrated."

"We do. This is the summer Saint Luke."

Owen's eyes narrowed. "And the name? Is your tribe part of the Church of Norisle?"

Kamiskwa shook his head. "Some are, but not many missionaries get out this far. My father just likes the name. He speaks your tongue a bit, and has confused Luke for luck. He likes that you have a god for luck."

Owen thought the name slightly blasphemous, but imagined Bishop Bumble's outrage if he knew the truth. That made him smile.

Nathaniel slapped him on the shoulder. "Just remember, Captain, this ain't Launston society."

Owen nodded, but straightened his coat. "I shall comport myself as befitting one of Her Majesty's officers."

The trio came down through the woods to the Altashee village. It had been laid out in a broad ravine with a stream running around the northern border. A long house with an arched roof dominated the center. The saplings that had been joined together to form the rafters had their branches braided together. Magick had been used because the trees bled into each other. Between them birch bark formed most of the roof and siding, save for where leather flaps allowed entry and exit.

Around the long house sat smaller structures, all domed, of varying sizes and ostentation. Made of pine and birch like the long house, these dwellings benefited from their owners' artistic talents. Images from children at play to men hunting a rhinoceros decorated them. Owen wondered if these pictures illustrated stories or might in some way serve as did a coat of arms, to identify the owner.

As they entered the camp, villagers took notice. Small children came running over to jabber at Kamiskwa. A couple took hold of Woods' hands, trying to drag him off toward one dwelling or another. He resisted their efforts and said things which had them shrieking or laughing or both.

One little girl, her green hair shining, clad in a buckskin dress with lovely beadwork, just stared shyly at Owen. He stopped, and dropped to a knee to smile at her. She returned the smile, then her eyes widened and she ran off screaming. It didn't sound like terror to him, nor was it that happy scream most children just couldn't contain.

He stood. "What did I do, Mr. Woods?"

"Your eyes. She's not seen that shade of green before. She ran off calling you 'Moss-eyes.' Not really a bad thing."

Owen frowned. "But not a good one, either."

"Ain't the worst."

A hand threw the long house door flap open and an older, heavyset Altashee emerged. He straightened up, showing streaks of hair so white amidst the green that it seemed to glow. He smiled at Kamiskwa and opened his arms. Kamiskwa flew to him and they embraced.

They parted, then the old man hugged Nathaniel. They exchanged comments and both of them laughed. Owen noticed the old man's left eye was milky-white, but saw no battle scar in or around the socket. The two men seemed quite familiar and Owen sensed the connection was more than just Nathaniel's being Kamiskwa's friend.

Finally, Nathaniel turned away and waved a hand toward Owen. "Great Chief Msitazi, this is Captain Owen Strake of the Queen's Own Wurm Guards."

Owen pulled himself to attention and saluted. He made a horrible sight, with his stockings and trousers shredded, coated in mud and with scratches bleeding beneath. Leaf litter, burrs, and bits of thorny branches clung to his jacket. His hat had faired the best, but salt stains rimmed the black felt.

The old Altashee drew himself up and returned the salute. "It has been a long time since the Queen has sent a man to me."

Owen wanted to immediately explain that he wasn't an official envoy, but there wasn't any way to do that without dishonoring the man's comment. Owen cleared his throat. "Her Majesty cherishes the friendship of the Great Chief Msitazi of the Altashee."

Msitazi laughed and made a comment that made both Kamiskwa and Nathaniel smile.

Owen opened his hands. "Did I...?"

The Chief shook his head. "Captain, I know your Queen has no idea who I am. But you are polite. I like this."

Nathaniel jerked a thumb at Owen. "You'll be liking the fact that Captain Strake here done killed hisself two Ungarakii back two-three walks of here. He'd a-killed more, but me and Kamiskwa was selfish and got a pair each ourselves."

Msitazi looked Owen up and down. "Never has your Queen sent a warrior to me. You must come inside." He turned, and reentered the long house.

Kamiskwa and Nathaniel began shucking off all their gear and piling it near the long house. Kamiskwa barked an order at two boys. They immediately plunked themselves down beside the equipment and warned others off.

Kamiskwa smiled. "Guards against curiosity. Please, Captain, take off your coat, trousers, stockings and shoes?"

Nathaniel was already stripping down, and Kamiskwa pulled off his leggings. They kicked them into a pile, adding their moccasins, and an Altashee maiden approached with a basket to gather them up.

Owen hesitated.

Woods slapped him on the back. "Don't be shy, Captain. Tain't nothing she hain't seen before."

The maiden giggled.

Owen blushed, then turned his back and stripped off his muddy clothes. Fortunately his blouse tails hung down far enough to protect his modesty. He gathered his things up and placed them in her basket, nodding his thanks.

He joined the others in the long house. Msitazi sat on a blanket with Kamiskwa at his right hand and Nathaniel at his left. Owen took up a place across from him. In the long house's dim interior the Twilight People's faces all but disappeared for eyes and teeth.

"Where did you find the Ungarakii?"

"They were in Longmeadow, Father. They were scouting for the Tharyngians."

Nathaniel nodded. "Had them a man with them, Pierre Ilsavont. Might could be he's a *wendigo*."

The elder sat back. "Did you destroy it?"

"Burned the head." Nathaniel shrugged. "Left the Ungarakii for the crows."

Msitazi's laughter filled the long house. "You warm my heart, Magehawk."

Magehawk? Owen killed the question on his lips. "Great Chief Msitazi, we found a ring on a corpse out there. Kamiskwa says he can feel strong magick on it. I believe that this magick could link back to a man Prince Vlad wishes us to hunt."

The Altashee closed his right eye and turned his face toward the long house's exterior wall. "I see the ring. It has a thread that extends to the dawn."

"But…" Owen frowned. Du Malphias had to be north and perhaps even west of them.

Msitazi held up a hand. "This man has the wiles of a fox. He has anchored his magick far away to deceive. Were you to track him by the ring, you would face disaster."

Nathaniel sat back. "I reckon then we're gonna be a-hunting him regular."

"Yes, of course, but we need to send the ring and the journal back to Prince Vlad."

Msitazi smiled. "I shall see to this, in honor of what you have done for the Altashee, Captain Strake. And tonight you will sleep over there, near the fire. It is a position of honor."

"You are most kind, Chief Msitazi."

The Chief's smile broadened. "I will send one of my daughters to sleep with you."

"Thank you, but I am married."

Nathaniel laughed. "Just to keep you warm, Captain."

"I think I will be fine, Mr. Woods. I have my blanket and my wool coat."

Msitazi nodded very solemnly. "That is a very fine coat. Very colorful. I like your coat."

"Thank you."

"I like your coat very much."

Owen was about to repeat his thanks, when Nathaniel kicked him in the shin. "What was that for?"

Nathaniel lowered his voice. "Give him the coat."

"What?" Owen leaned in toward him. "I can't. It's my uniform. I am on a mission. If I am caught on Tharyngian territory out of uniform, I shall be shot for a spy."

"You already been done shot at on account of that coat, Captain. Give him your coat."

Owen shot a sidelong glance at the elder Altashee. He smiled back.

"It would be an honor, Chief Msitazi, for you to have my coat."

The Altashee clapped his hands and a young woman went to fetch the coat.

She returned quickly and presented it to Owen. He, in turn, handed it to Msitazi, who immediately pulled it on.

Though about as broad of shoulder as Owen, the Altashee had a bit of a belly, so the coat fit awkwardly. Still, Msitazi smiled widely, happily toying with the brass buttons and running his fingers along the gold braid.

Owen handed across his hat as well, and the Chieftain clapped his hands. The Norillian officer could do nothing but smile. Not at the ridiculousness of a woodland savage dressing up in his uniform, but from the pure pleasure the man exhibited as he got up and strutted around. A couple of women deeper in the long house made comments, and Msitazi barked back at them, but they just laughed.

That little bit of byplay took Owen leagues away. He saw himself back in Launston, recounting his adventures before the Royal Geographical Society. Well-dressed men and handsomely draped women, all the cream of society, would titter and smile as he related this moment. They would feel superior, and yet, at the moment, Owen felt anything but.

And he found himself resenting his future audience's reaction.

Msitazi clung to the jacket's blue facings and smiled. "This is grand. You will wait here, Captain, for my return. You are a warrior, and I shall not let any of the Shedashee mistake you for anything less."

CHAPTER TWENTY-TWO

May 14, 1763
Saint Luke
Bounty, Mystria

Once the door flap had settled back into place, Owen glanced over at Kamiskwa. "Was your father serious about having one of your sisters sleep with me?"

"His offer was quite sincere, Captain. You are a warrior. You have killed Ungarakii. You are a powerful visitor from afar. To do less would have been rude."

Nathaniel smiled. "And Msitazi is a cagey one. Iffen you did get a child on one of his daughters, that child would be very powerful in the ways of magick."

Owen scrubbed a hand over his face. "I am mindful of our previous discussion, but this is so alien…"

Kamiskwa patted Owen's shoulder. "Your rules suit your land, Captain. Ours are for our land. Respect is more honorable than understanding, and politeness soothes misunderstanding."

Before the discussion continued, Msitazi returned and seated himself again. He offered Owen a bag similar to the ones the others used. The flap and the bag had been embroidered and set with beads and bits of shell depicting a bear sharpening his claws on a tree.

"I would not have it said that Msitazi allowed a friend to go naked. In here you will find clothing and moccasins. I will tell you of this clothing. These are the clothes that I wore many years ago when I stole my first wife from the Lanatashee. I was not a craven warrior, one to steal into their camp and sneak away like the weasel. I went as a man. I walked to her and took her by the hand and led her to my home. Some came to oppose me, their greatest warriors amongst them, but none could wrest her hand from mine."

Owen brushed his hand over the bag's surface. "You honor me greatly, Msitazi, but these clothes should go to your son."

"My son needs none of my glory. He makes his own." Msitazi smiled. "He simply needs good friends, and in these clothes, so shall you be known."

Owen dressed in Msitazi's clothing. The leggings, moccasins, and tunic were all made of soft doeskin so pale it approached white. Another beadwork bear decorated the chest. Fringe lined the sleeves and leggings. The material felt very warm against his skin. Wearing it he felt even more a part of Mystria.

For the first time he had to wear a loincloth. It wasn't terribly hard to figure out how to make it fit. He used his own belt to secure it. He played with it until the tails hung evenly front and back. It pleased him that the linen cloth itself had a broad blue stripe down the middle, and red stripes at the edges, mirroring the front of his regimental coat.

His donning the clothes brought a change in how the Altashee treated him. Children stared, but more in wonder at the honor bestowed upon him than the unusual sight he'd been coming into their village. The same little girl who had run away screaming came and sat quietly next to him as he wrote in his journal, playing with two corn husk and rag dolls. Every so often she would look up and smile, clearly feeling safe in his presence.

Again the contrast with his own people struck him as odd. He recalled a grand ball that had been given for a dowager aunt who had reached the age of seventy. Though Owen had not been adopted by his stepfather, his presence was still required. He'd been fitted for a proper set of clothes and given a wig that had been expertly prepared and powdered. He'd even suffered through a couple of rudimentary dancing lessons. The dance master decided he was beyond hope and should beg off dancing for an imagined "wound from the war, any war, anywhere."

And despite his having served the Queen honorably in a number of conflicts, women stared and laughed at him behind their fans. Men came up and greeted him, dropping names and clearly making fun of him with their airs and insinuations. He played dumb, taking some pleasure in their being too stupid to understand he couldn't be as obtuse as they thought him and still have done his job. That, however, formed just a tiny silver lining to the cloud of his being an outsider.

And then Catherine appeared. Young and very pretty, she was just growing out of the coltish stage marking the transition from adolescence to womanhood. She wore her dark hair up, but had teased three ringlets loose. The fashion of the day dictated that only two should have been present, but she flouted convention.

She passed by him once, her brown eyes studying him above the lace edge of her fan. Then she returned in her pale yellow gown and snapped that fan shut in a gloved hand. "I hope you can save me, Lieutenant?"

"I beg your pardon, Miss…"

"Catherine Litton. My grandmother is your aunt's best friend. I have lived with her since my parents, missionaries, died of cholera in the Punjar."

"My sympathies at your loss, Miss Litton."

She leaned in, smelling sweetly of apple blossoms. "I shall need you to rescue me. They shall begin the dancing soon, and Percy Harlington has already vowed to kill any man who dances with me. It frightens me, so I would ask you to walk with me through the gardens to save me."

Owen later discovered—after he and Catherine had wed—that she was seldom so timid at cotillions, receptions, or galas. She loved dancing, and gossiping, tittering laughter from behind a fan. Never cruel things, only pointing out how a person had failed, completely, to abide by social convention. The rules for proper seasonal dress seemed far more complex and less forgiving than the Military Code of Justice. Catherine, however, understood it all better than any barrister, and often corrected Owen's dress as they headed off for a night of fun.

That first night they walked in the gardens for a bit, then stopped outside the Ryngian windows and peered back in from the darkness at the gaily lit party. Catherine laughed and told him all sorts of things about the people inside. Owen learned which men were dancing with their mistresses while their wives glared, and watched a beautiful young widow playing three ardent suitors off against each other. Catharine layered meaning onto things he'd always noticed but had never understood. With her at his side, a world he had rejected because of how it treated him suddenly became oddly interesting and filled with new depths of hypocrisy.

And he recognized, later, that Catherine had set her heart on more than rescue. She told him she fell under his spell because of his gallantry that night. He had been her hero, and would forever love him for it.

Catherine accepted me just as this little girl has, but to the others of my own kind, I remained an outsider. Here, however, I am welcomed.

He would consign none of his memory about that dance to the journal. Instead he concentrated on the Altashee and how their opinion of him had changed. The fact that Msitazi and Kamiskwa lauded him as a great warrior meant the Altashee accepted him as such. When he went for a short walk, looking for a couple of plants on the Prince's list, six boys had followed him, walking as he did, then squatting in a group to study what he studied. He caught no mockery in how they acted, just the hope that they, too, by doing what he did, could become a great warrior.

He smiled as he wrote. He imagined Bethany reading the words, tracing her fingers over the ink, perhaps reading some passages to her younger siblings, and others to her father and mother. He doubted she would share much with Caleb; and suspected Caleb would have little interest in what Owen had to say.

As pen scratched on paper, Catherine came again to his thoughts. Her sidelong glances, her little smiles, the way she would sigh and take his hand in hers, wishing aloud for a day when he could leave the army and they could be free to live as they wished. He loved her for all those things, and more. *I cannot wait to have her in my arms again.*

He finished a passage, then sighed loudly, wishing she was at his side.

The little Altashee looked up, read his face, then handed him one of her dolls.

He smiled at her kindness and admired the doll before handing it back to her. And she smiled, as if all was well with the world, and for once, Owen thought, just for a little bit, such a judgment might have been right.

That evening passed uneventfully. The presentation of the wurmscales to Msitazi pleased the Altashee elder. He ran his hands over them, studying the underside with its mother-of-pearl sheen. He then placed him on his shoulders like epaulets, and Owen suspected he might see them affixed there in the future.

After a dinner of venison and vegetable in a stew, Owen spent time cleaning and oiling his musket and pistol, quietly observing everything going on around him. Life seemed anything but hurried among the Twilight People. For the most part they seemed happy, smiling and humming as they worked. On the rare occasion a child cried out, the closest adult came to his rescue, and peace was restored.

He didn't see much of Kamiskwa, but Nathaniel Woods had three children following him wherever he went. The two boys looked enough alike to be brothers and neither had reached his teens. The third, a little girl, appeared only a couple years older than the lass who had attached herself to Owen. The three of them got along well enough, with the two boys being solicitous of the young girl's needs.

Nathaniel played with the children a little, laughing and joking with them, admiring things they showed him. He let the girl sit in his lap and tousled the boys' hair. Though Owen couldn't understand a word they said, hand-gestures, pantomime, and growls led him to believe Nathaniel was relating some story about hunting a jeopard. Others stopped to listen, and broad smiles suggested the story was a well-known favorite.

Owen also noticed his spending a certain amount of time, both separately and together, with two of the Altashee women. Given the beadwork and motifs on their clothes, they'd made Nathaniel's clothing, the rifle-sheath, and bags. Owen also guessed that they were related to Kamiskwa, being the right age to be his sisters, largely because their clothes had bear paw prints beaded onto them.

And, because the children appeared to be a bit lighter in color than others in the camp, Owen came to the conclusion that they might well be Nathaniel's offspring. Their previous conversation about Altashee marriage and mating customs held Owen back from assuming that Nathaniel was a flagrant womanizer. Tenderness characterized the way he interacted with the women and Owen saw none of the predatory aggressiveness so common with lechers.

As they sat together rolling cartridges, Owen turned to Woods. "The children are yours, by those women."

"The boys is by Naskwatis and the girl by Gwitak. Ten, eight, and five." Nathaniel shook his head. "And we ain't married. Iffen you're of a mind to tell me I'm going to Hell, save your breath, save your teeth."

Owen measured out some brimstone. "Do you love them?"

"The kids, yes. Their mothers, sure, but not in Norillian thinking. Love is fine for fancy stories and songs. Ain't much of a place for it in the world." Nathaniel looked around the village. "You know the Altashee word for romantic love is the same word they use for madness."

"I thought that was their word for greed."

"The same. Romantic love is emotional greed. Lust the Altashee understand. Love between parent and child, that they understand. Being devoted to one person only, that they reckon is insane."

"But they allow people to marry."

"Guarantees children strong in magick."

Owen glanced at the mothers of Woods' children. "And they wanted your magick?"

Nathaniel nodded.

"This has something to do with why they call you 'Magehawk'?"

The other man twisted the ends of the cartridge paper, and tucked it away in his pouch. "Don't be setting much store in stories you hear in Temperance Bay."

"Didn't hear the term until Saint Luke."

Nathaniel raised an eyebrow. "Bethany Frost didn't fill your ear?"

Owen smiled in spite of himself. "I gathered she found you odious, but she did not speak ill of you. She just cautioned me against you. Were you a bad influence on her fiancé?"

"Ira, no. He was a good man. Didn't know him well. Seventh son of a seventh son. Strong in magick. Only ever met one man stronger. Always liked Ira. Sorry to hear he died."

Owen nodded, then glanced at Nathaniel. "Why do they call you 'Magehawk'?"

The Mystrian patted him on the shoulder. "You been in a fight or three? Heard men spin grand war stories?"

"I have."

"Grand's just another word for lie."

"That doesn't answer my question."

"Some men, they needed themselves some killing. I obliged 'em. Folks what wasn't there made something big out of it."

A little shiver ran down Owen's spine. "But that incident created this interest in your magick?"

Nathaniel slowly nodded. "The Twilight People understand the truth of things. Ain't nothing like a woman doing for you to get a man back on his feet. Kids'll do that, too. You got any?"

"No."

"Strong buck like you?"

"My wife is young. There will be time later."

"I reckon there's truth there." Nathaniel started working on another cartridge." You'll get started when you're back to Norisle, when we's just an adventure writ in a book."

"I didn't come for adventure." Owen frowned. "I came to do my duty."

Nathaniel chuckled. "And your wife, she didn't never suggest you getting rich out of this?"

Anger flashed through Owen. "She loves me. She wants the best for me, and I for her. The Altashee might think love to be madness, but I don't. Have you ever loved anyone?"

"I think, on this subject, Captain Strake, we ain't gonna be sharing no more words. I didn't mean to offend you concerning your wife. Needle you maybe, but offend, no. You've made your choices, I've made mine. Ain't no good our jawing about them."

"Agreed, and no offense taken."

"Thing you have to remember, Captain Strake, is that this here is a brand-new world. What-all they think across the ocean don't matter a whit here. Norillian tradition works, sure, but in a known land."

"Known land?"

Nathaniel smiled. "Norillians been in Mystria for two hundred fifty years or thereabouts?"

"That's about right."

"Now your family, your stepfather's family, they been around how long?"

"Since before the Invasion. Eight centuries."

"And afore that there was the Remian Empire, then the Mohammadeans and the Haxians. A good long time."

"Right."

"So all them kingdoms and empires, they've done fought over the same land for a long time. They make up rules. They keep the peace when they want peace. They make war when they desire war. All because they have a tiny land and everyone wants it."

Woods spread his arms. "Mystria is a big land. Bigger than you could imagine. We're ten walks from the coast. The Mystrian continent is three hundred more walks westward. Maybe five hundred, just east to west, and that many north to south. Don't nobody know. Ain't nobody ever made it all the way. So all them rules what keep people content in a tiny plot of land, they don't mean spit. Them rules is as useless as a law telling the sun, 'Don't shine.'"

"Then you think Mystria should become independent."

Woods smiled. "It's a notion. Keep things unspoiled, might be a good one."

Owen frowned. "You think people should be allowed to do what they want? No government? No authority?"

Woods tapped a finger to his temple. "This land is for strong people. You have a right to what you can do, what you can produce. Bountiful land, too. Give me shot, powder, a firestone, and some traps, me and mine will make out good. What I can't build, I trade for. Don't need money or taxes or some Fire Warden or other telling me what I can or cannot do."

"But what if a man comes along and decides to take what is yours? You're not suggesting that if you're not strong enough to hold it, he should have it."

"Ain't no need for a man to come take mine. Lots of empty hereabouts. He can just move on a-piece and make his own place."

"What if he's lazy? What if he doesn't want to move on? What if he decides to take a place from someone who is weaker than he is? What if he plunders and moves on?"

"I reckon he finds himself on the outside of a musket-ball."

"And if the shooter has made a mistake and hits the wrong target?"

Nathaniel shrugged. "Ain't saying things is perfect. It's just there ain't no government should come and take away everything you've worked for just on account of some voters decided they wanted it that way. Now you're gonna say that there's courts to deal with that. I'd allow as how you was right, if you could tell me a flash of gold might not influence a judge a time or three."

Owen laughed. "I will not argue that the current system is perfect, but at least it is a system. What you suggest is only a way that every man can die alone."

"Mayhap you're right, Captain Strake." Nathaniel shook his head. "But I'm thinking that sometimes that wouldn't be a bad thing at all."

CHAPTER TWENTY-THREE

May 15, 1763
Saint Luke
Bounty, Mystria

O wen slept in the long house alone, but close enough to the cook-fire and covered with a tanner pelt that he slept warm and comfortably. During the night he woke from two dreams in which he was talking to Bethany Frost. He couldn't remember the conversation, but in one of them they were walking hand in hand along the river near the Prince's wurmrest.

He wasn't certain what to make of that. He'd normally have dismissed the dream as meaningless. He'd told countless soldiers who'd suffered nightmares on the eve of battle that they meant nothing and predicted less. At the time he'd firmly believed that.

But all that was before he'd come to Mystria. Just the experience of the winding path pointed to more magick being alive in the world than he'd ever before imagined. Maybe it *was* just the land, with magick bubbling up like warm water from a spring. Maybe it was nothing at all, an illusion, but whenever he thought that, he recalled Kamiskwa's repairing the canoe and use of other magicks far more powerful than he'd been taught were possible.

He woke for the final time just after dawn and breakfasted on maize gruel. His hosts ground some maple sugar and mixed it into the gruel, turning the ordinary into a delight. The little girl sat next to him, eating as he did, smiling when he did, and giggling contentedly at nothing at all.

In the light of a cook-fire he wrote a letter to the Prince. He described the circumstances around the discovery of the journal and ring. He included his speculation that the circles represented phases of the moon. He added material on the background of Pierre Ilsavont, though found it difficult to code the name using *A Continent's Calling*.

Once that note had been completed, he wrote to the Frosts. He didn't want to alarm anyone so he stressed the amazing things he'd seen. He described the beauty of the falls and the friendliness of the Altashee. He refrained from mentioning much about magick. Given that the Frosts were members of Bishop Bumble's congregation, he wasn't certain how news that the Altashee could be so magickally powerful would go over. He thought Bethany would marvel at the fact, but others might not be so inclined.

He finished the note less because he was finished writing than that the village began to liven and he had to prepare to travel. He thanked Bethany for her help in obtaining the journals and pens, her father for *A Continent's Calling*, then folded and sealed the note. He addressed it to them and tucked it into the Ryngian journal.

As the three men packed, Owen discovered that Msitazi's family had worked through the night to prepare two gifts: a leather sheath for his musket and one for his pistol. Each had a long strap so he could carry the weapons across his chest, and a separate thong allowed him to bind the pistol to his belt so it wouldn't flap about while running.

Msitazi embraced Owen at the edge of the village, still proudly wearing the red coat. "May your walks be effortless, and may more Ungarakii die to build your legend."

Owen withdrew and gave him a salute. "I shall sing the praises of Great Chief Msitazi of the Altashee to my Queen."

Owen entrusted the journal, ring, and notes to Msitazi. "I will take your messages myself, Aodaga." The Chieftain nodded toward the eldest of Nathaniel's sons. "I shall have William accompany me. It is time he ventured out."

"Are you certain, Msitazi?"

The elder man laughed. "You now sound like all my children. I am old, I am not dead. And there is much magick left in me." His milky left eye sparkled as if it were not truly dead. "We will deliver your messages and I shall thank the Prince for his gifts."

Owen raised an eyebrow. "You want another look at Mugwump."

"The great warrior sees past the obvious." Msitazi slapped him on the arm. "When you next return, we shall share great stories of our adventures."

They each said their good-byes to those they were leaving behind. Nathaniel, who had not slept in the long house, hugged and kissed his children and their mothers. Kamiskwa made the rounds of the village.

The little girl came to Owen and offered him one of her dolls, the one she had given him when he seemed sad. He made ready to refuse it as politely as he could, but she remained adamant.

Kamiskwa intervened to explain. "She is giving you this to keep you safe. You will have to return it to her when you come back."

Owen crouched and gave the girl a kiss on the forehead. "Thank you, sweetheart."

Kamiskwa likewise crouched and gave the girl a hug and kiss. He spoke to her softly. She smiled, took a step back, stared at Owen for a moment, then ran off giggling.

"Who is she?"

Kamiskwa smiled. "Agaskan, my youngest sister."

Owen tucked the doll into the bag that had once contained his clothes and found himself smiling. It occurred to him then that Doctor Frost, Prince Vlad, and now an Altashee child had each given him a gift to speed him on his journey.

And that no one from Norisle had even made a pretense at doing the same.

Kamiskwa, Nathaniel, and Owen departed Saint Luke for Hattersburg by mid-morning. They traveled lightly laden with little more than guns, powder, shot, and supplies. The Altashee provided them with *pemikan*—dried meat combined with tallow and pressed into cakes. The food was packed into one pouch and the three of them alternated carrying it as they went.

The trio set off at an easy pace—what Kamiskwa called a hunting-walk. Owen considered it a stroll, and used the time to ask questions, make calculations, and even take notes. His companions pointed out a few more useful plants, stopped to harvest some tart red berries, and generally enjoyed the countryside.

The day's rising heat had them stripping off their tunics. By noon they cut onto a well-worn trail so they took off their leggings. Though not nearly wide enough for a modern army to move along, the track did allow them to make good time. By dusk they reached the shore of a small lake.

They made camp in a hollow a hundred yards or so from the shore. The area had clearly been used before—fire-blackened stones formed a circle at its heart. Nathaniel kneeled beside them. "Ryngians."

Owen picked his rifle up. "How can you tell?"

Nathaniel pointed to the hollow beneath a large stone canted to the side. "Not much wood there. Probably find bones and scat over other side of the hill. Lazy, good-for-nothing bastards the lot of them. Kamiskwa, best we check the canoe."

"Canoe?"

Nathaniel nodded. "Weren't thinking we was a-walking Hattersburg way did you?"

"You must have canoes hidden everywhere."

Nathaniel stood and waved Owen after him. They followed Kamiskwa over a small wrinkle of earth to the east and down into brushy ravine. Two trees had fallen across the ravine, providing a bridge for the brave, but the men ducked beneath them. There, half-hidden by bushes and the shadows of the log lay a birch-bark canoe approximately twelve feet long.

Kamiskwa brushed away some leaves. "Looks sound."

"Good." Nathaniel rubbed his nose. "We was happy to see Pierre dead on account of his joy in life was staving canoes in. He was just pure mean. Runs in the Ilsavont blood."

"People just leave these canoes out here?"

"This ain't Norisle. We ain't all thieves. We cooperate. Around these shores is dozens of canoes. You come up, you work. You make one. You take it across the lake and put it away. You tell another man where it is because, the next lake on, or the next river, he's got one you can use. Now there is those you don't use."

Owen worked his way out of the ravine behind Nathaniel. "Yes?"

"Ungarakii have several, most over to the eastern shore."

"And they'll kill you if you use them?"

"Nope." Mischief sparked in Nathaniel's brown eyes. "They make poor canoes."

Kamiskwa nodded. "Prone to leaking."

Owen stopped by the fire ring. "And that propensity, would it be something you help along a bit?"

Nathaniel laughed. "It's our way of encouraging Ungarakii to learn to swim."

"So, even if we'd not found the corpse, the Ungarakii would have been happy to kill us for sport?"

"Well, don't nobody out here kill just for sport. Don't mean they don't like killing, though. Ungarakii enjoy it an almighty lot."

The casual confidence with which Nathaniel made that statement sent a shiver down Owen's spine. He said nothing, choosing instead to gather firewood. He set the first pile near the ring, then gathered more to replenish the storage area beneath the leaning rock.

The fire offered light and warmth. The men took the opportunity to wash their loincloths and strung them from sticks to let them dry. Owen sat and wrote in his journal. He mostly recorded landmarks and basic information. The impressions he'd had from the day mostly involved Nathaniel's attitudes toward the Ungarakii and Ryngians. Recording them seemed to be a violation of trust.

The disgust with which Nathaniel had addressed the Ryngians' selfish use of the clearing echoed his earlier comments about the squatters they'd seen on the way to the Prince's estate. The idea that people might be wasteful offended him as much as absentee landlords controlling vast tracts of land.

Owen looked up. "If I might, Mr. Woods, ask you a question: When you look out at the land, when you travel through it, what is it you see?"

"Aside from the leaves and all, you mean?"

"Yes. I'm asking philosophically."

Nathaniel groaned. "You'll be a-wanting big words, then?"

"Not required. You love the land, clearly."

"Well, mostly, I reckon, I want it to be unspoilt." He sat silent for a moment, letting the crackle of the fire and the distant, mournful call of a loon fill the night. "I know men will bugger it all up. Chop down trees, make a farm, but that's soes they'll live. The Shedashee do that some, but they do it different. If they packed up Saint Luke tomorrow, how long before the land reclaimed it?"

"A year?"

"A season more like." Nathaniel's eyes narrowed. "How long for Temperance to vanish?"

"A generation?" Owen remembered marching along a portion of a Remian road in Tharyngia. "Much longer, maybe."

"Men is arrogant. Now their Good Book tells them that God made them out of mud just like everything else, but they reckon—on account of they disobeyed Him and got theirselves kicked out of that Paradise Garden—they is somehow better than the animals, plants, and dirt." The scout shook his head. "They go to making rules and laws what is for the benefit of themselves. Lets them get more. Lets them keep more. Don't matter they lie and cheat to get things."

Owen frowned. "You're not just talking about the land, are you?"

"Well, I don't reckon I am." Nathaniel hesitated, then smiled. "And I don't reckon I want to speak more on that particular point. Fact is, however, men and their society do more harm than good often as not. That's why I prefer keeping far from most folks."

"Is this a common theme among Mystrians?"

"I don't rightly know. Could be your little book will tell you. Don't care. I ain't a Mystrian." Nathaniel held a hand up. "Yep, I was born here. Probably die here, too, iffen there's a God who has a lick of sense. But I ain't a part of their society. Don't want nothing to do with it."

Owen frowned. "Then why not just live with the Altashee?"

"There's times, Captain Strake, when a man cain't do what he'd like to do. Cain't escape your history."

Kamiskwa snorted. "Not without trying."

"I reckon, Prince Kamiskwa, you've done forgot your original counsel in this matter."

Owen hadn't a clue as to what they were talking about, and was equally certain that he'd not get an explanation out of either of them. Nathaniel had seldom spoken about himself. Owen guessed that part of the poking and testing he did was to see how much he could trust Owen. Clearly he'd not made a decision one way or the other and, until then, whatever secrets he harbored would remain hidden.

The soldier couldn't help but smile. He'd been in the man's company for over ten days and could have written down all he knew about him on a single page. Catherine would have scolded him for not having learned more. He'd have explained that men don't talk about things the way women do, and she'd have countered that he was just afraid to ask.

Fear, however, had nothing to do with it. It was respect. He respected Nathaniel's right to privacy. Who he was, what he did, had no effect on the expedition. If it did, if Nathaniel was a drunkard, then they would have had words.

More importantly, the act of not asking built trust. Owen trusted Nathaniel to tell him anything that was important. So far Nathaniel had upheld his part of that bargain. Not asking personal questions became a silent vote of confidence in Nathaniel, engendering more trust.

Owen figured part of Nathaniel's attitude came from society's reaction to something he'd done. Just having children by two women—and Shedashee women at that—to whom he was not married would be enough to raise eyebrows and bring down condemnation. He would have been a right devil to men like Bishop Bumble. Many of those who spoke out against him would be hypocrites. Owen had heard countless superior officers lecture common soldiers on the sins of drink and debauchery, all the while themselves being drunk and just having departed a bordello.

Owen went to sleep thinking on that point and managed, unexpectedly, to sleep through to the last watch. Once the sun rose to splash gold over the lake, the men ate, scattered all signs of their camp, and launched their canoe. Owen sat in the middle as the others propelled the small boat across crystal water.

"I can paddle my share."

"Don't you be worrying about that. You just keep your eyes on the shore-line."

"We're beyond range for a shot."

"I reckon, but I want to know if there's folks watching us."

Owen retrieved his telescope from his pouch. He swept the shoreline but saw nothing aside from a moose grazing in shallow water. The placid surface reflected the blue sky, save near the shore where the trees' reflection rimmed the lake darkly.

"It looks clear."

Kamiskwa, from the front of the canoe, grunted a single word. "*Tekskog.*"

"Do you think, Kamiskwa? Hain't never been one in this lake afore." Nathaniel laughed. "Wouldn't do much good if he saw one."

Owen sighed. "Should I be looking for something specific?"

"Well, he's a-wanting you to be looking for a lake monster. Like a big snake, horse's head, lots of coils. The Prince probably put it on your list. He thinks it's a big otter. *Very* big. Get enough coats out of it for your army, I'm thinking."

"You're serious?"

"Can't honestly say I've seen one, but I've heard tell of plenty who have."

Owen would have dismissed the idea save for two things. First, he had seen creatures in Mystria he'd never seen before. Second, what they described—granted without the fur—was a wurm in its early life stage. *If there are wurms here and we can find them, we could raise and train them. The balance of Auropean power would forever be shifted.*

Over the next three and a half weeks they paddled over countless lakes and ponds, occasionally camping on islands, but only once making their way by canoe from one large body of water to the other. Mostly they stashed their canoe then trekked overland to the next lake to find another canoe and take a lend of it.

The journey thoroughly amazed Owen. Every day led him into territory completely devoid of any sign of man's passage. He knew it wasn't true, since they found canoes and campsites, but he saw no fences, no houses, and no roads. He had to look hard for places where trees had been cleared. More than once the forest had reclaimed a lot his guides said had been carved out twenty or thirty years before.

Owen studied the Prince's list as they went, but the animals proved elusive. He didn't regret not seeing a jeopard. At night wolves called to each other, competing with loons to be the loudest creatures around a lake. The noises had made him uncomfortable at first, but he learned to like them. Still, he never actually saw a wolf.

They took special notice when the forest went quiet. Kamiskwa and Nathaniel would immediately find cover, check their weapons, and wait to see what was in the vicinity. More than once they heard Ryngian trappers crashing through the brush, all the while remaining undetected themselves. At night, Owen made note of the interlopers' presence in his journal.

Finally they crossed over a low ridge that separated the Bounty and Lindenvale watersheds. They followed a chain of lakes and streams north and by noon, they stood on a hilltop looking down into the Hattersburg Valley. The town sat at the convergence of three rivers, the largest being the Tillie. The town began with a palisaded fort on the high ground nearest the confluence, and had grown out from there. Trees had been felled and all around the town small homesteads had been cleared.

Nathaniel slapped Owen on the back. "Hattersburg. Civilization as far west as allowed by law." Then he pointed off toward the east. "Of course, law done stopped back there to catch its breath, so watch your step. This ain't a place you want to be caught dead."

CHAPTER TWENTY-FOUR

June 7, 1763
Hattersburg
Lindenvale, Mystria

They raced the sun to Hattersburg and barely beat it. On the way in they went past several small farms all connected by a sorry excuse for a road. Cabins had been made from logs and outbuildings from roughly sawn boards. Grass and mud stuffed cracks, and shutters closed over empty openings that passed for windows.

"Glass is expensive out here?"

"A mite delicate to be transported." Nathaniel spit off to the side. "Folks born out here have a notion it don't truly exist. Lenses on that telescope of yours is the closest they've ever seen. A window pane is pure fancy."

"Is there an inn where we can purchase a room? I do have money."

"Well, I was being honest with you back there, Captain Strake. You'd best be keeping your mouth closed tight. Listen and learn." Nathaniel smiled and Owen didn't feel all that reassured. "Got to trod a slender board in Hattersburg to stay out of trouble."

Hattersburg looked unlike any town Owen had ever seen, and it was not simply the rustic nature of the buildings. Few had proper foundations, so more than one of them sagged. Several had log buttresses shoring them up. A couple had fallen to ruin and then been pilfered for building material and firewood.

The town itself started with the fort and had an irregular greensward to the side and around the front in an oddly angular crescent. Two roads paralleled it from one river and the other crossing it. They extended until they hit the Cool River coming down from the north. More roads ran at angles both irregular and convenient, dividing lots into unconventional shapes. The church stood inland from the fortress, as if balancing it, with houses, shops, and other buildings clustered haphazardly between. Some people had built on the eastern and southern sides of the river and had to rely on ferries and a single ford to get across.

The roads weren't much to speak of. They had sunken from much use and some half-hearted attempts to remove mud and pile it on the sides. The lack of recent rains made them dusty, yet any precipitation would reduce them to soup. Boards crossed the roads at various points, but lay mostly hidden in the dust while dry.

Nathaniel led them to one of the larger buildings. It had started small, but other construction had been grafted on to it. The roof appeared sound, especially above the main parts of the second floor, but some of the walls had gaping holes between boards.

He threw aside the leather curtain acting as the door and marched across the common room to the bar—two boards balanced on two kegs. Patrons sat at tables and benches of crude manufacture. A stone fireplace dominated the left wall, but no fire had been laid in it. Instead a man stood before it, a lamp on the mantle behind him, reading from a book.

Nathaniel slammed a fist onto the board, bringing the tavernkeeper's head around. "You done gawking?"

The owner, a rotund man with twice as many chins and half the hair normally allotted, raised his arms in alarm. "Nathaniel Woods! I heard you was dead."

"I know. Heard your daughters a-weeping all down Temperance way."

The barkeeper scratched at his left eye. "Should have known better. Heard it before and it ain't never been true."

"You'll hear it again." Nathaniel jerked a thumb back over his shoulder. "This here is Owen. He don't talk much. You remember Kamiskwa."

"What I remember is the last time you was here. You can stay in the stable."

"You really want to be more friendly to me, Samson Gates." He extended a hand back past Owen, and Kamiskwa put two of the Ungarakii bracelets in it. Nathaniel slapped them down on the bar. "Your finest room, a round of your horsepiss ale, and meat that died some time after the last thaw."

Gates leaned over, inspecting the bracelets closely. "Eight shillings for the both of them."

"Either your inn has got a might pricier or you're of a mind to be cheating me."

"I ain't a cheat." Gates folded his arms over his chest. "Parliament don't like we don't drink rum out here. They're putting a tax on whiskey. My still's going to cost me two hundred pounds in taxes."

"Now where did you hear a fool thing like that?"

Gates nodded toward the man before the fireplace. "Mr. Cotton Quince, up from Margaretstown. Said Parliament passed that law back middle of February. Here it is the start of June and the Queen's Agents are out and about." His eyes narrowed. "How do you know this Owen fellow?"

"I know him good enough. He ain't no agent of the Queen! He killed hisself two Ungarakii and Chief Msitazi done welcomed him as a guest. Ain't no redcoat could do all that."

"True words." Gates held his hands up. "Just have to be careful hereabouts. I'll get you your rooms. Kamiskwa still has to sleep in the stable. Food and drink, too. Just find yourself a seat."

Though most of the audience had given their rapt attention to the speaker, a few warily moved away from a corner table as Nathaniel approached. He sat with his back to the wall, and Kamiskwa kept his eye on the door. That left Owen with his back to the bar.

He leaned in, keeping his voice low. "Parliament never passed a tax on whiskey. They passed a tax on rum to cover the cost of a new season of fighting in Tharyngia."

"There's a lots of things get mixed up coming out here. Law stopped, common sense paused with him." Nathaniel sat back and smiled up at the comely lass who brought him a foaming tankard. "Thank you, Meg. I have a powerful thirst needs slaking."

The dark-haired woman giggled. "Like as much you have an itch needs scratching, too. You ever give up them city women, you'll know true pleasure."

"Take you for my wife and break the hearts of all these fine fellows? Won't do it." Nathaniel smiled. "Who is it overworking his jaw?"

"Not sure. Father says he comes from Margaretstown. He can read. Father likes him cause he brings people in to listen. He's reading from *A Continent's Calling*."

Owen slowly turned on his stool. Cotton Quince leaned casually against the fireplace, an elbow hooked on the mantle. He held the book in one hand down and out in front of him. His posture reminded Owen of upperclassmen lecturing the younger students at school. Quince's voice carried just a hint of the same superiority. Slender, with a long nose, blue eyes, and blond hair to his collar, Quince remained clean-shaven and, despite wearing homespun clothes, appeared dandified. His clothes showed little wear and no patches, and his frock coat had been recently brushed.

"And it says right here," he began, raising a finger to point at the ceiling, "'An eagle, no matter how grand and powerful, cannot dominate her offspring once they have departed her nest. No matter how powerful, no matter how lovely that nest, when her eaglets leave, they are free. They find their own nesting places. They find their own hunting grounds. They find their own destiny. And if she seeks to bring them under her domination again, they should, they must, they are *ordained* to destroy her.'"

"I'm not liking that look on your face, Owen."

He glanced at Nathaniel. "He's not reading it right. That last sentence, he added that." Owen dug for the book and thumbed through. "I read that passage when I prepared my message to the Prince. He's added a call for rebellion."

Quince snapped the book shut and held it up. "This book tells the truth, my friends. The Queen thinks we are her servants, her chattel. We're slaves to her. She doesn't send us troops to keep us safe, but she wants our gold to pay for her soldiers to play on the Continent. And those on the seaboard, they'll not protest. They don't drink our whiskey. They drink rum, just like the soldiers the Queen isn't sending us. This is a dire circumstance, gentlemen, and we need to act."

Owen shot to his feet. "You're lying."

Quince blinked, then let a serpentine smile slither onto his features. "Am I, sir? And you dispute the word of Samuel Haste?"

"I dispute your reading of it." Owen held up his copy of the book. "I have this book from Doctor Archibald Frost of Temperance. You added the sentence about the eagles needing to destroy their mother. It isn't in there."

"Ah, so you have a text published in *Temperance*." The man's voice layered disgust into the word. "We're to believe that your Doctor Frost didn't edit the text to make it protect his interests? He is of the coast. He doesn't care about us."

Over in the corner opposite, a huge man unfolded himself. Tall and broad, with a thick bushy beard and dark hair cut short, he dwarfed every man present. A most remarkable trio of scars started at his crown and extended down far enough that one bisected his left eyebrow. He loomed up out of his seat and took one lumbering step toward Quince.

"Now see here, Mister. You talk fancy good, but I don't know you. But my brothers and me, and my father and uncles before us, and my grandfather and his kin afore them, they's all traded with the Frosts. Ain't a manjack here will say he's been cheated by them Frosts. Might not paid what we wanted, but they paid fair."

Quince, who had paled, raised a finger. "You make a very good point. I may have misspoken. There are patriots everywhere, men who believe in Mystria and all it can become."

Owen cocked his head. "Why are you lying about the whiskey tax?"

"Again, sir, you accuse me of lying." Quince's chin came up. "How do you know they did not?"

Owen was about to answer, but Nathaniel stood. "On account of we was in Temperance. They got them this new printer who put out a broadsheet. Had all the news from Norisle. The man just got off the boat, sailed end-of-February. His paper didn't have no mention of no tax."

Another man snorted. "How would you know, Woods? You can't read."

"I read what I need to read, Hiram Marsh, so I don't get lost out in the woods. Unlike some other folks." Nathaniel slapped Owen on the shoulder, albeit a bit harder than necessary. "But I decided to get me some education, so I gots Owen here to be a-reading for me. And he'da read me of taxes since I asked special."

Quince opened his arms. "Perhaps my source on this was misinformed. Mark me, however, the day will come when the Queen turns to us to sustain her, when she has done nothing for us. We are the sons and daughters, grandsons and granddaughters of those Norisle cast aside. We owe the Queen nothing, yet we are fettered by her laws, enslaved by her nobles, impoverished by her merchants. And though there may be traitors among us, you all know in your heart of hearts, that someday, and someday soon, we too will need to fly the nest and extricate ourselves from her deadly talons."

Many of the men grumbled and banged tankards on the tabletops. A few whistled and two invited Quince to join them at a table on the far side of the fireplace. The giant walked over to Nathaniel's table and swung onto the wall bench, jamming Nathaniel into a corner.

"Good to see you again, Magehawk."

Nathaniel squirmed a bit. "Be buying you an ale, will we, Makepeace?"

"Your friend the reader will." The giant smiled and extended a hand. "Makepeace Bone."

"Owen Strake." His hand and half his forearm disappeared in Makepeace's grip. "Thank you for your intervention."

"Well, I was tired of his palaver. Easier to wrestle a wooly rhinocerbus to the ground than make sense of his talking." Makepeace gratefully accepted a tankard from Meg, drank, then licked foam from his lip. "Foul stuff this. His whiskey ain't much better."

Nathaniel leaned left and Makepeace slid over a bit to give him room. "Where are you and your brothers trapping these days?"

"Little north, little west."

"Seen Pierre Ilsavont?"

"He died two years ago. Planted yonder."

"True."

The giant leaned back, his voice a bass growl. "Did see some sign reminded me of him. He never did walk straight after that hip got busted up. It was just tracks though. Late spring, a piece west of here. What's your business with him?"

"He owed me money."

"That's a long line ain't moving fast."

"Heard he might not be dead." Nathaniel drank from his tankard. "We figured we'd see if we could scare him up."

Makepeace shook his head. "I hain't seen him. Trib said he seen Maurice a year back. Maurice weren't inclined to honor a debt."

Owen glanced at Nathaniel. "Trib?"

"His brother, Tribulation."

Makepeace smiled. "My family is Virtuan stock."

"I see."

"Let me ask you something, Mister Strake. You read that book you're carrying?"

"Parts of it."

"Are you believing any?"

"To be truthful, Mr. Bone, I've not read enough."

The big man pursed his lips, then nodded. "Ain't many men admit to ignorance. Weren't how Quince was inclined."

Nathaniel rolled his tankard between his hands. "Makes a man wonder why a man would be saying them sorts of things."

"Oh, I don't know, Magehawk, seems fair obvious. Men, they come out here, they cut a town from the wilderness, they have an edge to them. The ones that come after, though, ain't leaders. They's followers. Sheep. Every now and again comes a wolf looking for sheep. If it weren't Quince, it would be some minister or a messiah. Down Oakland I hear a man dug up his own Bible and has been preaching it. Says Mystria is the promised land and that the Good Lord wants us to make a Celestial City in the heart of the Continent. He says every man should have a dozen wives and they should bear a dozen children and God will come again to bless them all."

Nathaniel smiled. "You going?"

"Cain't find me one wife, so I don't reckon there's a point to it."

"Good." Nathaniel patted him on the shoulder. "Then you might want to help us with a errand tonight."

The man nodded. "What's that?"

Nathaniel chuckled. "We're going to rob us a grave."

CHAPTER TWENTY-FIVE

June 7, 1763
Hattersburg
Lindenvale, Mystria

It surprised Owen that Nathaniel's comment, delivered quietly, shocked neither Kamiskwa nor Makepeace. Both men nodded thoughtfully. Makepeace resumed drinking and Meg brought the others bowls of stew. She added a couple rounds of coarse-grain bread.

Owen waited until she'd departed before he spitted Nathaniel with a hard stare. "You can't be serious."

Nathaniel nodded, spooning stew into his mouth.

"But that's disturbing sacred ground. You can't…"

Nathaniel wiped his mouth on his sleeve. "Didn't none of us like Pierre. He didn't like God none. And if he *is* in that grave, we'll just be opening up a hole for him to get some cool air down in the Inferno."

Nathaniel's stressing the word *is* killed any argument. They already knew he wasn't in the grave, so they wouldn't be disturbing a body.

Makepeace chuckled. "Cain't be buried deep. Found him start of March. Ground was still frozen. Seth Plant ain't never been much for digging deep—in the earth or his pockets. We'll have him up right quick."

Neither that prospect nor the idea that they'd found Ilsavont so far from his grave gave Owen any comfort. He ate the stew and in thinking on how he would describe it, came up with the word *peculiar*. He didn't give himself too long to wonder what some of the vegetables floating around in the thick brown sauce actually were. He had no idea what the meat was and finally asked.

Nathaniel shrugged. "Squirrel or coon."

"Coon." Makepeace nodded toward the bar. "Out to the yard Gates' got a brining barrel. Got two-three in there. His wife does it up nice."

The meat held up well, but most of the flavor had been boiled out of it. Not the same as beef, just a bit more dark, closer to rabbit. Very lean, but needed a touch of pepper. Owen looked about to see if any was available, then realized it would be even more rare than glass this far west.

Nathaniel sopped up the last of the sauce with a piece of bread. "Needed onions. Done?"

Owen pushed the half-finished stew away. "I suppose."

Makepeace settled his hand on Nathaniel's neck. "Digging's going to be thirsty work. Another ale first."

The four of them stole over the stone fence and into the small churchyard. They worked toward the western end. They started down a small slope, with Nathaniel and Kamiskwa drifting left, while Makepeace went right. About a dozen paces apart they stopped and looked at each other.

Nathaniel pointed toward an oak tree. "It's over there. I was leaning up against that tree when I peed on his grave."

Makepeace leaned on the shovel. "Trib and me was over by that stone there doing the same."

"When?"

"This spring."

Nathaniel frowned. "We was the year before."

"Graves don't move." Owen walked past them and toward the oak tree. "Was it this one here?"

Kamiskwa nodded.

Owen read the carving on the wooden cross. "Mercy Heath born 1762, died 1763."

Makepeace grunted. "Girl caught the scarlet fever come new year. She weren't but three months old."

"She wasn't here two years ago." Nathaniel headed for the stones Makepeace had pointed out. A cross had been stuck in the ground reading "Pierre Ilsavont, died 1761. God Rest His Soul."

Owen folded his arms over his chest. "If he's resting, it's here."

Nathaniel took the shovel from the giant. "How far down?"

"Three feet, no more."

Nathaniel nodded, then began to dig. The wooden shovel had a steel edge that should have made digging easier. From the first, however, Nathaniel hit rocks. He scraped them away from the hole, but with the fourth strike, he hit the edge of a flat stone at least as big around as a dinner plate.

Owen crouched. "This earth's never been turned."

"I'm of a mind to be thinking you're right." Nathaniel leaned on the shovel. "So, if he was buried, it weren't here."

Owen pointed back toward the Church. "Perhaps the minister will have records. He must have kept them."

"Circuit preacher." Makepeace shrugged. "Be two weeks afore he's back."

"We don't need him." Nathaniel hung the shovel over his shoulders. "I reckon, come morning, we should visit the gravedigger. Mayhap we help with the morning chores, he'll have time to tell us exactly where Pierre went after all."

They returned to the inn. Kamiskwa slept in the stables. Owen and Nathaniel shared a bed. Makepeace stayed in the next room over. From the brief commotion coming through the wall Owen assumed that Makepeace took his share of that bed out of the middle, and roommates that complained found ample space on the floor.

He desperately hoped Cotton Quince was among them.

It took Owen a bit to fall asleep because questions about Quince's identity niggled. The man had a Mystrian name. He wore Mystrian clothes, but his manner suggested Norillian schooling. The Queen must have had agents throughout the colonies, but having one incite rebellion made no sense. Out here in the west the people had very little in the way of money or property. They couldn't mount a credible threat to Norisle. Even if the Queen sent troops in to smash a rebellion, she really had nothing to gain. There would be no treasure to be won.

Perhaps Quince was a Ryngian agent. Despite centuries of animosity between the two nations, there were those among the Norillian nobility that envied the Tharyngians. Their revolution, in which a despotic King had been overthrown in favor of the Laureates, promised rule by reason instead of whim. Many Norillians, especially those of means, disliked the influence of the Church at court. Since the Ryngian revolution had broken the Church's power in that nation, Ryngian sympathies grew up in places where they could inspire treason.

But what would the Ryngians gain by sparking a revolt in the west? Suggesting independence was not a way to gain political control over the region. It could be that the Ryngians intended to stir up unrest to force Norisle to deploy troops to the colonies. If a revolt succeeded, the Ryngians might even offer themselves as an alternate patron to a fledgling state. If they could stop Ungarakii raiding and provided other benefits the Queen did not, the westernmost colonies might even switch sides.

Is it what Makepeace suggested? Quince is just out here building his own empire? Aside from the fact that such a plan was pure foolishness and would never succeed, there was nothing to suggest that wasn't exactly what was going on. There doubtlessly were countless men who viewed the Mystrian continent as a place where dreams of avarice could be fulfilled.

There, Owen decided, was the flaw in Nathaniel's view of Mystria. If men were left to their own devices, they would seek to expand their own freedoms at the expense of others. Nathaniel pointed out that they'd do that no matter what society existed. Hypocrisy ran rampant within society—Owen accepted that as fact—but at least society limited it. When it got out of hand, society punished it. Without that pressure, however, a man could do anything he wanted and others—sheep—would follow. He'd seen soldiers follow inept officers into the mouth of cannon-fire without running or turning back, even though their sacrifice was meaningless and slaughter inevitable.

Imagine the power a man would wield if his followers thought God smiled upon them.

As unsettling as that thought should have been, Owen didn't have the energy to wrestle with it. He resolved to consider it when next writing in his journal. That brought him to thoughts of Bethany briefly, and then his wife at length, therefore he slept peacefully and with a smile on his face.

Seth Plant lived two miles upriver—they'd actually passed his farm on the trip down into Hattersburg. The four of them got out before dawn and reached his cabin about the same time his cock crowed. Nathaniel was of a mind to just barge in, but Makepeace advocated a more peaceful approach. He ambled into the side yard and started splitting and stacking wood.

Seth came out of his log cabin quickly enough. Owen found him to be an unremarkable man in size and intelligence. He neither smiled nor paled when he saw the four of them. He greeted them as if their presence was an everyday thing.

"Plenty of work to be done, plenty of work." Seth waved them after him as he grabbed a milking stool and a pail. He had to stoop to go through the makeshift barn door; Makepeace wouldn't have fit at all.

"Mr. Plant."

Seth poked his head back out of the barn. "You're a formal one, are you?"

Owen nodded. "We have a question for you."

Seth took another look at them and the split wood. Realization washed over his face, slowly, and in several waves. "So you didn't just have a hankering to split wood?"

"No, sir." Owen smiled. "I am Captain Owen Strake of The Queen's Own Wurm Guards. I've come to ask you what you did with the body of Pierre Ilsavont."

Seth dropped the pail. "I—I buried it. Right there in the church yard."

Nathaniel posted a hand on the doorjamb right beside Seth's head. "Now that ain't likely, is it, being as how his grave has moved. I don't reckon you wanted to bury him once, much less twice."

Seth moaned and slumped in the doorway. "Don't be telling the Reverend. I never should have done it, but I had no choice."

"We ain't telling nobody 'cepting the Queen, and she'll be sending you a medal."

The man's expression brightened. "You gotta understand. 1761, very cold.

Ground froze hard. Wasn't till late summer I could get down five feet. East side of some ravines never did get clear of snow. Now Pierre goes out, gets himself frozen solid. Two trappers brought him in. Reverend weren't around, so I just had them tuck the body up against the Church. Snow drifted on up over."

Seth looked down at his hands. "So one night me and Ef Park was having a dram. You know he got a new still a while back, makes the sweetest whiskey. And it were cold. And I told him that the trappers had two dogs they tied to Pierre's ankles to drag him in. No shroud, nothing, just him froze solid. And Ef said he had two dogs, he wanted to see it for himself.

"So we drank more, then got his dogs, and got Pierre and hitched him up. But the dogs, they wouldn't go. So Ef climbs right up there on Pierre's chest like he's a sled. And them dogs took off through the woods. Headed down into Fall's Ravine, got skewed around. We cut the dogs loose and the body just rode the snow crust down."

"Can you take us to that spot?"

"I can, but I ain't gonna." Seth's shoulders slumped. "I ain't slept good since that night. Ain't drunk much neither. Went looking for him spring of this year, after I planted Mercy. Didn't see no sign of him. When he thawed, animals ate him. Cain't say I am sorry about that."

Nathaniel frowned. "You're sure it was him?"

"When they first brought him in, we poured boiling water on the face. Bit of his nose went away. But it was him, no doubt."

Makepeace punched a barn slat, shattering it. "Damn you, Plant."

The little man cowered. "I'm sorry, I'm sorry."

"To think I wasted good ale on an empty grave."

Nathaniel scratched at his chin. "It was Gates' ale."

"You have a point."

Nathaniel slipped an arm over Seth's shoulders. "Well, you don't want to go and tell people we was asking questions."

"No, no, I won't, I promise."

"And you're going to do us a favor." Nathaniel nodded to Owen. "Captain Strake is going to write a message and you'll be taking it to Doctor Frost in Temperance."

"Oh, I can't go. I have Bessie here needs milking every day."

Kamiskwa unsheathed his musket.

"Now I'm thinking, Seth Plant, that the Gateses would be more than happy to watch your cow for her output for a month."

"I can't get to Temperance and back in a month."

Nathaniel cuffed him hard. "You let a man ride a frozen corpse through the woods. You tied dogs to it and you lost it. *Can't* ain't a word you want to be using right now."

"But, Nathaniel, that's too far."

"Well, then, we'll wait here for the preacher to come by on his circuit."

Seth looked from the musket to the cow, and then at all the stern faces surrounding him. "I guess I can catch a boat to the coast and another to Temperance."

"Good man." Nathaniel turned him toward the barn and gave him a shove. "Milk your cow. We'll be waiting."

Owen composed his messages quickly—a coded one for Prince Vlad, and a cover letter for the Frosts. In the Prince's note he outlined the mystery, reiterating everything from the identification of the *wendigo* down through discovering that the body never got buried. He described Ilsavont as "Mister Frozen Corpse." He wasn't sure what the Prince would make of that, and he hoped he didn't assume Owen had gone mad. The letter to Doctor Frost talked about trapping and mercantile issues. He referred to Ilsavont by name and suggested the letter could be communicated to the Prince. With any luck at all, the Prince would make the necessary connections, especially if Msitazi got to Prince Vlad before Plant delivered this note to the Frosts.

With the messages sealed up tight they gave Seth his instructions. Nathaniel made him repeat them back twice, then told him to get moving. Seth protested that he wanted to start in the morning, but Nathaniel remained adamant. "If I don't see your feet on the road now, we're finding dogs and Makepeace will ride you to Kebeton."

The big man smiled. "Always liked Kebeton."

Seth groaned and acquiesced. The four of them watched him leading his cow down to Hattersburg.

Nathaniel sighed. "Well, we cain't go back to town. Not sure what that idiot will tell them, but best to give them time to forget."

Owen opened his hands. "Everything points west. Du Malphias is out there somewhere. We don't know what he's doing, but we know whatever it is, it's going to be bad."

"I reckon you're right. Something terrible bad."

Owen nodded. Seth's story about Ilsavont confirmed the man had died. It just wasn't possible to thaw him out and have him live. *Or was it?* The Shedashee had magick he'd never seen before.

He looked at Kamiskwa. "It is possible to bring a man back from the dead?"

"A wise man knows nothing is impossible." The Altashee's eyes tightened. "There are stories of great warriors wrestling demons. Maybe one could have been used to make Ilsavont move again."

"But that wouldn't be life."

Nathaniel shook his head. "Does it matter? Dead men brought back to life or dead men filled with demons?"

Owen snarled. "There has to be a logical explanation."

"That would be a comfort." Nathaniel spat. "On account of the fanciful ones ain't bringing me no peace of mind at all."

CHAPTER TWENTY-SIX

June 9, 1763
Hattersburg
Lindenvale, Mystria

They spent the rest of the day and night at Seth Plant's place in case he decided to return. They also wanted to be there in case anyone came up from Hattersburg to investigate Plant's abrupt trip to Temperance. Owen used the time to copy the technical notes from one journal into the other, providing a very concise and direct compilation of useful military data.

He also took time to fire several shots through the Ryngian musket so he could evaluate it for his report. He carefully paced off forty yards and set out targets. He loaded half a charge and shot. The ball sailed out forty yards but missed low. Three shots later he'd determined that it could take a full charge and delivered the ball out to sixty yards with fair accuracy.

"Not a bad piece." Owen sucked at the tip of his shooting thumb. A little bead of blood appeared beneath the nail. It throbbed in time with his pulse—closer to annoyance than pain. He'd felt much worse in battle.

"Du Malphias' expecting a lot of action, I'm thinking. Nice vent spike there."

Owen nodded. The brass firestone assembly had a small triangular thorn off to the right side. It picked up heat from the brimstone combustion. If the blood under the nail became too much, the shooter could just press his nail to it. The metal would melt through and blood would spurt, relieving the pressure.

"The Ryngians make good weapons. Good soldiers, too." Owen shook his head. "You see them massed in those blue jackets, marching forward with bayonets fixed, it turns your guts to water."

"Good reason to leave war over there." Nathaniel stretched. "Or figure a way to end any war here fast."

For supper they harvested some onions and tomatoes from Plant's house garden. Makepeace mixed them with pemmican before frying it up. While he cooked, the others explained to Makepeace Bone what they were doing. He took it all in with a grunt here and there, then served up dinner at Seth's table.

Owen wanted to dig right in, but Makepeace wouldn't let them start unless they joined hands and bowed their heads as he offered grace. "Dear God, wonderful and terrible, we thank Thee for these gifts. May they strengthen us body and soul for to face the challenges Ye set before us. Amen."

The solemnity with which the giant offered the prayer surprised Owen. Based on the previous night's drinking and grave-robbing attempt, he hardly expected Makepeace to be pious to any degree.

"It's been a long time since anyone has offered to say grace."

Makepeace nodded. "Not many do. Most men out here only get churchy when the minister is looking their way. I was raised Virtuan. Kind of got away from it. Then the Good Lord got it in His mind to be reminding me of what I owes Him."

The man patted the top of his head. "In Second Kings God went and sent two she-bears to kill children who mocked his prophet Elijah. Well, I was mocking a man said he was a prophet. Mocked him for being bald, and an idiot, but mostly bald. 'Bout a day later a he-bear sent by the almighty came and near scalped me bald."

"What did you do?"

"Well, my scalp was flopping down over my eyes, so I just feeled about best I could. Me and the bear, we had a bit of a tussle. I heard tell you ain't supposed to kill the messenger, but that was long after and all."

Nathaniel kept his voice low. "Killed it with his bare hands."

"Only fair, really. Bear didn't have no gun. But when it was over, I was tore up a bit, clawed and gnawed. I went a-crawling, blind like Saul, and I was saying to myself 'The Lord is my shepherd,' over and over. Then a man was there, a shepherd out where there weren't no sheep. He done stitched me up, fed me the sweetest bread I ever did eat. And one morning I woke up, He was gone. No trace of Him around, neither, and I ain't second to nobody when it comes to tracking."

The giant glanced skyward. "Then I looked up and done seen His footprints in the clouds. Now I'm a sinner, but I sin lots less than before, and I take my praying serious."

Owen's eyes narrowed. "You don't wear any sign…"

Makepeace smiled broadly. "When you been touched by the Lord, or His surrogate, you ain't much in need of signs."

Nathaniel nodded. "I'm thinking we're seeing signs from diabolical forces, if you're wanting God's honest truth." He proceeded to outline what Prince Vlad had explained about Ryngian power and what he expected them to do in the west.

Makepeace Bone absorbed it all, then nodded solemnly. "I been a-wondering when God was going to call me to do His work. Sounds like this du Malphias feller is a Diabolist at the very least. Iffen you'll have me, I'll be going with you.

If not, I reckon I'll go anyway."

Owen smiled broadly. Right from the start, Makepeace's presence changed the expedition's dynamics. Even though Nathaniel and Kamiskwa had begun treating Owen as more than self-loading cargo after he killed the Ungarakii, they still shouldered more than their share of responsibility. Granted he had no wilderness experience, and they were willing to teach him, but there were some things they chose to do just because it was easier.

With four of them, and Makepeace being as big as he was, they could no longer travel in one canoe. Owen partnered with Makepeace in a second. This made their journeys a bit faster and, despite the aching shoulders and chest, Owen enjoyed the added work.

The giant's presence also made Nathaniel a little less reserved. He'd called Nathaniel "Magehawk," too, but Owen didn't press for that story. That would have violated the trust they'd been building up. Instead he would sit back at night, writing in his journal, as the other three men shared stories they'd obviously heard before but enjoyed nonetheless. And Makepeace, for all of his understatement, told as good a story as the other two.

Listening to them over the next several weeks Owen realized they all had a sense of freedom that he'd never known. One night Nathaniel told a story about his having been caught stealing eggs from an old woman's farm when he was a child. He'd tried for years and years to redeem himself in her eyes. He'd chopped wood in the winter, he'd brought her skins and meat, he'd carried messages, fetched packages, and always stopped in when he was near her home just to see if she needed anything.

"Then, 'bout five years ago, I came up on her farm and there weren't no smoke from the chimney, no chickens in the yard. I was thinking the worst, of course." Nathaniel rotated the spit on which he'd skewered a crow. "I went into Oaktown, asked. They said she was feeling poorly, been taken in by the Preacher and his wife. So I went to see her. She was in her bed and when she saw me, she started cussing a blue streak, calling me all kinds of thief.

"I reckon the Preacher he done read my face. I was disappointed to see her in such a state and all. And he says to her, 'Grannie Hale, you been hating this boy for nigh on to twenty years over a handful of eggs he didn't even get away with. Can't you forgive him, even now?'"

Nathaniel smiled. "So she looked up at him, all toothless grinning and says, "I don't hate him. I done forgive him twenty years ago, Reverend. I just hain't tole him I did. Iffen I had, who'd a-brung me venison and skins? Who'd a-been chopping my wood, hauling water, and patching my roof?'"

"And the Reverend said, 'Maybe he would have found it in his heart to do so anyway.' And she spitted him with a stare was clear-eyed and cold. 'You preach redemption, but it's at a word and a dunking. I make him work for it. It sticks that way.' And ain't no two ways about it, she was righter than rain."

Owen never could have told that sort of story on himself. It would have opened him to ridicule. He got enough of that just because of the circumstance of his birth. And yet the ease with which they shared such stories revealed an inner confidence that he craved.

Is it this place that breeds these men, or the freedom that encourages them? He jotted that question down. He stared at the empty page below it for a long while, and he found himself unable to compose a satisfactory answer.

Three weeks out of Hattersburg, as dusk was falling, they paddled across Pine Lake. Small, not particularly deep, it lay nestled in a small valley, with thick forest right down to the water. A few islands dotted it and fish jumped at bugs. The wind stirred the water a bit, but Owen felt that if he had to live out his days with that vista visible from his front porch, he could die happy.

The wind blew out of the north, slowing their progress, but brought the sound of voices. They came from a long, slender island running northwest to southeast. On the leeward side, where the island's central spine blocked the wind, a fire's golden hints glimmered.

Nathaniel and Kamiskwa immediately cut east. They headed out and around, approaching the island on the windward side. As they got close enough to land, Makepeace and Owen paddled toward the small, sandy beach on the island's lee side. They readied their muskets before they came within range then, fifty yards offshore, changed course to run parallel to the beach.

Makepeace cupped his hands around his mouth and shouted. "Hello, the fire. Bonsoir."

Brief movement eclipsed the fire. A voice called back cautiously. "Bonsoir. Who is it, please?"

"Makepeace Bone. That you, Jean?"

"Yes, my friend."

"Who's with you?"

"Etienne Ilsavont. You might like to choose another island, non?"

"Tain't very friendly, Jean."

"My friend, I will shoot if you try to land."

"You shoot, I'll be sore disappointed." Makepeace picked up his paddle and lowered his voice. "We go in easy. You shoot, then me, iffen they start a fight."

Owen, his mouth going dry, watched the island as they paddled closer. He'd long since learned better than to stare intently at any one spot. Instead he broadened his focus, watching for movement. Years as a skirmisher had taught him that motion was easier to see than men who wanted to be hidden.

Every stroke, the ripple of water around the bow, filled ears straining for any noise. Owen saw nothing. If they shot, he'd first see fire, then hear the blast. Every stroke brought them deeper into lethal range. Even the most inept shot had an even chance of hitting them. At that range, a .75 caliber ball would crush bone and blow right through a man, possibly even pitching him out of the canoe.

"Come on in. They're inclined to be peaceable."

At Nathaniel's call they sped up. While Makepeace and Owen had distracted the Ryngians, Nathaniel and Kamiskwa had slipped onto the island from the windward side. Having seen them move through the woods, Owen had no doubts that they'd taken the Ryngians completely by surprise.

Owen leaped clear of the canoe as it first touched sand, then dragged it forward. Makepeace climbed out into ankle-deep water and grabbed one of the crosspieces. Without grunt or grimace, he lifted the whole canoe out of the lake and carried it up to dry sand. He set it next to the smaller of two canoes that had been overturned to shelter a thick bale of pelts.

Carrying his rifle, Owen jogged up a slight incline to a flat spot where the Ryngians had built their fire. Nathaniel and Kamiskwa covered two men. The captives were seated on the ground; their muskets lay on the far side of the fire. Both weapons resembled Owen's carbine for length, but were much older and wanted for maintenance.

One man vaguely resembled Pierre. Owen figured him to be Etienne. Thick like his father, possibly brother, and not terribly tall, Etienne looked much younger and had a thick shock of brown hair. He looked more angry than sour, while his compatriot looked just the opposite. Jean looked as much like a drowned rat as he did a man, with his ears and nose warring for prominence. He had no chin to speak of, which he compensated for with a thick and droopy moustache. If not for a high forehead and decently spaced eyes, it would have been simple to dismiss him as a lower-class wastrel.

Makepeace circled around to stand to the right of and behind Jean. Nathaniel sat, but still kept his rifle leveled at their captives. "Now we don't mean you no discomfort or ill will. I pert near forgot that time when you and your pa were emptying my traps, Etienne. How so ever, I do have me some questions."

The younger man glared sullenly at Nathaniel.

Jean smiled half-heartedly. "My friend Nathaniel, you are not one to point a gun unless you mean to use it."

"Just as you was a-pointing at my friends."

"This is true. A misunderstanding, non?" Jean lowered his hands. "We shall start again. Welcome to our fire. Please, share with us."

"Ain't you a mite east of your normal range?" Nathaniel watched them closely. "I don't recall ever seeing you in these parts."

Jean shrugged. "The land, it is so beautiful. We just kept going."

"And I don't recall you traveling with the Ilsavonts."

"These are difficult times, my friend."

"Part of that difficult being your father up out of his grave, Etienne?"

Blood drained from Ilsavont's face. He started to say something, then his shoulders sagged and he began to cry.

Jean rested a hand on his shoulder and said something softly. He turned to look at Nathaniel and Owen. "Please, gentlemen, he has been tortured by this. This is why we are here."

Nathaniel pointed his rifle toward the sky. "Tell me."

Jean and Etienne exchanged glances, then the younger man nodded. Jean let his hand fall from his shoulder and hunched forward. "It is like this. Two months ago a ship arrives in Kebeton from Tharyngia. A man, tall, a scarecrow, a Laureate, they say, he comes with troops and many boxes of equipment. Big boxes, small, and he has servants who help unload, but only at night. He offers good money, much money, for scouts, and for other things. I just found paths for him, yes? I knew of the other things he wanted but he was a Laureate. Like your prince, *non?* Who can know their minds?"

"What did he want?" Owen dropped to a knee. "The *other* things?"

Jean stared into the fire. "He wanted bodies. He wanted to know where the Shedashee, they bury their people. He came to some of the resting grounds, but the bodies, they did not suit him. So he asked for other bodies. I hear, you know, men bring him murder victims. There was one small town where we hear there is a frozen body. They keep it in the ice house and charge for to look. And he sends for that body."

Nathaniel nodded. "And that would be Pierre?"

Jean shook his head. "I do not know."

"My father, yes." Etienne lifted his head, smearing dirt as he wiped away tears. "I fetched the body. I thawed it out. I saw it was my father. And a week later, I saw my father alive again."

CHAPTER TWENTY-SEVEN

June 27, 1763
Pine Lake
Lindenvale, Mystria

Owen ran a hand over his unshaven jaw. "No lie?"

"It was my father. The frostbite, it had nibbled, but no mistake." The young man hung his head. "And yet, you know, it was not my father."

"Meaning?"

Etienne closed his eyes tight. "His eyes. I saw some of him there, but very little. Hints of him. He was an echo, a faint echo, in his body. Physically able, yes, but mostly gone."

Jean looked up, fear etching lines around his eyes. "This is not possible, *non*? One cannot return from the grave."

"I reckon the Good Lord did."

"Yes, but if you believe such things, Nathaniel, he was the Son of God. No man can do this."

Makepeace spat. "That ain't exactly true. In the Good Book, Elisha done raised men from the dead, one man just on account of that man touched Elisha's bones. Saint Paul done raised a boy what fell out of a window and died. Saint Peter brought Saint Tabitha back."

Etienne's eyes opened again. "But the man from Tharyngia, he is no saint."

"Du Malphias."

Both the Ryngians looked up at Owen. Etienne shivered. Jean shook his head. "He is the Devil himself."

Nathaniel chuckled. "Here I thought, Jean, you didn't believe."

"He is enough to convert me. Gods, demons, evil thoughts in his head, I do not know, but I have seen what he has done."

Owen held a hand up. "What the boy said about echoes. I remember men who had head wounds. They didn't die, at least not immediately. They weren't in pain. They could remember some things. They were almost childlike."

Etienne nodded. "Yes, it was like that, a bit, but my father was not hurt in the head."

160

Nathaniel stood. "I'm a-wondering, Owen, why you's fighting what they're telling us. You said yourself this du Malphias robbed graves there on the Continent. Supposing he had found a way to raise the dead?"

He pointed at the Ryngians. "How many like Pierre did you see?"

Jean shrugged. "A dozen. Two."

"They eat much?"

"I never saw them eat. But when they would be broken, the devil would fix them." Jean glanced at Kamiskwa. "The *pasmortes*, he would use them to frighten the Ungarakii."

The Altashee nodded. "*Wendigo*. Very bad."

A chill puckered Owen's flesh. "Where is he?"

Etienne's eyes grew wide. "You are mad if you go there."

"Where is he?"

Jean's expression sobered. "You doom yourself. Nathaniel, Makepeace, you know Anvil Lake. The Green River flows from there to Lac Verleau—on the northern heights, he is building a fortress. He has cannon and soldiers. It cannot be taken."

Owen frowned. "Anvil Lake? How far?"

"Due west a week." Nathaniel scratched his jaw. "Anvil drains out the Roaring River south and into the Misaawa River south of Long Lake. It also drains east into the headwaters of the Tillie."

"He cuts us off from the interior and threatens Lindenvale." Owen lowered his musket. "How far built is his fortress?"

Etienne threw his arms wide. "It is huge. His workers are tireless. They shift stone, they chop wood."

"Can you draw me a picture of it?"

Jean shook his head. "It would do no good. He builds in pieces, tearing things down, putting things up. And he builds *down*, my friend. Deep. Into the depths are where these *pasmortes* go. From the bowels of the earth Pierre emerged."

Owen chewed his lower lip. "How reliable are these two?"

"Reliable? Not much."

"Can they be trusted to carry a message?"

Jean laughed. "If carrying it will get me far away from du Malphias, you shall have no better courier, my friend."

"There's a pound in it for you, a gold pound, if you get it to Temperance."

Jean nodded avidly, his partner dully.

Makepeace growled from behind them. "And a lead pound if you don't."

"Calm yourself, my friend Makepeace. I will be your most obedient servant." Jean smiled easily. "I live to serve, and if I serve you, I shall continue to live."

Owen wrote up two messages, coding the one to the Prince and another covering letter to Doctor Frost. He sealed the first, then sealed it inside the second. The four of them then split the night into watches and kept the Ryngians under guard. Finally, when morning arrived, they helped the Ryngians load their canoes and sent them on their way.

With the canoes a dozen yards offshore, Etienne turned back with a dripping paddle across his knees. "Monsieur Woods, have you seen my father?"

"Yup. Shot him dead. Burned his head. Ain't no more need for no nightmares."

"Yes, I see. Merci." He turned and drew deep water with the paddle.

Makepeace spat in the direction of the departing canoe. "By the Grace of God I hope that boy done learned a lesson."

"Wurms sooner to grow wings, I'm reckon." Nathaniel scratched at the back of his neck. "We're a week to Anvil. Another week to paddle our way across, give or take. Couple islands we could lay up on, ain't there?"

Makepeace squatted and drew a rough map in the dirt. The outline resembled an anvil with the top running north to south, and the beak pointing north. The lake narrowed toward the east, then broadened out again into the anvil's base. The Green River came in at the southwest quarter, and the Roaring River went out very close to it. The Tillie outflow split the eastern shore in half.

"Couple small islands near that fort. Jumbles of rocks mainly. Two big ones, one to the north, one straight east of that fort. North we won't see nothing. East we would have a good view, but your man would be an idiot iffen he didn't have no troops there."

"Why won't we see anything from the north?"

The giant traced a thick finger through the earth. "Jean called it the heights. Mess of hills."

"Could we get closer in the hills than the island?"

"We could up and just walk on in, but ain't likely your man will let us get back out again."

Owen nodded. "I understand, Mr. Bone, but I need to study that fortress. I need to make maps. Just drifting past and running away isn't enough.

"I know this is a very dangerous proposition. You are all courageous men but no amount of money could compensate you for this risk. I fully discharge you from any obligation. I'll write a note to the Prince and would ask you to bear it to him. I have no choice but to go there. I do not ask the same of you."

Nathaniel's eyes became slits. "Iffen there's not money enough to pay for anyone to go take a look-see, how come you're going?"

"I am a sworn officer in Her Majesty's Army. My orders are to survey Tharyngian positions in Mystria."

"Wouldn't no one know if you just didn't go. You'd not be the first to take a new name and adopt a new life."

"That would be true, Mr. Woods, but I would know." Owen lifted his chin. "I do not choose to live a dishonored life."

"Seems to me you think we would."

"No, not at all." Owen opened his hands. "Once we sail west of the shore, we will be in territory which, according to the 1760 Treaty of Mastrick, belongs to Tharyngia. Dressed as I am, I will be taken as a spy and shot. You will share my fate. And if a fraction of what we suspect is actually true, a fate worse than death may await us all."

Nathaniel arched an eyebrow. "This ain't you being all noble and Norillian and all?"

Owen shook his head ruefully. "You are my friends. I value your lives too much to put them in such obvious danger. I appreciate all you've done for me. I hope I've learned enough to let me complete my mission. I have no choice but to go."

Nathaniel stretched. "Well now, I is only speaking for me, but I don't reckon I have a choice neither. See, when all them Branches and Casks was a-wagering on how long you'd last out here, I done took their bets. And I doubled up on them, saying you'd be coming back alive. I reckon I have an investment to be protecting."

Kamiskwa nodded. "My sister wants you to bring her doll back. I go."

Makepeace rose, clapping the dust off his hands. "I been a-waiting for whatever that shepherd done saved me for. I'd be a durn fool iffen I thought this weren't it. Besides, last time I checked, killing Ryngians was more a virtue than a vice."

Owen nodded solemnly. "One more thing you'd best understand. We are going to be invading enemy territory. We're going to war. I understand war the way you understand the wilderness. From this point forward, I am in command. If I give an order, you obey. Is that understood?"

The other three exchanged glances, then nodded. Nathaniel tossed him a ragged salute. "Lead on, Captain Strake. Into the mouth of Hell and back out again."

Caution slowed their pace so that they reached Anvil Lake at noon a week later. It took them until mid-afternoon on the day of their arrival to locate and repair two canoes. Makepeace, using bark, some pitch and prayer managed to duplicate Kamiskwa's work. The patch held just as well, though did not blend seamlessly. When they launched Owen watched for any signs of leakage, but the canoe remained intact.

They kept to the northern shore and moved at night. They worked their away along carefully, never more than twenty yards out from shore. This afforded them some cover from the northern wind but, more importantly, made it harder for anyone in the fortress to see them.

They made good time on the water and by the third day, they stopped near the headland where the lake made a jog to the north into the anvil's beak. The northern island lay northwest of them. A sliver of moon provided them enough light to reach it undetected.

As they approached the island, Owen collected his thoughts and wrote his conclusions into his expedition journal. The trip from Pine Lake to Anvil Lake convinced him how difficult bringing an army up to assault the fortress would truly be. Transport ships could carry an army to Hattersburg, but from there they would have to go on foot. They would have to build a road through primeval forest, an undertaking that would take a month or more and that would be without bad weather or harassment by the Ryngian forces.

At Anvil Lake they'd need to create a flotilla of flat boats, since approaching by the southern shore would add fifty miles of road-building to the campaign. The forests would yield ample raw materials to build the fleet, but any hope of surprise evaporated. The fortress would have to be taken by siege, which required yet more men and supplies.

The smartest plan for the Norillians would be to build their own fortress at the outflow into the Tillie. The Ryngians would have to destroy it before moving down the river. That would buy ample time for Norisle to raise other defenses.

Owen made a solid case for that plan. Someone like Lord Rivendell would never see the wisdom in it. Owen's uncle, on the other hand, would. He would appropriate both the plan and the acclaim that came from it. Anger sparked at that idea; Owen smothered it.

Finally they reached the northern island. The rectangular plot of earth and stone rose up twenty yards, with a deep bowl in the middle. It had started life as a jumble of rocks, but over the years had grown up with trees and mosses, flowers and shrubs that completely hid the rocks beneath. They drew their canoes all the way up into the interior and made no fire. They kept watches, but aside from calling loons and a moose taking a shortcut across the island, they neither saw nor heard anything out of the ordinary.

In preparation for their scouting mission, each man put together a satchel with twenty-four rounds and changed their firestones for new. They assumed, quite rightly, that if they could not escape pursuit before they exhausted their ammunition, they were as good as dead or worse.

Owen left behind his journals, his pistol and pens. He included in his load two pencils and *A Continent's Calling*. He would jot his notes in it, then expand them into his journals. The other men likewise abandoned non-essentials. If all went well, they would make a trip to the western shore, take a look, return to retrieve their gear, then head east again.

Taking advantage of a low mist on the water, they struck out for the western shore in the early morning. They navigated up a small stream, then hid the canoes on the northern side. Kamiskwa pointed out a few other cached canoes on the way and holed one of Ungarakii manufacture. They crossed the stream and headed south. Kamiskwa found a game trail that brought them to a marsh between hills. They skirted the mire to the lake side, then headed directly up a wooded hill

Just beneath the crest Nathaniel smiled. "One more hill and we'll see what needs to be seen."

Makepeace, already at the crest, turned, his face ashen. "May God have Mercy on our souls."

Owen scrambled up the rest of the way, then flattened onto his belly.

To the south, where there should have been a wooded hill, construction had scraped a reddish scar in the earth. The hill at the lake's edge had been chopped in half, with the back hauled away, lumber, stones and all.

And beyond it, in all its dark and angular glory, stood the fortification that would soon become known as the Fortress of Death.

CHAPTER TWENTY-EIGHT

July 7, 1763
Anvil Lake
Lindenvale, Mystria

Owen had seen many fortresses during Continental campaigns. In medieval times stones walls had risen very high, but with the advent of cannon, such walls fell easily. As a result, engineers designed new fortifications that involved the creation of a glacis: a low slope rising ten feet or more. From the distant hilltop, the glacises gave the fortress an irregular, star-shaped footprint.

The glacises extended out from the walls for a hundred yards and came to a point. Their sides sloped gently back toward the fortress and stone faced them. Cannon-shot hitting the stone would bounce up over the fortress' wooden palisade wall. Getting cannons close enough that they could hit the walls directly, or moving mortars into range to lob shot over the walls, would be a long and laborious process. It involved digging endless trenches, working ever closer while under enemy cannon-fire from the fortress.

As bad as that was, other defenses made things worse. The ground above and below the glacises had been set with sharpened stakes. This would slow infantry assaults. Abatises made of logs with stout, sharpened branches crossed the only access near the two small gates on the west side. Those sally-ports would allow Ryngian troops to rush out to counterattack the Norillian trenchers.

Beyond the stakes, and a dozen feet before the wall, a berm had been thrown up, also strewn with stakes. Beyond it lay a trench which made the walls even taller. With the easternmost part of the fortress being built on the heights, flooding that trench wasn't possible, but down where the assault was likely to happen, sluice-gates by the river would fill it.

At the lake, the palisade wall came close to the edge of an eighty-foot-tall cliff. Naval gunfire could obliterate that narrowest portion of the fortress, but to get a ship of sufficient size into Anvil Lake would require a transit through Ryngian-controlled rivers and lakes. The final passage would take it past the Fortress of Death cannons.

The fortress formed a rough triangle, though the walls did boast a few projections that would allow troops to pour a murderous crossfire on any besiegers. With the high point on the east at the cliffs, the fortress spread out downhill to the base, which ran parallel to the Green River. As the scouting party moved west it became apparent that any ship trying to make it through the river would be under the fortress' batteries for five hundred yards. That sort of pounding would reduce the ship to a hulk before it ever made Anvil Lake.

And to complicate matters further, a smaller fort had been erected across the river on the western plain. Owen suspected chains could be strung between them to completely restrict transit.

Somehow, all of that wasn't the worst aspect. Pallid, shuffling human beings—or what he supposed once had been human beings—formed a different chain, one of constant motion to and from the hills. Some carried axes and shovels, felling trees and digging into hillsides. Others that moved haltingly carried sacks of earth on their backs, or were roped into teams that dragged trees from where they had been felled. These creatures performed labor that others might have reserved for oxen. While they did not move with great speed, they moved constantly and showed no sign of fatigue.

After the initial look, Owen signaled for a move to the west. Though the walls had not been completed, and work crews were refining trenches, the vision of what it would become blossomed full in Owen's mind. Without precise measurements and drawings, however, observations would be of little military value.

They went west and slowly worked their way back east to the shore. Owen made notes and maps in the back of his book. Kamiskwa stayed closest to him, with Makepeace and Nathaniel out and back to keep watch and provide cover. Owen used an average man's height to judge the length of logs, and then used them to provide a scale for the fortress.

It wasn't until they had returned to North Island, and he began transcribing information into his journals, that he found any reason to take the least bit of heart. "The one thing I didn't notice was enough cannon to destroy a ship."

"I reckon that's good." Nathaniel drew the fortress in the dirt with a stick. "They probably started with the fort on the hill, then expanded down. Second one down where the river meets lake. Put up a wall to link them. Then the third point, link that."

Owen nodded. "Makes perfect sense."

"Well now, we didn't see none of it because of where we was, but if they still have them internal fort walls up…"

Owen groaned. "You have smaller fortresses that still have to be taken."

Makepeace stirred their little fire. "'Member Jean saying du Malphias was digging down, too? If they build themselves tunnels and redoubts, that's a trap waiting to be sprung."

"Right. Tomorrow, then, we're going to have take a look from the hills on the other side of the Green River. We should be able to see from inside."

Nathaniel stood and rubbed his fort out with a foot. "If we're going to do that, best move now."

They took the expedient of hacking some branches off trees to decorate the right side of their canoes, then started back toward the narrows, then across. In the distance, in the stingy amount of light shed by a sliver-moon, they would look like nothing more than debris in the water. As they traveled, Owen watched the ramparts with his telescope, but he could see little. At best he thought he saw the silhouettes of a couple sentries marching along the high wall.

Once they reached the southern shore, they worked their way west and entered a small stream about a hundred yards shy of the Roaring River outlet. They dragged their canoes out of sight on the western shore, then found another hollow where they built a fire and stashed their gear.

Owen tore the maps he'd drawn from the back of *A Continent's Calling* and tucked them inside his journal. He secured them in their oilskin cases, and then stuffed them into his large pouch. In doing so he found the doll Agaskan had given him. He smiled and, on a whim, tucked it into his smaller pouch, along with the book and the pencils.

They got on the water again before dawn and used the mist to provide cover. They had to paddle out onto the lake to avoid being pulled in by the Roaring River. Though the mist largely hid it, Owen still made out dim rock teeth through which the water flowed. The river's thunder hinted at torturous cataracts below.

Once past, they made for the western shore, as close to the mouth of the Green River as possible. They brought their canoes in through a marshy area then stashed the canoes and went directly overland toward the fort.

The view confirmed what Nathaniel had suspected. The fortress' river wall bristled with cannon ports. Likewise, the river side of the smaller fort, a miniature of the larger fort, complete with glacises, trenches, and palisade walls. It had been built on an artificial hill created by taking the earth down all around it. While that provided a flat battlefield, it presented two problems. Trenches would end up running below the water-table, so would quickly become mires. Any army caught in the plain might also be subject to sudden flood if du Malphias could breach the riverbank.

Owen explained this to Nathaniel. The guide nodded and pointed at the river's southern bank, just east of the small fort. "I might just be seeing things, but looks like the bank was shored up there, by that little dock."

Owen studied it with his telescope. Pilings had been sunk along the bank. At a casual glance it looked like a wall erected on either side of the little jetty. "But there's no reason for a jetty there."

He collapsed the telescope. "A southerly breeze will shroud the field in smoke. Any army laying siege to the smaller fort would never see the bank collapse. Du Malphias must have the angles marked, the range measured. Blind men shooting at midnight could hit it with every shot."

"And see there, in the fort—you have your internal walls and that stone fort in the middle."

Owen nodded. What had once been tall external walls on the two lower forts had been chopped down to half their height, making the interior of the fortress a wonderful killing ground. Moreover, in the heart of it, du Malphias had created a stone star. Glacises and spikes protected it and the roof of the circular enclosure at its center only rose four feet high. Soldiers within could shoot out at all sides of the fortress, and the lack of doors hinted at tunnels that fed into it.

"Short of lobbing a mortar shell on top of it, there is no way to destroy it from outside." The soldier's shoulders slumped. "This is a lock on the heart of the Continent, and I cannot see that we have the key."

"Yep. And busting this lock will take more than a big rock."

A gunshot split the morning off to the left. Another, closer, followed. Both men snatched up their long guns and dashed toward the sound. Off to the south Kamiskwa paralleled them. Two more rifles fired in the distance, and a grunt prefaced a return shot.

At the edge of a clearing Makepeace sat with his back to the thick bole of a tree. Blood marked his left shoulder, but he still was using that arm to ram a bullet home. He saw them, jerked his head to the west. "Squad of blues. Ilsavont with 'em."

Owen took cover behind a tree, then ducked his head out. Ryngian regulars were moving forward. Three men advanced, three shot, three reloaded, and an officer marched behind with Etienne. The blue coats had gold facings, marking them as part of the Or Regiment.

"Nathaniel, the officer."

The Mystrian fired. The officer slammed off a tree and fell, a chunk of his face missing.

The Ryngians fired back. Makepeace's tree lost bark. The giant laughed, rose, and fired in one smooth motion. He didn't even bother to use his left arm, he just thrust the musket forward in one massive hand. The shot spun one of the Ryngians to the ground, but the rest kept coming up.

"Makepeace, Nathaniel, fall back. Kamiskwa and I will cover." Owen caught a glimpse of a Ryngian moving north to flank them. He waited for the man to poke his head out past a tree and fired. The shot gouged the tree and the man screamed.

Owen fell back twenty yards. He pulled out a cartridge and bit the bullet out of the paper. He upended the paper cylinder, pouring the brimstone down the barrel, then stuffed the paper after it. He pressed the bullet into the barrel, drew the ramrod, and forced it down. He hit it twice to pack it tightly, then withdrew the ramrod, reversed it, and slid it home beneath the barrel.

The Ryngians hesitated at the far end of the clearing, then darted across. Makepeace and Nathaniel both shot. Two men went down. One got back up and dove to the far side of Makepeace's tree.

Off to the left, Kamiskwa shot and dashed back through the trees, chased by a hail of bullets. Owen aimed for the man on the other side of Makepeace's tree. The man had crouched and his white-breeched bottom stuck out, made an inviting target. Owen shot. The man yelped.

Owen looked east and ran for a fallen log. He leaped, grabbing the top with his left hand to slow himself, and brought his legs over. He twisted in mid-air to face the enemy. His toes touched earth.

Then a Ryngian bullet skipped off a rock and slid through a gap between the log and ground. It caught Owen in the left thigh, midway between hip and knee. It shattered his femur, cutting his leg out from under him. He smashed face-first into the log. Lights exploded. Suddenly he was on his back, blood in his mouth, his leg twisted impossibly beneath him. Pain roared through him.

Nathaniel loomed over him. "Just a scratch."

"What?"

Nathaniel stood, tracked, and fired. Another man screamed. The Mystrian ducked down again. "Throw your arm over my shoulder."

"No." Owen grit his teeth against the pain. "Go. Get the journals to the Prince."

"You'll carry them yourself."

"No, Nathaniel. I can't travel. I'm likely dead already. Go. That is an order!"

"Now I ain't…"

Owen grabbed a fistful of Nathaniel's tunic. "You *promised*. The journals are how you save Mystria. Get them and go. *Go!*"

Nathaniel snarled, reloaded, and shot again. "You ain't seen the last of me, Owen Strake."

"I'll save you a seat in Hell, Nathaniel Woods."

Nathaniel ran and the other two shot to cover him. Owen tried to grab his musket, but it had fallen too far away. He did manage to catch hold of a rock and twist around so his leg straightened out a little. A wave of nausea washed over him and darkness nibbled at his eyesight, but he refused to pass out.

Shifting his leg didn't do anything to ease the pain. He pulled himself into a sitting position, then took his belt off and wrapped it around his thigh above the wound, yanking it tight.

Grabbing the rock again, he slid over to where a *mogiqua* fern grew. He stripped off leaves with a bloody hand and shoved them into his mouth. He chewed, welcoming the bitter taste, then spat the mulch out and stuffed it in the wound.

In the name of the Almighty, please work.

Owen tried not to whimper, but he couldn't keep silent. All the times he'd bit back cries when, in school, he'd been beaten all because remaining silent seemed the noble thing to do came back to him. *How silly.* Pain cut past nobility.

It cut past humanity.

A Ryngian came over the log and swung his musket around.

Owen opened his empty hands.

The man smiled coldly. About the point where Owen noticed the man's cheek had been opened by a splinter gouged from a tree, the solder reversed his rifle and slammed it into Owen's thigh.

Agony exploded in Owen's brain and mercifully snuffed out consciousness. As Owen's world faded to black, the man raised the rifle again and Owen forced himself to smile.

CHAPTER TWENTY-NINE

July 8, 1763
Prince Haven
Temperance bay, Mystria

Prince Vlad's lungs burned. His goggles had not leaked much; the gutta-percha sealed the glass well and the strip inside the leather mask molded tightly to his skin. The goggles provided amazing clarity beneath the waters of the Benjamin, though the lack of light past ten feet limited the view to the back of Mugwump's head.

His lungs demanded air. He pulled back on the reins and the wurm struck for the surface. Vlad grabbed the saddlehorn. The whipping of Mugwump's tail sent shivers through the beast's entire body. Combined with the water pressure, it would have been enough to tear him from the saddle. They rose swiftly, then shot into the air like an arrow, only to splash down again twenty yards upriver.

The Prince laughed in spite of himself. Back on shore his wurmwright and a servant waited, one anxiously, the other with a towel and robe. Baker, the wurmwright, had been dead set against the idea of letting the Prince swim with the wurm since that just was *not* done. Because wurms began their lives as large water-serpents, conventional wisdom had it that they would escape if allowed to swim freely. Vlad had watched Mugwump splash happily when the wurmrest flooded, so he took a chance.

Though the Prince had only been swimming the wurm for three weeks, Mugwump had taken commands more readily in water than in the field, and certainly seemed to enjoy himself more. The wurm showed greater speed in the water than on land, and proved adept at harvesting schools of fish. He looked forward to their daily swims, so much so that the Prince had even taken him out on a miserable, rainy day.

The Prince tugged on the reins, turning Mugwump toward shore. But the beast ducked his whole head beneath the water, then brought it up again. Water sheeted off the scales and down his snout. He refused to turn and instead, twitching his tail slowly but steadily, headed upriver. He tucked his legs in along his belly as he did so, moving serenely.

Vlad lifted his goggles and shaded his eyes with a hand. There in the distance, a canoe. *Mugwump heard the sound of their paddles that far away? That must be a half-mile.*

The Prince gave Mugwump a touch of his heels. Even if he'd worn spurs with foot-long spikes the beast would have felt no pain. Mugwump, however, responded, cruising up the river easily. The Prince rode tall in his saddle, aware that soaking wet he cut a ridiculous figure. Still, given the nature of his mount, he suspected his visitor would not much notice.

Within a hundred yards he recognized the man in the back of the canoe and raised a hand in greeting. The young boy in the bow pulled his paddle from the water and appeared ready to fend Mugwump off. The Prince pulled back on the reins and Mugwump slowed so that his propulsion matched the river precisely.

Msitazi, wearing the bright red coat of the Queen's Own Wurm Guards, brought the canoe in close. "Greetings, Great Prince Vladimir."

"I welcome your visit, Great Chief Msitazi. I am honored."

"I present to you my grandson, William."

Nathaniel's eldest, I would imagine. Despite the gray-green hue of the boy's flesh, there was no mistaking his lean frame and strong nose. *And his eyes, so wary, like his father.*

"Greetings, William."

"Thank you, Highness."

The Prince pointed back in the direction of his estate. "May I offer you hospitality? Unless, of course, you mean to make Temperance before nightfall."

"We have come to see you, Great Prince." Msitazi smiled broadly. "I bring you a message from Aodaga."

"Who?"

"The great killer of the Ungarakii." Msitazi straightened the jacket. "Captain Owen Strake."

Prince Vlad sped Mugwump back to the estate and let Baker return him to the wurmrest. He took the towel from the servant, then sent him off to gather food. Then he helped William drag the canoe into his back lawn. The trio of men moved up to where just two months before the Prince had entertained Kamiskwa, Nathaniel, and Owen. He waited for his guests to seat themselves, then he sat as they did, cross-legged.

Though he desperately wished to see Captain Strake's message, he prepared himself to observe Shedashee convention and allow the chief to get to the message in his own time. Though frustrating, the Prince had come to realize that the native Mystrians did not view time as Norillians did. For them time was measured as *sufficient* or not. While the need for urgency did not go unrecognized, haste was considered closer to a sin than a mere vice and often the height of foolishness. To suggest otherwise was to forfeit Shedashee respect, and this was a thing not easily regained.

Msitazi handed the Prince a gorgeously beaded belt four inches wide and a yard and a half long. "This my daughter Ishikis has made for you, Great Prince. I should consider it a great honor if you would take her for your wife."

Vlad accepted it. The shell and turquoise, coral, onyx, and malachite had all been worked into a beautiful mosaic that featured bears at either end and a creature much like Mugwump through the rest of the design. The colorful stones had come from afar and were of incalculable value to the Altashee. The gift was as much an honor as the offer of his daughter.

"I regret that I must refuse your daughter's hand, Great Msitazi. I sent notice of your previous offer to my aunt. She has not yet given me leave to marry. I shall write her again."

The elder Altashee smiled. "You men of Norisle, you mistake the true treasures of this land."

"I know you speak the truth." Vlad stroked the belt with a hand. "Captain Strake also refused a similar offer?"

"You shall write your aunt and ask her to send brave officers who do not have wives, please."

"I shall, indeed, do that. How is it that you wear Captain Strake's coat?"

"He gave it to me, and I gave him robes of great medicine. He has gone off on the great mission you have given him. He will need such medicine."

Msitazi opened a pouch and produced a sealed note. "Aodaga sent this for you. We brought it as directly as we could. We had a little adventure on the way."

Vlad accepted the note and broke the seal. He glanced at the date on the top of the first sheet. He traced a finger along through the numbers and did some figuring. His having committed *A Continent's Calling* to memory made swift translation possible. Strake modestly described their trip so far and informed the Prince of details about a man who might no longer be dead.

He read it over twice, just to make sure he was translating correctly, then looked up. "What did they say of this man who may have returned from the grave?"

Msitazi's face darkened. "Pierre Ilsavont. Magehawk did not like him. Shot him. They burned his head. He was supposed to have died during the bad winter. He was *wendigo*."

"Did they say anything of a man named Guy du Malphias?"

"No. The *wendigo* kept company with Ungarakii. My son said they were off to hunt great prey. They were bound for Hattersburg."

Vlad nodded slowly. "The note mentions a journal and a ring."

William glanced at his grandfather, then opened his pouch and produced both of them. "I would not have let anyone have them, Highness."

"They were entrusted to you wisely, William. Your duty has been nobly and well accomplished." The ring was, as noted in the message, unremarkable other than being of Tharyngian manufacture and very far from home. While it might excite some interest in Launston, likely it would be dismissed as indicating little or nothing.

The journal, on the other hand, greatly excited the Prince. He began leafing through and found the missive addressed to Bethany Frost. He set it aside and continued to study the writing. What he noticed first, aside from the dreadful spelling and questionable grammar, was that the entries deteriorated over time. Sentences became shorter. Punctuation disappeared. The hand itself became larger and sloppier, with lines sloping across pages. The phases of the moon remained obvious, but the orb's shape suffered mightily.

Vlad looked up. "I beg your pardon. I am being rude."

Msitazi held a hand up. "Your face is mine when I study a track. Watch him, William, for he is wise and can concentrate. A warrior who strikes fast is valued, but one who is wise enough to know *where* to strike, he will be the victor."

The Prince smiled. "And, William, you are fortunate enough to have a man who is both fast and wise in your grandfather. Study him."

The boy beamed.

The Prince stood and waved to his wurmwright. "Baker, come here."

The hefty man ran over, clearly afraid that the Shedashee might be somehow threatening the Prince. "Yes, Highness."

Vlad handed him the note to Bethany Frost. "Take my fastest horse and deliver this to the Frosts. Ask Doctor Frost, his wife, his daughter, and his son, Caleb, to be my guests this evening for dinner. They will return home in the morning. You will have Colonel Langford prepare a coach for them and an honor guard of his cavalry company. He'll tell you that you are an idiot. You will tell him I said he was not to lead the cavalry, which is how he will know the order comes from me. The cavalry carry something of value back tomorrow. Their escort duty shall be a ruse should the enemy be watching. Have the guards bring a small strong box with them, including all keys for it."

"Yes, Highness. Should I be going now, Highness, or in a bit since your wurm needs feeding."

"Go now. I think Great Chief Msitazi and his grandson would help me feed the wurm. And on your way, tell the kitchen we shall have seven for dinner. It should be memorable."

"Highness, it's a bit late in the day…"

"Tell them that if I have to cook, they will have to feed the wurm."

"I think they will understand, Highness."

Throughout the discussion Msitazi's face remained an emotionless onyx mask, but as Baker ran off, he smiled. "It is not power that enables one to rule, but the wisdom to know how much to employ and when."

"One always hopes for circumstances that allow for the deliberation that makes both power and wisdom possible." The Prince waved his guests toward the wurmrest. "You will, of course, dine with me this evening as my guests. But first, shall we see to Mugwump's comfort?"

The boy clearly enjoyed feeding the wurm at least after he got past his initial fear. Mugwump appeared to enjoy his presence even more, gently nudging him and bringing his tail around to corral him. The boy shrieked delightedly and jabbered away at his grandfather. Prince Vlad was certain some great tales were going to be heard in Saint Luke upon their return.

The Prince left the two of them to their own devices and retired to his laboratory to study the journal and ring. On closer examination, the only odd details he noted about the ring were some engraving and that a small sliver of brass had been carved from the band. It was possible the latter had happened by accident, but unlikely. The engraving inside the band was comprised, in part, of several symbols of arcane import. Compared with the crest on the outer face, these letters, like the sliver cut from the band, had been made very recently. The Prince accepted that both had been done deliberately and, therefore, had significance.

The journal itself presented the Prince with clues both tantalizing and frustrating. Inside the back cover he found the symbols from the ring repeated. That confirmed their use as some sort of indexing scheme. Still, simple numbers would have sufficed to please an accountant or quartermaster. The symbols themselves had their roots in magick, and Owen's suggestion in the letter that there was a magickal link to the ring suggested something rather sinister.

The journal entries began almost normally, and would have appeared to be nothing more than a travelogue, save that the author gave no sense of his impressions or feelings. He described hills and valleys in the sort of language a civilian might think would please a surveyor. He did make an attempt, at first, to write down the paces it took to cross a stream, but precise measurements soon vanished. In fact, save for the lunar observations that prefaced every entry, any semblance of order or science evaporated halfway through.

Toward the end, then, things became utter gibberish, the handwriting indecipherable. In two places the pencil's point had snapped off, but whole lines had been written before the author found a new pencil and continued on.

All in all, the journal entries were useless. They conveyed neither direction nor elevation. Vlad supposed that if one were familiar with the area being traveled, one might be able to correlate location to description. *But if one were that familiar with the area, he'd not need the journal's information.*

That fact, coupled with the idea that the ring could be tracked, started the Prince thinking. If one *could* track the ring and *know* where the person wearing it was at any given moment, then the person's travel would become a survey in and of itself. Moreover, if the ring could communicate more than just location, but conditions, even in the most rudimentary sense, then the journal would be used to confirm the observations made through the link.

The whole thing had the stink of Ryngian Thaumaturgy about it. Norillian magick built on long tradition, and Norillian mages were among some of the best in the world. Norillian magick was what made the Queen's armies so effective—her line troops were second to none in combat.

In the aftermath of the Tharyngian revolution, which elevated Science to the highest place in the Universe, magick had become yet one more area of study. While they had started with the same traditions as Norisle, the Ryngians had performed a systematic survey of magick to establish its underlying principles. This seemed a waste of time to many Norillians, and the newly published Tharyngian principles drew ridicule since it was well known that they just couldn't be true.

The necessity of touch in magick, for example, was indisputable. Folklore abounded with stories of mages laid low at the end of a spear, or of oracles able to read bones and identify who they had once belonged to. No one, until the Tharyngians, had bothered to ask *how* knowledge could be contained in those bones. They postulated the Laws of Similarity and Contagion to offer an explanation. In short, those things that looked similar had a link with each other, and those which had spent time in proximity to one another were similarly linked.

That would suggest, then, that the ring and the sliver taken from it would have a link. While the tradition that the Prince had studied suggested that the link would be too weak to be of use, he wasn't certain he accepted that anymore. The Shedashee appeared to be able to read links and, if Captain Strake's letter was to be believed, they could read them with no great difficulty. And if Strake had learned this, could not a Tharyngian have done so, too, and started his fellows studying the possibilities?

And worse yet, the letter hinted at necromancy. No Laureates endorsed it, and many decried it, but that didn't mean it did not exist.

The Prince sat back. If du Malphias had come to Mystria to study or employ magicks so foul his compatriots did not want him in their homeland, things had become dire indeed, and would become much worse.

CHAPTER THIRTY

July 7, 1763
Anvil Lake, New Tharyngia

O wen awoke naked and cold in a dark stone room, stretched out on a wooden slab. Thick leather straps secured his wrists, ankles, chest, and waist to the slab. Dull echoes of pain pulsed from his left thigh. A square of reddened cloth covered the hole. A glass vessel hung from the ceiling and dripped a greenish liquid on the cloth with maddening regularity.

Something shuffled through the shadows at his feet. He couldn't see what. He sensed the presence of at least one person, but whoever was there remained invisible. "Hello?" His voice came hoarse and ended in a cough. It shook his body and the pain increased marginally.

The sharp click of boots on stone filtered into the chamber. The shuffling chased it, then paused. A match scratched on the wall, bursting into flame. A slender-fingered hand applied it to one hanging lamp and then to another. The man raised the match to his lips and blew it out.

Du Malphias!

The Tharyngian Laureate looked much as he had when Owen had seen him before, though now, without a hat, black hair on his crown and grey hair at his temples became plainly visible. The pattern repeated itself in his goatee. He stood at the foot of the slab, studying Owen, then shifted to the left. He raised a hand and flicked a fingernail against the hanging glass. It rang and he seemed to take some satisfaction from it.

"You are a very fortunate man. Your perspicacity saved your life. The bullet had damaged your femoral artery, but the belt held things tight. Your packing the wound with that crude poultice likely has slowed infection. I should thank you for that. It has opened a new area of inquiry. I had no knowledge of the medicinal property of that plant and I am interested to see if it has uses beyond the obvious anesthetic qualities."

The man's words came with a soothing evenness that surprised Owen, and emphasized the lyrical quality of his Ryngian accent. It almost seemed as if the man cared whether or not Owen lived.

"Water."

"Perhaps, in a bit." Du Malphias disappeared for a moment, then returned, holding up a deformed hunk of lead. "This, then, was the bullet which struck you. It must have been a ricochet, no? It broke your leg, but I have set the bone. The break, she was clean. If you live, you will again be able to walk. If you do not, this is a problem we will deal with later."

The Tharyngian glanced past Owen's head. "Quarante-neuf, the stool, please, and the tray."

A large, shaved-headed man came around from the left and dragged a stool over to the slab's side. Du Malphias perched upon it, surrendering none of his height. He accepted a small silver tray with metal tools on it and rested it across Owen's ankles too far away for Owen to see what the tools were.

"And I shall need my apron."

Quarante-neuf became a silhouette, then returned to the circle of light and secured a blood-stained leather apron on du Malphias. The Tharyngian waved the servant back. He obediently retreated to the wall, barely visible, but staring forward.

Du Malphias took a small mirror from the tray, then peeled back the cloth covering Owen's injury. "If you care to look, the wound is relatively clean. I will sew it shut soon, but I wanted you to see the damage that has been done."

Owen didn't want to look, but found himself fascinated by his rent flesh and torn muscle. He wasn't certain because of the hanging lamp's weak light but he thought he caught an ivory flash of bone.

"You present for me a problem, sir." Du Malphias replaced the bandage. "I have examined your things. You have a rifle that has only been issued to men under my command. I have to assume that its previous owner is no more, his mission unsuccessful. He and his band sought property belonging to me. I shall assume you have some knowledge of this property and its current location. Do not bother to deny any of this. The pencils you carry were with the item I seek.

"I have made further deductions. You are friendly with the Altashee. You carry with you a child's doll, so you have deep connections with them. She is your daughter, the one who gave you this doll? And you carry a copy of *A Continent's Calling*. You are, therefore, literate and cognizant of fact that Mystria's future is not tied to the whims of Norisle's insane mistress."

Du Malphias plucked a blunt metal probe from the tray and used it to point at Owen's right thumb. "The blood under your nail and reports of my squad indicate you are brave and skilled at war. You were with others. I shall tell you that I have one of them in my custody, wounded worse than you. A shot through the bowels. He lost much blood, but he is a big man, no?"

Makepeace. Owen fought to keep any reaction from his face.

"He fares not as well as you. I am not certain I can save him." Du Malphias shrugged. "You know that if he does pass on, I will find uses for him."

Owen shivered.

Du Malphias smiled. "Good, you do understand. So, I shall tell you one more thing so you can make some decisions. You were betrayed by Etienne Ilsavont. He told me that you entrusted a message to him and his partner, promising a pound if they took it to Temperance. To Doctor Frost of the college. Etienne tried to convince his partner that if it was worth one pound to Frost, I should pay more. His partner disagreed, so they split, and Ilsavont returned here. He was out with the squad that discovered you. I shall assume, from the bullet I recovered from his chest, it was the one known as Magehawk who killed him."

He's dead. "Good."

The Laureate allowed himself a brief smile. "Etienne will serve us well, as did his father. The son has already identified your compatriots. You he did not know, but based on the conversation he related, you were keenly interested in what I am doing here. Now I am interested in what you are doing here, who you are, other mundane details of life. Will you share them with me, or must I convince you?"

"Owen Strake."

Du Malphias' grey eyes became slender crescents. "A Mystrian name. An alias? Perhaps. We shall determine this in due time." He peeled the bandage back and poked the probe into the wound.

It clicked off bone.

Owen jolted, half from the sound and half from pain shooting up his spine.

"Interesting. I grade reaction to pain on a decimal scale, zero to nine. Your reaction is a five. Your concoction and above is my own infusion of that fern in alcohol, far more effective in releasing chemicals than water or saliva is powerful. I imagine that your compatriot would benefit from it, even if only to ease his last hours. If you choose to speak freely, Monsieur Strake, I shall be kind to him."

Du Malphias tapped the bone again.

"And one more thing for you to consider. We never intended knowledge of this fortress to be hidden from Norisle. By the end of October, our ambassador will formally announce its presence to the Norillian government. It will confirm the rumors we have been feeding them for a short while. What I want to know is exactly *what* you have communicated about it."

Du Malphias reached up and turned a stopcock, curtailing the flow of anesthetic. "I will go tend to your friend now. I regret I only have one prepara-tion to use. I will test his level of pain, then administer it and see how much reduction there is. By then I hope it will have worn off you, and I shall resume testing here. All for the sake of science.

"Quarante-neuf will remain here to see to your needs."

Du Malphias put away the tray and snuffed the lamps before he left. His footsteps retreated down a corridor. Owen shivered, both from the damp cold, and from the man's lingering presence.

"Water, please."

The servant moved quietly through the darkness. Water poured. A hand slid beneath Owen's head, then a bowl touched his lips. Quarante-neuf fed him slowly, pausing, letting Owen catch his breath, before he resumed drinking.

"Thank you."

The other man lowered Owen's head to the slab again.

"Who are you? Can you speak? Why does he call you forty-nine?"

"This is my name."

Definitely Mystrian by his accent. "Who are you?"

"Quarante-neuf."

A thought puckered Owen's flesh. "Who *were* you?"

"I am Quarante-neuf."

A muffled scream echoed from nearby. Clearly a man, a big man in pain. *Makepeace.* Owen could not make out any words, but the tone of the sounds left no doubt that the screamer was begging for mercy. Another scream punctuated his request, then two more, shorter and weaker.

Owen's hands tightened into fists. Du Malphias had said all he wanted to know was the nature of the information that had been communicated. He knew of the note sent with Jean. Nathaniel and Kamiskwa had gotten away, so the Prince would have his journals and maps. Seth Plant's note really had nothing special in it, and Nathaniel or Kamiskwa could communicate all of that regardless.

Nothing he knew would prevent the Prince from requesting help from Launston. Jean's note would pinpoint the fortress. The maps would help planning a siege, but even the rough description Jean had supplied would tell Horse Guards what they were facing. The die had already been cast, and nothing Owen could reveal to du Malphias would benefit the Tharyngian in the least.

The man screamed again. Owen could imagine du Malphias jabbing the probe into his guts. Makepeace, strapped down as he was, his belly open, bleeding, stinking, suppurating. Stomach wounds always had seemed the most painful on the battlefield.

And the least survivable.

"Go. Tell du Malphias I will talk."

The large man drifted away silently. The screaming stopped, and du Malphias' footsteps returned. He struck another match, relit the lamps, and again hung the anesthetic above Owen. He did not, however, restart the flow.

Wet blood glistened on his apron and had stained his coat cuffs.

"You will understand that while I take you at your word that you will tell me the truth, I will test that truth, yes?"

"I am Captain Owen Strake of the Queen's Own Wurm Guards."

The Tharyngian's eyes widened. "This *is* a surprise. You do realize that since you are not in uniform, you are considered a spy, yes?"

"And you can have me shot."

"I can, and may yet. We shall see how useful you are." Du Malphias' brows arrowed together. "What are you doing so far from your home station, Captain?"

"I was sent on a mission to survey New Tharyngian territory. I did not know of your presence until after my arrival in Mystria." Owen winced as his leg throbbed. "Quite by chance we found the journals and the ring. They were sent to the Governor-General. The note Jean carried communicated the location of your fort. When my companions reach Temperance they will have a rough map of your fortifications."

The Laureate's face closed for a moment. "And of my experiments? Of Pierre Ilsavont?"

"We know he was frozen solid, but you revived him somehow."

"I prefer the word 'reanimate.' No matter." Du Malphias walked over to a table Owen could not see and brought the tray of tools back, setting them on the stool. "I do accept your general account. You do have more information, which I shall extract. I hope you will survive."

He picked up a sharp chisel probe and a small hammer. "Now, Captain Strake, if you will indulge me. Tell me your *real* name."

Owen passed out twice in the eternity that constituted du Malphias' questioning. He fought to hold back screams and was not wholly successful. He did mute them, however, in hopes Makepeace would not hear.

Du Malphias mixed his questions, asking about troop strengths in the colonies at one point, then shifting rapidly to questions about levels of pain and whether something felt hot or cold or just agonizing. The confusion as much as the pain prompted Owen to admissions he might otherwise not have made. He revealed his connection to the Ventnor family and spoke of the Frosts. Du Malphias detected something in the way he mentioned Bethany and questioned him closely about her.

Owen had replied curtly. "I am a married man, sir."

"A defense offered so often by a man willing to stray." Du Malphias cracked the hammer sharply against his femur. "You cannot lie to me, Captain, but please to lie to yourself."

The Tharyngian kept at it, asking the same questions from different angles and, eventually reached a certain level of satisfaction with the answers. He set his tools down, covered the leg wound again, and started the anesthetic drip. He removed his apron and handed it to Quarante-neuf, then dispatched the servant on a whispered errand.

Du Malphias loomed at his bedside. "I accept you at your word, Captain, in all you have told me. I am not yet determined what I shall do with you. But you appear a hearty specimen. You have some use."

Owen shook his head. "You will not make me into one of your *pasmortes*."

"I definitely hope not." Du Malphias tapped his finger against the hanging glass. "Curious properties, this fluid. I created something akin to it a number of years ago."

From the pocket of his black frock coat he produced a crusted bottle. "Others have conducted alchemical researches looking for the fabled Philosopher's Stone. They expect to find something that will turn dross to gold. Their dreams of avarice, while admirable, are pitiful in their lack of ambition. I sought something different, and I call it *vivalius*. After years of experimentation in my spare time, since you Norillians have required me to serve my country with my knowledge of military science, I have discovered and refined many of its more interesting properties. Creating the *pasmorte* is but one thing to which it is well suited."

He set the bottle between Owen's legs and turned toward the returning Quarante-neuf. The servant bore a wide, flat, wooden box, but du Malphias eclipsed it before Owen could get a good look. The Tharyngian opened it and fiddled with something, while looking back at Owen over his shoulder.

"Vivalius quickens healing and I would have used it on your leg, save that your application of the weed ruined any chance I had of truly testing the results. This is a pity because I think you would have done well under treatment." Du Malphias turned, a small pistol in his hand. "I should say, you *will* do well under treatment. One leg with *vivalius*, the other with the native preparation."

Du Malphias sighted down the pistol's barrel. "In the name of Tharyngia, Captain Strake, I thank you for your contribution to science."

The man's cold smile evaporated in the cloud of gunsmoke.

CHAPTER THIRTY-ONE

July 14, 1763
Prince Haven
Temperance Bay, Mystria

Prince Vlad sat in his laboratory. He'd cleared a place at his table and had laid out all three of Owen's letters, along with the journals and the best map of the surrounding colonies. He'd added to them several piles of books in a variety of languages, and had marked many passages with slender paper slips.

The third letter, the one brought by Jean Deleon, had arrived only that morning from Temperance. The letter covering it came from Doctor Frost, who indicated that Deleon said he had more information he would be pleased to sell in the event it would bring a good price. Deleon was certain the information would be very valuable.

The Deleon letter confirmed what had been suspected in the earlier two and expanded upon it. Du Malphias had indeed managed, somehow, to return a man to life. Ilsavont had been distant but clearly functional and the Prince was willing to assume the writer of the journal had been dead or dying or dying *again* as explanation for the journal's deteriorating reports.

It was after the receipt of the second letter that the Prince had begun his examination of the issue of necromancy. His library, though one of the largest on the Continent, had surprisingly few references to it. They generally fell into three categories. The first explored such rumors as a matter of folktales. The second condemned practitioners as diabolists and promised them an eternity in lakes of burning brimstone. These books, all written by learned Church fathers, claimed that practitioners, liars that they were, grossly exaggerated their success.

The third category's exemplars were the books on his desk. While the Prince confined his studies largely to those of the natural sciences, many reference books did touch upon the subject here and there. An anthropologist, in sorting a variety of avian bones found in a midden, used a magickal sense of which bones belonged to which grouping to help with his sorting. His subsequent re-construction of the skeletons proved accurate. This was taken as a confirmation of the Law of Contagion, and the anthropologist went on to speculate, based on impressions he'd gotten from the bones, as to the life-cycle of extinct birds. He went so far as to suggest that someday magicks might be able to reanimate the skeleton and verify his theory about the birds' locomotion.

Such was the nature of most mentions. No one claimed outright to have reanimated the dead, but they speculated that such a thing was possible. In other cases, certain magicks and magickally fashioned preparations had been effective in banishing ghosts and spirits from certain locations. If true, these reports suggested that magick could interact with the departed.

Had du Malphias dared do what others only speculated about?

Vlad steepled his fingers. Addressing that question would be the endpoint of an inquiry that had decidedly more humble beginnings. If reviving the dead were even possible, it would require great knowledge, great intelligence, and great power. There was no doubting du Malphias had the first two qualities, but great *power?* According to everything Prince Vlad had been taught about magick, such levels of power were simply unknown.

In the Old World.

The Shedashee were more adept at magick than any of the settlers. Whether or not they could raise the dead was a moot point. They were more skilled and powerful than Vlad had been led to believe was possible. That fact put the lie to that very proposition. Add to that the idea that the Crown granted charters for schools of magick, and anyone teaching outside the charter system would be decried by Crown and Church. Could it be that magicks more powerful than commonly believed were possible, and that the Crown was hiding this bit of reality from the people?

Vlad smiled. Though the peasantry might not think the Queen would ever lie, they were lied to every day. Official statements proclaimed the Villerupt campaign a victory for Norisle. Allies had been scapegoated for failures, every dead man had been declared a hero, and every officer had been elevated despite having had to retreat from the Continent. With so much ceremony attending the troops' return, one could not help but think they had been the victors.

The Prince accepted that greater and more powerful magicks existed. He based this on the evidence of the Shedashee and the fact that when he'd been taught to shoot, his instructor praised him for having taken to it more quickly than Princess Margaret's children had. "There will be more of this for the likes of you."

But, in fact, there had not been. The King had died childless while fighting on the Continent. Margaret was elevated to the throne, bypassing his father who, at that time, served as Governor-General of Mystria. He'd later been recalled to Launston and reentered the monastery from which he'd been drawn to marry Vlad's mother, and the Governor-Generalship fell to Vlad.

Whether or not du Malphias could raise the dead, heal those believed dead, or somehow cobble together bones and make them function, all three possibilities resulted in a single outcome. Du Malphias would have a superior supply of labor. Moreover, troops convinced of their functional immortality might abandon fear and good sense, fighting on in situations where they might otherwise flee. Such resolution would create an army that would deliver devastating casualties no matter how hopeless their situation.

He recognized, instantly, that his three conclusions amounted to the same thing: the balance of power in Mystria had shifted. While New Tharyngia had proved as wealthy a colony as Mystria, its smaller population and corresponding diminution of military power had curbed Tharyngian adventurism. More power, especially with du Malphias in charge of it, pointed to great trouble ahead.

Of course, anything wrought through magick could also be unmade by it. A spell could light brimstone afire. Another spell, applied quickly enough, could extinguish that fire. Granted, the mage would have to touch the fire to make the magick work—getting burned in the process—but the fire would go out. Touching a magickally enhanced soldier would likewise constitute a severe danger.

But iron is an anathema to all magick.

The Prince turned and snatched up the journal. He flipped halfway through, to where the pages became blank, and started making notes. He jotted a crude diagram and did some calculations. Then another idea popped into his head and he made another drawing.

He pushed his chair back and grabbed a measuring string. Looping it about his neck, he darted from his study and down across the lawn toward the wurmrest.

He never quite got there.

Nathaniel Woods waved from the shore as he pulled the canoe up. Kamiskwa jumped from the back and helped haul the canoe free of the water. Nathaniel produced a satchel and held it out to the Prince.

Vlad accepted it. "Where is Captain Strake? Is he?"

Nathaniel snarled. "He's alive, or I'll be killing him next I see him. These here are his journals. If you have some food, drink, and a place we can sleep for a bit, we'll be heading back for him."

The Prince nodded, relieved a bit, but still anxious. "Come with me, gentlemen. I shall see to your needs. You will tell me everything."

Their story matched the letters up to and including the Deleon message. After they had escaped the Ryngians, that being a harrowing adventure in and of itself, they'd traveled directly to Saint Luke. They left Makepeace Bone there to be mended, then hurried directly to the Prince. A journey that had taken Jean

Deleon two months, they had accomplished in five weeks and looked every bit as lean and exhausted as one might expect.

Nathaniel sliced an apple in half. "We would not have left Captain Strake, but it was an order. We had agreed. He said the journals was what you needed."

"My friends, this is the fourth time you've mentioned that order. I understand your anger and anguish, but your actions have not dishonored you in the least. I think more of you now, knowing what you have done, than I did before a feat I would have believed, until this moment, well nigh impossible."

The Prince rested his hand on the journals. "I will spend the night examining these journals and, in the morning…"

Nathaniel shook his head. "We'll be gone by then."

"You cannot go, Mr. Woods."

"All due respect being yours, Highness, I ain't one of your subjects to be ordered about."

"Precisely, Mr. Woods, which is why I need you here. The both of you." Prince Vlad looked from one man to the other. "Captain Strake was right. What you have uncovered is of more importance than you can even begin to imagine. What you have seen is critical if du Malphias is to be stopped. With your help I will construct a complete set of maps. We will work up plans and demands for troops. If that fortress stands, none of us are safe. Not Mystrians, not the Shedashee."

"I ain't leaving Captain Strake out there."

"Nathaniel, please." The Prince pressed his hands flat to the table. "If Captain Strake is alive, he is likely in du Malphias' custody. If dead, I fear he is as well. If alive, he will be held as a prisoner or shot. In Temperance and just up the coast at Truth Bay, there are two Ryngian agents. I shall order their apprehension and draft a letter to Guy du Malphias offering a prisoner exchange. This is the best chance Owen has."

Kamiskwa nodded. "Owen was shot in the leg. It needs time to heal. He could not escape for at least a month. And if they took his leg…"

Nathaniel hammered a fist against the table. "I know. I know. You're both right. Don't mean I like it."

"Nathaniel, had you been shot, you would have ordered him away. You don't like his having fallen and your still being alive."

"Ain't the first time I shouldered that burden, Highness. Don't need another ghost behind me." Nathaniel sighed. "Would you be letting me take that note to du Malphias?"

"I need you here. I'll send Jean Deleon." Vlad turned to Kamiskwa. "Prince Kamiskwa, how would the Confederation react if it is proved that du Malphias is creating *wendigo?*"

"It is enough that they hold Aodaga. If my father were to call for warriors, two hundred would answer. Many with guns, more with arrows and warclubs."

"That would be wonderful. I will have to raise what militia forces I can by next spring."

Nathaniel glowered again. "We leave Owen there over the winter, we ain't never getting him back."

"Please, Nathaniel, if du Malphias is raising the dead, we have more pressing problems. We need to know everything about his creatures. We have to know how to kill them."

"You shoot them." Nathaniel smiled. "It worked on Ilsavont."

"Yes, but *why* did it work? Was he bleeding? Did you hit a vital organ? Did you explode his heart? Did you shoot him in the head?"

Nathaniel looked at Kamiskwa, then back. "Caught him just above his paunch. Don't recall too much blood."

"And there was no sign of what had killed the one that possessed the journal, correct?"

Kamiskwa shook his head. "It looked as if he just lay down and died."

"These, gentlemen, are the things we need to know. We need to know how to kill them. Yes, you burned Ilsavont's head. This is good. But we do not know if the shot just rendered him unconscious and if he would have revived, or if your shot put him down."

The hunter smiled. "Onliest way to find this all out, Highness. You need you some specimens."

"Eventually, yes; and you'll have that job, Nathaniel. What I need first is your knowledge. I will go through these journals and the maps. I will need you to verify the maps, then I shall build a miniature." Vlad remembered the idea he'd just scratched into his journal. "Yes, I shall also need you to test something else. Perhaps not tomorrow, but soon, very soon."

"We will do that, Highness, but you'll be having to work with Kamiskwa tomorrow. And I'll need the lend of a horse."

"For?"

Nathaniel glanced down at a bone-strewn plate. "I reckon someone needs to ride into Temperance and tell the Frosts what happened. Since I know the blame will be settling on me, I might as well deliver the news."

Vlad slowly nodded. "Yes, of course. I should have thought of them first. I shall write a note. If you would deliver it for me, I should be most grateful."

"As you wish, Highness."

The Prince himself showed his guests to their quarters. He gave them rooms facing south with doors that opened onto a balcony. From previous experience he expected they would choose to sleep out there under the stars rather than in the beds.

He returned to his laboratory and began his study of the maps. Owen Strake had done a wonderful job, indicating heights and slopes as best possible, even sketching in little men to act as a scale. The Prince meticulously measured and transferred information from the journals to a larger sheet. With every wall and obstacle he increased the number of men that would be required to reduce the fort. He also increased his estimates of casualties.

At the end he made the final calculations and his stomach soured. *So many dead, and that is just if we are truly facing what I see here.*

He shook his head.

With du Malphias in charge, hidden horrors awaited. No man laying siege to that fortress would escape unharmed.

CHAPTER THIRTY-TWO

August 15, 1763
Anvil Lake, New Tharyngia

Owen ducked his head, shying from sunlight hitting him in the face. He wavered for a moment, taking enough weight on his right leg that he didn't topple over. He inched his left crutch forward, then the left foot, becoming steady again. His arms trembled. The crutches dug deep into his armpits, but he refused to fall or turn back.

But I would not be allowed to fall. Quarante-neuf hovered behind him, ready to catch him. Du Malphias had tasked the *pasmorte* to see to his every need. To the best of Owen's knowledge the creature never slumbered and, at least while he was awake, had never been far away. And whenever Owen had awakened from fever-dreams, Quarante-neuf had been there with cool compresses and gentle words.

The thin blouse Owen had been given did nothing to cushion the crutches. Du Malphias dictated he wear the loincloth he'd received from the Altashee, less as an honor, then it made inspecting the bandaged wounds much easier. The moccasins had likewise been returned to him and this was the first time he had worn them.

The gunshot to his right thigh had not opened so grievous a wound as the musket. The ball had been smaller and it missed the bone entirely. This did not please du Malphias. The lack of symmetry between the two wounds somehow ruined his experiment. So, with Quarante-neuf holding the leg steady, the Tharyngian used his hammer and chisel to break the femur.

When Owen resumed consciousness the Tharyngian was engaged in measuring both wounds by every means possible. He would call out numbers and comments, which another one of the *pasmortes* scribbled down. Then, apparently satisfied, du Malphias applied five drops of his *vivalius* along the length of the wound, and proceeded to stitch it up. He then closed the other wound and draped the first with a leather sheet so none of the dripping Shedashee potion would splash onto it.

Each day he would return, poking, prodding, taking his measurements and making notes. Owen had complained that his right leg did not feel as the left. It felt hot, and as if something was clawing into it. Du Malphias acknowledged his complaints with a nod, added an additional drop of *vivalius*, but his expression when he examined the wound from that point forward belied the confident noises he made.

Then the fever began. Owen had no idea how long it lasted because his nightmares never ended. Moments of wakefulness he had, but no true lucidity. He had distant memories of his own ravings echoing through his small prison as Quarante-neuf would bathe him in cool water.

The only relief from nightmares came in brief respites when Bethany Frost appeared. Her smile abated his fever and ended his torments. She would read to him in words that made no sense, but he listened only for her kind tone. She would reach a hand out to soothe his brow and, at times, would lean in for a kiss…

Only to be torn away from him screaming. Then he would find himself in the forest, running along the winding path. The stick creatures had faces, the faces of his wife and his relatives, dead comrades, and men like Lord Rivendell. They hounded him, nipping, tearing his flesh. He tried to run faster but bullets ripped through his legs. He stumbled and fell, feeling them ever close and drawing closer. He clawed at the earth, trying to drag himself along, and then, as a last resort, he burrowed into the earth for safety.

And he would awaken in his tiny prison, buried, and feel no safer.

Though du Malphias never explained what he had done, as Owen healed he came to certain conclusions. The Tharyngian clearly had reopened the wound in his right leg and drained it. He'd set up a second drip of the Shedashee preparation and left the wound open to drain more. Finally, when the heat and redness had vanished, he had reclosed the wound, all the while glaring at Owen as if he had somehow betrayed the Laureate.

Owen, thanks to Quarante-neuf's kind treatment and the wisdom of the Shedashee, recovered steadily. He no longer had to be restrained and du Malphias' stern expressions surrendered to looks of mild pleasure. He'd even brought the crutches and invited Owen to venture forth whenever he felt able.

I will hobble, then walk, then escape.

With this goal in mind, Owen forced himself to move. His legs protested mightily at first, but he pushed past this new pain. The stitches held and the wounds healed. Owen did notice that while they seemed to progress at the same rate, the right leg was closing without the puckered trace of a scar. The leg even felt a bit stronger than the left, though the difference in bullets might have accounted for that.

The things that interested du Malphias only concerned Owen in that as long as the Laureate found him worthy of study, he would remain alive. The look in the Laureate's eyes especially when he did not think Owen noticed revealed Owen's ultimate disposition. He was, after all, a spy and, therefore, had to be shot.

Ironically, of course, he'd wait until Owen healed. *Healed enough that* after *he kills me, he can make me into one of his* pasmortes.

Owen was determined that would not happen. He was not going to die in du Malphias' frontier fortress. He was going to return to Saint Luke and thank Agaskan for her doll keeping him safe. Then he would go to Temperance and complete his journals, finish his mission, and return home to his wife.

A cold chill ran down Owen's spine. During his fevered dreams, it had been Bethany Frost, not Catherine, who had comforted him. His wife did appear in his dreams, but she wore mourning and held back, staring at him in horror as if he were long dead. He reached out to her and she recoiled, calling him a *pasmorte*.

Owen did not trust dreams as did his wife, but he sought to make sense of them. His wife's reaction was perfectly in keeping with her character. She loved him dearly, but had no stomach for dealing with illness and infirmity. While she spent many hours reading to her grandmother as the old woman slowly sank into senility, blood, vomitus, or other leakage would send her running. He counted himself lucky that he had never been seriously wounded. Though many of his wife's friends volunteered in hospital sick-wards, Catherine never did.

The reasons Bethany comforted him were myriad. At the very least, she had been kind to him. During his short stay in Temperance, her laughter had put a smile on his face and she had been a very solicitous hostess. Add to that the fact that her mother had sewed his ear back on, and connecting healing with the Frosts was not hard to understand. Separated from his wife, in the throes of delirium, it was expected that his fevered brain might impose her as an image of hope.

He frowned. Regardless of it being an involuntary consequence of his illness, it was unseemly. He was a married man who loved his wife. He resolved that when he returned to Temperance, he would be cordial to and even friendly with Bethany Frost, but he would make certain there was no misunderstanding between them. He could not tell her of his dreams—this would make her uncomfortable. He would, however, show his gratitude, and hope that somehow she would understand his behavior.

Owen surveyed the fortress from the mouth of a tunnel set halfway between the upper fort and the stone star at the construction's heart. The *pasmortes* worked tirelessly—du Malphias noted that some of them had been worked to death and *still* worked—an oft-repeated joke in which the Laureate took great delight. Owen had concluded that the *pasmortes'* abilities and level of service corresponded to how badly damaged they were at resurrection. Quarante-neuf appeared to be quite high-functioning, able to carry on a conversation and even seeming to have emotions. He was a great deal more human than Etienne's description of his father.

Others, in various states of decay, functioned as beasts of burden. Du Malphias referred to them as his little "ants," capable of shifting mountains one tiny piece at a time. When one of the beasts became broken, du Malphias or a couple of the higher-functioning *pasmortes* like Quarante-neuf, would affect a repair via magick deep in the bowels of the fortress.

The ability of a *pasmorte* to use magick shocked Owen, but it made sense. They had become creatures of magick themselves, and the magicks they used were rather elementary. Just as Kamiskwa and Makepeace had repaired the canoes, so magick could reattach a severed arm, or strengthen a broken bone.

Du Malphias came walking down the path from the upper fort. "Good morning, Captain Strake. How are you feeling?"

"Pain is a three on your scale in my left leg, two in the right. Discomfort, but nothing insurmountable."

"Excellent." The Tharyngian frowned. "I regret the necessity of this. Come with me to the smith."

"Sir?"

"I cannot have you getting up to mischief."

Owen held his head up. "I pledge to you, sir, as an officer and a gentleman, that I have no intention of doing anything of that sort."

The slender man's grey eyes tightened. "You understand, sir, that you stand before me a *spy* whose life is under immediate threat of extinction. Please accept the honor I do you in treating you like a dangerous foe. I have determined that iron shackles will not impede your recovery, therefore this prudent precaution is one that must be employed now. Quarante-neuf, if he does not follow me, *drag* him."

Quarante-neuf took a step forward, but Owen started after du Malphias. "Please, sir, not so fast."

The Tharyngian glanced back, then slowed his pace.

"Thank you." Owen caught up with. "I have wanted to ask, sir, after my compatriot. How does he fare?"

"He perished. Sepsis. Everything I tried, failed."

Owen's stomach imploded. *Not Makepeace!* He scanned the lines of *pasmortes*. "Did you…?"

Du Malphias waved the question aside. "The infection did significant damage to his spine and brain. He was of no use to me."

"I should like to pay my respects."

"I imagine." Du Malphias pointed at a stool next to the smith's anvil. "It pleased me, however, to give him a Viking funeral. I laid him and his equipment in a canoe, lit it afire, and sent it sailing into the lake. The current caught it. His ashes will have washed down the Roaring River and into the Misaawa. On his last journey he shall see more of this continent than he did in life."

The smith, a burly man who wore a leather apron to protect a hirsute chest, took a pair of shackles from a burlap sack. He slid one on to Owen's right wrist, allowing the tabs from the upper and lower halves to stick through a thick, leather sheet. He wrapped the sheet around Owen's forearm, then drew a glowing red bolt of bronze from the fire. With tongs he slid it through the holes in the tabs, then hammered it flat against the anvil.

Sparks flew and the metal quickly grew hot. Hairs on Owen's arm melted into a sickly sweet smoke. The smith pulled the leather away, then yanked Owen forward, dunking his arm to the elbow in a water trough. The bolt bubbled, and steam rose.

Once the bubbling had stopped, he raised the wrist and showed it to du Malphias. The Laureate, who had a handkerchief over his nose and mouth, nodded. "Proceed."

The smith repeated the process with the other hand. Du Malphias studied the results. "We will try your native infusion on those burns, Captain."

"Most kind, sir." Owen smiled despite the throbbing burns.

"Almost done." From a pocket du Malphias drew a sharp metal stylus. He caught up each of Owen's hands in turn and inscribed an oddly angular series of symbols on the head of the bronze bolts. The Laureate then produced two brown leather bracers bearing a great resemblance to clerks'-sleeves. "You will wear these at all times over your shackles until directed to remove them. I would not have Quarante-neuf come to harm."

It made sense. The iron shackles restricted Owen's ability to use magick and especially fire a gun. The touch of iron or steel so disrupted magick that, in olden days, the inability to hold an iron nail for any length of time was enough to convict a person of being a warlock.

All of a sudden the mystery of the glove on Pierre Ilsavont's left hand became clear. He'd been given a left-handed glove because he had to grip the iron musket barrel to reload. For creatures like Quarante-neuf, iron could disrupt that which gave them a semblance of life.

Owen accepted the leather sleeves, pulled them on and secured them with buckles and belts at wrist and forearm. Du Malphias inspected his work and smiled.

"Very good, Captain Strake." The Laureate turned and spread his arms. "Though you would give me your word that you would be on your best behavior, I cannot grant you freedom of my camp. You are a most intelligent man…"

"You're afraid I'll learn something that will hurt you?"

Du Malphias looked at him incredulous, then laughed aloud. "Oh, dear me, no, monsieur. If I considered you that dangerous, I should have had you taken to pieces and used those pieces to repair my faithful servants. No, you will seek to learn much and you will exhaust yourself. Truly. You are barely able to work your crutches, and already you think of taking flight. I know this."

Owen half-closed his emerald eyes. "If I complain that you impugn my honor, you will point out, yet again, I am a spy and, therefore, untrustworthy."

"I believe we understand each other."

"Then why keep me alive?" Owen glanced down at his legs. "You surely have learned enough."

"An abundance of data is never a vice when it comes to science, Captain Strake." Du Malphias shrugged. "But this is not the only reason I keep you alive. Shall I be honest with you?"

"If you like."

"I have been given the resources to build all this. You've seen that to get a ship past my wall would be difficult and that is supposing the ship had gotten past Fort Cuivre and the other fortresses from here to the sea. Possible, but highly unlikely."

The Tharyngian turned and pointed toward the east. "The most intelligent plan for Norisle would be to make a fort of its own over there, at the Tillie headwaters. This would hold me back and protect your colonies. It would also accept, *de facto*, a division of the Continent, which traps you on the coast and leaves us free to exploit the interior."

Owen nodded.

"But neither your masters nor mine can abide that sort of division. My enemies are hoping that your country will raise an army that destroys this fortress and kills me. This would mean that Norisle would divert forces that otherwise would be used to attack Tharyngia. An admirable goal."

"And your goal, sir?"

Du Malphias chuckled again. "There, I told you that you were intelligent. It occurs to me that if Norisle is unable to project enough force to protect the interior of Mystria, and because I know Tharyngia is completely unable to do the same, the vast heart of this continent is open for the taking. There is no reason I should not take it and, with my magicks, no power in the world that can wrest it from me once I have."

CHAPTER THIRTY-THREE

August 16, 1763
Tanner and Hound, Temperance
Temperance Bay, Mystria

Nathaniel found Caleb Frost at the Tanner and Hound. The young man's surprise became delight. He rose from his table and shook Nathaniel's hand. Nathaniel could not but help return so broad a smile, even though he felt anything but joyous.

Caleb made room for him on the bench. "So Strake lasted a bit longer out there, did he? I made five shillings betting you'd keep him out for a month. Let me buy you a pint."

Nathaniel shook his head. "Tain't really a time for drinking. Not yet anyway. Ain't ale going to help."

Caleb's smile evaporated. "What's wrong?"

"I need to speak to your family." He produced the Prince's note.

Caleb took it, recognized the wax seal, and stood. "I'll fetch my father. You can talk with him."

"Has to be all of them. The adults, I'm thinking. Your sister included."

"But my mother won't…" Caleb stood. "You wait here. I will fetch my father home, then come get you."

Nathaniel rose to his feet. "You get your father. I shall be at your house by mid-afternoon. Be away before your mother feels obliged to offer me tea."

Caleb hesitated, then nodded. "Nathaniel, one thing you should know. Zachariah's gone down to Ashland. He hired in Esther Cask to be helping in the house. The girl may be a touch slow, but she's got keen eyes for her mistress' comings and going."

"Obliged. Ain't the time to be seeing Rachel." Nathaniel slapped the other man on the shoulder. "Go. I'll be finding you."

Nathaniel followed Caleb out of the tavern and felt a cold trickle twist down his spine. He'd spent a fair amount of time in taverns, and liked the Tanner and Hound as much as any, but being packed in close with bodies never suited him overmuch. He'd rather have a blizzard smothering him than a crush of men.

Caleb headed west and Nathaniel east, toward the waterfront. He nodded greetings to people on the street. Those that knew him either smiled or refused to meet his eye. A couple of men crossed to the other side of the street. Those new to Mystria often stared at his Altashee leathers, and the longer they stared told him how recently they'd arrived.

As much as he hated being crowded and confined and could never imagine being trapped on a ship for six hours much less six weeks, ships fascinated him. As a boy, when in Temperance, he'd come watch the ships unload. The mastheads, be they maidens, dragons, or something in between, just tickled him. At his youngest he thought they might come alive. As he grew older he wished they would, to tell the tales of what they'd seen. He was willing to swap wilderness adventure for sea story, but they remained mute, just bobbing and nodding either sage or senile, he could not determine.

He told himself he would go to the waterfront just to see if the ships had gotten bigger. They had, and the largest of them, a ship in the Royal Navy, had anchored out in the harbor. He watched for a bit as sailors struggled to decorously load a young noblewoman and her courtiers onto a barge. Sea breezes caught voluminous skirts, creating all manner of problems. The sailors worked on that problem on one side, while others brought up an ornate coach in pieces. He smiled at the cursing and shouting, and wondered if the ship also contained a team of horses.

Nathaniel watched the people, reading their faces as easily as he could read tracks in mud. Many looked unhappy. Most of them appeared tired. Worst of all, though, were the ones who just didn't care. They plodded along listlessly mostly redemptioneers with long years remaining on their service reminding him of du Malphias' *pasmortes*. He couldn't see much difference between them, and doubted the people could either.

He glanced at the Government House tower clock. He'd never learned his letters, but his father had taught him ciphering and to read time. Marking time by the sun suited Nathaniel just fine; the day, after all, ended when the sun went down, not at some point on a clock. Still, Temperance ran to the clock and while he refused to be enslaved by it, he was willing to abide by it temporarily.

I could go past, just to see if she is well. He thought about it for a long while, but refused. If he went to see Rachel, he'd not want to be leaving. Esther would report his presence to her master upon his return and, more like, to her kin in his absence. That would stir up a tussle Nathaniel'd not mind having a piece of, but not now.

He smiled, easily imagining Owen Strake standing with him on one side and Kamiskwa on the other. The Casks and Branches and anyone else could come for them and they'd run home all bleedy and whipped. Owen had been a good man—*still* is—and Nathaniel's guts hollowed out when he thought of him. That surprised the Mystrian, because he didn't make friends easily and never would have thought a Norillian could be a friend. The Prince came as close as possible, and he'd been raised in Mystria most all his life.

He and Kamiskwa had been having the Norillian on at the start, but not out of being cruel the way the Branches would have. Nathaniel had been prepared to take the man as far as he wanted. Nathaniel needed to see, however, what sort of man Owen was. The wilderness wasn't a place you could drag a man who couldn't carry his own weight. It was like a deer herd keeping the strong animals together and letting the weak pass. It was the natural order.

Nathaniel shook his head. "He was about the least complaining man I ever done met." There'd been fire in him, and times he wanted to take a poke at Nathaniel, no doubting that, but he'd held himself back. And then, in the fight with the Ungarakii, he'd done just fine. Despite being wounded, he'd killed two of them, and shooting that one in the face required a steady hand and ice in the veins.

But you still left him to die.

Nathaniel bristled, playing the scene through his mind again. He would've ignored Owen, excepting when he said that the journals would save Mystria. Owen had said it to get him to leave. They both knew it. They both knew that was the only thing that would have worked. And Owen had used it.

Another glance at the clock started Nathaniel on his trek up the hill to the Frost house. He smiled out of force of habit. He'd been welcome there from time to time, up until three years ago. He still remembered Mrs. Frost's towering anger. If Guy du Malphias ever came to Temperance, he'd meet his match with her in a rage.

His long legs ate up the distance, so he found himself at the gate, waiting, as the tower clock struck three. The house door opened and Caleb bounded down to the gate. His father came out onto the porch and his mother stood in the doorway, clearly intent on barring passage.

Caleb opened the gate. "She's not having it."

"I imagine." Nathaniel walked behind him, but remained at the bottom of the steps. "Doctor, ma'am, I do recall your telling me n'er to darken your doorstep again. I apologize for violating your wishes. Wouldn't do it if it weren't powerful important."

Doctor Frost turned to his wife. "It *is* about Captain Strake, Hettie."

Resolution made her face into a marble mask. "He is not coming through my house. If you must speak to him, it shall be in the kitchen yard." She stepped back and closed the door, trapping father and son outside.

Doctor Frost pointed to the path around the house. "After you, Mr. Woods."

Caleb led the way and Nathaniel imagined he was feeling what a man on the way to the gallows might. He didn't look toward the windows, not wanting to see any faces there. He recalled the Frosts had a whole passel of children and imagined Mrs. Frost would be shooing them somewhere safe while he was on the property.

Two chairs had been put into the yard. Caleb offered him one, but Nathaniel refused. "Go on, sit. Been thinking about this on my feet. Ain't sitting going to make it no easier for me." Nathaniel added a bit of volume to his voice so it would play on through the almost-closed kitchen door.

"The long and the short of it is this: Captain Strake ain't coming back for a spell. Not sure how long. Might be he's dead, but I'm fair sure he ain't."

The door opened and Bethany Frost slipped through it. "If *he's* not here, why are *you?*"

Her accusation sank straight into his heart. "Well, Miss, I reckon that's on account of he's a brave man. Braver than me. He charged me with a duty, and made sure I did it. I give him my word to obey his orders. And I give him my word I'd be returning for him."

Doctor Frost removed his spectacles and rubbed them on the hem of his coat. "Bethany, dear, get our guest a chair. Mr. Woods, I would have the whole of the story from you. As much as you can tell."

Nathaniel accepted the chair, but waited to speak until Caleb returned with yet another chair having given his to his sister. Bethany sat at her father's right hand, clutching it. Caleb leaned forward, expectant, and she hung back, fearful.

He told them of the trip in every detail, omitting only the idea that du Malphias could raise the dead. When he talked about the fighting, he showed them his thumb and the blood beneath the nail. He didn't need to embellish Owen's role or prowess. The Frosts took pride in their guest's abilities. Doctor Frost especially liked the endorsement his family's firm had gotten in Hattersburg and offered to send a note to the Bone family to tell them of Makepeace's situation.

The telling had gone through the pealing of four and five, but they didn't notice. At the bottom of the third hour, two younger boys hauled a small table out into the yard, and Mrs. Frost appeared with a tray, teapot and cups. She poured wordlessly, then departed, though the door did not close fully after her.

Bethany looked at her father. "They cannot just leave him out there, can they? Someone has to go after him."

Doctor Frost patted her hand. "Bethany, Mr. Woods had told us the Prince will make arrangements. This is how things are done between nations. It may be slower than we like, but we must be patient."

She looked at Nathaniel. "Couldn't you go in and get him?"

"Well, Miss, it is as your father says. The Prince, he has hisself a plan."

200 — MICHAEL A. STACKPOLE

Her eyes became slits. "In all the stories of the Magehawk, I've never heard cowardice mentioned as one of his characteristics."

"Bethany Frost!" Hettie Frost appeared through the doorway. "Mr. Woods may be an unrepentant sinner and a man of dubious moral character, but this gives you no right to insult him. As much as you might not care for him, and as little as I care for him, I will not tolerate such behavior. You will apologize this instant!"

Bethany looked down. "I beg your pardon, Mr. Woods."

"Ain't no apology needed, Miss." Nathaniel rested his hands on his knees. "I ain't a coward. Ain't no man alive what's been three days deep in the wilderness that is. But I reckon it does seem like I'm acting like one. I don't like it. Fact is, the Prince, he's one smart fellow. He reckons that anyone walking on in to Anvil Lake territory is a fool who is like to get hisself killed dead. And if they go to get Captain Strake out, they'll get him killed too." *And ain't none of us want to be dead there.*

"I will, however, tell you this: Captain Strake is a strong man. Stronger than you imagine. Stronger than I suspected. I know, God as my witness, he's going to come through your front gate. Afore long you'll all be having a laugh about things. Until that time, and preparing for the war that will come, me and Kamiskwa is going to be going back to learn what can be learned. I swear to you we'll be back to tell you all everything we know."

Nathaniel settled a reassuring smile on his face. "I'm thinking you should all know he set a great store by all of you. Didn't have anything but a kind word for you all. And plenty of them. The Prince is going to have the journal copied for you. Owen was looking forward to your reading it."

Distantly came the sound of the front door's heavy knocker. One of the younger children came out the door and spoke to Mrs. Frost. She turned on her heel and re-entered the house.

Bethany looked up, her eyes wet. "What did he say, Nathaniel, when he sent you away?"

"He said it was up to me to see that you were all safe." Nathaniel nodded. "That was important to him. Worth all the risk and pain."

Her gaze focused distantly, then Bethany produced a handkerchief and dabbed at her eyes. Her father slid his arm around her.

Nathaniel stood. "Please be thanking the Missus for the tea. Hain't never had better."

"Wait, Mr. Woods."

Hettie Frost had returned, and behind her came a man dressed very fancy, complete with a powdered wig, white hose, white gloves, and luxurious moustaches. Hettie turned to her guest. "This is Mr. Woods."

"Pleased to meet you, Mr. Woods." The man's Norillian came clipped and precise, with an accent he couldn't quite place. "I am pleased to be Count Joachim von Metternin."

"I imagine you are."

"We have just arrived today. We have asked after a team of horses for our coach. At the livery, I admired your mount and was told it belonged to Prince Vladimir. They said you had come to town to deliver a message to the Frost family."

Nathaniel nodded. "Done and delivered."

"Then I should beg of you an indulgence." From inside his white and gold brocade jacket, the man produced an envelope. "This is a message to the Prince. If you would deliver it, we would be most grateful."

Nathaniel accepted the sealed packet of papers. "I'll be putting it in the Prince's hand straight away."

"Very good, thank you." Von Metternin smiled. "And please tell him that my lady awaits his reply, and is very pleased to be his wife."

CHAPTER THIRTY-FOUR

"Che is my *what?*" The Prince stared at the packet Nathaniel offered. His mouth had gone dry and he didn't want to accept the packet. "Wait, just wait."

When Nathaniel found the Prince and Kamiskwa in the Prince's laboratory, the two of them were working on the miniature model of du Malphias' fortress. Kamiskwa was cutting and carving sticks into the right length for the palisade wall while the Prince was shaping clay into an approximation of the terrain. Grey-brown mud coated his hands and streaked his apron.

The Prince looked about for a cloth upon which he could wipe his hands, and settled for the hem of his apron. "You obviously know more than you're telling."

Nathaniel couldn't hide his smile. "Well, 'pears the packet boat *Swift* limped into North Portland up Summerland. Lost the main mast in a storm. Two weeks late or so. Boys down to the docks mentioned it. I figure the wedding notice must be on it."

"You're probably right." The Prince rubbed his forehead and realized too late he'd smeared clay on it. "Blast and damn. It's one thing to tell me I'm to be married, but to only send notice bare weeks before the woman sets sail?"

He looked at his hands and then wiped them on his pants. "Please, the missive."

Nathaniel handed it over and the Prince broke the seal. Inside he found three smaller packets, each similarly sealed. He opened the one from the Home Minister, Duke Marbury. It had been folded in thirds and thirds again, but imprecisely a mark of the slovenly attention to detail which described Marbury.

Vlad scanned it quickly. He groaned and tossed the other two onto his desk, hoping they would be disappear. "This is not good."

"I would never pry, Highness."

Vlad laughed. "Typical Marbury. 'If it pleases you, Highness...' Of course it does not please me, but I haven't anything of a choice in the matter. My aunt, in her wisdom, has decided that having the Kingdom of Kesse-Saxeburg join an alliance focused on Tharyngia is to her benefit. Granting that Kessians are the most martial of the Teutonic nations this might not be a bad idea, but she's determined to solidify this alliance by marrying me off to Princess Gisella. The child is half my age, doubtlessly has been schooled in needlepoint and blushing on cue, and has been raised in a world filled with creature comforts the like of which have never reached these shores."

Nathaniel cracked a sunflower seed and fed the meat to the Prince's caged raven. "Well, you could marry her to Kamiskwa here, and then take his sister as your wife. Your aunt would be getting two alliances instead of just one."

"Msitazi would demand Mugwump as a brideprice, so that would not work." He looked at the note again, then frowned. "Did you see her?"

"Not exactly, Highness. She was being loaded on a barge…"

"A barge!"

"Weren't like they was using a crane to unload her." Nathaniel smiled. "Never did get a clean look at her. Her carriage is a grand thing. Gold and white, like the man what delivered the note."

"What was he like?"

"Dressed fancy. Needed a barge just for his mustachios. Count Joachim von Metternin said his name was. Polite as can be." Nathaniel smiled. "Gave me a pound to deliver the message."

Vlad's eyes narrowed. He tapped a finger against his teeth, then tasted clay. "Von Metternin. The name is familiar."

"He was hoping for a return message fast."

"I'll have one in the morning. I'll send Baker. I need you here to help with the model." Vlad raked fingers back through his hair, streaking it. "My aunt seeks to save her empire by this marriage, but she distracts me from the real work that will preserve it."

Kamiskwa whittled a point on a stick. "This princess could bear you strong sons."

The Prince opened his arms wide. "I do not need children here. I am a man of science. Yes, the Tharyngian revolution has made that a most malevolent prospect, but their perversion of the process does not invalidate it. My studies have advanced our understanding of the world. I have identified plants with medicinal properties. I have found a strain of potato that grows larger than others and resists rot. I am learning things every day about wurms. I don't need a distraction."

Kamiskwa nodded, sliding his obsidian knife into its sheath. "Many a warrior has said the same. My father points out where they are wrong. They want to make the world safe. You want to make the world better. For whom? You try hard now. When it is for your child, you will try harder."

Vlad blinked.

Nathaniel smiled. "Annoying, ain't he, Highness?"

"Very." The Prince shook his head. "And, alas, he may be correct. I do not like this turn of events, but since I can do nothing to avert it, I shall have to hope for the best possible outcome."

The Prince, in order to better formulate his reply, opened the note from Count von Metternin. It had been folded with great precision. The script came in a strong hand and the lines ran straight across the page. Vlad used a square to confirm this. The Count had the pleasure of introducing the Princess, a relation of distant sanguinity, whom he had the pleasure of knowing for many years. The note went on to praise her in glowing but less than hyperbolic terms. Vlad felt this grew out of genuine affection for the girl instead of an attempt to cover up flaws.

Vlad turned to his library to track down why the name von Metternin seemed familiar. The family had been ennobled for many generations, the progenitor of which had performed a great service to the Holy Remian Emperor centuries past. It was in Rivendell's Villerupt, however, where Vlad found a direct reference to Joachim von Metternin. The Kessian had been an observer with Tharyngian forces and, on the fourth day, had assumed command of a battalion to which he had been attached. Their officer corps had been devastated, but he organized the battalion and put up stiff resistance. They fought their way free of the town of Planchain and a potential Norillian encirclement led by John Rivendell. Rivendell's book had nothing good to say of the man, which caused Vlad no end of comfort.

Vlad composed a cordial but formal reply, inviting the Count alone to visit him and spend the next night. He folded and sealed it, intending to dispatch Baker with it in the morning.

He stared at the missive the Princess had written, as yet unopened. He really didn't want to read it. It had been addressed in a very delicate but orderly hand, but he did not know if it belonged to her or one of her handmaidens. And the words inside might not have been hers, but those crafted by ministers and the aforementioned handmaidens, designed to obligate and ensnare him.

He told himself he wasn't going to read it because he wanted to be fair to the girl even though he knew this was not true. It was not that he wanted to be unfair to her either, but he was being given no choice in the matter. Neither was she, of course. The less he got to know her before meeting her, the less time he'd have to dislike her. Since they were going to spend the rest of their lives together, there would be ample time for that.

The Prince slept relatively well, though his miniature model filled his dreams.

He awoke and returned to the laboratory to find Kamiskwa and Nathaniel already there making piles of model palisade posts. They spent the morning and early afternoon planting, scraping, shaping, and reshaping the landscape until they'd created a match for the fortress that satisfied both witnesses and conformed to the maps.

So engrossed in their work were they that it came as a complete surprise when Baker appeared at the laboratory door and announced the arrival of Count von Metternin. The Kessian wore a light blue uniform, white breeches, buff facings and waistcoat, gold epaulets, and black cavalry boots. A jaunty cavalier's hat with a feather and a gold cockade holding the left part of the brim up against the crown completed his outfit. The cockade and epaulets had been fitted with a small, black metal lizard, marking the man as a Wurmrider.

The Count took one step into the laboratory and bowed deeply. "Prince Vladimir, it is the greatest of pleasures to meet you and on behalf of Princess Gisella…"

Vlad held up both clay-caked hands. "Count von Metternin, please, stop. Two things I require of you. The first is to realize that here, in Mystria, formality is appreciated, but sincerity is valued above form. This is a land that can be beautiful and harsh. We take it and people as presented."

The Count straightened, then nodded. "As you desire, Highness."

"And second, do not speak to me of the Princess unless I ask for word of her." Vlad opened his arms and looked around the laboratory. "I asked you here to see me as I am, so there will be no illusions. You will see me as my aunt and her ministers never have. Once you get to know me, then you will be better able to tell me of the Princess. Does that sound like a good idea?"

"It does, Highness, thank you." The man removed his hat and set it atop the raven's cage. "To be entirely truthful, Highness, the duty of transporting and presenting my cousin has been the most difficult I have ever been given. It has nothing to do with the girl, but bureaucracies and manners are not my forte."

"This, then, we have in common. May I present Prince Kamiskwa of the Altashee and Nathaniel Woods. They have obtained many of the specimens you see herein."

"Mr. Woods, a pleasure to see you again. Prince Kamiskwa, I am honored."

Kamiskwa bowed after the Shedashee fashion and Nathaniel sketched a friendly salute that daubed his forehead with gray.

The Count approached the model. "This is fascinating. Something you are planning to build?"

"No, it is under construction by the Tharyngians to the northwest of here, near the headwaters of the Tillie River."

The Kessian circled it, peering closely at some points, squatting to judge angles at others. "Quite formidable. The creator fears no assault from the lake side. On land, the only approachable route would be from the north. Once inside the fortress, any invading force would be slaughtered—provided the commander was not an idiot."

Vlad nodded. "It's being built by Guy du Malphias."

Von Metternin visibly shuddered. "He is an evil man. I met him, briefly, once. He offered me a place on his staff. I refused. He tried to have me killed, along with a battalion of the Fluor Regiment at Planchain. His Platine Regiment was supposed to support our flank, but he withdrew his forces in the night. I barely escaped with my life."

"Brilliantly, if Rivendell's account is at all accurate."

The Count smiled. "In few things was that book accurate. But if a man may be measured by the scorn of others, I am pleased he hates me so."

Vlad smiled. "We have just finished our model. We will send more scouts to see how it changes."

The Count's blue eyes narrowed. "If it is your intent to do harm to this place or its master, it would do me great pleasure to be of service in any way possible."

"I think," Vlad said as he untied his apron and slipped it off, "we should be most happy to accommodate your desire."

The Count waited patiently on the lawn as the other three men stripped to the flesh and washed themselves off in the river. They chatted about nonsensical things as the sun dried them off, then pulled their clothes back on and moved back up onto the lawn. The servants had set out a blanket and a meal of bread, cheese, tomatoes, and maize relish. They added a red wine, which the Count praised as "refreshing"—a polite way of saying it was far too young to be in a bottle and that it could not compare to Continental wines.

Vlad found himself inclined to like the Kessian and think better of him than his initial appearance had suggested. After lunch they returned to the model and studied it for an hour. Von Metternin offered insights about vulnerable points, couching them in realistic assessments of the necessary troop dispositions to affect a siege. His estimate amounted to more troops than the Crown had in all of Mystria, which cast the idea of ever being rid of du Malphias into doubt.

After that the Prince had taken him to see Mugwump. The Count marveled at the colors and lack of stench. The wurm splashed him and he did not react with the good graces Owen had exhibited. He'd stiffly retreated from the wurmrest, pulled off his boots, then marched into the river fully clothed and ridded himself of as much filth as he could.

Vlad watched him clean up, studying his sour expression. The man is vain, though fights to control it. This was good to know. There would be a point where vanity would trump sensibility and that would be a problem. That von Metternin chafed under non-military command spoke to that same vanity, but his willingness to follow orders nonetheless underscored the man's sense of loyalty.

Dinner—a ham from the cellar, applesauce, peas, and maize boiled on the cob—devolved, as it always will when shared by men only, into a symphony of serious discussions, grand stories, and laughter. The Count had never eaten maize from the cob before, and his luxurious moustaches did not aid him in this undertaking. The others laughed and he accepted it, though not so well.

As wine flowed and sherry followed, the Count offered his own version of war on the Continent. He stripped it of any sense of glory, reducing it to ground made muddy with blood, where what appeared to be white pebbles were fragments of bone, and where packs of wild dogs fought over the entrails of men who still lived. "I did not know if I should shoot the dog or the man."

"Not a choice I should want to have to make." Vlad held up his sherry glass. "To those who will have to choose. May God ease their decision and straighten their aim."

CHAPTER THIRTY-FIVE

August 21, 1763
Anvil Lake, New Tharyngia

I n the week since he'd first seen sunshine again, Owen had come to relish his daily outdoor sojourns. Quarante-neuf still hovered, but the *pasmorte* appeared confident in Owen's ability to navigate. Owen made certain not to stray off the gravel-covered paths, reducing his quiet companion's anxiety—*if* facial expression was any indication.

Owen had abandoned one crutch and bore weight on his right leg. It still hurt a bit. An ointment made of *mogiqua* and bear fat did nothing to help relieve the pain, though the act of massaging it in did help. Du Malphias offered a preparation of willow bark, noting that Owen's pain had not reached the level needed to be ameliorated by morphine.

His left leg healed more slowly. When out for his walks, Owen let it appear far stiffer than it truly was. In his cell, using the crutch more like a cane, he forced himself to walk daily, making more circuits around the room during each exercise period. He couldn't run—he could barely walk, and *totter* best described his gait—but he could move. Each day he got stronger.

Before long I can escape.

A breeze teased flame-colored leaves on distant trees. Summer was surrendering to autumn. The nights had been getting colder—cold enough that he'd been given two thin blankets. He'd offered one to Quarante-neuf, but his captor refused it. "Cold does not bother me."

Owen's gaze swept over the camp. Apparently satisfied with the basic construction, du Malphias had charged his army of *pasmortes* with engineering the landscape south of the river. They cleared the ground for five hundred yards back, increasing the potential flood zone. The collected stones had then been used to build several fences and—though of completely new construction—what appeared to be an abandoned farmhouse which had fallen into disrepair. The ground had been sown with grass seeds, some of which had already sprouted. Come spring it would look as if the Tharyngian forces had driven a farmer out, leaving his fields and fences to offer some cover for troops advancing on the southern fortress.

Owen studied the new construction because he knew du Malphias wanted him to. The new building, despite appearing to have been there for a long time, hadn't been included in Owen's original survey. No Norillian commander would pay it any attention and would recognize the killing field for exactly what it was: a trap.

That is *what they must see, isn't it?*

Owen shook his head. "But they never did on the Continent."

Quarante-neuf stepped forward. "Did you require something?"

"No, just made a comment." He pointed toward the new construction. "When you look out there, what do you see?"

"What is it you wish me to see?"

"I don't know." Owen frowned. "I see nine hundred men in red coats dying over there."

The *pasmorte* nodded slowly. "Blood, much blood." His voice grew uncharacteristically distant. "Thunder and metal."

Owen glanced at him. Quarante-neuf's face had flushed, but his expression had become one of profound sadness. "Are you well?"

The *pasmorte* blinked. "I am fine." He reached up and brushed away a tear, then looked at the wet stain on his finger as if it were something he had never seen before. "Are you fatigued? Shall I fetch you a blanket?"

The questions came more urgently than ever before, so Owen nodded. "A blanket, yes."

Quarante-neuf departed, and Owen returned to the real reason he enjoyed his time in the sun. Stumbling around as if looking for a place to sit, Owen studied the construction to the north. His only chance to escape lay in getting into the woods and locating one of the cached canoes. He could never outrun pursuit, but on the water his legs wouldn't make much difference.

He watched men and *pasmortes* walk by and compared their stride against the shadow of a flagpole he had previously measured. Counting their paces he obtained an accurate measurement of distances within the fortress. He committed those distances to memory and double-checked them as best he could. When he got out, he could supplement his maps. He would use that information and other things he had learned to make his escape and come back to crack the fortress.

Quarante-neuf returned with the blanket and settled it around Owen's shoulders. "Thank you, sir."

"Do not address him as 'sir,' Captain." Du Malphias emerged from the dungeon opening, eyes venomous. "A disobedient servant does not deserve praise."

"I had asked him to get me a blanket."

"And I had tasked him with keeping you always in his sight. He does not seem to realize, as I do, that you are a very dangerous man."

Owen laughed. "A cripple, dangerous?"

"Your legs are broken, not your mind." The Tharyngian snapped a telescope open. "Would you like a closer look at anything to refine your calculations?"

"I have no idea…"

"Captain Strake, do not insult my intelligence. If you were stupid, you would not have been given the job of finding me. You are a spy, yes, but perhaps also an assassin. I should fashion for you gauntlets. An iron mask, perhaps? How much magick can you use, Captain?"

Owen held up his shackled wrists. "Now, none. Without, read my nails if you wish an answer."

"You could read mine, monsieur, and learn nothing of my skill or power."

"But…"

Du Malphias laughed. "Smart, yet unworldly. What do you truly know of magick?"

"Few can do it, fewer can do it well. Blood is exacted for using magick. It is God's Gift, to be used in his service."

Du Malphias held up unblemished hands. "Enough. What you understand of magick is what a dog understands of thunder. It is enough to make you hide under a bed. You are a child, because your masters wish for you to be a child."

"And you know better?"

"Oh, I do. You were taught that magick was outlawed by the Remian Empire. This is the reason they exterminated Norisle's Druids. Did you know that the Remians believed your Savior to be a magician? Consider the stories of his miracles. Are they not the tales of the greatest magick the world has ever seen? And were not his disciples who displayed similar gifts also martyred?"

"Yes, but…"

The Laureate waggled a finger. "No objections. You would protest that to call your Lord a magician is to slander him, but consider two things. First, who is it who has told you, down through the ages, that to be a magician is bad, only to have them reverse that course when they realized they needed magicians to fill their armies and fire their cannon and guns? And, second, how is it that the Remian Emperors, who sought and wielded power with skill or abandon, would destroy magicians when, as their history proved, they were more willing to absorb conquered people and use them as part of their Legions?"

"You are trying to suggest that the crowned heads and the Church itself have suppressed magick while secretly hoarding it?"

"No suggestion, monsieur." Du Malphias shook his head. "Do you not find it curious that, with the advent of cannon and gun, all these noble houses were able, in a single generation, to suddenly manifest an ability to work magick? Let us assume you are a five. You would be powerful. Most troops in the ranks are twos, perhaps threes. Two volleys, then it is 'fix bayonets,' yes? And yet these nobles, they are, a six or a seven? Perhaps much more."

Owen shook his head. "That requires a conspiracy of silence lasting centuries. Someone would have confessed."

"Yes, but the Church, you must remember, found it very convenient to draw clergymen from the ranks of the nobility. A religion of magicians who control the common people. They direct witch hunts to destroy the powerful and disruptive. An upstart noble is declared a heretic or diabolist; is shunned, disbelieved, and killed. They have a perfect system using hatred and fear to enforce their rule. They would have maintained it forever, save for two things."

The Laureate clasped his hands behind his back. "The need for soldiers meant that they had to mitigate the sinfulness of magick. This gave people pride in their abilities. This is why, when we overthrew king and church, we had the mass support. Science had succeeded where a mad king had not. We made magick a science. No shame, only truth. And, in case you doubt me, let me assure you that hidden in the archives in Feris are ample documents—correspondence, confessions, and more—that verify this conspiracy. Had King Anselm not gone completely mad and broken with the Church, their united front would have concealed the conspiracy for good. In fact, there are those Laureates who believe we need to perpetuate it, saying the people of the world are not yet ready to understand."

"Hence your exile?"

"One reason among many, and all inconsequential." Du Malphias smiled quickly. "The second point is that every Old World power saw fit to ship their malcontents here. What they failed to consider was that many of them—perhaps even a majority—were able to work magicks. Being of the underclasses, or uneducated, they still lived in fear of witch hunts. And, quite by accident, Mystria has become a place where mages have bred with mages. You have seen what this does for the natives."

Owen nodded slowly. "Many of the redemptioneers were cursed."

"Now they are Auropa's bane. The governments so fear that the secrets of magick will be shared with common people, they dare not let anyone with knowledge of advanced magick come here. Still, there are other conspiracies that see the value in sharing the secrets. I do not know if they will be enough to counter the forces which wish to continue the people's suppression."

"You were allowed to come."

"They could not stop me from coming. It is a difference, a significant difference."

Echoes of Nathaniel's words thundered in Owen's head. He scrubbed his hands over his face. "You will forgive me, monsieur, but this makes my head hurt. I should rest."

Du Malphias nodded. "Of course, but I would have you indulge me for just a moment longer, please."

"Yes?"

"A different subject." The Laureate opened his arms. "You have studied my fortress. You are an intelligent man. How will your armies take it?"

Owen jerked a thumb to his right. "They will come from the north. That is the clearest line of attack. This is the way they will take this fortress of death."

"*La Fortresse du Morte.* Clever, but overwrought. Only an idiot would use it. I do appreciate, however, that you mean title in two ways." Du Malphias chuckled politely. "From the north, yes, rather obviously. I do plan additional construction. We will counter-tunnel, of course. But the north wall is not the weakest spot of my fortress, is it?"

"No. It's the high fort overlooking the lake. If we build a ship, load cannon on it, and float it out there, it can blast that wall into splinters. A concerted push by attacking troops—and suddenly we have the high ground. It will still be bloody, but this fort can be taken."

"Very good, monsieur. I do not disagree with your assessment." Du Malphias shrugged. "I also believe you have not been wholly forthcoming."

"I assure you…"

"Yes, yes, you will give me your word as an officer. Need we play this game again?"

Owen shook his head, hair rising on his arms. In an instant, he took a step forward, then swung his crutch at du Malphias.

The Laureate's eyes shrank to bare slits. His left hand came up, blocking the crutch with a puff of mist. His right hand thrust forward, palm out. A flash, some heat, more mist. Owen couldn't breathe. He flew back past Quarante-neuf, sprawling in the dirt. His breastbone throbbed.

"Fetch him to his cell. Strap him down."

"As you desire, monsieur."

Owen rubbed his chest. It ached. Something had cracked. He coughed, igniting more pain, then struggled ineffectually against Quarante-neuf's grasp.

Du Malphias shook his head. "Yes, I shall be extracting information from you, Captain Strake. But you did not listen to me. You expected torture. You shall have it. You have earned it. I shall enjoy it. But, know this: I have other means that would have proved just as effective, and would have saved you great pain."

Owen nodded, believing.

After all, in blocking the crutch and knocking Owen down, du Malphias had never actually touched him or the stick. Whatever he had done, it involved magick Owen had never seen before and had no immediate interest in ever seeing again.

CHAPTER THIRTY-SIX

August 24, 1763
Tanner and Hound, Temperance
Temperance Bay, Mystria

"I do declare, Caleb, you spend more time here than might be advisable." Nathaniel Woods pulled a chair back from Caleb's table. Nathaniel sniffed the man's bowl of stew. "Cain't be the food here is good."

"The summer ale's getting sour, and the raspberry-wheat beer isn't ready yet." Caleb closed a book. Not being able to read, Nathaniel had no idea what it was, but it bore a strong resemblance to the book he'd seen Owen carrying. "I'd go home but my mother is still upset about your visit the other day."

"Well, I reckon I'd apologize but I'm thinking that won't help much."

Caleb shook his head. "She's not upset with you—not that she's forgiven you, nor is she likely to. It's Beth. She took the news about Captain Strake hard."

Nathaniel recalled the tears and the quavering quality of her voice. "Your sister, she's a smart woman. Strong, too. Got steel in her spine, like your ma. Owen set a store by her."

"I know." Caleb took a spoonful of the stew, looked at it, then let it subside into the slowly congealing mass. "I was short with Captain Strake, you see. My mother and sister are afraid that he's thinking my attitude is their attitude. Makes things uncomfortable."

"I think you'd be finding that Owen didn't take no dislike to you. He weren't the kind of man to get a hate on all easy like."

"I know, still." Caleb sighed. "You and Kamiskwa are going to look for him. I want to go."

The woodsman sat back. "You might want to be taking a second to think on that."

"I've thought long and hard about it. I shoot good and have my own musket. I know the woods and I'm strong."

Nathaniel nodded. "You're still a mite young."

"Older than you were when you first went out."

Nathaniel raised his hands. "No disputing that. And I ain't saying you couldn't do it. What I am saying is that you don't know what you're taking on."

Caleb frowned. "You made it pretty plain."

"Nope." Nathaniel stood, waved Caleb toward the door. The young man followed. Outside, Nathaniel pointed to the sky. "What do you see there?"

Caleb rolled his eyes. "Geese, down from New Tharyngia heading south. I can also spot moose, tanner, bears, jeopards, and rabbits. I'll hit if I shoot, too."

Nathaniel sighed. "And the calendar date today?"

"Feast day of St. Bartholomew, the twenty-fourth of August."

"And that tells you?"

Caleb stared at him. "What do you mean?"

"Winter's coming. Early and bad." Nathaniel pointed west. "More bear sign and jeopard sign—they're coming out of the mountains early. Look at any of the dogs around about. Winter coats coming in. Smart young man like you ought to round up some friends, go chop a store of firewood. I'm thinking it'll sell dear inside a six weeks."

"I can dress warmly."

"It ain't I doubt you, Caleb Frost. I'd be happy to have you with me. Kamiskwa feels the same way. Fact is, though, the Prince gets his say on this."

"You'll mention me to him?"

"I will that." Nathaniel slapped him on the back. "Now, I was wanting to ask you a favor…"

"Get away from him, Caleb, he's a traitor."

Nathaniel turned slowly toward the sound of the voice. "You're looking a mite thinner, I reckon, than when I seen you last."

Cotton Quince spat at his feet. "You betrayed me."

"That so?" Nathaniel watched the slender man's hands curl into fists. "I reckon you don't got no idea what you is jabbering about."

Caleb moved between the two of them. "I'd suggest, gentlemen, that the street is not the place for this discussion."

"Ain't no cause for no discussion at all." Nathaniel nodded toward Quince, lowering his voice. "This here boy was off to Hattersburg adding words to that book your father gave Captain Strake. He called your father's honor into question. Owen took exception. Makepeace Bone likewise. That about did for Mr. Quince in Hattersburg."

"That did for me *everywhere*. I was made a laughingstock."

Caleb's eyes tightened. "You called my father's honor into question?"

Quince glanced at the ground. "I didn't realize who had given Strake that book."

"Ask him if he was adding things to it."

"Well?"

Quince shifted his shoulders. "I'd made a remark in a couple other places. People liked it." He stabbed a finger at Nathaniel. "But he should have stopped his friends. And would have, but he is working for the Queen's coin. He isn't one of us."

"No, I ain't." Nathaniel shook his head, looking from one young man to the other. "I hain't got no idea what you are up to, beyond being pure idiots. Ideas like you have are fine for your debating societies, but only mean trouble out on the frontier. People out there ain't got no time for that nonsense."

"It's not nonsense."

"It is, Caleb, iffen your circumstances is poor." Nathaniel opened his arms. "I just tole you that winter is a-coming fast and will be bad. Early winter means poor harvest. Livestock won't have fodder. They die. Men have to eat seed. Ain't going to be good hunting. Them folks out there ain't gonna be caring if some woman an ocean away gives a fig about them. They'll be hungry and cold, and filling their minds with airy thoughts ain't going to solve their problems."

Quince snorted. "You'll be fed and warm on the Queen's coin."

"I reckon that what I choose to do with my money is my choice." Nathaniel folded his arms over his chest. "And I reckon you should leave me out of your scheming."

Quince looked from Nathaniel to Caleb and back, then shook his head. "Very well. Caleb, good day. As for you, Mr. Woods, rot in Hell."

Quince stormed off.

Caleb turned to Nathaniel. "Why did you lie about being one of us?"

Nathaniel looked him straight in the eye. "I ain't. Curiosity done got the better of me. I attended a meeting. Two. But that don't mean I throwed-in with your 'Sons of Freedom.' And there ain't no cause for someone like Quince to be even knowing I was ever there."

Caleb held his hands up. "I never told him. I barely know him to speak to. Seen him at meetings is all."

"I'm thinking I believe you on that." Nathaniel smiled. "As for Quince, I reckon he needs beating with a smart-stick. I don't reckon nobody makes one big enough."

Caleb grinned. "I'll let the right people know he has been editing *A Continent's Calling.*"

"It *was* a pretty turn of phrase he used." Nathaniel nodded. "Might be he ought to be writing more than speaking."

The younger Frost nodded. "I'll mention that. Now you said you had a question for me? Back inside? I'll buy you a drink."

Nathaniel braced him on both shoulders. "Another time. Weren't terrible important."

"You'll ask the Prince about my going with you?"

"I shall. Tomorrow, maybe day after."

Caleb smiled. "You're back in town to escort the Princess to meet the Prince?"

"Could be." Nathaniel smiled. "My regards to your family, please."

"My pleasure."

The young man headed back into the Tanner and Hound. Nathaniel watched him go, then shivered. He'd wanted to ask if Zachariah Warren was still out of town, but now he was kind of hoping that he wasn't. A dust-up would suit Nathaniel just fine. If Warren wasn't in town, a Branch or a Cask might have to stand in.

He headed across Temperance toward the North End. On Generosity, where it curved toward the ocean, he came to Warren's Fine Wares. Wider and deeper than it was tall, the wooden building rose to three stories. The top two had rooms for rent and the taverns across the street did a lot of custom for the residents. The entire bottom floor consisted of an open room in which the various real goods had been arranged. Furniture mostly, with bolts of cloth, silver, and dinnerware in the back, it displayed the very best imported items from Norisle. Wide doors in the back allowed carts to load easily.

Nathaniel watched from across the street for a minute or three. He debated going in. Wasn't any reason he couldn't. Warren had never publicly told him to stay out. Wouldn't have really mattered if he had—at least Nathaniel didn't care about Zachariah's feelings on the matter.

Rachel's, on the other hand, mattered more than anything.

He raked fingers back through his hair and put a smile on his face before wandering across the street. He opened the door and a tiny bell jingled. Two people, a man and a woman, looked over. *New off a boat.* They studied him with surprise and interest, but they never glanced toward Rachel.

Locals would have.

She was engrossed in making an entry in a ledger book at the back counter. Nathaniel loved seeing her that way, concentrating. She wore her dark hair gathered into a bun, but wisps escaped at her temples. Full lips slightly parted, the pink tip of her tongue at the corner of her mouth, delicate fingers tracing along a page to the left. She wrote on the right page with a fluid and efficient motion as beautiful as a deer gliding through the woods.

Then she looked up, her hazel gaze meeting his eyes. She smiled brilliantly for a heartbeat, then caught herself. Her smile shrank. She set her pen back in the inkwell. She tugged at her grey dress, then came from behind the counter. "It is so very good to see you, Mr. Woods. Have you come for more trade scraps?"

"I have." He nodded to the couple admiring a silver service and crossed to the back corner near the rack with bolts of cloth. Next to it sat a box with scraps—too small for quilting in most cases, or oddly shaped and unsuited for much of anything.

"The box is almost full." Rachel smiled at him. "How much will you need?"

He smiled, his heart pounding faster. "I reckon I'd gladly take it all. I have gold." He fished in a pouch and pulled out three gold pounds, holding them above her outstretched palm. "This be enough?"

She nodded and caught the coins.

Oh, how he wanted to place each one in her hand, just to let his fingers brush her palm. He knew her flesh well, both as she had caressed him, and he had caressed her. He felt clumsy at times, for she was so small and soft, and he rangy, his hands calloused, his thumbnail usually rough and darkened beneath with blood.

She closed her hand, letting a fingertip touch his thumb. Just a tiny touch. No one watching could suggest impropriety or intimacy, no matter how strongly they suspected. And yet, for him, it was rain in a drought.

He nodded. "I don't reckon I can be taking it right now. Is there a better time?"

"This evening, if you wish. I shall bundle it up for you."

"Thank you most kindly."

The door's bell jingled again. "You can be leaving now, Woods."

Nathaniel turned. "Rufus, you're a-looking more vertical than the last time I seen you. Your brothers, on the other hand, is looking twice as stupid."

"Nathaniel…" Rachel laid a hand on his elbow.

"Don't you be worrying, ma'am. Ain't nothing going to happen in your store. That right, boys?"

Rufus nodded solemnly. "That's right."

Nathaniel turned back to Rachel. "It will be fine."

"I don't want you hurt, Nathaniel."

"I don't reckon I will be. Got to be coming back for them scraps." He nodded. "Good day to you, ma'am."

The door's bell jingled again and a man came in, pushing past Rufus. The larger man took offense, and grabbed the smaller man by the shoulder. The smaller man spun, a dagger appearing in his hand, the point drawing a single droplet of blood from Rufus' throat.

"Mister Woods, if you would do me the honor of an introduction to your friends. I like to know the names of men I will kill."

Nathaniel smiled. "Count Joachim von Metternin, that there is Rufus Branch."

"And the other two?"

"You don't need to be knowing their names. I'll do the killing on them."

"I think I shall come to appreciate the egalitarian notions of Mystria." The Count smiled over his shoulder at Rachel. "And you would be Mrs. Warren, the owner of this shop?"

Rachel curtsied. "How may I help you?"

Von Metternin grabbed a handful of Rufus' tunic and tugged him around so he could face Rachel without moving his dagger. "My mistress, the Princess Gisella, has heard of this thing called a 'picnic.' She is desirous of hosting one. So she will need a dinner service for twelve, table, chairs, all the necessaries for this. And if you know a kitchen which can prepare the correct foods, I should be thankful."

He glanced up at Rufus. "And you, my fine friend, shall I be killing you, or finding a use for your brawn? I shall need these goods carted to the place and taken away again. A crown per man for a day's service."

Rufus nodded while his brothers rubbed their hands together.

"Good. The bargain holds as long as I do not see you again until the appointed day and time. Otherwise, I shall have to kill you. Do you understand?"

"Yes, sir." Rufus gave Nathaniel a glare, then departed with his brothers.

"I reckon I owe you thanks, Count Joachim."

The Kessian shrugged, slipped the dagger back into the sheath on his forearm. "I have a service to request of you, too. And you, Mrs. Warren."

"Yes, Count Joachim?"

"This evening, the both of you shall attend dinner with my mistress and me. For the sake of propriety, our dinners must be chaperoned and I, quite frankly, have tolerated all the boring people I can abide. This evening it would have been Bishop Bumble and his family, save that his gout is acting up. If you should be so kind."

"A pleasure, sir." Rachel smiled.

"I shall send a carriage for you. No fancy dress. My mistress would get to know Mystria's people for who they are, not who they pretend to be." He clapped his hands. "This is wonderful. She shall be very happy. And then, tomorrow, Mr. Woods, you shall lead her to meet her husband, and all shall be well."

CHAPTER THIRTY-SEVEN

August 25, 1763
Prince Haven
Temperance Bay, Mystria

Prince Vlad waved as Nathaniel rode up to the estate. He and Kamiskwa had just finished supervising Mugwump's feeding. The Altashee had remained down by the river, tickling fish out, while the Prince had changed in anticipation of the Princess' arrival. He wore a blue velvet jacket with gold trim over a fresh white shirt, pants to match jacket, white hose, and black shoes with gold buckles.

"How far back of you are they?"

"Well, 'bout an hour. Maybe more. I set out before they had fully commenced coming." Nathaniel dismounted, flipped open a saddlebag, and handed the Prince a note sealed by Count von Metternin. "He said this would explain it all, and that you ain't got no worries."

The Prince accepted the note. "Will you tell me of her?"

Nathaniel smiled. "I was swore not to, and *I* keep my word on things confidential."

"Meaning?"

"Meaning I reckon we're going to have us a conversation." Nathaniel turned the horse over to a stablehand, having shucked his sheathed rifle from the saddle-scabbard. "The Princess said you was to wait for her in your laboratory. She respected what the Count tole her about you. That's where she's fixing on meeting you."

Interesting. Though the Count had not seemed horribly fixated on protocol, Vlad had assumed Princess Gisella would be. She'd certainly been schooled in it. She was being sent to him as an instrument of diplomacy, so all that truly mattered was that conventions be observed. *If she is not concerned with them, what* does *concern her?*

"And you will share no observations with me?"

"Nope. I do as I is told."

"I would be more inclined to believe you if you were not clearly so pleased with the situation."

Nathaniel grinned. "I might be taking some satisfaction in it."

"And on this matter you and I need to discuss?"

The woodsman frowned. "'Pears the Count got some notions in his head about Rachel and me. More than gossip notions."

"That would be because I told him about you after he asked."

Nathaniel's rifle rested easily in folded arms. "I'll grant you got spine to just up and say it that way. Said anything else, I'd a-thumped you."

The Prince opened his hands. "Nathaniel, you told me of your situation in confidence, and I do respect that."

"But you thought sharing it with the Count was just fine and dandy?" Anger gathered on Nathaniel's face.

Vlad did not back down. "I employ you as my agent. I am responsible for you. I am responsible for your actions. What you told me was told in confidence, because you trusted me. You trusted me not to hurt you, and I have not. The Count has his duties, and they require him to trust you, too. He could only do that if I disclosed things that would counteract any gossip he heard about you."

Nathaniel shook his head. "How do you know you can trust him?"

"Does he seem like the sort of man to gossip about another man's affairs?"

"Hain't seen nothing to suggest he is, but he could be fooling you and me."

"He could, but he knows the worth of a man. And he knows two things about you. One, I value you as the best woodsman in Mystria. Second, he knows that if social opprobrium was something you cared about, you would never go near Temperance again."

"You still oughtened to have said nothing."

Vlad blinked. "Do you think he could not have learned everything?"

"Not the truth of it."

"But close enough that he, being clever, could have figured it out." Vlad started ticking points off on his fingers. "Rachel Warren has two children. A son, six, Humble Warren, who looks nothing like his father and a daughter, three, Charity, who, poor thing, looks too much like her father. Her husband has hired people to watch you and watch his wife. He cannot prove anything, but there's scant few people in Temperance who aren't certain what is happening."

Nathaniel ran a hand over his mouth. "I reckon what you say is true and all, but you oughtened not to have said nothing."

"I am sorry I broke your confidence, Nathaniel. I would not have done so if matters of very great import did not hinge on it." The Prince squeezed the other man's shoulder. "One thing you may not understand is that most people who hear the stories don't think badly of you. They know what happened. If Zachariah Warren was shot dead in the middle of Sunday services, half the congregation would claim not to have seen anything, and the rest wouldn't agree on what had happened."

Nathaniel shook his head. "I wouldn't never murder him."

"I know." The Prince nodded solemnly. He believed Nathaniel, and even believed that Nathaniel believed his words, but then Nathaniel didn't know of the Prince's other violation of trust. Four years earlier, when Nathaniel and Kamiskwa had been out on a hunting expedition, word had come that Zachariah Warren, in a drunken rage, had beaten his wife and exerted his marital rights. Vlad had bought the silence of the two female servants in the Warren house and had sent them to his mother's plantation in Fairlee.

He also summoned Zachariah Warren to Government House and explained very carefully how, if he ever hit his wife again, his business would burn to the ground. The Prince informed him that no bank in Norisle would ever again grant him any sort of credit, and the Prince would see to it that he was driven into utter ruin. Vlad had assured him that the only way he would be able to care for his family was to kill himself so they could be awarded a private pension for widows and orphans.

Warren had blustered, claiming he had every right to use his wife as he desired. The Prince had countered that he would use his office to do to Warren whatever the merchant did to his wife. "Which do you wish to be happier, Mr. Warren—yourself or the Crown?"

After some deliberation, Warren saw the wisdom of Vlad's counsel.

Had Nathaniel ever learned what Warren had done, there would have been no stopping him from murder. The Prince valued the man too much to allow that to happen. *If he ever learns I knew…* It was a calculated risk keeping that secret from Nathaniel; but one the Prince had no choice but to make.

The Prince smiled. "I sometimes place too much importance on these affairs of state. Were I in Launston, I would be more used to them. And, truth be told, learning I am to wed is a bit confusing."

Nathaniel nodded, his anger apparently abated. "Packet boat got in with the tide. Had a letter from your father. The Princess asked to be allowed to bring it to you. Didn't figure it would hurt none."

"That's fine." Vlad smiled. It would doubtless be a letter of wise advice, urging calm, deliberation, and prayer. *Always prayer*. "Any other news?"

"None of importance soes I know." Nathaniel frowned. "Oh, one thing, if I could ask a favor, Highness."

"Yes?"

"You should be a-telling me and Kamiskwa to go off to hunt something."

"Because?"

Nathaniel's face soured. "On account of your Princess has got herself an idea about picnics. The Count, he has a good eye, so he's gone and got me and Kamiskwa measured for some fanciful clothes. You, too, mind, but you look a mite better in them than we do."

The Prince laughed. "Are you afraid of dressing for a dinner?"

"Not me, Highness. It's Kamiskwa." Nathaniel looked around, then lowered his voice. "He ain't never took to civilized clothes."

"I shall see if Her Highness will excuse your presence." The Prince brandished the note. "Let me go see to this, and then we can deal with your problem."

"Thank you, Highness."

Vlad retreated to his laboratory and cracked the letter's seal. Couched in very precise and flowery language, the Count had outlined the reason for the Princess' tardiness and the source of Nathaniel's anxiety. The Princess had determined to host a picnic and was supplying everything from furnishings to guests. In addition to herself and the Count, Mrs. Warren, Doctor Frost, his wife and daughter, would come Bishop Bumble, his wife and niece. She was supplying the food, wine, furnishings, and all other necessities to fulfill all social obligations.

He set the note down. The Frosts were most welcome. Likewise Rachel Warren, whom he had never met. Bishop Bumble, on the other hand, was someone the Prince tolerated in very small doses. To be specific, only on Easter and the Feast of the Nativity, when, as the Queen's representative in Mystria, he was required to attend Church services.

Bumble had gained some renown for his sermons. He'd even had them collected in a volume and had sent Vlad a copy. The man urged morality, fidelity, and adherence to the laws of God and the Crown. All good material, especially from the standpoint of someone desirous of maintaining societal stability.

And yet, whenever the Prince attended his services, the sermon became one directed at the ungodliness of Tharyngia. Bumble pointed out how that nation had once been great, but when it abandoned God and overthrew its rightful ruler, that all ended. In his thinking, science and its methods required the rejection of God. After all, anything God wished man to know could be found in the pages of the Good Book. If it was not there, it was unnecessary.

Bumble's one previous visit to the estate had left an indelible impression. Every other visitor stepped into the laboratory with a slack-jawed expression of wonder and amazement. That always delighted the Prince. Bumble proved the exception. His face closed, his words became clipped, and he sought to leave as quickly as possible.

If I abandoned this place while he was here, the laboratory would burn, I am certain of it. Men like Bumble could not separate ideology from methodology. Vlad walked over to the model of du Malphias' fortress. Careful measurements and other things demanded by science had created an invaluable tool for fighting the Ryngians; but to Bumble it would be fruit of a poisonous tree.

Vlad stared at the model, wishing that Bumble's God would decide to smite the real fortress. "It would certainly be convenient."

"What would be convenient, my lord?"

Her soft voice surprised him because of the hushed reverence and maturity in it. She had slipped through the door easily enough, being smaller than the average Teutonic woman. She wore her blonde hair long and loose. It had the warmth and glow of honey. Freckles distributed themselves playfully over a face that was a bit wider than Vlad expected, but her dark blue eyes were full of intelligence and curiosity. She wore a simple dress of local manufacture, quite modest and yet fetching upon her.

Vlad stepped to the side and bowed deeply. "Highness, you honor me."

She curtsied. "You did not hear me knock, Highness?"

Vlad glanced past her. "No, I fear..."

She shook her head, an insuppressible smile tugging at the corners of her mouth. "I have been told you are a man of great deliberation and concentration. Now I see it first hand. This pleases me, to know that unobserved you are as when you are observed."

Vlad looked at her curiously, his pulse quickening. "Thank you. I am as you see me, though usually not attired thusly."

"My lord looks very good in those clothes."

Vlad half-closed his eyes. "Please tell your tutors they have schooled you well."

"What do you mean?" Her brows arrowed up, not down.

Normally that question would have been asked in an offended tone but hers suggested consternation. "I mean that you are well schooled in the art of flattery, but I am not so much of a fool as to imagine that a girl like you could find me in the least attractive. We both understand this will be a diplomatic marriage."

She glanced down. "Is this how you see it?"

Vlad rubbed his chin. "Have I misjudged you?"

"I should think, my lord, that a man of your intelligence, one who reveres the scientific method, would consider more of an investigation before drawing a conclusion." Gisella's head came up. "If I believed this to be a marriage of convenience only, what reason would I have for any deception? Our fate is quite out of our hands. We would be wed, I would give you children, and everyone save ourselves would be satisfied."

Vlad nodded slowly. "You have a point, but this is still little from which to reach a conclusion."

She clasped her hands behind her back. "Count Joachim said you did not ask after me and, instead, wished him to observe you for me. He has, and has laughed much in reporting to me. He said that we could not have been better matched were we shaped by artisans for that purpose.

"You might ask why I was chosen for you. I have older sisters who could have been sent."

Vlad slowly smiled. *She has no trouble speaking her mind.* "Why you then?"

"To be rid of me." She turned and peered closely at the caged raven. "I have never had much tolerance for the court and nobles who have the intelligence bred out of them. I find stories of valor and courage boring. I find more beauty in a butterfly's wing than in all the world's jewelry. Neither my father nor any of his court can tolerate my asking 'why?' I much prefer reading to needlepoint or other female arts."

"And what do you read?"

She smiled, flashing even white teeth. "Norillian, Kessian, high and low, Remian, Archelian, and I even convinced my Norillian tutor to teach me Ryngian. I do not know your mother's native tongue, but I should wish to learn it."

"Very good on the languages. Subjects, girl."

Her eyes brightened. "The classics, of course, philosophy and science. I have read the Bible and will admit to being quite a reader of travelogues. I have long wanted to visit Mystria."

Vlad nodded, then opened his arms. "And what do you think of my laboratory?"

Gisella smiled. "It needs dusting."

He raised an eyebrow.

"And I should love to spend hours here studying everything, if my lord would permit it."

Vlad smiled. "I do believe, Princess Gisella, this could be arranged."

CHAPTER THIRTY-EIGHT

September 1, 1763
Anvil Lake, New Tharyngia

Owen awoke with a start, clutching his blankets tighter. He shivered, cold air finding him through both. A draft poured into his cell beneath the wooden door, flooding the dark room.

He rolled onto his side and drew his legs up. They protested, less from the wounds than those other things du Malphias had proved he could do. The man had studied enough anatomy to have charted nerve paths. A touch here, a caress there, and it felt as if he was scourging Owen's flesh. He body reacted, yet the flesh remained untorn and unbruised.

And it wasn't always a touch. As he had done in stopping the crutch, du Malphias was able to use magick at a distance. Owen didn't know how, and had been in too much pain to make any serious observations, but du Malphias had been able to affect him from at least a yard away. Perhaps more.

Owen groaned, his breastbone still aching.

Quarante-neuf loomed out of the shadows. He draped a heavy piece of canvas over Owen. "This may help."

Owen shook his head. "I need to move. If I lay here I shall die."

He threw back the covers and sat up. He wrapped a blanket around himself. He reached a hand out and Quarante-neuf took it, easing him to his feet. Owen chuckled.

The *pasmorte* cocked his head. "What amuses you, sir?"

"You're dead and yet your flesh is warmer than mine? How is that?"

"I do not know, sir."

Owen slowly straightened, his spine popping as he did so. "Did he give you *vivalius* recently?"

"I do not require it as often as the others."

That made sense. As nearly as Owen could determine, the *pasmortes* in the most advanced states of decay needed the most. To heal Owen's wounds, du Malphias employed mere droplets. He'd watched ragged collections of flesh and bones bathe in it. He had no idea if it warmed their flesh, but it did vitalize them.

Owen took a step, then another. In another demonstration of power, du Malphias hobbled him by magick. If Owen tried to take a full stride, pain shot up his hamstring, over his rump, and into his back. It hurt worse than being shot. Sometimes it left him breathless.

He forced himself to ignore the pain.

Owen clutched at Quarante-neuf's shoulder when his left leg buckled. The *pasmorte* caught him. "You must be careful, sir."

"I have a duty to escape."

"But, Captain Strake, the Laureate will have you killed if you defy him."

"I think, my friend, if I shall end up dead, I should like to die a man."

The *pasmorte* walked with him, supporting him. "You called me 'friend.'"

"You keep me alive." Owen looked up at him. "Your service is compelled. You are not my enemy."

"No."

Owen smiled. "I know, from your voice, you are Mystrian."

The *pasmorte* shook his head. "I do not recall."

Owen would have taken that as a blanket dismissal, but the words trailed off ruefully. Over the time he had been in Quarante-neuf's care, Owen had noticed subtle changes. Pierre Ilsavont, according to his son, had memories of his previous life. Quarante-neuf might have some as well. He might be hiding that information for a variety of reasons. *Do the dead desire privacy?*

"Please remember this, then: You are my friend. I cannot thank you enough for helping me, no matter what comes."

"You are welcome, sir."

They continued walking around the cell. Owen hissed when the pain spiked. Quarante-neuf would pause, ready to catch him. Owen leaned on him when his legs quivered so violently that he wasn't sure if he could take another step. Then he would push on.

Quarante-neuf nodded encouragingly. "You must continue. She is waiting for you, your wife."

Owen raised an eyebrow. "How did you…?"

"You spoke her name in your sleep."

Owen hesitated. He recalled the dream, when he was so cold. She had come with a thick blanket. She had laid it over him, then crawled beneath it. She held him, whispering that everything would be fine.

Bethany.

"That was not my wife." Owen struggled along several more steps. "It was a woman I met in Mystria. Another friend."

"I understand, sir."

"Not *that* sort of friend. She is a lovely young woman, is Bethany."

The *pasmorte* nodded. "It is a beautiful name."

"True, but we must never speak it aloud again." Owen glanced toward the door. "Your master is an evil man. If he suspects, he will find a way to harm her. I will not let that happen. Promise me."

"As best I am able, Captain." The dead man shook his head. "I would have no harm come to your friend."

Owen shivered again. He was fooling himself if he thought du Malphias did not already know about Bethany, about *everything*. Owen couldn't remember what he'd revealed under torture, but he'd have given *anything* up to stop it. He tried lying, repeatedly, and even kept one lie alive over three sessions, but finally broke down and admitted it had been a lie. All he'd done was purchase time and earn himself the thaumaturgical shackling.

I must escape. He labored under no illusion that his escape would protect his friends and his nation against du Malphias. The man was evil in ways beyond human comprehension, and incredibly powerful. The way he had assaulted Owen, the way he'd tortured him, implied depths of magick skill Owen had never even imagined could exist.

"To escape, Quarante-neuf, I will need your help."

"I do not know what I can do."

"I will need food and clothing. And I will need nails. Four nails, no, six. Maybe a dozen. Iron nails." Owen shuffled around to look at Quarante-neuf. "Can you get those things for me?"

The *pasmorte* considered for a moment, then nodded. "The Laureate has me under a compulsion to keep you safe."

"Then how can you can watch him torture me?"

"I am also constrained from harming *him*." Quarante-neuf shook his head. "It does not mean I cannot hate him. I just cannot harm him."

Owen nodded. "If you gather these things for me, you will be making me safe. Distancing me from du Malphias will keep *him* safe."

"Thank you, sir." The *pasmorte* smiled. "It shall please me to be of service to you both."

Quarante-neuf was good to his word. He collected everything Owen requested and concealed it somewhere in the fortress. He did not tell Owen where, so Owen could not reveal the location of the cache under torture.

As Owen identified new needs, he worded his requests carefully. "I would feel much safer if…" prefaced all of them. When Quarante-neuf told him of his success, Owen always thanked him with, "I feel much safer now."

The nails trickled in. Owen hid them inside the leather sleeves, sliding them between the shackle and his skin. It pleased him to carry the keys to his escape at all times and that du Malphias never noticed. When Owen was alone he'd pull one out and sharpen it against the cell's stone floor. He worked it until it was needle sharp, then started on another.

Du Malphias refrained from more torture, though he hardly became civil. He allowed Quarante-neuf to bring Owen out for some fresh air. He took great delight in the pain the hobbling caused. He seemed largely unconcerned about where Owen traveled, though Owen had no doubt that du Malphias catalogued every step.

The Laureate had taken to revising the fortress yet again, but his *pasmortes* worked with only a fraction of the industry they had previously exhibited. Du Malphias had begun the construction of a stone wall inside the north palisade wall. He offset it by four yards and was filling the space between the walls with smaller stones and debris. While cannon could destroy the outer wooden wall easily, the rubble would flow down to seal the breach immediately. Any troops trying to race in would find themselves at the bottom of a gravel slope staring up at soldiers on a stone wall.

And, clearly, if he had the time, du Malphias would replace the palisade wall with stone, forcing his enemies to expend more time and brimstone to bring it down.

Owen limped over to where du Malphias stood. "Do you know why they have slowed?"

The Laureate half-closed his eyes. "I have my theories."

"And you shall be testing them?"

"I may." He waved a hand toward a tattered crew dragging a large rock along. "It is their metabolism. When I first began my experiments, I chose the *vampyr* model—a creature that would feed on blood. Alas, they did not work well. Aside from an annoying tendency to scintillate in daylight, the *vampyr* created a logistical nightmare. In nature, a predator must consume forty times its own weight to sustain itself. The *vampyr*, then, would require a small city to make an army viable.

"The *pasmortes*, on the other hand, have a greatly reduced metabolism. They need to be fed very little, but it takes them a long time to process what they have consumed to repair themselves. Just keeping their muscles warm enough to function uses up most all of their energy. Thus they cannot repair themselves, so they move more slowly, have much less energy, and eventually break down."

"I see."

"Do you? What do you see, Captain Strake?" The Laureate smiled. "Is this place any less of a killing ground? Hardly. And lest you make a fearful mistake, you must remember that, as with the hardly lamented Monsieur Ilsavont, my *pasmortes* are capable of using muskets and cannon. Were Norisle to present an army to me here, even now, I could destroy it. And next spring, when I am reinforced with a more conventional force, your people will not be able to take this fortress."

He studied Owen's face for a moment. "You do not believe me."

"I believe this is a formidable fortress." Owen winced as he straightened up. "What I do not believe is that any fortress is unconquerable."

"Do you believe your God will smash this place? Or will He merely employ one of your generals as His agent to do so?" The Tharyngian laughed. "Ah, the shock on your face. If your God existed, would He not smite me for my insolence?"

"God moves in mysterious ways."

"Always the excuse when He fails you." Du Malphias clasped his hands at the small of his back. "This is what I find curious about you Norillians. You cling to superstition when it has clearly ceased to be of service. Tell me, Captain, were you motivated in war to do things because you feared Perdition?"

"No."

"Neither were our people. Aside from hopeful prayers before an attack, and the mournful petitions of the mortally wounded, God could easily be removed from warfare. For every man who claims he survived by a miracle, I can show you hundreds for whom a miracle failed to materialize. Shot and shell seem curiously indiscriminate when it comes to whom they kill."

"Perhaps God has a greater purpose which we cannot fathom."

"Another excuse. I would have thought better of you, Captain. You mouth platitudes which, I am certain, you do not believe." Du Malphias smiled cruelly. "So, I propose a test."

Owen's flesh puckered. "I am not a theologian."

"Nor am I, so we are well matched. You see that post over there?"

Forty yards uphill a post had been sunk into the ground. "Yes."

"Run to it. If your God speeds you before two of my *pasmortes* catch you, you are free to go. I swear this by your God." The Tharyngian shrugged. "If you fail, that is the end of you and this insipid notion of a God."

Du Malphias almost looks bored. "You can't be serious."

"But I am." Du Malphias yawned against the back of his hand, then nodded at a pair of *pasmortes* hauling on a stone. "You and you, kill him."

Two of the *pastorates* dropped their rope and began to shuffle toward Owen. One fell forward onto all fours and began to lope. Their jaws hung open, then snapped shut with solid clicks.

Fear jolted Owen. He turned to run. Pain ripped up the back of his legs. He cried out, slipping, dropping to a knee. He scrambled to get up again, more pain drilling into him.

Du Malphias laughed.

I will not give him the satisfaction! Owen heaved himself up and clawed at the ground. *No giving up. No losing!*

On came the *pasmortes*. As sluggish as they had been hauling on the rope, they picked up speed. One had an eye hanging by the stalk, bouncing off a cheek that was mostly bone. What was left of the other's tongue waggled out of its mouth.

Owen twisted around to keep an eye on them. He shuffled sideways up the hill. Pain continued with each step, but if he locked his knees, it didn't hurt as much. Teetering and tottering, he hopped along sideways. He dug at the ground with his hands, dirt impacting under his nails. One foot slipped. He almost fell, but he kept going. Pushing off with the other foot, he whipped his body around, dragging the recalcitrant leg.

Twenty yards. Ten. Owen kept on, gaining ground with his arms more than legs. The sharpened iron nails dug into his forearms. He ignored that pain and kept scrambling uphill. *I can make it.*

The *pasmortes* closed steadily. The one gnawed off half its tongue while the other took great leaps forward. The second closed the gap quickly. It gathered itself to pounce. Owen swung his body wide as it leaped. It crashed down, its forearms collapsing. It hit face first. Its neck snapped. The skull popped up, the eye whipping free, both bouncing back down the hill.

Owen whirled around and dove. He twisted in the air, his fingers outstretched. He felt wood. He grabbed it. His body hit the ground hard. "I won!"

Then the other *pasmorte* landed on his chest. It raised both hands, fingers clawed. A gobbet of tongue hit Owen in the face.

But before it could rake its boney fingers through his flesh, Quarante-neuf grabbed the other *pasmorte* around the waist and yanked. He lifted it over his head, holding on tightly despite the creature's angry snarling. Quarante-neuf shifted his grip to the thing's neck and leg, then hurled the creature down. Ribs shattered as the victory post punched through the *pasmorte*'s chest.

Quarante-neuf helped Owen to his feet. The Norillian soldier nodded toward du Malphias. "I reached the post, Monsieur. Will you honor your word?"

"Were I a man of God, you would be headed on your way." The Laureate shrugged. "I am a man of Science. Science demands repeatability. We shall test you again, in the coming days. If you succeed then, freedom will be yours."

Owen's eyes tightened. *To you it is testing. To me it is training for my escape.* "I believe it will, Monsieur, I believe it will.

CHAPTER THIRTY-NINE

September 11, 1763
Benjamin River
Temperance Bay, Mystria

Nathaniel waved good-bye to Prince Vlad and Princess Gisella, tossing free the tow-rope attached to Mugwump's saddle. Both royals wore goggles and laughed as the wurm turned back downstream. Nathaniel still felt uneasy around Mugwump, even after spending time around the creature. The wurm appeared a bit bigger and quicker than before, and the colors on its scales really stood out. But he could understand the Prince and Princess' attachment to the wurm.

Mugwump gave Nathaniel a sidelong glance, as if having read his thoughts, then ducked under the water as he passed back by the canoe.

Nathaniel dipped a paddle quickly, fighting the wake of the beast's passage. *Now, you'd not have been attempting to swamp us, would you?* He dug deep into the water to maintain the canoe's upstream momentum.

"I don't know about you, Kamiskwa, but I'm right happy 'bout getting shed of that place. I'm thinking I couldn'ta stood another week."

"You wanted to stay while Rachel was a guest."

"Well, now, that's true, though weren't as much smooth sailing as I'da preferred." His presence while Rachel was at the estate created some friction with the Frost family and the Bumbles. Doctor Frost had been cordial, but his wife and daughter had been as cold to him as they had been warm to Rachel. The Bumbles had been sour about everything, but Nathaniel was practiced in ignoring folks like them.

Nathaniel didn't get private time to speak with Doctor Frost. Overall Nathaniel's behavior had been courteous and circumspect, which led to a slight thawing on the part of the Frost women—and much of their continued reserve he put down to his being blamed, in part, for Captain Strake's disappearance.

"People is curious." Nathaniel glanced back over his shoulder. "What did you make of that Lilith Bumble?"

"Pretty, like a jeopard."

"Yep. Seemed like she had her sights set on the Count."

"I do not fear for him."

"No, I reckon he seen what we seen." Nathaniel paddled harder, pulling them up a small set of rapids. "He did manage to keep the Bumbles entertained."

Out of respect for the Prince, Nathaniel had been on his best behavior. He and Rachel had managed to slip away for walks in the fields and to go fishing. She'd always loved fishing, and that particular afternoon glowed warmly in his memory. Just the two of them by the river, letting lines tied to corks bob in the water, watching clouds roll by. For the first time in the longest while he'd felt completely relaxed.

The Prince had said nothing to him before or after those excursions, but he hadn't needed to. Since they had done nothing untoward, no dishonor could fall to the Prince. Moreover, if anyone did make false claims, they would be insulting the Prince. He used his prestige to provide Nathaniel and Rachel a chance to be alone, and Nathaniel owed him a debt of gratitude for that.

"Magehawk, I must ask."

"Yes?"

Kamiskwa pointed his paddle at a bundle in the middle of the canoe. "Why did you bring the fancy clothes?"

Nathaniel smiled. "Well, I was amembering how much of a shine your father took to Owen's coat."

The Altashee snorted. "You know that was so Captain Strake would have appropriate clothes for our journey."

"Well, I done noticed your father ain't taken that coat off since."

"Nor will he. Captain Strake killed Ungarakii."

"I need to ask you a question, brother mine."

"Yes, Magehawk?"

Nathaniel glanced back just for a heartbeat. "Did you be thinking I'd not notice that my bundle was a mite heavier than when I packed it? Heavier by the suit of clothes you was made to wear at that dinner."

"If you were to attire yourself in the proper Norillian style in Saint Luke, I would not want you to feel alone."

That brought Nathaniel full around, his paddle resting against his thighs. "You liked being all gussied up, didn't you?"

"*Natahe.*"

"Oh, now don't you go and be telling me you don't understand. You know right well what I was asking." Nathaniel turned back an applied himself to his paddle. "*Natahe,* my left foot."

He added outrage to his words, but was happy his friend couldn't see his smile. The simple fact was that Kamiskwa wore Mystrian clothes very well. He'd been given breeches and a long coat in black, with white hose and shirt.

Black shoes with silver buckles and a dark green neck-cloth had been added to finish his outfit. He'd found a string of malachite beads in his bag and used it to tie his hair back. The whole thing gave him a slightly diabolical cast, but one that looked good.

By contrast, Nathaniel had just looked awkward. His shoes had felt too short, or so he thought, until the Count took him aside and pointed out that he had them on the wrong feet. There didn't seem a way to know that, and Nathaniel had never heard of shoes meant for each specific foot—clear foolishness, that was. But when he switched them they did feel better. Still, the hose scratched. He managed to misbutton the coat, and the shirt sleeves ended in lace that only had one purpose—to soak up gravy faster than a biscuit.

He did count his blessings, however. Neither he nor Kamiskwa had been provided wigs, which had to have itched something awful. Nathaniel really couldn't see any purpose to the things since all the men but the Bishop had hair.

"I am thinking it is a good thing your father weren't there for that dinner else we'd be having nine-course meals in Saint Luke and then dancing after."

"No dancing."

Nathaniel's grin broadened. "You just ain't got no appreciation for culture."

"No. You dance for recreation. We dance for magick."

"Oh, there was some magick there." Nathaniel had enjoyed the dancing, despite not being good at it. The Princess had brought along a string quartet and a dance caller. The caller explained all the dances, which were danced by couples and groups of four. Mrs. Frost or Lilith Bumble ended up being partnered with him all of the time, but when the dance's progression would put him in league with Rachel and her partner, breaths were being held. Everyone watched them to see how they reacted, and those reactions and their impression had been a source of much mirth when Nathaniel and Rachel were out fishing.

"I do not think you appreciate how much magick there was, my friend."

"Prolly not." Nathaniel chuckled. "But I sure did enjoy it."

The fortnight following the dinner had been one with a bit of entertainment, but the guests left after four days, allowing the Prince, the Count, Nathaniel, and Kamiskwa to get down to work. The Prince and the Count drew up a list of facts they needed to know about the fortress. The Prince added to it a list of things he wanted to know about du Malphias' *pasmortes*. He even hoped they could capture one for him and bring it back.

Nathaniel had not liked that prospect. "Begging your pardon, Highness, but what if it gets all bitey or stabbity or otherwise unpeaceable? It's going to be a long trip back here."

The prince had allowed that might be a problem, and the next day borrowed Nathaniel's bullet mold and produced some special ammunition. They fired the bullets a few times, both being satisfied with the performance, and Nathaniel promised to report on their effect against *pasmortes*.

Nathaniel and Kamiskwa pushed their walks fast and reached the winter Saint Luke in a week and a half. They stopped long enough to get a good night's sleep, then picked up Makepeace Bone and made for to Hattersburg. Instead of heading into the town itself, they stopped at Seth's farm.

He didn't seem to bear them any grudge, but his new wife—Meg Gates—did. She would have made them sleep in the cow shed, but Seth explained how if it weren't for them making him go to Temperance, she'd never have taken care of his cow, they wouldn't have fallen in love, and wouldn't have gotten married. This mollified her a little, though Nathaniel figured she loved the cow more than Seth.

From there they made directly for Pine Lake, cutting the trip to three days. They reached the small island by mid-afternoon. The wind had shifted from east to north, so Makepeace suggested they stop for the day.

Kamiskwa disagreed. "Snow tomorrow. We should best get across now."

By the time they reached the far shore, the sun had set and the first few snowflakes began to drift down. They burned when they hit his flesh. He pulled his sleeves down to cover his hands. First snow of the year always made him happy. It was at first snow that he'd first kissed Rachel—albeit a bit later in that year and a long time before she ever became another man's wife.

The three men set up camp then pulled on heavy winter Altashee robes. They'd traded cloth scraps for them—as a formality since Msitazi wanted to help them succeed. Makepeace's robe and hood had been pieced together from two bearskins. Nathaniel's had only taken one, his hat a beaver, and his mittens an otter. Kamiskwa wore a robe of jeopard that his sister Ishikis made from animals he'd killed. All three of them had boots made from wolverine since the ice didn't stick to it, lined with rabbit to keep their feet warm. The winter clothes' bulk kept them warm, but could be shucked quickly enough if they had to start fighting.

Snowfall picked up and the wind howled through the night. They cut branches for snowshoes, stripped them of leaves and bent them into ovals. Using well-oiled leather thongs they wove a web in the center and created harnesses for their feet. The snowshoes would allow them to move across the snow pack.

Nathaniel tossed another log onto their fire. "Ain't going to be easy being that close to Owen and not going in to get him."

Kamiskwa shook his head. "We do not even know if he is alive."

"If he ain't, I'm going to dig him up and give him a right good talking to."

Makepeace grunted. "In du Malphias' hands, you ain't neither gonna need to dig him up. He'll be coming after you."

A low growl rolled from Nathaniel's throat. "Iffen he does, I don't know what I'll do."

Makepeace sat up. "You will do God's work. Ain't rightly nor natural the dead running around."

"But maybe this du Malphias can change things. Make him, you know…"

"Dead again?" Kamiskwa stirred the fire with a stick. "Bone is right. If he attacks, you have to kill him."

"And what if he don't? What if he is one of them *pasmortes* but ain't mean? If you cain't tell he ever died, how would you know he was dead?"

Makepeace held his hands out toward the fire. "I would reckon it's all in the bringing back. Now when the saints did it, they were godly men, so God would let them bring the original spirit back in. Man like du Malphias, that would be Satan putting a demon in."

Nathaniel raised an eyebrow. "But Pierre came back."

"And when he died, Satan got control of his soul, I am certain." Makepeace rubbed his hands together. "If the dead are walking, evil spirits is in 'em."

"*Wendigo.*"

"Well now, the two of you agreeing, that's a powerful argument. And it ain't that I don't believe there's a God in His Heaven, but I ain't had much church learning. Fair recent, though, Bishop Bumble up and lectured me on what the Good Lord says we ain't to be doing. Resurrecting folks weren't among the things mentioned. If God ain't commanding agin it, his prophets, saints, and Son is doing it, could be there's more to the issue than we know to be exploring."

Kamiskwa and Makepeace thought on that for a bit. Makepeace, his hands warmed enough, went back to making his snowshoes. "Could be you're right, Nathaniel. Could be. So what are you going to do when Captain Strake's looking at you from the other side of death?"

Nathaniel sighed and tapped his cartridge pouch. "Load up one of the Prince's special bullets. And if God has mercy, let Him visit it on Owen quick—before my bullet finds its mark."

The next day they set out by mid-morning heading due west, but the unseasonable cold slowed them down. After the better part of a week they worked their way upslope toward the southern bank of Anvil Lake. They kept back on the mountainside, well away from the open water. The north wind, blowing across it, kicked up a lot more snow. They were glad for the trees' shelter.

A new storm kicked up by the time they'd gotten close to the Roaring River. Given that the storm was intensifying and threatening to dump two feet of snow by midnight, pushing further would have been foolish. By early afternoon they built a lean-to in a sheltered hollow and lit a fire. They couldn't see the fort from the nearest ridge, so they figured du Malphias couldn't see their fire.

Despite the cold and the snow making every task laborious, each man cleaned, oiled, and charged his gun anew. They didn't change their firestones, but they rotated them so clean color rested beneath their thumbs. This close to the fort there was no sense in not being prepared to fight.

They debated taking watches. For a man to have an effective post, he'd have to be up on a ridge. He'd constantly have snow in the face and get cold fast. Since they couldn't see anything in the pitch dark, they opted to remain in their camp and trusted that any Ryngian scouts this far out would be hunkered down against the storm themselves.

As a precaution, however, no one talked much. They all kept an ear out for anything aside from howls of the north wind. By mutual agreement, two tried to sleep while the other stayed awake to feed the fire, but Nathaniel reckoned there was more trying going on than actual sleeping.

A couple hours past midnight, based on the stars that came out when the north wind died and the snow stopped, Nathaniel woke Kamiskwa. "Sleep any?"

"Very little. Did I hear thunder?"

"Might coulda been, not long ago. Wind snatched it away right quick." Nathaniel stretched. "I reckon I will lay me down, but I ain't 'specting sleep."

And before he even lay a blanket down, two gunshots rang out.

CHAPTER FORTY

October 15, 1763
Prince Haven
Temperance Bay, Mystria

S nowflakes sped on a shrieking gust of wind coming through the wurmrest's door and sizzled on the giant boiler. Vlad, down in the pit, tossed another log on the fire beneath the iron tank, then looked up toward the door. He smiled, despite being sweaty, mud-streaked, and soot-stained.

"You should not be in here, Highness."

Gisella pulled off a thick woolen cloak and hung it over the pit's railing. She stamped her feet, freeing them of snow, then returned his smile. She wore a baggy pair of riding breeches and a homespun shirt with a knitted sweater over it.

"I thought, Highness, you might value help on this bitterly cold night."

"Baker will be back after he gets some supper and a little sleep." Vlad tossed another piece of wood on the fire. "And while your help would be welcome, you know why you should not be here. We are unchaperoned."

"Not true, my Prince." She started down the ladder into the pit. "We have your Mugwump."

Vlad turned. The wurm had huddled himself into a circle with head and tail pointed away from the river. Wooden shutters had been closed over the river entrance, and a copper pipe ran from the boiler down into the pit. Steam came off of it and combined with the heat of the fire to render the wurmrest as warm as a windless August day.

"Though he seems to be tolerating the cold better than he has in the past, I am afraid, Princess, that Mugwump is not really much of a chaperone."

"It does not matter; wurms are known in all the medieval tales to be fine chaperones. Knights of great virtue have rescued princesses by the dozen, and the presence of the wurm was enough to ensure no loss of honor."

"Do you believe such tales are true?"

She came to his side and grabbed a piece of wood. "It matters only what others believe. You are an honorable man, so there is no question of my virtue being in jeopardy."

"I hope the Count agrees. I recall the joy with which he relates his dueling stories."

"The Count is unconscious, buried beneath many blankets." She tossed her log in.

The Prince grabbed another. "Ouch."

"What?"

Vlad tossed it onto the fire, then shook his right hand. "A splinter." He held out a grimy hand, then spat on his finger and wiped away the dirt. "Right there."

Gisella took his hand in hers. "Hold still." She ran a finger gently over his skin. When he jolted, she murmured, "Sorry." Then she deftly caught the splinter between two fingernails and yanked it free.

"Thank you."

"In Kesse-Saxeburg we have a superstition." The Princess raised his hand toward her lips and gave the wound a gentle kiss. "That will make it better."

Vlad smiled and reluctantly drew his hand from her grasp. That kiss—by its very gentle nature—stirred something in him. He found Gisella physically attractive, with his affection growing through all the time spent with her. She was, in many ways, more beautiful a woman than he had ever supposed he would have in his life.

Because of his bloodline, however, his destiny had never been his own. He had forced himself over the years to be cordial, but to reject the advances of many women who had dreams of someday being the Governor-General's wife or perhaps even Norisle's queen. He had learned to quickly turn away from the biological urgings such as those her presence encouraged.

She cocked her head. "What is it, Highness?"

"You are a conundrum, Princess Gisella, much akin to du Malphias' *pasmortes*."

"I assure you, my lord, that I am quite alive."

"You are wise enough to know that is not what I meant." He tossed another log on the fire. "You have been plucked from your father's domain and sent here to marry me, and you actually appear to *like* me."

"This would be because I do."

"This is what I find to be so peculiar." Vlad shook his head. "You are less than half my age and from another nation. You have told me, and I have seen, that you enjoy many things that other ladies at court loathe. You are in the midst of a grand adventure, one the equal of any in a variety of novels…"

"I do not read novels, Highness. They are persiflage that does not educate nor illuminate and seldom succeeds in amusing. Writers of such fanciful tales should find something useful and honorable to do with their lives, instead of filling their days writing lies."

Vlad laughed aloud. "Yes, perfect."

"What?"

"And you are a woman of strong opinions, not afraid to express them."

She tucked a strand of blonde hair behind her ear, then picked up a firerake and reduced a log to coals. "I should think, for Mystria, this would be preferred."

"I agree." Vlad smiled. "My father's most recent letter had explicit instructions for me to follow concerning my upcoming marriage. He began, of course, with the Church's teachings. He cannot help it. He's been a monk longer than he has been a father, but he tries at the latter. He told me that to marry someone I barely knew and didn't like was a duty. In time, he said, we would come to understand each other. We might even get to the point where we tolerated each other's company. If blessed, we might even be friends. He said our children would be a point of commonality and would reflect our shared values. But the idea of liking each other…"

"Or loving each other?"

Vlad looked down. "Yes, these were things, he said, dreamt of by fools and novelists."

"Because of what your father wrote, you cannot believe I like you?" Gisella smiled and stepped closer to him. "You cannot believe I might love you?"

"It is, I think, far too early to be speaking of love, Princess, lest you commit foolishness for which you would condemn a heroine and the novelist who created her."

"I should tell you, I do not think it is so." Gisella reached up and stroked the side of his face, then turned away. The fire flooded her hair with golden highlights. "I was raised at court, my lord, where I did not fit in because that which attracted others bored me. Like you, however, I was prepared to do my duty. I would come here and marry a man I did not know. I would bear him children and I would hope he would go off to wars or to tour his lands. I would hope he was an ambitious man and that his ambitions took him far from me. And this is why I hate ambition."

Vlad smiled. "Princess, I *am* an ambitious man."

She turned, her eyes alight. "Your ambition is practical. Your laboratory shouts it. You want to know things, to discover things, to learn. You seek to make the world a better place. Ambition can be selfish or selfless, and you are the master of the latter form. For that reason alone I would like you; and certainly do love you."

"But I am not…"

"Not what, my lord? Dashing and handsome like von Metternin? I would tell you that you are. Handsome, most certainly, and dashing, of course. Who else in all the world rides a wurm beneath the river? You enter worlds no other man has seen. Countless are the fools who charge into battle and think themselves brave because their enemies cannot shoot straight. Their foe's incompetence somehow becomes a shining sign of God's favor."

Her face lit up as she paced. Even Mugwump stirred at her words, sliding his tail out of her way as she paraded. "Shall I tell you, my lord, why it is I love you, for I do love you, and it does not matter to me if you do not return that love? Knowing I have found a man worthy of being loved is enough. But do you wish to know?"

Vlad met her gaze and nodded. "I should be honored."

"You are a man who deals in realities. You acknowledge that honor and glory exist, but you do not seek them as a hound seeks a fox. You see them for what they are. Glory will feed no one. Honor will keep no one warm on a night such as this. A bullet will kill the virtuous and brave as easily as the dissolute and craven—and often side by side with the same volley."

She pointed back toward the house and his laboratory. "The model you have created, the men you have sent to scout it, none of these things are matters for the Governor-General. Your responsibility would have ended with sending reports to Launston. That would be your duty as seen by the Crown, but you see more. You see what is *necessary* and you execute."

Gisella smiled. "And here, my lord, the fact that you have sent your wurm-wright to bed while you stoke these fires, it pleases me. I can imagine you sitting up the night with a coughing child or…"

"Or a wife entering labor?"

"A silly girl who is afraid of how her body is changing?"

Vlad reached out, resting his hands on her shoulders. "I do not believe you will ever be described as silly. And I would tell you that I would thrash any man who dared say so. I also believe, my dear, you would have thoroughly dealt with such a foolish man well before I had a chance to intervene."

She looked up, a tear glistening in an eye, but she smiled. "I have practiced my thumbs red with a dueling pistol, to my father's delight and disgust."

Vlad brushed the tear away, smudging her cheek. "Princess, my lack of belief in your feeling for me is no fault of your own. No, please, let me explain."

He smiled, suddenly warmed by the memory of her sitting behind him on Mugwump, her arms tight under and around his shoulders, as the wurm first slid beneath the river. She had laughed with surprise, killing the sound as she closed her mouth quickly. She clung to him, her breasts pressed to his back, her body shaking. Only after he surfaced, tugging Mugwump up quickly, did he find her shaking with delighted laugher. Drenched, her clothing hanging from her, she did not care about appearances, but she wished to take a deep breath and go under again and again.

"I have spent so many years, Princess, dreading the day a bride would be chosen for me. I had hoped, honestly hoped, that my aunt would see the possibility of my having children as a threat to the throne. I hoped, and fervently believed, that when she did send a wife for me, it would be some old Morvian dowager duchess who would hate me, hate everything I do, and resolve to remain on the Continent while I stayed here.

"And here she has chosen someone who is perfect for me, who is intelligent and beautiful, practical and witty." Vlad shook his head. "It is a dream which I fear will end."

Gisella hung her hands around his neck. "Kiss me, Highness. I promise this dream will not end."

His arms slipped around her, drawing her to him, pressing her tight to his chest. He lowered his mouth to hers. That first kiss, warm and firm, tightened his stomach. He held her closer, not wanting to let go, not wanting to break it, not wanting to even breath. And she held him tightly, not letting him go, not letting him break the kiss.

And she took his breath away.

He could not tell how long they kissed. Empirically he knew it had to have been less than two minutes, since he could only hold his breath that long. Realistically it didn't matter. It could have been a heartbeat, but might as well have been forever. In that moment, a part of himself that had been shut away for so long became free.

The look on her face as their lips parted said she read it all in his eyes. He had no words for the emotions racing through him. The freedom, the towering joy. It was every bit as exhilarating as the first time Mugwump had dived beneath the river with him. It was the complete satisfaction of having found something he never even knew he had lost. And he wondered how he could have survived so long without it.

He laughed silently, then kissed her again. *Is this love?* He knew lust was involved, certainly, for hungry were their kisses and hot their desires. But he found more there, more that was frustratingly elusive. He could not measure it nor describe it—an ability for which he had to grudgingly admire the much-disparaged novelists. And yet, even though it escaped measurement, it existed because it quickened his pulse and brought him such great joy he could not stop smiling.

Reluctantly he released her. "I fear, Princess, Mugwump is a very poor chaperone."

"This may be, my lord, but he is a silent one, which could make him a wonderful chaperone." She laughed lightly and he adored the sound of it. "But we shall not do anything which would besmirch von Metternin's honor."

"It's best we don't." He took her hand and led her back to the ladder. "And we need to refill the boiler."

He bled the steam off, then opened the boiler. They took turns pumping water and hauling it to the boiler. When they'd filled it two-thirds full, he sealed it again, then climbed back down into the pit to stoke the fire.

She remained above, leaning on the rail, smiling down at him. "I find your working this way very attractive."

He smiled, but stopped himself from preening foolishly. He raked the coals around and started laying in more wood.

"I have a question for you, Princess."

"Ask, my lord."

"In your family, the women bear strong children?"

She nodded, her golden hair shimmering. "Very, my lord."

"So then, by three or four, my sons will be able to tend the boiler on cold nights?"

She grinned. "Only if, my lord, you excuse them from hunting jeopards, which they will want to do from two."

"Very good, my dear, very good. We are splendidly matched. Perfectly." Vlad beamed for her sake and tossed more wood onto the coals. *And I wonder, when my aunt discovers this fact, what she will do to ruin us.*

CHAPTER FORTY-ONE

"It's time." Owen threw back his bedclothes. "Quarante-neuf, we go tonight."

The *pasmorte* shook his head. "It is too dangerous. It is too cold."

Owen stood and unlaced the leather covers over the shackles. "The wind will bury our tracks with snow. This is the only chance. I need your help."

"You can hardly move."

"This is why I need you to help me." Over the last six weeks du Malphias had taken great delight in having *pasmortes* chase Owen down. Because Quarante-neuf would stop them from harming him, the game really had no purpose, but Owen played it anyway. His clumsy efforts gave du Malphias data concerning the magick shackles.

Quarante-neuf had learned through the exercises as well. He broke other *pasmortes* instead of reintroducing them to death. Repair made more work for du Malphias. The Laureate, in turn, taught Quarante-neuf enough magick to affect basic repairs, mending bones and flesh.

He pulled the sharpened nails from beneath the shackles. "Pull on your glove. Now, pinch the flesh at the back of my thigh. Get a good handful. Yes, now, shove one of the nails all the way through the fold."

"I cannot. I would hurt you."

"No, you're preventing hurt." Owen held nails out. "Please, you have to do this. I can't."

The *pasmorte* sank to a knee behind him. He grabbed a hunk of flesh and drew it away from the muscle. The nail popped through and out again, more of a burning sensation than pain, but nothing in comparison to the magick hobbling. Quarante-neuf repeated the procedure on the other leg.

"How does that feel?"

Owen took a step. He felt the tug at the back of his leg, and some of the magickal pain triggering, but less. Another step and another, longer each time. "The iron mutes the magic. I need more nails. Another above the knee. One

244

below. One below the calf, and maybe at the small of my back. Please, my friend, hurry."

"Yes. Let me prepare things." The *pasmorte* quickly bent the nails into a gentle curve. He tore the shackle covers into rectangular strips and pierced them with the nails first. He used the strips to pinch the skin, then inserted the nails through Owen's flesh and the leather. The wounds burned, and blood welled up to stain the leather.

Once all the nails had been set in place, Owen made several circuits of his cell. He moved more easily, but couldn't run. Then again, with the deep snow, what could? *This will have to do.*

He dressed, careful not to catch clothes on the nails. He wrapped one thin blanket around him and saved a corner as a hood, then pulled on the leather tunic Msitazi had given him. They tore the other blanket into strips and bound his feet in several layers, then tied them in place with strips of canvas. The remaining canvas he pulled around him as a cloak, and used the last two nails to hold it closed.

Quarante-neuf nodded. "Ready?"

"Wait, I need Agaskan's doll."

The *pasmorte* produced it from a drawer and Owen tucked it inside his tunic. "Now I will be safe."

Owen followed the *pasmorte* from his prison, hunching himself over. He moved haltingly, imitating as best he could the *pasmortes* circulating as sentries. He mimicked their awkward gaits and ducked his head as he turned north. The full brunt of the storm battered him. He snarled defiantly and forced himself toward the wall.

Snow drifted against the walls' northern faces. He fought the wind and reached the stone wall construction inside the north wall. The open end and ragged line of stones allowed him to easily scramble up to the top. He crouched, searched through the blizzard for any sign of *pasmortes* nearby, but saw nothing.

He couldn't see a dozen feet in any direction, but that hardly made him feel safe. He imagined du Malphias had some arcane means of piercing the storm's curtain. *Or he might have a way to track me or Quarante-neuf.* That thought soured his mouth, but he dismissed it.

Knowing where I am and dragging me back are two different things in this blizzard.

He grabbed the wooden wall's points and hauled himself over. He fell for a yard, then sank into snowdrifts. He floundered for a moment, then another body crunched down beside him. Quarante-neuf grabbed his arm and pulled him from the snow. The *pasmorte* wore no heavy clothes, but did have a pack on his back. "Come."

Owen began wading through the snow. "You have to get me away from here.

I will kill du Malphias if I stay."

Quarante-neuf nodded. "Thank you, my friend…" His voice trailed off for a moment. "Is it that we are truly friends? Can it be?"

"Of course." Owen leaned heavily on the *pasmorte*'s arm. "Why would you think we are not friends?"

"I am dead, Captain. I may not remember much, but that cannot be forgotten. The dead have nothing to offer the living."

"Not so, Quarante-neuf, not so." They stepped free of the largest drift—which had totally filled the trench—and made their way across the wind-scoured glacis. They forded another drift, then pushed on straight north, toward the looming hill from which he had first scouted du Malphias' domain.

They paused in the lee of another drift. Quarante-neuf knelt with his back to the wind, providing Owen shelter. Snow caked the pack and his clothes, but he did not seem to notice. He did not shiver, he did not brush snow away. He remained untouched by the storm.

Then he grabbed Owen by the shoulders and hauled him to his feet. "Come, Captain, we must go."

"Just a moment longer."

"No. Every step away from here makes my master safer." The *pasmorte* nodded. "And it brings happiness one step closer for your Bethany."

Owen smiled and warmth coursed through him. "She is a good woman, kind and smart. You would like her. But I am bound for the reunion with my wife."

"That does not mean your Bethany will not be pleased to see you. I shall get you to her." Quarante-neuf dragged him through another drift, then they began the long, slow trek up a half-carved hill. They cut toward the lake halfway up and around into the forest, then started working down again.

Owen began to shiver. He tucked his hands up under his armpits, seeking some warmth, and feeling the lump that was Agaskan's doll. *I have more friends to see when I am safe.*

Already his nose and ears had begun to burn. He'd lost feeling in his cheeks for the most part. The wind whipping through the trees lost some of its intensity, but dumped snow from high branches that drifted down to coat his hair, melt, and freeze eyelashes together.

They crested the hill and Owen sagged against a tree. "Just a moment's rest."

"Be quiet, Captain." Quarante-neuf shucked his pack and leaped to the right. Snow half-blinded Owen, but could not hide three forms looming from within the woods. Quarante-neuf pounced upon one and bones cracked. He lunged at another and vanished into the storm.

A *pasmorte* appeared at Owen's side, reaching for him with boney fingers. The

Norillian lurched forward. A branch lashed him across the face. He twisted, his knees buckled. He went down and began sliding across the frozen snow on the hill's windswept face.

Owen could do nothing to slow himself. Snow sprayed into his face, then he barked a shin against a sapling. He spun and slammed his shoulder into another tree. Twisting forward and back, spinning helplessly, he caromed from one tree to another and finally, battered and aching, slid into a deep drift at the hill's base.

He huddled there, his hands drawn in. His body ached from the collisions, but he forced that away. He listened, waiting for sounds of an enemy's approach. He slipped one of the cloak-clasp nails into his right hand. *Crush the skull with a shackle or stab it with this nail. That has to work.*

The snow and howling wing mocked him. He couldn't have heard a cavalry charge above the wind. Anyone coming downhill for him would have the wind carrying away the sound of their approach. But if he moved he would give himself away. He shivered, despair seeping into him.

A hand grabbed his ankle.

He kicked at it, but it held tightly. "Captain Strake, I have found you."

"Quarante-neuf?"

The *pasmorte* dragged him from the drift and rolled him over. "Are you hurt?"

"Banged and bruised. Ready to go on." He looked to the north. "There has to be a canoe here. There *must* be."

Quarante-neuf smiled. "There is, my friend. We will find them closer to the lake."

Owen looked up at him. "You sound happy."

The *pasmorte*'s gaze drew distant. "Happier, I think. I am free. Destroying the others I did because I wanted to, not because I was compelled to."

"Good, my friend." Owen nodded, fighting against dread. *How long will you remain free?* Owen could not forget the first *pasmorte* they had found, all curled up and chewed, the journal showing evidence of deterioration. Quarante-neuf might be free, but there would come a point where the magick would run out.

"Tell me you have some *vivalius*."

"I chose not to steal any."

"What? The Prince could re-create it from a sample. He could keep you alive."

"Not possible, my friend, for I am dead." Quarante-neuf helped him over a fallen log. "I shall not fail you. But I would not have anyone else know what I know. The emptiness. Memories that hover just beyond remembering. I feel as if I am waiting, always waiting, but for what I do not know."

Owen grabbed him by the shoulder. "But…"

"I will return you to your Prince and your Bethany." The *pasmorte* smiled. "Then I shall return to the grave in peace."

The wind's shrieking and a blast of snow silenced any counter-argument Owen would have offered. As they struggled toward the lake, an emptiness grew in Owen. He did not want Quarante-neuf to die. *But if this is a fraction of what he feels, I understand.*

After a short time, Quarante-neuf leaned against a tree, letting the storm rage around him. The *pasmorte* slipped down into a small depression and drove his hands into the snow. He grunted, then straightened, flipping over a canoe. Two paddles lay in the hollow beneath it.

"Come, Captain Strake, get the paddles."

They put the canoe in the water. Owen got in the front. He knelt, sitting back on his haunches, which, oddly enough, quieted the lingering pain. Quarante-neuf launched the canoe, then waded out and climbed in.

The wind hit them immediately, driving them south toward the shore and the fortress. Owen had intended to go north and cut around the same route he'd taken to reach the fortress originally, but the wind made that impossible. They turned the canoe to the southeast and paddled hard. They heard nothing but the wind, which is why when the first cannon ball splashed beside them, it came as a complete surprise. Only after the second and third hit did a momentary lull in the wind let him hear a cannon's dying roar. They had drifted perilously close to the fortress.

Du Malphias does have a way to track me. His mind immediately flashed to the symbol du Malphias had cut into his shackle's bronze bolts. It had not been to mark Owen as chattel. It had been to allow du Malphias to locate him.

Owen looked back over his shoulder. "We have to go out and get past the river. We have to do it now. He knows where we are."

Quarante-neuf dug his paddle deep. The canoe surged forward. Another cannon ball sprayed water over them, but the *pasmorte* ignored the danger. Owen bent to the task of paddling, trying to match the *pasmorte*'s strength, but it took his utmost to keep the canoe headed deeper into the lake.

As the cannon balls splashed behind them, Owen surrendered a little to the wind and sent the canoe toward the southeast shore, just beyond the Roaring River outlet. The wind began to slacken, and Owen laughed aloud. "Just when we could use its push!"

Quarante-neuf laughed as well, for the very first time in Owen's memory. An aborted sound, like a burp from a child who has realized that burping was not allowed in polite company. The *pasmorte* broke his paddling rhythm, then laughed again, a bit longer. Owen looked back, reading surprise and a hint of delight on his companion's face.

"It's a good laugh, my friend. Let it out."

"I will. I remember laughing. I liked it."

Suddenly the wind died. Clouds cracked enough to allow moonlight to ignite the snow. The fortress menaced from atop its hill. Owen swore he could see a tall, slender man pacing the walls, but something else urged him to paddle with renewed vigor.

Behind them, in two large, broad boats the Tharyngians called *batteaux*, two dozen soldiers pursued them. A man in the lead boat stood and shouted, then raised a musket and fired. He moved too easily to be a *pasmorte*, but the tireless repetition of the oarsmen's strokes suggested they were.

"Make for shore. We need cover."

The two of them paddled harder, fervently wishing the wind would rise again. It didn't. Their hunters took turns shooting. As the two of them reached the shore, one ball skipped off the water and holed the canoe. Water gushed, but it didn't matter. Quarante-neuf's powerful strokes drove the canoe up onto the shore with such force that stones ripped the bottom out.

Another ball ricocheted off a rock as Owen scrambled to the treeline. Tharyngians shouted orders, looking for a place to beach their boats. Quarante-neuf shot past Owen, then grabbed him by the shoulders and dragged him further into the woods. Keeping the lake on their left, they plunged into the forest, seeking hollows to work their way up and in while remaining hidden.

They fought through deep drifts. The sound of pursuit came quickly. "They must have snowshoes." Quarante-neuf shoved Owen up to the crest of a small hill. "Go, I will delay them."

"No, I can't make it without you." Owen stood and turned, then a musket barked. A ball caught him in the left flank, pitching him backward. He spun, slammed into a tree, then started tumbling down the hillside.

Owen reached the bottom, new pain rippling through him. The bullet had only caught flesh and maybe a little muscle, but smashing into the tree had stunned him. Stars evaporated from his eyes, but the forest took on an odd quality. The snow had tinges of green and hints of deep blue. Stones began to shift shape and trees began to part. To the south a whole avenue opened, welcoming him.

Two more gunshots and Quarante-neuf crashed down beside him. "How bad, Captain?"

"I will live. Did they hit you?"

"Once, in the stomach." The *pasmorte* spasmed, as if to vomit, then spat the bullet into his hand. "It is nothing."

"We have to go." Owen struggled to get up. "South, there, can you see it?"

The *pasmorte* nodded. "The winding path. It will kill us."

"But it will not return us to du Malphias."

Quarante-neuf pulled Owen up. "Then the winding path it is."

CHAPTER FORTY-TWO

October 15, 1763
Anvil Lake, New Tharyngia

N athaniel would have laughed had the situation not been dire. With snowshoes strapped to his feet, Makepeace sailed down the hillside, taking huge long steps and leaps. His bear robe, which he'd peeled down to the waist, had sleeves flopping, making the man look like a four-armed nightmare creature.

Kamiskwa and Nathaniel followed quickly in his wake. The Altashee cut left well above the spot where Makepeace had stopped, and Nathaniel turned to the west two steps later. In parallel, they filed through the woods, coming on through the shore zone.

More guns fired before them, closer this time, and the trio broke into a run. They caught voices distantly, the words unintelligible, but recognized the cadence as Tharyngian. Then, as they came around a hill, three shots fired in volley. The muzzle-flashes revealed an infantry squad in blue jackets tearing up a hill, and over a dozen ragged *pasmortes* coming on through the snow.

Nathaniel raised his rifle, sighted, and pulsed magick into the firestone. Forty yards, at night, even with the moonlight, would be a tricky shot, but the Tharyngian soldiers silhouetted themselves against the snow. His rifle spat fire and metal. A man halfway up the hill, calmly reloading his musket, grunted and collapsed, snow dusting his corpse.

From his right and left his companions also fired. One man screamed and kept screaming. Two men shot back, one shot hitting the tree behind which Nathaniel had taken cover. The shot hit high. The Ryngians were shooting blindly. Then someone shouted orders and the Ryngian regulars returned no more fire.

Nathaniel ignored the bluebacks and crouched. He worked the lever, cleared the breech, reloaded and levered the assembly back into place. He peered out, saw two silhouettes still on the slope, and *pasmortes* on their way.

"Remember, the Prince wants one of them things."

Makepeace laughed. "I'll try to save him a piece, anyway."

Nathaniel tracked and shot. One *pasmorte* was loping forward on all fours. The bullet caught it high in the chest as it rose to spring ahead. It nearly stood like a man again, then flopped over onto its back, arms and legs spasmodically clawing at the sky.

A single gunshot answered him, chipping bark from the tree. "Careful. One has a gun."

"By the rock." Kamiskwa pointed due west, then raised his musket and shot. Another *pasmorte* went down, raising a cloud of snow. The Altashee ducked back, but didn't bother to reload his gun. Instead he unlimbered his warclub.

Makepeace shot. Nathaniel, just finishing a quick reload himself, didn't see if the big man hit anything or not. He came up, sighted the rock and, when he saw movement, fired. Whatever had been moving stopped, but that didn't matter much.

The *pasmortes* had reached them.

Kamiskwa screeched at the top of his lungs and lunged from behind the tree, his warclub held high. His first blow crushed a skull and the second caught a *pasmorte* in the chest. Ribs snapped and the creature flew off into the underbrush. The Altashee stalked forward, his club whirling, not waiting for them to close.

Makepeace similarly waded into battle, clubbing his musket. He brought it down sharply, bashing a skull in, then levered the body aside. Two more came at him, more by happenstance than planning. He smashed one with the rifle, but the other lunged and bit him on the thigh. Makepeace roared, dropped his rifle and ripped the thing away from his leg. "Back to Hell with you!" The very avatar of wrath, he hoisted the thing aloft, then slammed it down, snapping its spine over his knee.

Two of them had come for Nathaniel, but a snowdrift slowed them. Nathaniel buried his tomahawk in one's skull, then sidestepped the other. He smacked it in the head with his rifle's butt and it dropped, but only for a moment. It kept clawing at the snow. He hit it again, crushing the skull.

By the time he wrenched his tomahawk free of the first, only one of the *pasmortes* remained. It was a small man none of them recognized. The *pasmorte* didn't have any intelligence showing in the one eye he had left, but he crouched and hissed at them like a snake. He shifted to face each in turn, but Makepeace got behind and draped his bear robe over him. Makepeace gathered the whole bundle up and smiled. "Got your Prince a prize.

Nathaniel quickly reloaded. Kamiskwa retrieved his musket and followed suit. They watched the bundle while Makepeace got his gun and reloaded. The big man also produced some leather straps. He opened up the robe a bit, bound the *pasmorte*'s ankles together, then dabbed a loop around a loose hand. He stripped the robe off, forced the *pasmorte* face down in the snow, and tied his hands together. The thing still hissed, but wasn't moving much.

Makepeace, back in his robe again, dragged the thing along by its ankles as they approached the rock. Before they saw anything, they heard the sound of breathing—more angry than labored. Kamiskwa went up and around the hillside to cover, then waved Nathaniel forward.

The *pasmorte* behind the rock had taken the bullet high on the left side of his chest. He struggled to move his limbs. It almost looked as if he was drunk or asleep, but his eyes were open and he scowled when his eyes focused on Nathaniel. "This is the second time you have killed me."

"I'd do it a third, Etienne Ilsavont."

"This shot shouldn't have hurt me."

Nathaniel smiled. "Special bullets. Prince Vlad cast lead around an iron core. Figured if you was magicked up, iron might magick you down."

The thing snarled. "The soldiers will find them, the Norillian and the traitor, and kill them, you know. Then they will come for you."

"The Norillian? Owen?" Nathaniel looked up. "Makepeace, stay with him."

Kamiskwa had already turned. Nathaniel tracked after him and the squad of Ryngian soldiers who had struggled up the hill. The man he'd shot lay dead. The other was shivering and making mewing sounds. His eyes didn't focus and the red snow around him marked his time in minutes. Nathaniel crested the hill, found another Ryngian soldier dead, and Kamiskwa at the bottom of the hill.

The Altashee looked up from where he crouched. "Blood, and it goes that way."

Nathaniel looked. "The winding path. Owen knew better. Why would he…?"

Kamiskwa stood. "He knew to fear it, and hoped the others did not."

"We have to go after him."

"No."

"But your father and the bargain he struck. They could do us no harm."

Kamiskwa shook his head. "My father's bargain was that no innocents would be taken. If we step on that path, we knowingly violate the agreement."

"They wanted Owen once." Nathaniel sat down in the snow. "They ain't letting him go this time."

"I fear you are right." Kamiskwa turned from the winding path. "Tonight we have lost a brother. This is something for which the master of the *wendigo* will pay a dear price."

They returned to the battlefield and decapitated all the dead, including the Ryngian regulars. They put the soldiers and some of the *pasmortes* into one *batteau* and sent it drifting back west. They hoped the current would suck it down the Roaring River. They loaded their two captives and the ammunition from the dead soldiers into the other batteau and headed across the lake. Two days later they reached the outflow to the Tillie and were able to work the boat down quite a ways.

Iced-over rocks made the going treacherous the few times they had to get out and pull the *batteau* past obstacles, but they learned a few lessons in the doing. The smaller *pasmorte* fell into the river and, despite having been underwater for five minutes, had not drowned. And when the sun came out, both *pasmortes* became a bit more active, though Etienne remained very weak and palsied.

They brought the *batteau* almost into Hattersburg, but cached it west of the town and cut south to avoid the town itself. They visited Seth Plant just long enough to tell him where they had cached the boat and that he was welcome to it. From there they headed south, hoping to cut the Benjamin below Grand Falls. Etienne slowed them with his clumsiness, so they fashioned a travois and dragged him—a task actually made easier because of the snow.

The party detoured to Saint Luke to tell Kamiskwa's father of Owen's death. They made a separate camp outside the bounds of the Altashee village and kept the *pasmortes* fully restrained. The Altashee mourned Owen in a ceremony both solemn and sincere, with many tears shed. Little Agaskan, however, maintained Owen would bring her doll back.

The ceremony gave the men time to rest before heading out again. Once back on the trail they moved as quickly as was prudent, but the weather did not cooperate. Just over a month out from Anvil Lake, they camped below Great Falls and built a roaring fire. They let the little *pasmorte* huddle near it. The journey had not been kind to him, and the fire did little to revive him.

Makepeace finally said what Nathaniel had been thinking. "Hisser ain't long for this world."

"Nope."

The small *pasmorte*'s leathery skin had split and frayed. His fingertips were all white bone and one of his cheeks had opened beneath that empty eye socket. And something kept leaking out of that socket like tears, save that they were black and foul smelling.

Makepeace squatted next to him. "Got a notion what is ailing him?"

Nathaniel shook his head. "Ain't nothing wrong with him but he's dead and all."

Kamiskwa frowned. "The *wendigo* leaves the weak."

Etienne laughed, his jaw gaping open and out of his control. "You do not understand. Du Malphias could fix him easily. The man works miracles."

"He ain't 'zactly here." Nathaniel frowned. "I wonder iffen his magick gets weaker the further things get from him."

Makepeace grunted. "That would explain Hisser's problem. Don't look good for you, neither, Pierre."

Ilsavont laughed. "He will be coming soon enough. Over the winter he will have the dead of Kebeton shipped to him. He will leave them frozen like my *père* until spring. They will be thawed and finish the fort. Then he will come for you. You will all die, then you will serve him, too."

Makepeace snorted. "Good God willing that ain't a-going to be happening."

"Fools. Du Malphias does to us what your God did to His Son. The difference is that du Malphias does not seek salvation, but dominion, and he shall have it."

By morning Hisser had stopped moving. They built a pyre and laid him on it. Makepeace said a few words and they watched it burn down. It delayed them for half a day, but Nathaniel figured they owed it to Hisser or, at least, to whomever he'd been. They scattered the ashes into the river.

Using two canoes, they headed toward Temperance. Makepeace volunteered to be in the canoe with Ilsavont. They tied the *pasmorte* up for transportation, stuffing him into the bow. Nathaniel and Kamiskwa usually ranged ahead, but occasionally they were close enough to hear Makepeace speaking to the Ryngian.

"'Pears Makepeace ain't too happy with Etienne's Godlessness."

"Cutting out Ilsavont's tongue would be easier than enduring his cursing."

"Well now, I reckon the Prince will want to ask him some questions."

From the point where Makepeace had offered words over Hisser, Etienne had taken to speaking an endless stream of profanity. The words alternated through several Shedashee dialects: Norillian, Tharyngian, and a couple other tongues Nathaniel couldn't identify. Makepeace had countered with Scripture, starting from Genesis and working his way on up. Nathaniel couldn't swear Makepeace got everything right—he was fair certain a Remian Governor hadn't threatened to shoot the Good Lord—but the pure delight in Makepeace's voice disinclined Nathaniel to be asking any questions.

At night Makepeace would continue his recitations, volunteering to take the first watch so he could continue. After that, Etienne would beg Nathaniel to kill him.

"Oh, I reckon you'll be dying, don't you be worrying about that." Nathaniel smiled. "Prince Vladimir, he's a smart man. Does a powerful lot of thinking. He done wanted us to bring him back a *pasmorte*, and we have."

"You are a fool, Woods, if you think he wants to know how to kill me." Etienne looked disgusted enough to spit. "You know how. Crush a skull. Cut off the head. You knew that from my father."

"Then why is it he wants you?"

"To learn how to make more like me." The *pasmorte* shook his head. "You think I am stupid. That I always was stupid, no?"

"Weren't nothing you ever did took much thought."

"But I see things, no? I do. People everywhere. People dying. 'Such a waste,' they say when someone dies young. But du Malphias, he can make use of them. People, they will sell him their dead. He can use them to clear forests and till fields. We do not complain, we eat little, we do not sleep. And if one of us fails like my little friend, there will be more to take his place."

"Keep talking like that and I'll wake Makepeace."

"But you know I am right. A man, he comes out here, he clears a farm, he works it, he makes a life. This is good, no?"

"It is."

"Imagine the rich man, who buys the dead, has them work for him. When the single man has a bad harvest, his family suffers. He cannot repay debts, so the rich man, he buys the farm. He needs no food for his laborers. He can sell cheaply and still profit. But that is not the worst."

Nathaniel narrowed his eyes. "Do tell."

"That rich man, he fears only one thing. Death. And Monsieur du Malphias can ensure he will not die. How much will men pay for that, Woods, eh? You might be tempted yourself."

Nathaniel shook his head. "Not with you as an example. I'll take my God-given and count it as good."

"But so many others will not, monsieur." Etienne smiled. "Bring me to your Prince. Let him learn my secrets, and you guarantee the dead shall rule the living forever more."

Etienne appeared to have talked himself out, which was good. Saved Nathaniel putting a bullet through his skull. He didn't appreciate the *pasmorte* saying those things about the Prince. Nathaniel didn't believe a word of it, but the others things, they rang true. Nathaniel had no trouble making a list of wealthy men who would buy immortality—with Zachariah Warren at the top.

He smiled and patted his cartridge case. "I reckon I'll be saving a bullet or three for a good purpose."

The next day they started down the river in good spirits. Though snow still covered the ground, the sky started clear and the sun burned hot. Snow started melting off branches and a gentle, warm breeze came up from the south. The men stripped off their heavy robes and paddled only to steer, content to let the river bring them to the Prince's estate.

After two days they caught sight of the steam plume from the wurmrest. Coming around the last bend, Nathaniel put them on course so the breeze would guide them straight to the Prince's landing.

Up on the grounds, two figures stood wrapped in cloaks, with Mugwump nosing the snow out of his way. Nathaniel raised a paddle and one of them pointed. Smaller, with golden hair—it had to be the Princess.

Beside her the Prince raised hands to his mouth. He shouted something, but the breeze carried his words off. The Prince started toward the dock.

The wurm raised his head. Nostrils dilated, then his tail flicked. The beast whipped around and in two quick bounds, plunged past the Prince and through the shore ice. His tail lashed, spraying the Prince, then vanished without a trace. Nathaniel looked into the water but saw nothing until the wurm surfaced again.

Mugwump came up fast, right beneath Makepeace's canoe. The beast's nose flipped the fragile craft into the air, snapping it in two. Makepeace tumbled backward. The *pasmorte* spun upward, lazily, struggling ineffectively against the ropes binding him.

And Mugwump, hanging in the air for an impossibly long time, opened his jaws and devoured Etienne Ilsavont in one big gulp.

CHAPTER FORTY-THREE

November 23, 1763
Prince Haven
Temperance Bay, Mystria

Vlad stared disbelieving, a hand outstretched, as Mugwump snatched the man out of the air. The wurm's body slowly twisted, his tail all the way clear of the water. Mugwump splashed down on his back, sending spray and a wave that almost swamped the other canoe. And yet, despite the splash, there was no mistaking a second opening and closing of jaws, and a large lump moving down the wurm's throat.

Wurms had eaten riders before, or so the stories said. The riders had always been evil, unsavory men—again, according to the stories. It always seemed they had provoked the wurms into it and deserved their fates.

Then Mugwump surfaced again, a sputtering man draped across his muzzle. The Prince waited for the head flip that would propel the man into the air, then a quick snatch for another bite. The tail flicked and Mugwump sped toward the shore, a wave breaking high as he came up out of the water and straight onto the snowy lawn.

Vlad instinctively ran over, gathering Gisella behind him, shielding her with his body. "Don't run. He might see you as prey."

She held onto his shoulders, shivering. "Yes, my lord."

Mugwump lowered his head, letting the man roll to the ground. The wurm stared at the Prince, the golden eyes full of curiosity. The wurm nosed the man again, flipping him over onto his stomach, where he vomited and started muttering a psalm.

Vlad raised a hand, uncertain of what do to, but perceiving no threat. "What is it? What am I missing?"

The wurm's eyes half closed, then he turned and trundled off to the wurmrest, head held proudly high.

Is that it, or is that what I want to see?

Nathaniel and Kamiskwa, came running over, guns in hand. The Altashee knelt by the man Mugwump had rescued. The man vomited again, then gathered himself on all fours. "Ain't supposed to breathe drink. I will be fine."

Vlad looked at Nathaniel. "Who did Mugwump kill?"

"Ain't like he killed him. I done that. Twice." Nathaniel shook his head. "Etienne Ilsavont. He was a *pasmorte* like his father. Your bullet worked like a charm."

"You shall have to tell me everything. First, however, we should get inside and fetch your companion some dry clothes."

The large man's wet beard and clothes made him look like a half-drowned cat, though his smile attested to his good spirits. "I don't reckon you'll have much more than a sheet will fit me, but I would be obliged for a lend of one while these things dry."

"Nonsense. My father was a large man. There is a trunk in the attic. I am Prince Vladimir, by way of introduction, and this is Princess Gisella of Kesse-Saxeburg."

The large man's eyes widened, then he came up on one knee and bowed his head. "Pleased and honored, Your Highnesses."

Nathaniel slapped the man on a soggy shoulder. "This is Makepeace Bone."

"Ah, the man wounded at Anvil Lake."

Makepeace got up again. "T'weren't nothing, Highness. Just got all meat, no bone."

Nathaniel's smile slowly evaporated. "Anvil Lake's where we got the *pasmorte*."

"Any word of Captain Strake? I sent Jean off to trade for him."

"He'll be a bit late for that, Highness." The woodsman swallowed hard. "Captain Strake ain't coming back."

The Prince took them up to the main house and left Kamiskwa, Makepeace, and Nathaniel to build a roaring fire in the dining room's fireplace. Gisella set herself the task of arranging food and drink. Vlad dispatched Baker to close Mugwump in the wurmrest and watch him, firing up the boiler as the day drew to an end.

He took it upon himself to go to the attic and retrieve clothes. Without too much difficulty he located the wooden chest and opened it. He unfolded a shirt and held it up. It might barely fit. He also found trousers and doubted they could be buttoned closed, but they would have to do. Below them he found a folded blanket, which he also pulled out.

A small packet of letters fell to the floor. They had been tied with a ribbon, which had been sealed with wax. The seal bore the imprint of his mother's signet, and the letter on top had been addressed to his father in her hand. By riffling the corners, however, he saw other letters in his father's hand. The paper looked old and the date on the first letter marked it as being older than he was.

Blushing for reasons he could not fathom, he hid the letters back in the chest and returned to his guests. Makepeace's wet clothes got hauled into the kitchen to dry while the large man sat wrapped in a blanket, his feet perilously close to the fire.

Gisella and a serving girl arrived with mulled cider and stew, bread, and cheese. Vlad offered whiskey, which Nathaniel accepted, but Kamiskwa and Makepeace refused. They chatted pleasantly while the men ate, with Gisella effortlessly playing hostess. Once they had finished their stew, she cleared the bowls, then returned to sit quietly at Vlad's side.

Nathaniel reported on the expedition and confined himself to important facts—or the facts he thought the Prince wanted to hear. He described the battle with the *pasmortes* in a bit more sanitized detail than he might have in the past, occasionally glancing at the Princess as he did so, but Vlad understood what he was doing and found the information fascinating.

"You say Ilsavont acted as if palsied? Limbs would shake, overall weakness?"

"'Cepting his mouth, which ran just fine."

Vlad stroked his chin. "I had hoped the iron would kill them outright, but debilitating them also works. I wish I'd had a chance to examine him or even this Hisser."

Makepeace shook his head. "Poor little feller. He was scared most all the time. Didn't mind lugging the travois for a piece, though."

"That's interesting. You're saying the *pasmorte* followed your orders?"

"Just hitched him up, told him to follow."

"Told, or *commanded*?"

Makepeace tugged on his beard. "Come to think on it, my voice did rise a mite."

"Very good."

Nathaniel frowned. "But now Ilsavont, he didn't take no orders at all."

"No, I gathered that, and this is what I find interesting. We know the *pasmortes*, some of them at least, can work magick. Ilsavont and his father both maintained some of their personality and could shoot. I would hazard a guess that your Hisser could not have. Logic and reason are critical for doing complex tasks. Following orders, however, only requires obedience. Tell me truthfully, gentlemen, did Hisser exhibit any behavior that would mark him as being more intelligent than, say, a dog?"

"Cain't say as he did."

Makepeace smiled. "I reckon if he'd had fur, I might have even petted him."

"And there was a discernible difference between him and Ilsavont in terms of decay?"

Kamiskwa nodded. "None of the lesser *pasmortes* had been fresh from the grave. Ilsavont was killed when they took Aodaga."

Vlad's eyebrows knitted together. "Would you have known Ilsavont was *pasmorte* if he had not mentioned it?"

Nathaniel's eyes narrowed for a bit. "I don't reckon I would have. He was pink and warm, didn't have no bits fallen off."

"Most peculiar, and yet I wonder…"

Gisella squeezed his shoulder. "What is it, my lord?"

"Just a thought. I shall need to do some reading on it." His left hand rose and covered hers. "Your speculation about distance from du Malphias having an affect on his magic is also interesting. Enchantments have been known to diminish over time. Distance, then, would make sense, too—though the implication that he can work magick at range disturbs me."

Vlad sighed. "And to the other matter, there is no doubt Captain Strake is gone?"

"Him, someone who escaped with him, and seven Ryngians near as we can make out." Nathaniel looked down, refusing to meet the Prince's gaze. "Me and Kamiskwa should have gone after him. I was just scared. We lost him to the winding path."

Gisella leaned forward. "Please, what means this 'winding path'?"

"It's a place in the forest, many places, really. You see a path that goes on forever and you get lost in it."

She nodded. "We know these places. The forests of Kesse have them. *Die Dunkelheitplätze.* Children, they get lost. They say devils live there. There are stories of the children returning later, generations later, thinking they have been gone for no time at all."

"Ain't no returning from the winding path." Nathaniel glanced at Kamiskwa. "Lessen you're Chief Msitazi."

Kamiskwa's eyes tightened. "My friend says he was afraid. This is not so. I told him we could not go. He was brave. I was not."

"Now that ain't so, Kamiskwa."

"You know it is."

Vlad held his hands up. "Gentlemen, your courage is not to be questioned. The three of you killed four times your number in *pasmortes* and killed at least three Ryngians. Had the trail ended at a deep crevasse, you would not have leaped in. Death on the winding path would be just as certain. The spirits here are not so kind as they are in Kesse-Saxeburg. And your mission was not to rescue Captain Strake, but to gain information, which you have done admirably."

He stood. "Mr. Bone, I shall require from you a complete inventory of what you lost when your canoe was destroyed. I will replace everything. I shall even have Temperance Bay's finest gunsmith make a gun to your specification."

Makepeace smiled. "Well, Highness, if you make that Queensland, I been fancying—not coveting, mind you—fancying that there gun Nathaniel's been toting around."

"Done. Until it is finished, I shall offer you the lend of any piece I own." Vlad smiled. "Though I know it is an imposition, I should ask the three of you to remain here, as my guests, for however long you wish. A week at the minimum. I am certain there are questions I shall have, and details I wish to confirm."

Nathaniel nodded. "I reckon we can do that, though my fancy clothes are in Saint Luke."

"I promise you, gentlemen, you'll have no need for such. We'll not be having other guests any time soon."

"I need to be getting word to the Frosts." Nathaniel sighed. "I done promised them I'd bring Owen home. It's on me to deliver the truth."

"Agreed, but your trip can wait. I will need you, and the information we compile will make his sacrifice worth it."

The next day Vlad interviewed each man separately. He teased out extra details about *pasmortes,* which he compiled in a notebook. The idea that they could be killed by crushing the skull or shooting them in the head suggested du Malphias was stimulating something in the brain to *animate* the creatures. He carefully chose that word so as to avoid thinking of them as *alive.*

He'd torn through his library and found an interesting collection of treatises by a Tharyngian surgeon who had traveled with the army during the Tharyngo-Alandaluce War two decades earlier. He described, in clinical detail, the nature of head wounds in a variety of patients and the symptoms his patients exhibited. He coupled this with highly detailed descriptions of brain dissections where he purported to identify the structures that governed certain functions.

One, which lay lodged deep in the brain, above the stem, but not in the higher brain, he identified as the Gland of Miracles. He indicated that it, deeply set as it was, was the portion of the brain which enabled one to access magick. He included some tables that purported to show that magick users had larger Glands of Miracles than others, but his statistical sample had been ridiculously small. He so believed his thesis, however, that he had openly advocated inserting a needle through the ears of criminals to destroy that gland, assuring readers it could be done with minimal impairment of other functions.

Vlad's study led him to divide *pasmortes* into two classes. One were low-functioning creatures who were converted after an extended postmortem period. Their outer brain had decayed to the point where they were not capable of much more than following orders. If the Gland of Miracles, set deep inside, was one of the last portions of the brain to decay, it would allow for this sort of *pasmorte*.

The other *pasmortes* clearly had been brought back before much, if any, decay had set in. The Prince caught himself thinking about their being *alive* and not just reanimated. The fact was that very few people died *instantly*. Death was a process that look a long time, and ample were cases of people who had been believed dead and had later awoken to find themselves in a casket or being lowered into a grave.

What if du Malphias did not reanimate these people, but brought them back from the very brink of death? Some impairment consistent with their injuries made sense. The Laureate could have mistaken that for symptoms of brain damage, hence his belief they were actually dead. It could be that they were returned to life through magick healing, which was not unknown, but was rare and never before conducted so thoroughly.

But that can't be true. While Ilsavont's palsy was consistent with spinal cord injury, none of the three explorers had mentioned his being in pain or bleeding from the wound. That, coupled with the low-functioning *pasmortes* moving sluggishly in the cold, suggested a depressed metabolism. The things really were just reanimated corpses.

Or, at least, Ilsavont was.

A savage storm blowing in from the east prevented Nathaniel from heading into Temperance. Vlad did not envy his having to deliver the news and resolved to go with him to visit the Frosts. Given the nature of that visit, neither was anxious for the storm to end.

The storm did require the boiler to be fired up around the clock and Makepeace volunteered to help man it. "Well, now, I done some praying and thinking. Seems if Mugwump wanted to make a meal of me, I'd long since be et. I reckon God has plans for him and me, so this is God's work I'll be doing."

Mugwump, for his part, remained silent on matters of theology, but took to Makepeace's presence easily. He never splashed him and always looked up when the man came to relieve the Prince. Baker reported that Mugwump seemed sulky when Makepeace left and, as nearly as Vlad could figure out, he was hoping the big man would be bringing him another *pasmorte* as a snack.

Exactly *why* Mugwump had gone after the reanimated corpse remained a mystery. None of the Prince's books explained that behavior. Mugwump had resumed his normal diet and ate with his usual enthusiasm.

Three days after the storm had begun to blow, it broke. As the stablehands were hitching a team to the Prince's coach, a lone rider, his horse steaming, galloped into the yard. He leaped from the saddle, tossing Nathaniel his reins, and dropped to a knee. "Forgive me, Highness. I've just come from Temperance."

Vlad flicked a finger. "Up, please. You're Caleb Frost."

"I am, Highness." Caleb caught his breath. "Please, sir, I have a message. It's Captain Strake, sir."

The Prince nodded. "We know."

Caleb blinked in surprise. "You do?"

"Mr. Woods brought the news. Terrible thing. Tragedy." The Prince shook his head. "We were just heading into Temperance to let your family know he's dead."

"No, sir, that's not it." Caleb laughed aloud. "Captain Strake. He's come back to us. He's alive!"

CHAPTER FORTY-FOUR

Otherwhen
The Winding Path

One step onto the winding path and the world changed. The wind's whisper became the unceasing crash of breaking glass. With every footfall the powdery snow hissed and popped as if it were burning coals. The sky, where it peeked through between trees, became a luminous grey the likes of which Owen had only seen once before, on the voyage to Mystria. Sailors had pointed at the horizon, paled, and prayed.

Left arm tucked tightly against the hole in his side, he draped his right arm over Quarante-neuf's left shoulder. The *pasmorte* supported him with an arm across his back. Owen remembered to close his left eye. "Only use your right eye."

The *pasmorte's* voice came listlessly. "It doesn't matter. Their magick does not affect me."

Behind him came shouting and two more shots. One hit Quarante-neuf in the lower back. He grunted. He twisted, putting his body between the Tharyngian soldiers and Owen. Owen peeked past and continued sidling along the winding path.

The Tharyngians spread out, their faces serious. An officer snapped orders. The two men who had shot reloaded their muskets with quick and efficient motions. But as they came to reinsert their ramrods beneath their barrels they slowed. Their intensity slackened, their ferocity melted into wonder. Their hands opened and guns fell forgotten.

Owen dared not open his left eye for fear of being seduced by whatever the Ryngians saw. Small creatures with spindly limbs, woven from branches and decorated with moss and mushrooms, played coy games of hide and seek. They peered from behind trees, the light melody of giggles playing through the air. Men laughed and darted forward, stumbling. They emerged from the snow, faces covered, laughing all the more in that tone men reserve for acknowledging their foolishness before women they desire.

Military discipline vanished. The officer bowed, sweeping off his hat, then

264

straightening. He offered a gloved hand to a gnarled dryad. He took the creature into his arms as he might a Duchess at some grand Feris gala. They began to dance—he, surprisingly well for wearing snowshoes. His men scattered, chasing other phantom lovers further into the woods.

"We have to get away from them." Owen turned back south, then stopped.

Another of the creatures had emerged. Whereas the others had been made of sticks, this one had stout saplings for limbs and the bole of a tree for a body. Where branches might have topped it, lightning-blasted wooden spikes formed a crown. The creature sat there, knees drawn up, arms wide, eyeless and yet clearly watching them.

Words formed in low murmurs, seeming to vibrate up through the ground. "You *know* the dangers, yet you come. You do not *seem* stupid."

Owen removed his arm from Quarante-neuf's shoulder and stood as straight as he could. "There are things outside the path which are worse than whatever fate awaits me here."

"The abomination."

The creature referred to du Malphias' fortress, and a moment's thought revealed why. The walls were formed of this thing's bones, and its creation ate into his domain. The *pasmortes*, mindlessly pursuing directives, might well have carved into places men would have avoided by instinct alone.

"The abomination's creator is my sworn enemy." Owen chose his words carefully, not sure how Quarante-neuf would react. He wondered if du Malphias' magick could hold sway on the winding path, but Quarante-neuf's continued existence and the hints of pain in Owen's legs gave him a very clear answer. *Or did it?* He felt more the gunshot wound and the piercing of the nails than the shooting pains his steps had produced before.

"You came to my realm. What is it you wanted from me?"

"We came wanting nothing."

Bass notes thrummed through Owen. *Laughter?*

"Men always want something."

"I just want to go home."

"Of course you do." The creature climbed to one knee, towering over them. "You brought my children playthings."

Owen looked back, but aside from the dancing officer, he could see none of the other soldiers. Laughter echoed from the hillsides, and Owen braced himself for screams of terror.

"What will happen to them?"

"Do you care?"

"They are men like myself, I must care."

More deep laughter thrummed through Owen. "You say that because you think you must. You think yourself superior because you have risen above the other animals. Even though these men wished to kill you, you think you must care because you share a kinship. But, in truth, you do not care. You fear you will die as they will. Admit it."

Owen nodded. "And I pity them."

"You tell yourself it is pity, manling, but you disguise the true reason. Guilt. And this is what sets you apart from the animals, this feeling of guilt. Your most useless emotion, sour and bitter, yet one you are trained to accept as inescapable."

Owen *did* feel guilty. Whatever pain and terror the Tharyngians would know was the result of his leading them onto the winding path. But he had not forced them to follow. They were rational individuals who had made a decision to follow. They were fully responsible for their own actions, and the consequences fell fully on their heads.

The creature leaned forward. "You are a bright one, aren't you? You have figured it out."

Owen shook his head. "Guilt is not useless. Without it, we would do horrible things again and again. We would be lawless."

"You would be *wild*, as you once were, free to own the world. Free to be our favored pets again, instead of a pest which must be exterminated."

"I don't understand."

"No, you refuse to let yourself understand." The creature sat back. "You believe you know the way of things, the way things were intended. In your creation stories, man knows the forest—the *garden*—existed before he did. He places himself above it, to hide his fear of it.

"No matter. You wish to know what will become of them." The arms swung wide. "They will know the greatest pleasures, and then the greatest fears. They will be alone, and terrified, and after we have drained them of all emotion, they will die. Their flesh and blood will nourish our bodies as their emotions feed our souls."

Owen watched the Tharyngian officer and read the pure delight on his face. He turned away again. "It won't be fast, will it?"

"Excruciatingly slow."

"And us?"

The giant creature stood. "I find myself in your debt. Not sufficiently that I can release you, but if you would perform for me a service…"

"What? Lure more in?"

"You will do that, and more." The creature swept a branched hand down, clearing away snow and a layer of wet leaves. He revealed an oval sheet of ice. "I require a drop of your blood, and for you to peer into this frozen glass."

Owen nodded.

The creature extended a branch and probed his wound in a manner not wholly gentle. Owen winced. The creature offered no apology and dabbed a drop on the ice. The rest of the blood, as nearly as Owen could tell, sank into the branch and a green bud rose in its place.

"Look, manling."

Owen knelt beside the translucent ice, hands on either side, and stared down. It shifted to a mirror. For a heartbeat he did not recognize the reflection. Ragged beard, unkempt hair, sunken eyes. Captivity had not been kind. Then the ice cleared. He saw his wife, Catherine, standing, staring at him, her face full of hatred.

"No, Catherine!" He thrust a hand forward to touch her, but his fingers crumpled against the ice. It became translucent again, the droplet of blood having vanished.

Owen looked up. "She doesn't hate me."

"It is not what *is*, but what *will be*, because of choices you make." More laughter rippled up through the ground. "Her love withers, but you shall remain ignorant until too late."

Owen's stomach collapsed in on itself. He pounded his fist against the ice, trying to shatter it. Neither it nor his hand broke, but he fervently wished for either. He wanted to destroy that future, and if he hurt himself, so much the better.

Because, as the image became clear, and as he saw the woman's face emerge from shadows, for a heartbeat, just a heartbeat, he'd feared it was Bethany. And when it turned out to be his wife, just for another heartbeat, he felt relief.

Quarante-neuf pulled him back upright, then faced the creature. "You would have the same of me?"

"No." The creature reached out and touched the green bud to Quarante-neuf's forehead. In the space of three heartbeats the bud flowered fully, leaves sprouted green and huge, then became red and gold and dropped away.

Quarante-neuf staggered, sinking to his knees. "I understand."

Owen turned. The *pasmorte*'s face had become a lifeless mask. "What did you do to him?"

"Accelerated a process which you had begun." The creature stepped back. An avenue opened to the east. "I know you both. I know your lives will be full of misery. I shall enjoy that, therefore I shall let you live."

Owen stood and helped Quarante-neuf up. "You said that what I saw was the future. Is there a way to change it?"

"A few ways, if you choose carefully. If you remember what you truly are. But you won't. It is that friction, between what you want to think you are and your true nature, which will be the source of your misery." Laughter trembled up through the earth and snow. "You torture yourselves so well."

The creature pointed along the path. "Go. You will find your world different, but much the same. Go, sons of Mystria, knowing your future has earned your freedom."

Owen threw an arm around Quarante-neuf's waist and led the *pasmorte* up along the path. He didn't see any other dryads lurking around trees, and did not bother to look back. The creature would be gone, all traces of the Tharyngians would have vanished. All he had of the winding path was its truth—misery—not the illusion of peace.

"What did it do to you, Quarante-neuf? What did you see?"

"It does not concern you, Captain. As it said, it made faster what you had started."

"Are you dying?"

Quarante-neuf managed a short laugh. "Not a task that requires doing twice. No, my vitality is not ebbing."

"Good." Owen stopped and hunched over. "I'm afraid mine is."

The *pasmorte* straightened up. "I can carry you."

"No, my friend, just let me rest. A few more steps. Let us crest the hill and then I shall rest."

Quarante-neuf threw his left arm around Owen and looped the man's right over his shoulders again. The *pasmorte*'s steps remained strong. He held Owen up easily. With each step it seemed as if he was becoming stronger, showing no fatigue or consequences of having been shot.

Then Owen laughed. *It is because you are becoming weaker.*

They crested the hill and everything changed again. An east wind blasted them full in the face, driving wet snow. Owen staggered back a step, hoping to return to the winding path's sanctuary, but it no longer existed. Instead of being on the side of a hill, they had just emerged into a meadow.

"I don't understand." Owen shielded his face with a hand. He had to scream above the shrieking wind. "This can't be."

Quarante-neuf laughed. "Where we just were could not be, Captain. This place *is*. Luckily, I know where we are. Come."

They kept walking. Quarante-neuf, anyway, walked. He dragged Owen through drifts and kept him moving when Owen wanted to stop. "You cannot, Captain, you'll freeze. You will die if you do not keep moving."

"That's better, my friend, than causing what I saw. My wife hating me."

"Is that truly what you saw?"

"The expression on her face. My fault."

"But you can change it. He said that."

Owen collapsed, curling into a ball. "I can't take another step."

"And I can't let you come to harm."

Owen patted the *pasmorte*'s leg. "That is du Malphias' magick speaking. Save yourself. If you save me, I will kill him."

Quarante-neuf knelt, and gathered Owen into his arms. "What I feel is not his magick. It is the magick of what a friend feels for a friend."

How long he traveled in Quarante-neuf's arms Owen could not say. The blizzard had made the world a timeless, silver-grey tunnel. When night fell it became colder. He would have frozen to death, save for the *pasmorte*'s warmth.

Finally Quarante-neuf set him down. Owen opened his eyes and found his surroundings vaguely familiar. *This place. This is the Frost house.* "How did you know?"

Quarante-neuf did not answer. He stood over Owen and pounded on the door. He waited and pounded again, then backed down the steps.

Owen reached out even as he heard footsteps on the other side. "No, you cannot go."

The *pasmorte* shook his head. "I am dead, but I *remember*. For this reason, I *must* go."

The door cracked open, yellow light pouring into the storm. Of Quarante-neuf, Owen could only see a dim silhouette being devoured by the storm. Snow had filled his footsteps and, by the time Owen had been stripped of his clothes, bandaged and lowered to bed, there would be no sign of Quarante-neuf's passing.

1764

CHAPTER FORTY-FIVE

May 13, 1764
Government House, Temperance
Temperance Bay, Mystria

Prince Vladimir had always found the long delay in communications with Norisle to be a blessing. The swiftest response he had ever had to a missive had been three months, and that was on a matter of no consequence. In general, the more serious the request, the slower the response. And while that suggested due deliberation at the highest levels of government, the replies most often had an offhand quality that suggested no one read his reports nor did any sober thinking on the problem.

Within a day of Captain Strake's miraculous return, the Prince had interviewed him. Within a week, Owen had come to the estate and helped update the model of du Malphias' fortress. The Prince had written a fully detailed report with all cogent facts included—he left out specifics of Owen's escape since that would have undercut the reliability of his testimony—and sent it with Colonel Langford back to Launston on the tenth of December.

And then he had waited.

And waited.

News trickling in from Norisle had not been good. The war in Tharyngia did not go well. General Ahab Smalling had made Lord Rivendell look very much the master of war. Smalling had managed to squander the few advantages the Laureates had given him. Lord Rivendell had led through neglect; Smalling managed every tiny detail, demanding reports on powder and shot expenditure by soldier—expecting unit survivors to provide that data for their fallen comrades. He wasn't above flogging those who failed to comply. This included the dead sergeant of a squad that had been wiped out in a rearguard action.

The Prince learned those sorts of details through private correspondence. The official records praised the casualty figures. Smalling was given a knighthood and posted to Her Majesty's colony of Xue Vang, on the Han coast, where he would parade local levy troops before races and other events for Norillian expatriates.

The Mystrian winter was not passed unpleasantly. Though the weather was bitterly cold, with more snow than usual, Gisella's presence brought Vlad great pleasure. She purchased a home in Temperance and the Count took up residence nearby. She often entertained and required the Prince to attend her parties. She invited other friends, including Rachel Warren, for they had become quite close.

Watching Owen Strake's progress toward full recovery had been a joy. Owen had looked horrible when the Prince first saw him. A bullet had passed all the way through his flank and doctors thought bleeding him would help drain toxins from the blood. Prince Vlad outraged them when he dismissed them in favor of Chief Msitazi and Altashee medicines.

Of greatest concern was the magick that filled Owen's steps with pain. Msitazi had managed to unweave du Malphias' magick, but doing so had not been easy. The Altashee Chieftain suggested that had du Malphias been closer, or had chosen to fight him, he might not have been able to accomplish the job.

The gunshot wound responded well to poultices and unguents. Kamiskwa and Nathaniel supplied ample amounts of *mogiqua*. Because they'd had to dig it out from beneath the snow, it wasn't at full potency, but they made a poultice from the leaves and a bitter tea from mashed roots.

Bethany Frost made certain Owen drank the tea, and she changed his dressings. She also barred any visitors she felt would irritate Owen. The Prince credited her presence with much of Owen's recovery. She and the rest of the Frost family watched over him. Doctor Frost opened his library to Owen, and Caleb even came to treat him decently.

Within two weeks Owen had gained enough strength to walk without more than a cane. Now, in mid-May, one had to look to notice his limp, and that came only after a long day's walk. The Prince had seen pain occasionally on the man's face, but a decoction of pussy willow eased it quickly enough. The Prince admired how the man pushed himself, regaining the weight he had lost and refusing to give in to weakness.

The Prince had only seen Kamiskwa and Nathaniel briefly. This was not unusual, since they both wintered with the Altashee at Saint Luke. Vlad assumed that Zachariah Warren's presence in Temperance made meeting Rachel all but impossible. When they did come around the estate, they generally brought useful news, like that of a Tharyngian ship that had tried to sail up the Argent River to Lac Verleau. A blizzard drove it aground on a sandbar near Fort Dufresne on the east end of Salmon Lake. Before they could get it off again, the lake began to freeze over, crushing the ship's hull. Most of the cargo was saved, but if it was meant for du Malphias, it would take a very long time to reach him.

The nasty weather also worked against du Malphias' fortress in the spring. The Argent River took a long time to clear of ice, so any reinforcements from

Kebeton or Tharyngia had to wait. Flooding from abnormally high runoff had damaged port facilities in Kebeton and wiped out spring wheat crops. New Tharyngia's year had not started auspiciously.

Had troops and orders come from Norisle by April, an expedition could have been mounted that might well have taken the fortress. The prince had issued a call for militia units, placing Major Robert Forest in charge of them. He was due up from Fairlee with a levy of their famed sharpshooters. The Prince had resolved to head out on his own come the end of May if he heard nothing from Norisle.

But then a fast packet boat had arrived at the beginning of May, heralding a coming fleet. The message, for the sake of operational security, had been maddeningly vague, but the Prince followed its dictates. So it was that he'd remained in Temperance and even had Baker bring the model to Government House, so he could brief whomever the Crown had put in command.

A clerk found the Prince studying the model. "Highness, report from the headland: the HMS *Indefatigable* will reach port this morning."

Finally. "Very good, Mr. Chandler, thank you."

"Beg pardon, Highness, but will you be greeting the ship or receive the commander here?"

"Send my coach for him. Also ask Count von Metternin and Captain Strake if they can attend me."

"Yes, sire, very good, sire."

Vlad retired to the Captain's Walk with his telescope. He studied the ship. It came into the harbor under one sail only and dropped anchor well shy of the docks. This struck the Prince as curious, for unless the commander had reasons to keep his troops on board, he should have come directly to the wharves. The signal flags indicated no illness, which was the last thing they needed. An epidemic killing Mystrians and devastating troops would be an ill omen.

Count von Metternin waited for him in his office. The Kessian had dressed in his light blue uniform, having added a red sash with medals and a heavy cavalry saber. His hat he'd set on a chair, its previously jaunty plume replaced by a turkey feather.

They shook hands and the Count smiled. "I thought it would help our cause if I were properly attired."

"To be quite frank, I had hoped whomever they sent would not be overly impressed with uniforms and medals." Vlad sighed. He wanted someone who would take charge and destroy du Malphias instead of an indolent noble focused on his own advancement.

"I do find curious, Count von Metternin, your use of the word 'our.'"

"Do you?" The Kessian smiled. "I have taken to your Mystria. I find the openness and honesty refreshing. I stand ready to do what I can to preserve this special place, for its own sake, and that of the Princess."

"Good, a… *land* like Mystria needs good men." Vlad turned to the model to cover his surprise. He'd almost said *country*. Suggesting that Mystria could be its own nation was treasonous. Vlad put it down to his having already called up militia without Norillian authorization. He would have made war on a Tharyngian outpost. If successful, the assault would have been hailed as a Norillian victory and, if a failure, blamed entirely on the people of Mystria.

"Your land breeds good men." Von Metternin walked slowly around the model. "You may not notice these things, but I do. A man like Nathaniel Woods, for example, do you know what he would be on the Continent or in Norisle?"

Vlad smiled. "A highwayman?"

"Quite possibly. He certainly would not be the confidant to a prince. All the forces that could be brought to bear would keep him in his place. Yes, he might enlist in the army and would fight well, but rise to rank even as Captain Strake has? This could not happen. And it could not happen because if it did happen—on merit—men like me, men of the aristocracy, would have to destroy him. His existence threatens the system which exalts us."

"It sounds as if you do not hold the nobility to be special."

"You mistake me. I think many are. I am, you are, and there are many more examples. But I wonder if a man like Mr. Woods would not be even *more* special given the opportunities we have had. He is a very smart man, but he does not read. How much more would he understand and be able to offer if he did?"

The Count pointed at the model. "Do you not think, had Captain Strake not escaped, that Woods and his friends would have made an attempt to free him?"

"They might have."

"Defying a direct order is behavior that would lead one to be declared an outlaw in Kesse-Saxeburg—unless, of course, they were successful. Then they would just never be put in a situation to disobey again." The Count smiled. "This is not to say that Mystria is free of politics. It is just that the practitioners do not have centuries-long family traditions, memories, and vendettas to guide them."

Chandler appeared at the office door. "Prince Vladimir, I am to present Her Majesty's Military Governor, John Lord Rivendell."

Rivendell! Vlad managed to cover his surprise at first, then Rivendell walked through the door. Whereas he had been expecting an older man, stout and balding, using a cane, a much younger man entered, clad in a uniform of red and gold satin, with black shoes and gold buckles, red knickers and waistcoat, white shirt and hose. The man carried a cane, but as a baton, not anything useful. His hat had two feathers, both impossibly long, and his shirt had a lace collar and cuffs.

The man, long-faced and slender, save for a pouchy belly, paused just past the doorway. He swept his hat off in a grand gesture, bowing very low, his left foot pointed forward. He came back up, his face alight with a grin wide enough to almost touch his ears.

He barked a quick laugh. "I told you they'd be surprised, Langford. Ain't I right? Ain't I? That's three crowns you owe me."

Colonel Langford emerged from his shadow. "Yes, your lordship."

"Take it from the whist winnings, mind—no more cheating when you keep score. Love the game, can't be bothered with the numbers, you know." Rivendell turned back to the Prince. "You thought of my father when you heard the name. Everyone does. Died January, he did, God rest him. No worries—could have been worse. You could have had Smalling. See the look, Langford, they know how lucky they are having me here."

"Yes, my lord."

Rivendell tapped his stick on the floor. "Your troubles are over. I've read my father's book, of course, been part of his command for years. I'm as good as he was. Even better, I dare say. Much of Villerupt, that was me when his gout had him down."

"You are most welcome, Lord Rivendell."

"Just call me Johnny. All the troops do, even after I flog 'em. Want them to know I care, don't you know."

"I see." The Prince forced a smile. "I should like to present Count Joachim von Metternin."

"Keeping with the enemy, now, are we?" Rivendell laughed aloud. "You keep an eye on him here, Langford, the eye you should have had on him at Planchain. That's good. You gentlemen know my aide, Colonel Langford. Most useful to me. Bless me, what have we here?"

Vlad moved aside. "This is du Malphias' fortress. We built it from the maps and drawings I put in my report."

"Oh, very good. Capital." He glanced back at Langford. "You knew of this?"

"Yes, your lordship. I mentioned it to you."

"Did you? Very good. That's your job, ain't it? Ain't it?"

Vlad frowned. "Lord Rivendell…"

"Johnny."

"Johnny, you did read the report I sent, didn't you?"

"Read it? No, no, no. No time for that." Rivendell reached around and smacked Langford in the chest with his cane. "That's what I have Simon here for, ain't it? He read it. He told me everything I needed to know. We have the situation well in hand."

"You do?" Vlad glanced at von Metternin. The Kessian's expression was completely blank. "Do you have any information about what sort of troops Tharyngia has sent to invest the fortress?"

"This one, this one here?" Rivendell peered closely at it, then pulled back. "I think we have some documents, don't we, or are they coming on the other ships?"

"Other ships, my lord."

"Very good, you are right on top of things, Langford. Good to be home, ain't it? We won't tell your wife what you've gotten up to in Launston, will we? No, we won't." Rivendell smiled at the Prince. "All those troop things are coming on the other ships, along with the troops. We came in with supplies, don't you know. Guns, powder, firestones."

Vlad sighed, and didn't care that Rivendell saw him. "So you're here to prepare things, but you're not leading the expedition?"

"Ain't I? Ain't I?" The Norillian noble frowned. "Langford, this is my command, ain't it?"

"Yes, sir."

Vlad forced another smile. "No offense intended, Johnny, but I would have thought they would have chosen someone more senior."

"To wipe out a Ryngian bugger in the middle of God-knows-where? No. There was some panic at Horse Guards when your report first came through. I must say, Highness, no need to gin up the panic by saying du Malphias is a necromancer who has a legion of the dead to oppose us. Why, everyone knows that can't be true! Took some talking to make that point, of course, but cool heads prevailed, saw the truth of it."

Vlad clasped his hands behind his back. "I'm afraid, Lord Rivendell, the reports were the truth. Du Malphias has at least a battalion of these *pasmortes*."

"Really?"

"Really."

"Have you ever seen one?"

Vlad hesitated. "I have. Men in my employ brought a captive to my estate."

"Do you still have it? Heard you were a keen one for studying the Ryngian way. Got it in bottles do you, all pieced out?"

Vlad looked down. "No. My wurm ate it."

Rivendell laughed, holding his belly and doubling over. "Your *wurm* ate it. Oh, very good. Langford, remember that one. Have to tell it to the others when they arrive. His *wurm* ate it."

The Prince's cheeks flushed. "That misfortune not withstanding, I do have witnesses. Their statements were in my report. I can bring them before you."

"Now, now, Highness, I don't blame you for being taken in by these rustics. They're of inferior breeding, ain't they? Lying is in their blood. They couldn't explain why they ran from some scruffy Ryngians, so they made them into monsters. That you believe them goes to your heart, sir, and I commend you on it. But no need to worry now Johnny Rivendell is here."

He looked back at his aide. "That's good, Langford, get that down for the book."

"Book?"

"Yes, Highness, I'll write one just as my father did, once we deal with this fort of yours." He lowered his voice. "But you are not alone in your concerns. Some at Horse Guards thought I might want an advisor. Richard Ventnor, Duke Deathridge, is following with the troops. And his mistress, right pretty one, she. His niece, too, but don't let that get around."

Vlad blinked. "His *niece?*"

"Oh, ain't like that at all, Highness." Rivendell smirked. "Niece by law, not blood. Catherine Strake, she's what keeps him warm all through the night."

CHAPTER FORTY-SIX

May 13, 1764
Government House, Temperance
Temperance Bay, Mystria

"I believe, sir, you are mistaken."

Lord Rivendell turned toward the doorway, the wild smile still wide. "No, I ain't."

Owen glanced at Chandler, who withdrew, and stepped into the room. "The woman to whom you refer is my *wife*. I believe you are *mistaken*, sir."

Langford, who had blanched when he saw Owen's face, interposed himself between the soldier and Lord Rivendell. "So good to see you again, Captain Strake."

Owen spitted him with a stare. "Unless you are going to act for Lord Rivendell in a matter of honor, Colonel, I suggest you give ground."

Count von Metternin tugged off one of his gloves and proffered it. "If you require a second, Captain, it would be my honor to attend you."

Owen reached for the glove.

Rivendell's smile evaporated. "Could be I was mistaken, sir. Could be. The voyage, you see, takes its toll. That's right, Langford, ain't it? Ain't it?"

"Yes, my lord." Langford nodded enthusiastically. "Wasn't Deathridge's whore some Countess from Alandaluce? Dark hair, blue eyes, fiery temper, big woman."

"I do believe you are right, sir." Rivendell bowed in Owen's direction. "My apologies, sir, profound and sincere."

Owen let his hand drop. "Accepted. The voyage, I understand."

As Rivendell responded, his mood entirely changed and ice trickled down Owen's spine. He'd never met the younger Rivendell, but he had heard stories. Rivendell liked to lead from the rear, hated being in reserve, followed orders when it suited him and appealed to his father for absolution when he caused disaster. He whored on Saturday, prayed on Sunday, and schemed through the rest of the week.

Rivendell circled the model, forcing Prince Vlad and the Count to give way. Owen positioned himself at the fort's northeast corner and did not budge as

Rivendell approached. The other man slowed, then brought a hand up and tapped a finger against his teeth.

"Formidable little slice of nowhere, ain't it?" Rivendell nodded at the small fortress on the southwest side of the river. "First thing, first thing, I say, we take that. Walls give us cover; we can headquarters in the farm here… Something wrong, Captain?"

"That's where du Malphias wants you to attack. The whole area can be flooded. He'll staff the fortress with *pasmortes*. Your headquarters would be within mortar range of the small fortress."

"And you know this how, Captain?"

"I studied it while du Malphias' prisoner."

Rivendell nodded. "Colonel Langford mentioned that. Heroic escape and all, after he had given you free rein to explore as you wished."

"I wasn't his *guest*." Owen's head came up. "He tortured me."

"I'm sure he did, Captain, I'm sure he did. And then he let you escape so you would tell us a tale. He held you in no chains, he gave you a companion who aided and abetted your escape—though I share Langford's supposition that neither the aide nor escape existed."

"I didn't escape, sir?"

"No, of course not. You were deposited in Temperance by Ryngian traders. Drugged, I suppose. You *believe* you escaped. Since no one can verify your story, I must assume it is false."

Owen's face darkened. "You impugn my honor, sir."

"Oh Captain Strake, no need to be so sensitive. Not your fault you told the enemy everything under torture. I understand your mortification. Shame is leading you to dissemble about your experience, but you must ask yourself a question: Were you in my position, would you believe such fanciful tales without verification?"

Prince Vlad drew a step closer. "I have offered to bring witnesses forward, Johnny."

Rivendell waved that suggestion away. "A Colonial and his faithful native companion. Proper fodder for hysterical novels, but not to be relied upon for military science. And I know something of military science. I wrote the book. Well, I am *writing* the book. Langford's read it. Good stuff, ain't it?"

"Yes, my lord." Langford smiled politely. "It covers everything learned from Villerupt and more."

"And *more*, you see." Rivendell laughed happily. "This campaign shall complete my work. My crowning achievement, really, until the next one. Oh, that's good. Write that down, Langford."

Vlad bowed his head. "Perhaps, Johnny, you would like to tell us how you read this model."

"Of course. Watch and learn, gentlemen. Even you, von Metternin. You'll be thankful you're not facing us again." Rivendell's cane came up, the tip pointed at the northern wall. "Formidable defenses here, impervious to cannon, much open ground and obstacles. The river, of course, has his southwest flank, but he has overextended with this fortress. That clearly is his weak spot. The lakefront with the cliffs are unassailable."

The Prince pointed toward the fortress' heart. "And the internal defenses?"

Rivendell shrugged. "No matter. These are Tharyngians, remember. Once we shell them, they'll surrender. Always do."

Owen frowned. *That isn't how I remember Villerupt.*

Vlad nodded, gathering his hands behind his back. "And how many men did you bring to do this job?"

"Very good question. Two regiments, two capital regiments."

The Prince sighed. "1800 men."

"No—one regiment of horse, so it's more like 1350, provided they all make the passage, yes? Oh, and a company of cannon, must have those." Rivendell smiled broadly. "Handpicked the units myself. Many school chums leading them, you see, all tip-top. It's more than enough, I assure you."

"Your confidence pleases me." Irritation rippled through Vlad's voice, but his face betrayed none of it. "I should inform you that I have a regiment of local militia called up—companies from Summerland, Bounty, Temperance Bay, Blackwood, Oakland, and Queensland. In addition, Major Forest is bringing a company of Fairlee sharpshooters and we will supplement that with men drawn from the northland."

"Good, we'll need groomsmen and the like, splendid planning."

"If you would allow me to finish, Johnny."

"By all means, Highness." Rivendell began another unctuous bow, but he would have smashed his face into the model, so he aborted it. Instead he waved indulgently.

"I also have a company of lumberjacks and engineers who will be able to supplement your strength." The Prince turned and walked to a desk on which he had laid out a map of Anvil Lake. "As I noted in my report, the best strategy is to build our own fort here, at the Tillie outflow."

Rivendell smiled, not bothering to approach the map. "That might seem the thing, Highness, but defensive wars are never won. Hit him hard and hit him harder, that's the way it's done. By the first of June we'll be there, and the first of July right back here."

Vlad looked over at him. "Are you serious?"

"Quite."

The Prince's eyes tightened. "Let me understand you, Johnny. You've not read my report. Langford read you bits, and you dismissed the pieces you didn't like. You bring too few men, a third of them being cavalry which is worthless in the wilderness. You expect to make a six-week journey in two weeks, despite a complete lack of roads, lay siege to a fortress staffed with God alone knows how many and *what*, and be back here before August?"

"Precisely." Rivendell held his hands up. "Others thought it couldn't be done, but I convinced them. With your help, Highness, we could be done sooner."

"Without Mystrian troops, you will fail completely."

"We might be a little late…"

"Not fail getting there, fail to win the siege!" The Prince pounded his fist on the table. "You're not listening at all."

Rivendell's gaiety vanished. "Understand two things, Prince Vladimir. I am, by the will of the Parliament and with your aunt's blessing, the *Military* Governor of all Mystria. In the realm of military affairs I outrank you, sir. Do not force me to see how far my power extends in other matters."

Vlad stared at him, open-mouthed, then slowly closed it.

Rivendell thrust a finger at him. "Second, and most important, I will *not* be fighting Mystrian troops. I know very well their meager abilities and their complete lack of military discipline. I will not put them into the field because I cannot trust them. I would not disgrace the Tharyngians by exhibiting such troops before them."

Count von Metternin grasped Vlad by the elbow. "Perhaps, Highness, Lord Rivendell should be excused from further discussion. The voyage, after all—he shall be needing to rest."

The Prince slowly nodded. "Of course. When can we expect Duke Death-ridge?"

"Two weeks, three. Had a wager on the passage, you know." Rivendell's smile returned. "I do feel fatigued. I shall retire, then perhaps we shall dine together, Highness. Over wine and in good fellowship we can make things work."

"I am sure, my lord."

"That's the spirit, ain't it?" The man bowed again with great pomp, and withdrew with Langford trailing in his wake.

The Prince waited until the door closed behind them, then checked. He opened it, peered out, and closed it again. "I fear, Count von Metternin, that it will take much more than medals to impress *Johnny*. How the two of you restrained yourselves from challenging him to a duel, I do not know. You, Count, with his remark about the enemy and you, Captain, with that slander about your wife."

Owen shook his head. "I have endured asses such as him all my life. My wife would have been disappointed if I had slain him over such a thing as gossip."

The Count's eyes narrowed. "There are times, my friend, when these asses beg to be killed."

Vlad smiled. "Agreed."

Owen glanced down. "This may be true, but he is not the first to suggest untoward things out of spite and for sport."

Both men stared at him, questions on their faces but, mercifully, did not ask.

Owen hung his head. "I'm sorry, gentlemen. This is neither the time nor the place."

"Please, Owen, I would welcome a distraction before I turn around and challenge that insolent fool to a duel." The Prince turned a chair around from the desk. "Sit. Chandler! Whisky, now, a bottle and glasses."

Owen sat, slumping onto elbows planted on thighs. Frustration pounded at his temples. Chandler arrived with whisky and glasses on a tray and abandoned it quickly. The Prince poured, and Owen just stared down into the glass of amber liquid. The vapors reached him and he wanted to smile, but didn't have the strength.

"It is nothing of which I am proud, gentlemen. When my mother married Francis Ventnor, I was very young. I did not understand that I had become a bastard. I was the ugly stepchild who would not go away. That's it with the Ventnors. They didn't want me, but they fiercely guarded me. I was property—an unwitting redemptioneer with no expiration on my contract.

"Growing up, my cousins had everything. I told you, Highness, of the wurmwright who took me in. He did the family a service. They repaid him by firing him, once I had entered the army. That is the way my family is. They gave me nothing and sought to strip me of everything. They largely succeeded."

Owen sipped the whisky. "Then I found Catherine, who wanted me for me. And I wanted her. We wed and, during the Villerupt campaign, Catharine followed me to the war. My uncle's wife remained in Norisle. When I had duty on the line and he had a social function to attend, he would borrow her. I thought it most kind of him. She loved parties and she would weep in fear on my shoulder when we were together. I thought gaiety would please her. I wanted her happy."

The Count snorted with disgust. "And stories came to you of her and your uncle?"

Owen took a gulp of the whisky and enjoyed it burning its way down his throat. "Not of my uncle, but with everyone else. Officers who despised me took great delight in spinning tales of seeing her bedded by another. Never them, of course, just some elusive Major with another regiment, or some dashing officer from another nation."

The Prince raised an eyebrow. "Lies promulgated to hurt you."

Owen looked up. "I can see that now. One night, I drank too much and found a man who looked like a man the latest tale had been told about. I… I dishonored myself."

He looked at his hands, turning the right one over. White, wormlike scars striped his knuckles. Most of them had been earned fighting the Tharyngians, but Owen could see those he'd gotten beating a man senseless.

"I was going tell Catherine what I had done, but before I could she told me of her disgust for a friend's husband. He had fought a duel over similar gossip about his wife. She said the man dishonored his wife by believing the rumor and acting upon it. She clung to me, happy I would never believe such horrible lies about her."

Owen searched the men's faces. "How could I tell her after that? I love her and know she is not a whore. So, I maintained my silence. Ultimately, I accepted this posting so I could accomplish something grand enough that the two of us could escape my family's corrupting influences."

Von Metternin laughed gently. "Be proud of your restraint, Captain. You conquered your worst self and decided to reach for a lofty goal."

Prince Vlad swirled whisky in his glass. "You are even more admirable than I had imagined, Captain. Your wife was right, and your willingness to give Johnny a chance to escape is a mark of your character. Many other men kill because of their sense of honor—and their victims are not always the enemy. I fear our Johnny is one such man."

Owen tossed off the last of his whisky. "When you say that, Highness, I wonder if my having killed him would have been a virtue."

Vlad sighed. "I hope, Captain Strake, hindsight does not prove that judgment correct."

CHAPTER FORTY-SEVEN

May 16, 1764
Harper's Field, Temperance
Temperance Bay, Mystria

Nathaniel laughed quietly as Makepeace Bone reloaded the rifle Prince Vlad had bought for him. The large man had no trouble working the lever and twisting the gimbal. He blew into the socket, clearing it of unburned brimstone. He refilled the socket, then stuck a bullet on top, wedging it in place with the help of the cartridge paper.

Where the large man ran into trouble was positioning the bullet going back into the barrel. It fell out, or jammed. The frustrated giant looked ready to snap the rifle over his knee. "All well and good for you to be laughing, Nathaniel, but you've worked one of these for years and ain't got big thumbs."

"Two things to be amembering, Makepeace. First, don't be so all-fired hurried. With this here rifle you'll be shooting things far off. They cain't get you."

Makepeace nodded. "You're right."

"And second, if your durn thumb is too big, use your pinkie."

The giant laughed. "Still bigger around than your thumb."

"But it ain't gonna pull the bullet out of line so easy." Nathaniel nodded at him. "Go on, get this loaded, so the rest of them young bucks can see a real man shoot."

News that the famous Major Forest was coming from Fairlee with his Southern sharpshooters had inspired every man who owned a long gun in Temperance to head out to Harper's Field. Harper had planted clover, letting it lay fallow for the year, and boys had shooed cows off it before setting up targets. Mostly they made them out of a wooden post with a crossbar, and set clamshells as targets. Chances of them hitting anything and making it explode were minor, but a great cry went up when someone did.

Makepeace had come out to try his new rifle. Nathaniel and Kamiskwa had come out to watch. By far the rifle made Makepeace one of the better shots. He consistently hit the post at eighty yards. The rest of them, using smooth-bore muskets, could get a ball out that far, but few put it on target.

Still, the boys from town were having great fun. Caleb Frost stood in the middle of it all, happily barking orders. Nine of his college acquaintances had formed themselves up into a squad, loading in unison and firing on order. Caleb's voice had a calming quality. His men consistently managed three shots in a minute and displayed their thumbnails to each other, laughing as the purple stain grew beneath.

Kamiskwa came up to Nathaniel's side. "Young men, not yet warriors."

"I reckon. Ain't gonna be no sparing 'em."

Makepeace fired, shattering a shell at forty yards. He turned from the line and started to reload. "Ain't gonna be but a handful of 'em go. I seen my brothers over the winter. Trib and Justice figger they'll come with us."

Nathaniel nodded. As word had filtered out about the presence of the Tharyngian fortress, men began making decisions concerning it. They fell into three classes. First were the students who saw war as a place to win glory. A subset, Caleb Frost among them, saw the coming war as a chance to redeem the image of Mystrian fighters.

A more fool notion Nathaniel could not imagine.

After that came men like the Bone brothers who figured that having a Ryngian fort to the west meant more restrictions and danger for their livelihood. That fort would become a trade center for the Ryngians. Ryngian trappers and hunters would flood the area. Ungarakii would get bolder. They'd do more raiding against Mystrians and the 'Shee.

The last group, which accounted for the Branches, Casks, and others down at the north end of Harper's Field, came looking for money. They'd hire out for war. While Nathaniel wouldn't turn down the Queen's money, his understanding of the dangers and necessity of action meant he'd not be deserting when it rained too much or rations dwindled. Damnable thing was, Rufus Branch and his brothers would be a good addition to any local militia. They fought hard and had skills in the woods.

"I hain't seen your brothers in ages. Doing well?"

"Mostly."

"And Feargod?"

Makepeace frowned. "Hain't heard nothing since he went off to sea. Ma says he ain't dead, and I did see a tea chest hid in the barn. Onliest could have come from him."

Nathaniel smiled. Rumor had it that Feargod had gone pirating. He couldn't ask, and Makepeace would never tell. All the Bone brothers looked as if the same blacksmith had hammered them into shape, so whatever Feargod was doing, he'd be making his mark and making it large.

Down the line, Caleb put his men through another triple volley. The target survived without harm, but brimstone soot gave the boys a grim look. It aged them a bit, which was good, and that bitter taste would want ale for cutting it.

As they came off the line, four horses rode into view. Nathaniel picked out Count von Metternin and the Prince easily enough. The other two had to be the Norillian noble sent to lead the war against du Malphias and Colonel Langford. Though Nathaniel hadn't recently ventured into Temperance proper, he'd heard enough about the previous night's doings in the town to expect Langford to be sporting a black eye from his wife, and Lord Rivendell to be nursing a fierce hangover.

The Norillian vaulted from his saddle first, his red and gold satin clothes gleaming in the sunlight. He reached back and slid his own gun—a shortened cavalry carbine musket—and marched up to the line. He took his time, spreading his legs wider than shoulder width, pointing his body at the target, then raised his musket. He aimed down the barrel. His head came up for a moment and back down. He reset his feet, then fired.

The ball sailed past the forty-yard post harmlessly.

Rivendell, a smile on his thin face, set his musket butt on the ground and started to reload. "A fine first shot, Colonel Langford. Note that."

"Yes, my lord."

Nathaniel, his rifle resting easily across his right forearm, butt up in his armpit, nodded toward the target. "Which was you aiming for, my lord?"

Rivendell looked up, surprised at having been addressed, then nodded. "The shell at the head. Always want to hit them in the head, you know."

In one smooth motion, Nathaniel's rifle came up, he sighted, and fired. With the brimstone smoke he couldn't see if he'd hit, but Caleb's boys cheering set his mind at ease. He lowered his rifle and reloaded.

Rivendell looked from Nathaniel to the target and back. Nathaniel had hit at fifty yards. The Norillian smiled. "Was that luck, or are you a sporting man?"

Nathaniel shrugged. "Weren't luck."

Rivendell's smile grew. "A wager, then. A pound per shell shattered in a minute. You versus me. Langford, bring your timepiece."

Nathaniel shook his head. "I ain't got that kind of scratch."

Count von Metternin stepped forward. "I would be pleased to back you, Mr. Woods."

Rivendell's eyebrow went up. "So this is the man saw ghosts in the wood, is it? If you're backing him, von Metternin, two pounds per, then, shall it be? I will shoot first."

Nathaniel nodded, then turned away. He looked at Makepeace and Kamiskwa, keeping his voice low. "Seen ghosts, did we?"

Rivendell shouted from behind him. "Mark time *now*, Langford!"

Nathaniel watched Rivendell after the first shot, which had missed. The man loaded quickly enough. He bit the bullet from the paper cartridge, emptied the powder, and then spat the bullet into the barrel. Lots of men did that, thinking it was the fastest way to work, but spit was enough to cake brimstone on a ball or stop it burning clean.

Rivendell reloaded three times and got off four shots, though the fourth came right after Langford had yelled, "Time." The last two shots hit shell, so Rivendell turned to the Count and held out his hand. "Four pounds, sir."

"Shall we settle after Mr. Woods shoots?"

Caleb ran down and replaced the shells. Nathaniel levered his rifle closed. "Call it, Langford."

The Norillian Colonel glared at him. "Now!"

Nathaniel fired his first shot easily hitting the shell in the head position. He reloaded without any haste, brought the rifle up again and hit the shell at the right shoulder. Again and again he fired, missing once and hitting a third. Then his last shot came a heartbeat before Langford called, "Time."

Count von Metternin nodded in Nathaniel's direction, then extended his hand to Rivendell. "I believe that will be four pounds you owe me, my lord."

"Can't trust you Kessians at all, can I? Only two."

"But he hit four."

"Last one was after time was called. That's it, ain't it, Langford, ain't it?"

"Yes, my lord."

Makepeace started forward. "Now just see here…"

Nathaniel stopped him with a hand on his chest. "Don't make no nevermind, Makepeace. Never did reckon Langford knew what time it was."

The Mystrians, who had crowded in closer, all laughed. Langford's face flushed hotly. Rivendell looked around, then shook his head ruefully. "This is our fault, Prince Vladimir. We give them everything, but did not give them the proper respect for authority. You men really do not understand the way of the world. Colonel Langford, decorated veteran of many wars, is your superior and deserving of respect. He is a gentleman. He is an officer. He would never lie, cheat, or steal. If he says the last shot happened after time was called, that is that, and no man amongst you can question him."

Nathaniel frowned. "But he weren't the one what said it."

"I beg your pardon."

"What I am saying, your lordship, is that *you* said I shot after time had been called. Langford didn't say no such thing. He just barked yes when his master done give him the command to do so."

"Woods, isn't it, yes?" Rivendell handed his musket to Langford. "I can see by your attire you're a man who prides himself on his independence. You shoot well, I grant you, but this is a game. Have you ever gone to war, sir?"

"I've shot more than one man dead. That would be in the last year. You, sir?"

Langford stepped between them. "You mind your tongue, Woods."

"That will be enough, Colonel." Rivendell pulled Langford aside. "I ask, Mr. Woods, because you and your friends clearly do not understand the nature of war or what my troops will be facing out there. To be a true warrior, you must advance in the face of fire, closing with the enemy, to use your bayonet to gut a man. Have you any idea what that's like?"

"I don't reckon, your lordship, I ever been so foolish as to march on up to a man a-shooting at me." Nathaniel grinned. "I just as soon drop him as far away as possible."

Rivendell wheeled, pointing directly at Prince Vlad. "It is as I told you yesterday. I cannot fight these men. They are a rabble. They have no training and no discipline. They will shoot at range and run. They won't hold a line. We saw that at Artennes Forest."

The Prince raised his hands to quiet grumbling in the crowd. "My Lord Rivendell—Johnny—insulting these men will not help."

"Insulting them? I am paying them high praise by even speaking with them. That they dare to come out here and play at soldiering is a grand gesture. I welcome it. It reminds me why I and my men are here. So feeble a muster could never hope to defeat the Tharyngians. It is our charge, our sacred duty, to protect you all, and I mean to do that."

Makepeace muttered into his beard. "Is he crazy or drunk?"

Nathaniel glanced back. "I hope drunk. He might make sense sober."

Rivendell took his musket back from Langford and returned to his horse. Mounting it and sliding the musket home, he took up the reins and looked down at the Mystrians. "Fear not. The Queen has not forgotten you, nor abandoned you. She will save you. For this she has sent me. In the coming weeks, you will see how real troops act and fight. You will be amazed and you will be thankful. It will be a lesson for you to remember for as long as you live. Come along, Langford."

Langford mounted up and the two of them cantered back to town.

Prince Vlad looked around. "I hope, gentlemen, you understand that Lord Rivendell, first, is not the author of the history which vilifies us. That was his father."

"Apple din't fall far from the tree," someone quipped.

The Prince somehow kept himself from laughing aloud. "That not with-standing, he *is* here to deal with the Tharyngian threat. He's brought Norillian troops—veteran troops. It would please me, and ease things, if you would treat them with the utmost courtesy."

Rufus Branch spat. "I reckon they'll get what they give is all."

Nathaniel smiled. "I reckon that ain't very neighborly. They coming from so far away. Bound to feel odd here. Kind of like Captain Strake. He took some getting used to our ways, but look what he gone and done for us. I'm thinking we can be a mite more tolerant than otherwise."

"Thank you, Mr. Woods." The Prince nodded. "And, please, no matter what Lord Rivendell says, no matter any comments by his troops, I pray you continue your practice here. Four shots in a minute if you can, and see how long until you tire. We will need to know."

The Prince stared after Rivendell's retreating figure. "He says he won't fight you. Circumstances will say differently. I want you ready for that day. Hell will be to pay, and I rather it be accounted in shot and brimstone than our blood."

CHAPTER FORTY-EIGHT

May 19, 1764
Government House, Temperance
Temperance Bay, Mystria

Prince Vlad smiled cordially as Princess Gisella's servants brought sherry for the men at the table. The meal had been wonderful—pheasant, new potatoes, peas, and cornbread. It had begun with sliced tomatoes, which was a daring choice, since most Continentals took it as true that tomatoes were bright red as a warning against poison. The meal concluded with a wonderful pudding laced with sugar and brandy. Vlad had asked for a second helping, and was pleased when Major Forest joined him.

The Prince stood, lifting his glass to the Princess. "To you, my dear, a wonderful hostess. You, from so far away, make one feel welcome in Mystria."

The men lifted their glasses and sipped.

Gisella bowed her head. "I only reflect the hospitality my friends have showed me since coming to these shores."

The Prince smiled. "We shall abandon you ladies, if that is acceptable. I know Major Forest is fatigued, but I wish to give him a look at du Malphias' fortress."

The Major slid back his chair. While not a tall man, his solid build gave the impression of his being quite powerful. A full shock of white hair topped his head. It had been blond before Villerupt. A handsome man, he shared his sister's noble features, save that his nose clearly had been broken on at least one occasion, and Hettie Frost's had not. Aside from that, and his missing right hand, no other mark of misfortune made itself apparent.

"Splendid. I've heard so much about the model." He set his sherry glass down and grasped the knife blade protruding from his wooden prosthesis. He twisted it, then pulled, and the knife came free. He slipped it into a boot sheath, then produced a small hook and locked it into the hole. He nestled the sherry glass into the metal curl replacing his right hand.

Dr. Frost, his son Caleb, Count von Metternin, and Owen Strake all made their apologies to the women and headed for the Prince's office. Owen became noticeably formal, but he had been that way all night. He had been seated next to Bethany Frost, a pairing which had previously brought him some pleasure, but this evening it appeared to be a source of discomfort.

Discomfort the Prince had not seen reflected on Miss Frost's face.

Vlad led them straight to the model. The militia officer circled it. Fairlee had adopted a light green coat with buff facings and cuffs. Forest wore it well. Buff breeches and waistcoat matched, and he wore tall cavalry boots.

He took a good look, then sipped sherry. "And we have no idea how many troops will be opposing us?"

Vlad shook his head. "I am afraid not."

Caleb snorted. "Add one for that idiot, Rivendell."

The men chuckled, but Forest waggled a finger at his nephew. "Let that be the last time I hear that out of you, Caleb, or any of your boys, if you expect to be chosen to join my men. Ridicule erodes morale and discipline faster than the sun melts ice. As any veteran will tell you, when the cannons roar and guns thunder, you don't fight for country or leader. You fight for your friends in the ranks. If they don't understand the importance of standing with you, they won't, and you'll all die."

"Yes, sir."

The Prince pointed to the model. "Rivendell has one regiment of foot, one of horse, twelve guns, probably light. He couldn't recall the size."

"The man *is* an idiot, isn't he?"

Caleb laughed.

Forest raised an eyebrow. "Remember, when *I* say it, it is a judgment based on experience. I met him on the Continent a couple of times. He was insulting, short-sighted, and had an inflated sense of his own position in history. How is it he got this command?"

Vlad shrugged. "Correspondents of mine have hinted at a political fight in Parliament. The Foreign Ministry wishes to finish Tharyngia on the Continent and sees du Malphias as a distraction. Last year's campaign did not go well, and Rivendell was part of the reason why. Getting him away from Tharyngia is a way to give someone a chance at victory.

"The Home Office wants to protect Mystria to protect the Norillian economy. They point out that conquering New Tharyngia will destroy the Tharyngian economy and, ultimately, boost ours. Rivendell's enthusiasm for this venture made him easy to promote. Unfortunately, they underfunded and undermanned his expedition based on his manpower request. This leaves them sufficient resources to campaign on the Continent this year or next, regardless of what Rivendell does."

Forest turned to Owen. "I understand, Captain, that du Malphias indicated he wished to form his own nation?"

"Yes, sir. His fortress controls access to the west. Being south of New

Tharyngia, it has better growing seasons. The rivers and lakes let it get furs and other trade goods out." Owen sighed heavily. "If he can get settlers in, he could achieve his dream."

"This was all in the report you sent to Launston, Highness?"

"Every word." The Prince finished his sherry in a gulp. "And every one was dismissed as fantasy."

"Amazing." Major Forest turned back to the model. "There is, of course, only one way to take this fortress. Surely you all see it."

Count von Metternin set his sherry glass in the middle of the ruined farmhouse. "It is not to begin the assault from here?"

"No." Forest tapped the cliffs with his hook. "Two companies of men, hand-picked men, approach the cliffs under cover of darkness. They scale up, use grapnels to get over the wall, then take the upper fortress. From there they command the interior and can use Ryngian cannons to knock out the other artillery batteries along the north wall. The rest of the troops stage here, to the north, and concentrate on this point nearest the cliff fort. Once in, du Malphias' stone wall works *for* them. They eliminate the central fortress and clean out the other forts."

"Are you certain, sir?" Owen frowned. "Those cliffs are quite sheer."

"I appreciate your perspective, Captain, but I'll differ with you. While I cannot climb with my metal hand, I have plenty of men who climb like squirrels. Here in the Northlands are dozens like them."

Caleb nodded. "The Bone brothers, Nathaniel, Twilight People, could all get right up there."

"We would arm them with two guns. They would have their rifles for accurate shooting, and shotguns for closer work. From what you have said, Highness, iron pellets, bits of nails, and the like would be effective against the *pasmortes.*"

Vlad nodded. "Likely against other troops, too."

Owen drew closer to the model. "Shotguns would work well for cleaning out the warrens."

Forest nodded. For the first time since Vlad had begun work on the model, he felt hopeful. He had no doubt that taking the fortress would be a fierce and bloody affair, but prior to Major Forest's suggestion, the only solution seemed to be relentlessly pounding the fortress with cannon, then to throw men at it.

Which was exactly the sort of attack for which du Malphias had been prepared.

Doctor Frost circulated. He refilled the men's sherry glasses, then raised his in a toast. "To a Mystrian solution for a Mystrian problem."

They all laughed, then drank, the Prince included. As he set his glass down, however, he wondered if his *Norillian* problem would scuttle their solution.

Owen shook his head. "Rivendell will never allow this. Success would take away from his glory."

Count von Metternin smiled. "Do not be so dour, my friend. There is a way. I will suggest, perhaps, to Colonel Langford, that were I leading the assault, I would send a *diversionary* attack up the cliffs. I would use Mystrians. Keep them out of my way, you know, since they are not Norillians. I would give them a chance, but contain the danger. Langford will mention this to Rivendell. His lordship and I shall talk. I shall congratulate him on having had the same idea I did. Once he believes he came up with it, that I think it is brilliant—*and* that it will put an end to Mystrian complaints—he will adopt it."

Vlad smiled. "If it succeeds, it is his brilliance. If it fails, it is Mystrian weakness. Do you honestly believe Rivendell will fall for this?"

"He cheated to save himself two pounds, Highness. He thinks himself a military genius." Von Metternin smiled easily. "If I go and find Langford now, by noon tomorrow the plan will be set."

Forest laughed. "Then I think you should get to your work, my lord. I will get my quartermaster requisitioning the necessary arms, and we shall take a fortress."

Vlad closed the door to Government House as the Frosts, Major Forest, and Owen Strake left. Count von Metternin had headed out to find Colonel Langford, leaving him and Gisella alone save for servants. The Prince turned to her and bowed deeply.

"I cannot thank you enough, my dear. You made this evening delightful."

She moved to his side and slipped her hand inside his right elbow. "Though the social niceties were never of much interest, I am not ignorant of them. Your man, Chandler, has an excellent grasp of protocol. The rest is in making people feel important and, as you said, welcome."

"You do it very well."

"You are very kind." She paused, then stood on tiptoe and kissed him on the cheek. "And I notice a relief in you that has been absent since I first met you. Do I no longer make you nervous?"

"I think you always shall. No, my dear, I do not mean that in any bad way." Vlad glanced down, blushing. "When I see you, when you smile, I get that same flutter in my stomach that I did when we first met. And I feel hollow when you are away from me. That is a case of nerves, certainly, but one I would not be without."

She squeezed his arm, and his stomach fluttered.

"As for my relief, my darling," he continued, "it is because of Major Forest and your own Count von Metternin. Forest pointed out a way to take the fortress. The fact that it uses tactics you'd never see on the Continent means it could take du Malphias by surprise."

"But Rivendell will not approve." Gisella shivered. "He is an awful little man, your Johnny. He thinks you are a fool, but he is the fool. He did not even read your report. Please, Vladimir, promise me we shall no more have to entertain him."

"I wish I could." Vlad shook his head. "By the end of the month Duke Deathridge will be here with his troops."

"And Owen's wife."

"Yes. And we shall have to invite them, and Lord Rivendell, for dinner. You know this."

"Yes. I had just hoped it would be otherwise. I shall do all required to make the dinner successful."

"I am gathering this is a trait among those from Kesse-Saxeburg, and one I like. Your Count von Metternin is off planting the seed that will ensure Lord Rivendell believes Forest's plan is his own. A dangerous man, the Count."

Gisella laughed lightly and rested her head on Vlad's shoulder. "He is like me, not one who fits in at home. Here, he too is more relaxed. Had his duties not required him to attend me, he would have joined Prince Kamiskwa and Mr. Woods on their last expedition."

"I should like, very much, for him to accompany the mission to the fortress. You can attach him as an advisor to my command."

Gisella stopped and came around to face him. "You did not tell me you would be going." Her expression deadened. "I did not think you would abandon me."

Vlad reached out, resting hands on both her shoulders. *She's trembling.* "I have no choice, darling."

"You have Major Forest to lead them."

"I do, but he does not have the standing to be present as things are planned."

"Count von Metternin can speak for him."

"He could. I have no doubt he will, but I need to be there as well. No, please, my darling Gisella, do not look at me that way. You know me better. You know I do not desire glory."

She stroked his cheek. "My dearest, I know you do not seek military glory, but your mind seeks answers. Do you not think I know of the experiments you have been conducting with Mugwump? I marvel at your genius, but I fear for you. What you would see as just another experiment might put you in harm's way. I love you, I truly do, and I would not have you hurt for anything."

"And I have no desire to be hurt. But I do have responsibilities. The Crown may not recognize how important this is. Rivendell will not use our troops because he is stupid. I need to convince him that he must. For that I must go."

She slowly shook her head. "I understand your reasoning, but I also know you seek the adventure. Not of war, but of seeing places you have not seen. You have showed me the jeopard; Nathaniel shot it, but only after you *missed*, my darling. It was coming for you. And in all the times I have heard you tell that story, you marvel at the beauty of the beast, never mentioning the danger you were in. I love you for this, but I fear for you because of it. You will put yourself in a place where danger can find you."

"And if I promise you I will not? If I have the Count swear he will not let me do so?"

Gisella laughed. "You are both men. He will promise. You will plan. He will protest, but not too much, then join you. I know this. And, alas, I know there will be no gainsaying you."

Vlad pulled her to him. "And you will worry, and I would do anything to prevent that."

Her hands came up around his shoulders, one sinking into his hair. She looked up and kissed him softly. "If you were to do that, you would not be the man I love."

CHAPTER FORTY-NINE

May 19, 1764
Temperance
Temperance Bay, Mystria

To Owen's surprise, Bethany Frost slipped her arm through his as the six of them started the trip back to the Frost home. Bethany had slowed her pace so that her parents, uncle, and brother drew ahead of them. "You are completely lost in thought, Captain. What is it?"

"I don't think you want to know, Miss Frost."

"I should not have asked if I did not."

Owen sighed. "Would you think me a coward if I told you I feared returning to du Malphias' fortress?"

"No, Captain. I should think you very intelligent and brave, because I know you shall go regardless."

"You're very kind."

She looked up at him, her blue eyes flashing. "I read your journal. I know exactly how brave you are, both from what you wrote, and from what others have said."

He shook his head. "Mr. Woods exaggerated."

"Of course he did, but I could see the truth."

"When I think of du Malphias—and he invades my nightmares far too often—I see his face lit by the pistol backflash. He shot me cold-bloodedly. It wasn't that I was an enemy. I was just an experiment. If I lived or died, it meant nothing. The man's expression revealed neither anger nor pity. He showed no emotion whatsoever. He was wholly inhuman and I am not certain we know of a way to defeat such."

"He was arrogant, and his arrogance, then, will prove his downfall."

"I shall trust in your wisdom."

"Trust more in the humanity of your companions. He is a man surrounded by the dead. He is alone, and together you shall defeat him."

Bethany stopped at the crossroads of Diligence and Virtue to call out to her parents. "The night is pleasant. May Captain Strake escort me on an extended walk?"

298

Her father nodded his assent. Bethany directed him toward the west, along Virtue. "I hope you don't mind, Captain."

"Not at all."

"Good, because I need to speak with you." She looked up again, a kind smile on her face, but her eyes looking sad. "I fear this is the last I shall be able to walk with you."

Owen looked straight ahead. "I never meant to lead you on, Miss Frost."

She laughed. "You will do better, sir, to listen with your ears, rather than your mouth. You did not lead me on. You have been very direct, from the first, that you are married and you love your wife. I have known this from things you said about her, and things you have not said. I know you love her from things you wrote in your journals, and the letters you had me write for you during your convalescence."

"Miss Frost…"

"No, Captain, I beg you. Let me say my piece directly, or I shall never get through it."

"Very well."

She wet her lips with the tip of her tongue. "I am neither silly nor stupid. When you first came to stay with us, I knew you were different from the others. I enjoyed your company. I enjoyed seeing you argue with my brother and discuss with my father. I felt very much at ease around you. I had not known that sense since Ira had been taken from me. I thought certain I had made a fool of myself and I was pleased when you left with Nathaniel, as it gave me a chance to recover my dignity.

"And yet, while you were away, I found myself missing you. When a missive would arrive, my father would read it aloud, and I would take it and read it over to myself. More than once. Perhaps that was silly, but it gave me comfort."

Bethany's grip tightened on his arm. "And then when word came that you were lost, I felt the same pain I had at the news of Ira's death. It left me prostrate. I prayed for your safe return as I had for his—and told God that He had taken one from me, so He must deliver you to me. And yet, even as I did so, I remembered your wife. I remembered you belonged to her."

A hand rose to brush away a tear. "When you came back, God had answered my prayer. I made certain you would get well. That became my mission. For me, yes, but also because I knew your wife would feel as I did, and I would not have anyone know such grief. This is why I wrote those letters for you, why I reminded you to write her when your strength returned.

"But now she will be coming. I will lose you to her."

Owen's guts roiled. Bethany had been his angel during his captivity and during his recovery. The very fact that he feared her hating him more than his wife doing so had revealed the nature of his feelings for Bethany. Those feelings were wrong—he knew it, and her hatred would be just punishment. The pain in her voice lashed at his heart, for only by misleading her could they have reached this state of affairs.

He stopped and turned to face her. "Don't, Bethany, please. I…"

She pressed a finger to his lips. "You will tell me you have feelings for me, too. Of course you do. How could you not? I nursed you back to health. But you love your wife. She has your heart. I know that. I am content with that, with knowing I am your friend. But I shall have to be your friend at a distance."

"It does not have to be that way…" Owen stopped, not certain what he was saying. "I wish I had not done what I did."

"You did nothing, other than be yourself. And this is why I must put distance between us." She shook her head. "It will hurt, but to not do this will hurt more."

"Miss Frost…"

"No, Captain. You see, I know a woman who married a man she did not love because she thought her heart's desire was dead. She listened to rumors that were false. And even though those rumors had been spread by the man she married—spread because of his desire to win her heart—she is married nonetheless. Still, she yearns for her lover and sees him. And I see how it tears her apart when they cannot be together."

Owen clasped her hands to his chest. "There are so many things I wish to say that I cannot. You have been more of a friend to me than anyone I have ever known. You have treated me better than my family ever did. You tended me in a way that my wife never could have. You have made me welcome in Mystria. Miss Frost, were it not for you, I should board the next ship to Norisle and read of Rivendell's folly in a book."

"No, you would not."

"Yes, I would."

She lightly pushed him away. "You're lying. He will create disaster, and you want to be there to prevent it. As much as you might dread seeing du Malphias again, you dread more seeing him on the outskirts of Temperance."

Owen nodded. "You know me too well."

"And I am proud to know you. You are truly an amazing man." She slipped to his side, linked her arm through his, and steered him south again. "Due to you, Caleb is more reserved in his comments about Norillian soldiers. He's not been in a tavern scuffle since your return."

"Less his respect for me than his growing up." Owen glanced over at her. Moonlight gave her skin an alabaster tone, and let glisten the track of a tear. "You have changed the subject, however, and I must be given a chance to finish my thought."

"It does not matter, Captain, for I know what I must do, and nothing you can say will change that."

"It is not my intention to change it. I shall respect your wishes completely. Tomorrow I shall move out of your family's home. I will take apartments elsewhere. And I shall have to invite your parents to dine there. Catherine will want to entertain. She will want me to invite you as well."

"Captain, you do not understand women. She will tell you she wants me there, but she does not." Bethany's eyes tightened. "Were I to come, I should be made to feel the provincial cousin. She would be kind, while being cutting. She would be as Lilith Bumble is, but more gracious and subtle. No, you shall ask, and I shall be feeling ill. I will send my regrets, and at the thought of missing you, they shall be sincere."

"Catherine would not do that."

"It is no slight against your wife, Captain, just the reality of being a woman in love with a man such as yourself. She will show everyone that you are truly hers. That is her right as your wife. I truly am happy that you have someone."

They walked in silence, then turned west at Kindness. Thin clouds striped the sky, eclipsing stars, moving slowly. Crickets chirped and dogs barked here and there. From the upper floor of one house came soft singing of a lullaby, the words unintelligible, but the melody soothing.

Owen laid his hand on hers. "You mean that I shall never see you again."

"You will, at a distance. You will come to church, and I shall be there. In the crowd when you march off to destroy du Malphias, I will be there. You'll see me with my uncle and my brother. You'll see my hand in stitches sewn for uniforms. You will be able to find me, but I cannot find you."

"And if I wished to send you a letter?"

"Please, Captain, do not. I lost you once, then came you back. But now I cannot have you. Please do not make this more difficult." She looked up and smiled briefly. "You will have your wife, and you will go back to Norisle and forget me, almost completely. Perhaps when you see the scar on your side and notice the stitching, you'll remember, but memory of me will fade far sooner than that scar. No matter."

"You'll forget me as well."

"No." She shook her head, looking down. "Women do not forget the men… Do you remember the first girl you ever kissed?"

Owen thought for a moment, then nodded. "Her name was Jenny. Cook's daughter at Overton Park Academy."

"Very good. Do you remember the first kiss?"

His brow furrowed. "No. I mean, I can remember the circumstances, but…"

"You can *reconstruct* the circumstances, Captain, but you cannot remember the touch of her lips, can you?"

"No."

"I remember my first kiss. I recall the scent of clover and the warmth of the summer air. I remember butterflies in the field, and the hiss of grasses as a breeze sent waves through them. I remember him, Ira, taller than me, casting a shadow over me. The sun made a halo around his head. I remember him bending over and kissing me quickly, so no one would notice, though we were utterly alone. I remember my lips tingling and my stomach feeling as if a dozen butterflies had flown down my throat. I remember every detail, and this was before I ever knew I loved Ira.

"So, Captain Strake, you will come to forget me. You might be able to reconstruct me, but you will have no memory of me. Your wife, your family concerns, will bury me but, again, I do not mind. I shall remember you as tall and handsome, honorable and brave. And that will be quite enough for me."

They turned east on Generosity and headed back toward the Frost home. "Have you any idea how remarkable a woman you are, Miss Frost?"

"Remarkable rather than infuriating?"

Owen chuckled. "Remarkable will do. You have wisdom beyond your years."

"Not wisdom, truly, just the knowledge that life seldom unfolds as one wishes it would." She smiled up at him. "And that is not terribly cynical, just realistic. So many people grumble and complain, waiting for things to change instead of accepting them as they are, or working to change them. But changing things is very difficult, so only the brave attempt it."

Owen nodded. "Thank you."

"For?"

"For yet one more gift." His eyes narrowed. "If we are going to defeat du Malphias, the old way of doing things will not work. We will need to change. I will not allow Rivendell to resist change, but force him to address reality."

"It could cost you your career."

He shrugged. "And it will save men's lives. The risk is worth it."

"And that, my dear Captain Strake," she said as they stopped in the shadow of her parent's gate, "is why I love you."

CHAPTER FIFTY

May 22, 1764
Old Stone Face, Temperance
Temperance Bay, Mystria

"I reckon that's the ugliest troop of monkeys I ever did see." Nathaniel smiled as he greeted Major Forest. "Heard tell you was back."

Forest turned, his eyes sharpening. "Nathaniel Woods, there's a sight for sore eyes. I'd offer to shake your hand, but I've been a bit on the rude side since Villerupt."

Beyond the Major stood an open face of weathered rock. Quarrymen had been cutting into it from the west, but had left a hundred feet of old stone with pine trees on top and broken rock at the base. A couple stout men amid the trees—one being Makepeace Bone if Nathaniel's eyes weren't lying—hung on to ropes lashed to men making the ascent. The climbers each wore two long sticks across his back, and two pouches filled with stones.

Forest smiled. "You can take your turn next, Nathaniel."

"Iffen you think I can't climb that face…"

"If you want to be one of the picked men, you have to earn it. Kamiskwa, too, if he's going to join up."

"He's gone back to Saint Luke. Gonna see how many braves want to join us." Nathaniel surveyed the men gathered by the cliff. Most tended to be big, with Makepeace at the upper end, and his brother Tribulation being the only one taller. Weight-wise they ran about the same, with Trib being shaggy on top and clean-shaven otherwise. Others varied in height, but most carried a lot of muscle. Those tending toward leaner, like Nathaniel or Justice Bone, had a wolfish look about them.

Forest followed his gaze. "It's a good crew answered the call. Those boys over there, with the red caps, they're down from Summerland, town of Farmingtown. Were bringing in furs when they heard about the call. Those two over there, in the brown jackets, they came up with me from Fairlee. Uriah and Jubal Hill. As good shots as you are."

Nathaniel smiled. "They related to Colonel Hill?"

"Not soes I know. They muzzle-load their rifles, so they are not as fast as you, but they are as good."

"I reckon some wagering on that point might be in order."

Forest nodded. "Have the Count back you again?"

"That was his call." Nathaniel shrugged. "You serious 'bout me skinning that hill?"

"I am if you expect to be a captain of one of the companies."

Nathaniel folded his arms over his chest. "I don't think you'll be wanting me in command of no one."

"Command? Perhaps not. *Leading*, on the other hand, without question." Forest pointed toward where Caleb and another of the college boys were beginning their ascent. "Many of these men have fired shots in anger, but not all. Like it or not, you're a legend. They all know three things about you. First, you've been where we're going. Second, you embarrassed Lord Rivendell, which means, to most of them, you've redeemed Mystria. Third, you *are* Magehawk."

"You know better than most just how much that Magehawk talk is hooey."

Forest shook his head. "Better than most, I know how much isn't. You were younger than any of them here when you went off, and you're not the oldest here now. Lots of men have bragged about shooting jeopards, but you're the only one who has the Governor-General bragging for him."

"I ain't special. I just done what needed doing."

"And that's what you'll do here." Forest smiled. "Your quiet confidence, Nathaniel, will calm a lot of nerves before we go up that cliff. Any boy thinks of quitting won't for fear of disappointing you."

Nathaniel shook his head. "I ain't thinking I want that responsibility. I just want to get me a clean shot at du Malphias."

Forest stroked his chin. "Let me put this a different way, Nathaniel. Either you come as a Captain of the Northland Rangers, or you'll not be going at all."

"Now, I don't reckon…"

"No, you don't reckon at all if you interrupt me. The situation is simple. If I can't have you in a leadership position, I can't have you in the ranks. You will chafe under someone else's command. Men will follow you because you're a natural leader. That creates division. And if men refuse to follow orders—and we will have scant time to train them at anything—they will die. And while you and Kamiskwa have been to Anvil Lake, you're not the only men who know how to get there.

"If you are not under my command, you will still be a divisive force. You just want a shot at du Malphias. I understand this, but none of us can hazard you taking that shot regardless of our plans. If you're not with us, you won't be allowed on the expedition. Is this clear?"

Nathaniel's nostrils flared. "You're beginning to sound powerful close to that idiot come to lead us."

"No. He sounds the way he does because he supposes that is how he should sound. He has no real clue as to why he should insist on discipline. That others oppose him is an affront to his honor, and that is all he cares about, his honor and his glory." Forest tapped a finger against his own chest. "If I ever had such dreams, I was clutching them in the hand I left in the Artennes Forest. I'm commanding and demanding because that is what will keep men alive. You've seen the fortress. It will be a meat-grinder. As much as I admire you and want you with me, if it is not on my terms, you will do more harm than good."

"Some thinking needs doing." Nathaniel turned away and paced off, heading toward a barrel of water that had been filled from Sutler's Creek. Another man offered him a dipper, but Nathaniel waved it away, then plunged his head into the barrel. The cold water shocked him, then he came up and shook his head, spraying water all over.

Major Forest was right, of course. Nathaniel knew he didn't fit well within society's sense of order. That was why he spent so much time outside of it. Society looked askance at his carrying-on with Rachel—even though they knew that she was rightfully his. The hypocrites turned his stomach, and the less he had to do with them, the more he liked it.

Jumped-up idiots play-acting at soldiery, like Langford and Rivendell, were worse. Scolds might whisper about him, but those fools would get men killed. Nathaniel had already heard from various sources that Rivendell doubted most all of what they'd reported about du Malphias. He'd attributed their claims to "a certain Colonial propensity for hysteria when the subject of war with Tharyngia is at hand." Rivendell had cheated and stolen. Given three bullets and a choice of targets between Rivendell and du Malphias, Nathaniel would just as soon shoot Rivendell twice.

Major Forest was pretty much the only officer he'd met that he thought deserving of rank. Nathaniel checked himself. Owen Strake merited that honor, too. Both men thought a lot about how to win, not what they'd do after they won. Owen had his scars; Forest, too, obviously. If he had to guess, Nathaniel figured Rivendell's body would have fewer blemishes than a newborn baby's behind.

As much as he hated the thought of taking orders from someone else, his problem with Forest's offer went deeper. He could take orders from Forest. He had before—though he had been much younger—and respected the man enough to assume any service he asked was a service needed doing.

What he didn't want was being responsible for men, and for their feeling beholden to him. Nathaniel could take care of himself. Always had done, likely would do until the day he died. He'd already forgotten things Caleb Frost would need to learn if he was going to live. There wasn't any way, as Forest had said, that they'd be able to teach the men everything, and Nathaniel wasn't sure there was a way to even teach them *enough*.

He looked up as Caleb shouted for joy. He'd reached the top of the cliff. A few men below applauded; a couple threw caps in the air. Most of the hard men ignored his victory and, if he got chosen, many of them would figure it was because he was Forest's nephew.

Nathaniel knew that wasn't true. Caleb was a smart young man and a good shot. He was a leader, too. He stood up there on the cliff, urging on his college friends. The other men had come in by themselves, or in small clumps. Caleb had brought a squad and had them gamely doing things some of them likely never imagined doing.

"And like as not, they're the ones who end up dead." Nathaniel ran his hands back along his scalp, squeezing out barrel water, feeling it run down inside his leather shirt. That was the real trick of it. If men died, he'd end up carrying them with him forever. He'd do for their families what he'd done for Grannie Hale. He was sure he'd be thanked a lot, be told it wasn't his fault, but there would be those glances that told him otherwise. *Cuz ain't nobody, given a chance to shift blame off the sainted dead, won't do it.*

He hugged his arms around himself. There was the final point. If he didn't go, if he didn't lead, he'd still feel responsible. If any of them died, he'd think they wouldn't have had he been there. He didn't want responsibility, but he saddled himself with it anyway.

"I am pure-D doomed." He shook his head again, then smiled. "Least ways Kamiskwa ain't here to see this."

Nathaniel walked back over to Forest. "I got me one condition."

Forest raised an eyebrow.

"You pick Caleb, he's my Lieutenant. You take his squad, Makepeace Bone leads it."

The Major watched him warily. "Making Caleb your Lieutenant will not keep him out of danger."

"I know that, but means I have his smarts working for me. And you're gonna be most like putting orders in writing, which he's better at deciphering than I's ever going to become."

"I'll need time to think on this, Nathaniel. I favor your proposal at the moment. I'll decide in the time it takes for you to climb that cliff. Don't give me too long to change my mind."

Nathaniel laughed and kicked off his moccasins. "Step aside boys. Coming up for to show you how this oughtta be done."

Most men did part, though Rufus Branch made it his duty to get in the way while doing his best to pretend he was ignoring Nathaniel. Nathaniel darted around him, pulled on three pouches of stones and the two sticks as rifles.

The man tying the rope around his waist commented on the extra pouch of stones. "You only need two."

"Well, Rufus, he's carrying an extra stone or two. Ain't no reason I shouldn't."

Men laughed, and someone made the mistake of trying to slap Rufus on the belly. That man landed on his butt with a split lip, but had the sense not to get up right away.

Nathaniel began his climb. It came easy at the start, with hand- and footholds having been worn deep by boys who'd played on the cliffs for years. About twenty feet up a nice ledge afforded a view of the ocean past Temperance, and one could spot sails rounding the headland easily.

After that it got a bit trickier, but Nathaniel had long since learned the secrets of climbing. Never hug the rock, never get too spread out, and do all the lifting with your legs. Sudden moves, especially with stones swaying and sticks clacking, would throw a climber off balance more sure than a gallon of whisky drunk in a minute. And the fall from a cliff was worse than the fall from an alehouse stool.

Once he got past halfway, things became easy again because fewer climbers had made it that high. He ranged a little to the east, away from the quarry-side, and once he'd cleared some crumbling rock, made the run up fairly quickly. He climbed over the top and stood—even though he wanted to lay down and pant—and untied the belay line himself.

Major Forest cupped a hand to his mouth. "Glad to have you with us, Captain Woods."

Makepeace slapped him on the back, and Caleb offered him his hand as men below cheered and a couple fired off their guns. No bullets came close, but that was because Rufus wouldn't have dared do anything where folks could see, what with Makepeace above him and with his new Hill breech-loading rifle close by his side.

Nathaniel shook Caleb's hand. "You done right well, Caleb."

The younger man blushed. "Just hope my uncle thinks so. We, the boys and me, we want to go, do our part."

"Iffen he does choose you, be an honor to serve with you."

Caleb threw him a salute. "Yes, sir, Captain Woods."

Nathaniel hesitated. "I ain't thinking it's right me having the same rank as Captain Strake."

The younger man frowned. "Technically you don't. I mean, you'll be commanding the same number of troops as he does, doing the same things his troops do but in the command structure you'd only be a Subaltern."

"A what?"

"It's kind of a half-Lieutenant, and no Norillian trooper would have to obey your orders. It's because you're Colonial Militia."

"So, by that thinking, your uncle, he's below Captain Strake?"

"Yes."

Nathaniel shook his head. "Don't seem right being as how one man stops a bullet good as the next."

"Well, we are, after all, only redemptioneers."

"Uh huh. I reckon there's going to have to be some mind-changing along about that." Nathaniel patted Caleb on the shoulder. "You go and get the rest of your men on up here, Mr. Frost. Show them Branches and Casks that reading don't slow you down none."

"Yes, sir."

Nathaniel laughed, not sure he'd ever get used to being called "sir" in that manner; and positive he never wanted to get to liking it. He headed along the path that ran around the top of the quarry and north, down a hill to the creek.

Another man, medium height, lean build, rose from a stump and fell in step with him. "Nathaniel."

"Justice."

"How is it you ain't killed Rufus Branch yet?"

"Well, I reckon he's just smart enough to not rile me when I'm in a cutting mood."

Justice Bone nodded. "I amember a time you did cut him."

Nathaniel nodded. Back when they were all young, with Rufus being three years older than Nathaniel, and Justice two years younger, Rufus had taken to pounding on Justice for some offense or other. Nathaniel had taken exception to that, and one cut with his knife had sent Rufus running long enough to get Justice home and his scalp sewed up.

"He had it coming."

"Heard tell he was saying he hoped you was going to head out with the troops. Said lots of strange things could happen to a man in battle."

"Did he now?"

Justice nodded. "Noticed he and Zachariah Warren spent a long time whispering and drinking together afore Warren headed south Monday."

"Good thing to know."

"Might have even seen some money change hands."

Wasn't hard to figure out in which direction, since Branch never had any, and Warren had far too much.

"I'll watch my back."

"You do that, Captain. I will, too." Justice Bone nodded solemnly. "Time comes to settle accounts, Rufus will have his paid in full."

CHAPTER FIFTY-ONE

May 24, 1764
Government House, Temperance
Temperance Bay, Mystria

Prince Vlad made no attempt to hide his surprise. He'd been awakened by an urgent message from Lord Rivendell. The Military Governor took two pages of painfully pretty handwriting to request an urgent meeting. Vlad called together Count von Metternin, Major Forest, and Captain Strake. At the stroke of ten, Chandler ushered Rivendell into the Prince's office. Langford trailed in his wake, carrying two journals and several rolled maps.

Rivendell bowed deeply. He still wore red and gold, but linen garments which were more in keeping with Temperance's fashion sense. "Thank you, Highness, and you, Count von Metternin. I trust you have not spoiled my surprise."

The Kessian bowed and clicked his heels. "As we discussed over dinner last evening, I am merely honored to bask in your genius."

"Of course you are." Rivendell made directly for the model. "I have been devoting much time to thinking, gentlemen, thinking of a way to crack this nut. I've decided to call it the Fortress of Death. Brilliant, ain't it? Ain't it?"

Rivendell then hesitated, tapping his teeth with a finger. "Perhaps it should be 'du Morte' to honor the Tharyngians. You'd like that, wouldn't you, von Metternin? Note that, Langford. No matter. Cannons on all sides, no way for us to build a ship and keep it on station, many things here, save for a singular vulnerability."

The Prince peered closely at the model. "What would that be, Johnny?"

"The cliffs, Highness." Rivendell beamed. "None of you thought of the cliffs. You see, we send an elite force of men scaling these cliffs, and using ropes and grapnels, they can be inside the fort, capture this corner, and turn the guns on the inner compound. Sweep the northern walls—we take them, and the fort is ours. Brilliant, ain't it? Ain't it?"

Von Metternin clapped. "Bravo!"

Vlad shook his head. "A bold stroke, Johnny, very bold, but where could we find soldiers who could make that climb? It would have to be in the dark, or so close to dawn they could not be seen. Yes, Major Forest, you have

309

something to say?"

The Mystrian officer nodded. "Begging your pardon, Highness, I have two companies of Mystrian Rangers. One from Fairlee, one from the Northlands. My men could do it."

Vlad smiled. "Excellent."

Rivendell laughed. "Major, with all due respect, I have the perfect warriors for the job. The Fourth Heavy Horse. Horses can't go up that cliff, so we'll dismount 'em and let them climb."

The Prince chuckled lightly. "You jest, of course, my lord. Your cavalry has no experience scaling cliffs, do they?"

"Don't need it, Highness, don't need it." Rivendell sniffed. "These are the finest young men from the finest houses in all of Norisle. They've been defending the realm since 1066. They shed their blood in the Holy Lands and have fought the Tharyngians for centuries. They have the finest of breeding, upbringing and education. If I tell them to go up those cliffs, they will…"

"Fall back down again like the prats they are." An older man with thinning hair and disdain etched deep into his features flipped a coat off and draped it over Chandler's arms. "Dick Ventnor, Highness. Count von Metternin, Major Forest, I believe. Owen." His boot heels clicked crisply on the wooden floor as he made haste to the model. "Excellent, much as I imagined from reading your report, Highness."

Rivendell bowed. "Duke Deathridge, a pleasure."

"Straighten up, Johnny. You look every bit the popinjay."

Vlad glanced at Owen. The man's face had become an impassive iron mask. "Duke Deathridge, we were given to suppose your ship would not be here for a week."

"True, but the wager was whether or not I would be here, not my ship. Langford will pay my man when he arrives, Johnny. A packet boat overtook us, so I transferred to it, coming with the latest dispatches." The dark-eyed man stared at the model. "Southwest is a trap, of course. North is the only true avenue of assault. Cliff is a nice idea, but the cavalry would never make it. The Fourth has a hard enough time climbing out of bed."

"You impugn their honor, sir."

"And you would use them like tin soldiers, Johnny, but you cannot reset them for play when things do not turn out as you wish."

Vlad pointed to Major Forest. "We have two companies of Mystrian Rangers, sharpshooters, and hand-picked men who can and will make that climb."

Deathridge nodded, his eyes narrowing. "Two full companies?"

"Yes, Duke Deathridge."

"Fully capable woodsmen, Robert? The best Mystria has to offer?"

"Yes."

"And you'll be leading them?"

Forest smiled. "I still have a thumb, so I will be leading them."

"Very good."

Rivendell blinked. "You cannot mean to have them go up the cliff, Dick. These are *Mystrian* troops. Have you forgotten the lessons of the Artennes Forest?"

Deathridge's lip curled into a sneer. "I will ask you only once, Johnny, to remember who was there actually *fighting* the Mystrian troops on that day."

"Then you should know better than anyone…"

"I do, you ass, I know better than you or your father." Deathridge's voice lowered and slowed. Vlad visualized every word as an inch of steel sliding into Rivendell's guts. "If I had my druthers, I'd take Major Forest's men and send them to deal with du Malphias. I'd let your men eventually get to Anvil Lake, let them occupy the ruins of the fort, and hope they forget how to find their way back."

Rivendell sniffed. "You do not have that option, sir. Parliament chose *me* to lead this expedition. You are here to observe."

"And advise." Deathridge looked to the Prince. "What I would advise you, Highness, is to make Major Forest's Rangers an independent command. I have a mission for them of the utmost importance."

"Yes, my lord?"

Deathridge glanced at Rivendell's aide. "Langford, make yourself useful. You have a map of Mystria there? Yes, on that table. *Now*, man, we do not have all day."

Langford, flustered, dropped journals and two maps, then dropped two more as he bent over to recover one of the first. He took it to a table and spread it out.

The smoldering expression on Deathridge's face killed any humor in Langford's distress. Vlad realized that such was the force of Deathridge's personality that he, himself, was ready to spring into action had the man commanded it. Though he knew of the man only from histories and cryptic mentions in letters, Deathridge in the flesh surged past all legend. Descriptions that had seemed hyperbolic in the reading failed in comparison to the man's dark energy.

With Rivendell bringing up the rear, the assembly moved to study the map once Langford laid it out.

Deathridge pointed to the mouth of the Argent River. "Just before we sailed, agents on the Continent sent word that two Ryngian regiments of foot set off for Mystria. One regiment is bound for this Fortress of Death."

"Du Morte," Rivendell corrected him.

Deathridge fixed him with a stare that would have melted an anvil. "We believe du Malphias will be reunited with the Platine Regiment. The Silicium

Regiment—finally rebuilt after Villerupt —will reinforce cities in Kebeton. They will place one battalion, here, at Fort Cuivre on Lac Verleau's eastern shore, at the Upper Argent outflow."

The Prince's expression tightened. "Whoever controls that fort can pinch off supplies heading for du Malphias, as well any trade goods heading for Kebeton."

"Exactly. Cuivre is the cornerstone to eliminating much of Tharyngia's trade." Deathridge looked up. "Major Forest, can your men take it?"

"You'd be asking us to cover near three hundred miles as the crow flies, most all of it through Seven Nations land. The Tharyngians will know we are coming. We will have no artillery and will be outnumbered by the fort's garrison."

Deathridge nodded. "Now you see why I won't ask Johnny's playmates on horseback to attempt it."

Forest smiled slowly. "We can do it. I'll get to drawing up requisitions and all."

"Good. You will be going out in advance of the main army, a scouting party in force. You will divert later. I shall write out full orders."

"Thank you, my lord."

Deathridge nodded. "As for you, Highness, I will want you to take charge of the Colonial Militia. I understand you have a regiment available. You will be our reserve, but I shall also need you to prepare roads through the wilderness. You have men who know their way around an ax?"

The Prince laughed. "Every man in Mystria owns one and keeps it sharp. I have a militia company specifically…"

"Militia! Never!" Rivendell protested. "I will not be fighting them. I will never deploy them."

"Then you are a fool, but I suspect this is apparent. Your influence at court and in Parliament has put you in charge of this expedition. I am able, however, to advise the militias, which I am doing. If you choose to ignore my advice, you do so at your peril."

"My *peril*? We shall see about this, my lord."

"Get off your high horse, Johnny. This is not a game." Deathridge waved Rivendell to the side. "I shall get this buffoon out of your way so you may do your planning. Captain Strake, I would dine with you this evening at my lodgings. I shall send a man with the details. I expect you will be here as a liaison until then."

"Yes, sir." Owen hesitated. "If I might ask after my wife?"

"Hardly the time, not the place." Deathridge's expression eased ever so slightly. "She was well last I saw her, and is anxious for your reunion."

"Thank you, my lord."

Deathridge nodded, then glanced again at the model. "Plan well, gentlemen.

The fate of Mystria depends upon what you do. Now, Johnny, get you and your shadow out of here, and let real men work."

Rivendell looked nothing so much like a sulking child as he walked out stiff-legged, head down, trailing Deathridge. Langford hurriedly gathered maps and the journals, leaving the Mystrian map on the desk, and scuttled after the other two.

Vlad sighed when Chandler closed the door behind the visitors. "That, gentlemen, was fascinating. It may yet be early, but could I offer you a restorative drink? Chandler, whisky and water, please, all around."

The Prince looked at Owen. "Your uncle makes quite an impression."

"He's had years of practice." Owen shook his head. "He almost made me pity Rivendell."

The Count accepted a drink from the servant. "Not looking forward to dining?"

"I would sooner dine with the Laureate."

"We all may get that chance." Vlad studied the map. "How fast can we realistically expect to travel? Ten miles a day?"

Forest shook his head. "I'll get that out of my men, maybe twelve. Decent rivers for part of the way. Heading to Anvil, you should get six."

"Do you concur, Owen? You've been there."

Owen cupped his drink in both hands, but did not sample it. "Depends on how many wagons we need for supplies. I would send as much as I could ahead to Hattersburg up the Tillie. Definitely ship the cannon. The horses, too. Not that they will do any good at the fortress."

"If we leave on the thirty-first, we will arrive at Anvil around the second of July. This gives us two months, perhaps three, for a siege." The Prince shook his head. "Getting the necessary food and fodder out there alone will be incredibly difficult. It is a logistical nightmare."

The Count chuckled. "An idiot for a leader, an unrealistic timetable, insufficient forces to do the job: If one were not acquainted with the ways of royalty, one might think there was no intention for this effort to succeed."

Rivendell closed the coach door before Langford could climb in. "Walk, Langford, and hurry. I shall join you presently after the Duke and I have our chat."

Langford made to salute automatically, started to drop things, failed to catch them, and blushed.

Deathridge pounded the coach roof with a fist. "Go!"

The driver snapped a whip, and the black coach lurched into motion. Rivendell smiled. "Oh, Dick, I think we fooled them. They haven't a clue. That's right, ain't it? Ain't it?"

"Yes, of course, as planned." Deathridge smiled every so slightly. "You played your part well."

"And you, sir, and you." Rivendell smiled broadly. "Your arriving early was brilliant. Packet boat, you say."

"Yes, and I shall want my twenty pounds, too."

"Of course." Rivendell nodded. He had first met Deathridge on the Continent and had not liked him at all. Not much to like, since the man did not socialize as others did. Yet he always seemed to have someone's ear. The younger Rivendell, unlike his father, always did notice those who moved in the background and seemed to weather any storm without upset. When he found himself on the other side of the Mystrian argument from Deathridge, he had been apprehensive; and wholly terrified when the man had sent word he wished to speak with him in Launston.

Deathridge tucked himself into the carriage's corner. "You *will* fight the Mystrian troops."

"I shall not, sir. Wholly unreliable."

"Of course they are, you fool. We need them destroyed so the Queen understands the idiocy of leaving her colonies without a strong garrison. You will take them to Anvil Lake, you will lay siege to the fortress, you will kill the Colonials and withdraw to build a fort at the outflow of the Tillie River, as planned. We prevent du Malphias from forming his own nation and keep him alive as a threat."

Rivendell nodded. "I hate that it will appear that I lost the siege."

Deathridge shook his head. "You only lose if we allow them to say that in Parliament. And we will not. Yours will be a 'strategic redeployment.' You will be hailed as a genius, and given more troops to destroy him next summer. And all of Mystria will see you as its savior. Tharyngia sends more troops to Mystria, we attack the Continent, and end the Laureate tyranny forever."

"Yes, yes, of course." Rivendell's smile shrank a little. "Why was it you sent Forest's men off to that other place?"

"If you had them at Anvil Lake, you would have been forced to use them. By sending them off to be killed, we make Mystria much more vulnerable. The whispers of independence will die." Deathridge's eyes half-closed. "The Prince will be removed as Governor-General. I believe you will be offered that post."

Rivendell rubbed his hands together. "I get so much, and you ask so little in return."

Deathridge shrugged. "See to it that my nephew dies, and I shall consider us more than even."

CHAPTER FIFTY-TWO

May 24, 1764
Duke Deathridge's Residence, Temperance
Temperance Bay, Mystria

Owen slowly mounted the steps to his uncle's apartments. Duke Deathridge had taken rooms from Zachariah Warren. The shop's location proved convenient to the docks and the garrison armory. The choice made perfect sense *and* managed to offend Lord Rivendell, since renting from a shopkeeper was hardly suitable for a man of Deathridge's status.

Owen felt as if he were a child again. His father had never been a disciplinarian, so those duties devolved to his grandfather or uncle. Grandfather simply had the help beat him. His uncle greatly relished his role and, it had often seemed to Owen, was intent on bleeding him dry of Mystrian blood.

His uncle had never just inflicted pain. He always threw in humiliation. Owen's cheeks burned at the memory of the time his uncle had appeared at his Academy, had him strip off his breeches in the courtyard, then applied a riding crop to his buttocks and thighs for an imaginary offense. As it turned out, Richard Ventnor had actually committed that particular offense thirty years earlier, and his father had beaten him as he beat Owen.

Owen doubted the invitation to dinner would include a beating. Still, he was willing to bet humiliation and mental torture would be on the menu. Owen knocked at the apartment door, wondering why he had even come.

Harlmont, a wizened prune of a man whose subservient attitude had left him perpetually hunched, opened the door. The servant said nothing by way of greeting. He took Owen's hat, then waved him through to the sitting room.

Richard Ventnor stood before a modest fire, holding a book in his left hand. He snapped it shut and set it on the mantle, then looked Owen up and down. "I have, I fear, grossly misjudged you."

Owen hesitated. "I beg your pardon."

"Harlmont, two whiskies. My best. Be generous and quick." Deathridge moved to a chair beside the fire, and nodded Owen toward its mate opposite. "I read the Prince's report—twice, in fact. The level of detail, the things you learned about these *pasmortes,* impressed me."

Owen sat. "Lord Rivendell believes they are ghosts to frighten children."

"Rivendell could not find east even if you started him at the dawn."

"He will get men killed."

Deathridge accepted a whisky and raised his glass to his nephew. "To men who see what is."

Owen took his whisky and sipped. "Thank you."

"To you goes the thanks. And an apology." Deathridge set his glass on a side table. "Had not your wife so eloquently pled your case, I would never have considered you for this assignment. I had little expectation of success. Certainly nothing on this level. You justified her faith in you, and opened my eyes."

Owen frowned. "Did you know du Malphias was on his way when you sent me?"

"It had been rumored, but he sailed after you did. Had I guessed at the depths of his depravity I would have…" His uncle's head came up. "No. I was going to say I would have informed you, but the truth is, I would have chosen someone else. I never imagined you to be as clever as you are."

Owen shivered. "Are you well, Uncle?"

The man laughed, and openly so. It had to have been the first time Owen had heard that sound. "I deserve that. I treated you poorly, Owen, for reasons that, I guess, you should know.

"My brother, your stepfather, is a drunkard and a horrible gambler. Your maternal grandfather, Earl Featherstone, had lent Francis a great deal of money—more than our father was willing to repay. When your father died, your grandfather purchased Francis' marriage to your mother at the price of his debts. I, and my father, had hoped to use Francis to secure some other alliance. My discomfort at being thwarted was something I took out on you. I convinced myself you were a stupid boy and that if you were dead, it would be the best thing for all involved. I do not, however, stoop to murder."

Owen gulped a decent slug of the whisky, letting it burn his throat so he would not scream. *My existence thwarted his ambition, so that justifies how I was treated?*

Deathridge steepled his fingers. "So I have several things to tell you. The first, which will be made public when you return to Norisle, is that the Queen is going to make you a Knight of the Norillian Empire. With that shall come a modest land grant here. You know what you have seen and what you like; please choose a place. A thousand acres. You might name it after the family estate."

"A knighthood. Do not tease me."

"No, it is quite true. Her Majesty recognizes the threat these *pasmortes* represent. Du Malphias had been rumored to be collecting bodies and looting graves back in the days of Villerupt. We saw no evidence of anything untoward, so suggestions of necromancy had been dismissed."

Owen raised an eyebrow. "What about his ability to use magick beyond the realm of touch?"

Deathridge recovered his glass and drank. "That I find the most disturbing of all. There are always rumors of magick that powerful."

"The Shedashee can do it, after a fashion."

"This gives the rumors more credence, certainly." Deathridge put the glass down again. "This brings me to one charge I have for you, one that you must reveal to no one else."

"Yes?"

Deathridge closed his eyes for a moment. "When you take the fortress, du Malphias will attempt to burn his papers. You must, at all costs, prevent this. We need his documents, to analyze and determine what breakthroughs he has made. The very future of Norisle will depend upon it."

"That is a very important job, Uncle. I should think you save it for your-self."

"I would, but I will not be joining you on the expedition."

Owen frowned. "But you said your job was to advise… You're not going with Forest's troops, are you?"

"As much as I might like to, no." His uncle sighed and almost seemed to shrink. "The packet boat did have the information I informed the Prince of concerning Tharyngian troops. It also contained a letter directing me to return to Launston with all haste. One of my political allies—one of Rivendell's enemies—suffered a public scandal. I will remain here long enough to organize supplies for the expedition, then I will return to Launston to salvage what I can."

Deathridge covered his face with his hands, then looked up. "How smart is Prince Vlad? Is he sane? He seemed so, but many fear he has adopted Tharyngian ways."

"He's very smart, and very sane."

"Ambitious?"

"Not in any way you might think." Owen smiled. "His ambition extends only to his studies. He gave me a list of plants and animals to bring back for him. He understands politics, but only uses that knowledge to do what the Crown wants."

His uncle nodded thoughtfully. "Good. And he is not too much under the influence of the Kessian?"

"Von Metternin? He uses the Count as an advisor, but even the Count is in awe of the Prince."

"This is important, Owen." His uncle's expression sharpened. "What did they think of du Malphias' plan to create his own nation?"

"The Prince laughed when I told him. He said it was impossible. Aside from

Tharyngia lacking the necessary number of people, Mystria is too large, with too many regions and interests. The Continent would sooner be united than Mystria."

"Very good." His uncle smiled quickly. "And the Kessian's thoughts?"

"He feels the same, as best I know."

"Good." Deathridge stood and plucked the book from the mantle. He handed it to Owen. "Do you know this book?"

Owen ran his fingers over the cover. "*A Continent's Calling.* "Yes. I used it as a key for coded messages to Prince Vladimir."

Still standing, Deathridge took up his glass and sipped more whiskey. "Did you know that the author, Samuel Haste, does not exist? It is a *nom de plume.*"

"I wasn't aware of that fact."

"If you knew who had written it, you would tell me, yes?"

Owen nodded despite goosebumps puckering of his flesh. It occurred to him in a flash that the book's true author might be Doctor Frost. *I would never betray him.* "Of course. Is there a problem?"

"The document is seditious. Be careful. Do not let Rivendell know you have read it."

"I won't."

"One last matter."

Owen looked up. "Yes?"

"If Lord Rivendell were to lose his mind and lead the expedition to ruin, do you think Prince Vladimir could take over? Allowing that he would use Count von Metternin as an aide. Would you be able to command troops in his name?"

"Yes, to the first. A conditional yes to the second, since colonels will be commanding the regiments."

Deathridge smiled coldly. "I yet have it within my power to do certain things, Owen. Before I leave, I shall write out a sealed order and give it to the Prince. It will grant you a field promotion to General in the event that Rivendell is relieved of command. I will brief the Prince on this matter."

Owen blinked. "Are you certain, Uncle?"

"I am. You have to be my man here, Owen. You have to be Norisle's man here. If we fail to deal with du Malphias, our position in the world is compromised. My enemies do not see it that way, but it is quite clear. I know it, and I know their will is such that when adversity strikes, they will withdraw and merely hasten a collapse that never need happen.

"You, Owen Strake, have seen the evil that is Guy du Malphias. It falls to you to eliminate him. It is our family duty to thusly serve the Crown."

Owen shook his head as if to clear it. *Is this truly my uncle?*

He knew there had to be more going on than he was seeing. Before he could even begin to puzzle it out, his uncle set the whisky down and extended his hand. "I must be leaving."

Owen stood and shook his hand. "But I thought… Dinner?"

"One last ruse, and you will understand." Deathridge smiled curiously. "You will still have dinner, and you will enjoy the company."

Deathridge exited to the foyer. Owen made to follow, but a voice from behind, from the dining room, stopped him. "Owen."

He turned, his heart instantly in his throat. There she stood, perfect and smiling, a gown of white reminding him of the day they wed. "Catherine!"

She flew to him and he gathered her into his arms. She clung to him, burying her face against his chest, her body wracked with sobs. She grabbed handfuls of his coat. She seemed so small and delicate. All he could do was hold her and stroke her hair.

"Shhhhh, nothing is wrong, beloved."

She pulled back and looked up, her cheeks wet. "I thought I had lost you."

"No, darling, no."

"Owen, I sent you from me and then when you were hurt, when you almost died. It was my fault. I had hurt my husband, my love."

"Hush. I am fine."

"You don't know, Owen. But for the kindness of your Uncle Richard, I should have been undone." She stroked his face, holding it in both hands. "It really is you, isn't it?"

He smiled and turned his face to kiss her palms each in turn. "You never lost me. You never came close to losing me."

"Oh, you are such a frightful liar." She closed her eyes and rested her forehead against his breastbone. "Your uncle, too. He would not tell me how close to death you were, not for the longest time. But I was inconsolable, Owen. I love you so much."

He tipped her head up, then kissed her. She melted into his arms, her hands running beneath his jacket, holding him tightly. She broke the kiss, then kissed his chest. "I thought I should never have you in my arms again."

"I am here, now, Catherine."

"Yes, you are." She pulled back and took both his hands in hers. She led him into the hallway and deeper into the apartments. On the left, toward the back, she brought him into a bedroom and bade him sit on the bed. She knelt and tugged his boots off, then stripped him of hose.

"Your uncle brought me to Mystria because I could not bear to be without you. He said nothing of my passage on the packet boat to surprise you. I had to go with him, of course, since it would not do for me to be left alone on a troop transport. You soldiers can be such a randy lot."

Owen stared at her. "If one of them touched you…"

"Calm yourself, Owen. None of them did, beloved. None of them touched me as you have, as you will." She peeled his coat off him and slowly unbuttoned his waistcoat. Both of them she deposited on a spindly chair, pausing then to kiss him again and press herself to him. Smiling, she unbuttoned his shirt, teasing, kissing exposed flesh.

His hands rose to hers, stopping her halfway.

"There are new scars, Catherine."

"They are part of you, husband, so I love them." She opened his shirt and shivered, but just for a moment. Her smile grew wide again. She leaned in and kissed the bullet wound on his left flank.

Owen gasped. Until the heat of her kisses flowed into his flesh, he had not realized how alone he felt. Part of his captivity had remained with him, grown out of the dreams where Catherine held herself apart. She had feared losing him, and deep down, he had feared losing her. One kiss, a kiss which was but the harbinger of many more, was enough to banish that fear.

Sinking to her knees in a rustle of linen, Catherine unbuttoned his breeches and stripped him naked. She ran her hands from his waist along his thighs, her thumbs brushing over his bullet wounds, her fingers tracing the splinter scars on his hip. Her breath warmed his skin as she kissed the wounds on his thighs.

She looked into his eyes. "I have missed you so, Owen, you cannot know my agonies, my fears." She kissed his flesh again. "But now they have all evaporated."

He drew her to her feet. He began to fuss with the knotted lacings of her gown, but she pushed his hands away. She gathered pillows on the bed and directed him to lay against them, kissing him once, then pressing a finger to his lips.

She loosened the ties that bound her into her gown and let the dress slip to the floor. She was as he remembered her, slender with full breasts and large nipples. He smiled, and she blew out the bedside candle. Then she slid onto the bed and straddled him.

Catherine unfastened her hair. It cascaded down about her shoulders. She leaned forward, kissing him again, then whispered, "I feared I had lost you, Owen. I will now rediscover you, every inch of you, and show you how so completely I missed you."

CHAPTER FIFTY-THREE

May 30, 1764
Temperance
Temperance Bay, Mystria

"Truth be told, sir, I ain't too proud to acknowledge I am pleased to be leaving Temperance behind." Nathaniel walked beside Major Forest. "Every foot between me and Bishop Bumble makes me happy."

Forest smiled. "It was good he gave us that blessing before we headed out. His heart is in the right place."

Nathaniel frowned, unsure he believed Bumble had a heart. The Bishop had offered an hour-long sermon on the horrors of Tharyngian society, telling the men that their mission was really God's plan. He offered numerous scriptures to underscore this opinion, even mentioning the Good Lord wandering for forty days and forty nights in the wilderness. "Not sure I find tales of the Lord wandering and lost much of a good omen, Major."

"Your feelings not withstanding, Captain Woods, I'm sure the sermon was a comfort to some." Forest's eyes narrowed. "Everyone fell out properly."

"True, sir, with a few exceptions."

By rule both companies of the Mystrian Rangers carried a hundred rounds of ball or bullet per man. The riflemen among them had an added twenty of the prince's *pasmorte* killers. All of them had their long guns in a deer- or moose-skin case. Most all the men had decorated them with beads, buttons, bits of shell, or fancy stitching. They carried hatchets or tomahawks and knives.

Each carried two types of packs. The first, consisting of a blanket wrapped in bearskin, had a strap looped through its middle. That loop settled over the man's shoulders and across his chest rather high. A few men tucked some notions in the blanket, but nothing too heavy. A canvas cloth rolled up and tied on either end into a loop made up the second pack. It closely resembled a big sausage. The men carried rice, beans, some salt, some sausage and salt pork in it, as well as eating utensils, some ginger, sugar, and tea.

In a separate satchel they kept bullet molds, lead, spare firestones, and tools. Because these things tended to be heavy, four or five men would share them, passing the satchel around every couple of miles. Nathaniel had his own satchel with the molds, but Makepeace offered to haul it since they both used the same rounds.

Nathaniel smiled as the troops marched along. No one would mistake them for Norillian troops, as they looked far more raggedy than professional soldiers. In general, the Rangers all dressed alike, wearing moccasins and leather leggings, breeches, leather tunics or homespun shirts, with short jackets over them, and caps. The similarity ended there, however, as colors marked the men as different. Caleb and his college friends all wore sashes of maroon and gold around their middles. The men from Summerland had their red caps. The Branches and Casks all wore foxskin caps, while the southerners had adopted the Fairlee militia's green coat.

Nathaniel hadn't been immune to sprucing up his appearance. He decorated his slouch-brimmed, black felt hat with a band of jeopard fur. William's mother had made him a necklace with bear and jeopard claws—the bear claws for his relationship to Msitazi, and the jeopard claws to celebrate his warrior nature. Just seeing that made some men smile and soured Rufus Branch's expression right quick.

Caleb's men—whom the others had taken to calling the Bookworms—had made a point of carrying a diary, pencils or pens, and at least one other book. They planned, during pauses in the marches, to read to each other, continuing their education on the way. Not to be outdone, Makepeace had managed to find himself a copy of the Bible and threatened to read the entire thing to every Tharyngian left alive at Fort Cuivre.

"I reckon them books will get heavy, Major."

"I believe you are correct. I suggested they read from one of them until it was finished, then move to the next. I suspect some will be abandoned in Hattersburg."

"We'll be leaving more than books." Nathaniel pointed to a skinny man whose buckskin clothes hung on him like mammoth hide on a mouse. "It was kindly of Bishop Bumble to give us Mr. Beecher to tend to our spiritual needs, but he ain't gonna make it."

"It could be worse."

Nathaniel smiled. At the end of his sermon, Bishop Bumble announced that he would accompany Lord Rivendell and his army. This appeared to surprise his wife, who began crying and had to be comforted by Lilith and Mrs. Frost. Mrs. Frost appeared a bit weepy, too, but she put on a brave face when she said her good-byes to Caleb.

"True enough, Major." Justice Bone, who got himself elected Corporal in charge of the third squad, had picked Beecher as part of his squad. The other men split up his heavier gear, leaving him with a knife, his Bible, and his blanket pack. The squad would eat their way through his supplies first, then let him carry his empty canvas pack until they resupplied at Hattersburg.

"I reckon I will head back and see to the first squad."

"Thank you, Captain."

Forest had deployed his hundred and forty men well for traveling. A pair of men headed out in front of the column, a pair flanked it either side, and two followed it, rotating the duty through all the men in whichever squad had that particular assignment. Since the northerners knew the area better, they got the honor of guaranteeing the unit's safety.

The Bookworms had won the job of rearguard for the march from Temperance. As Nathaniel fell back, he greeted men and pet a number of the dogs traveling with the column. A few men had fitted their dogs with packs, but most just muzzled them. Dogs made sniffing out ambushes much easier, and the muzzles prevented a lot of barking from alerting the enemy to their location.

The Bookworms appeared to be in high spirits by the time Nathaniel reached them. They clearly were enjoying their new clothes—they had outfitted themselves in buckskins head to toe, having bartered clothes from Norisle in some cases for soiled and ratty skins. Nathaniel was pretty sure none of them had killed any of the animals whose skins they'd pulled on. They walked with a swagger the long miles would burn out of them. He expected half would remain in Hattersburg, but it pleased him to have them along.

Makepeace had dropped all the way back to school whichever Bookworm marched beside him. Nathaniel fell in beside Caleb, who traveled with his fellows despite being in charge of the fifth squad. Caleb, himself wearing a black felt, slouch-brimmed hat, gave Nathaniel a nod.

"How does it look up front, Captain?"

"Moving right along." Nathaniel acknowledged the Bookworms with a nod. "How are your boys holding up?"

"We've barely gotten a mile, Captain. They will be fine."

"Going's easy now."

Caleb nodded. "Most all of them know it."

"Way I see it, you have two jobs, Lieutenant Frost." A long line of men walking two abreast wound its way down the road. "First is to see to the fifth squad. Makepeace will see to your Bookworms."

"I understand."

"Second, don't be preaching no glory and duty." Nathaniel smiled. "Leave all the preaching to Mr. Beecher."

"I don't believe I understand your point, Captain."

"Men will talk themselves into all manner of stupid things. See it mostly when they been drinking. But speechifying, that will make some men drunk.

And glory-seeking is stupid. On this here long walk we will be wet, bug bit, snake bit, thorn-scratched, hot, cold, hungry, thirsty, sore, shot at, and just plain tired. A man what figgers he's doing all that for glory, he's a man who will run when he learns there ain't no glory. Man who won't run is one who looks on down inside and knows he's doing this for himself and his kin, the ones he loves."

"My men won't run."

"I will accept your word on that. Just soes you know that you need to treat them like men. Make 'em believe they can do it and they will. Tease them with a reward that don't mean nothing, and they won't."

"Thank you, Captain."

"And you *can* get through this, Caleb."

The younger man smiled. "I know. Captain, I hope you won't mind, but I did something for you, back in Temperance."

"What would that be?"

"I know you didn't get a chance to see Rachel before we marched. So I told my sister to tell her that you wished Rachel well."

Nathaniel nodded slowly. "You know you oughten not poke your nose into a man's affairs."

"I know, but…"

"And you know your sister ain't going to cotton to delivering that message."

"Yes, but…"

Nathaniel looked at him. "I appreciate it, Lieutenant Frost. Might be, as we go along, you could scratch down some words for me. You'll be sending things back to Temperance from Hattersburg, most like."

"I'd be happy to."

"I would be obliged." Nathaniel smiled easily. "And just to ease your mind, I did sit a spell with Rachel, making my good-byes."

Caleb stared at him, mouth open. "But Rufus' Foxtails, they were guarding her. How could you sneak in to see her?"

"I reckon that's something for you to be thinking on for the nights the boys in them fox-caps is having sentry duty." Nathaniel nodded and started working his way back up the line. "Or be happy about when we come to Fort Cuivre and we need me to take a peek inside."

By the end of the day the column made camp on the banks of the Benjamin River, several miles east of the Prince's estate. Nathaniel had gone ahead with the Summerland boys to pick out exactly where they would camp. The eldest of them, Thomas, had been in logging camps for a few years, so he laid out where the privies would go, while Nathaniel placed sentries.

Before darkness had fallen, Kamiskwa appeared from the river along with twenty Shedashee braves. Half were Altashee, the other half Lanatashee. They'd brought down the river large war canoes suitable for carrying thirty men each.

Nathaniel looked the Shedashee party over. "That's a powerful lot of canoes."

"The Lanatashee made two more than we did, though ours are better."

"I reckon. None of the other Confederation tribes sent warriors?"

Kamiskwa shook his head. "They see this as a white-man's war."

"Probably wise to stay out of it." Nathaniel sighed. "Seven Nations?"

"They've heard the Ryngians are dealing with *wendigo*. Only the Ungarakii are crazy enough to act for them."

"Better only one tribe than all seven."

Nathaniel took Kamiskwa around through the camp, introducing him to the various officers. Most of the men had met Shedashee before and, despite the fact that the men of Fairlee had fought a couple wars against the Chokashee and Ishannakii, they mostly accepted the Twilight People. Their dogs sniffed and yelped, as they had been trained, but their owners held them back.

Major Forest greeted Kamiskwa warmly and invited him to dine at the Major's tent along with the unit's captains and lieutenants. Forest's enthusiastic acceptance of the Shedashee silenced most protests, save those from the Foxtails. Rufus, who had been elected as their Corporal, bristled at serving under Caleb and Nathaniel, so nothing would make him happy.

Nothing shy of my dying. Nathaniel laughed. *So they is just going to go on being disappointed.*

After supper the Shedashee made their own camp on the far side of the river. It gave the dogs a chance to settle down and saved Forest from having to post a guard across the water. Forest set his sentries up in units of six, with a pair of men chosen from various companies. He posted them far enough away from the main camp that discovering a sentry post would not put an enemy on top of his force. Two sentries would be awake at all times at each post. If they heard anything, they would wake others who would alert the main camp.

A runner found Nathaniel and asked him to report to Major Forest. He found Benjamin Beecher with the Major. "Reporting as ordered, sir."

"Mr. Beecher has a problem. I cannot seem to make him understand our situation."

Nathaniel nodded to the minister. "Reverend."

"With all due respect, Major Forest, I'm not certain Captain Woods can help. He never attends church and is, well, how can I say this? He is a notorious fornicator."

Nathaniel eased his shoulders back and his spine slowly popped. "That sounds like something bad, Mr. Beecher."

"It is, and you know it."

"I reckon that if you're gonna damn me for that, there's more than half the men here would be in the same boat."

Major Forest held up his good hand. "That is immaterial to the problem at hand. Mr. Beecher, if you will."

"Yes, Major." Beecher frowned mightily, his expression mocked by the face of the raccoon staring down from his cap. "These Twilight People are unbaptized. We cannot have the godless on this expedition."

"Would you be caring to make sense, Mr. Beecher?"

Beecher clasped his hands behind his back. "The Tharyngians have rejected our God. They are our enemies. The Shedashee have not embraced our God. It is the same in His eyes."

"Well now, Mr. Beecher, being as how I am a notorious fornicator and hain't never stepped into a church where you was able to see me, ain't I just as bad as any Ryngian?"

"You, I have been told, were baptized. Your foot has been set on the road to redemption. Those men in our company who have not been baptized will be baptized tomorrow morning, right here, in the river. I should like the Shedashee to join them."

"Iffen they don't, they's enemies?"

Beecher looked skyward. "It's God's judgment, not mine."

Nathaniel could see where Beecher was headed, and it wasn't good. "Well, I don't reckon you need to be crying your eyes out over all this. The Altashee live in the village of Saint Luke."

The minister blinked. "They do?"

"I ain't lying. Their Chief Msitazi declared it so after welcoming missionaries. Your fears is just silly."

"I didn't know." Beecher frowned. "Why didn't you just tell me this?"

"Why did you go and call me a fornicator?" Nathaniel looked at him hard. "Some folks don't take kindly to be being judged."

The man glanced down. "I see. I beg your pardon, Captain Woods."

"Forgiven and forgotten. But now don't go a-mentioning baptism to the Twilight People. They's strong in their faith, but silent about it. Probably over there in a prayer circle now."

Beecher turned and looked over across the river. "God bless them."

"I reckon he has." Nathaniel nodded. "If you'll excuse me, I'm thinking I could use some saving, and I'll be over there getting it. Sir."

Forest held his hand up. "Wait, Captain. That's all, Mr. Beecher."

The preacher withdrew.

Nathaniel raised an eyebrow. "Major?"

"There might be a problem when Beecher finds out you've lied."

"From who? The Shedashee?" Nathaniel shook his head. "I reckon they've had more experience dealing with men of the cloth trying to save them than all the rest of us combined. I don't expect they'll have a problem. And if Beecher does, well, I hear tell the Good Lord done spent forty days and forty nights wandering the wilderness. Mr. Beecher might find hisself doing the same thing, doing everyone some right powerful good."

CHAPTER FIFTY-FOUR

May 31, 1764
Government house, Temperance
Temperance Bay, Mystria

"You're up very early, my lord." Prince Vlad greeted Count von Metternin happily. "Did you get any sleep?"

"Almost none." The Count bowed his head. He wore his complete uniform, including spurs and a cavalry saber. The boots had been polished until they glowed, the same with the gold buttons and the sword's silver scabbard. He wore white leather gloves, white breeches, and a waistcoat that matched the gold facings on his light blue coat. He'd even added his sash with medals. "And, yes, I know I look as ridiculous as you do."

The Prince laughed. "Well, you see, these are the clothes I wore on the jeopard expedition. A gift from Msitazi." The buckskin shirt, with fringed sleeves, had been decorated with a beadwork wurm curled over his heart. The red loincloth had a similar design woven in black, and the leather leggings repeated the design at the shin. "They were auspicious on the hunt."

"One can never have too much luck at war." Von Metternin nodded. "I am sorry to come to you so early…"

"No matter, I am awaiting Duke Deathridge."

"Very good. There is a disciplinary matter which I feel must be referred to you. An individual was caught leaving…"

"A deserter?" Vlad shook his head. "I should have thought…"

"Please, Highness." The Count walked back to the door and ushered in a slender young man in homespun with a slouch-brimmed hat. The youth looked at his feet, the brim hiding his face. The Count nodded and exited, closing the door behind himself.

Vlad approached the deserter. "What do you have to say for yourself?"

The deserter shook his head. Tears dappled the floor.

The Prince sighed. "There is no shame in being afraid, you know. I will admit to being afraid myself, but we have duty to do, and we will do it."

The deserter looked up and Vlad caught the flash of familiar eyes. He reached out and tugged off the hat. "Gisella!"

She nodded, her lips pressed flat together. She'd raggedly chopped off her hair and had smudged her face with soot. Tears had worn tracks through it.

Vlad cast the hat aside and gathered her into his arms. "You weren't deserting—you were coming with us?"

She nodded, sniffing.

He stroked her hair and cupped the back of her neck. "What were you thinking?"

"I do not want to lose you."

Vlad laughed. "You have no fear of that, my darling." He kissed the crown of her head, and hugged her more tightly. "I am no military man. I have no place in battle."

"But you will bring your wurm on the expedition."

"Only because I must." His hands on her shoulders, he eased her back. "Most of our men have never been to war. Having the wurm come along will give them heart. More importantly, Mugwump is stronger than any five teams of oxen. He will be invaluable getting us there."

"You must promise me: no heroics."

He studied her face, her resolution, then slowly shook his head. "I cannot make that promise."

"You must, or with God as my witness, I shall join your army. Joachim caught me because he suspected, but he will not find me again. If I do not march today, I go tomorrow, or the next day. I will ship with your supplies to this Hattersburg. Your army will have a long tail. I will travel unseen."

There was no denying the validity of her claim. Forty Norillian women—wives of officers and enlisted men—had sailed with their husbands. Another twenty Mystrian had fallen in with them, all intent on following their men to war. Almost twice as many women, a few with children in tow, had joined the Mystrian militia units. In addition to them would come tinkers and other tradesmen, tailors, seamstresses, and laundresses to tend to the soldiers needs. Teamsters and skinners along with a ragged gaggle of other people would follow all of them.

"Princess Gisella, I cannot promise I will remain constantly out of harm's way. I do not know the enemy's mind. I do not know God's mind. I could as easily be struck by lightning as I could a ball fired from ambush. Such a fate would be a matter of chance. But I also cannot tell you that if a man is wounded, I will not run to help him. Those decisions are made not with the mind, but the heart. While I promise you I shall always think, I do not believe you wish me to close my heart."

She brushed a lock of brown hair out of his eyes. "No, I would not have that."

He took her hand in his and kissed her palm. "I need you to promise me that you shall remain here. I need you, though you are not yet my wife, to act bravely and give others courage. You and Mrs. Frost, Mrs. Bumble, Owen's wife: you will be the heart of Temperance. Others will look to you for hope. They will need you as much as I do."

Gisella nodded, then pulled her hands back over her head. "I shall be quite the sight with my hair so short."

"No. You will tell them you cut a lock for me. You wished it to be the most beautiful lock, and found none suitable until the last."

She glanced up at him. "You have the soul of a poet, my love."

"No." He turned from her and pulled a small pair of thread snips from his desk. He handed them to her. "Take a lock of my hair, please."

She slipped behind him and snipped one. Then she ran her arms around his middle and hugged him fiercely. "You will come back to me, Vladimir, a hero, I am certain."

He turned within her arms and kissed her. "I will count the days, the hours, the seconds. I love you, Gisella. Nothing will stop me coming back."

Vlad finished sealing the second of two letters as Chandler showed Duke Deathridge into the office. He rose and smiled. "Good to see you this morning, Duke Deathridge."

"And you, Highness. And when it is just us, please, call me Dick. So much easier, don't you think?"

"Quite." He handed the man the two letters. "One to my father and one for my aunt. The letter to my father is just our normal correspondence. The letter to my aunt is requesting immediate permission to marry Princess Gisella."

Deathridge raised an eyebrow. "She's not...?"

"No." Vlad shook his head. "Despite our affection and attraction, neither of us wished to spark an international incident by proceeding without sanction."

"Very wise, Highness." Deathridge tucked the letters inside his frock coat. "I shall see these are delivered immediately upon my landing."

The prince's eyes tightened. "You're determined to go, then?"

"I really have no choice. I would much prefer to go with you. Since Rivendell will most likely not fight your troops, you should use them to build the fort at the Tillie outflow. He can retreat to it and winter there. I will argue in Parliament that we need more troops to smash the Tharyngians. And you can gather proof of these *pasmortes* which even the most obstinate minister will have to recognize."

"You'll have that proof, I guarantee it."

"Excellent." The smaller man nodded. "I will remain in Temperance to see to the shipping of supplies up to Hattersburg. I may even travel up to Margaretstown before catching a packet ship to Norisle."

"I expect us to be in Hattersburg a month from now." Vlad ran a hand over his chin. "We'll be carrying forty days of rations, so we shall need our supplies."

"More than enough time to get them there. Two weeks at most." Deathridge smiled. "Supplies in first, then the cavalry. Everyone should be there and waiting for you."

Vlad glanced at the model. "We need twice the number of regulars, and more than a company of artillery to destroy that place."

"And next year we will have it." Deathridge folded his arms over his chest. "Rivendell's retreat will destroy his coalition in Parliament. He'll be relieved. I would hope I am appointed in his place."

"What if Rivendell takes the Fortress of Death?"

"I do not believe he can. For him to succeed would require our enemy to be a fool. Guy du Malphias may be any number of things, but fool is not numbered among them. I expect Rivendell to mass troops to the north, get his cavalry destroyed and, in a sulking fit, retreat to your fortress. Have you decided on a name?"

"I was thinking 'Hope.'"

"Auspicious. Excellent choice. From Fort Hope we will sweep the Tharyngians from Mystria."

Vlad nodded. "I just wish we did not have to wait a year."

Deathridge's dark eyes narrowed. "The price of haste is blood. Quick action, when successful, crowns heroes. When unsuccessful, it creates unimaginable slaughter. For every hero, there are ten thousand victims. Never tempt those odds."

The Prince joined Count von Metternin at the head of the First Colonial Regiment. Of the five infantry battalions, three had been recruited solely from single colonies: Fairlee, Blackoak, and Temperance Bay. The other two were the Southlands Battalion and the Battalion of the North. They split all the other recruits between them. Each had its own regimental flag, and Blackoak had actually brought along a band including bagpipers, fife-players, and drummers.

An elderly tuba-player had tried to join the Temperance Bay Battalion, but he could barely walk carrying his instrument. The men voted him a corporal's commission and bought him a cap. He stood at their staging area, ready to play them off. And he was not alone in wishing the troops well.

Mounted on a grey mare, the Prince surveyed the crowd. Families had turned out, all dressed in their Sunday-best. Fathers stoically embraced their sons. Mothers and sisters wept while forcing cloth-wrapped bundles of food on the soldiers. Small children ran about, little boys snapping to attention when the soldiers were given orders. Dogs barked. The Prince even saw some Twilight

People watching the assembly—Blue Hand Lanatashee if he read the markings on their clothes correctly—and wondered what they were making of it all.

A rotund man made his way through the crowd to the Prince's left foot. "Care to make a comment for *Wattling's Weekly,* Highness?"

"I could, Mr. Wattling, but wouldn't you be more comfortable making something up yourself?"

"Highness, I…"

The Prince smiled. "You've carried two interviews—*long* interviews—with Lord Rivendell. Is there anything more to be said on this matter?"

Wattling's face puckered. "Lord Rivendell says you will smash the Godless Ryngians and be back the first of August."

Count von Metternin laughed. "Rivendell is more of an optimist than he is a geographer."

Wattling scribbled.

The Prince tapped him with his foot. "Please quote me: The bravest men in Norisle and Mystria will see to the safety of all. We will miss our families and cannot wait to rejoin them."

Wattling wrote, then frowned. "Not very encouraging, Highness."

"Reality seldom is, Mr. Wattling. Good day." The Prince nudged his horse forward, making his way to the head of the column. Rivendell and his troops would leave later in the day, allowing the Mystrians to head off first and cut roads where necessary. The Norillians would pick up any stragglers and keep things organized.

Once he and the Count reached the mounted officer corps, a captain gave a signal. The Blackoak band began to play a stirring march, and the column, marching four abreast, moved out. Down the line the tuba bellowed, and a few men fired muskets into the air. Applause and shouts filled the city and the Prince's heart swelled.

The determined expressions on the Mystrians' faces made Vlad smile. "I think, von Metternin, if du Malphias had a look at these men, he might abandon his fortress right away."

The Kessian smiled. "Long marches drain the hero out of every soldier, alas. But these men, they have heart."

"And we will give them more." Vlad set spurs to his horse's flank, and von Metternin joined him. They raced ahead to the Prince's estate to prepare their surprise for the Mystrian militia.

Bright and early the next morning, Prince Vlad sat astride Mugwump on the road near his estate, waiting for the militia troops to march past. Ribbons of red and green fluttered in the breeze from the wurm's tack. The Prince rode on a saddle at the wurm's shoulders; Count von Metternin was mounted at the wurm's hips. Bulging oilskin satchels lined the beast's flanks, stretched between the saddles, each one of them decorated with more ribbons.

The soldiers, whose line of march drifted toward the other side of the road, smiled and laughed. A few shouted: "He'll be having the Ryngians running," or "He'll win us the war all by himself!" Others just nodded as if a wurm was something they saw every day—those being more of the northerners than the men from the south. The Prince figured the northerners would have also gaped, but the Blackoaks had seen Mugwump first, and no northerner was going to let a southerner believe he was surprised by anything.

The Prince could not help but smile and wave. "You still think the march will drain the hero from them?"

The Kessian laughed aloud. "Half of them do not have shoes, most of them are ragged, and clearly they have not been trained. But, that fire in their eyes. These are men, sir, with which I should be willing to assault the gates of Hell itself."

"Let's hope it doesn't come to that, my lord." The Prince smiled as more men passed. "Alas, I think it may."

CHAPTER FIFTY-FIVE

May 31, 1764
Temperance
Temperance Bay, Mystria

"Who is she, Owen?"

Catherine's question took Owen completely by surprise. He'd been laying on his left side and his wife had snuggled in behind him, her naked body molding itself to his. She'd kissed his shoulder and the back of his neck, then licked at his earlobe.

And then the question.

"Who is whom?"

She grabbed his shoulder, pulling him onto his back, then threw her right leg over his hip. She loomed over him, her face warded by shadows as the first tendrils of dawn lightened the white curtains. "You know who."

Owen frowned. "I really don't." He raised his head to kiss her, but she pulled back. *This is serious.*

"You do, Owen. The woman who wrote those letters for you."

"Bethany Frost?"

"Yes."

Owen pulled himself up against the headboard. "I was billeted at her family's home. She wrote you at my request, when I could not write. You know that."

"Yes, but who *is* she?" Catherine's voice rose and her eyes sharpened. "Who is she, Owen?"

"I don't understand the question, Catherine."

She whirled away from him, dragging the sheet after her. She wrapped herself in it, then sat in a chair, hunched, weeping. "You've stopped loving me, haven't you?"

Owen stared after her, completely puzzled. The past week had been nothing short of fantastic. They had enjoyed Temperance and the surrounding area. She had taken immediate charge of his life. Their first stop had been to a tailor who fashioned for him a brand new uniform of the Queen's Own Wurm Guards, including two sets of breeches, three shirts, two waistcoats, and a heavy oilskin coat to cover the uniform jacket.

After that they had spent their time exploring both the city and each other intimately. She had always been curious, inventive, hungry, and insatiable. She wanted him fiercely—even when they'd ridden into the countryside for a picnic, she had wanted him. Right there, under the sun, in the open, wanton and brazen, she had reminded him that he was her husband.

Her ardor erased memories of their separation. She laughed heartily and lustily, reminding him of the girl he'd fallen in love with. She was full of plans—things they could do with his estate in Mystria, things they could do upon his return to Norisle. She knew of dozens of societies that wished him to speak to them, and dozens of others that wanted to give him honors. Her face glowed as she spoke, and the way she clung to his arm and smiled proudly as they walked through Temperance had stoked the fire in his heart.

He climbed from bed and went to her, standing over her, his hands on her shoulders. "Catherine, I love you completely. You're my whole world."

"I am such a fool. Oh, Owen, I forced you into her arms. I should have been brave enough to come with you. And then, when I got word that you were hurt, I wanted to come. I begged your uncle to arrange my passage. I wanted to be here, to nurse you back to health, but then your letter arrived, the one telling me not to come. Telling me you would send for me when the time was right. And I waited."

Owen frowned. "What letter? I never said that."

"Yes, Owen, you did." Her hands came away from her face and she looked up. "In that first letter, in her hand, you told me not to come."

He shook his head. "I never said that."

"It was there, Owen." Her tears began anew. "I would show you the letter, but, oh, I am such a silly girl. I carried it with me and was reading it on the ship. The wind tore it from my grasp. I thought God was giving me a sign that you had been torn from me. I was inconsolable. I did not leave my cabin for days."

Owen went to his knees and took her in his arms. "Hush, Catherine. You have not lost me. I am yours, and yours alone." He stroked her hair and kissed her cheek. *Bethany wouldn't have added that, would she?*

"Oh, Owen." She pressed her forehead to his. "When you did not mention her to me, or introduce me to her, when she was not present when her parents had us to dinner, what was I to think? Have I been silly, Owen? Please tell me I have been silly."

He took her face in both hands and kissed her. "You have been silly, Catherine, but that is no vice."

She sniffed. "Then the reason you want me to remain in Temperance is not because *she* is going off on campaign?"

"What? No." Owen shook his head. "If she *is* going—and I do not believe she is at all—I know nothing of it and want nothing to do with her."

"Then why don't you want me to go with you? You let me come to war on the Continent."

Owen rose and scooped her in his arms, then deposited her on the bed. "On the Continent, my lovely wife, there were comforts like this bed; and other women to organize balls and social events. On this campaign all those things shall be here, in Temperance."

"What about this Hattersburg?"

He snorted. "You would hate it. Social life is a tavern and if you can find a bed, you're sleeping three or four to it."

She rested a hand on his hip. "I would endure it gladly, Owen, to be close to you."

"And I would not put you through that."

She sat up, the sheet falling away, and licked his stomach. "Come, Owen, be my husband one more time. One more time before you are away. Show me how much you love me, and give me reason to believe you will return."

Owen took leave of Catherine privately, in their rooms. She had insisted on dressing him while remaining naked. She said it was a duty she owed him as his wife. Then she kissed him and clung to him, finally letting him go, her hand in his until he descended the stairs.

He made his way to the green before Government House, where the Fourth Foot was assembling. Because he was not a member of the Regiment, he found himself in a curious position. His rank entitled him to command a battalion, but the Regiment had no need for him. Ostensibly he was attached to the unit's command company as a liaison with the Colonial forces, but he and Rivendell wanted little to do with each other. Rivendell had made this apparent by denying him a horse. Rivendell likewise showed his disdain for the Colonials by refusing to allow Owen to march with them.

He found Lieutenant Palmerston and picked up his pack and musket. The Lieutenant gave him a wink, and Owen smiled. Despite having had a new uniform created for him, Owen had arranged that his Altashee kit would be packed for his use in the field.

"Gone native, have you, Nephew?"

Owen turned. "What, sir?"

Deathridge pointed to the tomahawk hanging from his pack. "Not standard issue."

"No, sir, but useful." Owen smiled. "There are a lot of things that we consider standard that won't be here."

Deathridge nodded solemnly. "I am aware of that, and aware that Rivendell will studiously avoid anything that requires thought. He really has no idea what he will find out there."

"Agreed."

"Owen, I need to ask a favor."

He'd never heard that tone in his uncle's voice before. "Yes, sir."

"I need you to refrain from doing more than requested."

"I am not sure I understand."

"It's really rather simple. I've told Prince Vladimir the same thing. Our best outcome here is for Rivendell to realize conquering the Fortress of Death just is not possible. I would prefer he build Fort Hope and go no further. I hope just getting to Anvil Lake will take the fire out of his belly. If this happens, please, let it be so."

Owen nodded. This was one of his uncle's political games. Owen loathed that sort of thing, but agreed with the goal. "Yes, Uncle, I understand."

"Good." Deathridge embraced Owen. "Go with God. Fight with honor and return home safely."

Owen, quite thrown off guard, retreated from the embrace, then tossed his uncle a crisp salute. The older man returned it, added a quick nod, and made his way off toward where Rivendell was speaking with his officers.

Owen shook his head. Before seeing his uncle, he had been feeling isolated. He did not fit in with the Regiment. Wearing a Norillian uniform, he no longer felt as if he fit with Mystria. People did not look at his face, just his coat, and based their reaction to him on it alone.

And now he asks me to work against the wishes of the Crown.

"Captain Strake."

Owen turned and smiled. "Doctor Frost, good to see you, sir."

"And you, looking very fierce in your uniform."

"Thank you." Owen looked past him for any sign of his wife or daughter. "And thank you for seeing me off."

"Had to. My wife wished to be here, but seeing Caleb off yesterday…"

"I understand, sir."

The older man smiled. "And Bethany, I think she would have been here, but she is a very stubborn girl. She's made her mind up about you and is unbending."

"Please remember me to her."

"I shall. Were she here, she would wish you Godspeed and safety, as do I." The man dug into his pocket and produced a small book. "It is a journal. I hope you will keep it as you did the others. I should be happy to read of your expedition."

"Very thoughtful, sir."

Frost laughed. "Not me, sir. I had thought to give you another copy of Haste's *A Continent's Calling*. My daughter took my coat for a brushing, and I found this in my pocket instead. I suspect I shall not be alone in reading about your adventures."

"I shall be happy to share them." Owen tucked the book in his coat pocket. "If I might impose on you, sir. My wife, she will be remaining here in Temperance. She knows no one save…"

"Say no more, my boy. I will arrange introductions." Doctor Frost offered his hand. "Godspeed, sir, there and back again."

"Good health to you and yours, sir."

Up and down the line, whistles blew. Owen shook Dr. Frost's hand, then found his position in the rear of the formation. A drummer set a pace, and the Fourth Regiment of Foot set out for the Fortress of Death.

Deathridge found Rivendell in a gaggle of officers and caught his eye. The mission's commander excused himself and drew back into an alley. The man made an elaborate charade of being cautious which guaranteed that he, being clad in red satin, would draw attention.

Idiot. Deathridge followed and hissed at him. "My lord! Discretion, if you please."

"Of course, Dick, of course. Are things set?"

"Completely. I've issued the necessary orders." Deathridge smiled. "Provided these Colonials can do anything at all correctly, you will have what you need to complete your mission."

"Oh, I shall, and return showered in glory." Rivendell raised his face to the sky, stretching his throat, and Deathridge imagined the satisfaction of drawing a razor across it. "New Tharyngia shall be a thing of the past."

"Very good. I have instructed my nephew to do nothing helpful on this expedition. I expect you will give him the most onerous duty, find fault with him whenever possible, and produce scurrilous reports about him."

Rivendell clapped his hands. "He'll be digging every slit trench between here and *La Fortresse du Morte.*"

"No, you fool, you can't do that. He is an officer. He is a skirmisher. Use him as a messenger to the Colonials. Have him scouting ahead. Use him as he is meant to be used. Give him the impossible to accomplish and he will fail."

"Of course, Dick, absolutely." Rivendell's eyes narrowed. "I'll work him to death, then get him killed, as you desire."

"Make sure he dies bravely. We don't want his wife disgraced."

"No, no, of course not."

"Good." Deathridge offered the man his hand. "I would wish you luck, but I know you need none of it."

"No, sir, Dick. It's all about brains and courage, ain't it? Ain't it? No need for luck when you have both of those."

Deathridge shook Rivendell's hand, then retreated down the alley and back between buildings. Whistles blew and drums rattled. Shouted orders faded into the distance, then the thunder of marching feet rumbled through Temperance.

For Deathridge, it had been almost too easy. The Mystrians were simple to beguile. Approach them with confidence, speak openly and honestly and they believed everything you told them. Validate ideas they had suggested, like the building of Fort Hope, and they took it as a sacred duty that such a thing should be done. They treated with him with the avidity of a younger brother trying to appease an older brother. *And with more facility than Francis ever showed.*

Rivendell, on the other hand, had been easier. The product of an inferior family, sent to inferior schools, his vanity was the key. His father's publication of self-congratulatory books, the son's desire for ostentatious clothing, his overweening pride: these were traits Deathridge had seen in countless of his peers. Play to their fears that conspiracies exist and invite them to participate, and you had them. To doubt what you told them was to be excluded, and since they sought inclusion above anything else, they would comply no matter how outrageous the task given to them.

Rivendell's entire expedition had been Deathridge's doing. All he needed to do was to let slip to friends that he could destroy du Malphias' fortress with two regiments of foot and one of horse, and Rivendell was forced to suggest he could do the same thing with even less. Influencing which units would go had been even easier. Before Rivendell had even felt the first sea breeze, his fate had been sealed.

Deathridge returned to his apartments and smiled as Catherine opened the door. "And how did it go, dearest Niece?"

"Exactly as you predicted, dearest Uncle."

"You are a wonder." He kissed her fully on the lips. "You make it so I almost wish that Owen would live to see you once more."

"So do I." She draped her arms around his neck. "After all, the fool still loves me, and would easily believe our child is his."

CHAPTER FIFTY-SIX

June 26, 1764
Hattersburg
Lindenvale, Mystria

"See, Nathaniel, see? What did I tell you?"

"I see, Seth." Nathaniel wasn't quite certain what he was seeing, but it wasn't right. It wasn't the Hattersburg he'd last seen. "Been here two weeks, have they?"

"Two and a half, more like." Seth looked at him with pleading eyes. "I love my wife, but iffen her kin gots to stay with me another day longer, I'll kill them all."

"You run on home. Tell Gates come back to his tavern." Nathaniel, standing at the center point of the bridge spanning the Tillie, waved Caleb forward. "Lieutenant, I reckon second, fifth, and sixth squads need to come up and hold this bridge."

Caleb, dark circles under his eyes, nodded. "Three ranks, lying, kneeling, and standing?"

"Aim low. Don't let Rufus give you no trouble."

"No, sir."

"Makepeace, Justice, bring the first and fourth up, on me." Nathaniel waited for the two squads to assemble. "Casual like, but have your guns clear."

The Bone brothers arrayed the squads into three smaller groups, with Tribulation guiding the third. They wandered into Hattersburg, walking along the muddy North road. Two hundred yards further on sat Gates' Tavern.

Nathaniel had never liked Hattersburg, but he'd always found something to look at on the streets. Not so this time. Some folks would be out at their summer homes, farming, so it made sense that half the homes should have been empty. The fact that they all had smoke coming from chimneys surprised him. Likewise that three dogs lay dead in the street with visible gunshot wounds, and that civilians were nowhere to be seen. From between houses the breezes produced flashes of scarlet coats hung on drying lines. Even the docks appeared empty and the stockyard didn't have but one scrawny old dairy cow in it.

Nathaniel wandered into town and right up to Gates' Tavern. He made a

340

hand signal and Justice took the fourth squad around toward the back while Makepeace brought the Bookworms in tight. He pulled open the door and entered, but got only four feet in.

A blond-haired young man in the 31st Horse Guards uniform barred his passage. "This headquarters is off limits to your kind." Beyond him a squad and a half of men sat at tables drinking and playing cards. From above came sounds of laughter, giggles, and creaking beds.

"I reckon I best speak to your commanding officer."

"I reckon," the man began, slowing his speech to affect a Mystrian accent, "you'd best sod off."

Nathaniel smiled, then drove his right knee into the man's groin. The cavalryman jackknifed forward, clutching himself. Nathaniel grabbed a handful of his hair and slammed his head into the wall, then pitched him back into the room, upsetting a table. Cards flew and before a one had fluttered to the floor, Nathaniel had his rifle's muzzle nestled between the downed man's chin and silver gorget.

"A one of you makes a move or a sound, and he dies."

Justice and Makepeace led their men into the room and spread them out. The Summerland boys gathered all the cavalry carbines and then directed the men to crowd into the narrow end of the room. Justice looked to Nathaniel. "Fix bayonets?"

"I reckon."

The cavalrymen paled, with more than one having occasion to pee on himself. Infantry bayonets added eighteen inches of spade-shaped steel to a six-foot long musket. Every single one of the Queen's soldiers had seen the grisly damage done by bayonets. All would sooner be hit by a cannon ball than have that much steel twisting in his guts.

"Makepeace, with me." They headed outside, and took the back stairs to the second floor. They ignored the guest rooms and instead headed for the commotion in the Gates' living quarters. They made enough noise coming through the door that anyone with half a mind would have known something was wrong, but the cavalry commander was firmly in the saddle and, therefore, distracted.

Distraction that ended when Makepeace grabbed him by an ankle and yanked him off the bed.

Nathaniel tugged the brim of his cap to the lady. "Sorry to be bothering you, ma'am. Got a need for the, uh, Captain, ain't you?"

The officer had pulled his hat to him, using it to cover his rampant embarrassment. "Captain Percival Abberwick. I should warn you, sir, that Her Majesty does not tolerate brigandry. You will be hung from the nearest tree."

"Brigandry? I'm thinking you mean thieving, right?"

"You know what I mean." He reached out for a pair of breeches, but Makepeace slapped his hand away. "Really, man, this is outrageous."

"I reckon outrageous is a regiment of horse-sitters coming here to Hattersburg and just eating and drinking and stealing as they like."

The Norillian snorted. "It is all right and proper. We are here at the Queen's command. All good citizens of Mystria are required to give aid and comfort to Her Majesty's soldiers. Once our Colonel gets here with our horses and our treasury, the people will be reimbursed at a proper rate for the provisions we have taken."

"I will be powerful pleased to see that, Captain." Nathaniel smiled. "Now you go and get dressed, then get your men out of here on account of Mister Gates is coming back in residence. This here is going to be Major Forest's headquarters."

"Now see here, a Colonial Major does not outrank me. I will not give up my headquarters."

Nathaniel squatted. "Well, I reckon this is how I sees things. You got fifteen men downstairs with five carbines between them. I'm gonna reckon more than your horses is being sent on upriver. I got a hundred forty of the hardest fighting, best shooting men in all of Mystria. They ain't had a drink in two weeks. They are going to be powerful sore angry if you done drunk this town dry. They ain't gonna let you stand between them and this tavern."

Abberwick stared at him incredulous. "Do you mean to tell me you would attack soldiers of Her Majesty's government?"

"No. I am just telling you that out here there are places where your children and your grandchildren could search every day of their lives, and they'd not find hide nor hair of you. We'd just tell folks the Ryngians got you. Now I reckon that any Mystrian here in Hattersburg would back us up on that. Ain't that right, ma'am?"

The woman, who was buttoning up her dress, nodded emphatically.

"So you see, Captain, you are going to make the right choice."

"You have not heard the end of this."

"No, but I reckon I've seen more of your end than I want. Get dressed. Give orders. You'll want your men on parade to welcome Major Forest when he gets in."

Forest eyed Nathaniel curiously as he sat at a table in the tavern. "Do I want to know how you organized that welcome, Captain?"

"I don't reckon you do." Nathaniel half-filled an earthenware cup with whisky and slid it across the table before filling one for himself. "Drink up. You ain't gonna like the news."

Forest picked up the cup, sniffed, then set it down again. "Tell me."

"Supplies ain't made it up from Temperance. They was supposed to go first, but Colonel Thornbury got it stuck in his craw that supplies going afore his men was disrespectful. He done changed orders, sent his men with no grub nor money, and here they be. They's waiting for horses and all. And they're thinking that will be slow as there ain't enough barges for to ship it all upriver."

Forest shot the whisky, wiped tears from his eyes, then held the mug out for more. "So you're telling me we have no food, no spare shot or brimstone?"

Nathaniel refilled his cup. "Well, these here cavalry ain't the first raiders Hattersburg ever done seen. Last winter came early and spring wheat weren't much, but folks did put some stuff by. Makepeace done tole folks we was part of the Prince's procession, so that loosened up some provisions. Shot and brimstone not as much, but we will be fine."

"I trust you are correct." Forest sipped at the whisky, wincing as he did. "We have decisions to make. Men to leave here."

Nathaniel nodded. The journey out had been arduous. Major Forest had chosen two extra squads because he assumed that sickness, injury, accident, and desertion would deplete his numbers. He was not disappointed as much as he might have hoped to be. Two men had broken legs and three broken arms or wrists. Two men had simply vanished and Nathaniel figured they'd gone off on the winding path. Many more, however, were feeling the effects of the long journey, including most of the Bookworms.

"How long we gonna stay here to Hattersburg?"

"Not as long as I would have liked." Forest ran his good hand over his stubbly jawline. "I wanted at least a week, but I expected us to be here a week ago."

"'Cept for the rain slowing us down, we woulda been."

"I can only imagine it caused more problems for those following us. I don't like it that no runners have come forward."

"Kamiskwa will find them."

"I hope. I want him and his men to be leading us from this point forward." Forest shook his head. "If we had powder and shot we could try some close order drills. We've got good men. Many of them hard men, but I need them acting together. I can still drill them, but resting would do them more good."

"I reckon."

"The question remains: Who will we be drilling?" Forest reached inside his jacket pocket and produced a small notebook and the stub of a pencil. "We have five casualties who can go no further. Two men are missing. Second company has three more men who are hurting badly."

"You counting Benjamin Beecher?"

Forest sighed. "I was rather hoping he would choose to remain behind here of his own accord."

"He cain't even tote his own Bible, Major. You should leave him here to tend to the spiritual needs of our wounded."

"I'll have a talk with him."

Nathaniel looked into the whisky cup. "I reckon 'bout half the Bookworms is close to done in. Them what hasn't had their boots rot off their feet has raw blisters."

"Reason enough to leave them behind."

"Well, now, I ain't saying it ain't. What I is saying is what you said. You need men acting together, that's them Bookworms." Nathaniel smiled, remembering them fixing their bayonets and giving the cavalry savage stares. "And I reckon the rest of the men is gonna have to do more iffen they don't want the Bookworms to be the better of 'em."

"Are you saying that, Captain, because you believe it, or because you know Caleb is one of the ones I'd have to leave behind?"

"You'd be making a big mistake leaving him here."

Forest arched an eyebrow. "Nathaniel, he's exhausted. He can barely stand up."

"On account of he's doing more than anyone else, you and me included." Nathaniel drank, letting the raw whisky torch his throat. "He's the last one asleep, first one up, doing all the duty anyone could ask of him, and volunteering for more. Ain't a man in that column don't owe him a favor or three."

"I'm not in an easy position here, Nathaniel. If I keep him on and he cannot do the job, it will be seen as favoritism."

"And iffen you leave him behind, he ain't gonna be right the rest of his life." Nathaniel gave Forest a nod. "You go make up your list, but give me a week. I reckon with a little work, things will come together just fine."

Supplies still had not come upriver by the second of July, when Forest determined his force would leave Hattersburg. The locals, happy for the relief from the Norillian cavalry, opened their larders and magazines to the Rangers. Each man was able to refill his supplies and add another fifty rounds of ammunition and powder. Every squad carried an additional two pounds of brimstone, the burden of which rotated through the squad.

During the week Nathaniel had a course of discussions with men in both companies. Looking the force over, it wasn't too difficult to pick out men who were the natural leaders, even if they'd not been the ones who had been voted an officer. All the soldiers looked up to these men, for their leadership, their encouragement, and their favor.

Nathaniel found a way to have a conversation that, in part, got around to pointing out just how hard-working Lieutenant Caleb Frost really was. Nathaniel allowed as how Caleb was working himself to death, doing all the things that other men ought to be doing. He suggested that a man who let another man do all that wasn't really a man, and it was a shame to let a young buck like Caleb ruin himself.

Things began to change. Men started doing all the things Caleb had done, and without being asked. Squads took it upon themselves to pitch his tent for him, or invite him to share their supper. Men always brewed an extra cup of tea or found an extra pinch of salt for him.

The week in Hattersburg did Caleb well. He managed to catch up on his sleep and let his feet heal. When Kamiskwa and the Shedashee returned, they fashioned new moccasins for the Bookworms and shared supplies of salve that brought most of the young men back into marching shape.

When it came time to move on, two of the Bookworms couldn't continue. That morning the men were all but in tears, even though they were having a hard time standing up straight for review. Major Forest gave them courier duty. He put them in charge of writing letters for those that wanted them written, and to carry them back to Temperance. He also dictated an account of events so far, and asked for that to be passed to Mr. Wattling and Doctor Frost.

The rest of the Bookworms got shuffled into other squads and Makepeace was given the hardest men in the unit to call his own. The Bookworms started as mascots, but the men came to appreciate them for their intelligence. The Bookworm journals became squad journals, and the burden of carrying them passed around as did the spare brimstone.

The Rangers even made room for Reverend Beecher. Though Nathaniel cared little for him, and he did make maddening demands on individuals, a solid core of Rangers took solace in his reading Scripture aloud. Beecher, when he wasn't actually trying to preach, had a good voice and managed to calm fears.

The news that Kamiskwa brought of the Prince's group was not good. By the time Major Forest's unit left Hattersburg, the Colonials were still a week back, and Rivendell a day behind them. Cutting a road through the wilderness had left the Colonials exhausted and furious with Rivendell's constant entreaties for more speed.

Forest fell in beside Nathaniel as they headed northwest out of Hattersburg. "If I calculate things right, we will reach Fort Cuivre about the same time they get to Anvil Lake. End of July is going to be very busy."

"I reckon." Nathaniel nodded easily. "And as long as I see August, I am right fine with that."

CHAPTER FIFTY-SEVEN

July 1, 1764
Lindenvale, Mystria

Prince Vlad swiped a forearm over his face, smearing mud, then put his floppy-brimmed hat back on. He leaned back against Mugwump's flank, cool stream water flowing around his knees. The wurm, his head upstream, lowered his muzzle and let water flow into him.

"Prince Vladimir, you can postpone things no longer."

The Prince looked toward the shore, where the stream had overflowed its banks. Bishop Bumble stood there, hands on hips, his face reddened beneath a black hat, his white hose mud-stained, and his feet slowly sinking into the ooze. How the man had managed, from the knees up, to remain spotless, Vlad could not imagine.

Bumble wagged a finger. "You are jeopardizing men's souls, sir. You have them working on the Sabbath. You refuse to give me time to conduct a proper service."

Vlad dropped to a knee, letting the water swirl up around his waist and scrubbed his hand clean. He scooped up a double handful of water and drank.

"Are you listening to me, Highness?"

Vlad looked up, water dripping from his unshaven chin. "I hear you very clearly, Bishop. I explained this morning that you could have a half-hour."

"I said *proper* service, sir." Bumble twisted to point back at the work crews and nearly toppled when a foot came free of a shoe. "It is bad enough that they are working on the Lord's Day!"

Vlad, exhausted, knew he shouldn't say anything, but he couldn't hold himself back. "I would submit to you, Bishop Bumble, that if the Good Lord didn't want us working on this particular Sunday, He'd not have had it raining Wednesday, Thursday, Friday, and Saturday. He's given us, in His infinite wisdom, a perfect day to get some construction done."

Bumble's eyes narrowed. "Is this how it is, Prince Vladimir? You think yourself higher than God?"

"No, sir. I gave you your time for a service. This is now my time. We have a *purpose* here, sir. It is to build a road so that our army can go and smite a godless enemy."

Bumble raised a hand toward Heaven. "You blaspheme, sir. God will smite His enemies, and you shall be among them. I shall report your behavior to God and to Lord Rivendell! I demand you give me an escort back to the *real* army."

I'd rather give you an escort to Heaven. Vlad, standing again, nodded. "Find Captain Strake and send him to me, please."

Bumble snorted and started to walk away dramatically, but having to reach down and dig his shoes out of the muck robbed the gesture of its vehemence.

Vlad leaned back again and patted Mugwump on the flank. "Humbling duty for you, my friend, but without you we would be no where near this close."

The wurm glanced back, blinked a golden eye, and went back to drinking.

The road-building enterprise had been one huge frustrating exercise. The Colonials were called upon to build tracks eight feet wide whenever *necessary*, but no one thought that would be for the entire two hundred miles to Hattersburg. Unfortunately the long winter had produced greater snowfall and huge runoff. Major Forest's men had worked around things like marshes, but Rivendell insisted that these detours unacceptably lengthened the route.

Even under the best of circumstances, the work would have been grueling. Spade-and-pick crews would carve their way into the sides of hills to widen paths to the required eight feet. Woodsmen would chop down the nearest trees and hack them into eight-foot lengths. These would get laid down on the bare earth, and dirt would be shoveled over them to smooth things out. The resulting "corduroy roads" lived up to their bumpy reputations.

Rains, which had plagued them since the start, simply made things worse. What had been a perfectly good stretch of road suddenly became a sodden mess. Earth eroded, logs slipped, and crews that should have been cutting the path further ahead had to go back and do repair work, all the while being derided by redcoats.

The friction between forces led the Colonials to work at a more leisurely pace, especially when it meant the Norillians camped on the edge of ponds from which great black fly populations rose. Despite being warned against it, troops drank from brackish pools, resulting in chronic cases of the trots. While Kamiskwa and the Altashee had pointed out useful plants for combating such things, the Norillians didn't trust them, and the Mystrians, who were busy brewing up *mogiqua* syrup by the gallon, kept suggesting the Twilight People cures were witchcraft.

Mugwump had proved invaluable to the effort at road construction. Whereas everyone else seemed worn down by the work, he thrived and grew stronger.

He seemed to take it as a personal affront that the earth defied his master's wishes. He also grew in size, bulking up muscles, but also getting bigger. Vlad had to mount via an elbow before he could reach the saddle, and did his best to record measurements when he had time.

Mugwump faced every challenge without reluctance. He dragged logs toward the road and then, chained to a massive log, would smooth the bed before other trees got laid down. At one stream he spat large stones further down stream. Later, at a marsh, they used that strategy to dam the marsh's outflow. They raised the water level and set up a ferry to carry wagons while the soldiers marched around. The Mystrians named it Mugwump Pond and cheered as the wurm swam across, dragging the first ferry rope.

The few ravines that needed bridging resulted in the hardest work, but there Count von Metternin displayed his worth. He culled the smartest of the Mystrians from the work crews and had them range ahead to locate problem areas. They quickly designed bridges, blazed the trees with specific cuts to show where they would fit in the plan, and left one man behind to oversee construction. Work crews would come up, cut wood as needed, and build the bridges even before the road had reached them.

The crews averaged just over four miles a day, and at the start had hit eight. The early success caused all of the disappointment later. Granted that circumstances had turned against them, and the work was grinding them down, but everyone thought they should be doing more. They pushed themselves, but Norillian derision sapped their strength. Most grumbled that the redcoats should hold their tongues and hold some spades. A few suggested they'd be happy digging graves for the soldiers.

"You sent for me, Highness?"

Vlad tipped his hat back and smiled. "I did. I have onerous duty for you."

Owen waded into the stream in his Altashee leathers, knelt and dunked his head. The water washed away mud. His head came up, his hair dripping as he cleared it from his face. "The Bishop told me. I am to take him back, not just a message."

"Can you possibly convince him to go off on the winding path?"

"I have a feeling the spirits wouldn't want him." Owen got up on his feet again. "Long walk will do him good."

"Give him one of our draft horses. I'll need it returned immediately. Give you an excuse to come back."

Owen nodded. "If we leave now, I should get him there in time for Lord Rivendell's Sunday supper with his officers. Couple of his men are old poachers. They got pheasant and deer. He will eat well, off hanware plates with a silver service."

"Can you suggest to him that he ask Rivendell to let him deliver his sermon to the troops?"

"I'll do my best, sir." Owen sighed. "And since Rivendell will ask…"

Vlad shrugged. "We have another week to Hattersburg, weather permitting. Two bridges, one ferry, twenty-nine miles uphill, three down. I hope we have a week's rest before we push on."

Owen sloshed forward and patted Mugwump on the flank. "Lord Rivendell believes we have surprise on our side."

"Rivendell is an ass." Vlad shook his head. "I'm sure someone has let du Malphias know about the brimstone, shot, and other supplies piling up in Hattersburg. Depending on how his forces are arrayed, he could just raid the town and burn everything."

"Or cart it back to his fortress." Owen nodded. "I'd do it. He won't. He wants us to come to his fortress and be destroyed."

"A great victory here would win him much support among the other Laureates." Vlad folded his arms over his chest. "Raiding Hattersburg is not his only option."

"Agreed. I fear he might build his own Fort Hope. He would block our access to Anvil Lake."

"Another wise strategy, and a contingency for which we should be prepared. I will have von Metternin scout ahead when we are in Hattersburg. You will go with him." The Prince pulled of his hat, soaked it in water, then put it back on. "Have you shared your thoughts with Lord Rivendell?"

Owen opened his arms. "I would have to be invited into his counsels to have a chance to offer an idea."

"He doesn't realize that you actually have experience out here?"

"He does, but he is invested in proving me wrong. Colonel Langford, for obvious reasons, as well." Owen unslung a canteen, unstoppered it, and sank it, bubbling, into the stream. "A couple of sergeants have spoken with me. The soldiers will fight and fight hard, but they have a flock of featherbrains to lead them."

"That is a lament often heard among soldiers."

Owen shot him a sidelong glance. "Did my uncle give you a packet of sealed orders to be opened in the event Lord Rivendell loses his mind?"

Vlad shook his head. "Why do you ask?"

"He told me he did. He asked if you were sane and ambitious. And he asked if you would be able to take over the expedition and lead it militarily if Rivendell's sanity were in question."

Vlad's eyes narrowed. "He said nothing of this to me. He encouraged me to use our men to build Fort Hope, since Rivendell will not use us in the battle. Your uncle never suggested a combat command, and, quite frankly, I am not suited to it."

"He said you could use the Count as an advisor."

"And I'm sure he would be most able. What are you thinking, Owen? There's a look in your eye."

The soldier blinked. "I'm thinking that I've not been thinking. My uncle only ever does things for his own benefit. So his speaking to me as he did was for his benefit. He said nice things and apologized to me. I thought it was sincere, but how would I know? He's never been sincere before."

Vlad nodded. "He told me that Rivendell would fail, and that next year he would be back with enough troops and artillery to destroy du Malphias. Fort Hope would be a stepping-off place. He would lead them, reap the glory."

"That's part of it." Owen frowned. "But it makes me wonder, given what he told you and me, what has he told Rivendell?"

"That's a very good question." Vlad glanced down, shielding his eyes with a hand from the sun's shifting reflection in the water. "Your uncle succeeds if Rivendell fails. This explains the paltry number of troops in Rivendell's command. A victorious du Malphias is a threat, so Norisle must increase the troops and resources sent next year."

Owen's jaw dropped open. "Which would give my uncle the largest and most formidable force in Mystria. He could do what du Malphias' has threatened: make his own nation."

"Possible, though a grateful queen could easily grant him a holding of the land he has secured, allowing him the benefit he seeks *and* giving him more power in Norisle."

Owen chewed his lower lip. "There was another thing, Highness. He instructed me, when we take du Malphias' fortress, to secure possession of all du Malphias' papers. My uncle wants the secret of how to control the *pasmortes*."

Vlad's head began to hurt. "So the only way to thwart your uncle is to see to it that Rivendell is successful, and that du Malphias' secrets never fall into your uncle's hands."

"Impossibility stacked on impossibility."

"So it would seem." The Prince nodded, then pointed back to the roadway. Bishop Bumble, clad in new white hose and with silver buckles gleaming on his shoes, waited impatiently. "Go, relieve me of this tiring cleric, and I shall see if I can find a way to unstack these impossibilities."

CHAPTER FIFTY-EIGHT

July 6, 1764
Lindenvale, Mystria

Owen Strake remaining crouched, turned back toward Lieutenant Marnhull. "For the last time, shut your mouth. Your babbling will get us killed."

The blond officer sniffed. "I am not a coward, Strake! And this sentry duty is ridiculous."

Owen could have taken Rivendell's little provocations easily. Picket duty had never bothered him, but to be stationed in the woods with a chatterbox put him over the edge. Shifting his musket to his left hand, he filled his right with his tomahawk. He darted forward, not certain if he just wanted to scare the man or murder him.

Because of his sudden move an Ungarakii warrior's warclub only grazed his right shoulder instead of crushing his skull. Owen twisted from the impact, pain shooting down his arm. As he came around, he whipped his musket up and across the Ungarakii's painted face. Though deerskin sheathed it, the heavy steel barrel still cracked bone and spun the man away. A second warrior darted in from beyond the first, his warclub raised high for a heavy blow. Owen lunged, driving the musket's muzzle into his stomach. As the Ungarakii doubled over, Owen buried his tomahawk in the man's skull.

"Sound the alarm!" Owen abandoned the tomahawk, and stripped the cover from his musket. He had no time to shift hand or aim. He simply thrust the musket at another Ungarakii, pressed his left thumb to the firestone and invoked magick.

The brimstone's flash lit the small sentry post. The ball blew through the middle of the closest attacker and caught the one behind him on the hip. Flipping the musket around, Owen clubbed the wounded man to the ground. Another step and he smashed the butt into the first Ungarakii's head, crushing his skull.

He glanced toward the others. Lieutenant Marnhull sat on a bed of rusty pine needles, his hat gone, his right ear missing as well. His right shoulder, shattered by a warclub, sank lower than the left. He rocked side to side, mumbling a lullaby and staring at nothing.

The third sentry lay face down, his hair matted with blood, not moving.

Owen tossed his own rifle aside and snatched up the dead soldier's. "Be quiet."

The Lieutenant's voice shrank, obeying as if he were a scolded child.

There has to be more out there. Owen kept slowly turning, not wanting to present his back to any direction for very long. He peered out into the darkness, waiting, listening as best he could. Nothing.

His heart pounded and sweat stung his eyes. One of the Ungarakii grunted his last breath. Something snapped in the darkness. Owen turned, thumb on firestone. Silence again fell, broken only by the soft whisper of Owen's moccasins on dry pine needles.

Then a new set of sounds arose. A squad of troopers came crashing through the woods to the sentry post. A Sergeant entered the clearing. Blood drained from his face. "What happened here?"

"Sergeant, deploy your men in a square. They may still be out there."

"Yes, sir." The Sergeant pointed at various men in his command. "You heard the Captain. Fix bayonets. Form square. Keep your eyes open."

Owen crossed to the Lieutenant. His mangled hat lay next to him, with the ear inside. An Ungarakii warclub had torn off his ear, then mangled the shoulder. How badly it had scrambled the man's brains would remain to be seen

Lord Rivendell arrived with his shadow, Langford. "My God. What have we here?"

Owen stood. "Ungarakii war party. I killed the four over here. The pair that attacked the Lieutenant and the Private got away."

Rivendell frowned. "You say you killed four?"

Owen nodded. "Clubbed the two at your feet, shot one, and my tomahawk is still in the head of the fourth."

"And you say they killed none?"

Owen sighed. "You have the evidence before you, sir."

"I do, sir, and I know how to read it." Rivendell glanced at Langford. "Get this down, Colonel. Captain Strake claims to have shot one of the raiders, but you will note that his rifle is unfired."

"This isn't my rifle. I picked it up from the dead trooper."

"What happened here is very clear. The Twilight People killed the Private. Lieutenant Marnhull grabbed his rifle and shot one of the raiders before being gravely wounded himself. Citation for bravery. Captain Strake killed one man who had stumbled, and the cause of death of the fourth is still under investigation. Note that Captain Strake attempted to claim credit for all four dead men, clearly out of guilt at having led the raiders to this very post."

"I must protest, my lord, this is not what happened."

Rivendell's eyes narrowed. "I think you would do well to understand, Captain Strake, that this is *my* expedition. I am the sole arbiter of truth. I have rendered my decision and, depending on how things proceed from here, I might be called upon to revise my view. I might find that in the excitement of the event, you *misremembered* what happened."

Owen tossed the Private's rifle down and recovered his own. He made a show of wiping blood from the brass butt-plate. "I'd be remiss in my duty, *sir*, if I did not point out that hostiles are still in the area and killing you would go a long way to destroying *your* expedition."

Rivendell quickly shot glances into the darkness, but did not immediately retreat. "Sergeant, have two men conduct Lieutenant Marnhull to an aid station. Bring his ear. And you, Captain Strake. I have a message to go to Prince Vladimir immediately. Tonight."

Owen looked at him. "Tonight, through these woods, knowing the Ungarakii are out there?"

"Yes, he must be warned. You are his liaison officer. You will bear the message."

At least, out there, I can kill my enemies. "Permission to reload my musket, sir?"

"It should already be loaded, sir, but I shan't write you up for that breech this time." Rivendell sniffed with indignation. "The message shall be ready in an hour."

After an hour's wait, Owen made it through to the Mystrian camp without difficulty. He had not traveled on the road, but nearby so as to avoid ambushes. Upon arrival he reported to the Prince and handed him the hastily scrawled note. Though Rivendell requested a reply to be sent back immediately by the same courier, the Prince declined to provide one and ordered Owen to remain with his party until they reached Hattersburg.

This gave Rivendell two days of apparent joy at Owen's death. It evaporated when he spied Owen in the frontier town on the ninth. His fury should have evaporated in the face of an even larger difficulty, but he immediately convened a court-martial with Langford at its head. Charges were disobeying a superior officer's direct order.

Prince Vladimir immediately invalidated the charge. "The *order* was never issued to Captain Strake by Lord Rivendell. The order was included in a confidential communication to me. I know his lordship would not presume to give *me* an order, nor did his message instruct me to instruct Captain Strake on what the message read. Since no order was issued, no order could have been disobeyed."

Even with that direct evidence, the panel deliberated long enough for a work crew to set up a flogging cross. None of the men were happy to see that, and the Mystrians became restive. Owen might be a Norillian, but there was no disguising the fact that the charges were personal. Their general dislike for Rivendell worked in Owen's favor and the tribunal returned a verdict of not guilty, forestalling a general mutiny.

Rivendell sulked for a while, then returned to high spirits when reunited with his school chums from the cavalry. The fact that their horses had not yet arrived did not seem to cause him much concern. Nor did the more distressing fact that the supplies that were supposed to be in Hattersburg had not made it in the promised quantities. The cavalry had done its best to eat their way through much of what had arrived—save for the horse fodder, which had come upriver in abundance.

The evening of the ninth consisted of two basic operations. The troopers—Mystrians and Norillians—reported to the warehouses to draw rations. By Lord Rivendell's order, rice, beans, and other staples were doled out by a curious formula by which each Mystrian was only counted as two-thirds of a person. His rationale had been that since official ration tallies were set for Norillian *fighting men*, and that the Mystrians were not of that caliber, they should not need a full ration. This rationale also got applied to supplies of brimstone and shot, prompting one Mystrian to wonder how it was that his musket would be less hungry, being as how it was bigger than the cavalry carbines.

The Mystrians did not complain too loudly, however. Hattersburgians learned of the injustice and opened their larders to their fellow citizens. Word circulated quietly, along with a guarantee by Prince Vlad in which he indemnified all Mystrians for the supplies they gave the troops. He even sent an order down-river with the Bookworms to send more supplies to Hattersburg to cover the donations.

The supply barges had been able to bring the dozen light artillery pieces, their powder, and shot up to Hattersburg, but the horse teams needed to haul them still had not made it. Local farmers, again with an agreement through the Prince, supplied teams of oxen to drag the guns along. Given the painfully slow pace of the column, the oxen's lack of speed was not an issue.

While the troopers collected their meager rations, Lord Rivendell invested Gates' Tavern and demanded a feast to celebrate his reunion with the cavalry. Two steers and a dozen chickens, a cask of whisky and a tun of ale, three dozen loaves of bread and a dozen puddings laden with sugar—sugar drawn from the warehouse before rations were issued—went into the meal. As an afterthought the Prince and Count were invited to join the festivities.

Music, laughter, and cheers lasted late into the night.

Owen didn't mind not having been included. Seth Plant had found him shortly after his arrival. He'd filled Owen in on the details of what had happened when Nathaniel and the others had come through two weeks earlier. He'd also managed to snag two letters that had come upstream from Temperance and presented them to Owen.

"Thought these should get to you first thing."

Owen thanked him and turned the first over. It had been addressed in a clean, feminine hand. *Catherine.* He read it quickly, the scent of her perfume rising from the page.

She told him she missed him terribly. She felt so horribly alone since his uncle had departed—leaving his loathsome servant behind to help her—but Mrs. Frost had come to the rescue, having all but adopted her. Catherine said that her sewing skills had progressed admirably and that she had been appointed, along with Mrs. Langford, to the Citizen's Committee for the Homecoming of the troops. All the women were planning many festivities and she could not wait for his return because she had wonderful news.

He had no idea what she meant, and she promised more details in her next missive. He glanced at the date, which was 15 June, almost a month previous.

The second letter had also been addressed in a feminine hand. It bore a faint resemblance to Bethany's writing. He opened it. Hettie Frost had written it on 21 June.

Dear Captain Strake,

Two days ago your wife had quite a fright. One of the Twilight People spied in the window of her room. Your wife screamed and fainted, but Rachel Warren heard and ran to her aid. She got your wife into bed and we, the women of Temperance, have been seeing to her care.

I am writing you to let you know that she is well, if a bit weak. She promises to write you when she is able. She says you should not worry about her, that she will be fine, and should not cause you the least bit of concern.

We all hope you are doing well and we look forward to your home-coming as soon as the Good Lord permits.

Sincerely,

Mrs. Archibald Frost

"Seth, no other letters?"

"Just orders to the cavalry and some things to local folks."

"How often have supplies come in?"

"Some here and there. Bargers say normal traffic coming in and out of Margaretstown. Horses is waiting on a boat to bring them up from Temperance."

"Why didn't they just use the *Bellepheron?*"

"Heard tell she got loose of her moorings in the bay. Ran aground."

Tharyngian agents or… Owen shook his head. His uncle wouldn't have engineered the ship running aground. It was unnecessary. Rivendell already had insufficient troops and the cavalry were the least of them. In fact, since the Fortress of Death would be especially difficult for the cavalry to attack, having them on foot made them *better.*

Or is he hoping that Rivendell will see the impossibility of the attack and just build Fort Hope? Any other commander might have done that, but Rivendell? His grasp on reality was tenuous at best. If he went ahead with the attack, using dismounted cavalry as infantry, he would kill off the scions of many noble houses. This would poison their blood against Rivendell. The lack of horses *did* play to the outcome his uncle desired, no matter what Rivendell decided.

"Seth, I will have two letters to head back in the morning. Will you see to it they get to Temperance?"

The man nodded. "Be needing some time to myself after all the doings here. Glad to, Captain."

"Thank you." Owen sighed. "First, I have to talk to the Prince. He needs to know what's been going on. Then, my friend, we have to pray he can fix it."

CHAPTER FIFTY-NINE

July 24, 1764
Fort Cuivre
Lac Verleau, New Tharyngia

Nathaniel handed Major Forest back his spyglass. "I reckon that is near the damnedest thing I have ever seen."

"It is, and us with a hundred and then some men and no cannon to destroy it."

"Least ways we got here." Nathaniel smiled. "Mayhap that'll have been the toughest part of it all."

Forest snapped the spyglass shut. "It will be as nothing to what comes. Tough as that journey was, cracking this nut will be tougher."

"Has the looks of a jeopard lair to it, does Fort Cuivre."

The Tharyngians had built Fort Cuivre on Lac Verleau's eastern shore, at the outflow of the Argent River. The river was two hundred yards wide at the outlet, and flowed strongly as well as deep. The fort's wharves had two corvettes and numerous canoes moored there. To the west, the lake's blue-green waters stretched on as far as the eye could see.

The fort itself had been dug down into a small hill. The hill's west and south sides had been faced in stone. A tall palisade wall protected the fort on the north, east, and south side. The west remained open toward the wharves, but had a small stone wall with two cannon placements and two other stations where small swivel-guns had been rigged. The guns had been set up to discourage Shedashee raids.

The fort itself ran fifty yards on a side, with walls rising on average a dozen feet above the hilltop. A minimal amount of work had been done to prepare glacises to the north and east. Trees had been cleared for approximately sixty yards around the fort. Undergrowth remained save to the north where some fields had been plowed. This far north, the maize crop was barely waist-high compared to being over a man's head down south in Bounty.

Fort Cuivre boasted a dozen more cannon neatly split into three groups of four on the north, east, and south walls. Towers at the corners gave lookouts good vantage points, but the men on duty appeared to be bored. A dozen men who were off duty, and not assigned to farming or gathering wood, spent their time fishing. When one of them landed a big salmon, a general cheer went up. The fisherman cleaned it, kindled a fire and, in short order, was parceling out steaming filets to his friends.

To prevent a ship of the line getting into the lake, a smaller stone tower had been built on the southern bank. That put it on ground claimed by Norisle. A heavy chain stretched between the two buildings. Two Ryngian soldiers stood guard in the small tower and Nathaniel guessed two more were crowded in below. Around the tower the woods had been chopped back only twenty yards and no one had made an attempt at clearing brush.

Forest rubbed at his eyes. "The troops are wearing blue coats, green facings with gold trim. They're part of the Silicium Regiment, probably Second battalion. They outnumber us by a company."

"I reckon we can even them odds."

"No doubt about it." Forest pointed with his hook. "The cannon can fire into the woods all around, but muskets can barely reach. The fort's cannon can cover the small tower, but musket-fire cannot. The small tower is ours when we want it, but taking it gives us no advantage."

"I reckon they might want to recover it."

"They might, but a commander with half a brain would just knock the tower down, and us in it. Set out pickets. Let them know I want no shots fired."

"I'll be picking men with sharp knives."

"Good, and it will be a cold camp. Can't afford fires alerting the Ryngians. If we are to take that fort, our only ally will be surprise."

They studied the Ryngians for a full day and learned some useful facts. The tower garrison consisted of six soldiers. To change the garrison, six men paddled a canoe across the river at dawn and the garrison hopped into it and paddled back. The exchange took ten minutes at a landing a mere twenty yards from the woods. During the exchange the tower remained unoccupied.

Fort Cuivre sent out hunting parties and wood-gathering parties several times a day, beginning at dawn. The hunters carried muskets, but the soldiers sent to gather firewood only carried axes. Both groups disappeared into the forest in the course of executing their duties.

At noon on the twenty-fifth, Forest gathered his officers together. "Fort Cuivre's garrison probably has three men for every two of us. Tomorrow morning we'll capture a dozen of them. From them we'll learn more about the garrison's condition. They look a bit scrawny, but no less so than we."

Nathaniel smiled. He'd always been on the lean side, but Makepeace had complained he could see his own ribs. Most everyone else had clothing hanging looser on them. Benjamin Beecher had become positively skeletal. He sat quietly and looked as if he'd stop breathing at any time.

"Now we really can't lay a proper siege to the fort because of those corvettes. They can sail on down, get supplies, and come back. There's nothing we can do to stop them."

Thomas Hill—one of the Summerland boys—raised a hand. "Me and some of the others sailed a mite. Get us aboard one and we can deal with the other."

"Getting your ship out of the docks before the landward cannons and the other corvette sink it? I would not want to risk your life on that." Forest frowned. "Unless the Ryngian commander is a complete idiot, he has no reason to come out and engage us. He has the fort and we have to come take it."

Caleb raised a hand. "Permission to speak, Major."

"Yes, Lieutenant?"

Caleb stood, picking up a stick. "What if we give him a reason?"

Forest nodded. "How would we do this?"

Caleb drew a diagram in the dirt. "Fact is, we have one advantage. All of our men are sharpshooters. Over half of us have rifles. They've left us plenty of cover to shoot from. We could, fairly easily, snipe sentries and gunners."

"Interesting, but he can just keep his people under cover."

"The point, Major, is that it's like the Battle of Ajiancoeur, when King Henry defeated the best of the Ryngian knights. His Kyr longbowmen peppered the Ryngians at long range. That made them angry, so they had to come out. If they don't come after us, more of them will die."

"I suspect, Caleb, the Ryngian commander has read many of the same histories as you. He may have learned from them." Forest nodded kindly. "Still, this idea might work."

Benjamin Beecher roused himself. "You cannot possibly consider that strategy, Major!"

Confusion flashed over Forest's face. "You have an opinion, Reverend Beecher?"

"That is not how warfare is waged, sir." Beecher climbed unsteadily to his feet, one of his holed-hose slipping down to mid-calf. "I may be Mystrian, but I have been to Norisle. There are rules to warfare, proper rules and proper conduct. You should form up and offer the Ryngians proper combat."

Nathaniel snorted. "And what if he ain't about accepting our invitation?"

Caleb shook his head. "What if he declines it by blasting us with his cannons?"

"Well, then, he would be in violation of the rules. The moral victory would be ours."

Makepeace laughed. "I don't reckon that would stop us from bleeding."

"Gentlemen, please, Reverend Beecher's argument deserves respect." Major

Forest took the stick from his nephew. "Many of you have killed other men, but not in cold blood. And that's what it will be. You'll be laying in wait, timing that sentry as he walks his watch. You'll see him come to the end, pause and turn. Right there, right where he slows down, you'll make his wife a widow, his babies orphans. Chances are he's just hungry, lonely, and scared—and would have surrendered given the chance. Are you ready to murder men who would rather be an ocean away?"

A chill ran up Nathaniel's spine. He'd killed his share. *Hell, I've killed enough to account for all the Bookworms* and *double for Beecher.* Damned few were the ones he'd regretted. All the men he'd killed needed killing, but some of them only needed it a little bit. If someone had talked sense into them, they might be on the green side of grass even today.

What surprised Nathaniel was that while Caleb had been speaking, he'd been looking at the problem the way Prince Vlad would have. It was all a matter of angles and powder, elevation and wind. Nathaniel even figured that wounding a man was better than killing him, since there wasn't quite anything like a grown man shrieking to take the steel out of other men's spines.

He hadn't been thinking about morality. Sure, the men were *men*, but they were men whose existence threatened his. The connection might be slender, but if the Ryngians had their way, they'd sweep all Mystrians off the continent. What he was doing might have been pre-emptive, but there wasn't any denying the Ryngian threat.

Nathaniel stood. "Well now, Major, you done given me something to be thinking on for a bit."

"Good. I don't want any men who aren't willing to think, and who aren't willing to take responsibility for their actions." Major Forest nodded slowly. "I want you all to think about it. We'll reconvene at dusk but, in the meantime, get crews together to make canoes to get us across that river."

Kamiskwa, the Altashee, and Lanatashee worked with the Mystrians to shape canoes. The Shedashee had lost four warriors, two from each tribe. In entering Seven Nations territory, Kamiskwa had met with representatives of the Waruntokii, whose land they were moving through. The Waruntokii were wary of du Malphias because of his close association with the Ungarakii. The Waruntokii would do nothing to help the Rangers, and demanded four hostages against any hostilities by the Rangers on the Waruntokii.

As evening fell they completed five large war canoes that could carry ten men each. The plan was to move downriver, out of site of Fort Cuivre, and string a line across. In an hour or two they could ferry their complete force north.

Major Forest studied the faces of his officers as they met in a hollow. A few logs burned in a fire pit, casting red illumination that made everyone appear as if dwelling in Hell. "Your thoughts, gentlemen?"

Makepeace nodded. "I done me some cogitating and praying, more one than the other, truth be told. Begging the Reverend's pardon, but seems to me that the Good Lord done used a lot of trickery in war in the Good Book. Now iffen He wanted to give one of us a horn what would bring down the walls of that there fort, we'd be counting it a miracle, nothing more be said. Just because a bunch of men put laws to warfare don't go amending God's Laws. I reckon as long as we treat honorable what surrenders, I'm willing to drop those as don't."

Beecher blinked several times. "But, gentlemen, this will put your immortal souls in jeopardy."

Rufus Branch spat into the fire. "Ain't like it ain't there already. I'll kill those opposing me. If they're gonna surrender, best do it right quick, or I'll kill them, too."

Nathaniel stood and ran a hand across his jaw. "I reckon you all 'spect me to be agreeing with Makepeace. I ain't saying I don't. I also ain't saying Reverend Beecher don't have a point. Seems to me that iffen we all agree on shooting all the Ryngians we can, we still got us a problem. As the Major said, ain't no reason the Ryngians cain't all just stay hunkered down. And, see, here's where Caleb and Reverend Beecher has their points."

He got a stick and redrew the fort. "Now iffen they keep their heads down, they cain't see what we is doing. That works to our advantage. And if they's angry with us, they ain't gonna be thinking straight if they do see something. And they is Ryngians, so they is going to be worried about their honor. Iffen we did form up, they might come out after us, accepting that battle when they see how pitiful we is."

Major Forest watched him, a smile fighting its way onto his face. "You have something in mind, Captain Woods?"

"I do, sir. Glimmerings, anyway. I reckon that in three days we can have them Ryngians so confused they ain't got no idea what's happening. I reckon that's when surrendering will sound good. One quick trick, and that fort will be ours."

"I await your plan, Captain Woods." Forest chuckled. "Let's hope your trick saves a lot of blood."

Beecher shook his head. "Duplicity is not honorable! I forbid this."

Forest's expression tightened. "You need to understand two things, Mr. Beecher. The first is that you are here as a courtesy to Bishop Bumble. Your duties consist of providing spiritual comfort. Second, war itself is not honorable. There is no honor in slaughtering men. Moral right, perhaps, especially when your family and your freedom are under attack, but never honor. Dying with honor is a myth promulgated to ease the grief of survivors, nothing more."

Beecher stiffened. "I shall write the Bishop about this."

"Please do. Do it now, in fact." Forest nodded to the cleric. "My men and I have a war to plan."

CHAPTER SIXTY

July 25, 1764
On the Shores of Anvil Lake, Mystria

Though it remained high summer and Prince Vlad had pulled a blanket around himself, he could not shake the chill. The Mystrian contingent arrived at Anvil Lake by mid-morning. The whole of the space in which he had considered putting Fort Hope had already been cleared. Stumps had been pulled, holes filled, and ground leveled. The lumber had been trimmed and stacked neatly, waiting for construction.

The Tharyngians had even supplied a sign proclaiming the site to be Fort Hope. Prince Vlad had not confided that name to but a handful and the enemy already knew it. The Ryngian's skill at ferreting out information impressed the Prince.

And it explains why we faced so little harassment on the way here.

Clearing the site of Fort Hope was not the lone improvement the Ryngians had supplied. They cut a fifteen-foot-wide road to the southwest, presumably running all the way past the Roaring River outlet and right up to the Fortress of Death. Count von Metternin and Owen had already traveled a ways upon it and returned to report that excess wood had been split into firewood and stacked for their use.

Vlad had immediately sent runners back to fetch Lord Rivendell. He dispatched work parties to clear campsites well away from the foundation of Fort Hope. While it would have been easier to let the men set up camp there, it was also possible that du Malphias had positioned mortar emplacements in the woods and had them angled to drop explosives on the cleared ground. Vlad organized hunting parties to scour the hills looking for those sites and set pickets out along the road.

He wished he had Nathaniel or Kamiskwa on site. Either of them could have told him how long ago the work had been done. He was guessing, given that bare shoots were the only undergrowth at Fort Hope, that the ground had been prepared two weeks previously. He also suspected the road had been cut at fifteen feet to mock their meager eight-foot effort.

The Prince left Mugwump to Baker's care and found Owen. "Why would he do this?"

Owen frowned. "Winter slowed the *pasmortes* down. All this work means they are revitalized. I would bet that the winter's dead from Kebeton City never made it into the ground. He will have the Platine Regiment, and whatever dead he could ship west."

Count von Metternin joined them. "This is a foul business. The road extends fifty miles and is twice as wide as ours. In two weeks he has cut what it would have taken us a month *and* cleared this space. When we come to the Roaring River, I am certain there will be a bridge."

Lord Rivendell and Colonel Langford rode up. Rivendell surveyed the area and smiled broadly. "Bravo, Highness. This is splendid. Splendid. Your men have outdone yourselves."

"Not our work, Lord Rivendell." The Prince nodded toward the sign. "Du Malphias did this. He even cut us a lovely path to his domain."

"Doubtless thinking I will be merciful in my gratitude. Excellent. A broad boulevard—that's their word, ain't it—for our victory march. Even Harry's men won't be too sad to march it."

"I believe you are missing my point."

"Trying to think like a soldier, are you, Highness? Leave that to the professionals." Rivendell stood in his stirrups and looked at the road. "He's not the sort to ambush us."

Vlad frowned. "But he *did* send the Ungarakii to attack you on the road."

"He's not responsible for the actions of his heathen allies, Highness. They don't understand our ways of war. But we showed them." Rivendell turned to his aide. "Make a note of that, Langford. Du Malphias showed me the honor due for my actions at Villerupt. We'll have an entire chapter about such honor in my book."

"Yes, sir."

"Canoe approaching, under a white flag."

The Mystrian sentry's shout brought all eyes to the shore. A birch-bark canoe glided over placid water reflecting the blue sky and high clouds. A soldier in the Platine Regiment's uniform held a white flag aloft, while two civilians provided propulsion. Sentries ran knee-deep to help drag the boat ashore, but only the soldier alighted.

He marched stiffly up the beach, then saluted. "I am Major Lebouf. Do I have the honor of addressing Prince Vladimir?"

"You do."

Rivendell rode forward. "I am the commander of this expedition. Anything you have to say you should address to me."

The Major smiled politely. "And you would be Lord Rivendell?"

"I would."

"Then my master has a special greeting for you. He says he looks forward to meeting you face to face, since the last time you met, he only saw your back."

Rivendell blanched, then lashed out with his riding crop. He caught Langford across the chest. "Do *not* write that down, you idiot."

Langford snapped the journal shut.

Prince Vlad waved the sentries back to their posts while they could still contain their mirth. "You have a message, Major?"

"Yes. The Esteemed Laureate Guy du Malphias requests the pleasure of your company, under a white flag, for dinner this evening. If you proceed up the road for ten miles, you will find the pavilion he has created. He asks that you join him by seven. He said he would be pleased if you brought Lord Rivendell, Colonels Langford, Thornbury, and Exeter with you. With apologies, he did not include Count von Metternin."

"I see."

Rivendell swept off his hat. "Please convey to your master that we accept his invitations. We shall be pleased to discuss terms of surrender as well."

The Major smiled. "He has anticipated you, sir. He said he would decline your kind offer, as he is not prepared to accept your surrender yet."

"My surrender? My surrender?" The color which had previously left Rivendell's face flushed back swiftly. "It is not *our* surrender of which I speak."

Vlad held up a hand. "Please tell the Laureate that we will join him."

"I shall, thank you." The Major bowed, then turned toward Owen. "And you, sir, would be Captain Strake?"

"I am."

The Ryngian officer reached inside his coat pocket and withdrew a sealed missive. "I was asked to give this to you."

Owen accepted it, but did not break the seal. "You've done your duty."

The Major returned to the canoe, and Owen shoved it back into the lake. The paddlers steadied the boat as the Major sat, then bent to the task of propelling it across the water.

Rivendell pointed his crop at Owen. "I will have that note from the enemy, Captain Strake."

Owen ignored him, broke the seal and read. He grunted. "Just an apology for not including me in the dinner. Given the circumstances of my previous departure, he found me an ungracious guest."

"Give it here."

Owen's face darkened. "Are you calling me a liar?"

"You are a man who is known to be familiar with ciphers and who, beyond all belief, escaped to Temperance with two broken legs."

"So you believe I am du Malphias' agent?"

"I think it is also curious that his native allies killed our soldiers, but let you live." Rivendell sneered. "Langford, you *are* getting this down, are you not?"

The scratch of a pencil on paper answered him.

Vlad sighed and held his hand out. Owen gave him the note. The Prince read it, then looked up at Rivendell. "I should remind you, sir, that *I* am the expert in ciphers. This note contains none, and is exactly what Captain Strake reported it to be. Now, unless you want to call me a liar or suggest I am in the Laureate's employ, I think you should get to your wardrobe and prepare yourself for this evening's dinner."

The Prince looked at himself in the small hand mirror von Metternin held up. "This will have to do."

The Kessian shook his head. "You will be the vulture at a peacock ball, highness. I have waistcoats and shoes that will fit you."

Vlad laughed. "I appreciate the offer, but homespun will be fine. I represent the people of Mystria—as Rivendell is oft wont to remind me—so I shall be attired as they are. I do appreciate, however, the loan of clean hose."

"I would lend you one more thing." The Count withdrew a small, double-barreled, over-and-under pistol. "Take this. Kill the Laureate. We will be done with this business."

The Prince stared at the weapon. "But that would be murder, and under a white flag."

"My friend, you are smarter than to believe that. Du Malphias will be waging war under the white flag. He will scare Rivendell, or make him overconfident. This campaign will be won over dinner this evening. You can win it with one shot."

"I can't do it."

"Of course you can. It is easy. Point. Shoot. It is never hard."

Vlad glanced down. "You are a soldier."

"By the blood of God, you have never killed a man, have you?"

The Prince met the man's incredulous stare. "I've seen them die. I've never killed one."

Von Metternin returned the pistol to his pocket. "How I envy you, and pity you. Firing the shot is easy. Living with the consequences is not. I do not think, however, I would lose sleep over killing du Malphias."

Vlad smiled. "Then I hope, my friend, that the opportunity falls to you."

The Prince remained silent on the ride to the dinner simply because he did not want to invite his companions to speak. Langford and Rivendell led the way. Colonel Harry Thornbury of the Cavalry and Colonel Anthony Exeter of the Fourth Foot came next. The Prince rode in the back next to a self-invited guest, Bishop Bumble. The Bishop bore the white flag.

Vlad contented himself with studying the landscape. Wildflowers splashed color into tiny spots where the sun managed to knife its way through the leafy green canopy. In the darker spots lichens and mosses, mushrooms and shelf-fungus took over, with wonderful golds and reds to contrast with the flowers' blues and yellows. Just enough of a breeze came off the lake to make the flowers and leaves dance, animating a mosaic of color and light.

Blue jays chattered and a couple of squirrels scolded from on high. He saw signs of where bears had climbed trees, or moose and tanners had scraped their horns against them. Rabbits scampered through the brush almost unseen and ravens watched them pass, offering haunting commentary.

Any other time, I would have enjoyed this ride. The source of his displeasure was his companions. He would have welcomed them looking about, too, knowing that they were searching for tactical advantages even while he was studying beauty. They were not even doing that. Taking their cue from Rivendell, they sat their horses with straight spines, eyes forward, faces tilted up, and remained that way as if posing for portraits.

Not even sight of the pavilion broke their composure. Vlad had expected a large tent erected in the middle of the road, but du Malphias had other ideas. His pavilion had been fashioned from a stand of birches. A dozen of the trees bent inward, curving softly to form a high ceiling. A wooden floor had been fitted together tightly, with the wood sanded, lacquered and polished until it glowed from the sun's dying light. A long table had six chairs set at it, likewise shaped of native woods and left blonde in keeping with the nature of the pavilion. Cloth streamers of blue, red, and green to honor the various military units floated playfully in the breeze.

Back a bit, deeper in the woods, a large tent had been erected to serve as the cooking station.

Soldiers of the Platine Regiment took charge of their mounts and conducted them to the pavilion. The Laureate stood at the head, dressed in white and gold. He opened his arms and smiled.

"Welcome, gentlemen. Highness, I would have you here at my right hand and Lord Rivendell opposite me. Lieutenant Laforge, we will need another place setting, down there, on the other side of Colonel Langford. And you are, sir?"

Bumble tried to look imposing. He failed. He had shed thirty pounds. His clothing hung on him poorly and when he further sucked in his stomach, his breeches threatened to fall to his knees. "I am the Right Reverend Bishop Othniel Bumble of the Church of Norisle, Temperance."

"This could be more interesting than I expected. Please, gentlemen, sit."

The moment they had pulled their chairs up to the table, service began.

While soldiers stood all around, civilians served them. A comely lass had been assigned to attend to Prince Vlad; nondescript men to deal with the middle of the table, and a beautiful young boy attended to Rivendell's every pleasure. As the sun's light began to die, and the soldiers lit lanterns, Vlad could not be certain, but the pallor of the girl's skin suggested she was a *pasmorte. Which would make all of the servants* pasmortes.

As hosts went, du Malphias had to be the greatest on the continent in spite of the rustic nature of his banquet hall. Each course had its own wine, and each wine had its own glass, which the servants presented and kept filled. They began the evening with fresh-caught salmon, followed by roasted duck with mushrooms and wild rice, then moose with a quince compote and fresh peas. Each course arrived on its own plate, covered with a silver turtle, which the servants removed with a flourish when the Laureate gave them the sign.

In addition to providing fine fare, du Malphias likewise encouraged discussion among his guests. He skillfully set the military men to refighting the Villerupt campaign through their anecdotes, while speaking to Vlad of a variety of experiments he'd conducted in Mystria. The man had no trouble following multiple conversations and offering cogent commentary on all.

Vlad's chill returned. *He is a genius. The Count is right. The battle is being won even now.*

When it came time for dessert and cognac poured into glasses, du Malphias stood. "Before we reveal the dessert—and I assure you it shall be a surprise—I should offer a toast to the brave men who will serve in the battle to come. Serve now and serve forever."

The others raised their glasses and drank.

Rivendell rose, raising his glass. "And a toast to those who will lose the battle. May they never fear treatment at the hands of an honorable foe."

The Laureate smiled and drank, but his eyes became cold.

Rivendell meant his toast one way, but du Malphias read it another. And Rivendell will rue his comments.

Du Malphias seated himself after Rivendell had returned to his chair, then nodded. The servants lifted the silver domes from the dessert plates.

Vlad stared down. A small, single-barreled pistol similar to Count von Metternin's, sat centered on the plate and garnished with a sprig of rosemary.

Rivendell picked the pistol up. "What is the meaning of this?"

The Laureate smiled. "I mean to show you something. Please, all of you, take your pistol and shoot your servant."

Bumble's eyes grew wide. "Are you mad?"

"No, not at all." Du Malphias smiled. "Highness, if I might."

Vlad nodded.

Du Malphias appropriated the Prince's pistol and shot the serving girl in the stomach. She flew back into one of birches, then struggled to her feet, still holding the silver plate cover. She approached the table, a black hole burned in her blouse, and smiled. "Will that be all, Highness?"

Vlad, his hands shaking, could not answer.

The three colonels picked up their pistols and shot their servants. Rivendell made a great show of aiming, then fired. The pretty boy spun away. It looked as if, unlike the others, he might stay down. Rivendell brandished the pistol triumphantly, then his expression soured as the young man regained his feet.

Bumble refused to touch the pistol. "I never learned that magick."

"You may all keep your pistols as my gift. I have boxes for them, along with bullet molds and measuring tools. You will understand if I decline to provide brimstone, but the firestones are new and of the highest Tharyngian quality."

He nodded toward the servants. "Captain Strake has told you of my *pasmortes*. All of them can and do use firearms. In addition to the regiment-and-a-half of regular soldiers in my command, I have hundreds of my *pasmortes*. They never tire, they do not eat, they do not sleep, they know no fear. And any of my soldiers who fall shall return as *pasmortes*. Your efforts to destroy my fortress are futile."

He picked up his cognac glass and smiled. "To the health of your troops, gentlemen. May they remain hardy, or else they will be *mine*."

CHAPTER SIXTY-ONE

July 25, 1764
La Fortresse du Morte
On the Shores of Anvil Lake, Mystria

Owen watched with the forward pickets for the leaders' return. *If du Malphias had intended to unsettle Lord Rivendell with his dinner, he succeeded very well.* All of the officers appeared subdued and even a bit queasy. Rivendell didn't even rouse himself to abuse Owen. He just looked at him with haunted eyes and rode on past.

Prince Vlad settled in near Fort Hope and invited Owen and von Metternin to join him in his tent. He poured three small tots of brandy and offered one to each man. "I should have taken your pistol, Count Joachim."

"Indeed? Why?"

The Prince proceeded to describe the evening's finale. He pointed to the wooden box on his camp desk. "The pistol is yours, Captain Strake. You'll doubtlessly have better use for it than I will."

Owen nodded. "Thank you, Highness."

"Don't thank me. Were I you, I would keep it to blow my own brains out, guaranteeing I won't become a *pasmorte*." The Prince shot his brandy, growled, and poured himself another. "Rivendell and the others now believe *pasmortes* exist. On the ride back they even rejoiced in the fact that the things could be shot. Exeter suggested that du Malphias used a small caliber bullet and light charges to trick us into believing his *pasmortes* are immortal. Not enough recoil to the shot, you see."

Von Metternin sipped his brandy. "Did no one shoot one in the head or spine?"

"No. Du Malphias shot my servant off-center and in the abdomen." The Prince arched an eyebrow. "Why the smile, my lord?"

"He took your pistol to forestall your turning it on him. None of the others would dare." Count von Metternin laughed. "It was a calculated gamble on his part."

"If only I had followed your advice." Prince Vlad shook his head. "I could have ended all this with one shot."

"That was clearly not meant to be, Highness." Von Metternin shrugged. "He won this time, but that does not mean he shall win every time."

Owen remained with the Mystrian contingent when it set off next morning for the Fortress of Death. They made very good time along du Malphias' road. They delayed only twice. Once, for a short while, Mugwump went off the road at the birch pavilion. He rooted through the surrounding area like a pig hunting truffles, snorting disgustedly when he came up with nothing. He glanced back at the Prince and Owen would have sworn he saw regret at failure in those gold eyes.

The other pause came during the second day's march at the Roaring River. As had been predicted, a tall, arching bridge spanned the river. Men marveled, but the sight of it made Owen's stomach roil. Yes, it was a wonder, but a wonder created by creatures that should have long ago been in the grave. He could imagine *pasmortes* crawling all over the bridge, hunting troops as they had once chased him.

Mugwump went over it first, sniffing as he went. It didn't move an inch beneath his bulk. Mystrian soldiers swarmed over it then, testing what they could, reinforcing other bits, and determining it was safe. They then deployed to forestall any attack that would disrupt the crossing.

The Mystrians had welcomed the shift from shovels and axes to muskets. Knowing the Norillian troops would be watching their every move, they did their best to comport themselves as fighting men. They moved quickly and took up good cover positions. They even supported each other as troops moved deeper along the road.

The problem was, of course, that when the Norillian troops got to crossing, the Mystrians had not arrayed themselves in proper order for Continental combat. It didn't matter that they weren't on the Continent, it just looked for all the world to the Norillians as if they were timid and amateur.

Owen smiled proudly as the Mystrians took up their positions. They reminded him of the Mystrian Rangers preparing to defend the Artennes Forest. Eager and fresh-faced many of them, they had no idea the sort of Hell they'd be marching into. Stories of *pasmortes* had filtered through the ranks, but the Mystrians dismissed them as stories intended to frighten Norillians. No Mystrian, whether or not he believed the stories, would ever show signs of fear around Rivendell's troops.

The regular soldiers came up quickly. They came across the bridge in column, five men abreast, their footsteps sounding as thunder, cadence perfect. The infantry came in two battalions first, their red coats brilliant in the summer sun. Tall, implacable and imposing, they came in a mass that should have frightened even *pasmortes*. At forty yards they could volley out a wall of lead balls that would rip through the enemy, and then their steel bayonets would finish them off.

The cavalry marched in the middle of the formation. They looked a bit footsore, but no less proud. They marched with carbines slung across their backs and their sabers drawn. For men unaccustomed to marching, they came on in good order and pushed to the fore on the west side of the bridge. Drawn mostly from the ranks of lesser nobility and the second sons of greater nobility, they moved to the lead since that was their station in life.

As the column moved further west, Owen found himself constantly thirsty. He stared at his hands to see if the flutter in his stomach had translated itself into a palsy. Though the forest hid the fortress, Owen could feel it there, brooding, waiting to devour him again. He wanted nothing more to do with it but duty demanded his presence, and if Rivendell were to even guess at the fear in his heart, he'd find a way to humiliate Owen.

Owen would do anything to deny him that pleasure.

Originally Rivendell had intended to take the small tower, but du Malphias' dessert surprise had alerted him to the possibility of duplicity. He allowed himself to be convinced that keeping a Mystrian battalion back in the woods would threaten the tower and allow him an anchor on the Green River's western shore. It would forestall du Malphias' trickery and give Rivendell a way to retreat.

The Norillian formation hooked west and north through the forests and cleared area while remaining outside of the fortress' guns' range. Northwest of the fort itself they came to a ferry and sent the cavalry across first. They unlimbered the dozen cannon on the west bank to cover the cavalry. Mystrians then crossed and returned to their ax and shovel duties outside the range of the Tharyngian guns. They dug emplacements and trenches and chopped trees, which they transformed into redoubts and mantlets.

Owen and Count von Metternin crossed at the head of the Mystrians. The Kessian pointed toward the southwest face of the fortress, about even with the tower across the river. "If he opens those gates and deploys the Platine Regiment, he can cut us in half. A river crossing—any sort of amphibious operation—should be contested."

"He's not the sort to make so simple a mistake."

"Well, he is arrogant. But then, he is Tharyngian." Von Metternin laughed quickly. "He sees that Rivendell has been thinking. We declined to take the tower. Rivendell will see his failure to oppose the crossing as a tactical error. Rivendell will begin to believe he has won two battles already."

Lord Rivendell came splashing through the river and reined his horse up in the middle of the cavalry salient. He raised a spyglass to his eye, then laughed. "I see you, du Malphias, and I know your game. You thought I'd take your tower, didn't you? Didn't you?"

Von Metternin chuckled. "I don't believe he can hear you, my lord."

"But he can see me." Rivendell took off his hat and waved it. "He has to know we won't be cowed. It ain't the thing."

One cannon replied. Flames shot from the rampart and smoke jetted. Twelve pounds of iron sphere flew from the cannon's mouth. Three hundred yards out it hit the ground and bounced. It bounced again and again, slowing as it came. One of the cavalrymen laughed and stood, making as if to catch the slow-moving ball.

His right hand evaporated in a red mist. He stared at the gushing stump, then began to scream.

Rivendell's horse shied from the ball, and other men parted to let it through. Owen darted forward, yanked the cavalryman's saber sash off. He looped it around the man's right forearm, then stuck a stick into it and twisted until the arterial flow trickled to a slow drip. The man raised his pulverized wrist toward his face, then fainted.

"Captain Strake, get some of your Mystrians up here to dig us a trench!"

Owen shook his head. "If they come forward, my lord, your bunker won't be ready for nightfall. Colonel Thornbury should get his men to digging their own trenches."

The Count stepped between Owen and Rivendell's raised crop. "I might suggest, my lord, that you draw the men back another hundred yards. The ridge there, if they get on the other side of it, will protect them."

"Yes, of course. Colonel Thornbury, move your men back to that ridge." Rivendell donned his hat again. "Langford, come here. Captain Strake shall be written up for insubordination!"

Owen's shoulders and back ached from digging holes and chopping wood. Being an officer, he could have been spared that duty, but he pitched in. Had anyone asked, he'd have said he intended to set a good example. The simple fact was, however, that he wanted to put as much wood and earth between himself and the fortress as possible.

By evening of the twenty-ninth, Rivendell had arrayed his forces in prepara-tion for the siege. He placed his artillery in a single battery in the middle of his line. That tactical placement actually made sense. The Mystrians wove together and filled fascine, which they installed around the front of the emplacement. The guns could cover most of the field and could scatter any attack coming from the fortress, should it round the corner by the river.

The cavalry remained nearest the river, but pulled back so the fortress' cannon could not harass them. East of them came the Fourth Regiment of Foot. They dug in and threw up ramparts, but did it casually. The infantry expected no assault, and wasn't keen on having to cross their own trenches to get going at the enemy. They believed the siege would end quickly, and Owen did not take that as a good sign.

Further east, between the Norillians and the lake, the Mystrians set up. Prince Vlad headquartered on the heights nearest the lake, with his men dug in all along that front. Despite being exhausted from the preparation of Rivendell's headquarters, they dug a good trench line, letting it slither across the landscape in keeping with the natural formations. Their camp was built to last through the winter.

The greatest bit of construction came at the Prince's headquarters. The men felled a number of trees and bound them crosswise, then linked them to several central beams. They sank them into the earth, creating an A-frame wurmrest to which Mugwump took easily. The building dwarfed Lord Rivendell's tent complex, and the Mystrians took to joking about that fact.

Owen sat in the shadows outside the Prince's tent. He caught sight of Rivendell and Langford marching toward him, with an honor guard of six men. He considered standing, but saw little sense in it. *If it is another court-martial, an additional charge of conduct unbecoming an officer can't hurt.*

To his surprise they marched past him and into the Prince's tent. Greetings between the officers, the Prince, and Count von Metternin passed tersely.

Rivendell cleared his throat. "Langford, just hold down that edge of the map. As you can see, Highness, we have our plan. Your men will begin to dig trenches here and here, so we can move the guns forward and begin our assault."

Silence reigned for a moment, then the Prince spoke. "Forgive me if I read this map incorrectly, but with the cavalry pulled back here, you've only got cannon to discourage raiders. My men will be vulnerable to both cannon and direct assault. Am I misreading things, Count von Metternin?"

Before the Kessian could offer an opinion, Rivendell huffed. "Need I remind you, I am in command of this expedition. Your concern for your men is commendable, but I shall not be asking them to fight, just do work for which they are suited."

Mugwump's roar, full of fury and urgency, killed the conversation. The sound thrummed through Owen's chest, causing him to spring to his feet. To the west, by the river, muskets fired. Owen snatched his up and started in that direction. Prince Vlad raced from the tent and past him toward the wurmrest. Owen trailed him, intent on seeing to the Prince's safety. Mugwump thrust his muzzle from the building, roaring again. The Prince leaped for the wurm and caught part of the baggage harness. He got one foot into a stirrup and hauled himself into the saddle as the wurm darted forward.

Owen jumped and hooked a hand into the harness and clung there. Mugwump hurtled down the hill. He raced through the middle of the Fourth's tents, his tail flicking a number into the air like sails shredded in storms. His repeated roar scattered men, then he was past the Fourth's lead elements.

He burst into the cavalry camp. They didn't need to see him to scatter. They were already in full retreat, screaming, throwing their carbines down. Men fled, eyes wide, throats already raw from screams of terror.

Owen stared into the night and knew why they ran.

As they reached the edge of the camp, Owen leaped free of the wurm and rolled to his left. Mugwump's tail whistled above his head. Owen came up on one knee, shouldered his musket and fired.

The ball hit a soaking wet *pasmorte* in the throat, blowing its head off. Owen tossed his gun aside and picked up a carbine. He tracked again, then shot, knocking a young boy down. He tossed that gun aside and groped for another. Instead of a gun, he found the hilt of a fine steel cavalry saber and shucked it from its scabbard.

No one would ever describe the heavy blade as elegant. It had been designed for butchery, with a solid blade and full brass hilt. Owen slashed, opening a *pasmorte* from shoulder to hip. Not only did the saber cut well, but the steel blade disrupted magick. Any serious slash was enough to palsy the *pasmorte* into a twitching mass on the ground.

He ran forward, trying to get to where Prince Vlad and Mugwump fought. The Prince had ridden into battle unarmed, putting himself at great risk. Owen slashed the head from one *pasmorte*, then opened another across the belly. "Hold on, Highness!"

Owen might as well have saved his breath. Mugwump's tail swatted *pasmortes* into piles of broken bone and rent skin. He reached out with one clawed hand, pulling a *pasmorte* to him, then biting it in half. Two more struggled beneath his other foreclaw. He reared up and swatted as a bear might have done, scattering a trio into throbbing gobbets.

A squad from the Fourth came running up. Owen turned. "Fix bayonets. Use your steel!"

The troopers did as commanded and drove into the last of the *pasmortes*. They hacked and stabbed, clubbed them, and shattered skulls. A couple men hesitated when faced with children, but their Sergeant picked up another discarded saber and put them to rest.

Owen ran to the Prince, slowing as Mugwump eyed him. The wurm drew *pasmortes* to him, whole and in pieces, and devoured them. Prince Vlad sat astride him, tugging on the reins, to no avail.

"Highness, are you unhurt?"

"Yes, quite." He dug a heel in against Mugwump's flank.

The beast burped, then shoved more of the undead into his maw and swallowed. Mugwump's thick tongue pulled an arm from between his teeth.

Owen turned back to the infantry. "Cut off their heads, then drag them into a pile."

A trooper looked at him. "We going to burn them?"

Owen glanced at the wurm. "I think Mugwump has other ideas." He sighed and looked toward the fortress. *And I'm certain the Laureate does as well.*

CHAPTER SIXTY-TWO

July 31, 1764
Fort Cuivre
Lac Verleau, New Tharyngia

Nathaniel dipped his paddle quietly into the lake's still water, and slowly drew the canoe forward. The war canoe, one of four they'd launched pre-dawn, drifted through the morning mist toward Fort Cuivre. Kamiskwa, bow in hand, arrow nocked, knelt behind him.

The Mystrian held his breath. The sun had begun to lighten the sky off to the east, but the forest yet cast shadows over their route. They kept close to the shore, hoping the sound of trout rising to snap up flies might disguise their approach. If the Ryngians guessed they were coming, the sloop's cannon and the fort's swivel-guns would sink the flotilla before they could ever fire a shot.

Major Forest had identified the docks as the fortress' weakest point. The low stone wall with loopholes made for a great defense against Shedashee raiders. The Ryngian commander kept six soldiers on duty at the wharves, and had six men crewing each corvette, which was all he could spare given the other to Fort Cuivre.

Nathaniel narrowed his eyes, trying to see through the mist. The current was enough to draw them toward the river; all he had to do was steer. The fort's angular outline loomed in the darkness, silhouetted against a starry sky. The sliver moon cast wan light that shimmered in a long stripe further into the lake.

He turned to Kamiskwa. "Short walk now."

The Altashee nodded, and cupped a hand over his mouth. He gave a soft loon-call. Something splashed behind them—the Summerland canoe heading off for the sloop. The other three headed for the wharves to deliver the Northern Rangers.

Major Forest had put together a pretty little campaign, all leading up to this point. They captured the tower's garrison, then picked off every hunting, wood-gathering, and search party the Ryngians had sent out. Then sniping began at dawn and sunset, so regular the Ryngians could safely duck away. The sniping toll had been fearful that first day, but the Mystrians only harvested the foolishly brave and the stupid thereafter.

Nathaniel had done his fair share of shooting. He figured he had killed one and wounded two. He'd not have killed any, but the one man fell from the wall and broke his neck. Nathaniel wasn't sure how he felt about the killing. He'd not lost any sleep over it yet, but wasn't certain that would be a constant state of affairs.

The sloop loomed out of mist and the Summerland canoe slipped past. They headed for the ship's aft, intent on going around and boarding on the starboard side. Nathaniel nodded, watching, his ears straining for any sound that might alert the enemy.

From behind came the groan of an arrow being drawn.

There, on the sloop, a sentry had paused amidships. The shifting mist half-hid his silhouette. Nathaniel couldn't tell how far he was from the port gunwale, but that ceased to matter. The man unlimbered the musket he'd worn over his shoulder.

Kamiskwa's bow thrummed. The arrow arced through the air. The Ryngian's hands came up to his throat. He tried to stem the spurting blood. The arrow had passed clean through his neck, so he was already dead, but instead of dropping, he staggered forward and collapsed, smashing into the ship's bell as he went down.

A single clean peal shattered the morning quiet.

Nathaniel dug hard at the water. The canoe, with men paddling furiously with gun butts and paddles, surged toward the wharf. Nathaniel vaulted from the boat as it hit the dock. He whipped the paddle around, catching a running Ryngian across the face. That man went down screaming before Nathaniel kicked him into the water.

Rangers poured onto the dock, sprinting toward the fort. They came on grim and silent, knowing they'd lost the advantage of surprise. When they'd volunteered, they each acknowledged that without surprise, theirs was a forlorn hope. Their only chance of survival lay in wresting a fort from a garrison that outnumbered them four to one.

Kamiskwa handed Nathaniel his rifle. "Good hunting, Magehawk."

Ryngian voices called out to them. They started fearful, became angry, then rose to panic when no one replied. A Ryngian sentry fired blindly toward the sloop. His muzzle-flash revealed the raiders' presence. A second sentry shot and one of the Rangers went down, curled in around his belly.

Nathaniel knelt beside him, then raised the rifle. He caught a flash of movement through a loophole and dropped his thumb onto the firestone. The rifle roared, vomiting fire and lead. Hot smoke and little particles of burning brimstone blew back into his face, stinging his eyes. The rotten scent of brimstone filled his nose and caked his throat.

Makepeace Bone hefted two muskets, one in each hand. In his titanic hands they might as well have been long pistols. He fired both toward the loopholes, never slowing down. Men screamed, others shot, and Makepeace charged straight ahead.

He hit the wooden gate with a shoulder, roaring as he went. The gate exploded off its leather hinges. Makepeace rolled into the darkness beyond it. Rangers followed. More muskets lit the dawn with fire.

Nathaniel came through the door two steps behind Kamiskwa. He pointed toward the fort's ramparts. "Justice, get your boys up there. Trib, the other side. Caleb, your boys sweep the courtyard! Move it!"

Muzzle flashes came like lightning, freezing combatants for one quick second. Under Caleb's command, the first squad crouched and shot at anything moving in the compound. The second and third squads cut right and left respectively, heading up to the ramparts with the Bone brothers. The fourth and fifth squads inched forward, taking cover behind storage sheds and a longboat undergoing repairs.

Shots echoed from the sloop. A ball ricocheted off the gatepost near Nathaniel's head as he crouched to reload. The Ryngians returned scattered fire from the fort's far end, where they'd been waiting the dawn firing.

Which was what we was waiting for, too. So much for the Major's diversion! Nathaniel levered the rifle's breach closed. *I reckon we're the diversion now!*

A door opened on the compound's central building. A man silhouetted himself against a lantern. Nathaniel moved right, lifted his own rifle and shot. Smoke blinded him and by the time tears had washed his eyes clear again, all he could see was light pouring through a hole in the door.

Nathaniel reloaded again, then tapped one of the Bookworms on the shoulder. "Be pleased iffen you'd tell them Summerland boys we'd enjoy them cannons helping out with the barracks and all."

The man nodded. "Which one?"

"Either, for a start. Go!"

The Ryngians had built the barracks against the north and south walls respectively. The central building cut the compound in half. Nathaniel reckoned the Prince could explain the math they used for designing the layout, but no matter the numbers; it made things awkward for the Rangers. Already Ryngians had knocked loopholes in the barracks walls and were shooting back. Nathaniel also figured they'd be forming up on the other side of the headquarters for a charge that would sweep the Rangers right out into the lake.

Nathaniel's heart pounded. The Ryngians would come running around that building, bayonets gleaming. They'd fire maybe one volley. Maybe they'd not even bother. Twenty-five yards and they'd be on the Mystrians like cats on mice.

What am I going to do? If the Rangers stayed, the Ryngians would slaughter them. If they ran, they'd die. He glanced at Caleb, not seeing the soldier the man had become, but the boy he'd been. *Damned foolish thing, war.*

Nathaniel drew his tomahawk and laid it on the ground by his knee. "Fix bayonets, boys. Give 'em one volley on my order. Shoot low."

Muskets clanked with the haunting sound of bayonets being slid over the barrel and locked down. From the compound's far side, a whistle shrilled. A Ryngian voice shouted orders. Booted feet stamped in unison, the crisp sound smothering the occasional crack of a musket. The whistle blasted again.

From twenty-five yards away, the Second Company of the Silicium Regiment streamed around their headquarters, sharp steel forward, shrieking with outrage and fury.

Nathaniel stood. "Hold it, boys. Hold it! Fire!"

The Rangers fired, but thirty muskets against sixty men didn't matter much. Here and there a Ryngian went down, but their fellows just galloped over them. A couple Rangers stared, frozen. A couple more ran. Others looked around, defiance melting into fear as uniformed soldiers drove at them.

Nathaniel fired quickly, smashing the whistle and the face of the man blowing it. He stood there, loading as quickly as he could, but he knew there wasn't time. The rolling thunder of the Ryngians' pounding feet confirmed it. He fumbled with his bullet, but caught it before it hit the ground. He drove it home and levered the breech shut.

Too late!

The Ryngians had closed to where he could see their wide eyes and glinting bayonets.

Then hands yanked him backward as Makepeace Bone yelled, "Get down!"

Makepeace swung one of the swivel-guns around and slapped his palm over the egg-sized firestone. White teeth showed in a smoke-stained grimace. A heartbeat later, the small cannon erupted.

Compared to the sloop's cannon, swivel-guns hardly presented a threat. They could fire a small, two-pound cannonball, which would have bounced off the sloop's hull. But men do not have oaken flesh, and these swivel-guns had been loaded with grape shot: twelve balls to the pound, two pounds to the load.

The Ryngians had crossed all but the last ten yards to the dock when Makepeace fired.

Hot metal balls blasted out in a volcano of brimstone. They shredded the front rank. Flying metal instantly transformed running soldiers into screaming piles of bleeding meat, broken bone, and smoldering uniforms. Men flew backward, impaling themselves on Ryngian bayonets. The balls blew through the leading soldiers and hit others, taking legs off at the knee and perforating bowels. High shots blasted skulls into shrapnel, piercing men with bits of their comrades.

And still Ryngians came on. Some slipped in blood. Others tripped over screaming compatriots. Their comrades dripped from their uniforms, but they closed with the Rangers, thrusting bayonets, howling at the top of their lungs.

Nathaniel fired, dropping one man, then parried a thrust with his rifle. The Ryngian, insensate with fury, still rushed forward. He caught Nathaniel with a shoulder and knocked him back.

The Mystrian smashed his head against the stone rampart. Stars exploded before his eyes. His rifle bounced away as he hit the ground. The Ryngian, straddling him, raised his rifle for a killing thrust.

Kamiskwa's warclub whistled. Bones cracked. Teeth scattered. The Ryngian whirled away, flopping into a loose pile of flesh. Kamiskwa dodged a second soldier's thrust, then crushed his shoulder with another blow. The Altashee shoved him back into a third man, then dropped him with a swing that spun him full around.

Nathaniel grabbed a musket and shoved the foot-and-a-half of spade-shaped steel through a man's chest. The soldier, who had already knocked Caleb down and stabbed him through the thigh, opened his mouth to say something, but blood replaced words.

The man slid off the bayonet with a shove.

Nathaniel dropped to a knee beside Caleb. He pulled a sash off the dead Ryngian. "Wrap it tight, Lieutenant Frost. I ain't losing you."

Nathaniel never head Caleb's reply.

The sloop's cannon thundered. Heavy iron balls ripped through the headquarters roof, shattering the main beam. The roof collapsed, but the balls carried on into the fort's eastern half. Hardly spent by blasting through shingles, they caromed through the courtyard. Men screamed and a half-dozen fell when a ball undercut a rampart support.

A volley of musketry echoed from the east. More Ryngians dropped, falling inside the compound. Recovering his rifle, Nathaniel ran forward. The Bone brothers advanced their squads along the ramparts. Kamiskwa darted ahead, warclub at the ready.

By the time they reached the headquarters building, the first of the Southern Rangers had gained the wall. Using scaling ladders they'd hacked out of logs, they came through the embrasures. The Ryngians, trapped between two forces, quickly laid down their arms and threw open the gates for Major Forest.

The Tharyngian commander, Colonel Pierre Boucher, surrendered his sword to Major Forest. Forest, in keeping with Continental etiquette, returned the sword in exchange for a promise of parole and good conduct. The Colonel agreed and at Colonel Boucher's orders, with Major Forest's agreement, the

Ryngians formed up details to collect their wounded and then bury their dead.

Nathaniel slid the deerskin sheath over his rifle. "I reckon, Major, we done surprised you a mite."

"I have learned not to be surprised by war, Captain Woods. Things never go as one plans and, alas, there is always a butcher's bill to be paid." The older man looked around, his eyes hardening. "Caleb?"

"Has himself a scar to go with any story he wants to tell." Nathaniel nodded. "Commanded his boys fine."

"Good. Thank you."

"And you, sir, for coming to the rescue." Nathaniel sighed, the back of his head aching. "I reckon it's time to figure that bill. Begging your leave, Major, I'll get at it."

The Summerland boys had two men killed and two seriously wounded in taking the sloop. One of the dead was a Lanatashee. The Northern Rangers lost a total of fifteen men; five more were wounded. A third of the dead had been Bookworms. There would have been a sixth, but a copy of *A Continent's Calling* stopped a ball at page two-fifty. The Southern Rangers had no one killed. Their only injury came from a man breaking his leg when he fell off a siege ladder.

Major Forest reunited the Ryngians with the captives, then had each man sign a parole document stating that he would not fight against Mystrians again. The Rangers helped them build rafts and canoes, then sent the survivors down the river to Kebeton.

Makepeace should have been counted among the injured, but he wouldn't hear of it. He'd never used a cannon before and assumed it was just like a big musket. He invoked the magick and the larger firestone pulled more out of him than he expected. He turned black and blue up to the elbow. He told everyone he was just fine, but he got more quiet than usual, and took to reading Bible verses to Ryngians his shot had wounded.

Nathaniel reported to Major Forest, meeting him on the wall over the east gate. "Caleb will be good. Packed the wound with *mogiqua*, bound it up tight. Blade got meat, not anything vital."

Forest nodded. "I will write letters to the families of the fallen."

Nathaniel frowned. "Reckon I might have to learn some letters to do that myself."

"It's not something you will enjoy."

"Don't expect it is. Needs doing." Nathaniel sighed. "Part of my responsibility to my men."

"Your men?" Forest smiled. "Strike me, but I never thought I'd hear you utter those words."

"Ain't saying they come easy, but I reckon you know that. And you knowed this was a-coming when you made me an officer."

"I might have at that." The Major rested his living hand on Nathaniel's shoulder. "I knew you would make a good officer."

"Not sure your trust is entirely placed right." Nathaniel glanced back toward the wharf. "Truth be told, when they was charging, fear took a mighty hold of me. I could have run."

"But you didn't."

"No, sir."

"Do you know why you didn't?"

"Got it narrowed down to being too ornery or just a damned fool."

Forest laughed, an incongruous sound in the fort, but no less a welcome one. "You didn't run because, if you did, your men would have run and died. Their only chance was to stand and fight. And they would do that for you, because of their trust in you. You didn't betray that trust. As an officer, you can never do that. Your men will die and, even if you survive, you'll be dead inside."

Nathaniel glanced down. "I reckon I need to do some more thinking on that, but thank you, sir."

"You're more than welcome, Captain." Forest nodded solemnly. "And you might as well rejoice. The Mystrian Rangers have defeated a larger Ryngian force and put a lie to the story of Villerupt."

"I reckon that's true." Nathaniel smiled for a moment, then his brows arrowed together. "Occurs to me now that didn't nobody tell us what we was supposed to do once we took this place."

"That's because we weren't supposed to take it." Forest's eyes narrowed. "Colonel Boucher told me that he'd had word from Kebeton that a hundred fifty men were on their way to capture his fort. He refused to believe because the very idea was outrageous. I think he's still waiting for the rest of our force to come out of the woods."

"I reckon his being warned means Deathridge wanted us dead."

"Or Rivendell, or their enemies." Forest shook his head. "Perhaps they didn't want us dead, just out of the way."

"And being here accomplishes that, don't it?"

"It does." The Major stared out to the east. "If we cut back the woods and use the lumber to give this place a back wall, we could hang on to it for a good long time. And absent other orders, that's as good a plan as any."

CHAPTER SIXTY-THREE

August 1, 1764
La Fortresse du Morte
Anvil Lake, Mystria

Prince Vlad read Rivendell's brief note again, then looked at the Lieutenant who had delivered it. "Lord Rivendell is in a meeting and cannot be disturbed? And yet he has summoned my Colonel Daunt to his meeting?"

The Lieutenant, a slender young man who had developed none of an adult's angles to his body or face, shook his head. "I do not know what the message said, Highness. I was told to give it to you and report back to Lord Rivendell immediately."

"You'll wait here." Vlad stalked from his tent. "Count von Metternin! Captain Strake! To me immediately!"

The Prince ground his teeth. Rivendell had consistently played the fool, but his conduct in the last forty-eight hours had gone beyond the pale. On July thirtieth Rivendell had sent the Laureate an invitation to dine in his headquarters in honor of Tharyngia's Liberation Day. Rivendell had even ordered Blackoak's band to practice the Ryngian anthem.

Du Malphias declined regretfully, citing a need to celebrate with his men, but extended an invitation for the officers from the other evening's festivities to join him in his fort. Rivendell and his command staff accepted. Bumble did not. Prince Vlad offered Count von Metternin in his place, but du Malphias' envoy had politely declined.

I knew nothing good would come of that dinner. He half-hoped du Malphias would poison the Norillians. Prince Vlad would then take command, retire and build Fort Hope solidly. He'd add a smaller fort atop the hills on either side, thereby guaranteeing control of the high ground.

The Tharyngians had celebrated enthusiastically, firing off cannons. Chemicals added to the brimstone produced bright red and green flames. Ryngian mortars launched fused charges that exploded in the air, providing dazzling displays of light. Ever courteous, the Ryngians aimed the mortars over the lake, so no errant charge could explode among the besieging army.

The Mystrians had worked day and night digging trenches and moving their cannon forward. They'd gotten to within eight hundred yards of the fort. They controlled the battlefield, but the glacises prevented them from hitting the walls. That would require them to be two hundred yards closer. Vlad imagined that du Malphias would use his cannon to discourage those efforts.

Owen found the Prince first. "Yes, Highness?"

"What do you know of Rivendell's doings?"

The younger man shook his head. "Not much. The diners started working yesterday after their hangovers eased. Everyone else was kept away. What has he done?"

"He's undone us all, I am sure." The Prince nodded as the Kessian joined them. "Come, gentlemen. Lord Rivendell requires a visit."

Von Metternin's eyes tightened. "Rivendell has taken du Malphias' bait?"

"I believe so." Vlad had been afraid of trickery ever since the invitation had been extended. Rivendell's contempt for du Malphias would blind him to whatever the Laureate sought to hide.

The Norillian commander assumed du Malphias was every bit the gentleman he was. Since Rivendell would never stoop to trickery, he assumed that du Malphias would likewise eschew deception. Rivendell and his subordinates would accept the Laureate's word that things were as they appeared to be. They would note things of interest within the fort, and think themselves far cleverer than their host for having gotten inside to take a look.

They just would never imagine that what they saw was exactly what du Malphias wanted them to see.

As they marched, Vlad glanced toward the fortress. In no time shot and shell would shred the green, grassy expanse between camps. It would destroy the men fighting their way across it. Though Prince Vlad had never witnessed warfare on this scale before, he'd read enough and talked to enough men, that he had no trouble imagining the bleeding ruin Rivendell's foolishness would foster.

"I cannot let Rivendell's folly kill men." Vlad stared at the soldier blocking the entrance to the tent. "Stand aside, soldier."

Stone-faced and silent, the man remained rigidly in place.

Owen slipped past him and slashed through the tent's wall with his Altashee obsidian knife. "This way, Highness."

Owen stepped aside as Vlad passed through the slit. He had never seen that level of resolution on the Prince's face before. Count von Metternin followed him, then Owen squeezed through. The tent had been divided into three parts, with the largest—Rivendell's headquarters—taking up nearly two-thirds. The smaller two areas were centered one around a bunk and the other a small dining table.

Langford abandoned the map table around which Rivendell and three other colonels had gathered, moving to intercept the Prince. "You should not be here, Highness."

Vlad stopped him with a glare. "Your saying that is precisely why I must be."

Rivendell's head came up. "Leave us, Highness. You, too, von Metternin. Colonel Langford, place Captain Strake under arrest."

"What deviltry are you up to, Johnny?"

"This is a military matter, Highness. I command you to leave."

The Prince hammered a fist on the table. Colonel Thornbury jumped back, giving Owen a glance at the map. Rivendell and his colonels had altered Owen's original survey map significantly. They'd placed a small sheet of paper over the central stone roundhouse and had drawn flowers and a tree upon it. The gun emplacements remained correctly positioned, but instead of four cannon at each, they'd only placed two. Beside the barracks buildings they'd made notes indicating that only battalions of the Platine Regiment were on station. Other notes indicated that a hundred civilians functioned as laborers.

"What is this travesty?"

Rivendell's nostrils flared. "It is the proper map of *La Fortresse du Morte*. We were given a complete tour. It is woefully understaffed and vulnerable. We will press our attack today and destroy du Malphias."

Vlad stared, his mouth open. "What did he do to you in there?"

"He offered brilliant conversation on military strategy. He fully understood that for a defender to be successful, he must have at least a third of the attacking force's numbers under arms. He remained confident that he would be able to hold us off, but he lacked the resources necessary to do so."

The Kessian studied the map. "You show two cannon at each battery."

"That is how many there are, sir, no more."

"But you show a pair at each battery, including the lake wall. Cannot du Malphias just transfer those cannon to the north wall?"

"He does not have enough personnel to operate them. Six batteries of four, with four men each to serve them. This places one of his battalions at the guns, leaving only two more to man the walls—and he has a great deal of wall to cover."

The Kessian frowned. "He will strip men from other walls to defend."

Rivendell shook his head. "We keep Thornbury's cavalry in reserve as a threat to strike at a weak point."

The Prince leaned forward and tapped the troop estimate notes. "You did not account for the Ungarakii he has under arms."

"There are no Twilight People in there."

"Yes, there are." Vlad pointed off toward the lake. "I have had men watching the water. We counted nearly two hundred warriors coming in. I sent you reports."

"Langford, did I get any such reports?"

"Yes, sir. You deemed them unreliable and insignificant."

Rivendell smiled. "Satisfied?"

"What about the *pasmortes*. You know they can't be killed."

Thornbury stepped back to the table. "The civilians were women and children, with a few old men. They are non-combatants."

Owen couldn't contain himself. "Those civilians attacked your cavalry!"

"The wurm devoured the bodies, so we don't know what they were."

Vlad rubbed a hand over his forehead. "Why have you eliminated the central stronghold?"

"It has trees and flowers on it. It is nothing."

The Prince tapped another part of the map, where the opening to the underground chambers should have been. "And this building here?"

"Storage." Rivendell preened. "I demanded to see within. And I did find a chamber dug into the hillside. It was the Laureate's wine cellar. From there I shall choose the vintage with which to toast our victory."

The Prince stared at him. "And your grand plan is to walk our men up and storm the walls?"

"Precisely. We have more than three times his numbers."

Count von Metternin rested a hand on the Prince's shoulder. "My Lord Rivendell, the three-to-one ratio is accepted minimum needed to defeating a foe, but it does not guarantee victory."

"But, my lord Count, we are speaking of Norillian troops."

Vlad again hammered a fist against the table. "No, you fool, you are speaking about men! Men who are going to be ripped to bits as they march forward. Grapeshot will rake any siege ladders you create, and blow apart you trench bridging."

Rivendell laughed. "This is precisely why command of this operation was given to a military man, Prince Vladimir. Anthony, tell him what you saw."

Colonel Exeter replied with a smug half-smile. "While I was examining one of the batteries, I measured both the carriage height and the height of the embrasures. I did the basic geometry. It is impossible for the guns to depress far enough to shoot anything atop the glacises."

"My God, man, do you think he doesn't know that?" Vlad thrust a finger toward the fortress. "Do you think he has no axes to cut the embrasures down?"

Exeter chuckled. "We'll hit him so fast he won't have time to chop."

The Prince sighed. "Your enemy is not a fool."

Lord Rivendell smiled proudly. "Nor am I, Highness. I am a genius. Ain't it,

Langford, ain't that a fact?"

"Yes, sir."

"And a genius will win this day, Highness. We go at one."

Vlad shook his head. "I won't allow it."

"You are a civilian. I am in command of your people. Colonel Daunt, you will have your men make siege ladders and bridges. Exeter, give him some of your engineers to help."

Exeter saluted smartly. "Yes, sir."

Owen watched the Prince's face deaden. Disaster loomed; there was no getting away from that. Owen's guts twisted. He choked vomit back down. *I have to do something.* "Permission to be assigned to Colonel Daunt's command, my lord."

Rivendell's sneer gushed ice through Owen's bowels. "Denied. You are under arrest."

Vlad's head came up. "On what charges?"

"Insubordination. Conduct unbecoming an officer. Destroying Her Majesty's property." Rivendell produced a pocket watch, flicked the cover open and then snapped it shut again. "I should convene a court-martial, but we've not enough time. Anthony, have a squad of the Fourth take charge of Captain Strake. Clap him in irons and stick him outside my tent. Let him watch and wish he had his place in the line of glory."

The Prince snarled. "This is outrageous, sir!"

"It is necessary, sir." Rivendell slid the watch home in his waistcoat. "Perhaps, in victory, I shall be magnanimous. I think not, but that is the joy of genius—I am unpredictable. Good day, Highness."

The Prince began to say something else, but the count grabbed his arm and steered him back out through the slit. He took a last look at Owen, but Owen just shook his head. "I will be fine."

"The prisoner will remain silent!"

Owen met Rivendell's gaze openly, and the other man smiled. "You have your orders, gentlemen. We have three hours. Please be ready."

Exeter, Thornbury, and Daunt departed. Langford glanced at Lord Rivendell. "Should I stay, sir?"

"No, Colonel. The words I have for Captain Strake are for his ears alone."

Langford retreated quickly. Rivendell began to slowly circle Owen. Clearly he meant to walk with a predatory mien, trying to be intimidating. The fact that he was so thoroughly proud of himself—being unable to hide a smile—robbed the attempt of its intent. He made two circuits and spoke on the third.

"You know, Captain Strake, you could have been where I am. Well, not truly, since you don't have the blood; but you had the backing of a very powerful family. Had you proven yourself worthy, you would have succeeded in the

Army. You might have risen to Major or Colonel. You could be one of the officers out there going to glory."

Owen lifted his head. "Said as if you mean to lead from the front, sir."

"Oh, lead I shall, lead I shall. I'm a Rivendell, ain't I?" The man came around and squared up in front of Owen. "People like you can't understand someone like me. You are incapable of fathoming genius. You fear what you do not understand. That fear marks you as a coward."

Rivendell walked back around his table. "After we had dinner, the Laureate and I had a private conversation. About you, in fact. He said he had forgiven you for spying and had fully intended, once you were well, to return you to Temperance. He said he was relieved to learn you had made it back safely, and said you completely misunderstood the search parties he had sent out after you. He was concerned that in a blizzard, in your weakened state, you would have perished."

Owen's flesh puckered. He wanted to ask if Rivendell believed du Malphias but the man's expression made the question unnecessary. Fatigue washed over Owen. He wanted to lay down and die.

No, you have to be strong, for Catherine.

"You should know, Captain, that I would have put you in the front lines and given you a chance to redeem yourself, but the Laureate himself asked that I refrain. He said he considered you a friend. He did not want to be the cause of your death. He asked me this one indulgence."

"Of course, he did."

"You have not been given leave to speak, Captain!"

"Permission to speak, sir!"

"No, Captain, you shall only impugn the honor of a man who is many times your superior."

Owen met Rivendell's stare and held it until the other man looked away.

"Please yourself, Captain."

"Du Malphias made his request to show me that he still had control over my life. If I die, it will be by his hand, not ill luck in battle. He means to shame me and, after you're defeated, he'll kill me in his own good time."

"That," said Rivendell, "is not something that should concern either of you. By this evening, the *Fortresse du Morte* shall be mine, and the two of you shall pass into obscurity."

Vlad, furious, yanked his arm from von Metternin's grasp. "I am not a child, my lord!"

"Then you should not act like one, Highness."

The Prince shot von Metternin a venomous glance. "Is it childish to act as if this idiot and his plans won't kill hundreds of my people? Du Malphias has filled his warrens with Ungarakii, *pasmortes,* and the rest of the Platine Regiment. The stronghold still exists despite having flowers and trees on it. You yourself pointed out that cannon can be redeployed. Can't you see the slaughter that is coming? Or don't you care because these are not your people?"

Count von Metternin's face froze and Vlad knew he had overstepped. "If you believe, Prince Vladimir of Norisle, that I am not as concerned for the lives of men I have spent the last month and a half sweating, toiling, living, and laughing beside, then you are a singularly poor judge of character and perhaps no smarter than the moron whose tent we have just departed."

Vlad nodded. "Forgive me, my lord. Perhaps I am acting childishly. But what am I to do?"

"There is nothing for you to do, my lord."

"How can you say that?"

Von Metternin laughed. "We have been in a trap since the moment your report went to Norisle, Highness. Parliament made decisions based on internal power struggles, not the wisdom of your report. Deathridge and his faction were willing to allow Rivendell this mission because they knew it would fail. And Rivendell, short of his dying in battle, wins. Just getting here is a victory. His failure will be blamed on the inadequacy of Mystrian troops. His career will become retrograde, but none of his backers will be demoted. He was a piece both sides welcomed as a sacrifice."

The two men trudged up the hill toward the wurmrest. "But my people, real people will die because of their game-playing."

"But you must understand that the powerful do not see things as we do. They keep score differently. If they lose a scion here, it is no matter. The death will be honorable, and they will be in mourning—as society dictates. For the common men who will die on the field, they care not. Most are from the underclasses, are thieves and drunkards with no future anyway. Many—and this would apply to your Mystrians—are not even from Norisle. Why should they care if Mystrian blood is spilled?"

"You're saying they have no stake in the game."

"It is worse, my friend." The Count stopped at the top of the hill and looked toward the Fortress of Death. "They already know the outcome. In one way, Norisle has already won because you cut the road to get here. They will use it next year, or the year after, to finally eliminate this threat. But when the battle is lost here and Mystrians die, two things take on new life. One is the myth that Mystrians cannot fight. It will take root here as well as grow even more wild in Norisle. News of Major Forest's failure to take Fort Cuivre will just exacerbate things. The second, and far more important to Deathridge, is the myth of Mystrian vulnerability. People here will feel the threat, and will believe that only Norillian troops can save them. They will welcome more troops, and the presence of these troops will enable Deathridge to crush nascent notions of independence. Publication of books like *A Continent's Calling* will be outlawed, and anyone who thinks of independence will be labeled as a Malphian sympathizer. It is a simple process that will destroy Mystria's future."

Vlad shook his head. "This isn't even a game. It is merely their preparation of the board for the next round."

"Elegantly put, Highness."

The Prince looked out at the battlefield. He had no difficulty seeing it reduced to maps in a book. Squares with unit designations would replace flesh and blood. Giant arrows would show lines of attack. Dotted lines would show lines of retreat. Somewhere a chart would total the casualties. He could write a report detailing why the disaster occurred, but Rivendell would commission another book. Vlad's criticism would be dismissed as an attempt to, once again, cover up for the Mystrian inability to wage war.

"So, my only choices are to either march back down there and shoot Rivendell dead, or remain here and use my skills at observation to create a complete and accurate chronicle of what happens?"

"I am as frustrated as you are, Highness, perhaps more." Von Metternin's eyes narrowed. "What Rivendell will create is a disaster, but there might be a way to avert it. We've known it all along."

"Yes?"

The Kessian pointed toward the highest part of the fortress. "The cliff fort. If we were to concentrate forces there in a direct assault, du Malphias could not bring all of his cannon to bear on our flank. You force one section of his wall, get into that fort, and then use that position to attack down into the Fortress of Death."

"Back to the original plan, but without our climbers." Vlad sighed. "Deathridge saw to that."

"So, Highness, back to your choices. Shall I drag a table and chairs out here so we may make notes as we observe, or do I charge a pistol and fashion an alibi?"

Owen gave Sergeant Unstone a withering glance. "And I have given you my word, as an officer and a gentleman, that I will not run off."

The non-commissioned officer held the shackles out. "Please, sir, I don't mean you no disrespect."

"Have you forgotten the other evening, Sergeant? Who was it told you how to kill the Ryngians? Who stood there side by side with you?"

"You, sir."

"Exactly." Owen exposed a wrist. "See these scars, Unstone? When I was in that very fortress, the Ryngians put me in shackles. They did that to humiliate me. That's what Rivendell wants you to do to me now."

"Sir, I have my orders."

"You won't be charged with insubordination, Sergeant. I will be charged with escape. I'll make that clear to his lordship. You'll testify to that fact and all will be well."

The Sergeant, whose face bore more than one battle scar, looked at his squad and then dropped the shackles. "I ain't going to lie, sir."

"You're a good man, Sergeant."

Owen drew his hands to the small of his back and watched the troops assembling. He couldn't help but shiver as disaster loomed. The Fourth formed up by battalion, with four on the line and one held in reserve. The cavalry held the right flank, anchored against the river but, dismounted, only mustered two battalions of foot. Armed with carbines, their effective kill range was only thirty yards, which made them especially weak. Since they were not drilled in infantry tactics, they were even less useful. An intelligent commander would have pulled one of their battalions back into reserve and used the Fifth infantry battalion to fill out the line.

The Mystrians likewise had four battalions on the front and one held in reserve. Owen shook his head. The Mystrians had no real uniforms to speak of. They looked more a rabble than a military force. Their ranks remained ragged, though they did cover four hundred yards of front, same as the Fourth Foot.

Sixteen hundred souls marching into Hell. Two squads in every battalion carried siege ladders and bridging material. Those men would have to reach the wall first. Even if Rivendell's fantasy about the cannon being unable to depress far enough were true, many men would die in the approach.

Off to the left, Rivendell emerged from his tent, wearing his red satin uniform. Bishop Bumble flanked him. Exeter and Thornbury greeted him, saluted, and reported to their commands. Rivendell advanced to where a bugler stood and gave the man an order.

He started playing an alert, which buglers for the line units matched. Drummers—young boys mostly—started beating a steady, measured cadence. Norillians unfurled unit colors and voices rose to cry "Hurrah!" The Mystrians, lacking regimental colors, just cheered and waved their hats. The Blackoak Pipers began a squealing tune and all the Mystrians held their heads a little higher.

The bugler's call changed. Advance. The strident notes echoed from the Fortress of Death. On that signal, the battalions marched forward. The Norillian artillery fired a volley. Iron balls flew, but hit the glacises and bounced high, passing over the walls. Owen could but hope that some would come down within the fortress environs and smash through waiting troops.

The Tharyngian response scythed through the Norillian lines at the point where the Fourth Foot and the cavalry met. Iron balls smashed through the ranks. A dozen men went down. The lucky ones died instantly, their heads splashed over their comrades, or torn in twain. The wounded clawed at the ground futilely trying to crawl to where their severed legs lay, or sat there unable to understand why a sleeve ended wetly at the elbow.

Even at that distance, the screams echoed sharply through Owen's skull.

All six Ryngian batteries concentrated on the Norillians. Du Malphias had reinforced each with two extra cannon, and did not seem at a loss for crews. Owen would have taken their choice of target as a sign of contempt for the Mystrians, but the Fourth Foot were the most formidable force on the field. If du Malphias concentrated on them, he could blast the Mystrians close up with grape shot. Chances were they would break before they reached the wall.

But it wasn't the Mystrians whose courage flagged first. Owen pointed toward the cavalry. A gap had opened between them and the infantry. "Thornbury isn't driving his men forward."

Sergeant Unstone stepped up beside Owen. "Gap only hurts if the Tharyngians have troops to push into it. Colonel says…"

"The Colonel doesn't believe du Malphias has spare troops. If he's right, filling that gap now won't hurt. If he's wrong, the battle's lost."

Suddenly gunfire echoed from the woods west of the river, where a battalion of Mystrians had been left to hold the flank. Owen stood on tiptoes to see what was going on, but only saw smoke rising from the woods. You were even craftier than we imagined.

Owen turned to one of the privates. "Take this message to Rivendell. There is firing on the right. The Mystrians are fighting in the woods. Du Malphias has a force he'll cross at the ferry to flank the cavalry."

The man looked at the Sergeant. Unstone sent him off with a curt nod.

Responding to the fighting across the river, the cavalry shifted its facing. Thornbury ordered his reserve unit to the river's edge. The line unit reshuffled and withdrew to become a reserve for the river defenders. Their maneuver, executed poorly and in complete confusion, completely opened the Fourth's flank.

The Private reached Rivendell's station, but Langford never let him get to the man. The Colonel dismissed the soldier and then turned to Rivendell. They shared a laugh, then went back to watching the Tharyngian cannon ravage the men under their command.

The Mystrians had bravely moved up the slope toward the high fort, the Blackoak Pipers driving them forward. Then the high fort's battery opened up. Grapeshot killed men several ranks deep in the Third battalion, but the survivors kept moving forward. A man on the formation's edge kept shouting, and the men of the Third surged ahead.

The other battalions faltered and began to pull back. The cannon spoke again, nibbling at the Second battalion. A dozen of their men went down. Their rear ranks began to turn and run. The First and the Fourth slowed, then stopped.

Count von Metternin shook his head. "You cannot blame them."

"I know." Vlad snapped a pencil in half. "But I have to stop them."

The Kessian looked at him. "What can you do? If you go down there, you'll die."

"But I have to do something. Look." Vlad stood and pointed toward the Third. "The hill, the glacises, the guns in front can't get them. But others will sweep them once they've destroyed the Norillians. The Third is trapped, and I can't leave them there."

The Count reached across the table and grabbed Vlad's arm. "You are going to do something stupid and get yourself killed. And I shall have to inform Princess Gisella."

"Come with me." Vlad gave the man a confident smile. "If you agree to go, it can't be stupid."

The Count came out of the chair. The two of them ran to the wurmrest and the Count gasped. "This is insane, completely insane. No one has…"

In accord with the experimentation the Prince had been conducting through the spring, a second assembly had been fitted snuggly to the saddles, forward of them. It consisted of a steel post a foot and a half high, with a semicircular bar fixed to it by four spokes. The semicircle and spokes lay parallel to the ground. A six inch spike rose in the center of the arc.

A one-pound swivel-gun had been mounted on the post, secured with a water-tight leather sheath and cork plug. The ramrod had been fitted with a gimbaled guide, so it couldn't go missing in the heat of the battle. The center spike prevented the cannon being fired straight forward—hence the rear gunner could not shoot the rider, and the rider could not shoot Mugwump. Oilskin saddle-bags before and behind the rider's legs contained premeasured charges and rounds for the guns.

The Prince hauled himself into the saddle. "Baker, find Colonel Daunt. Tell him to charge the high fort on my signal."

The wurmwright gaped up at him. "Signal, Highness?"

"He'll know it. Go."

Vlad turned in the saddle and smiled at von Metternin. "Use the spike to gash the charges when you reload. It's all grape, and designed to kill *pasmortes*."

Von Metternin laughed. "This is not stupid, Highness, it is spectacularly stupid."

"Only if we die, my lord." Vlad smiled and touched Mugwump's flank with his heel. "We're off to save Mystrians. The devil can take all else!"

By the time the Private returned, the battle had deteriorated. The Mystrians had stalled on the left flank. One battalion had been trapped near the hill's summit. Whenever a squad tried to advance, cannon blew them to pieces. The survivors hunkered down, unaware that once the Tharyngian cannon had finished with the Fourth Foot and smoke had thinned enough for gunners to aim, it would rake their flank and clear them off the hillside.

More firing came from the right, sporadic but steady. Owen couldn't make any sense of the noise. The smoke drifting up from the battlefield made seeing anything difficult.

In the Norillian center, the Second company had pushed forward and had actually reached the walls. The Third slid right, breaking contact with the Mystrians, to follow the Second through the forest of spikes. Bridging went over the trenches. Siege ladders leaned against walls. Soldiers started to climb, and then the Platine Regiment mounted the battlements. With deadly precision they opened fire. Musket balls blasted men from the ladders. Bayonets stabbed down. Norillian gunfire slew Ryngians—several bodies hung lifeless from the top of the palisade wall, but far more Redcoats fell.

Then Owen saw it, on the right. "There, Tharyngian troops mustering at the corner."

Unstone looked toward Rivendell. "His lordship is gone, sir."

"What?" Owen turned just in time to see Langford disappearing into Rivendell's tent. "Sergeant, send a man back down there."

"Won't do no good, sir. Smoke. He can't see a thing."

Owen grabbed Unstone's lapels. "Then we have to do it, Sergeant. We have to get the reserve battalion over there."

"Sir, I can't give those orders." The Sergeant shook his head adamantly. "It's not my place. I will be court-martialed and shot."

"Listen to me. All of you." Owen looked at the entire squad. "It's your friends who are going to die, and you know damned well that Rivendell couldn't care less. Do you think they will survive if we don't act?"

Unstone glanced at his feet. "We won't survive if we do."

"I'd rather die saving friends than live watching them die." Owen shoved the man away and started off down the hill. "Shoot me for escaping, or come with me and be a hero. Your choice. Me, I'm going to kill some Ryngians."

Mugwump charged from the wurmrest, then paused on the crest of the hill. His head came up and nostril slits flared. He turned, looking back at the Prince. Vlad could have sworn great intelligence burned in that golden eye.

The Prince nodded. "Yes, it's into that Hell we're going. Plenty of *pasmortes*. All you care to eat."

The wurm blinked slowly, then loped down the hill as cannons boomed. They rode down into a cloud of gunsmoke, then appeared in the valley as if conjured. Soldiers who had been pulling back stopped. Mugwump curled his tail around to corral a few more.

The Prince looked down at astonished faces. "Done already? By God, I've just gotten to the fight."

Mystrians stood there, dumbfounded, not even bothering to duck when another cannon roared. One man pointed back up the hill. "Highness, you can't go up there. You'll be killed!"

"I'm not abandoning the Third!" Vlad pointed at the fortress. "I'll meet you at the top!"

The man who'd spoken stared at him as if he was mad, but another man raised his musket and shouted. "To the top! To the top." Mugwump roared and more men took up the cry. "To the top! To the top!"

Vlad pumped a fist into the air. "To the top!"

The men turned, heading back toward the battle. Vlad tugged on the left rein. Mugwump looked back as if to ask, "Are you serious?"

"We're meeting them at the top."

The wurm growled, then set off to the east, running parallel to the line of battle. He began to gallop, exhibiting more fluidity and speed than Vlad had ever imagined he could. The Prince shouted to von Metternin. "By God, he knows he's going to war!"

"He was trained to it." The Kessian laughed as his hat blew off.

Vlad had a heartbeat to consider pulling back on the reins when Mugwump reached the lakeshore. The wurm didn't bother to slide down the embankment, he just leaped. His legs, fore and back, came in. The Prince drew in a deep breath and ducked down, holding tight to the swivel-gun. The wurm's dive carried them deep. A wall of water hit Vlad hard, almost tearing him from the saddle. Water rushed in, booming against his body.

Mugwump took them deeper. The water went from warm to cold, then the wurm's nose came up. His tail twitched once, sending a powerful shudder through his body. They exploded from the depths. Water sheeted off as they flew upward, then stopped hard.

Mugwump's claws sank into the cliff face. Stones cracked and fell away but the wurm's grip remained strong. Effortlessly Mugwump climbed up the rock face, and swiftly enough that Vlad almost didn't have enough time to pull the plug from his swivel-gun's muzzle. Mugwump came up over the cliff edge with enough velocity that he grabbed the top of the palisade wall and hung there. He surveyed the interior as if he were a dog peering over a picket fence.

Vlad stripped off the leather sheath, swung his swivel-gun around to the right, and angled it up at the cannon batteries blasting away at the Mystrians. He clapped his right hand over the firestone, feeling cool smoothness beneath it. His hand tingled as he triggered the spell firing the small cannon.

The swivel-gun's load was the Prince's own creation. It consisted of pea-sized bits of lead and iron, meant in equal parts for the living and the dead. The shot expanded in a cloud, raking the crews. Pieces pinged off cannons. Perfect uniform coats tattered. Hats flew. Men spun and a loader pitched back over the wall, taking his waxed-paper cylinder of grapeshot with him.

Mugwump's weight snapped lumber. He clawed away more of it and a portion of the palisade wall collapsed. Supports for two small gunnery platforms snapped, spilling cannons and crews into the main compound. The wurm landed atop the debris and scrambled forward, his claws shredding a trooper.

Vlad yanked open a saddle bag and pulled out a cloth cylinder knotted at both ends. A musket ball glanced off Mugwump's scaled head, hissing past the Prince. Vlad tipped the gun up, gashed the lower half of the cylinder on a spike at the cannon's muzzle, and let a little brimstone pour into the barrel before he jammed the entire bag into the weapon. The ramrod came around and down, slamming things home. He retracted it, then swung the gun around, aiming toward that battery again.

His next shot went low, cutting men's legs from beneath them. It blasted one gunnery carriage wheel to bits. That cannon sagged. Carriage locks ripped free of shattered wood. The heavy bronze gun rolled, crushing the gunner and snapping another man's leg.

The Prince's hand stung as if attacked by a dozen wasps. Numbness nibbled at his fingers, and color bled into his skin. I bleed, they bleed. Two shots had sent nearly a dozen men to Perdition. Is this all it takes to kill?

Count von Metternin fired to the left, sweeping a Platine squad from the fort's inner wall. Half of one man went back over the wall while his legs fell inside. Others just sagged, suddenly boneless and leaking. A few desperately clung to the wall as if remaining upright would hold death at bay.

The Prince loaded and fired mechanically, scattering soldiers, but giving no thought to directing Mugwump. The wurm darted toward the north and up onto the top of the stone wall. He raised his muzzle and repeated the roar he'd offered in response to the cry of "To the top!" Then his tail whipped around, sheering off the top of the palisade wall.

"To the top!" men screamed from below. Had Prince Vlad not been so busy reloading, he would have thrust a fist in the air. He rammed the powder and shot home, then looked west, seeking a target.

And he saw one, a grand one, but one too far away to target. There, by the river, two battalions of the Platine Regiment had crashed into the Norillian line. And to make things worse, a sloop under a Ryngian flag sailed down the Green River and had run its guns out to fire.

Every instinct urged Owen to sprint away from the battle. Straight ahead, through curtains of gunsmoke, two Platine battalions formed up. The cavalry had pulled back and faced the river, exposing its flank to the Ryngians. Their maneuver gave the Ryngians a boulevard into the heart of the Norillian formation wider than the road du Malphias had cut through the woods. On the left, the Fourth Foot had no idea of the danger. If the Ryngians split their forces, they could likely roll up both sides. And if they concentrate them...

Owen marched straight to the Captain commanding the artillery. "Compliments of Lord Rivendell. He wonders if it would trouble you too much to shift your guns forty-five degrees to the west. We have some Tharyngians forming up there."

The artillery commander raised his telescope and dropped his jaw. "By God, that gap!"

"Fill it with fire, Captain, fill it with fire." Owen turned and stalked toward the gap.

"Where the devil are you going?"

Owen turned, throwing his arms wide and laughed. "You fill it with fire, I'll fill it with me. Shoot high, man, so I can watch you knock them down."

The artilleryman shouted at his crews. Owen spun again, then dropped to a knee and pulled a musket and ammunition pouch from a dead body. A bit further along he recovered another musket and a bayonet, which he slung over his shoulder. He went to pull the cartridge case from another corpse, but the fallen man clung to it.

Owen looked at the soldier. Not a drop of blood. "On your feet soldier!"

The man—really just a boy—opened his eyes wide. "I don't want to die."

"Not like any of us have a choice, son. What's your name?"

"Private Hodge Dunsby, sir."

Owen tugged him to a sitting position. "You can sit here and weep, or laugh at Death and feed him Ryngians. It's better to laugh. Move it."

The young man stared up at him. "But, sir."

"Son, if you don't move, your friends will die. Come with me, and we might save a few."

Hodge's eyes focused distantly for a moment, then he wiped away tears and stood, bringing his musket to hand. "As you say, laughing's better. Lead on, sir."

Owen felt ridiculous. Dressed in his Altashee leathers, one musket over his shoulder, another in his right hand. He thumbed the firestone, rotating it. He felt it grind. The musket had been loaded and never fired. With Hodge at his back, Owen marched into the gap as Ryngian drummers started in.

"Hodge, grab two more muskets." Owen bent to get himself a third. "Sixty, forty, and twenty, then it's steel on steel."

"Yes, sir."

Just looking at the Ryngians gave Owen gooseflesh. The enemy formed a solid wall of blue coats with white facings, silver-white buttons, and tall bearskin hats with silver crests. When he'd faced them in Artennes Forest he'd joked that one should aim for that badge. No need to aim now. At that range he couldn't miss, but even killing two with every shot wouldn't slow them.

The drums began a steady beat. Cannons roared from behind him. Balls slammed into the formation, plowing red furrows through it. The Platine just closed ranks, drawing closer, ever closer, step by step, their iron will and discipline revealing why they were the masters of the battlefield. An officer shouted an order and the front rank lowered muskets to the hip, then thrust them forward. Bayonets at the ready, they came on, with the second rank's bayonets gleaming at shoulder height.

"You still with me, Hodge?"

"Got a couple more, sir."

Owen looked to his side. Two other men, one bleeding from the shoulder and the other wounded in the thigh, raised their muskets. "If you can find an officer, drop him."

More cannonballs hammered the Tharyngian forces, but the Norillian cannon were slow to reload. They might get one more volley in before the Ryngians overran Owen's position. More Ryngians filled the gaps, leaving the line seamless. A hundred yards. Eighty. Owen raised his musket. Seventy. Sixty.

His thumb brushed the firestone. The musket spat fire. A second later the other three soldiers shot. Three Ryngians went down, their bodies instantly hidden behind the advancing line.

Then the drumbeats sped up, hammered more quickly.

The Ryngians charged.

Owen brought a second musket to his shoulder. Seeing a man with a sword shouting orders, he shifted right and tracked. He aimed for the badge, then invoked a spell. Gunsmoke hid the line, but it blew away quickly and the officer had vanished.

The solid wall of blue raced on and Owen braced himself to receive the charge.

Then a volley roared from behind him and the Ryngians staggered. Unstone and the Third had come to plug the gap. The first two Ryngian ranks went down, but rest of the Platine came on hard. Owen screamed defiantly and met their charge. He parried the first thrust, then drove his own bayonet home, plunging it deep into a man's belly. The soldier vomited blood and sagged. Owen ripped the bayonet free and swung the butt up, catching another soldier in the face, shattering bone and scattering teeth.

The first wave passed by him, intent on the Third. The Ryngians flowed into the gap beyond Owen, leaving him free in the rearward ranks. Soldiers there weren't yet prepared to meet the enemy in the sea of blue coats before them. Owen's lack of a bright red uniform bought him a heartbeat before they realized he was the enemy.

One man lunged. Owen parried the bayonet wide. He brought his musket butt up with a stroke that should have snapped the man's head back. Unfortunately his target stumbled, ducking beneath the attack. As Owen's blow slipped past the man's shoulder, the Ryngian whipped his musket's butt around and caught Owen square in the stomach. Owen, his gun lost, sprawled on the ground.

The Tharyngian rose up on one knee, raising his musket high for a killing thrust.

Then another bayonet stabbed forward, catching the Ryngian high in the chest. Hodge! The bantam Private yelled as he thrust, driving the other man back. He yanked his bayonet free and a single geyser of blood shot into the air.

Owen rolled to his feet and grabbed the dying Ryngian's musket. He spun it around, leveling it at another Tharyngian soldier. He thumbed the firestone. The musket roared. The soldier fell, his waistcoat growing dark. Another butt-stroke, another lunge and, with Hodge beside him, Owen broke through to the back of the Ryngian formation.

For a heartbeat he felt relief, then he glanced toward the river and felt as if he'd again been struck in the stomach.

The First Cavalry battalion had collapsed. Its colors fell as bluecoats swarmed. The best Tharyngian troops in the world had taken the Norillians in the flank. The scions of Norillian nobility loved playing at parade or riding down fleeing infantry. War had been more a sport for them than a serious pursuit, but the Ryngians had brought them blood and fire. Such intensity had never been inflicted on them before. Not for the first time did it occur to Owen that horsemen on foot had surrendered the smarter part of their partnership. Fleeing soldiers, their panic infective, ran headlong into their Second battalion, destroying any hope of defending against the pursuing Platine battalion.

And to make matters worse, a Ryngian sloop had appeared on the river drawing parallel to the cavalry position. It had run its cannons out. Nothing could save the Norillian right, and once those men had been scoured from the field, nothing could stop du Malphias from winning the day.

CHAPTER SIXTY-FOUR

August 1, 1764
La Fortresse du Morte
Anvil Lake, Mystria

The ship's cannon—sixteen pounders every one—erupted with fire and iron. They'd been loaded with grapeshot and lit off inside thirty yards of their target. All four spoke in unison. A hail of hot metal jetted from the billowing smoke clouds. Men vanished in a bloody mist. Balls sailed through them, their speed unabated, tearing legs off or blowing open chests, revealing hearts as red birds fluttering furiously in shattered ivory cages.

Nathaniel Woods and a company of Mystrian Ranger sharpshooters crouched at the gunwales. "Officers first! Officers first!" He turned to the Summerland boys. "Run those guns out again, boys. Give them another taste of Hell!"

The sharpshooters poured more fire into the Platine battalion's flank. Scattered return shots splintered oak planking. Thomas Hill brought the bow swivel-gun around and pounded the battalion's back ranks. Nathaniel twisted, tracking a man with a saber and braid. He caressed the firestone.

Gunnery crews hauled on ropes and ran the reloaded cannon out again. The sloop rolled as they fired. Where there had been ranks of blue-backed soldiers now existed a red swamp dotted with bone and dying things writhing in the mire.

One of the fortress' batteries fired at the sloop. Grapeshot mostly rattled off the hull, though a few balls careened over the deck. Several men went down—two clearly dead and one with a long splinter through his leg.

Nathaniel ran to the bow, reloading as he went. He cranked the lever forward, sealing the bullet into the barrel, then steadied the rifle on the gunwale. If it's a duel you want...

The smoke cleared, revealing a gunner standing on his cannon's carriage, hand shielding his eyes from the sun. Nathaniel dropped the sights on him, then invoked magick. The rifle boomed and bucked. The gunner staggered back, holding his stomach, before pitching down into the fort.

Without thinking, Nathaniel cranked the lever to the side, flipped the gimbaled chamber up, dropped another round into it, and worked the lever to send the bullet home. By the time he aimed again, a loader was just shoving the ramrod into the gun. Another man held a small cylinder full of grape. Nathaniel hit the firestone again.

The loader, his ramrod still stuck in the cannon's throat, hung draped over the gun. The sloop's swivel-gun roared and grapeshot scattered another cannon's crew. The remaining two cannon fired back, killing three more on deck, while the sloop's guns tore deeper into the Tharyngian formation.

Nathaniel shrieked delightedly. "More boys, faster! Until they's bled out or running." Smiling, he worked the lever and began his search for more prey.

Vlad couldn't be certain at that range with all the smoke, but it appeared as if the sloop had somehow fired on Ryngian troops! Before he had a chance to double-check, Mugwump leaped from the parapet down into the fort. He landed with the élan of a cat, his right flank to the fort's open interior doors. He flashed his fangs and hissed, defiant and angry.

Vlad brought his swivel-gun around. *Pasmortes* and Ungarakii filled the gateway. The Prince fired, and von Metternin immediately after him. Smoke thinned as it swirled out through the gate. Some *pasmortes* still came on but many had fallen, convulsing as the iron shot inhibited magick. A handful of Ungarakii lay on the ground. More slithered away trailing blood, but a knot of warriors sprinted forward.

Mugwump lashed out with his tail. An Ungarakii's thighs snapped. The man screamed, but the wurm's hiss overrode the sound. The other Ungarakii stopped, and when Mugwump snatched up a *pasmorte* child and swallowed it whole, they broke and ran.

The Prince reloaded as quickly as he could. Numbness had spread up to his right elbow, making the task difficult. His swollen hand throbbed. Purple seeped into his fingers and past his wrist. He loaded with his left hand, jamming the shot home.

Mugwump sidled back as the men fired again. Their shots raked the *pasmortes*, scattering them like toys in a child's tantrum, yet others came. Had they been thinking creatures—had they but one scintilla of self-preservation yet left in them—they would have fled with the Ungarakii.

It occurred to the Prince that perhaps they wanted to die.

And then, visible through the gateway, a company of bluebacks came running up hill. "Reinforcements, my lord. Theirs, I'm afraid."

"Then, Highness, we shall just have to shoot faster."

Vlad leaned on the swivel-gun's aiming lever to tip it upright. He grabbed another charge and dumped it into the barrel. He worked the ramrod as Mugwump gobbled down another *pasmorte*. Bringing the gun down, Vlad hunched forward and hooked his right elbow around the aiming lever. He pulled it tight against his ribs, and pressed his left palm to the firestone.

As a wave of blackness swept his sight from him for a moment, and his left hand tingled, Prince Vlad realized he'd made a grave error. With both hands numb, reloading would be that much more difficult. *And I can't grab the reins…*

He twisted back and watched von Metternin slowly loading again, his right hand dark enough that it might have been gloved in purple leather. "I am done, my lord."

The Kessian laughed defiantly as a Platine company filled the gateway. "It was a grand gesture, Highness! We will live forever in the annals of war." He brought the gun down, and spelled a blast that trimmed the left edge of the Tharyngian line.

Mugwump came around to face the Tharyngians, his mouth gaping wide, hissing again. His muzzle eclipsed the Prince's view of the soldiers. "No, Mugwump!" The wurm might shrug shot off his scales, but his mouth and tongue would get shredded.

Muskets roared.

Tharyngians fell.

The men of the Mystrian Third streamed over the wall, firing as they came. "To the Top!" they yelled as if it would protect them from shot and steel. Men captured the nearest Ryngian battery with a bayonet charge, then levered the functional cannon around to the west. A Mystrian clapped a hand over the firestone. Golden-red flame exploded from its muzzle. The load of grapeshot slashed through the next battery below on the wall. The Mystrian gunner shook his hand as if it had been hit by a hammer, but urged men to reload as quickly as they could.

Another Mystrian crew levered a cannon all the way around. They aimed at the Platines. The Tharyngian ranks fired on the Mystrian troops and then evaporated after the cannon spoke. Mystrians, dead and wounded, filled the courtyard. The survivors pressed on, taking the gate. They fired into the main compound while even more Mystrians lined the upper fort's parapet and fired on the Platine troops defending the north wall.

Mugwump leaped forward, pouncing on a moving *pasmorte* and devouring it. He seemed almost playful. He'd dig his nose beneath a body, flip it into the air, and snatch it with his mouth. His tongue gathered in arms and legs, then he'd swallow them whole, ambulatory or not.

More Mystrians poured over the wall in a muddy river of men. They didn't organize themselves in ranks as much as they did small teams of three or four. As one man reloaded, another would spot targets and the third would shoot. While their musket-fire was not terribly accurate, the sheer volume of it, aided by the occasional cannon blast of grape, cleared a length of parapet.

Vlad slipped from the saddle and, hugging his arms to his chest, staggered up to the captured battery. "You see that small hill there, in the middle of the fort?"

The Mystrian crew stared at him for a moment, then followed his line of sight. "Yes, Highness."

"Put some solid balls on it, as many as you can." Vlad smiled. "It's a hornets' nest and I want it smashed."

Only with the second broadside could Owen confirm what he'd thought had happened. The Ryngian sloop had somehow fired into its own formation. When sharpshooters started sniping, the fort fired on the sloop, and a familiar figure ran toward the bow, the truth became apparent.

"By God, Hodge, the ship is ours!"

Hodge, his face streaked with powder, spat a ball into his musket's muzzle. "Not so loud, sir, because they ain't ours."

The Platine Guards rear ranks pulled back from the sloop's assault. Men ran for the fort. Owen picked up a Ryngian musket, then grabbed Hodge by the shoulder. "Come on!"

They ran with the retreating Ryngians, hidden plainly in the midst of unreasoning men with fear-filled eyes. A Ryngian pulled ahead of Hodge, casting his musket away, and held his hands out as if asking to be bound. Hodge shouldered him out of the way. The man tumbled to the ground and other men stampeded over him.

"Are you sure this is wise, sir?"

"Stay with me, Hodge."

Owen rounded the corner through the gate. Ungarakii were in full retreat from the upper fort. On the left, cannon-fire swept the ramparts. Another cannon launched a ball from the high fort. It overshot the hill and bounced through the troops packed in the gate. Men screamed.

Through the chaos Owen ran, and Hodge came hot on his heels. Another cannonball sailed over their heads and hit the grassy stronghold. A couple of soldiers moved to stop them, but Owen shot one and Hodge charged with his bayonet. The remaining Ryngian soldier read the determination on his face and fled screaming.

Owen ran past the flagpole and straight to the small shack Rivendell had drawn on his map. He kicked the door in. The room beyond it did indeed appear to house a wine cellar, but the back panel had slid open, revealing the passage Owen had limped through almost a year before.

"Follow me and shut this panel. No one gets out."

"Yes, sir." Hodge shouldered the panel closed and panicked screams dulled, but not so the full-throated cannon roars.

Owen entered the passage, sparing a glance at his old prison. Blankets, neatly folded, showed where troopers had waited while Rivendell and the others feasted. Owen moved past, going deeper, passing the dark doorway where he'd once believed Makepeace had been imprisoned. He didn't know who du Malphias had tortured in there to break him down, and could only hope it had been someone like Etienne Ilsavont.

He turned left at the end of the corridor, down another, toward a doorway to a larger room from which came a shifting orange glow. He advanced slowly, his bayonet at the ready. He hesitated at the opening, confused by what he saw.

The room had been dug out and down, with steps at the doorway. A large table dominated the room. Maps, many of them, created an overlapping mosaic. Small bronze disks with what looked like firestones set in them all gathered at one spot and jockeyed for position. Some, toward the east, had stopped moving.

A huge orange glass sphere hung in a bronze helix lattice above the table. It looked akin to a firestone, but was clearly hollow. It rotated as a light burned inside. Though it gave off light, it put out no heat and, instead, seemed to be sucking warmth from the room.

And at the edge of the orange glow stood du Malphias. He'd raised his right hand toward the sphere, not even close to touching it. Still, the fire quickened in response to his gesture.

The Laureate smiled at Owen. "Captain Strake, you look well."

"I am very well."

The Laureate shook his head. "This pleases me. You know, Rivendell never would have found his way here without you. I am glad you didn't let his capricious whim keep you from this meeting."

Owen, with the bayonet held firmly in both hands, descended the stairs. "Thanks to you, he put me under arrest. He will court-martial me."

Du Malphias laughed. "How little you truly understand of the world. He will do nothing of the sort. You have captured me. You will be inviolate. He will, if he survives, write scurrilous things about you. Few will believe him."

Owen came around the table. "But what if I don't intend to capture you?"

Du Malphias raised an eyebrow. "Kill me? You won't." He reached for one of the brass disks at the table's edge and slid it across to Owen. "Quarante-neuf."

"What?"

"The disks represent *pasmortes*. That disk is Quarante-neuf."

Quarante-neuf's firestone had a glimmer of light. Others, those that did not move, had blackened, like spent firestones.

"Is he alive or dead?"

"He's quite dead, Captain." Du Malphias' smile grew. "You should ask if he is strong or weak."

"Well?"

"Strong, for now."

The Laureate traced a fiery sigil in the air. The sphere's light flared, then the glass blackened and sagged inward. Like candle wax, it flowed onto the maps, which began to smolder. And the disk firestones melted along with it.

Except for Quarante-neuf's.

Owen looked up. "His firestone glows. What does it mean?"

"I wish I knew." Du Malphias' eyes tightened. "I fear I shall not have time to study the matter, for now I am your prisoner. Will you treat me as I treated you?"

Owen shook his head. "Not that you deserve better."

"Not that you could inflict worse." The Tharyngian gently waved his left hand as if dismissing a rebuke. Owen's musket moved to the right, trailing steam, offline of the man's slender chest. "I promise I shall go as any man would go, with you, to surrender my forces and my fortress. The *pasmortes* cannot be raised again."

"You could raise more."

"I shall not." He smiled easily. "That line of research bores me. There are other things I wish to investigate."

Owen looked around the room. "Notes on your experiments? Journals? Books?"

He laughed. "Concerning the *pasmortes?* All gone. As for those on the healing concoctions, they are in my private quarters. But do not be in haste to get them. A copy of my research has already been sent to Feris to be published in the Tharyngian Science Journal. You are mentioned as Patient Ten. I shall have a copy sent to you."

"You're so kind."

"You know that is manifestly untrue." Du Malphias raised his hands above his head. "Now, shall we go stop this battle? I have no more use for corpses and I imagine there are a few men you should like to see yet alive."

CHAPTER SIXTY-FIVE

August 1, 1764
La Fortresse du Morte
Anvil Lake, Mystria

W hat in Heaven's name? Prince Vlad stared, disbelieving.
As if they were all puppets controlled by the same strings, the
pasmortes jerked suddenly in unison. Their backs bowed as if
their shoulders were being drawn to the earth. Their mouths gaped open.
Those that had eyes stared at the sky. Some even seemed surprised. And then,
all at once, they snapped upright for a heartbeat before collapsing in a tangle
of limp limbs.

The Prince shook his head, not certain if in his fatigue he had slipped into
some malaise where he was dreaming. He could not believe his eyes. Then
Mugwump shuddered beneath him, and vomited forth a black puddle of
quickly dissolving bones. The wurm shied from the steaming mire and scraped
dirt over it with his tail.

The Mystrians, finding themselves with no *pasmortes* to fight, flew to the
battlements and angled fire into the fort's heart. The Fourth Foot finally came
over the north wall's top, toward the middle. They quickly formed up by squads,
five men crouching in front, five standing, and hammered the Ryngians with
deadly volleys.

Mystrian cannon-fire smashed the central stronghold. As men would discover
as they dug through it for survivors, cleverly hidden tunnels fed into it. What
Owen had once seen as shooting ports had been shuttered with planking and
planted over. Inside had been three swivel-guns and enough room for two
squads to take turns firing. Taking the stronghold by storm would have been
a bloody affair.

The battling raged for another five minutes, then du Malphias emerged from
his wine cellar. He ordered his men to lay down their arms and had the colors
struck from the flagpole. Aside from a few shots on the battlefield, and a few
more across the river, all hostilities ceased by mid-afternoon.

Prince Vlad rode Mugwump down and then slid out of the saddle. He nodded
toward Owen and the stocky little redcoat holding a gun on du Malphias. "Well

done, Captain Strake."

"Thank you, Highness. May I present Guy du Malphias, Laureate of Tharyngia."

The tall Ryngian bowed crisply. "It is an honor, Prince Vladimir. I much enjoyed your paper on the relation between ursine hibernation cycles and formations of geese flying south at winter. With your permission, I should undertake a proper translation."

Vlad's eyes narrowed. "You'll forgive me, sir, but that's hardly what I expected from you." The Prince turned and beckoned Count von Metternin forward with a purple hand. "You know Count von Metternin."

"Too well." The Laureate's head came up with the barest trace of a smile. "If you wish, I could heal your hands."

Vlad shook his head. "Thank you, but no. Prior to this, battle has always been an intellectual exercise. I would not be soon without my reminder."

The Count snorted. "To a Kessian, this is nothing."

"You disguise your distrust well, gentlemen." Du Malphias drew his hands together at the small of his back. "At the very least I can offer you an unguent made from bear tallow and the *mogiqua* to which I was introduced by Captain Strake. It will ease the discomfort."

"Very kind."

"And I wish it noted that I surrendered to Captain Strake and his companion, Mr. Dunsby. If you will dispatch Mr. Dunsby to my quarters in the southern fort, he can fetch my saber for a formal presentation. I would send one of my servants but..." He glanced toward a withered *pasmorte* and shrugged.

The Prince nodded to the redcoat. "Go."

Dunsby ran off and returned with du Malphias' sword. The Laureate smiled, then handed it to the Prince. "There. The formalities have been satisfied."

Vlad accepted it, then extended it back. "I have your parole?"

"Of course." Du Malphias accepted the blade and leaned on it as if it were a walking stick. "I have quite tired of war."

Lord Rivendell finally forced his way through the circle of soldiers surrounding the Laureate. The Norillian commander had come up over the wall once the shooting had stopped, his appearance spoiled only by the bloody mud on his boots. He drew his own sword, gold tassel dancing playfully, and leveled it at du Malphias.

"In the name of her most Holy and Terrible Majesty, the exalted Queen Margaret of Norisle, I, John Lord Rivendell, demand your surrender, unconditionally, and that of your troops and possessions." Rivendell made certain his voice carried, and filled his words with gravity to underscore the moment's drama. "Your sword, sir."

Vlad held up a hand. "He surrendered to me, my lord, and I returned it. I have his parole."

Rivendell's blade quivered. "Your sword, sir."

"As Prince Vladimir has said, I surrendered it to him."

"He is not a military man. He has no authority to accept your surrender!" Spittle frothed at the corners of his mouth. "For the third time, sir, and the last, your sword."

Du Malphias, gracing Rivendell with a stare that could have etched steel, turned and presented his sword to Captain Strake. "I surrender."

Owen accepted the blade, then gave it back.

Count von Metternin stepped forward, brushing Rivendell's blade aside. "I suggest the men attend to their wounded and comfort the dying."

His suggestion, delivered in a calm but firm voice, fell as a command into all ears but those of Lord Rivendell. Men peeled away, forming squads. Many Mystrians headed back up and out the way they'd come in, to get their picks and shovels for grave-digging duty. They walked as men proud, heads held high, with the cry "To the top!" going up to cheers from time to time.

Colonel Langford, ever Rivendell's amanuensis, followed his master doggedly, recording copious notes. Von Metternin, to Rivendell's displeasure, found a Ryngian from the Valmont region near the Kessian border who could read and write, and used him to record the Count's recollections. The Count shadowed Rivendell, driving him to distraction.

Vlad wanted to record his thoughts as well, but because of his hands, had to employ a secretary. He chose Caleb Frost, who had come down from Fort Cuivre on the sloop. He found Caleb gifted at not only recording his thoughts faithfully, but adding quick sketches which enhanced the text.

Recollections of the battle varied highly with the author—something which came as no surprise to the Prince. In Rivendell's account, no mention of *pasmortes* graced the page. He explained the myriad *pasmorte* bodies as simply being those of civilians who expired of fright when they looked upon a wurm for the first time. Langford did add a note that suggested the civilians were suffering from an unknown malady, which contributed to their diminished capacity.

Rivendell's description of the surrender, of course, made no mention of anyone but Rivendell and du Malphias. It read as if Rivendell had taken the *Fortresse du Morte* all by his lonesome, and tracked du Malphias down in his hidden lair. Rivendell noted that he'd been aware of du Malphias' duplicity the whole of the time at Anvil Lake and, therefore, had not been surprised by it.

The various battle reports most closely agreed when it came to matter of casualties. The Fourth Foot suffered 54 percent killed or wounded. The Third battalion, which had closed the gap, had suffered 83 percent casualties, with over half of those dead. The cavalry's cowardly First battalion had escaped lightly. The Second took 57 percent casualties, including Colonel Thornbury. Survivors within the First claimed that when the sloop had appeared under Ryngian colors, Thornbury had ordered them to withdraw, but no physical evidence of that order was ever found.

The Mystrians came off the best on the Norillian side of things, having only one in five men killed or wounded. Among historians, this worked against them because military experts assessed unit performance based on casualties, rather than objectives gained. Thus historians deemed the Fourth Foot's effort as the most critical. They tied the Tharyngians up, freeing the Mystrians to do what they did. As for the sloop's crew, their advancing under the enemy flag was seen as contemptible conduct. Norillian politicians seized upon that fact to besmirch the Mystrian effort and salve the wounded egos of those who had wished for a cleaner victory.

The Ryngians were given muskets and sufficient shot and powder to defend themselves on the long trip home. They gave their parole that they would not fight against Norillian interests in the new world and headed up the Green River. Du Malphias traveled on the sloop along with a company of the Fourth Foot, led by the newly promoted Lieutenant Unstone, to take over the garrison of Fort Cuivre. From there the Laureate would be given passage to Kebeton.

The Ungarakii melted into the wilderness and the Seven Nations announced their neutrality in all wars of the white men.

The Fourth Foot garrisoned the Fortress of Death, which they renamed Fort Hammer—the name based on the fort's location at Anvil Lake. The Mystrians, the cavalry, and Lord Rivendell all headed back to Hattersburg, making the return trip in half the time.

They could have made better time, but despite wanting to be home again in time for harvest, the men remained reluctant to break apart their company. Vlad understood and agreed. Combat had brought together men from all over Mystria. They had faced crack troops from Tharyngia and beaten them.

The grumbling from the cavalry limping at the end of the column only made them feel better.

In their absence, Hattersburg had been transformed. They returned on August twelfth to a town largely unlike the one they'd left a month earlier. Horses filled brand new corrals. Warehouses nearly burst with supplies. Men wearing Kessian blue sashes—locals with Seth Plant at their head—stood guard. They herded the redcoat cavalry away from the horses at gunpoint, and the Prince was directed to Gates' Tavern.

He'd barely dismounted Mugwump when the door flew open and Gisella, her golden hair flashing, threw herself into his arms. He caught her as best he could, but she still knocked him back into the wurm's flank. His betrothed wrapped him up in a hug so tight that he gasped for breath, then she kissed him and clean took his breath away.

She pulled back quickly. "I love you, my darling. The days without you have been agony."

Vlad laughed. "It is the same for me, but what are you doing here?"

Gisella smiled, then looked down. "I knew your timetable, yes, and I saw there were delays. When messages came from Hattersburg saying you were going on and supplies had not arrived, I had to do something. Mrs. Frost and the others, we made men work. We shamed them and set things to right. And the people here said they gave you their supplies and wanted these, but I would not let them take them until you gave me leave."

The Prince drew her into his arms and kissed her heartily. A great cheer arose from among the Mystrians, though the few who dared shout, "To the top!" were buffeted into silence by more sensible companions. Colonel Daunt directed men to the warehouses to relieve the Hattersburgians.

Shortly after they broke that second kiss, Gisella noticed Vlad's discolored right hand. She took hold of it and he winced.

She rolled his sleeve up. "What have you done?"

"It was nothing."

Her head whipped around. "And where are you going, Count von Metternin?"

The Kessian smiled, his hands hidden behind his back. "I thought, Highness, I should see to a table within where the Prince and I, with your permission, could recuperate from our long and arduous journey."

Gisella's eyes narrowed. "Your hands."

Von Metternin held them out.

"Remove your gloves and roll up your sleeves."

He complied. "You will not accept we were arm wrestling and hurt ourselves?"

"I thought I told you to keep him safe."

"Is he not safe?"

She stamped her foot. "Do not mock me, my lord."

Vlad reached out, gently taking hold of her chin, and turned her face to him. "You will come to understand why we did what we did. It may seem reckless and foolish, but had we not acted, many women in Mystria would be widows, and children without their fathers." He patted Mugwump with his free hand. "Mugwump kept us alive. Save your ire, and be pleased he brought us home."

Gisella looked hard into his eyes for a handful of heartbeats, then turned and walked to the wurm's muzzle. She kissed him beneath an eye and stroked his skin. "Thank you."

The wurm raised his head, his lower jaw dropping open ever so slightly, as if smiling.

She came around again. "As for the two of you, there is a place in the tavern by the fire. We have even taught them to brew a good beer."

Gisella took his left hand and led him inside. The Count, Owen Strake, and others joined them. The Prince ordered the distribution of food to the people of Hattersburg. The entire town erupted into a spontaneous celebration, lessened not at all by Rivendell and his cavalry claiming their horses and setting off on the ride back to Temperance.

Gisella had not been wrong. Gates' beer had lost the sour edge. The tavern-keeper roasted two steers, slicing off thick slabs of meat which the men devoured happily—all the while jesting about how they missed road rations. Stories began to be told about what had happened at Fort Hammer, and many a mug was raised in the Prince's honor.

Through it all, Gisella held his hand, and when men cheered for him, she squeezed. She listened intently as the recollections flowed. "And then alls I knew," claimed one man, "the guns had stopped and Mugwump done smashed the wall. To the top it was!"

Vlad had looked at her. "They exaggerate."

"Not enough by half." She took his hand in both of hers and raised it to her mouth for a kiss. "But I understand. What you did was for them, not for yourself. That is the man I love."

CHAPTER SIXTY-SIX

August 12, 1764
Hattersburg, Lindenvale, Mystria

"Ain't you gonna come celebrate?" Nathaniel, standing in front of Gates' Tavern as dusk crept over the town, gave Kamiskwa a puzzled look. "Ain't no reason you shouldn't."

"Prince Vladimir has already made his thanks to the Shedashee known." Kamiskwa smiled. "Each warrior has two horses, even those who fell, and all the grain those horses can carry. It is not far from here to Saint Luke and the Lanatashee villages. Our people will be very grateful. He also allowed us each two jackets from the fallen Ryngians, and shot and brimstone to replace what we used."

Nathaniel frowned. "That ain't telling me why you won't be celebrating. I know you gots something on your mind."

"My brother is very perceptive." Kamiskwa glanced down. "You know our ways. We celebrate great victories. We mourn our losses. We recount great courage in songs and stories."

"As do we."

"And for you, this is a great victory." The Altashee smiled. "And I shall sing of Prince Vlad's courage, and Mugwump's effort. There shall be much joy at hearing these things. My father will again ask the Prince to take my sister Ishikis as his wife."

"I reckon Princess Gisella ain't going to be having none of that."

"No. My brother, I honor the effort of this army, and yet I fear it." Kamiskwa pointed toward men wandering through the town, musket in one hand, bottle in the other. "You have taught farmers and shopkeepers that they can travel into the wilderness and kill other men. They will come to see the Shedashee as enemies, for we deny them land as the Tharyngians did. Old alliances will be forgotten, old prejudices will rise, and more blood will flow."

Nathaniel frowned. "I reckon you're more right than I care to admit." It wasn't so much what Nathaniel had heard in stories about the battle, but how the stories got told. Among the men there wasn't room for great amounts of exaggeration. That would come later, the further distant they were from the fight and others who could keep them honest. Three thousand men had taken part on the Mystrian side of the battle, but there'd be three or four times that many claiming to have been there in a year or two.

He caught himself. It hadn't been the Mystrian side of the battle; it had been the Norillian side, but men were already casting it as a Mystrian victory. And that wasn't that far from the truth, given that Mystrians had taken Fort Cuivre, had sailed the sloop down the river, and had taken the upper fort. Men were beginning to see themselves as Mystrians, not Norillians, and they weren't ever going to see the Shedashee as Mystrians.

He scratched at the back of his neck. "I reckon I'm going to need to do some thinking on this. I can tell you, I ain't gonna let it happen."

Kamiskwa braced him on both shoulders. "I know you could do this, my brother, but how much of yourself are you willing to sacrifice?"

"That don't really matter, do it?" Nathaniel shrugged. "Iffen I don't do something, people I love will suffer."

"But to make the changes in your people, you will have to become part of them. You have a start, as Captain Woods. They respect you and will listen to you. If you remain apart, your influence will dry up and blow away."

The Mystrian shifted his shoulders uneasily. "I ain't never going to be citified."

"I know this, but you might have to become more Mystrian."

"That stings more than getting shot."

Kamiskwa shook his head. "You would sacrifice yourself for the Altashee. And I would sacrifice our future for you to remain as you are."

"'Praps there is some room in the middle for meeting."

The Altashee thought for a moment, then nodded. "If there is not, we will create it."

"I like that. We make the choice and others have to live with it." Nathaniel laughed. "Ain't gonna be a lot that likes it, but I reckon they will get over it."

Kamiskwa pulled Nathaniel into a hug. "Be well, brother mine, and not too long away."

Nathaniel returned the hug, then pulled back. "Need to get down to Temperance, let folks know I done survived."

"My regards to Rachel." Kamiskwa smiled. "I have packed the two small uniforms you took for William and Thomas; and the silver gorgets for their mothers, and the silver buckles for your daughter."

"Thank you. Tell them I will see them soon." Nathaniel looked up at the sky and thin streams of clouds. "Early winter, you reckon?"

"Late, but cold."

"Good." Nathaniel smiled. "I gots me some ideas about getting the Prince one of them wooly rhinocer-whatevers he wants. Might have time to get it before the snow flies."

"If it can be done, Magehawk can do it." Kamiskwa took a step back, half disappearing into the twilight. "I look forward to hearing your plans. Soon."

"Soon." Nathaniel watched Kamiskwa go, and almost headed out after him. He would have, too, save for his friend having reminded him that he was Captain Woods. He had responsibilities. He had men who looked up to him, some figuring he'd even somehow saved their lives. If he were just to abandon them, it would rob them of part of their pride. It was as if his being there and treating them as if he liked them, kept all the fear they'd felt on the battlefield at bay.

He did like his men—the ones he'd gone to Fort Cuivre with and then brought down on the ship. The others, well, they'd gotten it into their minds that a lucky shot that had killed someone trying to kill them had come from his rifle. Pure nonsense, and he'd tried to convince a few of the absurdity of their notions, but they weren't having it. Their belief connected them to him—same as men were connected to the Prince through what he did.

Nathaniel sighed. He'd been willing to accept the responsibility of leading men into battle, but he'd not figured that the responsibility would extend beyond that. He'd made a lifetime commitment, and it wasn't one that would go away just because it would make his life easier.

The Mystrian made his way into Gates' Tavern, shaking hands and getting his back slapped. He smiled, nodded to men, called a few by name. Someone shoved a mug of ale into his hand and he took a gulp. It surprised him. He figured Gates must have gone and gotten a new, young horse for pissing into his casks, and he hoped it was one of the best stolen from Captain Percy Abberwick.

He moved deeper into the room, raised his mug toward the Bone brothers. The three of them had come through things without a scratch, though Makepeace was still nursing his bruised arm. He hadn't wanted anything to do with the swivel-guns on the sloop, even after the Summerland boys offered to teach him the proper spell. When he learned of what the Prince and Count had done on Mugwump, he'd been in absolute awe.

The Prince and the Count book-ended Princess Gisella. The rest of the men took note of her, of course. As they told their stories, they played up to her and were certain to let her know that Prince Vlad and Count Joachim had been the heroes. She seemed to delight in every story, even though it was the same story told over and over again. She looked up at Vlad with pure worship on her face at the end of each one.

Wasn't a man in the place who wouldn't have killed a whole Tharyngian regiment to have a woman look at him that way.

Me, included. Nathaniel smiled, thinking of Rachel. The cavalry would arrive in Temperance long before the rest of the soldiers. She'd know he survived. Word would get to her somehow, despite her husband's doing his best to hide it from her. That had worked once, and she'd vowed that it never would again.

Nathaniel would see her when he got to Temperance. She'd be there, somewhere, in a crowd, and he'd see her. Her husband would be watching her like a hawk, but it wouldn't matter. He could have all the Branches and Casks in the world set between Nathaniel and his wife, and it couldn't keep them apart.

He laughed to himself. Nathaniel never had been much of a one for what-iffing, but Zachariah Warren had done him more of a service than he could have imagined, and likely had saved many lives. Had he not tricked Rachel into marrying him, she would have married Nathaniel. He would have moved to town and probably would have gotten fat. He'd have learned a trade, turned his back on the wilderness and hunting and trapping and exploring.

I'da become one of them men what looks up to me. He shivered and felt a bit of an ache in his belly. He wasn't a hundred percent sure that he'd have been saddle-broke so easily, but the prospect scared him. Both because of who it meant he would have become and because his inability to be broken meant he'd be denied certain pleasures in his life.

It struck him that here he was, in a room jammed with people, and yet he found himself utterly alone. They thought sure they knew him—and some did, far better than most. Yet men like the Bone brothers had a bond with each other that he really didn't have with anyone else. Maybe Owen, there near the Prince; sort of with the Prince, but otherwise, his closest connection had headed off to Saint Luke as the sun went down.

Realizing he was alone among many didn't provoke melancholy. Nathaniel wasn't inclined that way, and certainly wasn't going to tolerate that sort of a mood. A man gave in to melancholy, he figured, if he wanted to, or he wasn't smart enough to figure out what it was that made him happy.

Right now that would be getting some fresh air, relieving my bladder, and figuring out where I'm going to bed down for the night. He wasn't really feeling that tired, but it was getting to the time in August when shooting stars would pour through the night sky. He'd enjoyed watching that ever since he was a boy, when his father had shared that wonder with him. Even with the full moon and thin clouds, the show would be grand.

He squeezed back through the crowd and went out the back door. He headed toward the privy, but all of a sudden the ache in his belly stabbed front to back. He doubled over and dropped to a knee. His guts had gone liquid and he clenched his teeth against the pain. Then something slammed hard against his head and he pitched forward.

He blacked out, but for how long he couldn't really tell. Couldn't have been long because his stomach still hurt and he stank. His bowels had let go and his arms and legs trembled. He'd been poisoned. In the ale. He tried to remember who had given it to him, but it was just a hand through the crowd.

Rough hands jerked him into a sitting position against a wall. A dark silhouette backlit by the full moon hovered above him, then a stinging slap snapped his head around. "Wake up, Woods."

Nathaniel forced himself to focus. "Rufus."

"Mr. Warren, he don't want his wife mooncalfing after you no more. Kinda hoped you'd get it in the fighting, but you is damned lucky. Have to do it myself." Rufus straightened up, swimming out of focus. Two more silhouettes stood center and off to the right. "Now you die, sitting in your own shit. Make it easy to forgit you."

Nathaniel tried to get to his feet, but Rufus hit him with the butt of his musket square in the chest. Nathaniel sank back, smacking his head on the wall. "You hurtin'?"

Nathaniel spat. "Not 'specially."

"Too bad." Rufus reversed the musket and pressed the muzzle to his belly. "Mr. Warren, he wanted you to die in pain."

Nathaniel forced a smile onto his face. "When I get my hands on you, I'm going to learn you all about pain. Him, too."

"Ain't gonna happen. Your time on this earth is up."

Nathaniel's vision began to dim as Rufus dropped his thumb on the firestone. The pain in his stomach spiked. Nathaniel screamed. The musket boomed, and Nathaniel's world went black.

Nathaniel had never attended much church, and when he had, he'd not paid particular attention to what was being said from the pulpit. Most of it involved Hell and damnation, so as he returned to consciousness, he was expecting demons to be stabbing him and lakes of fire and the unending cries of souls in torment.

What he got was the creak of a bed and the crunch of fresh straw. He opened an eye and while the preaching hadn't much talked about Heaven, what he did remember gave him cause to be thinking that it wouldn't much look like a room in Gates' Tavern.

And Justice Bone, he wasn't looking much like an angel. He sat at the foot of the bed, a small pistol in each hand, watching the door. He glanced over when Nathaniel shifted his weight, then nodded. "Water there in the mug iffen you is thirsty."

Nathaniel groaned and rubbed his hands over his belly. "I ain't shot."

"Nope."

"Mouth tastes like I been eating burned leather and bitterroot."

"Yep."

Nathaniel eased himself on to his right side and took the mug of water. He sipped, ready for his guts to protest, but they tolerated the water well enough. He took a mouthful but let it slowly trickle down.

He rolled onto his back again. "Morning?"

"Afternoon."

"Want to be telling me what happened?"

Justice nodded. "Noticed you going out. The weaselly little Branch followed. Time I got out, you'd been drug off a-ways. Rufus was a-jawing at you. He went to shoot you, but I shot him first."

"Kill him?"

"Hit him in his sit-down parts. He done run off while I took care of his brothers. The weasel's dead. Gutted him. Other one will probably live, but ain't going to be using his right arm none." Justice shrugged. "Men choosing up a squad to be going after Rufus."

"Tell 'em no." Nathaniel had to catch his breath. "I will be finding him."

"I reckoned you'd say that. Trib told them all we was having to wait for you to give your blessing." Justice smiled. "The Prince, he done figured what they poisoned you with. Make you drink a tea of crushed charcoal and bitterroot. Stunk to heaven. You threw up a bit. Got you cleaned up and put to bed."

"Thank you."

"I told you I would be watching out."

"You did." Nathaniel nodded slowly. "You hear what Rufus said?"

"Didn't need to. I seen enough to know. What you want to do about it is your business. Want help, I'm in."

Nathaniel nodded. He could lay charges against Zachariah Warren and most all folks would believe him. But a jury would hear Warren deny he had ever hired Rufus to do anything. Some would think that Warren was defending his wife's honor against Nathaniel's advances. Even those who knew the true story would still be thinking Nathaniel had brought this on himself.

"I reckon I will be thinking on that for a bit." He smiled. "Which cheek?"

"Left."

"I once shot him in the right." Nathaniel laughed. "Next time, more to the center, and a lot higher."

CHAPTER SIXTY-SEVEN

September 17, 1764
Temperance, Temperance Bay, Mystria

With their desire to be home swiftly, the Mystrian troops set out from Hattersburg on the fourteenth and made very good time along the road they had previously hacked out of the wilderness. The wounded—including Caleb Frost and escorted by Princess Gisella—traveled ahead down the river on barges and then by ship to Temperance. The wounded reached Temperance before the bulk of the Norillian cavalry, though Rivendell and his staff joined them on board.

Owen remained in Prince Vlad's party, on orders from Rivendell. Rivendell even gave him Hodge Dunsby as his aide, as the bantam soldier had been by his side constantly. Rivendell clearly intended to write up reports casting Owen in an extremely negative light, but Owen had moved past caring.

He had come to Mystria in hopes of doing his duty and perhaps winning enough fame and glory that he and his wife could become free of his family. He had accomplished his goal and more, but not in the way he had hoped. He realized this as he walked with men—some of whom, though wounded, refused to admit they were hurt—and sail home. These men had taken up arms against an enemy even though fighting was neither their profession, nor had they trained at it. They responded to a call to handle a situation that threatened everyone. For them, it wasn't a quest for personal glory or treasure or fame. That wasn't to say that some hadn't also hoped to prove something to themselves or others, but those personal motives had been subordinated to the betterment of all.

What struck him most strongly was the affection he felt for these men. The Mystrians had accepted him and Dunsby not because of Owen's connection to the Prince, but because of what they had done in the fight. He and Dunsby had bearded the lion in his den. They had forced du Malphias to surrender. And Owen had done it dressed like one of them, not some arrogant, no-good Norillian officer!

My future, if it is anywhere, is here, in Mystria.

That realization filled him with dread. Catherine loved him, but he wasn't sure she could come to love Mystria. The land demanded more of its people than she could ever give. If he wanted to keep her, he would have to return to Norisle and a life he hated. It would tear his heart out. *Here I am home.*

The idea that he had to choose between his wife's happiness and his own filled Owen with melancholy. He feared she was slipping away—and the haunting vision he'd had of her while on the winding path seemed likely. While letters from their loved ones in Temperance had caught up with soldiers in Hattersburg, she had sent him nothing. *Does she know what I am thinking?*

Nathaniel caught up to him, still looking gaunt. "Bit of a long face you have there, Captain."

Owen forced a smile. "Never a good moment when a man's on the horns of a dilemma. No matter what choice I make, it will hurt."

"My pap said them choices is what puts hair on your chest."

"And white into your hair." The Norillian frowned. "My wife will never stay in Mystria. I don't want to leave. I see now what you see in this land, Nathaniel, thanks to you."

Nathaniel snorted. "You'da gone done and see it for yourself, Captain. You're a smart fellow."

"But not smart enough to make this choice." Owen sighed. "What would you do?"

"I wouldn't be so damned foolish as to ask romantical advice from me." The man's eyes tightened. "You love someone and you love this land. I love this land and another man's wife. Don't knows I could make a choice 'tween 'em. Tough choice."

"That isn't much help."

"Iffen you don't mind me asking, why is it you love your wife?"

That question gave Owen a start. "She's my wife."

"That's saying a fish likes water on account of he's wet."

"Why do I love her?" Owen smiled. "Her smile. The way she makes me feel wanted and included. She loves me, makes me smile when I think of her."

"All positive points, I reckon. And you think she won't take to Mystria?"

"She might eventually come to see its beauty." Owen shook his head. "But that would require her getting out into the country. That will never happen.

"Might not. But I reckon you need to ask yourself if she would ever want to see the beauty. Nothing against your wife, but iffen she can't see it, or won't see it, yours ain't a fight can be won. Most all us redemptioneers came here because we had nothing back there." Nathaniel shrugged. "Iffen her life is back there, ain't never she gonna be happy here."

Owen chuckled. "That's fairly insightful romantical advice."

"Just talking about human nature." Nathaniel pointed to the men marching in front of them. "They all went and fought Queen Margaret's war here. They figure they done earned some praise and a reward. Ain't gonna get it, on account of the Queen and men like Rivendell have their lives over there. What we see they cain't. They don't want to. You have seen, and you is going to have to decide where your life is."

The Norillian nodded. He wanted to stay, and divorce wasn't an option. At best he could send her back to Norisle and visit, but what kind of a life would that be for either of them? If he remained he would never take another wife. He would never dishonor Catherine that way.

Owen signed. "I made my commitment to Catherine before I ever came to Mystria. I shall hate leaving this beautiful country."

Nathaniel patted him on the shoulder. "Leastways your wife is nearly as pretty."

"Yes, she is." Owen sighed again. If his uncle had been telling the truth about the land grant and title, he'd opt for a place in Temperance Bay, as close to the Prince's estate as he could get. He'd keep it as a preserve and every three years or so would come for a season or two. Catherine would doubtlessly choose to remain in Norisle. But I can bring my children, and they can grow to love Mystria.

That thought brought a smile to his face. He had come to win glory, and yet in Mystria had found something else to love. The sheer physical beauty and fecundity of the land could not be matched anywhere in Norisle. The people's spirit had a positive nature. Half the troops were barefoot, wearing clothes that were worn through at knees and elbows despite multiple patchings. Their condition didn't bother these people at all. They honestly believed, one way or another, that better times and a brighter future were around the corner. They marched toward it with a child's wide-eyed curiosity and sense of wonder.

And even if he would have to absent himself from Mystria, the thought that his children, and his legacy, would be here, pleased him. The Old World, hidebound as it was, would smother him.

Owen took a deep breath, filling his lungs with fresh air, and fought to memorize every detail, so even in his dotage, he wouldn't forget the time he truly felt free.

On the sixteenth the troops returned to the camping ground they'd occupied on that first day out. They re-created their camps and spent one last night together. On the morrow they'd march into Temperance and would never again assemble as one unit, so they sang songs and spun stories and extracted promises of correspondence and visits.

Many men wished Owen well. They assumed that on his return to Norisle he'd run for Parliament. They said he'd be their representative "...being as how you know Mystria, Captain, sir." They offered him lodging were he ever to visit, and promised to find him if they ever traveled back to the mother country.

And they said it with sincerity and a bit of deviltry.

The Prince brought Mugwump back to his wurmrest and the beast seemed content to return. Vlad then spent the evening circulating among the troops, thanking them all for their service. On the trip home, Vlad had made a couple of side-trips searching for things on Owen's list. Many men picked up on that and promised him a fine hunting expedition whenever he chose to visit them.

The next morning they marched early for Temperance. Folks from farmsteads came out to greet them. Huge smiles blossomed all around. And then, when only a half-hour outside the city, the troops gathered themselves into the same column in which they'd marched onto the battlefield. Solemn and proud, with heads high and steps in unison, they gave their people a look at the warriors who had defeated the Tharyngians at Anvil Lake.

Everyone had come out to line the parade route. The troops threaded between thick, cheering throngs. Someone had created a flag of green, with a black and red wurm claw at the heart of it. The talons pointed down, transforming it into an M for Mystria. Copies fluttered from hands and hung from windows. Owen's uncle would have seen it as a sign of incipient rebellion, and he vowed there would be no mention of it in his reports.

The column wended its way to the city green, where the troops assembled. The Lord Mayor took his place, welcoming the Prince. Doctor Frost and other local luminaries joined him on the stage. Frost wore a green armband, marking him as someone who had a relative who served on the expedition.

The Lord Mayor invited Prince Vlad to address the assembly, which he did with the customary reluctance that had marked the man since Owen first met him.

Vlad smiled. "Thank you, Lord Mayor, and the people of Temperance. You honor us today in ways we never would have imagined. It is so good to be home. I will not speak very long because I know all of us want the company of our families. So I only wish to say this: Know that your friends and kin are the bravest men on the continent. Know that even if they tell stories that seem outrageous, they could exaggerate them a hundred times and would not even come close to the truth of what they endured. And understand that as happy as we are to be home again and reunited with you, we mourn the passing of our brothers in arms, and honor their sacrifices, which made it possible for each of us to be here.

"I look out over this sea of faces and I see two thousand brothers I never knew I had, and two thousand brothers whom I shall never forget."

Cheers rose, hats flew, and many tears fell. The Prince dismissed the men with a salute and the orderly formations dissolved into chaos. Owen went toward the stage, having seen Doctor Frost head off to the left. And as he got close, the crowd opened and there stood Bethany with her family not twenty feet away.

His heart leaped.

Then Catherine spoke. "At least pretend, my husband, that you were looking for me."

Owen spun. "Catherine!" He smiled, his arms going wide. "I was looking for you. I assumed you would be with the Frosts."

Weariness flashed over her drawn and haggard face. Then her expression softened and she forced a brave smile. "I'm sorry, Owen. It has just been so trying a time without you." She opened her arms, spreading the cloak she wore, then let a hand stroke her swollen belly. "You see why I have missed you so?"

Owen's jaw dropped. "A baby? Our baby?"

"Ours, yes, of course. You are my husband."

"Catherine, I dreamed of this on the march." He clapped his hands and laughed. "This is perfect. We can make a new life here for our child."

"A new life here?" She shook her head, her eyes narrowing. "Did I hear you correctly?"

Owen hesitated. "A slip of the tongue, darling. I mean… for us to return home, of course. It is just… with the land grant, we will have lands here, too."

She reached out and caressed his cheek. "Of course. The land here shall make our life in Norisle perfect."

Owen drew her to him, holding her tightly. "It will be perfect. I might, you know, wish to visit…"

She stiffened slightly within his embrace. "I understand, husband. I much prefer you coming here to visit than your going off to war." She pulled back and smiled. "I shall remain in our home, caring for our children, while you adventure and bring back more glory and wealth."

Owen kissed her forehead. "Nothing could induce you live here?"

"Remain here. Are you joking?" She looked up at him, her brown eyes intently studying him. "No power under Heaven could convince me to stay a moment longer than absolutely necessary."

"I hope, Mrs. Strake, this is not completely true." Prince Vlad, his complexion ashen, gave them a wan smile. "I would ask of your husband a personal service which would delay your departure."

Catherine, surprised, turned and curtsied. "Highness, please, I did not mean…"

Owen's eyes narrowed. "What is it?"

The Prince sighed heavily, shrinking, shoulder sagging. "Baker sent word from my estate. It's Mugwump." The man looked up, stricken. "He's dying.

CHAPTER SIXTY-EIGHT

September 17, 1764
Prince Haven, Temperance Bay, Mystria

"Owen, you can't abandon me."

He looked at his wife. "I'm not."

"You just returned from war." Catherine's eyes began to brim with tears. "I need you."

Prince Vlad held his hands up. "Forgive me making so unseemly a request."

Owen shook his head. "No, Highness, your request is anything but. I have my duty to you and my desire to help Mugwump." He turned to his wife. "And I am not abandoning you. With the Prince's permission, I will have Mr. Dunsby get a coach and convey you to the Prince's estate. There you can get some peace and we will have time together."

Vlad smiled. "Yes, of course. Mrs. Strake, I would have you renew your acquaintance with Princess Gisella, and I would love for you to be my guest. I would be honored."

Catherine sniffed. "Really?"

"Sincerely."

Owen kissed her. "I want you with me, Catherine. We have been too long apart and now that we are a family, I do not want you away from my side. Were this not an emergency…"

She wiped away tears. "Go. I am so silly. Do not think of me thus. I shall be with you as fast as possible, beloved husband."

Owen signaled Dunsby and explained what he needed. The Private accepted the orders with a smile and led Catherine off to gather her things. Owen then followed the Prince to the garrison stable where Nathaniel Woods had already gotten three horses saddled. The three of them mounted up and made haste for the estate.

The lack of conversation gave Owen time to think. On the road he had been ready to return to Norisle, but his blurted admission to Catherine had relieved pressure that had been building in his chest. He really didn't want to leave Mystria. He really had nothing back in Norisle, but here, in the land of his father, he had a future.

He recalled Mr. Wattling accusing him of being a Mystrian. At that time he'd taken it as a grand affront, but now, he would find it high praise. While no Mystrians would see him as one, they would come to accept him as one. The reverse, no matter how great the service one performed for the Crown, would never be true in Norisle.

The words I spoke to Catherine came from my heart. Owen smiled as they sped over the unspoiled landscape. Can a man live with his heart an ocean away?

Their horses lathered thickly and flagging, they rode straight through the yard to the wurmrest. Owen leaped from the saddle and glanced at Baker, who sat listlessly near the wurmrest's door. He looked up as Owen approached, his eyes red, dark circles beneath them and his complexion sallow.

Owen dropped to a knee. "What's happened, Mr. Baker?"

The wurmwright shrugged. "I don't really know. He was fine, just fine, last evening. He ate. He swam, he came back in. Nothing unusual and then…" Baker opened the wurmrest. "He's dying."

Owen preceded the Prince and his wurmwright into the stable. The stench staggered him. Not only did it wreak of wurm—a cloying, musky scent that lodged deep in the sinuses and started them weeping—but heat blasted him. The heat radiated from the wurm, rising so sharply that every step closer felt as if he were walking into an inferno.

The wurm, or what Owen had to presume was the wurm, lay nestled inside a fat, twenty-foot-long cocoon spun of black and red silk, with hints of gold, reflecting the colors of the creature beneath it. The silk alone would be worth a fortune, but it came with a high price. The cocoon would kill the wurm, though slight movement suggested Mugwump hadn't died yet. Owen took this as a good sign.

Owen leaned on the railing. "I've never seen a molt like this. The scales are outside, as if the cocoon grew beneath the wurm's flesh and exfoliated them."

The Prince nodded. "Normally a cocoon's fibers grow over the scales?"

"Yes. You cut the wurm out of the cocoon, then help him shed." Owen pointed at the far side of the wurmrest. "Baker, what's that?"

"His tail, sir. He chewed it off." As long as the cocoon itself, the tail had already begun to putrefy, contributing to the fierce odor. "I wanted to drag it out, but it's too hot for me to get it."

Vlad grabbed Owen's upper arm. "I have pruning hooks. We might be able to cut him free. Do you think we should do that? Can we save him?"

A lump rose in Owen's throat. He clasped the man by both shoulders and swallowed past it. "I don't know, Highness. I've never seen colored silk. I've never seen shed scales nor a chewed-off tail. I've never heard of a wurm having a fever. Fact is, he's breathing. If we interfere…"

Vlad glanced down at the wurm, then nodded. "Right, right, of course. Fever means metabolism. Same with breathing. Part of a natural process. It must be something natural. I need to make some notes."

"Good idea." Owen pointed to the tail. "I'll see if we can drag it out."

"Rope and tackle might help."

"I think I can find it, Highness."

Vlad gave him a wan smile. "I am sorry for intruding on your reunion with your wife, Captain. I'm very glad you're here."

"As am I."

"And congratulations on your child."

Owen beamed. "Thank you. Of recent times I've seen a lot of death. Having life brought into the world will be good. And since I want my child to be able to swim with a wurm, we'll make sure Mugwump lives, too."

The Prince's smile broadened. "Your children shall ride, Captain. This I promise you."

Between the three of them, Owen, Nathaniel, and Baker were able to get some rope around the severed tail and drag it out of the wurmrest. Owen's guess that it was the source of the stink had been right. Nathaniel wanted to burn it. Baker suggested burying it. The Prince insisted on dissecting it, which he did using the aforementioned pruning hook and a highway-man's mask heavily laden with oil of eucalyptus.

Though the dissection did not thrill Owen, it kept Vlad busy. He would cut open a portion of the tail, make sketches of what he saw, then weigh flesh and bone before separating them. He noted that fish did not take the wurmflesh for bait and that birds seem reluctant to pick at it. Based on tracks they found the next morning, neither wolverine nor bear had difficulty eating the meat, and by the second day a family of raccoons waited in the woods for that day's dissection to end.

Vlad did make some interesting discoveries. In one of the tail bones he found an old arrowhead entirely encrusted with bone. "I checked Mugwump's history and in 1162, at the battle of Verindan, an arrow penetrated his tail. They could not dig it out, so they snapped it off."

Nathaniel and Baker took the wurmskin and set about cleaning and tanning it. The fact that Vlad was able to discover a variety of new things appeared to keep his anxiety at bay, and this made the waiting more endurable.

Princess Gisella did her best to make everyone feel at ease, especially Catherine. Owen's wife had taken to bed for two days after the rough coach ride from Temperance. Gisella waited upon her as if a servant. Owen apologized profusely to her Highness, but Gisella simply smiled and promised to care for her as Owen was caring for Mugwump.

On the third day, the Prince came to relieve Owen. "I believe, Captain, I know why this molt is different from others."

"Yes, Highness?"

"Mugwump made the cocoon very quickly—in less than five hours. That requires a great deal of energy. Mugwump does many things differently from wurms on Norisle or the Continent. He consumes a variety of flora and fauna that are unknown on the other side of the ocean. I am certain that has contributed to his health and his colors being so bright. But he's been doing that for fifty years, without this sort of molt. So I looked for something else, some way he might have gotten access to energy."

The Prince's expression tightened. "I think it comes down to his eating *pasmortes*."

Owen's eyes narrowed. "You're suggesting he consumed the magickal energy in them?"

"It's just a theory and yet, when du Malphias destroyed the magick, Mugwump vomited back corpses and showed no more interest in anything that had been *pasmorte*. He stored that energy up and then when back here, in his lair, feeling safe, he entered a molt."

For the next week and a half things settled into a routine. Owen, the Prince, and Baker divided the day into three watches. One of them was with Mugwump at all times, with Dunsby and Count von Metternin helping out as needed. Nathaniel hunted and fished, as well as continued to process the wurmleather and bones, happy with the distance between himself and the cocoon.

On the twenty-fifth of September, surprise visitors arrived on the river. Msitazi, still wearing Owen's jacket, accompanied by Kamiskwa and William, beached the canoe. After greetings and introductions—Msitazi doing Owen the great honor of offering to buy Catherine, that being an honor his wife neither understood or liked—William fetched a package from the canoe. Unwrapping it, he proudly bore one of the wurmscales filled with a small fortune of salt mixed with bear grease into a thick paste.

The Prince accepted the gift. "What is this?"

Msitazi chuckled. "It is for Mugwump. It is to celebrate his birth."

"I fear I don't understand, Chief Msitazi."

The older man dispatched William to fetch one of the scales from the wurm's tail. The chief squatted and planted the scale on the ground upside down. The inside shined with a wavy mineral rainbow akin to mother of pearl. The Altashee oriented the attachment point toward the north.

Msitazi pointed to a dark dot near the southern edge of the scale. "This marks his birth." His finger traveled over to the western side of the scale and tapped a small, thorn-like projection. "This is his nativity bump. When the sun sets, and its shadow touches the dot, it is his day of birth."

"I find your idea intriguing, sir, but the date of Mugwump's hatching was in April, many centuries ago."

The Altashee chuckled. "You are born once of your mother, and again born a man. If a man is lucky, he is again born into wisdom. If this is true of men, why is it not true of Mugwump?"

Vlad ran a hand over his jaw. "When?"

"Soon. Very soon."

"Then we shall have to be ready." Vlad looked over at Owen. "Though how we prepare for the birthing of a wurm, I have no idea."

After the evening's dinner, Owen found Catherine standing on the balcony overlooking the lawn. Below, the Altashee had constructed a domed hut and sat around a small campfire in front of it. Nathaniel sat with his son and the four of them all laughed.

He slipped his arms around her and kissed her neck. "You should come down, Catherine. They tell very good stories."

"No. You can go."

"Not without you."

"I know you want to go, Owen. I know you'd rather be with them."

He straightened up and turned her around. Tear-tracks glistened in moonlight. "I want to be in your company, Catherine. I like these men. They saved my life."

"They abandoned you to du Malphias."

"They did what I ordered them to do, and they returned for me. Had they not been there, I never should have escaped." He tipped her face up. "What is it?"

"You've changed, Owen. Sometimes I wonder if I know you anymore. I wonder if you still love me and want to return to our home with me."

He kissed her forehead. "I love you, and wherever we are together is our home, be it in Norisle, or here."

"Here?"

"Would that be so terrible?"

Before she could answer, a rumbling screech burst from the wurmrest. Baker bolted through the door. "It's happening. Come quick!"

Without a second thought, Owen vaulted the railing and sprinted to the wurmrest. The others came as well—including Nathaniel. Msitazi marched proudly into the dark confines, bearing his gift.

The wurmrest's temperature had dropped sharply. This would have worried Owen, save that movement from within the cocoon had increased. Though the silk still shrouded Mugwump, there was no mistaking him for dead.

Another shriek ripped through the night, with enough hints of Mugwump's battle-cry that none who had heard it before could help but smile.

Owen grabbed a pruning hook from the rack on the wall. "Shall I cut him out?"

The Prince considered for a moment, then glanced at Msitazi. "No. If Mugwump is emerging into wisdom, he'll get himself out."

Msitazi moved off to the side on the catwalk and sat down with his offering in his lap. He began to rock back and forth, singing in a low voice, a huge smile on his face. He clearly had no concerns for the wurm's health, and that calmed everyone save for Baker, who decided to keep an eye on both the wurm and the Altashee.

Nathaniel nodded. "I think I'd be liking to know how Msitazi knows what he knows about these wurms."

Kamiskwa tapped his own left eye. "I accept that he knows."

The grumblings from the cocoon became more consistent and louder. Activity within the cocoon became more deliberate. Before Mugwump could have been an infant moving within a dream, but now the motions had direction and purpose, not the fluid aimlessness of slumber.

And then, just as Princess Gisella entered the wurmrest, it happened.

Mugwump's tail slashed through the silk. It emerged slender and sinewy, but strong, with an arrowhead point at the tip. It uncoiled and waved about, like a snake preparing to strike. It chopped down toward the wurm's hip, opening another great rent.

Mugwump's head reared up through that hole on a long, slender neck. Though still wedge-shaped, his head was smaller than before. Small horns started at the tip of the nose and worked themselves up between the eyes, then split into two trios that angled back along the skull. His great golden eyes had shifted forward, peering out over the muzzle. It made him appear more equine, though the scales and horns had never been seen on a horse. Two pointed ears with tiny golden tufts topping each, flicked forward and back.

Talons clawed through the cocoon front and back, tugging on the silk and enlarging holes. They exposed him fully, his flesh gleaming, muscles visible, but with a new serpentine leanness to his shape.

"'Pears you'll be needing some new tack, Highness." Nathaniel scratched at the back of his head. "He done shrank a mite."

"That, or let him grow into the old, Mr. Woods."

The wurm bit at portions of the cocoon, pulling it away, but before he had fully freed himself from the black and red blanket, his nostrils flared. He extended his head toward Msitazi. The Altashee raised the scale. A forked tongue flicked out, snatching it from between his hands, and sucked it back into the wurm's mouth. Mugwump raised his head toward the roof and the offering slid down his throat.

The Prince smiled. "Magnificent."

Mugwump turned and stared at them, then stood. The last of the cocoon fell away.

"Oh my." The Prince pointed. "He has wings."

Owen nodded, smiling. "You, Highness, are in possession of a dragon."

"It would appear, Captain Strake, you are correct." Vlad smiled, then Gisella wrapped her arms around him and gave him a kiss.

Owen looked over, seeking Catherine's reaction to Mugwump's rebirth, but she'd not joined them. He started to the wurmrest's door, but hesitated. He wanted to look out, but there was no need. The winding path had showed him her expression, her hatred, as she stood out there on the lawn, alone, glaring at the wurmrest.

He looked back at Mugwump and just for a heartbeat, their gazes met. Owen understood.

He, like the dragon, truly was home again.

Night Shade Books Is an Independent Publisher of Quality SF, Fantasy and Horror

WINGS OF FIRE

DRAGON STORIES BY

HOLLY BLACK   GEORGE R.R. MARTIN

ORSON SCOTT CARD   ANNE MCCAFFREY

CHARLES DE LINT   NAOMI NOVIK

C.J. CHERRYH   MICHAEL SWANWICK

URSULA K. LE GUIN   ROGER ZELAZNY

AND MANY OTHERS

Edited by Jonathan Strahan and Marianne S. Jablon

ISBN 978-1-59780-187-4, Trade Paperback; $15.95

Dragons: fearsome fire-breathing foes, scaled adversaries, legendary lizards, ancient hoarders of priceless treasures, serpentine sages with the ages' wisdom, and winged weapons of war. *Wings of Fire* brings you all these dragons, and more, seen clearly through the eyes of many of today's most popular authors, including Peter S. Beagle, Holly Black, Orson Scott Card, Mercedes Lackey, Charles de Lint, Diana Wynne Jones, Ursula K. Le Guin, George R. R. Martin, Anne McCaffrey, Garth Nix, and many others.

Edited by Jonathan Strahan (*The Best Science Fiction and Fantasy of the Year*) and Marianne S. Jablon, *Wings of Fire* collects the best short stories about dragons. From writhing wyrms to snakelike devourers of heroes; from East to West and everywhere in between, *Wings of Fire* is sure to please dragon lovers everywhere.

Night Shade Books Is an Independent Publisher of Quality SF, Fantasy and Horror

FEATURING STORIES BY

STEPHEN BAXTER
HOLLY BLACK
PAT CADIGAN
ANDY DUNCAN
ALEX IRVINE
DIANA WYNNE JONES
ELLEN KUSHNER
KELLY LINK
KAREN JOY FOWLER
BRUCE STERLING
ROBERT REED
GEOFF RYMAN
JO WALTON
AND MANY OTHERS

THE BEST
SCIENCE FICTION
AND FANTASY
OF THE YEAR
VOLUME FOUR

EDITED BY JONATHAN STRAHAN

ISBN 978-1-59780-171-3, Trade Paperback; $19.95

A ruthless venture capitalist finds love—or something chemically similar—in an Atlanta strip club; a girl in gray conjures a man from a handful of moonshine; a rebellious young woman suffers a strange incarceration; an astronaut shares a lifeboat—and herself—with an unfathomable alien; an infected girl counts the days until she becomes a vampire; a big man travels to a tiny moon to examine an ancient starship covered with flowers....

The depth and breadth of science fiction and fantasy short stories continues to change with every passing year. The twenty-nine stories chosen for this book by award-winning anthologist Jonathan Strahan carefully map this evolution, giving readers a captivating and always-entertaining look at the very best the genre has to offer.

Night Shade Books Is an Independent Publisher of Quality SF, Fantasy and Horror

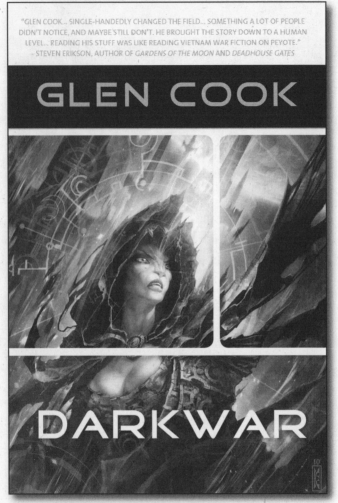

"GLEN COOK... SINGLE-HANDEDLY CHANGED THE FIELD... SOMETHING A LOT OF PEOPLE DIDN'T NOTICE, AND MAYBE STILL DON'T. HE BROUGHT THE STORY DOWN TO A HUMAN LEVEL... READING HIS STUFF WAS LIKE READING VIETNAM WAR FICTION ON PEYOTE."
— STEVEN ERIKSON, AUTHOR OF *GARDENS OF THE MOON* AND *DEADHOUSE GATES*

GLEN COOK

DARKWAR

ISBN 978-1-59780-201-7, Trade Paperback; $16.99

The world grows colder with each passing year, the longer winters and ever-deepening snows awakening ancient fears within the Dengan Packstead: fears of invasion by armed and desperate nomads, attack by the witchlike and mysterious Silth, able to kill with their minds alone, and of the Grauken, that desperate time when intellect gives way to buried cannibalistic instinct, when meth feeds upon meth. For Marika, a young pup of the Packstead, times are dark indeed, for against these foes, the Packstead cannot prevail. But stirring within Marika is a power unmatched in all the world, a legendary power that may not just save her world, but allow her to grasp the stars themselves...

From Glen Cook comes *Darkwar*, collecting for the first time the stunning science fantasy epic that originally appeared as *Doomstalker, Warlock,* and *Ceremony.*

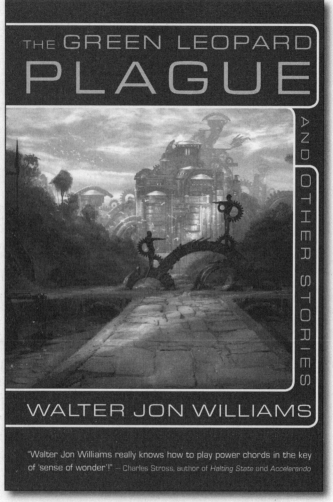

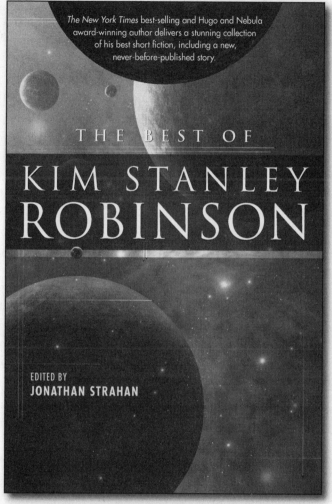

About the Author

Michael A. Stackpole is an award-winning novelist, graphic novelist, podcaster, screenwriter, game designer, computer game designer, and editor who is best known for his *New York Times* bestselling novels, *Rogue Squadron* and *I, Jedi*. Since 1988, he's published more than forty novels and was the first author to have work available in Apple's Appstore. He's the driving force behind the Chain Story Project (chainstory.stormwolf.com). He lives in Arizona, and enjoys indoor soccer and swing dancing during his spare time.

To learn more about Mike and to find other stories about the characters of the Crown Colonies, please visit his website at www.stormwolf.com. You can also find him in Second Life, where he holds weekly chats about writing and publishing issues (and where an earlier version of this novel was read aloud to raise money for the American Cancer Society's Relay for Life).